6

· ·

These half dozen short novels are as different from each other as any great works of fiction can be. From Melville we get an unforgettable tale of good and evil in conflict on the high seas. Joyce, the great genius of modern prose, gives us a touching and realistic story of lost love. Nobel Prize winner William Faulkner writes the stark drama of a young boy's savage awakening to life. From Katherine Anne Porter comes a penetrating study of Southern tragedy; from Gogol, a masterful narrative of man's quest for dignity; from Glenway Wescott, a sensitive and poignant picture of individual isolation. ... But despite these differences, all share that one element—the unmistakable ring of human truth—that marks each of them as a masterpiece. . . .

SIX
GREAT
MODERN
SHORT
NOVELS

. . . .

Published by

DELL PUBLISHING COMPANY, INC.

261 Fifth Avenue

New York 16, N. Y.

Library of Congress Catalog Card No. 54-12209

Designed and produced by
Western Printing and Lithographing Company
Printed In U.S.A.

TABLE OF CONTENTS

THE DEAD

• •

James Joyce

James Joyce

· ·

James Joyce, one of the great writers of our time
and one of the great masters of language, was
born near Dublin in 1882. He lived most of his life,
in exile, in France and Switzerland (where he died
in 1941) fighting blindness and poverty and writing the books that were to influence so strongly the
literature of the twentieth century. His work ranges
from a slim volume of verse: *Chamber Music* (1907);
to a great volume of stories: *Dubliners* (1914) (from
which "The Dead" is taken); to an autobiographical
novel: *A Portrait of the Artist As a Young Man*
(1916); to his masterpiece of modern man: *Ulysses*
(1922; 1933 in the U.S.); and, finally, to one of the
great experiments in literature: *Finnegan's Wake*
(1939). All of the above are published by The Vik-
ing Press, New York, except *Ulysses*, which is published by Random House, New York.

THE DEAD

LILY, the caretaker's daughter, was literally run off her feet. Hardly had she brought one gentleman into the little pantry behind the office on the ground floor and helped him off with his overcoat than the wheezy hall-door bell clanged again and she had to scamper along the bare hallway to let in another guest. It was well for her she had not to attend to the ladies also. But Miss Kate and Miss Julia had thought of that and had converted the bathroom upstairs into a ladies' dressing-room. Miss Kate and Miss Julia were there, gossiping and laughing and fussing, walking after each other to the head of the stairs, peering down over the banisters and calling down to Lily to ask her who had come.

It was always a great affair, the Misses Morkan's annual dance. Everybody who knew them came to it, members of the family, old friends of the family, the members of Julia's choir, any of Kate's pupils that were grown up enough, and even some of Mary Jane's pupils too. Never once had it fallen flat. For years and years it had gone off in splendid style, as long as anyone could remember; ever since Kate and Julia, after the death of their brother Pat, had left the house in Stoney Batter and taken Mary Jane, their only niece, to live with them in the dark, gaunt house on Usher's Island, the upper part of which they had rented from Mr. Fulham, the corn-factor on the ground floor. That was a good thirty years ago if it was a day. Mary Jane, who was then a little girl in short clothes, was now the main prop of the household, for she had the organ in Haddington Road. She had been through the Academy and gave a pupils' concert every year in the upper room of the Antient Concert Rooms. Many of her pupils be-

longed to the better-class families on the Kingstown and
Dalkey line. Old as they were, her aunts also did their
share. Julia, though she was quite grey, was still the leading soprano in Adam and Eve's, and Kate, being too feeble
to go about much, gave music lessons to beginners on the
old square piano in the back room. Lily, the caretaker's
daughter, did housemaid's work for them. Though their
life was modest, they believed in eating well; the best of
everything: diamond-bone sirloins, three-shilling tea and
the best bottled stout. But Lily seldom made a mistake in
the orders, so that she got on well with her three mistresses.
They were fussy, that was all. But the only thing they
would not stand was back answers.

Of course, they had good reason to be fussy on such a
night. And then it was long after ten o'clock and yet there
was no sign of Gabriel and his wife. Besides they were
dreadfully afraid that Freddy Malins might turn up
screwed. They would not wish for worlds that any of Mary
Jane's pupils should see him under the influence; and
when he was like that it was sometimes very hard to manage him. Freddy Malins always came late, but they wondered what could be keeping Gabriel: and that was what
brought them every two minutes to the banisters to ask
Lily had Gabriel or Freddy come.

"O, Mr. Conroy," said Lily to Gabriel when she opened
the door for him, "Miss Kate and Miss Julia thought you
were never coming. Good-night, Mrs. Conroy."

"I'll engage they did," said Gabriel, "but they forget
that my wife here takes three mortal hours to dress herself."

He stood on the mat, scraping the snow from his
goloshes, while Lily led his wife to the foot of the stairs
and called out:

"Miss Kate, here's Mrs. Conroy."

Kate and Julia came toddling down the dark stairs at
once. Both of them kissed Gabriel's wife, said she must be
perished alive, and asked was Gabriel with her.

"Here I am as right as the mail, Aunt Kate! Go on up.

I'll follow," called out Gabriel from the dark.

He continued scraping his feet vigorously while the three women went upstairs, laughing, to the ladies' dressing-room. A light fringe of snow lay like a cape on the shoulders of his overcoat and like toecaps on the toes of his goloshes; and, as the buttons of his overcoat slipped with a squeaking noise through the snow-stiffened frieze, a cold, fragrant air from out-of-doors escaped from crevices and folds.

"Is it snowing again, Mr. Conroy?" asked Lily.

She had preceded him into the pantry to help him off with his overcoat. Gabriel smiled at the three syllables she had given his surname and glanced at her. She was a slim, growing girl, pale in complexion and with hay-coloured hair. The gas in the pantry made her look still paler. Gabriel had known her when she was a child and used to sit on the lowest step nursing a rag doll.

"Yes, Lily," he answered, "and I think we're in for a night of it."

He looked up at the pantry ceiling, which was shaking with the stamping and shuffling of feet on the floor above, listened for a moment to the piano and then glanced at the girl, who was folding his overcoat carefully at the end of a shelf.

"Tell me, Lily," he said in a friendly tone, "do you still go to school?"

"O no, sir," she answered. "I'm done schooling this year and more."

"O, then," said Gabriel gaily, "I suppose we'll be going to your wedding one of these fine days with your young man, eh?"

The girl glanced back at him over her shoulder and said with great bitterness:

"The men that is now is only all palaver and what they can get out of you."

Gabriel coloured, as if he felt he had made a mistake and, without looking at her, kicked off his goloshes and flicked actively with his muffler at his patent-leather shoes.

He was a stout, tallish young man. The high colour of his cheeks pushed upwards even to his forehead, where it scattered itself in a few formless patches of pale red; and on his hairless face there scintillated restlessly the polished lenses and the bright gilt rims of the glasses which screened his delicate and restless eyes. His glossy black hair was parted in the middle and brushed in a long curve behind his ears where it curled slightly beneath the groove left by his hat.

When he had flicked lustre into his shoes he stood up and pulled his waistcoat down more tightly on his plump body. Then he took a coin rapidly from his pocket.

"O Lily," he said, thrusting it into her hands, "it's Christmas-time, isn't it? Just . . . here's a little. . . ."

He walked rapidly towards the door.

"O no, sir!" cried the girl, following him. "Really, sir, I wouldn't take it."

"Christmas-time! Christmas-time!" said Gabriel, almost trotting to the stairs and waving his hand to her in deprecation.

The girl, seeing that he had gained the stairs, called out after him:

"Well, tha̶n̶k̶ ̶y̶o̶u̶, sir."

He waited outside the drawing-room door until the waltz should finish, listening to the skirts that swept against it and to the shuffling of feet. He was still discomposed by the girl's bitter and sudden retort. It had cast a gloom over him which he tried to dispel by arranging his cuffs and the bows of his tie. He then took from his waistcoat pocket a little paper and glanced at the headings he had made for his speech. He was undecided about the lines from Robert Browning, for he feared they would be above the heads of his hearers. Some quotation that they would recognise from Shakespeare or from the Melodies would be better. The indelicate clacking of the men's heels and the shuffling of their soles reminded him that their grade of culture differed from his. He would only make himself ridiculous by quoting poetry to them which they could not understand. They would think that he was airing his superior education. He would fail with them just as he had failed with the girl in the pantry. He had taken up a wrong tone. His whole speech was a mistake from first to last, an utter failure.

Just then his aunts and his wife came out of the ladies' dressing-room. His aunts were two small, plainly dressed old women. Aunt Julia was an inch or so the taller. Her hair, drawn low over the tops of her ears, was grey; and grey also, with darker shadows, was her large flaccid face. Though she was stout in build and stood erect, her slow eyes and parted lips gave her the appearance of a woman who did not know where she was or where she was going. Aunt Kate was more vivacious. Her face, healthier than her sister's, was all puckers and creases, like a shrivelled red apple, and her hair, braided in the same old-fashioned way, had not lost its ripe nut colour.

They both kissed Gabriel frankly. He was their favourite nephew, the son of their dead elder sister, Ellen, who had married T. J. Conroy of the Port and Docks.

"Gretta tells me you're not going to take a cab back to Monkstown tonight, Gabriel," said Aunt Kate.

"No," said Gabriel, turning to his wife, "we had quite enough of that last year, hadn't we? Don't you remember, Aunt Kate, what a cold Gretta got out of it? Cab windows rattling all the way, and the east wind blowing in after we passed Merrion. Very jolly it was. Gretta caught a dreadful cold."

Aunt Kate frowned severely and nodded her head at every word.

"Quite right, Gabriel, quite right," she said. "You can't be too careful."

"But as for Gretta there," said Gabriel, "she'd walk home in the snow if she were let."

Mrs. Conroy laughed.

"Don't mind him, Aunt Kate," she said. "He's really an awful bother, what with green shades for Tom's eyes at night and making him do the dumb-bells, and forcing Eva to eat the stirabout. The poor child! And she simply hates the sight of it! . . . O, but you'll never guess what he makes me wear now!"

She broke out into a peal of laughter and glanced at her husband, whose admiring and happy eyes had been wandering from her dress to her face and hair. The two aunts laughed heartily, too, for Gabriel's solicitude was a standing joke with them.

"Goloshes!" said Mrs. Conroy. "That's the latest. Whenever it's wet underfoot I must put on my goloshes. Tonight even, he wanted me to put them on, but I wouldn't. The next thing he'll buy me will be a diving suit."

Gabriel laughed nervously and patted his tie reassuringly, while Aunt Kate nearly doubled herself, so heartily did she enjoy the joke. The smile soon faded from Aunt Julia's face and her mirthless eyes were directed towards her nephew's face. After a pause she asked:

"And what are goloshes, Gabriel?"

"Goloshes, Julia!" exclaimed her sister. "Goodness me, don't you know what goloshes are? You wear them over your . . . over your boots, Gretta, isn't it?"

"Yes," said Mrs. Conroy. "Guttapercha things. We both have a pair now. Gabriel says everyone wears them on the Continent."

"O, on the Continent," murmured Aunt Julia, nodding her head slowly.

Gabriel knitted his brows and said, as if he were slightly angered:

"It's nothing very wonderful, but Gretta thinks it very funny because she says the word reminds her of Christy Minstrels."

"But tell me, Gabriel," said Aunt Kate, with brisk tact. "Of course, you've seen about the room. Gretta was saying . . ."

"O, the room is all right," replied Gabriel. "I've taken one in the Gresham."

"To be sure," said Aunt Kate, "by far the best thing to do. And the children, Gretta, you're not anxious about them?"

"O, for one night," said Mrs. Conroy. "Besides, Bessie will look after them."

"To be sure," said Aunt Kate again. "What a comfort it is to have a girl like that, one you can depend on! There's that Lily, I'm sure I don't know what has come over her lately. She's not the girl she was at all."

Gabriel was about to ask his aunt some questions on this point, but she broke off suddenly to gaze after her sister, who had wandered down the stairs and was craning her neck over the banisters.

"Now, I ask you," she said almost testily, "where is Julia going? Julia! Julia! Where are you going?"

Julia, who had gone half way down one flight, came back and announced blandly: "Here's Freddy."

At the same moment a clapping of hands and a final flourish of the pianist told that the waltz had ended. The drawing-room door was opened from within and some couples came out. Aunt Kate drew Gabriel aside hurriedly and whispered into his ear:

"Slip down, Gabriel, like a good fellow and see if he's all right, and don't let him up if he's screwed. I'm sure he's screwed. I'm sure he is."

Gabriel went to the stairs and listened over the banisters. He could hear two persons talking in the pantry. Then he recognised Freddy Malins' laugh. He went down the stairs noisily.

"It's such a relief," said Aunt Kate to Mrs. Conroy, "that Gabriel is here. I always feel easier in my mind when he's here. . . . Julia, there's Miss Daly and Miss Power will take some refreshment. Thanks for your beautiful waltz, Miss Daly. It made lovely time."

A tall wizen-faced man, with a stiff grizzled moustache

and swarthy skin, who was passing out with his partner, said:

"And may we have some refreshment, too, Miss Morkan?"

"Julia," said Aunt Kate summarily, "and here's Mr. Browne and Miss Furlong. Take them in, Julia, with Miss Daly and Miss Power."

"I'm the man for the ladies," said Mr. Browne, pursing his lips until his moustache bristled and smiling in all his wrinkles. "You know, Miss Morkan, the reason they are so fond of me is—"

He did not finish his sentence, but, seeing that Aunt Kate was out of earshot, at once led the three young ladies into the back room. The middle of the room was occupied by two square tables placed end to end, and on these Aunt Julia and the caretaker were straightening and smoothing a large cloth. On the sideboard were arrayed dishes and plates, and glasses and bundles of knives and forks and spoons. The top of the closed square piano served also as a sideboard for viands and sweets. At a smaller sideboard in one corner two young men were standing, drinking hopbitters.

Mr. Browne led his charges thither and invited them all, in jest, to some ladies' punch, hot, strong and sweet. As they said they never took anything strong, he opened three bottles of lemonade for them. Then he asked one of the young men to move aside, and, taking hold of the decanter, filled out for himself a goodly measure of whisky. The young men eyed him respectfully while he took a trial sip.

"God help me," he said, smiling, "it's the doctor's orders."

His wizened face broke into a broader smile, and the three young ladies laughed in musical echo to his pleasantry, swaying their bodies to and fro, with nervous jerks of their shoulders. The boldest said:

"O, now, Mr. Browne, I'm sure the doctor never ordered

anything of the kind."

Mr. Browne took another sip of his whisky and said, with sidling mimicry:

"Well, you see, I'm like the famous Mrs. Cassidy, who is reported to have said: 'Now, Mary Grimes, if I don't take it, make me take it, for I feel I want it.' "

His hot face had leaned forward a little too confidentially and he had assumed a very low Dublin accent so that the young ladies, with one instinct, received his speech in silence. Miss Furlong, who was one of Mary Jane's pupils, asked Miss Daly what was the name of the pretty waltz she had played; and Mr. Browne, seeing that he was ignored, turned promptly to the two young men who were more appreciative.

A red-faced young woman, dressed in pansy, came into the room, excitedly clapping her hands and crying:

"Quadrilles! Quadrilles!"

Close on her heels came Aunt Kate, crying:

"Two gentlemen and three ladies, Mary Jane!"

"O, here's Mr. Bergin and Mr. Kerrigan," said Mary Jane. "Mr. Kerrigan, will you take Miss Power? Miss Furlong, may I get you a partner, Mr. Bergin. O, that'll just do now."

"Three ladies, Mary Jane," said Aunt Kate.

The two young gentlemen asked the ladies if they might have the pleasure, and Mary Jane turned to Miss Daly.

"O, Miss Daly, you're really awfully good, after playing for the last two dances, but really we're so short of ladies tonight."

"I don't mind in the least, Miss Morkan."

"But I've a nice partner for you, Mr. Bartell D'Arcy, the tenor. I'll get him to sing later on. All Dublin is raving about him."

"Lovely voice, lovely voice!" said Aunt Kate.

As the piano had twice begun the prelude to the first figure Mary Jane led her recruits quickly from the room. They had hardly gone when Aunt Julia wandered slowly into the room, looking behind her at something.

"What is the matter, Julia?" asked Aunt Kate anxiously. "Who is it?"

Julia, who was carrying in a column of table-napkins, turned to her sister and said, simply, as if the question had surprised her:

"It's only Freddy, Kate, and Gabriel with him."

In fact right behind her Gabriel could be seen piloting Freddy Malins across the landing. The latter, a young man of about forty, was of Gabriel's size and build, with very round shoulders. His face was fleshy and pallid, touched with colour only at the thick hanging lobes of his ears and at the wide wings of his nose. He had coarse features, a blunt nose, a convex and receding brow, tumid and protruded lips. His heavy-lidded eyes and the disorder of his scanty hair made him look sleepy. He was laughing heartily in a high key at a story which he had been telling Gabriel on the stairs and at the same time rubbing the knuckles of his left fist backwards and forwards into his left eye.

"Good evening, Freddy," said Aunt Julia.

Freddy Malins bade the Misses Morkan good-evening in what seemed an offhand fashion by reason of the habitual catch in his voice and then, seeing that Mr. Browne was grinning at him from the sideboard, crossed the room on rather shaky legs and began to repeat in an undertone the story he had just told to Gabriel.

"He's not so bad, is he?" said Aunt Kate to Gabriel.

Gabriel's brows were dark but he raised them quickly and answered:

"O, no, hardly noticeable."

"Now, isn't he a terrible fellow!" she said. "And his poor mother made him take the pledge on New Year's Eve. But come on, Gabriel, into the drawing-room."

Before leaving the room with Gabriel she signalled to Mr. Browne by frowning and shaking her forefinger in warning to and fro. Mr. Browne nodded in answer and, when she had gone, said to Freddy Malins:

"Now, then, Teddy, I'm going to fill you out a good glass of lemonade just to buck you up."

Freddy Malins, who was nearing the climax of his story, waved the offer aside impatiently but Mr. Browne, having first called Freddy Malins' attention to a disarray in his dress, filled out and handed him a full glass of lemonade. Freddy Malins' left hand accepted the glass mechanically, his right hand being engaged in the mechanical readjustment of his dress. Mr. Browne, whose face was once more wrinkling with mirth, poured out for himself a glass of whisky while Freddy Malins exploded, before he had well reached the climax of his story, in a kink of high-pitched bronchitic laughter and, setting down his untasted and overflowing glass, began to rub the knuckles of his left fist backwards and forwards into his left eye, repeating words of his last phrase as well as his fit of laughter would allow him.

. . . .

Gabriel could not listen while Mary Jane was playing her Academy piece, full of runs and difficult passages, to the hushed drawing-room. He liked music but the piece she was playing had no melody for him and he doubted whether it had any melody for the other listeners, though they had begged Mary Jane to play something. Four young men, who had come from the refreshment-room to stand in the doorway at the sound of the piano, had gone away quietly in couples after a few minutes. The only persons who seemed to follow the music were Mary Jane herself, her hands racing along the key-board or lifted from it at the pauses like those of a priestess in momentary imprecation, and Aunt Kate standing at her elbow to turn the page.

Gabriel's eyes, irritated by the floor, which glittered with beeswax under the heavy chandelier, wandered to the wall above the piano. A picture of the balcony scene in *Romeo and Juliet* hung there and beside it was a picture

of the two murdered princes in the Tower which Aunt
Julia had worked in red, blue and brown wools when she
was a girl. Probably in the school they had gone to as girls
that kind of work had been taught for one year. His mother had worked for him as a birthday present a waistcoat
of purple tabinet, with little foxes' heads upon it, lined
with brown satin and having round mulberry buttons. It
was strange that his mother had had no musical talent
though Aunt Kate used to call her the brains carrier of
the Morkan family. Both she and Julia had always seemed
a little proud of their serious and matronly sister. Her
photograph stood before the pierglass. She held an open
book on her knees and was pointing out something in it to
Constantine who, dressed in a man-o'-war suit, lay at her
feet. It was she who had chosen the names of her sons for
she was very sensible of the dignity of family life. Thanks
to her, Constantine was now senior curate in Balbriggan
and, thanks to her, Gabriel himself had taken his degree
in the Royal University. A shadow passed over his face as
he remembered her sullen opposition to his marriage.
Some slighting phrases she had used still rankled in his
memory; she had once spoken of Gretta as being country
cute and that was not true of Gretta at all. It was Gretta
who had nursed her during all her last long illness in their
house at Monkstown.

He knew that Mary Jane must be near the end of her
piece for she was playing again the opening melody with
runs of scales after every bar and while he waited for the
end the resentment died down in his heart. The piece
ended with a trill of octaves in the treble and a final deep
octave in the bass. Great applause greeted Mary Jane as,
blushing and rolling up her music nervously, she escaped
from the room. The most vigorous clapping came from
the four young men in the doorway who had gone away
to the refreshment-room at the beginning of the piece but
had come back when the piano had stopped.

Lancers were arranged. Gabriel found himself partnered with Miss Ivors. She was a frank-mannered talkative young lady, with a freckled face and prominent brown eyes. She did not wear a low-cut bodice and the large brooch which was fixed in the front of her collar bore on it an Irish device and motto.

When they had taken their places she said abruptly:

"I have a crow to pluck with you."

"With me?" said Gabriel.

She nodded her head gravely.

"What is it?" asked Gabriel, smiling at her solemn manner.

"Who is G. C.?" answered Miss Ivors, turning her eyes upon him.

Gabriel coloured and was about to knit his brows, as if he did not understand, when she said bluntly:

"O, innocent Amy! I have found out that you write for *The Daily Express.* Now, aren't you ashamed of yourself?"

"Why should I be ashamed of myself?" asked Gabriel, blinking his eyes and trying to smile.

"Well, I'm ashamed of you," said Miss Ivors frankly. "To say you'd write for a paper like that. I didn't think you were a West Briton."

A look of perplexity appeared on Gabriel's face. It was true that he wrote a literary column every Wednesday in *The Daily Express,* for which he was paid fifteen shillings. But that did not make him a West Briton surely. The books he received for review were almost more welcome than the paltry cheque. He loved to feel the covers and turn over the pages of newly printed books. Nearly every day when his teaching in the college was ended he used to wander down the quays to the second-hand booksellers, to Hickey's on Bachelor's Walk, to Webb's or Massey's on Aston's Quay, or to O'Clohissey's in the by-street. He did not know how to meet her charge. He wanted to say that literature was above politics. But they were friends of many years' standing and their careers had been parallel, first at the University and then as teachers: he could not risk a grandiose phrase with her. He continued blinking his eyes and trying to smile and murmured lamely that he saw nothing political in writing reviews of books.

When their turn to cross had come he was still perplexed and inattentive. Miss Ivors promptly took his hand in a warm grasp and said in a soft friendly tone:

"Of course, I was only joking. Come, we cross now."

When they were together again she spoke of the University question and Gabriel felt more at ease. A friend of hers had shown her his review of Browning's poems. That was how she had found out the secret: but she liked the review immensely. Then she said suddenly:

"O, Mr. Conroy, will you come for an excursion to the Aran Isles this summer? We're going to stay there a whole month. It will be splendid out in the Atlantic. You ought to come. Mr. Clancy is coming, and Mr. Kilkelly and Kathleen Kearney. It would be splendid for Gretta too if she'd come. She's from Connacht, isn't she?"

"Her people are," said Gabriel shortly.

"But you will come, won't you?" said Miss Ivors, laying her warm hand eagerly on his arm.

"The fact is," said Gabriel, "I have just arranged to go—"

"Go where?" asked Miss Ivors.

"Well, you know, every year I go for a cycling tour with some fellows and so—"

"But where?" asked Miss Ivors.

"Well, we usually go to France or Belgium or perhaps Germany," said Gabriel awkwardly.

"And why do you go to France and Belgium," said Miss Ivors, "instead of visiting your own land?"

"Well," said Gabriel, "it's partly to keep in touch with the languages and partly for a change."

"And haven't you your own language to keep in touch with—Irish?" asked Miss Ivors.

"Well," said Gabriel, "if it comes to that, you know, Irish is not my language."

Their neighbours had turned to listen to the cross-examination. Gabriel glanced right and left nervously and tried to keep his good humour under the ordeal which was making a blush invade his forehead.

"And haven't you your own land to visit," continued Miss Ivors, "that you know nothing of, your own people, and your own country?"

"O, to tell you the truth," retorted Gabriel suddenly, "I'm sick of my own country, sick of it!"

"Why?" asked Miss Ivors.

Gabriel did not answer for his retort had heated him.

"Why?" repeated Miss Ivors.

They had to go visiting together and, as he had not answered her, Miss Ivors said warmly:

"Of course, you've no answer."

Gabriel tried to cover his agitation by taking part in the dance with great energy. He avoided her eyes for he had seen a sour expression on her face. But when they met in the long chain he was surprised to feel his hand firmly pressed. She looked at him from under her brows for a moment quizzically until he smiled. Then, just as the chain was about to start again, she stood on tiptoe and whispered into his ear:

"West Briton!"

When the lancers were over Gabriel went away to a remote corner of the room where Freddy Malins' mother was sitting. She was a stout feeble old woman with white hair. Her voice had a catch in it like her son's and she stuttered slightly. She had been told that Freddy had come and that he was nearly all right. Gabriel asked her whether she had had a good crossing. She lived with her married daughter in Glasgow and came to Dublin on a visit once a year. She answered placidly that she had had a beautiful crossing and that the captain had been most attentive to her. She spoke also of the beautiful house her daughter kept in Glasgow, and of all the friends they had there. While her tongue rambled on Gabriel tried to banish from his mind all memory of the unpleasant incident with Miss Ivors. Of course the girl or woman, or whatever she was, was an enthusiast but there was a time for all things. Perhaps he ought not to have answered her like that. But she had no right to call him a West Briton before people, even in joke. She had tried to make him ridiculous before people, heckling him and staring at him with her rabbit's eyes.

He saw his wife making her way towards him through the waltzing couples. When she reached him she said into his ear:

"Gabriel, Aunt Kate wants to know won't you carve the goose as usual. Miss Daly will carve the ham and I'll do the pudding."

"All right," said Gabriel.

"She's sending in the younger ones first as soon as this waltz is over so that we'll have the table to ourselves."

"Were you dancing?" asked Gabriel.

"Of course I was. Didn't you see me? What row had you with Molly Ivors?"

"No row. Why? Did she say so?"

"Something like that. I'm trying to get that Mr. D'Arcy to sing. He's full of conceit, I think."

"There was no row," said Gabriel moodily, "only she wanted me to go for a trip to the west of Ireland and I said I wouldn't."

His wife clasped her hands excitedly and gave a little jump.

"O, do go, Gabriel," she cried. "I'd love to see Galway again."

"You can go if you like," said Gabriel coldly.

She looked at him for a moment, then turned to Mrs. Malins and said:

"There's a nice husband for you, Mrs. Malins."

While she was threading her way back across the room Mrs. Malins, without adverting to the interruption, went on to tell Gabriel what beautiful places there were in Scotland and beautiful scenery. Her son-in-law brought them every year to the lakes and they used to go fishing. Her son-in-law was a splendid fisher. One day he caught a beautiful big fish and the man in the hotel cooked it for their dinner.

Gabriel hardly heard what she said. Now that supper was coming near he began to think again about his speech and about the quotation. When he saw Freddy Malins coming across the room to visit his mother Gabriel left the chair free for him and retired into the embrasure of the window. The room had already cleared and from the back room came the clatter of plates and knives. Those who still remained in the drawing-room seemed tired of dancing and were conversing quietly in little groups. Gabriel's warm trembling fingers tapped the cold pane of the window. How cool it must be outside! How pleasant it would be to walk out alone, first along by the river and then through the park! The snow would be lying on the branches of the trees and forming a bright cap on the top of the Wellington Monument. How much more pleasant it would be there than at the supper-table!

He ran over the headings of his speech: Irish hospitality, sad memories, the Three Graces, Paris, the quotation from Browning. He repeated to himself a phrase he had written in his review: "One feels that one is listening to a thought-tormented music." Miss Ivors had praised the review. Was she sincere? Had she really any life of her own behind all her propagandism? There had never been any ill-feeling between them until that night. It unnerved him to think that she would be at the supper-table, looking up at him while he spoke with her critical quizzing eyes. Perhaps she would not be sorry to see him fail in his speech. An idea came into his mind and gave him courage. He would say, alluding to Aunt Kate and Aunt Julia: "Ladies and Gentlemen, the generation which is now on the wane among us may have had its faults but for my part I think it had certain qualities of hospitality, of humour, of humanity, which the new and very serious and hypereducated gen-

eration that is growing up around us seems to me to lack."
Very good: that was one for Miss Ivors. What did he care
that his aunts were only two ignorant old women?

A murmur in the room attracted his attention. Mr.
Browne was advancing from the door, gallantly escorting
Aunt Julia, who leaned upon his arm, smiling and hanging
her head. An irregular musketry of applause escorted her
also as far as the piano and then, as Mary Jane seated herself on the stool, and Aunt Julia, no longer smiling, half
turned so as to pitch her voice fairly into the room, gradually ceased. Gabriel recognised the prelude. It was that
of an old song of Aunt Julia's—*Arrayed for the Bridal.* Her
voice, strong and clear in tone, attacked with great spirit
the runs which embellish the air and though she sang very
rapidly she did not miss even the smallest of the grace
notes. To follow the voice, without looking at the singer's
face, was to feel and share the excitement of swift and secure flight. Gabriel applauded loudly with all the others
at the close of the song and loud applause was borne in
from the invisible supper-table. It sounded so genuine that
a little colour struggled into Aunt Julia's face as she bent
to replace in the music-stand the old leather-bound song-
book that had her initials on the cover. Freddy Malins,
who had listened with his head perched sideways to hear
her better, was still applauding when everyone else had
ceased and talking animatedly to his mother who nodded
her head gravely and slowly in acquiescence. At last, when
he could clap no more, he stood up suddenly and hurried
across the room to Aunt Julia whose hand he seized and
held in both his hands, shaking it when words failed him
or the catch in his voice proved too much for him.

"I was just telling my mother," he said, "I never heard
you sing so well, never. No, I never heard your voice so
good as it is tonight. Now! Would you believe that now?
That's the truth. Upon my word and honour that's the
truth. I never heard your voice sound so fresh and so . . .
so clear and fresh, never."

Aunt Julia smiled broadly and murmured something about compliments as she released her hand from his grasp. Mr. Browne extended his open hand towards her and said to those who were near him in the manner of a showman introducing a prodigy to an audience:

"Miss Julia Morkan, my latest discovery!"

He was laughing very heartily at this himself when Freddy Malins turned to him and said:

"Well, Browne, if you're serious you might make a worse discovery. All I can say is I never heard her sing half so well as long as I am coming here. And that's the honest truth."

"Neither did I," said Mr. Browne. "I think her voice has greatly improved."

Aunt Julia shrugged her shoulders and said with meek pride:

"Thirty years ago I hadn't a bad voice as voices go."

"I often told Julia," said Aunt Kate emphatically, "that she was simply thrown away in that choir. But she never would be said by me."

She turned as if to appeal to the good sense of the others against a refractory child while Aunt Julia gazed in front of her, a vague smile of reminiscence playing on her face.

"No," continued Aunt Kate, "she wouldn't be said or led by anyone, slaving there in that choir night and day, night and day. Six o'clock on Christmas morning! And all for what?"

"Well, isn't it for the honour of God, Aunt Kate?" asked Mary Jane, twisting round on the piano-stool and smiling.

Aunt Kate turned fiercely on her niece and said:

"I know all about the honour of God, Mary Jane, but I think it's not at all honourable for the pope to turn out the women out of the choirs that have slaved there all their lives and put little whipper-snappers of boys over their heads. I suppose it is for the good of the Church if the pope does it. But it's not just, Mary Jane, and it's not right."

She had worked herself into a passion and would have continued in defence of her sister for it was a sore subject with her but Mary Jane, seeing that all the dancers had come back, intervened pacifically:

"Now, Aunt Kate, you're giving scandal to Mr. Browne who is of the other persuasion."

Aunt Kate turned to Mr. Browne, who was grinning at this allusion to his religion, and said hastily:

"O, I don't question the pope's being right. I'm only a stupid old woman and I wouldn't presume to do such a thing. But there's such a thing as common everyday polite-ness and gratitude. And if I were in Julia's place I'd tell that Father Healey straight up to his face . . ."

"And besides, Aunt Kate," said Mary Jane, "we really are all hungry and when we are hungry we are all very quarrelsome."

"And when we are thirsty we are also quarrelsome," added Mr. Browne.

"So that we had better go to supper," said Mary Jane, "and finish the discussion afterwards."

On the landing outside the drawing-room Gabriel found his wife and Mary Jane trying to persuade Miss Ivors to stay for supper. But Miss Ivors, who had put on her hat and was buttoning her cloak, would not stay. She did not feel in the least hungry and she had already overstayed her time.

"But only for ten minutes, Molly," said Mrs. Conroy. "That won't delay you."

"To take a pick itself," said Mary Jane, "after all your dancing."

"I really couldn't," said Miss Ivors.

"I am afraid you didn't enjoy yourself at all," said Mary Jane hopelessly.

"Ever so much, I assure you," said Miss Ivors, "but you really must let me run off now."

"But how can you get home?" asked Mrs. Conroy.

"O, it's only two steps up the quay."

Gabriel hesitated a moment and said:

"If you will allow me, Miss Ivors, I'll see you home if you are really obliged to go."

But Miss Ivors broke away from them.

"I won't hear of it," she cried. "For goodness' sake go in to your suppers and don't mind me. I'm quite well able to take care of myself."

"Well, you're the comical girl, Molly," said Mrs. Conroy frankly.

"Beannacht libh," cried Miss Ivors, with a laugh, as she ran down the staircase.

Mary Jane gazed after her, a moody puzzled expression on her face, while Mrs. Conroy leaned over the banisters to listen for the hall-door. Gabriel asked himself was he the cause of her abrupt departure. But she did not seem to be in ill humour: she had gone away laughing. He stared blankly down the staircase.

At the moment Aunt Kate came toddling out of the supper-room, almost wringing her hands in despair.

"Where is Gabriel?" she cried. "Where on earth is Gabriel? There's everyone waiting in there, stage to let, and nobody to carve the goose!"

"Here I am, Aunt Kate!" cried Gabriel, with sudden animation, "ready to carve a flock of geese, if necessary."

A fat brown goose lay at one end of the table and at the other end, on a bed of creased paper strewn with sprigs of parsley, lay a great ham, stripped of its outer skin and peppered over with crust crumbs, a neat paper frill round its shin and beside this was a round of spiced beef. Between these rival ends ran parallel lines of side-dishes: two little minsters of jelly, red and yellow; a shallow dish full of blocks of blancmange and red jam, a large green leaf-shaped dish with a stalk-shaped handle, on which lay bunches of purple raisins and peeled almonds, a companion dish on which lay a solid rectangle of Smyrna figs, a dish of custard topped with grated nutmeg, a small bowl full of chocolates and sweets wrapped in gold and silver

papers and a glass vase in which stood some tall celery
stalks. In the centre of the table there stood, as sentries to
a fruit-stand which upheld a pyramid of oranges and
American apples, two squat old-fashioned decanters of
cut glass, one containing port and the other dark sherry.
On the closed square piano a pudding in a huge yellow
dish lay in waiting and behind it were three squads of
bottles of stout and ale and minerals, drawn up according
to the colours of their uniforms, the first two black, with
brown and red labels, the third and smallest squad white,
with transverse green sashes.

Gabriel took his seat boldly at the head of the table
and, having looked to the edge of the carver, plunged his
fork firmly into the goose. He felt quite at ease now for he
was an expert carver and liked nothing better than to find
himself at the head of a well-laden table.

"Miss Furlong, what shall I send you?" he asked. "A
wing or a slice of the breast?"

"Just a small slice of the breast."

"Miss Higgins, what for you?"

"O, anything at all, Mr. Conroy."

While Gabriel and Miss Daly exchanged plates of goose
and plates of ham and spiced beef Lily went from guest
to guest with a dish of hot floury potatoes wrapped in a
white napkin. This was Mary Jane's idea and she had also
suggested apple sauce for the goose but Aunt Kate had
said that plain roast goose without any apple sauce had
always been good enough for her and she hoped she might
never eat worse. Mary Jane waited on her pupils and saw
that they got the best slices and Aunt Kate and Aunt Julia
opened and carried across from the piano bottles of stout
and ale for the gentlemen and bottles of minerals for the
ladies. There was a great deal of confusion and laughter
and noise, the noise of orders and counter-orders, of knives
and forks, of corks and glass-stoppers. Gabriel began to
carve second helpings as soon as he had finished the first
round without serving himself. Everyone protested loudly

so that he compromised by taking a long draught of stout for he had found the carving hot work. Mary Jane settled down quietly to her supper but Aunt Kate and Aunt Julia were still toddling round the table, walking on each other's heels, getting in each other's way and giving each other unheeded orders. Mr. Browne begged of them to sit down and eat their suppers and so did Gabriel but they said there was time enough, so that, at last, Freddy Malins stood up and, capturing Aunt Kate, plumped her down on her chair amid general laughter.

When everyone had been well served Gabriel said, smiling:

"Now, if anyone wants a little more of what vulgar people call stuffing let him or her speak."

A chorus of voices invited him to begin his own supper and Lily came forward with three potatoes which she had reserved for him.

"Very well," said Gabriel amiably, as he took another preparatory draught, "kindly forget my existence, ladies and gentlemen, for a few minutes."

He set to his supper and took no part in the conversation with which the table covered Lily's removal of the plates. The subject of talk was the opera company which was then at the Theatre Royal. Mr. Bartell D'Arcy, the tenor, a dark-complexioned young man with a smart moustache, praised very highly the leading contralto of the company but Miss Furlong thought she had a rather vulgar style of production. Freddy Malins said there was a Negro chieftain singing in the second part of the Gaiety pantomime who had one of the finest tenor voices he had ever heard.

"Have you heard him?" he asked Mr. Bartell D'Arcy across the table.

"No," answered Mr. Bartell D'Arcy carelessly.

"Because," Freddy Malins explained, "now I'd be curious to hear your opinion of him. I think he has a grand voice."

"It takes Teddy to find out the really good things," said

Mr. Browne familiarly to the table.

"And why couldn't he have a voice too?" asked Freddy Malins sharply. "Is it because he's only a black?"

Nobody answered this question and Mary Jane led the table back to the legitimate opera. One of her pupils had given her a pass for *Mignon*. Of course it was very fine, she said, but it made her think of poor Georgina Burns. Mr. Browne could go back farther still, to the old Italian companies that used to come to Dublin— Tietjens, Ilma de Murzka, Campanini, the great Trebelli, Giuglini, Ravelli, Aramburo. Those were the days, he said, when there was something like singing to be heard in Dublin. He told too of how the top gallery of the old Royal used to be packed night after night, of how one night an Italian tenor had sung five encores to *Let me like a Soldier fall,* introducing a high C every time, and of how the gallery boys would sometimes in their enthusiasm unyoke the horses from the carriage of some great *prima donna* and pull her themselves through the streets to her hotel. Why did they never play the grand old operas now, he asked, *Dinorah, Lucrezia Borgia?* Because they could not get the voices to sing them: that was why.

"O, well," said Mr. Bartell D'Arcy, "I presume there are as good singers today as there were then."

"Where are they?" asked Mr. Browne defiantly.

"In London, Paris, Milan," said Mr. Bartell D'Arcy warmly. "I suppose Caruso, for example, is quite as good, if not better than any of the men you have mentioned."

"Maybe so," said Mr. Browne. "But I may tell you I doubt it strongly."

"O, I'd give anything to hear Caruso sing," said Mary Jane.

"For me," said Aunt Kate, who had been picking a bone, "there was only one tenor. To please me, I mean. But I suppose none of you ever heard of him."

"Who was he, Miss Morkan?" asked Mr. Bartell D'Arcy politely.

"His name," said Aunt Kate, "was Parkinson. I heard him when he was in his prime and I think he had then the purest tenor voice that was ever put into a man's throat."

"Strange," said Mr. Bartell D'Arcy. "I never even heard of him."

"Yes, yes, Miss Morkan is right," said Mr. Browne. "I remember hearing of old Parkinson but he's too far back for me."

"A beautiful, pure, sweet, mellow English tenor," said Aunt Kate with enthusiasm.

Gabriel having finished, the huge pudding was transferred to the table. The clatter of forks and spoons began again. Gabriel's wife served out spoonfuls of the pudding and passed the plates down the table. Midway down they were held up by Mary Jane, who replenished them with raspberry or orange jelly or with blancmange and jam. The pudding was of Aunt Julia's making and she received praises for it from all quarters. She herself said that it was not quite brown enough.

"Well, I hope, Miss Morkan," said Mr. Browne, "that I'm brown enough for you because, you know, I'm all brown."

All the gentlemen, except Gabriel, ate some of the pudding out of compliment to Aunt Julia. As Gabriel never ate sweets the celery had been left for him. Freddy Malins also took a stalk of celery and ate it with his pudding. He had been told that celery was a capital thing for the blood and he was just then under doctor's care. Mrs. Malins, who had been silent all through the supper, said that her son was going down to Mount Melleray in a week or so. The table then spoke of Mount Melleray, how bracing the air was down there, how hospitable the monks were and how they never asked for a penny-piece from their guests.

"And do you mean to say," asked Mr. Browne incredulously, "that a chap can go down there and put up there as if it were a hotel and live on the fat of the land and then come away without paying anything?"

"O, most people give some donation to the monastery when they leave," said Mary Jane.

"I wish we had an institution like that in our Church," said Mr. Browne candidly.

He was astonished to hear that the monks never spoke, got up at two in the morning and slept in their coffins. He asked what they did it for.

"That's the rule of the order," said Aunt Kate firmly.

"Yes, but why?" asked Mr. Browne.

Aunt Kate repeated that it was the rule, that was all. Mr. Browne still seemed not to understand. Freddy Malins explained to him, as best he could, that the monks were trying to make up for the sins committed by all the sinners in the outside world. The explanation was not very clear for Mr. Browne grinned and said:

"I like that idea very much but wouldn't a comfortable spring bed do them as well as a coffin?"

"The coffin," said Mary Jane, "is to remind them of their last end."

As the subject had grown lugubrious it was buried in a silence of the table during which Mrs. Malins could be heard saying to her neighbour in an indistinct undertone:

"They are very good men, the monks, very pious men."

The raisins and almonds and figs and apples and oranges and chocolates and sweets were now passed about the table and Aunt Julia invited all the guests to have either port or sherry. At first Mr. Bartell D'Arcy refused to take either but one of his neighbours nudged him and whispered something to him upon which he allowed his glass to be filled. Gradually as the last glasses were being filled the conversation ceased. A pause followed, broken only by the noise of the wine and by unsettlings of chairs. The Misses Morkan, all three, looked down at the tablecloth. Someone coughed once or twice and then a few gentlemen patted the table gently as a signal for silence. The silence came and Gabriel pushed back his chair and stood up.

The patting at once grew louder in encouragement and

then ceased altogether. Gabriel leaned his ten trembling fingers on the tablecloth and smiled nervously at the company. Meeting a row of upturned faces he raised his eyes to the chandelier. The piano was playing a waltz tune and he could hear the skirts sweeping against the drawing-room door. People, perhaps, were standing in the snow on the quay outside, gazing up at the lighted windows and listening to the waltz music. The air was pure there. In the distance lay the park where the trees were weighted with snow. The Wellington Monument wore a gleaming cap of snow that flashed westward over the white field of Fifteen Acres.

He began:

"Ladies and Gentlemen,

"It has fallen to my lot this evening, as in years past, to perform a very pleasing task but a task for which I am afraid my poor powers as a speaker are all too inadequate."

"No, no!" said Mr. Browne.

"But, however that may be, I can only ask you tonight to take the will for the deed and to lend me your attention for a few moments while I endeavour to express to you in words what my feelings are on this occasion.

"Ladies and Gentlemen, it is not the first time that we have gathered together under this hospitable roof, around this hospitable board. It is not the first time that we have been the recipients—or perhaps, I had better say, the victims—of the hospitality of certain good ladies."

He made a circle in the air with his arm and paused. Everyone laughed or smiled at Aunt Kate and Aunt Julia and Mary Jane who all turned crimson with pleasure. Gabriel went on more boldly:

"I feel more strongly with every recurring year that our country has no tradition which does it so much honour and which it should guard so jealously as that of its hospitality. It is a tradition that is unique as far as my experience goes (and I have visited not a few places abroad) among the modern nations. Some would say, perhaps, that with us it is rather a failing than anything to be boasted of. But granted even that, it is, to my mind, a princely failing, and one that I trust will long be cultivated among us. Of one thing, at least, I am sure. As long as this one roof shelters the good ladies aforesaid—and I wish from my heart it may do so for many and many a long year to come—the tradition of genuine warm-hearted courteous Irish hospitality, which our forefathers have handed down to us and which we in turn must hand down to our descendants, is still alive among us."

A hearty murmur of assent ran round the table. It shot through Gabriel's mind that Miss Ivors was not there and that she had gone away discourteously: and he said with confidence in himself:

"Ladies and Gentlemen,

"A new generation is growing up in our midst, a generation actuated by new ideas and new principles. It is serious and enthusiastic for these new ideas and its enthusiasm, even when it is misdirected, is, I believe, in the main sincere. But we are living in a sceptical and, if I may use the phrase, a thought-tormented age: and sometimes I fear that this new generation, educated or hypereducated as it is, will lack those qualities of humanity, of hospitality, of kindly humour which belonged to an older day. Listening tonight to the names of all those great singers of the past it seemed to me, I must confess, that we were living in a less spacious age. Those days might, without exaggeration, be called spacious days: and if they are gone beyond recall let us hope, at least, that in gatherings such as this we shall still speak of them with pride and affection, still cherish in our hearts the memory of those dead and gone great ones whose fame the world will not willingly let die."

"Hear, hear!" said Mr. Browne loudly.

"But yet," continued Gabriel, his voice falling into a softer inflection, "there are always in gatherings such as this sadder thoughts that will recur to our minds: thoughts of the past, of youth, of changes, of absent faces that we miss here tonight. Our path through life is strewn with many such sad memories: and were we to brood upon them always we could not find the heart to go on bravely with our work among the living. We have all of us living duties and living affections which claim, and rightly claim, our strenuous endeavours.

"Therefore, I will not linger on the past. I will not let any gloomy moralising intrude upon us here tonight. Here we are gathered together for a brief moment from the bustle and rush of our everyday routine. We are met here as friends, in the spirit of good-fellowship, as colleagues, also to a certain extent, in the true spirit of *camaraderie*, and as the guests of—what shall I call them?— the Three Graces of the Dublin musical world."

The table burst into applause and laughter at this allusion. Aunt Julia vainly asked each of her neighbours in turn to tell her what Gabriel had said.

"He says we are the Three Graces, Aunt Julia," said Mary Jane.

Aunt Julia did not understand but she looked up, smiling, at Gabriel, who continued in the same vein:

"Ladies and Gentlemen,

"I will not attempt to play tonight the part that Paris played on another occasion. I will not attempt to choose between them. The task would be an invidious one and one beyond my poor powers. For when I view them in turn, whether it be our chief hostess herself, whose good heart, whose too good heart, has become a byword with all who know her, or her sister, who seems to be gifted with perennial youth and whose singing must have been a surprise and a revelation to us all tonight, or, last but not least, when I consider our youngest hostess, talented, cheerful, hard-working and the best of nieces, I confess, Ladies and Gentlemen, that I do not know to which of them I should award the prize."

Gabriel glanced down at his aunts and, seeing the large smile on Aunt Julia's face and the tears which had risen to Aunt Kate's eyes, hastened to his close. He raised his glass of port gallantly, while every member of the company fingered a glass expectantly, and said loudly:

"Let us toast them all three together. Let us drink to their health, wealth, long life, happiness and prosperity and may they long continue to hold the proud and self-won position which they hold in their profession and the position of honour and affection which they hold in our hearts."

All the guests stood up, glass in hand, and turning towards the three seated ladies, sang in unison, with Mr. Browne as leader:

> *For they are jolly gay fellows,*
> *For they are jolly gay fellows,*
> *For they are jolly gay fellows,*
> *Which nobody can deny.*

Aunt Kate was making frank use of her handkerchief and even Aunt Julia seemed moved. Freddy Malins beat time with his pudding-fork and the singers turned towards one another, as if in melodious conference, while they sang with emphasis:

> *Unless he tells a lie,*
> *Unless he tells a lie,*

Then, turning once more towards their hostesses, they sang:

> *For they are jolly gay fellows,*
> *For they are jolly gay fellows,*
> *For they are jolly gay fellows,*
> *Which nobody can deny.*

The acclamation which followed was taken up beyond the door of the supper-room by many of the other guests and renewed time after time, Freddy Malins acting as officer with his fork on high.

.   .   .   .

The piercing morning air came into the hall where they were standing so that Aunt Kate said:

"Close the door, somebody. Mrs. Malins will get her death of cold."

"Browne is out there, Aunt Kate," said Mary Jane.

"Browne is everywhere," said Aunt Kate, lowering her voice.

Mary Jane laughed at her tone.

"Really," she said archly, "he is very attentive."

"He has been laid on here like the gas," said Aunt Kate in the same tone, "all during the Christmas."

She laughed herself this time good-humouredly and then added quickly:

"But tell him to come in, Mary Jane, and close the door. I hope to goodness he didn't hear me."

At that moment the hall-door was opened and Mr. Browne came in from the doorstep, laughing as if his heart would break. He was dressed in a long green overcoat with mock astrakhan cuffs and collar and wore on his head an oval fur cap. He pointed down the snow-covered quay from where the sound of shrill prolonged whistling was borne in.

"Teddy will have all the cabs in Dublin out," he said.

Gabriel advanced from the little pantry behind the office, struggling into his overcoat and, looking round the hall, said:

"Gretta not down yet?"

"She's getting on her things, Gabriel," said Aunt Kate.

"Who's playing up there?" asked Gabriel.

"Nobody. They're all gone."

"O no, Aunt Kate," said Mary Jane. "Bartell D'Arcy and Miss O'Callaghan aren't gone yet."

"Someone is fooling at the piano anyhow," said Gabriel.

Mary Jane glanced at Gabriel and Mr. Browne and said with a shiver:

"It makes me feel cold to look at you two gentlemen muffled up like that. I wouldn't like to face your journey home at this hour."

"I'd like nothing better this minute," said Mr. Browne
stoutly, "than a rattling fine walk in the country or a fast
drive with a good spanking goer between the shafts."

"We used to have a very good horse and trap at home,"
said Aunt Julia sadly.

"The never-to-be-forgotten Johnny," said Mary Jane,
laughing.

Aunt Kate and Gabriel laughed too.

"Why, what was wonderful about Johnny?" asked Mr.
Browne.

"The late lamented Patrick Morkan, our grandfather,
that is," explained Gabriel, "commonly known in his
later years as the old gentleman, was a glue-boiler."

"O, now, Gabriel," said Aunt Kate, laughing, "he had
a starch mill."

"Well, glue or starch," said Gabriel, "the old gentleman had a horse by the name of Johnny. And Johnny used
to work in the old gentleman's mill, walking round and
round in order to drive the mill. That was all very well;
but now comes the tragic part about Johnny. One fine day
the old gentleman thought he'd like to drive out with the
quality to a military review in the park."

"The Lord have mercy on his soul," said Aunt Kate
compassionately.

"Amen," said Gabriel. "So the old gentleman, as I said,
harnessed Johnny and put on his very best tall hat and his
very best stock collar and drove out in grand style from
his ancestral mansion somewhere near Back Lane, I
think."

Everyone laughed, even Mrs. Malins, at Gabriel's manner and Aunt Kate said:

"O, now, Gabriel, he didn't live in Back Lane, really.
Only the mill was there."

"Out from the mansion of his forefathers," continued
Gabriel, "he drove with Johnny. And everything went on
beautifully until Johnny came in sight of King Billy's

statue: and whether he fell in love with the horse King Billy sits on or whether he thought he was back again in the mill, anyhow he began to walk round the statue."

Gabriel paced in a circle round the hall in his goloshes amid the laughter of the others.

"Round and round he went," said Gabriel, "and the old gentleman, who was a very pompous old gentleman, was highly indignant. 'Go on, sir! What do you mean, sir? Johnny! Johnny! Most extraordinary conduct! Can't understand the horse!' "

The peal of laughter which followed Gabriel's imitation of the incident was interrupted by a resounding knock at the hall door. Mary Jane ran to open it and let in Freddy Malins. Freddy Malins, with his hat well back on his head and his shoulders humped with cold, was puffing and steaming after his exertions.

"I could only get one cab," he said.

"O, we'll find another along the quay," said Gabriel.

"Yes," said Aunt Kate. "Better not keep Mrs. Malins standing in the draught."

Mrs. Malins was helped down the front steps by her son and Mr. Browne and, after many manoeuvres, hoisted into the cab. Freddy Malins clambered in after her and spent a long time settling her on the seat, Mr. Browne helping him with advice. At last she was settled comfortably and Freddy Malins invited Mr. Browne into the cab. There was a good deal of confused talk, and then Mr. Browne got into the cab. The cabman settled his rug over his knees, and bent down for the address. The confusion grew greater and the cabman was directed differently by Freddy Malins and Mr. Browne, each of whom had his head out through a window of the cab. The difficulty was to know where to drop Mr. Browne along the route, and Aunt Kate, Aunt Julia and Mary Jane helped the discussion from the doorstep with cross-directions and contradictions and abundance of laughter. As for Freddy Malins he was speechless with laughter. He popped his head in and out

of the window every moment to the great danger of his
hat, and told his mother how the discussion was progressing, till at last Mr. Browne shouted to the bewildered
cabman above the din of everybody's laughter:

"Do you know Trinity College?"

"Yes, sir," said the cabman.

"Well, drive bang up against Trinity College gates,"
said Mr. Browne, "and then we'll tell you where to go.
You understand now?"

"Yes, sir," said the cabman.

"Make like a bird for Trinity College."

"Right, sir," said the cabman.

The horse was whipped up and the cab rattled off along
the quay amid a chorus of laughter and adieus.

Gabriel had not gone to the door with the others. He
was in a dark part of the hall gazing up the staircase. A
woman was standing near the top of the first flight, in the
shadow also. He could not see her face but he could see
the terra-cotta and salmon-pink panels of her skirt which
the shadow made appear black and white. It was his wife.
She was leaning on the banisters, listening to something.
Gabriel was surprised at her stillness and strained his ear
to listen also. But he could hear little save the noise of
laughter and dispute on the front steps, a few chords
struck on the piano and a few notes of a man's voice singing.

He stood still in the gloom of the hall, trying to catch
the air that the voice was singing and gazing up at his wife.
There was grace and mystery in her attitude as if she were
a symbol of something. He asked himself what is a woman
standing on the stairs in the shadow, listening to distant
music, a symbol of. If he were a painter he would paint
her in that attitude. Her blue felt hat would show off the
bronze of her hair against the darkness and the dark panels
of her skirt would show off the light ones. *Distant Music*
he would call the picture if he were a painter.

The hall-door was closed; and Aunt Kate, Aunt Julia

and Mary Jane came down the hall, still laughing.

"Well, isn't Freddy terrible?" said Mary Jane. "He's really terrible."

Gabriel said nothing but pointed up the stairs towards where his wife was standing. Now that the hall-door was closed the voice and the piano could be heard more clearly. Gabriel held up his hand for them to be silent. The song seemed to be in the old Irish tonality and the singer seemed uncertain both of his words and of his voice. The voice, made plaintive by distance and by the singer's hoarseness, faintly illuminated the cadence of the air with words expressing grief:

> *O, the rain falls on my heavy locks*
> *And the dew wets my skin,*
> *My babe lies cold . . .*

"O," exclaimed Mary Jane. "It's Bartell D'Arcy singing and he wouldn't sing all the night. O, I'll get him to sing a song before he goes."

"O, do, Mary Jane," said Aunt Kate.

Mary Jane brushed past the others and ran to the staircase, but before she reached it the singing stopped and the piano was closed abruptly.

"O, what a pity!" she cried. "Is he coming down, Gretta?"

Gabriel heard his wife answer yes and saw her come down towards them. A few steps behind her were Mr. Bartell D'Arcy and Miss O'Callaghan.

"O, Mr. D'Arcy," cried Mary Jane, "it's downright mean of you to break off like that when we were all in raptures listening to you."

"I have been at him all the evening," said Miss O'Callaghan, "and Mrs. Conroy, too, and he told us he had a dreadful cold and couldn't sing."

"O, Mr. D'Arcy," said Aunt Kate, "now that was a great fib to tell."

"Can't you see that I'm as hoarse as a crow?" said Mr.

D'Arcy roughly.

He went into the pantry hastily and put on his overcoat. The others, taken aback by his rude speech, could find nothing to say. Aunt Kate wrinkled her brows and made signs to the others to drop the subject. Mr. D'Arcy stood swathing his neck carefully and frowning.

"It's the weather," said Aunt Julia, after a pause.

"Yes, everybody has colds," said Aunt Kate readily, "everybody."

"They say," said Mary Jane, "we haven't had snow like it for thirty years; and I read this morning in the newspapers that the snow is general all over Ireland."

"I love the look of snow," said Aunt Julia sadly.

"So do I," said Miss O'Callaghan. "I think Christmas is never really Christmas unless we have the snow on the ground."

"But poor Mr. D'Arcy doesn't like the snow," said Aunt Kate, smiling.

Mr. D'Arcy came from the pantry, fully swathed and buttoned, and in a repentant tone told them the history of his cold. Everyone gave him advice and said it was a great pity and urged him to be very careful of his throat in the night air. Gabriel watched his wife, who did not join in the conversation. She was standing right under the dusty fanlight and the flame of the gas lit up the rich bronze of her hair, which he had seen her drying at the fire a few days before. She was in the same attitude and seemed unaware of the talk about her. At last she turned towards them and Gabriel saw that there was colour on her cheeks and that her eyes were shining. A sudden tide of joy went leaping out of his heart.

"Mr. D'Arcy," she said, "what is the name of that song you were singing?"

"It's called *The Lass of Aughrim*," said Mr. D'Arcy, "but I couldn't remember it properly. Why? Do you know it?"

"*The Lass of Aughrim*," she repeated. "I couldn't think of the name."

"It's a very nice air," said Mary Jane. "I'm sorry you were not in voice tonight."

"Now, Mary Jane," said Aunt Kate, "don't annoy Mr. D'Arcy. I won't have him annoyed."

Seeing that all were ready to start she shepherded them to the door, where good-night was said:

"Well, good-night, Aunt Kate, and thanks for the pleasant evening."

"Good-night, Gabriel. Good-night, Gretta!"

"Good-night, Aunt Kate, and thanks ever so much. Good-night, Aunt Julia."

"O, good-night, Gretta, I didn't see you."

"Good-night, Mr. D'Arcy. Good-night, Miss O'Callaghan."

"Good-night, Miss Morkan."

"Good-night, again."

"Good-night, all. Safe home."

"Good-night. Good night."

The morning was still dark. A dull, yellow light brooded over the houses and the river; and the sky seemed to be descending. It was slushy underfoot; and only streaks and patches of snow lay on the roofs, on the parapets of the quay and on the area railings. The lamps were still burning redly in the murky air and, across the river, the palace of the Four Courts stood out menacingly against the heavy sky.

She was walking on before him with Mr. Bartell D'Arcy, her shoes in a brown parcel tucked under one arm and her hands holding her skirt up from the slush. She had no longer any grace of attitude, but Gabriel's eyes were still bright with happiness. The blood went bounding along his veins; and the thoughts went rioting through his brain, proud, joyful, tender, valorous.

She was walking on before him so lightly and so erect that he longed to run after her noiselessly, catch her by the shoulders and say something foolish and affectionate into her ear. She seemed to him so frail that he longed to

defend her against something and then to be alone with
her. Moments of their secret life together burst like stars
upon his memory. A heliotrope envelope was lying beside
his breakfast-cup and he was caressing it with his hand.
Birds were twittering in the ivy and the sunny web of the
curtain was shimmering along the floor: he could not eat
for happiness. They were standing on the crowded platform and he was placing a ticket inside the warm palm of
her glove. He was standing with her in the cold, looking
in through a grated window at a man making bottles in a
roaring furnace. It was very cold. Her face, fragrant in
the cold air, was quite close to his; and suddenly he called
out to the man at the furnace:

"Is the fire hot, sir?"

But the man could not hear with the noise of the furnace. It was just as well. He might have answered rudely.

A wave of yet more tender joy escaped from his heart
and went coursing in warm flood along his arteries. Like
the tender fire of stars moments of their life together, that
no one knew of or would ever know of, broke upon and
illumined his memory. He longed to recall to her those
moments, to make her forget the years of their dull existence together and remember only their moments of ecstasy.
For the years, he felt, had not quenched his soul or hers.
Their children, his writing, her household cares had not
quenched all their souls' tender fire. In one letter that he
had written to her then he had said: "Why is it that words
like these seem to me so dull and cold? Is it because there
is no word tender enough to be your name?"

Like distant music these words that he had written years
before were borne towards him from the past. He longed
to be alone with her. When the others had gone away,
when he and she were in the room in the hotel, then they
would be alone together. He would call her softly:

"Gretta!"

Perhaps she would not hear at once: she would be un-
dressing. Then something in his voice would strike her.

She would turn and look at him. . . .

At the corner of Winetavern Street they met a cab. He was glad of its rattling noise as it saved him from conversation. She was looking out of the window and seemed tired. The others spoke only a few words, pointing out some building or street. The horse galloped along wearily under the murky morning sky, dragging his old rattling box after his heels, and Gabriel was again in a cab with her, galloping to catch the boat, galloping to their honeymoon.

As the cab drove across O'Connell Bridge Miss O'Callaghan said:

"They say you never cross O'Connell Bridge without seeing a white horse."

"I see a white man this time," said Gabriel.

"Where?" asked Mr. Bartell D'Arcy.

Gabriel pointed to the statue, on which lay patches of snow. Then he nodded familiarly to it and waved his hand.

"Good-night, Dan," he said gaily.

When the cab drew up before the hotel, Gabriel jumped out and, in spite of Mr. Bartell D'Arcy's protest, paid the driver. He gave the man a shilling over his fare. The man saluted and said:

"A prosperous New Year to you, sir."

"The same to you," said Gabriel cordially.

She leaned for a moment on his arm in getting out of the cab and while standing at the curbstone, bidding the others good-night. She leaned lightly on his arm, as lightly as when she had danced with him a few hours before. He had felt proud and happy then, happy that she was his, proud of her grace and wifely carriage. But now, after the kindling again of so many memories, the first touch of her body, musical and strange and perfumed, sent through him a keen pang of lust. Under cover of her silence he pressed her arm closely to his side; and, as they stood at the hotel door, he felt that they had escaped from their lives and duties, escaped from home and friends and run away together with wild and radiant hearts to a new adventure.

An old man was dozing in a great hooded chair in the hall. He lit a candle in the office and went before them to the stairs. They followed him in silence, their feet falling in soft thuds on the thickly carpeted stairs. She mounted the stairs behind the porter, her head bowed in the ascent, her frail shoulders curved as with a burden, her skirt girt tightly about her. He could have flung his arms about her hips and held her still, for his arms were trembling with desire to seize her and only the stress of his nails against the palms of his hands held the wild impulse of his body in check. The porter halted on the stairs to settle his guttering candle. They halted, too, on the steps below him. In the silence Gabriel could hear the falling of the molten wax into the tray and the thumping of his own heart against his ribs.

The porter led them along a corridor and opened a door. Then he set his unstable candle down on a toilet-table and asked at what hour they were to be called in the morning.

"Eight," said Gabriel.

The porter pointed to the tap of the electric-light and began a muttered apology, but Gabriel cut him short.

"We don't want any light. We have light enough from the street. And I say," he added, pointing to the candle, "you might remove that handsome article, like a good man."

The porter took up his candle again, but slowly, for he was surprised by such a novel idea. Then he mumbled good-night and went out. Gabriel shot the lock to.

A ghastly light from the street lamp lay in a long shaft from one window to the door. Gabriel threw his overcoat and hat on a couch and crossed the room towards the window. He looked down into the street in order that his emotion might calm a little. Then he turned and leaned against a chest of drawers with his back to the light. She had taken off her hat and cloak and was standing before a large swinging mirror, unhooking her waist. Gabriel paused for a few moments, watching her, and then said:

"Gretta!"

She turned away from the mirror slowly and walked along the shaft of light towards him. Her face looked so serious and weary that the words would not pass Gabriel's lips. No, it was not the moment yet.

"You looked tired," he said.

"I am a little," she answered.

"You don't feel ill or weak?"

"No, tired: that's all."

She went on to the window and stood there, looking out. Gabriel waited again and then, fearing that diffidence was about to conquer him, he said abruptly:

"By the way, Gretta!"

"What is it?"

"You know that poor fellow Malins?" he said quickly.

"Yes. What about him?"

"Well, poor fellow, he's a decent sort of chap, after all," continued Gabriel in a false voice. "He gave me back that sovereign I lent him, and I didn't expect it, really. It's a pity he wouldn't keep away from that Browne, because he's not a bad fellow, really."

He was trembling now with annoyance. Why did she seem so abstracted? He did not know how he could begin. Was she annoyed, too, about something? If she would only turn to him or come to him of her own accord! To take her as she was would be brutal. No, he must see some ardour in her eyes first. He longed to be master of her strange mood.

"When did you lend him the pound?" she asked, after a pause.

Gabriel strove to restrain himself from breaking out into brutal language about the sottish Malins and his pound. He longed to cry to her from his soul, to crush her body against his, to overmaster her. But he said:

"O, at Christmas, when he opened that little Christmas-card shop in Henry Street."

He was in such a fever of rage and desire that he did not

hear her come from the window. She stood before him for an instant, looking at him strangely. Then, suddenly raising herself on tiptoe and resting her hands lightly on his shoulders, she kissed him.

"You are a very generous person, Gabriel," she said.

Gabriel, trembling with delight at her sudden kiss and at the quaintness of her phrase, put his hands on her hair and began smoothing it back, scarcely touching it with his fingers. The washing had made it fine and brilliant. His heart was brimming over with happiness. Just when he was wishing for it she had come to him of her own accord. Perhaps her thoughts had been running with his. Perhaps she had felt the impetuous desire that was in him, and then the yielding mood had come upon her. Now that she had fallen to him so easily, he wondered why he had been so diffident.

He stood, holding her head between his hands. Then, slipping one arm swiftly about her body and drawing her towards him, he said softly:

"Gretta, dear, what are you thinking about?"

She did not answer nor yield wholly to his arm. He said again, softly:

"Tell me what it is, Gretta. I think I know what is the matter. Do I know?"

She did not answer at once. Then she said in an outburst of tears:

"O, I am thinking about that song, *The Lass of Aughrim.*"

She broke loose from him and ran to the bed and, throwing her arms across the bed-rail, hid her face. Gabriel stood stock-still for a moment in astonishment and then followed her. As he passed in the way of the cheval-glass he caught sight of himself in full length, his broad, well-filled shirt-front, the face whose expression always puzzled him when he saw it in a mirror, and his glimmering gilt-rimmed eye-glasses. He halted a few paces from her and said:

"What about the song? Why does that make you cry?"

She raised her head from her arms and dried her eyes with the back of her hand like a child. A kinder note than he had intended went into his voice.

"Why, Gretta?" he asked.

"I am thinking about a person long ago who used to sing that song."

"And who was the person long ago?" asked Gabriel, smiling.

"It was a person I used to know in Galway when I was living with my grandmother," she said.

The smile passed away from Gabriel's face. A dull anger began to gather again at the back of his mind and the dull fires of his lust began to glow angrily in his veins.

"Someone you were in love with?" he asked ironically.

"It was a young boy I used to know," she answered, "named Michael Furey. He used to sing that song, *The Lass of Aughrim*. He was very delicate."

Gabriel was silent. He did not wish her to think that he was interested in this delicate boy.

"I can see him so plainly," she said, after a moment. "Such eyes as he had: big, dark eyes! And such an expression in them—an expression!"

"O, then, you are in love with him?" said Gabriel.

"I used to go out walking with him," she said, "when I was in Galway."

A thought flew across Gabriel's mind.

"Perhaps that was why you wanted to go to Galway with that Ivors girl?" he said coldly.

She looked at him and asked in surprise:

"What for?"

Her eyes made Gabriel feel awkward. He shrugged his shoulders and said:

"How do I know? To see him, perhaps."

She looked away from him along the shaft of light towards the window in silence.

"He is dead," she said at length. "He died when he was only seventeen. Isn't it a terrible thing to die so young as that?"

"What was he?" asked Gabriel, still ironically.

"He was in the gasworks," she said.

Gabriel felt humiliated by the failure of his irony and by the evocation of this figure from the dead, a boy in the gasworks. While he had been full of memories of their secret life together, full of tenderness and joy and desire, she had been comparing him in her mind with another. A shameful consciousness of his own person assailed him. He saw himself as a ludicrous figure, acting as a pennyboy for his aunts, a nervous, well-meaning sentimentalist, orating to vulgarians and idealising his own clownish lusts, the pitiable fatuous fellow he had caught a glimpse of in the mirror. Instinctively he turned his back more to the light lest she might see the shame that burned upon his forehead.

He tried to keep up his tone of cold interrogation, but his voice when he spoke was humble and indifferent.

"I suppose you were in love with this Michael Furey, Gretta," he said.

"I was great with him at that time," she said.

Her voice was veiled and sad. Gabriel, feeling now how vain it would be to try to lead her whither he had purposed, caressed one of her hands and said, also sadly:

"And what did he die of so young, Gretta? Consumption, was it?"

"I think he died for me," she answered.

A vague terror seized Gabriel at this answer, as if, at that hour when he had hoped to triumph, some impalpable and vindictive being was coming against him, gathering forces against him in its vague world. But he shook himself free of it with an effort of reason and continued to caress her hand. He did not question her again, for he felt that she would tell him of herself. Her hand was warm and moist: it did not respond to his touch, but he continued to caress it just as he had caressed her first letter to him that spring morning.

"It was in the winter," she said, "about the beginning of the winter when I was going to leave my grandmother's and come up here to the convent. And he was ill at the time in his lodgings in Galway and wouldn't be let out, and his people in Oughterard were written to. He was in decline, they said, or something like that. I never knew rightly."

She paused for a moment and sighed.

"Poor fellow," she said. "He was very fond of me and he was such a gentle boy. We used to go out together, walking, you know, Gabriel, like the way they do in the country. He was going to study singing only for his health. He had a very good voice, poor Michael Furey."

"Well; and then?" asked Gabriel.

"And then when it came to the time for me to leave Galway and come up to the convent he was much worse and I wouldn't be let see him so I wrote him a letter saying I was going up to Dublin and would be back in the summer, and hoping he would be better then."

She paused for a moment to get her voice under control, and then went on:

"Then the night before I left, I was in my grandmother's house in Nuns' Island, packing up, and I heard gravel thrown up against the window. The window was so wet I couldn't see, so I ran downstairs as I was and slipped out the back into the garden and there was the poor fellow at the end of the garden, shivering."

"And did you not tell him to go back?" asked Gabriel.

"I implored of him to go home at once and told him he would get his death in the rain. But he said he did not want to live. I can see his eyes as well as well! He was standing at the end of the wall where there was a tree."

"And did he go home?" asked Gabriel.

"Yes, he went home. And when I was only a week in the convent he died and he was buried in Oughterard, where his people came from. O, the day I heard that, that he was dead!"

She stopped, choking with sobs, and, overcome by emotion, flung herself face downward on the bed, sobbing in the quilt. Gabriel held her hand for a moment longer, irresolutely, and then, shy of intruding on her grief, let it fall gently and walked quietly to the window.

She was fast asleep.

Gabriel, leaning on his elbow, looked for a few moments unresentfully on her tangled hair and half-open mouth, listening to her deep-drawn breath. So she had had that romance in her life: a man had died for her sake. It hardly pained him now to think how poor a part he, her husband, had played in her life. He watched her while she slept, as though he and she had never lived together as man and wife. His curious eyes rested long upon her face and on her hair: and, as he thought of what she must have been then, in that time of her first girlish beauty, a strange, friendly pity for her entered his soul. He did not like to say even to himself that her face was no longer beautiful, but he knew that it was no longer the face for which Michael Furey had braved death.

Perhaps she had not told him all the story. His eyes moved to the chair over which she had thrown some of her clothes. A petticoat string dangled to the floor. One boot stood upright, its limp upper fallen down: the fellow of it lay upon its side. He wondered at his riot of emotions of an hour before. From what had it proceeded? From his aunt's supper, from his own foolish speech, from the wine and dancing, the merry-making when saying good-night in the hall, the pleasure of the walk along the river in the snow. Poor Aunt Julia! She, too, would soon be a shade with the shade of Patrick Morkan and his horse. He had caught that haggard look upon her face for a moment when she was singing *Arrayed for the Bridal*. Soon, perhaps, he would be sitting in that same drawing-room, dressed in black, his silk hat on his knees. The blinds would be drawn down and Aunt Kate would be sitting be-

side him, crying and blowing her nose and telling him
how Julia had died. He would cast about in his mind for
some words that might console her, and would find only
lame and useless ones. Yes, yes: that would happen very
soon.

The air of the room chilled his shoulders. He stretched
himself cautiously along under the sheets and lay down
beside his wife. One by one, they were all becoming shades.
Better pass boldly into that other world, in the full glory
of some passion, than fade and wither dismally with age.
He thought of how she who lay beside him had locked in
her heart for so many years that image of her lover's eyes
when he had told her that he did not wish to live.

Generous tears filled Gabriel's eyes. He had never felt
like that himself towards any woman, but he knew that
such a feeling must be love. The tears gathered more
thickly in his eyes and in the partial darkness he imagined
he saw the form of a young man standing under a dripping
tree. Other forms were near. His soul had approached that
region where dwell the vast hosts of the dead. He was
conscious of, but could not apprehend, their wayward and
flickering existence. His own identity was fading out into a
grey impalpable world: the solid world itself, which these
dead had one time reared and lived in, was dissolving and
dwindling.

A few light taps upon the pane made him turn to the
window. It had begun to snow again. He watched sleepily
the flakes, silver and dark, falling obliquely against the
lamplight. The time had come for him to set out on his
journey westward. Yes, the newspapers were right: snow
was general all over Ireland. It was falling on every part
of the dark central plain, on the treeless hills, falling softly
upon the Bog of Allen and, farther westward, softly falling
into the dark mutinous Shannon waves. It was falling, too,
upon every part of the lonely churchyard on the hill where
Michael Furey lay buried. It lay thickly drifted on the
crooked crosses and headstones, on the spears of the little

gate, on the barren thorns. His soul swooned slowly as he heard the snow falling faintly through the universe and faintly falling, like the descent of their last end, upon all the living and the dead.

BILLY BUDD, FORETOPMAN
What befell him in the year
of the Great Mutiny etc.

· ·

Herman Melville

Herman Melville

• •

Herman Melville was born in New York City in 1819 and died there in 1891. *Billy Budd, Foretopman* was his final work, except for a few poems. During the past ten years an extraordinary amount of critical and scholarly work has been devoted to Melville, particularly to those books which made him a failure as a selling author, and which were the best work of his life, beginning with *Mardi* and *Moby Dick* and continuing to *Billy Budd*. This Melville "revival" has caused the reappearance of much of Melville's work and has produced many interesting and valuable insights into one of America's great writers. (Three of them of particular interest are: *American Renaissance* by F. O. Matthiessen; *Herman Melville* by Newton Arvin; and *The Melville Log* edited by Jay Leyda, who also edited the fine general volume *The Portable Melville*.)

Note: The text of *Billy Budd, Foretopman* used in this book is the definitive transcription of F. Barron Freeman published by the Harvard University Press, corrected in accordance with the Corrigenda later issued with that volume. Omitted only are the editor's footnotes and indications of the editor's insertions, which make Professor Freeman's book so valuable for textual study but tend to hinder the general reader.

Dedicated to

Jack Chace

Englishman

*Wherever that great heart may now be
Here on Earth or harbored in Paradise
Captain of the main-top in the year 1843
in the U. S. Frigate "United States"*

Preface

THE YEAR 1797, the year of this narrative, belongs to a period which as every thinker now feels, involved a crisis for Christendom not exceeded in its undetermined momentousness at the time by any other era whereof there is record. The opening proposition made by the Spirit of that Age, involved the rectification of the Old World's hereditary wrongs. In France to some extent this was bloodily effected. But what then? Straightway the Revolution itself became a wrongdoer, one more oppressive than the kings. Under Napoleon it enthroned upstart Kings, and initiated that prolonged agony of continual war whose final throe was Waterloo. During those years not the wisest could have foreseen that the outcome of all would be what to some thinkers apparently it has since turned out to be, a political advance along nearly the whole line for Europeans.

Now, as elsewhere hinted, it was something caught from the Revolutionary Spirit that at Spithead emboldened the man-of-war's men to rise against real abuses, long-standing ones, and afterwards at the Nore to make inordinate and aggressive demands, successful resistance to which was confirmed only when the ringleaders were hung for an admonitory spectacle to the anchored fleet. Yet in a way analogous to the operation of the Revolution at large the Great Mutiny, though by Englishmen naturally deemed monstrous at the time, doubtless gave the first latent prompting to most important reforms in the British Navy.

BILLY BUDD
SAILOR
(An inside narrative.)

1

IN THE TIME before steamships, or then more frequently than now, a stroller along the docks of any considerable sea-port would occasionally have his attention arrested by a group of bronzed mariners, man-of-war's men or merchant-sailors in holiday attire ashore on liberty. In certain instances they would flank, or, like a body-guard quite surround some superior figure of their own class, moving along with them like Aldebaran among the lesser lights of his constellation. That signal object was the "Handsome Sailor" of the less prosaic time alike of the military and merchant navies. With no perceptible trace of the vainglorious about him, rather with the off-hand unaffectedness of natural regality, he seemed to accept the spontaneous homage of his shipmates. A somewhat remarkable instance recurs to me. In Liverpool, now half a century ago I saw under the shadow of the great dingy street-wall of Prince's Dock (an obstruction long since removed) a common sailor, so intensely black that he must needs have been a native African of the unadulterate blood of Ham. A symmetric figure much above the average height. The two ends of a gay silk handkerchief thrown loose about the neck danced upon the displayed ebony of his chest; in his ears were big hoops of gold, and a Scotch

Highland bonnet with a tartan band set off his shapely head.

It was a hot noon in July; and his face, lustrous with perspiration, beamed with barbaric good humor. In jovial sallies right and left his white teeth flashing into view, he rollicked along, the centre of a company of his shipmates. These were made up of such an assortment of tribes and complexions as would have well fitted them to be marched up by Anacharsis Cloots before the bar of the first French Assembly as Representatives of the Human Race. At each spontaneous tribute rendered by the wayfarers to this black pagod of a fellow—the tribute of a pause and stare, and less frequent an exclamation,—the motley retinue showed that they took that sort of pride in the evoker of it which the Assyrian priests doubtless showed for their grand sculptured Bull when the faithful prostrated themselves.

To return.

If in some cases a bit of a nautical Murat in setting forth his person ashore, the handsome sailor of the period in question evinced nothing of the dandified Billy-be-Dam, an amusing character all but extinct now, but occasionally to be encountered, and in a form yet more amusing than the original, at the tiller of the boats on the tempestuous Erie Canal or, more likely, vaporing in the groggeries along the tow-path. Invariably a proficient in his perilous calling, he was also more or less of a mighty boxer or wrestler. It was strength and beauty. Tales of his prowess were re-cited. Ashore he was the champion; afloat the spokesman; on every suitable occasion always foremost. Close-reefing topsails in a gale, there he was, astride the weather yard-arm-end, foot in the Flemish horse as "stirrup," both hands tugging at the "earring" as at a bridle, in very much the attitude of young Alexander curbing the fiery Bucephalus. A superb figure, tossed up as by the horns of Taurus against the thunderous sky, cheerily hallooing to the strenuous file along the spar.

The moral nature was seldom out of keeping with the

unembarrassed officer deliberately diluting his grog a little, then tossing it off in three swallows, pushing the empty tumbler away, yet not so far as to be beyond easy reach, at the same time settling himself in his seat and smacking his lips with high satisfaction, looking straight at the host.

These proceedings over, the Master broke the silence; and there lurked a rueful reproach in the tone of his voice: "Lieutenant, you are going to take my best man from me, the jewel of 'em."

"Yes, I know" rejoined the other, immediately drawing back the tumbler preliminary to a replenishing; "Yes, I know. Sorry."

"Beg pardon, but you don't understand, Lieutenant. See here now. Before I shipped that young fellow, my forecastle was a rat-pit of quarrels. It was black times, I tell you, aboard the *'Rights'* here. I was worried to that degree my pipe had no comfort for me. But Billy came; and it was like a Catholic priest striking peace in an Irish shindy. Not that he preached to them or said or did anything in particular; but a virtue went out of him, sugaring the sour ones. They took to him like hornets to treacle; all but the buffer of the gang, the big shaggy chap with the fire-red whiskers. He indeed out of envy, perhaps, of the newcomer, and thinking such a 'sweet and pleasant fellow,' as he mockingly designated him to the others, could hardly have the spirit of a game-cock, must needs bestir himself in trying to get up an ugly row with him. Billy forebore with him and reasoned with him in a pleasant way—he is something like myself, lieutenant, to whom aught like a quarrel is hateful—but nothing served. So, in the second dog-watch one day the Red Whiskers in presence of the others, under pretence of showing Billy just whence a sirloin steak was cut—for the fellow had once been a butcher—insultingly gave him a dig under the ribs. Quick as lightning Billy let fly his arm. I dare say he never meant to do quite as much as he did, but anyhow he gave the burly fool a terrible drubbing. It took about half a minute,

I should think. And, lord bless you, the lubber was astonished at the celerity. And will you believe it, Lieutenant, the Red Whiskers now really loves Billy—loves him, or is the biggest hypocrite that ever I heard of. But they all love him. Some of 'em do his washing, darn his old trousers for him; the carpenter is at odd times making a pretty little chest of drawers for him. Anybody will do anything for Billy Budd; and it's the happy family here. But now Lieutenant, if that young fellow goes—I know how it will be aboard the '*Rights.*' Not again very soon shall I, coming up from dinner, lean over the capstan smoking a quiet pipe—no, not very soon again, I think. Ay, Lieutenant, you are going to take away the jewel of 'em; you are going to take away my peacemaker!" And with that the good soul had really some ado in checking a rising sob.

"Well," said the officer who had listened with amused interest to all this, and now waxing merry with his tipple; "Well, blessed are the peacemakers especially the fighting peacemakers! And such are the seventy-four beauties some of which you see poking their noses out at the port-holes of yonder war-ship lying-to for me" pointing through the cabin window of the *Indomitable*. "But courage! don't look so downhearted, man. Why, I pledge you in advance the royal approbation. Rest assured that His Majesty will be delighted to know that in a time when his hard tack is not sought for by sailors with such avidity as should be; a time also when some shipmasters privily resent the borrowing from them a tar or two for the service; His Majesty, I say, will be delighted to learn that *one* shipmaster at least cheerfully surrenders to the King, the flower of his flock, a sailor who with equal loyalty makes no dissent.— But where's my beauty? Ah," looking through the cabin's open door "Here he comes; and, by Jove—lugging along his chest—Apollo with his portmanteau!—My man," stepping out to him, "you can't take that big box aboard a war-ship. The boxes there are mostly shot-boxes. Put your duds in a bag, lad. Boot and saddle for the cavalryman, bag and hammock for the man-of-war's man."

The transfer from chest to bag was made. And, after seeing his man into the cutter and then following him down, the lieutenant pushed off from the *Rights-of-Man*. That was the merchant-ship's name; though by her master and crew abbreviated in sailor fashion into *The Rights*. The hard-headed Dundee owner was a staunch admirer of Thomas Paine whose book in rejoinder to Burke's arraignment of the French Revolution had then been published for some time and had gone everywhere. In christening his vessel after the title of Paine's volume the man of Dundee was something like his contemporary shipowner, Stephen Girard of Philadelphia, whose sympathies, alike with his native land and its liberal philosophers, he evinced by naming his ships after Voltaire, Diderot, and so forth.

But now, when the boat swept under the merchant-man's stern, and officer and oarsmen were noting—some bitterly and others with a grin,—the name emblazoned there; just then it was that the new recruit jumped up from the bow where the coxswain had directed him to sit, and waving his hat to his silent shipmates sorrowfully looking over at him from the taffrail, bade the lads a genial good-bye. Then, making a salutation as to the ship herself, "And good bye to you too, old *Rights of Man*."

"Down, Sir!" roared the lieutenant, instantly assuming all the rigor of his rank, though with difficulty repressing a smile.

To be sure Billy's action was a terrible breach of naval decorum. But in that decorum he had never been instructed; in consideration of which the lieutenant would hardly have been so energetic in reproof but for the concluding farewell to the ship. This he rather took as meant to convey a covert sally on the new recruit's part, a sly slur at impressment in general, and that of himself in especial. And yet, more likely, if satire it was in effect, it was hardly so by intention, for Billy though happily en-

dowed with the gayety of high health, youth, and a free
heart, was yet by no means of a satirical turn. The will to
it and the sinister dexterity were alike wanting. To deal
in double meanings and insinuations of any sort was
quite foreign to his nature.

As to his enforced enlistment, that he seemed to take
pretty much as he was wont to take any vicissitude of
weather. Like the animals, though no philosopher, he was,
without knowing it, practically a fatalist. And, it may be,
that he rather liked this adventurous turn in his affairs,
which promised an opening into novel scenes and martial
excitements.

Aboard the *Indomitable* our merchant-sailor was forthwith rated as an able-seaman and assigned to the starboard
watch of the fore-top. He was soon at home in the service,
not at all disliked for his unpretentious good looks and a
sort of genial happy-go-lucky air. No merrier man in his
mess: in marked contrast to certain other individuals included like himself among the impressed portion of the
ship's company; for these when not actively employed were
sometimes, and more particularly in the last dog-watch
when the drawing near of twilight induced revery, apt to
fall into a saddish mood which in some partook of sullen-
ness. But they were not so young as our foretopman, and
no few of them must have known a hearth of some sort,
others may have had wives and children left, too probably,
in uncertain circumstances, and hardly any but must have
had acknowledged kith and kin, while for Billy, as will
shortly be seen, his entire family was practically invested
in himself.

2

Though our new-made foretopman was well received in
the top and on the gun-decks, hardly here was he that
cynosure he had previously been among those minor ship's

companies of the merchant marine, with which companies only had he hitherto consorted.

He was young; and despite his all but fully developed frame in aspect looked even younger than he really was, owing to a lingering adolescent expression in the as yet smooth face all but feminine in purity of natural complexion but where, thanks to his seagoing, the lily was quite suppressed and the rose had some ado visibly to flush through the tan.

To one essentially such a novice in the complexities of factitious life, the abrupt transition from his former and simpler sphere to the ampler and more knowing world of a great war-ship; this might well have abashed him had there been any conceit or vanity in his composition. Among her miscellaneous multitude, the *Indomitable* mustered several individuals who however inferior in grade were of no common natural stamp, sailors more signally susceptive of that air which continuous martial discipline and repeated presence in battle can in some degree impart even to the average man. As the *handsome sailor* Billy Budd's position aboard the seventy-four was something analogous to that of a rustic beauty transplanted from the provinces and brought into competition with the high-born dames of the court. But this change of circumstances he scarce noted. As little did he observe that something about him provoked an ambiguous smile in one or two harder faces among the blue-jackets. Nor less unaware was he of the peculiar favorable effect his person and demeanor had upon the more intelligent gentlemen of the quarter-deck. Nor could this well have been otherwise. Cast in a mould peculiar to the finest physical examples of those Englishmen in whom the Saxon strain would seem not at all to partake of any Norman or other admixture, he showed in face that humane look of reposeful good nature which the Greek sculptor in some instances gave to his heroic strong man, Hercules. But this again was subtly modified by another and pervasive qual-

ity. The ear, small and shapely, the arch of the foot, the
curve in mouth and nostril, even the indurated hand dyed
to the orange-tawny of the toucan's bill, a hand telling
alike of the halyards and tar-bucket; but, above all, something in the mobile expression, and every chance attitude
and movement, something suggestive of a mother eminent-
ly favored by Love and the Graces; all this strangely indicated a lineage in direct contradiction to his lot. The
mysteriousness here, became less mysterious through a mat-
ter-of-fact elicited when Billy at the capstan was being
formally mustered into the service. Asked by the officer, a
small brisk little gentleman as it chanced among other
questions, his place of birth, he replied, "Please, Sir, I
don't know."

"Don't know where you were born?—Who was your
father?"

"God knows, Sir."

Struck by the straightforward simplicity of these replies,
the officer next asked "Do you know anything about your
beginning?"

"No, Sir. But I have heard that I was found in a pretty
silk-lined basket hanging one morning from the knocker
of a good man's door in Bristol."

"*Found* say you? Well," throwing back his head and
looking up and down the new recruit; "Well it turns out
to have been a pretty good find. Hope they'll find some
more like you, my man; the fleet sadly needs them."

Yes, Billy Budd was a foundling, a presumable bye-blow,
and, evidently, no ignoble one. Noble descent was as evident in him as in a blood horse.

For the rest, with little or no sharpness of faculty or any
trace of the wisdom of the serpent, nor yet quite a dove,
he possessed that kind and degree of intelligence going
along with the unconventional rectitude of a sound human creature, one to whom not yet has been proffered the
questionable apple of knowledge. He was illiterate; he
could not read, but he could sing, and like the illiterate

nightingale was sometimes the composer of his own song.

Of self-consciousness he seemed to have little or none, or about as much as we may reasonably impute to a dog of Saint Bernard's breed.

Habitually living with the elements and knowing little more of the land than as a beach, or, rather, that portion of the terraqueous globe providentially set apart for dance-houses doxies and tapsters, in short what sailors call a "fiddlers' green," his simple nature remained unsophisticated by those moral obliquities which are not in every case incompatible with that manufacturable thing known as respectability. But are sailors, frequenters of "fiddlers'-greens", without vices? No; but less often than with landsmen do their vices, so called, partake of crookedness of heart, seeming less to proceed from viciousness than exuberance of vitality after long constraint; frank manifestations in accordance with natural law. By his original constitution aided by the cooperating influences of his lot, Billy in many respects was little more than a sort of upright barbarian, much such perhaps as Adam presumably might have been ere the urbane Serpent wriggled himself into his company.

And here be it submitted that apparently going to corroborate the doctrine of man's fall, a doctrine now popularly ignored, it is observable that where certain virtues pristine and unadulterate peculiarly characterize anybody in the external uniform of civilization, they will upon scrutiny seem not to be derived from custom or convention, but rather to be out of keeping with these, as if indeed exceptionally transmitted from a period prior to Cain's city and citified man. The character marked by such qualities has to an unvitiated taste an untampered-with flavor like that of berries, while the man thoroughly civilized even in a fair specimen of the breed has to the same moral palate a questionable smack as of a compounded wine. To any stray inheritor of these primitive qualities found, like Caspar Hauser, wandering dazed in any Christian capital

of our time the good-natured poet's famous invocation,
near two thousand years ago, of the good rustic out of his
latitude in the Rome of the Cesars, still appropriately
holds:—

> "Honest and poor, Faithful in word and thought
> What has thee, Fabian, to the city brought."

Though our Handsome Sailor had as much of masculine
beauty as one can expect anywhere to see; nevertheless,
like the beautiful woman in one of Hawthorne's minor
tales, there was just one thing amiss in him. No visible
blemish indeed, as with the lady; no, but an occasional
liability to a vocal defect. Though in the hour of elemental
uproar or peril, he was everything that a sailor should be,
yet under sudden provocation of strong heart-feeling his
voice otherwise singularly musical, as if expressive of the
harmony within, was apt to develop an organic hesitancy,
in fact more or less of a stutter or even worse. In this particular Billy was a striking instance that the arch inter-
ferer, the envious marplot of Eden still has more or less to
do with every human consignment to this planet of earth.
In every case, one way or another he is sure to slip in his
little card, as much as to remind us—I too have a hand
here.

The avowal of such an imperfection in the Handsome
Sailor should be evidence not alone that he is not presented
as a conventional hero, but also that the story in which he
is the main figure is no romance.

3

At the time of Billy Budd's arbitrary enlistment into the
Indomitable that ship was on her way to join the Mediterranean fleet. No long time elapsed before the junction
was effected. As one of that fleet the seventy-four partici-

pated in its movements, though at times on account of her superior sailing qualities, in the absence of frigates, despatched on separate duty as a scout and at times on less temporary service. But with all this the story has little concernment, restricted as it is to the inner life of one particular ship and the career of an individual sailor.

It was the summer of 1797. In the April of that year had occurred the commotion at Spithead followed in May by a second and yet more serious outbreak in the fleet at the Nore. The latter is known, and without exaggeration in the epithet, as the Great Mutiny. It was indeed a demonstration more menacing to England than the contemporary manifestoes and conquering and proselyting armies of the French Directory.

To the British Empire the Nore Mutiny was what a strike in the fire-brigade would be to London threatened by general arson. In a crisis when the kingdom might well have anticipated the famous signal that some years later published along the naval line of battle what it was that upon occasion England expected of Englishmen; *that* was the time when at the mast-heads of the three-deckers and seventy-fours moored in her own roadstead—a fleet, the right arm of a Power then all but the sole free conservative one of the Old World, the blue-jackets, to be numbered by thousands ran up with huzzas the British colors with the union and cross wiped out; by that cancellation transmuting the flag of founded law and freedom defined, into the enemy's red meteor of unbridled and unbounded revolt. Reasonable discontent growing out of practical grievances in the fleet had been ignited into irrational combustion as by live cinders blown across the Channel from France in flames.

The event converted into irony for a time those spirited strains of Dibdin—as a song-writer no mean auxiliary to the English Government at the European conjuncture—strains celebrating, among other things, the patriotic devotion of the British tar:

"And as for my life, 'tis the King's!"

Such an episode in the Island's grand naval story her
naval historians naturally abridge; one of them (G. P. R.
James) candidly acknowledging that fain would he pass
it over did not "impartiality forbid fastidiousness." And
yet his mention is less a narration than a reference, having
to do hardly at all with details. Nor are these readily to
be found in the libraries. Like some other events in every
age befalling states everywhere including America the
Great Mutiny was of such character that national pride
along with views of policy would fain shade it off into the
historical background. Such events can not be ignored, but
there is a considerate way of historically treating them. If
a well-constituted individual refrains from blazoning
aught amiss or calamitous in his family; a nation in the like
circumstance may without reproach be equally discreet.

Though after parleyings between Government and the
ringleaders, and concessions by the former as to some glaring abuses, the first uprising—that at Spithead—with difficulty was put down, or matters for the time pacified; yet
at the Nore the unforeseen renewal of insurrection on a
yet larger scale, and emphasized in the conferences that
ensued by demands deemed by the authorities not only
inadmissible but aggressively insolent, indicated—if the
Red Flag did not sufficiently do so, what was the spirit
animating the men. Final suppression, however, there was;
but only made possible perhaps by the unswerving loyalty
of the marine corps a voluntary resumption of loyalty
among influential sections of the crews.

To some extent the Nore Mutiny may be regarded as
analogous to the distempering irruption of contagious
fever in a frame constitutionally sound, and which anon
throws it off.

At all events, of these thousands of mutineers were some
of the tars who not so very long afterwards—whether wholly
prompted thereto by patriotism, or pugnacious instinct,

or by both,—helped to win a coronet for Nelson at the Nile, and the naval crown of crowns for him at Trafalgar. To the mutineers those battles and especially Trafalgar were a plenary absolution and a grand one: For all that goes to make up scenic naval display, and heroic magnificence in arms those battles especially Trafalgar stand unmatched in human annals.

4

Concerning "The greatest sailor since the world began." Tennyson?

In this matter of writing, resolve as one may to keep to the main road, some by-paths have an enticement not readily to be withstood. I am going to err into such a by-path. If the reader will keep me company I shall be glad. At the least we can promise ourselves that pleasure which is wickedly said to be in sinning, for a literary sin the divergence will be.

Very likely it is no new remark that the inventions of our time have at last brought about a change in sea-warfare in degree corresponding to the revolution in all warfare effected by the original introduction from China into Europe of gunpowder. The first European fire-arm, a clumsy contrivance, was, as is well known, scouted by no few of the knights as a base implement, good enough peradventure for weavers too craven to stand up crossing steel with steel in frank fight. But as ashore knightly valor though shorn of its blazonry did not cease with the knights, neither on the seas though nowadays in encounters there a certain kind of displayed gallantry be fallen out of date as hardly applicable under changed circumstances, did the nobler qualities of such naval magnates as Don John of Austria, Doria, Van Tromp, Jean Bart, the long line of British Admirals and the American Decaturs of 1812 become obsolete with their wooden walls.

Nevertheless, to anybody who can hold the Present at its worth without being inappreciative of the Past, it may be forgiven, if to such an one the solitary old hulk at Portsmouth, Nelson's *Victory,* seems to float there, not alone as the decaying monument of a fame incorruptible, but also as a poetic reproach, softened by its picturesqueness, to the *Monitors* and yet mightier hulls of the European iron-clads. And this not altogether because such craft are unsightly, unavoidably lacking the symmetry and grand lines of the old battle-ships, but equally for other reasons.

There are some, perhaps, who while not altogether inaccessible to that poetic reproach just alluded to, may yet on behalf of the new order, be disposed to parry it; and this to the extent of iconoclasm, if need be. For example, prompted by the sight of the star inserted in the *Victory's* quarter-deck designating the spot where the Great Sailor fell, these martial utilitarians may suggest considerations implying that Nelson's ornate publication of his person in battle was not only unnecessary, but not military, nay savored of foolhardiness and vanity. They may add, too, that at Trafalgar it was in effect nothing less than a challenge to death; and death came; and that but for his bravado the victorious Admiral might possibly have survived the battle, and so, instead of having his sagacious dying injunctions overruled by his immediate successor in command he himself when the contest was decided might have brought his shattered fleet to anchor, a proceeding which might have averted the deplorable loss of life by shipwreck in the elemental tempest that followed the martial one.

Well, should we set aside the more disputable point whether for various reasons it was possible to anchor the fleet, then plausibly enough the Benthamites of war may urge the above.

But the *might-have-been* is but boggy ground to build on. And certainly, in foresight as to the larger issue of an

encounter, and anxious preparations for it—buoying the
deadly way and mapping it out, as at Copenhagen—few
commanders have been so painstakingly circumspect as
this same reckless declarer of his person in fight.

Personal prudence even when dictated by quite other
than selfish considerations surely is no special virtue in a
military man; while an excessive love of glory, impassion-
ing a less burning impulse the honest sense of duty, is the
first. If the name *Wellington* is not so much of a trumpet
to the blood as the simpler name *Nelson,* the reason for this
may perhaps be inferred from the above. Alfred in his
funeral ode on the victor of Waterloo ventures not to call
him the greatest soldier of all time, though in the same
ode he invokes Nelson as "the greatest sailor since the
world began."

At Trafalgar Nelson on the brink of opening the fight
sat down and wrote his last brief will and testament. If
under the presentiment of the most magnificent of all victories to be crowned by his own glorious death, a sort of
priestly motive led him to dress his person in the jewelled
vouchers of his own shining deeds; if thus to have adorned
himself for the altar and the sacrifice were indeed vainglory, then affectation and fustian is each more heroic line
in the great epics and dramas, since in such lines the poet
but embodies in verse those exaltations of sentiment that
a nature like Nelson, the opportunity being given, vitalizes
into acts.

5

Yes, the outbreak at the Nore was put down. But not every
grievance was redressed. If the contractors, for example,
were no longer permitted to ply some practices peculiar
to their tribe everywhere, such as providing shoddy cloth,
rations not sound, or false in the measure; not the less
impressment, for one thing, went on. By custom sanctioned

for centuries, and judicially maintained by a Lord Chancellor as late as Mansfield, that mode of manning the fleet, a mode now fallen into a sort of abeyance but never formally renounced, it was not practicable to give up in those years. Its abrogation would have crippled the indispensable fleet, one wholly under canvas, no steam-power, its innumerable sails and thousands of cannon, everything in short, worked by muscle alone; a fleet the more insatiate in demand for men, because then multiplying its ships of all grades against contingencies present and to come of the convulsed Continent.

Discontent foreran the Two Mutinies, and more or less it lurkingly survived them. Hence it was not unreasonable to apprehend some return of trouble sporadic or general. One instance of such apprehensions: In the same year with this story, Nelson, then Vice Admiral Sir Horatio, being with the fleet off the Spanish coast, was directed by the Admiral in command to shift his pennant from the *Captain* to the *Theseus;* and for this reason: that the latter ship having newly arrived on the station from home where it had taken part in the Great Mutiny, danger was apprehended from the temper of the men; and it was thought that an officer like Nelson was the one, not indeed to terrorize the crew into base subjection, but to win them, by force of his mere presence back to an allegiance if not as enthusiastic as his own, yet as true. So it was that for a time on more than one quarter-deck anxiety did exist. At sea precautionary vigilance was strained against relapse. At short notice an engagement might come on. When it did, the lieutenants assigned to batteries felt it incumbent on them, in some instances to stand with drawn swords behind the men working the guns.

6

But on board the seventy-four in which Billy now swung his hammock, very little in the manner of the men and nothing obvious in the demeanor of the officers would have suggested to an ordinary observer that the Great Mutiny was a recent event. In their general bearing and conduct the commissioned officers of a war-ship naturally take their tone from the commander, that is if he have that ascendancy of character that ought to be his.

Captain the Honorable Edward Fairfax Vere, to give his full title, was a bachelor of forty or thereabouts, a sailor of distinction even in a time prolific of renowned seamen. Though allied to the higher nobility his advancement had not been altogether owing to influences connected with that circumstance. He had seen much service, been in various engagements, always acquitting himself as an officer mindful of the welfare of his men, but never tolerating an infraction of discipline; thoroughly versed in the science of his profession, and intrepid to the verge of temerity, though never injudiciously so. For his gallantry in the West Indian waters as flag-lieutenant under Rodney in that Admiral's crowning victory over De Grasse, he was made a post-captain.

Ashore in the garb of a civilian scarce anyone would have taken him for a sailor, more especially that he never garnished unprofessional talk with nautical terms, and grave in his bearing, evinced little appreciation of mere humor. It was not out of keeping with these traits that on a passage when nothing demanded his paramount action, he was the most undemonstrative of men. Any landsman observing this gentleman not conspicuous by his stature and wearing no pronounced insignia, emerging from his cabin retreat to the open deck, and noting the silent deference of the officers retiring to leeward, might have taken him for the King's guest, a civilian aboard the King's-ship, some highly honorable discreet envoy on his way to an important post. But in fact this unobtrusiveness of demeanor may have proceeded from a certain unaffected modesty of manhood sometimes accompanying a resolute nature, a modesty evinced at all times not calling for pronounced action, and which shown in any rank of life suggests a virtue aristocratic in kind.

As with some others engaged in various departments of the world's more heroic activities, Captain Vere though practical enough upon occasion would at times betray a certain dreaminess of mood. Standing alone on the weather-side of the quarter deck, one hand holding by the rigging he would absently gaze off at the blank sea. At the presentation to him then of some minor matter interrupting the current of his thoughts he would show more or less irascibility; but instantly he would control it.

In the navy he was popularly known by the appellation—Starry Vere. How such a designation happened to fall upon one who whatever his sterling qualities was without any brilliant ones was in this wise: A favorite kinsman, Lord Denton, a free-hearted fellow, had been the first to meet and congratulate him upon his return to England from his West Indian cruise; and but the day previous turning over a copy of Andrew Marvell's poems had lighted, not for the first time however, upon the lines entitled *Appleton House,* the name of one of the seats of their common ancestor, a hero in the German wars of the seventeenth century, in which poem occur the lines,

> "This 'tis to have been from the first
> In a domestic heaven nursed,
> Under the discipline severe
> Of Fairfax and the starry Vere."

And so, upon embracing his cousin fresh from Rodney's great victory wherein he had played so gallant a part, brimming over with just family pride in the sailor of their

house, he exuberantly exclaimed, "Give ye joy, Ed; give
ye joy, my starry Vere!" This got currency, and the novel
prefix serving in familiar parlance readily to distinguish
the *Indomitable's* Captain from another Vere his senior,
a distant relative an officer of like rank in the navy, it remained permanently attached to the surname.

7

In view of the part that the commander of the *Indomitable*
plays in scenes shortly to follow, it may be well to fill out
that sketch of him outlined in the previous chapter.

Aside from his qualities as a sea-officer Captain Vere was
an exceptional character. Unlike no few of England's renowned sailors, long and arduous service with signal devotion to it, had not resulted in absorbing and *salting* the
entire man. He had a marked leaning toward everything
intellectual. He loved books, never going to sea without a
newly replenished library, compact but of the best. The
isolated leisure, in some cases so wearisome, falling at intervals to commanders even during a war-cruise, never
was tedious to Captain Vere. With nothing of that literary
taste which less heeds the thing conveyed than the vehicle,
his bias was toward those books to which every serious
mind of superior order occupying any active post of authority in the world, naturally inclines: books treating of
actual men and events no matter of what era—history,
biography and unconventional writers, who, free from
cant and convention, like Montaigne, honestly and in the
spirit of common sense philosophize upon realities.

In this love of reading he found confirmation of his own
more reserved thoughts—confirmation which he had vainly sought in social converse, so that as touching most
fundamental topics, there had got to be established in him
some positive convictions, which he forefelt would abide
in him essentially unmodified so long as his intelligent

part remained unimpaired. In view of the troubled period in which his lot was cast this was well for him. His settled convictions were as a dyke against those invading waters of novel opinion social political and otherwise, which carried away as in a torrent no few minds in those days, minds by nature not inferior to his own. While other members of that aristocracy to which by birth he belonged were incensed at the innovators mainly because their theories were inimical to the privileged classes, not alone Captain Vere disinterestedly opposed them because they seemed to him incapable of embodiment in lasting institutions, but at war with the peace of the world and the true welfare of mankind.

With minds less stored than his and less earnest, some officers of his rank, with whom at times he would necessarily consort, found him lacking in the companionable quality, a dry and bookish gentleman, as they deemed. Upon any chance withdrawal from their company one would be apt to say to another, something like this: "Vere is a noble fellow, Starry Vere. Spite the gazettes, Sir Horatio" meaning him with the Lord title "is at bottom scarce a better seaman or fighter. But between you and me now don't you think there is a queer streak of the pedantic running through him? Yes, like the King's yarn in a coil of navy-rope?"

Some apparent ground there was for this sort of confidential criticism; since not only did the Captain's discourse never fall into the jocosely familiar, but in illustrating of any point touching the stirring personages and events of the time he would be as apt to cite some historic character or incident of antiquity as that he would cite from the moderns. He seemed unmindful of the circumstance that to his bluff company such remote allusions however pertinent they might really be were altogether alien to men whose reading was mainly confined to the journals. But considerateness in such matters is not easy to natures constituted like Captain Vere's. Their honesty prescribes to

them directness, sometimes far-reaching like that of a
migratory fowl that in its flight never heeds when it crosses
a frontier.

8

The lieutenants and other commissioned gentlemen forming Captain Vere's staff it is not necessary here to partic-
ularize, nor needs it to make any mention of any of the
warrant-officers. But among the petty-officers was one who
having much to do with the story, may as well be forthwith
introduced. His portrait I essay, but shall never hit it. This
was John Claggart, the Master-at-arms. But that sea-title
may to landsmen seem somewhat equivocal. Originally
doubtless that petty-officer's function was the instruction
of the men in the use of arms, sword or cutlas. But very
long ago, owing to the advance in gunnery making hand-
to-hand encounters less frequent and giving to nitre and
sulphur the preeminence over steel, that function ceased;
the Master-at-arms of a great war-ship becoming a sort of
Chief of Police charged among other matters with the duty
of preserving order on the populous lower gun-decks.

Claggart was a man of about five and thirty, somewhat
spare and tall, yet of no ill figure upon the whole. His
hand was too small and shapely to have been accustomed
to hard toil. The face was a notable one; the features all
except the chin cleanly cut as those on a Greek medallion;
yet the chin, beardless as Tecumseh's, had something of
strange protuberant heaviness in its make that recalled
the prints of the Rev. Dr. Titus Oates, the historic depo-
nent with the clerical drawl in the time of Charles II and
the fraud of the alleged Popish Plot. It served Claggart
in his office that his eye could cast a tutoring glance. His
brow was of the sort phrenologically associated with more
than average intellect; silken jet curls partly clustering
over it, making a foil to the pallor below, a pallor tinged

with a faint shade of amber akin to the hue of time-tinted marbles of old. This complexion, singularly contrasting with the red or deeply bronzed visages of the sailors, and in part the result of his official seclusion from the sunlight, though it was not exactly displeasing, nevertheless seemed to hint of something defective or abnormal in the constitution and blood. But his general aspect and manner were so suggestive of an education and career incongruous with his naval function that when not actively engaged in it he looked like a man of high quality, social and moral, who for reasons of his own was keeping incog. Nothing was known of his former life. It might be that he was an Englishman; and yet there lurked a bit of accent in his speech suggesting that possibly he was not such by birth, but through naturalization in early childhood. Among certain grizzled sea-gossips of the gun-decks and forecastle went a rumor perdue that the master-at-arms was a *chevalier* who had volunteered into the King's navy by way of compounding for some mysterious swindle whereof he had been arraigned at the King's Bench. The fact that nobody could substantiate this report was, of course, nothing against its secret currency. Such a rumor once started on the gun-decks in reference to almost anyone below the rank of a commissioned officer would, during the period assigned to this narrative, have seemed not altogether wanting in credibility to the tarry old wiseacres of a man-of-war crew. And indeed a man of Claggart's accomplishments, without prior nautical experience entering the navy at mature life, as he did, and necessarily allotted at the start to the lowest grade in it; a man too who never made allusion to his previous life ashore; these were circumstances which in the dearth of exact knowledge as to his true antecedents opened to the invidious a vague field for unfavorable surmise.

But the sailors' dog-watch gossip concerning him derived a vague plausibility from the fact that now for some period the British Navy could so little afford to be squeamish in the matter of keeping up the muster-rolls, that not only were press-gangs notoriously abroad both afloat and ashore, but there was little or no secret about another matter, namely that the London police were at liberty to capture any able-bodied suspect, any questionable fellow at large and summarily ship him to the dock-yard or fleet. Furthermore, even among voluntary enlistments there were instances where the motive thereto partook neither of patriotic impulse nor yet of a random desire to experience a bit of sea-life and martial adventure. Insolvent debtors of minor grade, together with the promiscuous lame ducks of morality found in the Navy a convenient and secure refuge. Secure, because once enlisted aboard a King's-Ship, they were as much in sanctuary, as the transgressor of the Middle Ages harboring himself under the shadow of the altar. Such sanctioned irregularities which for obvious reasons the Government would hardly think to parade at the time and which consequently, and as affecting the least influential class of mankind, have all but dropped into oblivion, lend color to something for the truth whereof I do not vouch, and hence have some scruple in stating; something I remember having seen in print though the book I can not recall; but the same thing was personally communicated to me now more than forty years ago by an old pensioner in a cocked hat with whom I had a most interesting talk on the terrace at Greenwich, a Baltimore negro, a Trafalgar man. It was to this effect: In the case of a warship short of hands whose speedy sailing was imperative, the deficient quota in lack of any other way of making it good, would be eked out by draughts culled direct from the jails. For reasons previously suggested it would not perhaps be easy at the present day directly to prove or disprove the allegation. But allowed as a verity, how significant would it be of England's straits at the time confronted by those wars which like a flight of harpies rose shrieking from the din and dust of the fallen Bastille. That era appears measurably clear to us who look back at it, and but read of it. But to the grandfathers of us gray-beards, the more thoughtful of them, the genius of it presented an aspect like that of Camoens' Spirit of the Cape, an eclipsing menace mysterious and prodigious. Not America was exempt from apprehension. At the height of Napoleon's unexampled conquests, there were Americans who had fought at Bunker Hill who looked forward to the possibility that the Atlantic might prove no barrier against the ultimate schemes of this French portentous upstart from the revolutionary chaos who seemed in act of fulfilling judgment prefigured in the Apocalypse.

But the less credence was to be given to the gun-deck talk touching Claggart, seeing that no man holding his office in a man-of-war can ever hope to be popular with the crew. Besides, in derogatory comments upon anyone against whom they have a grudge, or for any reason or no reason mislike, sailors are much like landsmen, they are apt to exaggerate or romance it.

About as much was really known to the *Indomitable's* tars of the master-at-arms' career before entering the service as an astronomer knows about a comet's travels prior to its first observable appearance in the sky. The verdict of the sea quidnuncs has been cited only by way of showing what sort of moral impression the man made upon rude uncultivated natures whose conceptions of human wickedness were necessarily of the narrowest, limited to ideas of vulgar rascality,—a thief among the swinging hammocks during a night-watch, or the man-brokers and land-sharks of the sea-ports.

It was no gossip, however, but fact, that though, as before hinted, Claggart upon his entrance into the navy was, as a novice, assigned to the least honorable section of a man-of-war's crew, embracing the drudgery, he did not long remain there.

The superior capacity he immediately evinced, his constitutional sobriety, ingratiating deference to superiors, together with a peculiar ferreting genius manifested on a

singular occasion, all this capped by a certain austere patriotism abruptly advanced him to the position of master-
at-arms.

Of this maritime Chief of Police the ship's-corporals, so
called, were the immediate subordinates, and compliant
ones; and this, as is to be noted in some business departments ashore, almost to a degree inconsistent with entire
moral volition. His place put various converging wires of
underground influence under the Chief's control, capable
when astutely worked through his understrappers of operating to the mysterious discomfort if nothing worse, of
any of the sea-commonalty.

9

Life in the fore-top well agreed with Billy Budd. There,
when not actually engaged on the yards yet higher aloft,
the topmen, who as such had been picked out for youth
and activity, constituted an aerial club lounging at ease
against the smaller stun'sails rolled up into cushions, spinning yarns like the lazy gods, and frequently amused with
what was going on in the busy world of the decks below.
No wonder then that a young fellow of Billy's disposition
was well content in such society. Giving no cause of offence
to anybody, he was always alert at a call. So in the merchant
service it had been with him. But now such a punctilious-
ness in duty was shown that his topmates would sometimes
good-naturedly laugh at him for it. This heightened alacrity had its cause, namely, the impression made upon him
by the first formal gangway-punishment he had ever witnessed, which befell the day following his impressment.
It had been incurred by a little fellow, young, a novice an
after-guardsman absent from his assigned post when the
ship was being put about; a dereliction resulting in a
rather serious hitch to that manœuvre, one demanding
instantaneous promptitude in letting go and making fast.

When Billy saw the culprit's naked back under the scourge
gridironed with red welts, and worse; when he marked the
dire expression on the liberated man's face as with his
woolen shirt flung over him by the executioner he rushed
forward from the spot to bury himself in the crowd, Billy
was horrified. He resolved that never through remissness
would he make himself liable to such a visitation or do
or omit aught that might merit even verbal reproof. What
then was his surprise and concern when ultimately he
found himself getting into petty trouble occasionally about
such matters as the stowage of his bag or something amiss
in his hammock, matters under the police oversight of the
ship's-corporals of the lower decks, and which brought
down on him a vague threat from one of them.

So heedful in all things as he was, how could this be?
He could not understand it, and it more than vexed him.
When he spoke to his young topmates about it they were
either lightly incredulous or found something comical in
his unconcealed anxiety. "Is it your bag, Billy?" said one
"well, sew yourself up in it, bully boy, and then you'll be
sure to know if anybody meddles with it."

Now there was a veteran aboard who because his years
began to disqualify him for more active work had been
recently assigned duty as main-mast-man in his watch,
looking to the gear belayed at the rail roundabout that
great spar near the deck. At off-times the foretopman had
picked up some acquaintance with him, and now in his
trouble it occurred to him that he might be the sort of
person to go to for wise counsel. He was an old Dansker
long anglicized in the service, of few words, many wrinkles
and some honorable scars. His wizened face, time-tinted
and weather-stained to the complexion of an antique
parchment, was here and there peppered blue by the
chance explosion of a gun-cartridge in action. He was an
Agamemnon-man; some two years prior to the time of this
story having served under Nelson when but Sir Horatio
in that ship immortal in naval memory, and which dis-

mantled and in part broken up to her bare ribs is seen a grand skeleton in Haydon's etching. As one of a boarding-party from the *Agamemnon* he had received a cut slant-wise along one temple and cheek leaving a long pale scar like a streak of dawn's light falling athwart the dark visage. It was on account of that scar and the affair in which it was known that he had received it, as well as from his blue-peppered complexion that the Dansker went among the *Indomitable's* crew by the name of "Board-her-in-the-smoke."

Now the first time that his small weazel-eyes happened to light on Billy Budd, a certain grim internal merriment set all his ancient wrinkles into antic play. Was it that his eccentric unsentimental old sapience primitive in its kind saw or thought it saw something which in contrast with the war-ship's environment looked oddly incongruous in the handsome sailor? But after slyly studying him at intervals, the old Merlin's equivocal merriment was modi-fied; for now when the twain would meet, it would start in his face a quizzing sort of look, but it would be but mo-mentary and sometimes replaced by an expression of spec-ulative query as to what might eventually befall a nature like that, dropped into a world not without some man-traps and against whose subtleties simple courage lacking experience and address and without any touch of defensive ugliness, is of little avail; and where such innocence as man is capable of does yet in a moral emergency not always sharpen the faculties or enlighten the will.

However it was the Dansker in his ascetic way rather took to Billy. Nor was this only because of a certain phil-osophic interest in such a character. There was another cause. While the old man's eccentricities, sometimes bor-dering on the ursine, repelled the juniors, Billy, unde-terred thereby, revering him as a salt hero would make advances, never passing the old Agamemnon-man without a salutation marked by that respect which is seldom lost on the aged however crabbed at times or whatever their station in life.

There was a vein of dry humor, or what not, in the mast-man; and, whether in freak of patriarchal irony touching Billy's youth and athletic frame, or for some other and more recondite reason, from the first in addressing him he always substituted Baby for Billy. The Dansker in fact being the originator of the name by which the foretopman eventually became known aboard ship.

Well then, in his mysterious little difficulty going in quest of the wrinkled one, Billy found him off duty in a dog-watch ruminating by himself seated on a shot-box of the upper gun-deck now and then surveying with a some-what cynical regard certain of the more swaggering prom-enaders there. Billy recounted his trouble, again wonder-ing how it all happened. The salt seer attentively listened, accompanying the foretopman's recital with queer twitch-ings of his wrinkles and problematical little sparkles of his small ferret eyes. Making an end of his story, the fore-topman asked, "And now, Dansker, do tell me what you think of it."

The old man, shoving up the front of his tarpaulin and deliberately rubbing the long slant scar at the point where it entered the thin hair, laconically said, "Baby Budd, *Jimmy Legs*" (meaning the master-at-arms) "is down on you."

"*Jemmy Legs!*" ejaculated Billy his welkin eyes expand-ing; "what for? Why he calls me *the sweet and pleasant young fellow,* they tell me."

"Does he so?" grinned the grizzled one; then said "Ay Baby Lad a sweet voice has *Jimmy Legs.*"

"No, not always. But to me he has. I seldom pass him but there comes a pleasant word."

"And that's because he's down upon you, Baby Budd."

Such reiteration along with the manner of it, incompre-hensible to a novice, disturbed Billy almost as much as the mystery for which he had sought explanation. Something less unpleasingly oracular he tried to extract; but the old sea-Chiron thinking perhaps that for the nonce he had sufficiently instructed his young Achilles, pursed his lips, gathered all his wrinkles together and would commit himself to nothing further.

Years, and those experiences which befall certain shrewder men subordinated life-long to the will of superiors, all this had developed in the Dansker the pithy guarded cynicism that was his leading characteristic.

10

The next day an incident served to confirm Billy Budd in his incredulity as to the Dansker's strange summing up of the case submitted. The ship at noon going large before the wind was rolling on her course, and he below at dinner and engaged in some sportful talk with the members of his mess, chanced in a sudden lurch to spill the entire contents of his soup-pan upon the new scrubbed deck. Claggart, the Master-at-arms, official rattan in hand, happened to be passing along the battery in a bay of which the mess was lodged, and the greasy liquid streamed just across his path. Stepping over it, he was proceeding on his way without comment, since the matter was nothing to take notice of under the circumstances, when he happened to observe who it was that had done the spilling. His countenance changed. Pausing, he was about to ejaculate something hasty at the sailor, but checked himself, and pointing down to the streaming soup, playfully tapped him from behind with his rattan, saying in a low musical voice peculiar to him at times "Handsomely done, my lad! And handsome is as handsome did it too!" And with that passed on. Not noted by Billy as not coming within his view was the involuntary smile, or rather grimace, that accompanied Claggart's equivocal words. Aridly it drew down the thin corners of his shapely mouth. But everybody taking his remark as meant for humorous, and at which therefore as coming from a superior they were bound to laugh, "with counterfeited glee" acted accordingly; and Billy tickled, it may be, by the allusion to his being the handsome sailor, merrily joined in; then addressing his messmates exclaimed "There now, who says that Jimmy Legs is down on me!" "And who said he was, Beauty?" demanded one Donald with some surprise. Whereat the foretopman looked a little foolish recalling that it was only one person, Board-her-in-the-smoke who had suggested what to him was the smoky idea that this master-at-arms was in any peculiar way hostile to him. Meantime that functionary resuming his path must have momentarily worn some expression less guarded than that of the bitter smile, and, usurping the face from the heart, some distorting expression perhaps, for a drummer-boy heedlessly frolicking along from the opposite direction and chancing to come into light collision with his person was strangely disconcerted by his aspect. Nor was the impression lessened when the official impulsively giving him a sharp cut with the rattan, vehemently exclaimed "Look where you go!"

11

What was the matter with the master-at-arms? And, be the matter what it might, how could it have direct relation to Billy Budd with whom prior to the affair of the spilled soup he had never come into any special contact official or otherwise? What indeed could the trouble have to do with one so little inclined to give offence as the merchant-ship's *peacemaker,* even him who in Claggart's own phrase was "the sweet and pleasant young fellow?" Yes, why should *Jemmy Legs,* to borrow the Dansker's expression, be *down* on the Handsome Sailor? But, at heart and not for nothing, as the late chance encounter may indicate to the discerning, down on him, secretly down on him, he assuredly was.

Now to invent something touching the more private career of Claggart, something involving Billy Budd, of which something the latter should be wholly ignorant, some romantic incident implying that Claggart's knowledge of the young blue-jacket began at some period anterior to catching sight of him on board the seventy-four—all this, not so difficult to do, might avail in a way more or less interesting to account for whatever of enigma may appear to lurk in the case. But in fact there was nothing of the sort. And yet the cause, necessarily to be assumed as the sole one assignable, is in its very realism as much charged with that prime element of Radcliffian romance, *the mysterious*, as any that the ingenuity of the author of the *Mysteries of Udolpho* could devise. For what can more partake of the mysterious than an antipathy spontaneous and profound such as is evoked in certain exceptional mortals by the mere aspect of some other mortal, however harmless he may be? if not called forth by this very harmlessness itself.

Now there can exist no irritating juxtaposition of dissimilar personalities comparable to that which is possible aboard a great war-ship fully manned and at sea. There, every day among all ranks almost every man comes into more or less of contact with almost every other man. Wholly there to avoid even the sight of an aggravating object one must needs give it Jonah's toss or jump overboard himself. Imagine how all this might eventually operate on some peculiar human creature the direct reverse of a saint?

But for the adequate comprehending of Claggart by a normal nature these hints are insufficient. To pass from a normal nature to him one must cross "the deadly space between." And this is best done by indirection.

Long ago an honest scholar my senior, said to me in reference to one who like himself is now no more, a man so unimpeachably respectable that against him nothing

was ever openly said though among the few something
was whispered, "Yes, X—— is a nut not to be cracked by
the tap of a lady's fan. You are aware that I am the ad-
herent of no organized religion much less of any philos-
ophy built into a system. Well, for all that, I think that to
try and get into X——, enter his labyrinth and get out
again, without a clue derived from some source other than
what is known as *knowledge of the world*—that were hardly possible, at least for me."

"Why," said I, "X—— however singular a study to some,
is yet human, and knowledge of the world assuredly im-
plies the knowledge of human nature, and in most of its
varieties."

"Yes, but a superficial knowledge of it, serving ordinary
purposes. But for anything deeper, I am not certain whether to know the world and to know human nature be not
two distinct branches of knowledge, which while they may
coexist in the same heart, yet either may exist with little
or nothing of the other. Nay, in an average man of the
world, his constant rubbing with it blunts that fine spiritual insight indispensable to the understanding of the essential in certain exceptional characters, whether evil ones
or good. In a matter of some importance I have seen a girl
wind an old lawyer about her little finger. Nor was it the
dotage of senile love. Nothing of the sort. But he knew
law better than he knew the girl's heart. Coke and Black-
stone hardly shed so much light into obscure spiritual
places as the Hebrew prophets. And who were they? Mostly recluses."

At the time my inexperience was such that I did not
quite see the drift of all this. It may be that I see it now.
And, indeed, if that lexicon which is based on Holy Writ
were any longer popular, one might with less difficulty
define and denominate certain phenomenal men. As it is,
one must turn to some authority not liable to the charge
of being tinctured with the Biblical element.

In a list of definitions included in the authentic translation of Plato, a list attributed to him, occurs this: "Natural Depravity: a depravity according to nature." A definition which though savoring of Calvinism, by no means involves Calvin's dogma as to total mankind. Evidently its intent makes it applicable but to individuals. Not many are the examples of this depravity which the gallows and jail supply. At any rate for notable instances, since these have no vulgar alloy of the brute in them, but invariably are dominated by intellectuality, one must go elsewhere. Civilization, especially if of the austerer sort, is auspicious to it. It folds itself in the mantle of respectability. It has its certain negative virtues serving as silent auxiliaries. It never allows wine to get within its guard. It is not going too far to say that it is without vices or small sins. There is a phenomenal pride in it that excludes them from anything mercenary or avaricious. In short the depravity here meant partakes nothing of the sordid or sensual. It is serious, but free from acerbity. Though no flatterer of mankind it never speaks ill of it.

But the thing which in eminent instances signalizes so exceptional a nature is this: though the man's even temper and discreet bearing would seem to intimate a mind peculiarly subject to the law of reason, not the less in his heart he would seem to riot in complete exemption from that law having apparently little to do with reason further than to employ it as an ambidexter implement for effecting the irrational. That is to say: Toward the accomplishment of an aim which in wantonness of malignity would seem to partake of the insane, he will direct a cool judgement sagacious and sound.

These men are true madmen, and of the most dangerous sort, for their lunacy is not continuous but occasional evoked by some special object; it is probably secretive, which is as much to say it is self-contained, so that when moreover, most active it is to the average mind not distinguishable from sanity, and for the reason above suggested that whatever its aims may be, and the aim is never declared—the method and the outward proceeding are always perfectly rational.

Now something such an one was Claggart, in whom was the mania of an evil nature, not engendered by vicious training or corrupting books or licentious living, but born with him and innate, in short "a depravity according to nature."

12

Lawyers, Experts, Clergy
An Episode

By the way, can it be the phenomenon, disowned or at least concealed, that in some criminal cases puzzles the courts? For this cause have our juries at times not only to endure the prolonged contentions of lawyers with their fees, but also the yet more perplexing strife of the medical experts with theirs?—But why leave it to them? why not subpoena (?) as well the clerical proficients? Their vocation bringing them into peculiar contact with so many human beings, and sometimes in their least guarded hour, in interviews very much more confidential than those of physician and patient; this would seem to qualify them to know something about those intricacies involved in the question of moral responsibility; whether in a given case, say, the crime proceeded from mania in the brain or rabies of the heart. As to any differences among themselves these clerical proficients might develop on the stand, these could hardly be greater than the direct contradictions exchanged between the remunerated medical experts.

Dark sayings are these, some will say. But why? Is it because they somewhat savor of Holy Writ in its phrase "mysteries of iniquity"? If they do, such savor was far enough from being intended for little will it commend these pages to many a reader of to-day.

The point of the present story turning on the hidden nature of the master-at-arms has necessitated this chapter. With an added hint or two in connection with the incident at the mess, the resumed narrative must be left to vindicate, as it may, its own credibility.

13

Pale ire, envy and despair

That Claggart's figure was not amiss, and his face, save the chin, well moulded, has already been said. Of these favorable points he seemed not insensible, for he was not only neat but careful in his dress. But the form of Billy Budd was heroic; and if his face was without the intellectual look of the pallid Claggart's, not the less was it lit, like his, from within, though from a different source. The bonfire in his heart made luminous the rose-tan in his cheek.

In view of the marked contrast between the persons of the twain, it is more than probable that when the master-at-arms in the scene last given applied to the sailor the proverb *Handsome is as handsome does;* he there let escape an ironic inkling, not caught by the young sailors who heard it, as to what it was that had first moved him against Billy, namely, his significant personal beauty.

Now envy and antipathy passions irreconcilable in reason, nevertheless in fact may spring conjoined like Chang and Eng in one birth. Is Envy then such a monster? Well, though many an arraigned mortal has in hopes of mitigated penalty pleaded guilty to horrible actions, did ever anybody seriously confess to envy? Something there is in it universally felt to be more shameful than even felonious crime. And not only does everybody disown it but the better sort are inclined to incredulity when it is in earnest imputed to an intelligent man. But since its lodgement is in the heart not the brain, no degree of intellect supplies a guarantee against it. But Claggart's was no vulgar form of the passion. Nor, as directed toward Billy Budd did it partake of that streak of apprehensive jealousy that marred Saul's visage perturbedly brooding on the comely young David. Claggart's envy struck deeper. If askance he eyed the good looks, cheery health and frank enjoyment of young life in Billy Budd, it was because these went along with a nature that as Claggart magnetically felt, had in its simplicity never willed malice or experienced the reactionary bite of that serpent. To him, the spirit lodged within Billy, and looking out from his welkin eyes as from windows, that ineffability it was which made the dimple in his dyed cheek, suppled his joints, and dancing in his yellow curls made him preeminently the Handsome Sailor. One person excepted the master-at-arms was perhaps the only man in the ship intellectually capable of adequately appreciating the moral phenomenon presented in Billy Budd. And the insight but intensified his passion, which assuming various secret forms within him, at times assumed that of cynic disdain—disdain of innocence—To be nothing more than innocent! Yet in an aesthetic way he saw the charm of it, the courageous free-and-easy temper of it, and fain would have shared it, but he despaired of it.

With no power to annul the elemental evil in him, though readily enough he could hide it; apprehending the good, but powerless to be it; a nature like Claggart's surcharged with energy as such natures almost invariably are, what recourse is left to it but to recoil upon itself and like the scorpion for which the Creator alone is responsible, act out to the end the part allotted it.

14

Passion, and passion in its profoundest, is not a thing demanding a palatial stage whereon to play its part. Down among the groundlings, among the beggars and rakers of the garbage, profound passion is enacted. And the circumstances that provoke it, however trivial or mean, are no measure of its power. In the present instance the stage is a scrubbed gun-deck, and one of the external provocations a man-of-war's-man's spilled soup.

Now when the Master-at-arms noticed whence came that greasy fluid streaming before his feet, he must have taken it—to some extent wilfully, perhaps—not for the mere accident it assuredly was, but for the sly escape of a spontaneous feeling on Billy's part more or less answering to the antipathy on his own. In effect a foolish demonstration he must have thought, and very harmless, like the futile kick of a heifer, which yet were the heifer a shod stallion, would not be so harmless. Even so was it that into the gall of Claggart's envy he infused the vitriol of his contempt. But the incident confirmed to him certain tell-tale reports purveyed to his ear by *Squeak,* one of his more cunning Corporals, a grizzled little man, so nicknamed by the sailors on account of his squeaky voice, and sharp visage ferreting about the dark corners of the lower decks after interlopers, satirically suggesting to them the idea of a rat in a cellar.

From his Chief's employing him as an implicit tool in laying little traps for the worriment of the Foretopman—for it was from the Master-at-arms that the petty persecutions heretofore adverted to had proceeded—the corporal having naturally enough concluded that his master could have no love for the sailor, made it his business, faithful understrapper that he was, to foment the ill blood by perverting to his Chief certain innocent frolics of the good natured Foretopman, besides inventing for his mouth sundry contumelious epithets he claimed to have overheard him let fall. The Master-at-arms never suspected the veracity of these reports, more especially as to the epithets, for he well knew how secretly unpopular may become a master-at-arms at least a master-at-arms of those days zealous in his function, and how the blue-jackets shoot at him in private their raillery and wit; the nickname by which he goes among them (*Jimmy Legs*) implying under the form of merriment their cherished disrespect and dislike.

But in view of the greediness of hate for patrolmen it hardly needed a purveyor to feed Claggart's passion. An uncommon prudence is habitual with the subtler depravity, for it has everything to hide. And in case of an injury but suspected, its secretiveness voluntarily cuts it off from enlightenment or disillusion; and, not unreluctantly, action is taken upon surmise as upon certainty. And the retaliation is apt to be in monstrous disproportion to the supposed offence; for when in anybody was revenge in its exactions aught else but an inordinate usurer. But how with Claggart's conscience? for though consciences are unlike as foreheads, every intelligence, not excluding the Scriptural devils who "believe and tremble," has one. But Claggart's conscience being but the lawyer to his will, made ogres of trifles, probably arguing that the motive imputed to Billy in spilling the soup just when he did, together with the epithets alleged, these, if nothing more, made a strong case against him; nay, justified animosity into a sort of retributive righteousness. The Pharisee is the Guy Fawkes prowling in the hid chambers underlying the Claggarts. And they can really form no conception of an unreciprocated malice. Probably, the master-at-arms' clandestine persecution of Billy was started to try the temper of the man; but it had not developed any quality in him that enmity could make official use of or even pervert into even plausible self-justification; so that the occurrence at the mess, petty if it were, was a welcome one to that peculiar conscience assigned to be the private mentor of Claggart; And, for the rest, not improbably it put him upon new experiments.

15

Not many days after the last incident narrated something befell Billy Budd that more gravelled him than aught that had previously occurred.

It was a warm night for the latitude; and the Foretopman, whose watch at the time was properly below, was dozing on the uppermost deck whither he had ascended from his hot hammock one of hundreds suspended so closely wedged together over a lower gun-deck that there was little or no swing to them. He lay as in the shadow of a hill-side, stretched under the lee of the *booms,* a piled ridge of spare spars amidships between foremast and mainmast and among which the ship's largest boat, the launch, was stowed. Alongside of three other slumberers from below, he lay near that end of the booms which approaches the foremast; his station aloft on duty as a foretopman being just over the deck-station of the forecastlemen, entitling him according to usage to make himself more or less at home in that neighborhood.

Presently he was stirred into semi-consciousness by somebody, who must have previously sounded the sleep of the others, touching his shoulder, and then as the Foretopman raised his head, breathing into his ear in a quick whisper, "Slip into the lee forechains, Billy; there is something in the wind. Don't speak. Quick I will meet you there;" and disappeared.

Now Billy like sundry other essentially good natured ones had some of the weaknesses inseparable from essential good nature; and among these was a reluctance, almost an incapacity of plumply saying *no* to an abrupt proposition not obviously absurd, on the face of it, nor obviously unfriendly, nor iniquitous. And being of warm blood he had not the phlegm tacitly to negative any proposition by unresponsive inaction. Like his sense of fear, his apprehension as to aught outside of the honest and natural was seldom very quick. Besides, upon the present occasion, the drowse from his sleep still hung upon him.

However it was, he mechanically rose, and sleepily wondering what could be in the wind, betook himself to the designated place, a narrow platform, one of six, outside of the high bulwarks and screened by the great dead-eyes and multiple columned lanyards of the shrouds and backstays; and, in a great war-ship of that time, of dimensions commensurate to the hull's magnitude; a tarry balcony in short overhanging the sea, and so secluded that one mariner of the *Indomitable*, a non-conformist old tar of a serious turn, made it even in daytime his private oratory.

In this retired nook the stranger soon joined Billy Budd. There was no moon as yet; a haze obscured the star-light. He could not distinctly see the stranger's face. Yet from something in the outline and carriage, Billy took him to be, and correctly, for one of the afterguard.

"Hist! Billy," said the man in the same quick cautionary whisper as before; "You were impressed, weren't you? Well, so was I;" and he paused, as to mark the effect. But Billy not knowing exactly what to make of this said nothing. Then the other: "We are not the only impressed ones, Billy. There's a gang of us.—Couldn't you—help—at a pinch?"

"What do you mean?" demanded Billy here shaking off his drowse.

"Hist, hist!" the hurried whisper now growing husky, "see here;" and the man held up two small objects faintly twinkling in the nightlight; "see, they are yours, Billy, if you'll only—"

But Billy broke in, and in his resentful eagerness to deliver himself his vocal infirmity somewhat intruded: "D-D-Damme, I don't know what you are d-d-driving at, or what you mean, but you had better g-g-go where you belong!" For the moment the fellow, as confounded, did not stir; and Billy, springing to his feet, said "If you d-don't start I'll t-t-toss you back over the r-rail!" There was no mistaking this and the mysterious emissary decamped, disappearing in the direction of the mainmast in the shadow of the booms.

"Hallo, what's the matter?" here came growling from a forecastleman awakened from his deck-doze by Billy's raised voice. And as the foretopman reappeared and was recognized by him; "Ah, *Beauty*, is it you? Well, something must have been the matter for you st-st-stuttered."

"O," rejoined Billy, now mastering the impediment; "I found an afterguardsman in our part of the ship here and I bid him be off where he belongs."

"And is that all you did about it, foretopman?" gruffly demanded another, an irascible old fellow of brick-colored visage and hair, and who was known to his associate forecastlemen as *Red Pepper;* "Such sneaks I should like to marry to the gunner's daughter!" by that expression meaning that he would like to subject them to disciplinary castigation over a gun.

However, Billy's rendering of the matter satisfactorily accounted to these inquirers for the brief commotion, since of all the sections of a ship's company the forecastlemen, veterans for the most part and bigoted in their sea-prejudices, are the most jealous in resenting territorial encroachments, especially on the part of any of the afterguard, of whom they have but a sorry opinion, chiefly landsmen, never going aloft except to reef or furl the mainsail, and in no wise competent to handle a marlin-spike or turn in a *dead-eye,* say.

16

This incident sorely puzzled Billy Budd. It was an entirely new experience; the first time in his life that he had ever been personally approached in underhand intriguing fashion. Prior to this encounter he had known nothing of the afterguardsman, the two men being stationed wide apart, one forward and aloft during his watch, the other on deck and aft.

What could it mean? And could they really be guineas, those two glittering objects the interloper had held up to his (Billy's) eyes? Where could the fellow get guineas? Why even buttons spare buttons are not so plentiful at sea. The more he turned the matter over, the more he was non-plussed, and made uneasy and discomforted. In his disgustful recoil from an overture which though he but ill comprehended he instinctively knew must involve evil of some sort, Billy Budd was like a young horse fresh from the pasture suddenly inhaling a vile whiff from some chemical factory and by repeated snortings tries to get it out of his nostrils and lungs. This frame of mind barred all desire of holding further parley with the fellow, even were it but for the purpose of gaining some enlightenment as to his design in approaching him. And yet he was not without natural curiosity to see how such a visitor in the dark would look in broad day.

He espied him the following afternoon in his first dog-watch below one of the smokers on that forward part of the upper gun deck allotted to the pipe. He recognized him by his general cut and build, more than by his round freckled face and glassy eyes of pale blue, veiled with lashes all but white. And yet Billy was a bit uncertain whether indeed it were he—yonder chap about his own age chatting and laughing in free-hearted way, leaning against a gun; a genial young fellow enough to look at, and something of a rattle-brain, to all appearance. Rather chubby too for a sailor even an afterguardsman. In short the last man in the world, one would think, to be overburthened with thoughts, especially those perilous thoughts that must needs belong to a conspirator in any serious project, or even to the underling of such a conspirator.

Although Billy was not aware of it, the fellow, with a

sidelong watchful glance had perceived Billy first, and then noting that Billy was looking at him, thereupon nodded a familiar sort of friendly recognition as to an old acquaintance, without interrupting the talk he was engaged in with the group of smokers. A day or two afterwards chancing in the evening promenade on a gun deck, to pass Billy, he offered a flying word of good-fellowship as it were, which by its unexpectedness, and equivocalness under the circumstances so embarrassed Billy that he knew not how to respond to it, and let it go unnoticed.

Billy was now left more at a loss than before. The ineffectual speculations into which he was led were so disturbingly alien to him that he did his best to smother them. It never entered his mind that here was a matter which from its extreme questionableness, it was his duty as a loyal blue-jacket to report in the proper quarter. And, probably, had such a step been suggested to him, he would have been deterred from taking it by the thought, one of novice-magnanimity, that it would savor overmuch of the dirty work of a tell-tale. He kept the thing to himself. Yet upon one occasion, he could not forbear a little disburdening himself to the old Dansker, tempted thereto perhaps by the influence of a balmy night when the ship lay becalmed; the twain, silent for the most part, sitting together on deck, their heads propped against the bulwarks. But it was only a partial and anonymous account that Billy gave, the unfounded scruples above referred to preventing full disclosure to anybody. Upon hearing Billy's version, the sage Dansker seemed to divine more than he was told; and after a little meditation during which his wrinkles were pursed as into a point, quite effacing for the time that quizzing expression his face sometimes wore,—"Didn't I say so, Baby Budd?"

"Say what?" demanded Billy.

"Why, *Jemmy Legs* is *down* on you."

"And what" rejoined Billy in amazement, "has *Jemmy Legs* to do with that cracked afterguardsman?"

"Ho, it was an afterguardsman then. A cat's-paw, a cat's-paw!" And with that exclamation, which, whether it had reference to a light puff of air just then coming over the calm sea, or subtler relation to the afterguardsman, there is no telling, the old Merlin gave a twisting wrench with his black teeth at his plug of tobacco, vouchsafing no reply to Billy's impetuous question, though now repeated, for it was his wont to relapse into grim silence when interrogated in skeptical sort as to any of his sententious oracles, not always very clear ones, rather partaking of that obscurity which invests most Delphic deliverances from any quarter.

Long experience had very likely brought this old man to that bitter prudence which never interferes in aught and never gives advice.

17

Yes, despite the Dansker's pithy insistence as to the Master-at-arms being at the bottom of these strange experiences of Billy on board the *Indomitable*, the young sailor was ready to ascribe them to almost anybody but the man who, to use Billy's own expression, "always had a pleasant word for him." This is to be wondered at. Yet not so much to be wondered at. In certain matters, some sailors even in mature life remain unsophisticated enough. But a young seafarer of the disposition of our athletic Foretopman, is much of a child-man. And yet a child's utter innocence is but its blank ignorance, and the innocence more or less wanes as intelligence waxes. But in Billy Budd intelligence, such as it was, had advanced, while yet his simplemindedness remained for the most part unaffected. Experience is a teacher indeed; yet did Billy's years make his experience small. Besides, he had none of that intuitive knowledge of the bad which in natures not good or incompletely so foreruns experience, and therefore may pertain, as in some instances it too clearly does pertain, even to youth.

And what could Billy know of man except of man as a mere sailor? And the old-fashioned sailor, the veritable man-before-the-mast, the sailor from boyhood up, he, though indeed of the same species as a landsman is in some respects singularly distinct from him. The sailor is frankness, the landsman is finesse. Life is not a game with the sailor, demanding the long head; no intricate game of chess where few moves are made in straightforwardness, and ends are attained by indirection; an oblique, tedious, barren game hardly worth that poor candle burnt out in playing it.

Yes, as a class, sailors are in character a juvenile race. Even their deviations are marked by juvenility. And this more especially holding true with the sailors of Billy's time. Then, too, certain things which apply to all sailors, do more pointedly operate here and there, upon the junior one. Every sailor, too is accustomed to obey orders without debating them; his life afloat is externally ruled for him; he is not brought into that promiscuous commerce with mankind where unobstructed free agency on equal terms—equal superficially, at least—soon teaches one that unless upon occasion he exercise a distrust keen in proportion to the fairness of the appearance, some foul turn may be served him. A ruled undemonstrative distrustfulness is so habitual, not with business-men so much, as with men who know their kind in less shallow relations than business, namely, certain men-of-the-world, that they come at last to employ it all but unconsciously; and some of them would very likely feel real surprise at being charged with it as one of their general characteristics.

18

But after the little matter at the mess Billy Budd no more
found himself in strange trouble at times about his hammock or his clothes-bag or what not. While, as to that
smile that occasionally sunned him, and the pleasant passing word, these were if not more frequent, yet if anything
more pronounced than before.

But for all that, there were certain other demonstrations
now. When Claggart's unobserved glance happened to
light on belted Billy rolling along the upper gun-deck in
the leisure of the second dog-watch exchanging passing
broadsides of fun with other young promenaders in the
crowd; that glance would follow the cheerful sea-Hyperion
with a settled meditative and melancholy expression, his
eyes strangely suffused with incipient feverish tears. Then
would Claggart look like the man of sorrows. Yes, and
sometimes the melancholy expression would have in it a
touch of soft yearning, as if Claggart could even have loved
Billy but for fate and ban. But this was an evanescence,
and quickly repented of, as it were, by an immitigable
look, pinching and shrivelling the visage into the momentary semblance of a wrinkled walnut. But sometimes catching sight in advance of the foretopman coming in his direction, he would, upon their nearing, step aside a little to
let him pass, dwelling upon Billy for the moment with the
glittering dental satire of a Guise. But upon any abrupt
unforeseen encounter a red light would flash forth from
his eye like a spark from an anvil in a dusk smithy. That
quick fierce light was a strange one, darted from orbs which
in repose were of a color nearest approaching a deeper
violet, the softest of shades.

Though some of these caprices of the pit could not but
be observed by their object, yet were they beyond the con-
struing of such a nature. And the *thews* of Billy were hard-

ly compatible with that sort of sensitive spiritual organisation which in some cases instinctively conveys to ignorant innocence an admonition of the proximity of the malign. He thought the Master-at-arms acted in a manner rather queer at times. That was all. But the occasional frank air and pleasant word went for what they purported to be, the young sailor never having heard as yet of the "too fair-spoken man."

Had the foretopman been conscious of having done or said anything to provoke the ill will of the official, it would have been different with him, and his sight might have been purged if not sharpened. As it was innocence was his blinder.

So was it with him in yet another matter. Two minor officers—the Armorer and Captain of the Hold, with whom he had never exchanged a word, his position in the ship not bringing him into contact with them; these men now for the first began to cast upon Billy when they chanced to encounter him, that peculiar glance which evidences that the man from whom it comes has been some way tampered with and to the prejudice of him upon whom the glance lights. Never did it occur to Billy as a thing to be noted or a thing suspicious, though he well knew the fact, that the Armorer and Captain of the Hold, with the ship's-yeoman, apothecary, and others of that grade, were by naval usage, mess-mates of the master-at-arms, men with ears convenient to his confidential tongue.

But the general popularity that our *Handsome Sailor's* manly forwardness upon occasion, and irresistible good nature indicating no mental superiority tending to excite an invidious feeling; this good will on the part of most of his shipmates made him the less to concern himself about such mute aspects toward him as those whereto allusion has just been made.

As to the afterguardsman, though Billy for reasons already given necessarily saw little of him, yet when the two did happen to meet, invariably came the fellow's off-hand cheerful recognition, sometimes accompanied by a passing pleasant word or two. Whatever that equivocal young person's original design may really have been, or the design of which he might have been the deputy, certain it was from his manner upon these occasions, that he had wholly dropped it.

It was as if his precocity of crookedness (and every vulgar villain is precocious) had for once deceived him, and the man he had sought to entrap as a simpleton had, through his very simplicity ignominiously baffled him.

But shrewd ones may opine that it was hardly possible for Billy to refrain from going up to the afterguardsman and bluntly demanding to know his purpose in the initial interview, so abruptly closed in the fore-chains. Shrewd ones may also think it but natural in Billy to set about sounding some of the other impressed men of the ship in order to discover what basis, if any, there was for the emissary's obscure suggestions as to plotting disaffection aboard. Yes, the shrewd may so think. But something more, or rather, something else than mere shrewdness is perhaps needful for the due understanding of such a character as Billy Budd's.

As to Claggart, the monomania in the man—if that indeed it were—as involuntarily disclosed by starts in the manifestations detailed, yet in general covered over by his self-contained and rational demeanor; this, like a subterranean fire was eating its way deeper and deeper in him. Something decisive must come of it.

19

After the mysterious interview in the fore-chains, the one so abruptly ended there by Billy, nothing especially German to the story occurred until the events now about to be narrated.

Elsewhere it has been said that in the lack of frigates (of

course better sailers than line-of-battle ships) in the English squadron up the Straits at that period, the *Indomitable* was occasionally employed not only as an available substitute for a scout, but at times on detached service of more important kind. This was not alone because of her sailing qualities, not common in a ship of her rate, but quite as much, probably, that the character of her commander, it was thought, specially adapted him for any duty where under unforeseen difficulties a prompt initiative might have to be taken in some matter demanding knowledge and ability in addition to those qualities implied in good seamanship. It was on an expedition of the latter sort, a somewhat distant one, and when the *Indomitable* was almost at her furthest remove from the fleet that in the latter part of an afternoon-watch she unexpectedly came in sight of a ship of the enemy. It proved to be a frigate. The latter perceiving through the glass that the weight of men and metal would be heavily against her, invoking her light heels crowded sail to get away. After a chace urged almost against hope and lasting until about the middle of the first dog-watch, she signally succeeded in effecting her escape.

Not long after the pursuit had been given up, and ere the excitement incident thereto had altogether waned away, the Master-at-Arms ascending from his cavernous sphere made his appearance cap in hand by the mainmast respectfully waiting the notice of Captain Vere then solitary walking the weather-side of the quarter-deck, doubtless somewhat chafed at the failure of the pursuit. The spot where Claggart stood was the place allotted to men of lesser grades seeking some more particular interview either with the officer-of-the-deck or the Captain himself. But from the latter it was not often that a sailor or petty-officer of those days would seek a hearing; only some exceptional cause, would, according to established custom, have warranted that.

Presently, just as the Commander absorbed in his reflections was on the point of turning aft in his promenade,

he became sensible of Claggart's presence, and saw the
doffed cap held in deferential expectancy. Here be it said
that Captain Vere's personal knowledge of this petty-officer
had only begun at the time of the ship's last sailing from
home, Claggart then for the first, in transfer from a ship
detained for repairs, supplying on board the *Indomitable*
the place of a previous master-at-arms disabled and ashore.

No sooner did the Commander observe who it was that
now deferentially stood awaiting his notice, than a peculiar
expression came over him. It was not unlike that which
uncontrollably will flit across the countenance of one at
unawares encountering a person who though known to
him indeed has hardly been long enough known for thorough knowledge, but something in whose aspect nevertheless now for the first provokes a vaguely repellent distaste.
But coming to a stand, and resuming much of his wonted
official manner, save that a sort of impatience lurked in
the intonation of the opening word, he said, "Well? what
is it, Master-at-Arms?"

With the air of a subordinate grieved at the necessity of
being a messenger of ill tidings, and while conscientiously
determined to be frank, yet equally resolved upon shun-
ning overstatement, Claggart at this invitation or rather
summons to disburthen, spoke up. What he said, conveyed
in the language of no uneducated man, was to the effect
following if not altogether in these words, namely, that
during the chace and preparations for the possible encounter he had seen enough to convince him that at least
one sailor aboard was a dangerous character in a ship mustering some who not only had taken a guilty part in the
late serious troubles, but others also who, like the man in
question, had entered His Majesty's service under another
form than enlistment.

At this point Captain Vere with some impatience interrupted him: "Be direct, man; say impressed men."

Claggart made a gesture of subservience, and proceeded.

Quite lately, he (Claggart) had begun to suspect that

on the gun-decks some sort of movement prompted by the sailor in question was covertly going on, but he had not thought himself warranted in reporting the suspicion so long as it remained indistinct. But from what he had that afternoon observed in the man referred to the suspicion of something clandestine going on had advanced to a point less removed from certainty. He deeply felt, he added, the serious responsibility assumed in making a report involving such possible consequences to the individual mainly concerned, besides tending to augment those natural anxieties which every naval commander must feel in view of extraordinary outbreaks so recent as those which, he sorrowfully said it, it needed not to name.

Now at the first broaching of the matter Captain Vere taken by surprise could not wholly dissemble his disquietude. But as Claggart went on, the former's aspect changed into restiveness under something in the witness' manner in giving his testimony. However, he refrained from interrupting him. And Claggart, continuing, concluded with this:

"God forbid, your honor, that the *Indomitable's* should be the experience of the ——"

"Never mind that!" here peremptorily broke in the superior, his face altering with anger, instinctively divining the ship that the other was about to name, one in which the Nore Mutiny had assumed a singularly tragical character that for a time jeopardized the life of its commander. Under the circumstances he was indignant at the purposed allusion. When the commissioned officers themselves were on all occasions very heedful how they referred to the recent events, for a petty-officer unnecessarily to allude to them in the presence of his Captain, this struck him as a most immodest presumption. Besides, to his quick sense of self-respect, it even looked under the circumstances something like an attempt to alarm him. Nor at first was he without some surprise that one who so far as he had hitherto come under his notice had shown considerable

tact in his function should in this particular evince such
lack of it.

But these thoughts and kindred dubious ones flitting
across his mind were suddenly replaced by an intuitional
surmise which though as yet obscure in form served practically to affect his reception of the ill tidings. Certain it
is, that long versed in everything pertaining to the complicated gun-deck life, which like every other form of life,
has its secret mines and dubious side, the side popularly
disclaimed, Captain Vere did not permit himself to be
unduly disturbed by the general tenor of his subordinate's
report. Furthermore, if in view of recent events prompt
action should be taken at the first palpable sign of recurring insubordination, for all that, not judicious would
it be, he thought, to keep the idea of lingering disaffection
alive by undue forwardness in crediting an informer even
if his own subordinate and charged among other things
with police surveillance of the crew. This feeling would
not perhaps have so prevailed with him were it not that
upon a prior occasion the patriotic zeal officially evinced
by Claggart had somewhat irritated him as appearing rather supersensible and strained. Furthermore something even
in the official's self-possessed and somewhat ostentatious
manner in making his specifications strangely reminded
him of a bandsman, a perjurous witness in a capital case
before a court-martial ashore of which when a lieutenant
he Captain Vere had been a member.

Now the peremptory check given to Claggart in the matter of the arrested allusion was quickly followed up by
this: "You say that there is at least one dangerous man
aboard. Name him."

"William Budd. A foretopman, your honor—"

"William Budd" repeated Captain Vere with unfeigned
astonishment; "and mean you the man that Lieutenant
Ratcliff took from the merchantman not very long ago—
the young fellow who seems to be so popular with the men
—Billy, the Handsome Sailor, as they call him?"

"The same, your honor; but for all his youth and good looks, a deep one. Not for nothing does he insinuate himself into the good will of his shipmates, since at the least all hands will at a pinch say a good word for him at all hazards. Did Lieutenant Ratcliffe happen to tell your honor of that adroit fling of Budd's, jumping up in the cutter's bow under the merchantman's stern when he was being taken off? It is even masqued by that sort of good humored air that at heart he resents his impressment. You have but noted his fair cheek. A man-trap may be under his ruddy-tipped daisies."

Now the *Handsome Sailor* as a signal figure among the crew had naturally enough attracted the Captain's attention from the first. Though in general not very demonstrative to his officers, he had congratulated Lieutenant Ratcliffe upon his good fortune in lighting on such a fine specimen of the genus homo, who in the nude might have posed for a statue of young Adam before the Fall. As to Billy's adieu to the ship *Rights-of-Man,* which the boarding lieutenant had indeed reported to him, but in a deferential way more as a good story than aught else, Captain Vere, though mistakenly understanding it as a satiric sally, had but thought so much the better of the impressed man for it; as a military sailor, admiring the spirit that could take an arbitrary enlistment so merrily and sensibly. The foretopman's conduct, too, so far as it had fallen under the Captain's notice had confirmed the first happy augury, while the new recruit's qualities as a *sailor-man* seemed to be such that he had thought of recommending him to the executive officer for promotion to a place that would more frequently bring him under his own observation, namely, the captaincy of the mizzen-top, replacing there in the starboard watch a man not so young whom partly for that reason he deemed less fitted for the post. Be it parenthesized here that since the mizzen-top-men having not to handle such breadths of heavy canvas as the lower sails on the main-mast and fore-mast, a young man if of the right stuff not only seems best adapted to duty there, but in fact is generally selected for the captaincy of that top, and the company under him are light hands and often but striplings. In sum, Captain Vere had from the beginning deemed Billy Budd to be what in the naval parlance of the time was called a *"King's bargain"* that is to say, for His Britannic Majesty's navy a capital investment at small outlay or none at all.

After a brief pause during which the reminiscences above mentioned passed vividly through his mind and he weighed the import of Claggart's last suggestion conveyed in the phrase "pitfall under the clover," and the more he weighed it the less reliance he felt in the informer's good faith. Suddenly he turned upon him and in a low voice: "Do you come to me, Master-at-Arms, with so foggy a tale? As to Budd, cite me an act or spoken word of his confirmatory of what you in general charge against him. Stay," drawing nearer to him "heed what you speak. Just now, and in a case like this, there is a yard-arm-end for the false-witness."

"Ah, your honor!" sighed Claggart mildly shaking his shapely head as in sad deprecation of such unmerited severity of tone. Then, bridling—erecting himself as in virtuous self-assertion, he circumstantially alleged certain words and acts, which collectively, if credited, led to presumptions mortally inculpating Budd. And for some of these averments, he added, substantiating proof was not far.

With gray eyes impatient and distrustful essaying to fathom to the bottom Claggart's calm violet ones, Captain Vere again heard him out; then for the moment stood ruminating. The mood he evinced, Claggart—himself for the time liberated from the other's scrutiny—steadily regarded with a look difficult to render,—a look curious of the operation of his tactics, a look such as might have been that of the spokesman of the envious children of Jacob deceptively imposing upon the troubled patriarch the blood-dyed coat of young Joseph.

Though something exceptional in the moral quality of Captain Vere made him, in earnest encounter with a fellow-man, a veritable touch-stone of that man's essential nature, yet now as to Claggart and what was really going on in him his feeling partook less of intuitional conviction than of strong suspicion clogged by strange dubieties. The perplexity he evinced proceeded less from aught touching the man informed against—as Claggart doubtless opined—than from considerations how best to act in regard to the informer. At first indeed he was naturally for summoning that substantiation of his allegations which Claggart said was at hand. But such a proceeding would result in the matter at once getting abroad, which in the present stage of it, he thought, might undesirably affect the ship's company. If Claggart was a false witness,—that closed the affair. And therefore before trying the accusation, he would first practically test the accuser; and he thought this could be done in a quiet undemonstrative way.

The measure he determined upon involved a shifting of the scene, a transfer to a place less exposed to observation than the broad quarter-deck. For although the few gun-room officers there at the time had, in due observance of naval etiquette, withdrawn to leeward the moment Captain Vere had begun his promenade on the deck's weatherside; and though during the colloquy with Claggart they of course ventured not to diminish the distance; and though throughout the interview Captain Vere's voice was far from high, and Claggart's silvery and low; and the wind in the cordage and the wash of the sea helped the more to put them beyond ear-shot; nevertheless, the interview's continuance already had attracted observation from some topmen aloft and other sailors in the waist or further forward.

Having determined upon his measures, Captain Vere forthwith took action. Abruptly turning to Claggart he asked "Master-at-arms, is it now Budd's watch aloft?"

"No, your honor." Whereupon, "Mr. Wilkes!" summoning the nearest midshipman, "tell Albert to come to me." Albert was the Captain's hammock-boy, a sort of sea-valet in whose discretion and fidelity his master had much confidence. The lad appeared. "You know Budd the foretopman?"

"I do, Sir."

"Go find him. It is his watch off. Manage to tell him out of earshot that he is wanted aft. Contrive it that he speaks to nobody. Keep him in talk yourself. And not till you get well aft here, not till then let him know that the place where he is wanted is my cabin. You understand. Go.— Master-at-Arms, show yourself on the decks below, and when you think it time for Albert to be coming with his man, stand by quietly to follow the sailor in."

20

Now when the foretopman found himself closeted there, as it were, in the cabin with the Captain and Claggart, he was surprised enough. But it was a surprise unaccompanied by apprehension or distrust. To an immature nature essentially honest and humane, forewarning intimations of subtler danger from one's kind come tardily if at all. The only thing that took shape in the young sailor's mind was this: Yes, the Captain, I have always thought, looks kindly upon me. Wonder if he's going to make me his coxswain. I should like that. And maybe now he is going to ask the master-at-arms about me.

"Shut the door there, sentry," said the commander; "stand without, and let nobody come in.—Now, master-at-arms, tell this man to his face what you told of him to me;" and stood prepared to scrutinize the mutually confronting visages.

With the measured step and calm collected air of an asylum-physician approaching in the public hall some

patient beginning to show indications of a coming paroxysm, Claggart deliberately advanced within short range of
Billy, and mesmerically looking him in the eye, briefly
recapitulated the accusation.

Not at first did Billy take it in. When he did, the rose-
tan of his cheek looked struck as by white leprosy. He
stood like one impaled and gagged. Meanwhile the accuser's eyes removing not as yet from the blue dilated
ones, underwent a phenomenal change, their wonted rich
violet color blurring into a muddy purple. Those lights
of human intelligence losing human expression, gelidly
protruding like the alien eyes of certain uncatalogued
creatures of the deep. The first mesmeric glance was one
of serpent fascination; the last was as the hungry lurch of
the torpedo-fish.

"Speak, man!" said Captain Vere to the transfixed one
struck by his aspect even more than by Claggart's, "Speak!
defend yourself." Which appeal caused but a strange dumb
gesturing and gurgling in Billy; amazement at such an
accusation so suddenly sprung on inexperienced nonage;
this, and, it may be, horror of the accuser, serving to bring
out his lurking defect and in this instance for the time
intensifying it into a convulsed tongue-tie; while the intent head and entire form straining forward in an agony
of ineffectual eagerness to obey the injunction to speak
and defend himself, gave an expression to the face like that
of a condemned Vestal priestess in the moment of being
buried alive, and in the first struggle against suffocation.

Though at the time Captain Vere was quite ignorant of
Billy's liability to vocal impediment, he now immediately
divined it, since vividly Billy's aspect recalled to him that
of a bright young schoolmate of his whom he had once
seen struck by much the same startling impotence in the
act of eagerly rising in the class to be foremost in response
to a testing question put to it by the master. Going close
up to the young sailor, and laying a soothing hand on his
shoulder, he said: "There is no hurry, my boy. Take your

time, take your time." Contrary to the effect intended, these words so fatherly in tone, doubtless touching Billy's heart to the quick, prompted yet more violent efforts at utterance—efforts soon ending for the time in confirming the paralysis, and bringing to his face an expression which was as a crucifixion to behold. The next instant, quick as the flame from a discharged cannon at night, his right arm shot out, and Claggart dropped to the deck. Whether intentionally or but owing to the young athlete's superior height, the blow had taken effect full upon the forehead, so shapely and intellectual-looking a feature in the master-at-arms; so that the body fell over lengthwise, like a heavy plank tilted from erectness. A gasp or two, and he lay motionless.

"Fated boy," breathed Captain Vere in tone so low as to be almost a whisper, "what have you done! But here, help me."

The twain raised the felled one from the loins up into a sitting position. The spare form flexibly acquiesced, but inertly. It was like handling a dead snake. They lowered it back. Regaining erectness Captain Vere with one hand covering his face stood to all appearance as impassive as the object at his feet. Was he absorbed in taking in all the bearings of the event and what was best not only now at once to be done, but also in the sequel? Slowly he uncovered his face; and the effect was as if the moon emerging from eclipse should reappear with quite another aspect than that which had gone into hiding. The father in him, manifested towards Billy thus far in the scene, was replaced by the military disciplinarian. In his official tone he bade the foretopman retire to a state-room aft (pointing it out) and there remain till thence summoned. This order Billy in silence mechanically obeyed. Then going to the cabin-door where it opened on the quarter-deck, Captain Vere said to the sentry without, "Tell somebody to send Albert here." When the lad appeared his master so contrived it that he should not catch sight of the prone one.

"Albert," he said to him, "tell the Surgeon I wish to see him. You need not come back till called." When the Surgeon entered—a self-poised character of that grave sense and experience that hardly anything could take him aback,—Captain Vere advanced to meet him, thus unconsciously intercepting his view of Claggart and interrupting the other's wonted ceremonious salutation, said, "Nay, tell me how it is with yonder man," directing his attention to the prostrate one.

The Surgeon looked, and for all his self-command, somewhat started at the abrupt revelation. On Claggart's always pallid complexion, thick black blood was now oozing from nostril and ear. To the gazer's professional eye it was unmistakably no living man that he saw.

"Is it so then?" said Captain Vere intently watching him. "I thought it. But verify it." Whereupon the customary tests confirmed the Surgeon's first glance, who now looking up in unfeigned concern, cast a look of intense inquisitiveness upon his superior. But Captain Vere, with one hand to his brow, was standing motionless. Suddenly, catching the Surgeon's arm convulsively, he exclaimed, pointing down to the body—"It is the divine judgment on Ananias! Look!"

Disturbed by the excited manner he had never before observed in the *Indomitable's* Captain, and as yet wholly ignorant of the affair, the prudent Surgeon nevertheless held his peace, only again looking an earnest interrogation as to what it was that had resulted in such a tragedy.

But Captain Vere was now again motionless standing absorbed in thought. But again starting, he vehemently exclaimed—"Struck dead by an angel of God! Yet the angel must hang!"

At these passionate interjections, mere incoherences to the listener as yet unapprised of the antecedents, the Surgeon was profoundly discomposed. But now as recollecting himself, Captain Vere in less passionate tone briefly related the circumstances leading up to the event.

"But come; we must despatch" he added. "Help me to remove him (meaning the body) to yonder compartment," designating one opposite that where the foretopman remained immured. Anew disturbed by a request that as implying a desire for secrecy, seemed unaccountably strange to him, there was nothing for the subordinate to do but comply.

"Go now" said Captain Vere with something of his wonted manner—"Go now. I shall presently call a drumhead court. Tell the lieutenants what has happened, and tell Mr. Mordant," meaning the captain of marines, "and charge them to keep the matter to themselves."

21

Full of disquietude and misgiving the Surgeon left the cabin. Was Captain Vere suddenly affected in his mind, or was it but a transient excitement, brought about by so strange and extraordinary a happening? As to the drumhead court, it struck the Surgeon as impolitic, if nothing more. The thing to do, he thought, was to place Billy Budd in confinement and in a way dictated by usage, and postpone further action in so extraordinary a case, to such time as they should rejoin the squadron, and then refer it to the Admiral. He recalled the unwonted agitation of Captain Vere and his excited exclamations so at variance with his normal manner. Was he unhinged? But assuming that he is, it is not so susceptible of proof. What then can he do? No more trying situation is conceivable than that of an officer subordinate under a Captain whom he suspects to be, not mad indeed, but yet not quite unaffected in his intellect. To argue his order to him would be insolence. To resist him would be mutiny.

In obedience to Captain Vere he communicated what had happened to the lieutenants and captain of marines; saying nothing as to the Captain's state. They fully shared

his own surprise and concern. Like him too they seemed
to think that such a matter should be referred to the
Admiral.

22

Who in the rainbow can show the line where the violet
tint ends and the orange tint begins? Distinctly we see the
difference of the colors, but when exactly does the one
first blendingly enter into the other? So with sanity and
insanity. In pronounced cases there is no question about
them. But in some supposed cases, in various degrees supposedly less pronounced, to draw the exact line of de-
markation few will undertake though for a fee some professional experts will. There is nothing namable but that
some men will undertake to do it for pay.

Whether Captain Vere, as the Surgeon professionally
and privately surmised, was really the sudden victim of
any degree of aberration, one must determine for himself
by such light as this narrative may afford.

That the unhappy event which has been narrated could
not have happened at a worse juncture was but too true.
For it was close on the heel of the suppressed insurrections,
an after-time very critical to naval authority, demanding
from every English sea-commander two qualities not readily interfusable—prudence and rigor. Moreover there was
something crucial in the case.

In the jugglery of circumstances preceding and attending the event on board the *Indomitable* and in the light of
that martial code whereby it was formally to be judged,
innocence and guilt personified in Claggart and Budd in
effect changed places. In a legal view the apparent victim
of the tragedy was he who had sought to victimize a man
blameless; and the indisputable deed of the latter, navally
regarded, constituted the most heinous of military crimes.
Yet more. The essential right and wrong involved in the

matter, the clearer that might be, so much the worse for
the responsibility of a loyal sea-commander inasmuch as
he was not authorized to determine the matter on that
primitive basis.

Small wonder then that the *Indomitable's* Captain
though in general a man of rapid decision, felt that cir-
cumspectness not less than promptitude was necessary. Until he could decide upon his course, and in each detail;
and not only so, but until the concluding measure was
upon the point of being enacted, he deemed it advisable,
in view of all the circumstances to guard as much as possible against publicity. Here he may or may not have erred.
Certain it is however that subsequently in the confidential
talk of more than one or two gun-rooms and cabins he was
not a little criticized by some officers, a fact imputed by his
friends and vehemently by his cousin Jack Denton to professional jealousy of *Starry Vere.* Some imaginative ground
for invidious comment there was. The maintenance of
secrecy in the matter, the confining all knowledge of it for
a time to the place where the homicide occurred, the quarter-deck cabin; in these particulars lurked some resem-
blance to the policy adopted in those tragedies of the
palace which have occurred more than once in the capital
founded by Peter the Barbarian.

The case indeed was such that fain would the *Indomitable's* captain have deferred taking any action whatever
respecting it further than to keep the foretopman a close
prisoner till the ship rejoined the squadron and then sub-
mitting the matter to the judgement of his Admiral.

But a true military officer is in one particular like a true
monk. Not with more of self-abnegation will the latter
keep his vows of monastic obedience than the former his
vows of allegiance to martial duty.

Feeling that unless quick action was taken on it, the
deed of the foretopman, so soon as it should be known on
the gun-decks would tend to awaken any slumbering embers of the Nore among the crew, a sense of the urgency

of the case overruled in Captain Vere every other consideration. But though a conscientious disciplinarian he was no lover of authority for mere authority's sake. Very far was he from embracing opportunities for monopolizing to himself the perils of moral responsibility none at least that could properly be referred to an official superior or shared with him by his official equals or even subordinates. So thinking he was glad it would not be at variance with usage to turn the matter over to a summary court of his own officers, reserving to himself as the one on whom the ultimate accountability would rest, the right of maintaining a supervision of it, or formally or informally interposing at need. Accordingly a drum-head court was summarily convened, he electing the individuals composing it, the First Lieutenant, the Captain of marines, and the Sailing Master.

In associating an officer of marines with the sea-lieutenants in a case having to do with a sailor the Commander perhaps deviated from general custom. He was prompted thereto by the circumstance that he took that soldier to be a judicious person, thoughtful, and not altogether incapable of grappling with a difficult case unprecedented in his prior experience. Yet even as to him he was not without some latent misgiving, for withal he was an extremely good-natured man, an enjoyer of his dinner, a sound sleeper, and inclined to obesity. A man who though he would always maintain his manhood in battle might not prove altogether reliable in a moral dilemma involving aught of the tragic. As to the First Lieutenant and the Sailing Master Captain Vere could not but be aware that though honest natures, of approved gallantry upon occasion their intelligence was mostly confined to the matter of active seamanship and the fighting demands of their profession. The court was held in the same cabin where the unfortunate affair had taken place. This cabin, the Commander's, embraced the entire area under the poop-deck. Aft, and on either side was a small state-room the one room tem-

porarily a jail and the other a dead-house and a yet smaller
compartment leaving a space between, expanding forward
into a goodly oblong of length coinciding with the ship's
beam. A skylight of moderate dimension was overhead
and at each end of the oblong space were two sashed port-
hole windows easily convertible back into embrasures for
short carronades.

All being quickly in readiness, Billy Budd was arraigned, Captain Vere necessarily appearing as the sole
witness in the case, and as such temporarily sinking his
rank, though singularly maintaining it in a matter apparently trivial, namely, that he testified from the ship's
weather-side with that object having caused the court to
sit on the lee-side. Concisely he narrated all that had led
up to the catastrophe, omitting nothing in Claggart's accusation and deposing as to the manner in which the prisoner had received it. At this testimony the three officers
glanced with no little surprise at Billy Budd, the last man
they would have suspected either of the mutinous design
alleged by Claggart or the undeniable deed he himself had
done.

The First Lieutenant taking judicial primacy and turning toward the prisoner, said, "Captain Vere has spoken.
Is it or is it not as Captain Vere says?" In response came
syllables not so much impeded in the utterance as might
have been anticipated. They were these: "Captain Vere
tells the truth. It is just as Captain Vere says, but it is not
as the Master-in-Arms said. I have eaten the King's bread
and I am true to the King."

"I believe you, my man," said the witness his voice indicating a suppressed emotion not otherwise betrayed.

"God will bless you for that, Your Honor!" not without
stammering said Billy, and all but broke down. But immediately was recalled to self-control by another question,
to which with the same emotional difficulty of utterance
he said "No, there was no malice between us. I never bore
malice against the Master-at-arms. I am sorry that he is

dead. I did not mean to kill him. Could I have used my tongue I would not have struck him. But he foully lied to my face and in presence of my Captain, and I had to say something, and I could only say it with a blow, God help me!"

In the impulsive above-board manner of the frank one the court saw confirmed all that was implied in words that just previously had perplexed them coming as they did from the testifier to the tragedy and promptly following Billy's impassioned disclaimer of mutinous intent—Captain Vere's words, "I believe you, my man."

Next it was asked of him whether he knew of or suspected aught savoring of incipient trouble (meaning mutiny, though the explicit term was avoided) going on in any section of the ship's company.

The reply lingered. This was naturally imputed by the court to the same vocal embarrassment which had retarded or obstructed previous answers. But in main it was otherwise here; the question immediately recalling to Billy's mind the interview with the afterguardsman in the forechains. But an innate repugnance to playing a part at all approaching that of an informer against one's own shipmates—the same erring sense of uninstructed honor which had stood in the way of his reporting the matter at the time though as a loyal man-of-war-man it was incumbent on him and failure so to do if charged against him and proven, would have subjected him to the heaviest of penalties; this, with the blind feeling now his, that nothing really was being hatched, prevailed with him. When the answer came it was a negative.

"One question more," said the officer of marines now first speaking and with a troubled earnestness, "You tell us that what the Master-at-arms said against you was a lie. Now why should he have so lied, so maliciously lied, since you declare there was no malice between you?"

At that question unintentionally touching on a spiritual sphere wholly obscure to Billy's thoughts, he was non-plussed, evincing a confusion indeed that some observers, such as can readily be imagined, would have construed into involuntary evidence of hidden guilt. Nevertheless he strove some way to answer, but all at once relinquished the vain endeavor, at the same time turning an appealing glance towards Captain Vere as deeming him his best helper and friend. Captain Vere who had been seated for a time rose to his feet, addressing the interrogator. "The question you put to him comes naturally enough. But how can he rightly answer it? or anybody else? unless indeed it be he who lies within there" designating the compartment where lay the corpse. "But the prone one there will not rise to our summons. In effect, though, as it seems to me, the point you make is hardly material. Quite aside from any conceivable motive actuating the Master-at-arms, and irrespective of the provocation to the blow, a martial court must needs in the present case confine its attention to the blow's consequence, which consequence justly is to be deemed not otherwise than as the striker's deed."

This utterance the full significance of which it was not at all likely that Billy took in, nevertheless caused him to turn a wistful interrogative look toward the speaker, a look in its dumb expressiveness not unlike that which a dog of generous breed might turn upon his master seeking in his face some elucidation of a previous gesture ambiguous to the canine intelligence. Nor was the same utterance without marked effect upon the three officers, more especially the soldier. Couched in it seemed to them a meaning unanticipated, involving a prejudgement on the speaker's part. It served to augment a mental disturbance previously evident enough.

The soldier once more spoke; in a tone of suggestive dubiety addressing at once his associates and Captain Vere: "Nobody is present—none of the ship's company, I mean, who might shed lateral light, if any is to be had, upon what remains mysterious in this matter."

"That is thoughtfully put" said Captain Vere; "I see

your drift. Ay, there is a mystery; but, to use a Scriptural phrase, it is 'a mystery of iniquity,' a matter for psychologic theologians to discuss. But what has a military court to do with it? Not to add that for us any possible investigation of it is cut off by the lasting tongue-tie of—him—in yonder," again designating the mortuary state-room. "The prisoner's deed,—with that alone we have to do."

To this, and particularly the closing reiteration, the marine soldier knowing not how aptly to reply, sadly abstained from saying aught. The First Lieutenant who at the outset had not unnaturally assumed primacy in the court, now overrulingly instructed by a glance from Captain Vere, a glance more effective than words, resumed that primacy. Turning to the prisoner, "Budd," he said, and scarce in equable tones, "Budd, if you have aught further to say for yourself, say it now."

Upon this the young sailor turned another quick glance toward Captain Vere; then, as taking a hint from that aspect, a hint confirming his own instinct that silence was now best, replied to the Lieutenant, "I have said all, Sir."

The marine—the same who had been the sentinel without the cabin-door at the time that the foretopman followed by the master-at-arms, entered it—he, standing by the sailor throughout these judicial proceedings, was now directed to take him back to the after compartment originally assigned to the prisoner and his custodian. As the twain disappeared from view, the three officers as partially liberated from some inward constraint associated with Billy's mere presence, simultaneously stirred in their seats. They exchanged looks of troubled indecision, yet feeling that decide they must and without long delay. For Captain Vere, he for the time stood unconsciously with his back toward them, apparently in one of his absent fits, gazing out from a sashed port-hole to windward upon the monotonous blank of the twilight sea. But the court's silence continuing, broken only at moments by brief consultations in low earnest tones, this seemed to assure him and encourage him. Turning, he to-and-fro paced the cabin athwart; in the returning ascent to windward, climbing the slant deck in the ship's lee roll; without knowing it symbolizing thus in his action a mind resolute to surmount difficulties even if against primitive instincts strong as the wind and the sea. Presently he came to a stand before the three. After scanning their faces he stood less as mustering his thoughts for expression, than as one inly deliberating how best to put them to well-meaning men not intellectually mature, men with whom it was necessary to demonstrate certain principles that were axioms to himself. Similar impatience as to talking is perhaps one reason that deters some minds from addressing any popular assemblies.

When speak he did, something both in the substance of what he said and his manner of saying it, showed the influence of unshared studies modifying and tempering the practical training of an active career. This, along with his phraseology now and then was suggestive of the grounds whereon rested that imputation of a certain pedantry socially alleged against him by certain naval men of wholly practical cast, captains who nevertheless would frankly concede that His Majesty's navy mustered no more efficient officer of their grade than *Starry Vere*.

What he said was to this effect: "Hitherto I have been but the witness, little more; and I should hardly think now to take another tone, that of your coadjutor, for the time, did I not perceive in you,—at the crisis too—a troubled hesitancy, proceeding, I doubt not from the clash of military duty with moral scruple—scruple vitalized by compassion. For the compassion how can I otherwise than share it. But, mindful of paramount obligations I strive against scruples that may tend to enervate decision. Not, gentlemen, that I hide from myself that the case is an exceptional one. Speculatively regarded, it well might be referred to a jury of casuists. But for us here acting not as casuists or moralists, it is a case practical, and under martial law practically to be dealt with.

"But your scruples: do they move as in a dusk? Challenge them. Make them advance and declare themselves. Come now: do they import something like this: If, mindless of palliating circumstances, we are bound to regard the death of the Master-at-arms as the prisoner's deed, then does that deed constitute a capital crime whereof the penalty is a mortal one. But in natural justice is nothing but the prisoner's overt act to be considered? How can we adjudge to summary and shameful death a fellow-creature innocent before God, and whom we feel to be so?—Does that state it aright? You sign sad assent. Well, I too feel that, the full force of that. It is Nature. But do these buttons that we wear attest that our allegiance is to Nature? No, to the King. Though the ocean, which is inviolate Nature primeval, though this be the element where we move and have our being as sailors, yet as the King's officers lies our duty in a sphere correspondingly natural? So little is that true, that in receiving our commissions we in the most important regards ceased to be natural free-agents. When war is declared are we the commissioned fighters previously consulted? We fight at command. If our judgements approve the war, that is but coincidence. So in other particulars. So now. For suppose condemnation to follow these present proceedings. Would it be so much we ourselves that would condemn as it would be martial law operating through us? For that law and the rigour of it, we are not responsible. Our vowed responsibility is in this: That however pitilessly that law may operate, we nevertheless adhere to it and administer it.

"But the exceptional in the matter moves the hearts within you. Even so too is mine moved. But let not warm hearts betray heads that should be cool. Ashore in a criminal case will an upright judge allow himself off the bench to be waylaid by some tender kinswoman of the accused seeking to touch him with her tearful plea? Well the heart here denotes the feminine in man, is as that piteous woman, and hard though it be, she must here be ruled out."

He paused, earnestly studying them for a moment; then resumed.

"But something in your aspect seems to urge that it is not solely the heart that moves in you, but also the conscience, the private conscience. But tell me whether or not, occupying the position we do, private conscience should not yield to that imperial one formulated in the code under which alone we officially proceed?"

Here the three men moved in their seats, less convinced than agitated by the course of an argument troubling but the more the spontaneous conflict within.

Perceiving which, the speaker paused for a moment; then abruptly changing his tone, went on.

"To steady us a bit, let us recur to the facts.—In wartime at sea a man-of-war's-man strikes his superior in grade, and the blow kills. Apart from its effect the blow itself is, according to the Articles of War, a capital crime. Furthermore—"

"Ay, Sir," emotionally broke in the officer of marines, "in one sense it was. But surely Budd purposed neither mutiny nor homicide."

"Surely not, my good man. And before a court less arbitrary and more merciful than a martial one, that plea would largely extenuate. At the Last Assizes it shall acquit. But how here? We proceed under the law of the Mutiny Act. In feature no child can resemble his father more than that Act resembles in spirit the thing from which it derives—War. In His Majesty's service—in this ship indeed—there are Englishmen forced to fight for the King against their will. Against their conscience, for aught we know. Though as their fellow-creatures some of us may appreciate their position, yet as navy officers, what reck we of it? Still less recks the enemy. Our impressed men he would fain cut down in the same swath with our volunteers. As regards the enemy's naval conscripts, some of whom may even share our own abhorrence of the regicidal French Directory, it is the same on our side. War looks but to the frontage, the appearance. And the Mutiny Act, War's child, takes after the father. Budd's intent or non-intent is nothing to the purpose.

"But while, put to it by those anxieties in you which I can not but respect, I only repeat myself—while thus strangely we prolong proceedings that should be summary —the enemy may be sighted and an engagement result. We must do; and one of two things must we do—condemn or let go."

"Can we not convict and yet mitigate the penalty?" asked the junior Lieutenant here speaking, and falteringly, for the first.

"Lieutenant, were that clearly lawful for us under the circumstances consider the consequences of such clemency. The people" (meaning the ship's company) "have native-sense; most of them are familiar with our naval usage and tradition; and how would they take it? Even could you explain to them—which our official position forbids—they, long moulded by arbitrary discipline have not that kind of intelligent responsiveness that might qualify them to comprehend and discriminate. No, to the people the fore-topman's deed however it be worded in the announcement will be plain homicide committed in a flagrant act of mutiny. What penalty for that should follow, they know. But it does not follow. *Why?* they will ruminate. You know what sailors are. Will they not revert to the recent outbreak at the Nore? Ay. They know the well-founded alarm—the panic it struck throughout England. Your clement sentence they would account pusillanimous. They would think that we flinch, that we are afraid of them—afraid of practising a lawful rigor singularly demanded at this juncture lest it should provoke new troubles. What shame to us such a conjecture on their part, and how deadly to discipline. You see then, whither prompted by duty and the law I steadfastly drive. But I beseech you, my friends, do not take me amiss. I feel as you do for this unfortunate boy. But did he know our hearts, I take him to be of that generous nature that he would feel even for us on whom in this military necessity so heavy a compulsion is laid."

With that, crossing the deck he resumed his place by the sashed port-hole, tacitly leaving the three to come to a decision. On the cabin's opposite side the troubled court sat silent. Loyal lieges, plain and practical, though at bottom they dissented from some points Captain Vere had put to them, they were without the faculty, hardly had the inclination to gainsay one whom they felt to be an earnest man, one too not less their superior in mind than in naval rank. But it is not improbable that even such of his words as were not without influence over them, less came home to them than his closing appeal to their instinct as sea-officers in the forethought he threw out as to the practical consequences to discipline, considering the unconfirmed tone of the fleet at the time, should a man-of-war's-man's violent killing at sea of a superior in grade be allowed to pass for aught else than a capital crime demanding prompt infliction of the penalty.

Not unlikely they were brought to something more or less akin to that harassed frame of mind which in the year 1842 actuated the commander of the U.S. brig-of-war *Somers* to resolve, under the so-called Articles of War, Articles modelled upon the English Mutiny Act, to resolve upon the execution at sea of a midshipman and two petty-officers as mutineers designing the seizure of the brig. Which resolution was carried out though in a time of peace and within not many days sail of home. An act vindicated by a naval court of inquiry subsequently convened ashore. History, and here cited without comment. True, the circumstances on board the *Somers* were different from those on board the *Indomitable*. But the urgency felt, well-warranted or otherwise, was much the same.

Says a writer whom few know, "Forty years after a battle it is easy for a non-combatant to reason about how it ought to have been fought. It is another thing personally and under fire to direct the fighting while involved in the obscuring smoke of it. Much so with respect to other emergencies involving considerations both practical and moral, and when it is imperative promptly to act. The greater the fog the more it imperils the steamer, and speed is put on though at the hazard of running somebody down. Little ween the snug card-players in the cabin of the responsibilities of the sleepless man on the bridge."

In brief, Billy Budd was formally convicted and sentenced to be hung at the yard-arm in the early morning-watch, it being now night. Otherwise, as is customary in such cases, the sentence would forthwith have been carried out. In war-time on the field or in the fleet, a mortal punishment decreed by a drum-head court—on the field sometimes decreed by but a nod from the General—follows without delay on the heel of conviction without appeal.

23

It was Captain Vere himself who of his own motion communicated the finding of the court to the prisoner; for that purpose going to the compartment where he was in custody and bidding the marine there to withdraw for the time.

Beyond the communication of the sentence what took place at this interview was never known. But in view of the character of the twain briefly closeted in that stateroom, each radically sharing in the rarer qualities of our nature—so rare indeed as to be all but incredible to average minds however much cultivated—some conjectures may be ventured.

It would have been in consonance with the spirit of Captain Vere should he on this occasion have concealed nothing from the condemned one—should he indeed have frankly disclosed to him the part he himself had played in bringing about the decision, at the same time revealing his actuating motives. On Billy's side it is not improbable

that such a confession would have been received in much
the same spirit that prompted it. Not without a sort of joy
indeed he might have appreciated the brave opinion of
him implied in his Captain making such a confidant of
him. Nor, as to the sentence itself could he have been insensible that it was imparted to him as to one not afraid
to die. Even more may have been. Captain Vere in the
end may have developed the passion sometimes latent
under an exterior stoical or indifferent. He was old enough
to have been Billy's father. The austere devotee of military
duty letting himself melt back into what remains primeval
in our formalized humanity may in the end have caught
Billy to his heart even as Abraham may have caught young
Isaac on the brink of resolutely offering him up in obedience to the exacting behest. But there is no telling the sacra-
ment, seldom if in any case revealed to the gadding world
wherever under circumstances at all akin to those here
attempted to be set forth two of great Nature's nobler
order embrace. There is privacy at the time, inviolable
to the survivor, and holy oblivion the sequel to each di-
viner magnanimity, providentially covers all at last.

The first to encounter Captain Vere in act of leaving the
compartment was the senior Lieutenant. The fact he beheld, for the moment one expressive of the agony of the
strong, was to that officer, though a man of fifty, a startling
revelation. That the condemned one suffered less than he
who mainly had effected the condemnation was apparently
indicated by the former's exclamation in the scene soon
perforce to be touched upon.

24

Of a series of incidents within a brief term rapidly following each other, the adequate narration may take up a term
less brief, especially if explanation or comment here and
there seem requisite to the better understanding of such

incidents. Between the entrance into the cabin of him who never left it alive, and him who when he did leave it left it as one condemned to die; between this and the closeted interview just given less than an hour and a half had elapsed. It was an interval long enough however to awaken speculations among no few of the ship's company as to what it was that could be detaining in the cabin the master-at-arms and the sailor; for a rumor that both of them had been seen to enter it and neither of them had been seen to emerge, this rumor had got abroad upon the gun-decks and in the tops; the people of a great warship being in one respect like villagers taking microscopic note of every outward movement or non-movement going on. When therefore in weather not at all tempestuous all hands were called in the second dog-watch, a summons under such circumstances not usual in those hours, the crew were not wholly unprepared for some announcement extraordinary, one having connection too with the continued absence of the two men from their wonted haunts.

There was a moderate sea at the time; and the moon, newly risen and near to being at its full, silvered the white spar-deck wherever not blotted by the clear-cut shadows horizontally thrown of fixtures and moving men. On either side the quarter-deck the marine guard under arms was drawn up; and Captain Vere standing in his place surrounded by all the ward-room officers, addressed his men. In so doing his manner showed neither more nor less than that properly pertaining to his supreme position aboard his own ship. In clear terms and concise he told them what had taken place in the cabin; that the master-at-arms was dead; that he who had killed him had been already tried by a summary court and condemned to death; and that the execution would take place in the early morning watch. The word *mutiny* was not named in what he said. He refrained too from making the occasion an opportunity for any preachment as to the maintenance of discipline, thinking perhaps that under existing circumstances in

the navy the consequence of violating discipline should
be made to speak for itself.

Their captain's announcement was listened to by the
throng of standing sailors in a dumbness like that of a
seated congregation of believers in hell listening to the
clergyman's announcement of his Calvinistic text.

At the close, however, a confused murmur went up. It
began to wax. All but instantly, then, at a sign, it was
pierced and suppressed by shrill whistles of the Boatswain
and his Mates piping down one watch.

To be prepared for burial Claggart's body was delivered
to certain petty-officers of his mess. And here, not to clog
the sequel with lateral matters, it may be added that at a
suitable hour, the Master-at-Arms was committed to the
sea with every funeral honor properly belonging to his
naval grade.

In this proceeding as in every public one growing out
of the tragedy strict adherence to usage was observed. Nor
in any point could it have been at all deviated from, either
with respect to Claggart or Billy Budd without begetting
undesirable speculations in the ship's company, sailors,
and more particularly men-of-war's men, being of all men
the greatest sticklers for usage.

For similar cause, all communication between Captain
Vere and the condemned one ended with the closeted interview already given, the latter being now surrendered to
the ordinary routine preliminary to the end. This transfer
under guard from the Captain's quarters was effected without unusual precautions—at least no visible ones.

If possible not to let the men so much as surmise that
their officers anticipate aught amiss from them is the tacit
rule in a military ship. And the more that some sort of
trouble should really be apprehended the more do the
officers keep that apprehension to themselves; though not
the less unostentatious vigilance may be augmented.

In the present instance the sentry placed over the prisoner had strict orders to let no one have communication

with him but the Chaplain. And certain unobtrusive measures were taken absolutely to insure this point.

25

In a seventy-four of the old order the deck known as the upper gun-deck was the one covered over by the spar-deck which last though not without its armament was for the most part exposed to the weather. In general it was at all hours free from hammocks; those of the crew swinging on the lower gun-deck, and berth-deck, the latter being not only a dormitory but also the place for the stowing of the sailors' bags, and on both sides lined with the large chests or movable pantries of the many messes of the men.

On the starboard side of the *Indomitable's* upper gun-deck, behold Billy Budd under sentry lying prone in irons in one of the bays formed by the regular spacing of the guns comprising the batteries on either side. All these pieces were of the heavier calibre of that period. Mounted on lumbering wooden carriages they were hampered with cumbersome harness of breechen and strong side-tackles for running them out. Guns and carriages, together with the long rammers and shorter lintstocks lodged in loops overhead—all these, as customary, were painted black; and the heavy hempen breechens tarred to the same tint, wore the like livery of the undertakers. In contrast with the funereal hue of these surroundings the prone sailor's exterior apparel, white *jumper* and white duck trousers, each more or less soiled, dimly glimmered in the obscure light of the bay like a patch of discolored snow in early April lingering at some upland cave's black mouth. In effect he is already in his shroud or the garments that shall serve him in lieu of one. Over him but scarce illuminating him, two battle-lanterns swing from two massive beams of the deck above. Fed with the oil supplied by the war-contractors (whose gains, honest or otherwise, are in every land

an anticipated portion of the harvest of death) with flickering splashes of dirty yellow light they pollute the pale
moonshine all but ineffectually struggling in obstructed
flecks through the open ports from which the tompioned
cannon protrude. Other lanterns at intervals serve but to
bring out somewhat the obscurer bays which like small
confessionals or side-chapels in a cathedral branch from
the long dim-vistaed broad aisle between the two batteries
of that covered tier.

Such was the deck where now lay the Handsome Sailor.
Through the rose-tan of his complexion, no pallor could
have shown. It would have taken days of sequestration
from the winds and the sun to have brought about the
effacement of that. But the skeleton in the cheek-bone at
the point of its angle was just beginning delicately to be
defined under the warm-tinted skin. In fervid hearts self-
contained some brief experiences devour our human tissue
as secret fire in a ship's hold consumes cotton in the bale.

But now lying between the two guns, as nipped in the
vice of fate, Billy's agony, mainly proceeding from a generous young heart's virgin experience of the diabolical
incarnate and effective in some men—the tension of that
agony was over now. It survived not the something healing
in the closeted interview with Captain Vere. Without
movement, he lay as in a trance. That adolescent expression previously noted as his, taking on something akin to
the look of a slumbering child in the cradle when the
warm hearth-glow of the still chamber at night plays on
the dimples that at whiles mysteriously form in the cheek,
silently coming and going there. For now and then in the
gyved one's trance a serene happy light born of some wandering reminiscence or dream would diffuse itself over his
face, and then wane away only anew to return.

The Chaplain coming to see him and finding him thus,
and perceiving no sign that he was conscious of his presence, attentively regarded him for a space, then slipping
aside, withdrew for the time, peradventure feeling that

even he the minister of Christ though receiving his stipend from Mars had no consolation to proffer which could result in a peace transcending that which he beheld. But in the small hours he came again. And the prisoner now awake to his surroundings noticed his approach and civilly, all but cheerfully, welcomed him. But it was to little purpose that in the interview following the good man sought to bring Billy Budd to some godly understanding that he must die, and at dawn. True, Billy himself freely referred to his death as a thing close at hand; but it was something in the way that children will refer to death in general, who yet among their other sports will play a funeral with hearse and mourners.

Not that like children Billy was incapable of conceiving what death really is. No, but he was wholly without irrational fear of it, a fear more prevalent in highly civilized communities than those so-called barbarous ones which in all respects stand nearer to unadulterate Nature. And, as elsewhere said, a barbarian Billy radically was; as much so, for all the costume, as his countrymen the British captives, living trophies, made to march in the Roman triumph of Germanicus. Quite as much so as those later barbarians, young men probably, and picked specimens among the earlier British converts to Christianity, at least nominally such and taken to Rome (as today converts from lesser isles of the sea may be taken to London) of whom the Pope of that time, admiring the strangeness of their personal beauty so unlike the Italian stamp, their clear ruddy complexion and curled flaxen locks, exclaimed, "Angles" (meaning *English* the modern derivative) "Angles do you call them? And is it because they look so like angels?" Had it been later in time one would think that the Pope had in mind Fra Angelico's seraphs some of whom, plucking apples in gardens of the Hesperides have the faint rose-bud complexion of the more beautiful English girls.

If in vain the good Chaplain sought to impress the young

barbarian with ideas of death akin to those conveyed in
the skull, dial, and cross-bones on old tombstones; equally
futile to all appearance were his efforts to bring home to
him the thought of salvation and a Saviour. Billy listened,
but less out of awe or reverence perhaps than from a certain natural politeness; doubtless at bottom regarding all
that in much the same way that most mariners of his class
take any discourse abstract or out of the common tone of
the work-a-day world. And this sailor-way of taking clerical
discourse is not wholly unlike the way in which the pioneer
of Christianity full of transcendent miracles was received
long ago on tropic isles by any superior *savage* so called—
a Tahitian say of Captain Cook's time or shortly after that
time. Out of natural courtesy he received, but did not appropriate. It was like a gift placed in the palm of an out-
reached hand upon which the fingers do not close.

But the *Indomitable's* Chaplain was a discreet man possessing the good sense of a good heart. So he insisted not
in his vocation here. At the instance of Captain Vere, a
lieutenant had apprised him of pretty much everything as
to Billy; and since he felt that innocence was even a better
thing than religion wherewith to go to Judgement, he
reluctantly withdrew; but in his emotion not without first
performing an act strange enough in an Englishman, and
under the circumstances yet more so in any regular priest.
Stooping over, he kissed on the fair cheek his fellow-man,
a felon in martial law, one who though on the confines of
death he felt he could never convert to a dogma; nor for all
that did he fear for his future.

Marvel not that having been made acquainted with the
young sailor's essential innocence (an irruption of heretic
thought hard to suppress) the worthy man lifted not a
finger to avert the doom of such a martyr to martial discipline. So to do would not only have been as idle as invoking the desert, but would also have been an audacious
transgression of the bounds of his function, one as exactly
prescribed to him by military law as that of the boatswain

or any other naval officer. Bluntly put, a chaplain, is the minister of the Prince of Peace serving in the host of the God of War—Mars. As such, he is as incongruous as that musket of Blücher etc. at Christmas. Why then is he there? Because he indirectly subserves the purpose attested by the cannon; because too he lends the sanction of the religion of the meek to that which practically is the abrogation of everything but brute Force.

26

The night so luminous on the spar-deck but otherwise on the cavernous ones below, levels so like the tiered galleries in a coal-mine—the luminous night passed away. But, like the prophet in the chariot disappearing in heaven and dropping his mantle to Elisha, the withdrawing night transferred its pale robe to the breaking day. A meek shy light appeared in the East, where stretched a diaphanous fleece of white furrowed vapor. That light slowly waxed. Suddenly *eight bells* was struck aft, responded to by one louder metallic stroke from forward. It was four o'clock in the morning. Instantly the silver whistles were heard summoning all hands to witness punishment. Up through the great hatchways rimmed with racks of heavy shot, the watch below came pouring overspreading with the watch already on deck the space between the mainmast and fore-mast including that occupied by the capacious *launch* and the black booms tiered on either side of it, boat and booms making a summit of observation for the powder-boys and younger tars. A different group comprising one watch of topmen leaned over the rail of that sea-balcony, no small one in a seventy-four, looking down on the crowd below. Man or boy none spake but in whisper, and few spake at all. Captain Vere—as before, the central figure among the assembled commissioned officers—stood nigh the break of the poop-deck facing forward. Just below him on the quarter-deck the marines in full equipment were drawn up much as at the scene of the promulgated sentence.

At sea in the old time, the execution by halter of a military sailor was generally from the fore-yard. In the present instance, for special reasons the main-yard was assigned. Under an arm of that weather or lee ? yard the prisoner was presently brought up, the Chaplain attending him. It was noted at the time and remarked upon afterwards, that in this final scene the good man evinced little or nothing of the perfunctory. Brief speech indeed he had with the condemned one, but the genuine Gospel was less on his tongue than in his aspect and manner towards him. The final preparations personal to the latter being speedily brought to an end by two boatswain's-mates, the consummation impended. Billy stood facing aft. At the penultimate moment, his words, his only ones, words wholly unobstructed in the utterance were these—"God bless Captain Vere!" Syllables so unanticipated coming from one with the ignominious hemp about his neck—a conventional felon's benediction directed aft towards the quarters of honor; syllables too delivered in the clear melody of a singing-bird on the point of launching from the twig, had a phenomenal effect, not unenhanced by the rare personal beauty of the young sailor spiritualized now through late experiences so poignantly profound.

Without volition as it were, as if indeed the ship's populace were but the vehicles of some vocal current electric, with one voice from alow and aloft came a resonant sympathetic echo—"God bless Captain Vere!" And yet at that instant Billy alone must have been in their hearts, even as he was in their eyes.

At the pronounced words and the spontaneous echo that voluminously rebounded them, Captain Vere, either through stoic self-control or a sort of momentary paralysis induced by emotional shock, stood erectly rigid as a musket in the ship-armorer's rack.

The hull deliberately recovering from the periodic roll

to leeward was just regaining an even keel, when the last signal a preconcerted dumb one was given. At the same moment it chanced that the vapory fleece hanging low in the East, was shot through with a soft glory as of the fleece of the Lamb of God seen in mystical vision and simultaneously therewith, watched by the wedged mass of upturned faces, Billy ascended; and, ascending, took the full rose of the dawn.

In the pinioned figure, arrived at the yard-end, to the wonder of all no motion was apparent, none save that created by the ship's motion, in moderate weather so majestic in a great ship ponderously cannoned.

27

A Digression

When some days afterward in reference to the singularity just mentioned, the Purser a rather ruddy rotund person more accurate as an accountant than profound as a philosopher, said at mess to the Surgeon, "What testimony to the force lodged in will-power" the latter, saturnine, spare and tall, one in whom a discreet causticity went along with a manner less genial than polite, replied, "Your pardon, Mr. Purser. In a hanging scientifically conducted—and under special orders I myself directed how Budd's was to be effected—any movement following the completed suspension and originating in the body suspended, such movement indicates mechanical spasm in the muscular system. Hence the absence of that is no more attributable to willpower as you call it than to horse-power—begging your pardon."

"But this muscular spasm you speak of, is not that in a degree more or less invariable in these cases?"

"Assuredly so, Mr. Purser."

"How then, my good sir, do you account for its absence

in this instance?"

"Mr. Purser, it is clear that your sense of the singularity in this matter equals not mine. You account for it by what you call will-power a term not yet included in the lexicon of science. For me I do not, with my present knowledge pretend to account for it at all. Even should we assume the hypothesis that at the first touch of the halyards the action of Budd's heart, intensified by extraordinary emotion at its climax, abruptly stopt—much like a watch when in carelessly winding it up you strain at the finish, thus snapping the chain—even under that hypothesis how account for the phenomenon that followed?"

"You admit then that the absence of spasmodic movement was phenomenal."

"It was phenomenal, Mr. Purser, in the sense that it was an appearance the cause of which is not immediately to be assigned."

"But tell me, my dear Sir," pertinaciously continued the other, "was the man's death effected by the halter, or was it a species of euthanasia?"

"*Euthanasia,* Mr. Purser, is something like your *will-power:* I doubt its authenticity as a scientific term—begging your pardon again. It is at once imaginative and metaphysical,—in short, Greek. But" abruptly changing his tone "there is a case in the sick-bay that I do not care to leave to my assistants. Beg your pardon, but excuse me." And rising from the mess he formally withdrew.

28

The silence at the moment of execution and for a moment or two continuing thereafter, a silence but emphasized by the regular wash of the sea against the hull or the flutter of a sail caused by the helmsman's eyes being tempted astray, this emphasized silence was gradually disturbed by a sound not easily to be verbally rendered. Whoever has heard the freshet-wave of a torrent suddenly swelled by pouring showers in tropical mountains, showers not shared by the plain; whoever has heard the first muffled murmur of its sloping advance through precipitous woods, may form some conception of the sound now heard. The seeming remoteness of its source was because of its murmurous indistinctness since it came from close-by, even from the men massed on the ship's open deck. Being inarticulate, it was dubious in significance further than it seemed to indicate some capricious revulsion of thought or feeling such as mobs ashore are liable to, in the present instance possibly implying a sullen revocation on the men's part of their involuntary echoing of Billy's benediction. But ere the murmur had time to wax into clamor it was met by a strategic command, the more telling that it came with abrupt unexpectedness.

"Pipe down the starboard watch Boatswain, and see that they go."

Shrill as the shriek of the sea-hawk the whistles of the Boatswain and his Mates pierced that ominous low sound, dissipating it; and yielding to the mechanism of discipline the throng was thinned by one half. For the remainder most of them were set to temporary employments connected with trimming the yards and so forth, business readily to be got up to serve occasion by any officer-of-the-deck.

Now each proceeding that follows a mortal sentence pronounced at sea by a drum-head court is characterised by promptitude not perceptibly merging into hurry, though bordering that. The hammock, the one which had been Billy's bed when alive, having already been ballasted with shot and otherwise prepared to serve for his canvas coffin, the last offices of the sea-undertakers, the Sail-maker's Mates, were now speedily completed. When everything was in readiness a second call for all hands made necessary by the strategic movement before mentioned was sounded and now to witness burial.

The details of this closing formality it needs not to give. But when the tilted plank let slide its freight into the sea, a second strange human murmur was heard, blended now with another inarticulate sound proceeding from certain larger sea-fowl whose attention having been attracted by the peculiar commotion in the water resulting from the heavy sloped dive of the shotted hammock into the sea, flew screaming to the spot. So near the hull did they come, that the stridor or bony creak of their gaunt double-jointed pinions was audible. As the ship under light airs passed on, leaving the burial-spot astern, they still kept circling it low down with the moving shadow of their outstretched wings and the croaked requiem of their cries.

Upon sailors as superstitious as those of the age preceding ours, men-of-war's men too who had just beheld the prodigy of repose in the form suspended in air and now foundering in the deeps; to such mariners the action of the sea-fowl though dictated by mere animal greed for prey, was big with no prosaic significance. An uncertain movement began among them, in which some encroachment was made. It was tolerated but for a moment. For suddenly the drum beat to quarters, which familiar sound happening at least twice every day, had upon the present occasion a signal peremptoriness in it. True martial discipline long continued superinduces in average man a sort of impulse of docility whose operation at the official sound of command much resembles in its promptitude the effect of an instinct.

The drum-beat dissolved the multitude, distributing most of them along the batteries of the two covered gun-decks. There, as wont, the guns' crews stood by their respective cannon erect and silent. In due course the First Officer, sword under arm and standing in his place on the quarter-deck formally received the successive reports of the sworded Lieutenants commanding the sections of batteries below; the last of which reports being made the summed report he delivered with the customary salute to the Commander. All this occupied time, which in the present case, was the object of beating to quarters at an hour prior to the customary one. That such variance from usage was authorized by an officer like Captain Vere, a martinet as some deemed him, was evidence of the necessity for unusual action implied in what he deemed to be temporarily the mood of his men. "With mankind" he would say "forms, measured forms are everything; and that is the import couched in the story of Orpheus with his lyre spell-binding the wild denizens of the wood." And this he once applied to the disruption of forms going on across the Channel and the consequences thereof.

At this unwonted muster at quarters, all proceeded as at the regular hour. The band on the quarter-deck played a sacred air. After which the Chaplain went through the customary morning service. That done, the drum beat the retreat, and toned by music and religious rites subserving the discipline and purpose of war, the men in their wonted orderly manner, dispersed to the places allotted them when not at the guns.

And now it was full day. The fleece of low-hanging vapor had vanished, licked up by the sun that late had so glorified it. And the circumambient air in the clearness of its serenity was like smooth white marble in the polished block not yet removed from the marble-dealer's yard.

29

The symmetry of form attainable in pure fiction can not so readily be achieved in a narration essentially having less to do with fable than with fact. Truth uncompromisingly told will always have its ragged edges; hence the conclusion of such a narration is apt to be less finished than an architectural finial.

How it fared with the Handsome Sailor during the year of the Great Mutiny has been faithfully given. But though

properly the story ends with his life, something in way of
sequel will not be amiss. Three brief chapters will suf-
fice.

In the general re-christening under the Directory of the
craft originally forming the navy of the French monarchy,
the *St. Louis* line-of-battle ship was named the *Athéiste*.
Such a name, like some other substituted ones in the Revolutionary fleet while proclaiming the infidel audacity of
the ruling power was yet, though not so intended to be,
the aptest name, if one consider it, ever given to a war-ship;
far more so indeed than the *Devastation,* the *Erebus* (the
Hell) and similar names bestowed upon fighting-ships.

On the return-passage to the English fleet from the detached cruise during which occurred the events already
recorded, the *Indomitable* fell in with the *Athéiste*. An
engagement ensued; during which Captain Vere in the
act of putting his ship alongside the enemy with a view
of throwing his boarders across her bulwarks, was hit by
a musket-ball from a port-hole of the enemy's main cabin.
More than disabled he dropped to the deck and was carried
below to the same cock-pit where some of his men already
lay. The senior Lieutenant took command. Under him
the enemy was finally captured and though much crippled
was by rare good fortune successfully taken into Gibraltar,
an English port not very distant from the scene of the
fight. There, Captain Vere with the rest of the wounded
was put ashore. He lingered for some days, but the end
came. Unhappily he was cut off too early for the Nile and
Trafalgar. The spirit that spite its philosophic austerity
may yet have indulged in the most secret of all passions,
ambition, never attained to the fulness of fame.

Not long before death while lying under the influence
of that magical drug which soothing the physical frame
mysteriously operates on the subtler element in man, he
was heard to murmur words inexplicable to his attendant—
"Billy Budd, Billy Budd." That these were not the accents
of remorse, would seem clear from what the attendant said

to the *Indomitable's* senior officer of marines who as the most reluctant to condemn of the members of the drumhead court, too well knew though here he kept the knowledge to himself, who Billy Budd was.

30

Some few weeks after the execution, among other matters under the head of *News from the Mediterranean,* there appeared in a naval chronicle of the time, an authorized weekly publication, an account of the affair. It was doubtless for the most part written in good faith, though the medium, partly rumor, through which the facts must have reached the writer, served to deflect and in part falsify them. The account was as follows:—

"On the tenth of the last month a deplorable occurrence took place on board H.M.S. *Indomitable.* John Claggart, the ship's master-at-arms, discovering that some sort of plot was incipient among an inferior section of the ship's company, and that the ringleader was one William Budd; he, Claggart in the act of arraigning the man before the Captain was vindictively stabbed to the heart by the suddenly drawn sheath-knife of Budd.

"The deed and the implement employed, sufficiently suggest that though mustered into the service under an English name the assassin was no Englishman, but one of those aliens adopting English cognomens whom the present extraordinary necessities of the Service have caused to be admitted into it in considerable numbers.

"The enormity of the crime and the extreme depravity of the criminal, appear the greater in view of the character of the victim, a middle-aged man respectable and discreet, belonging to that minor official grade, the petty-officers, upon whom, as none know better than the commissioned gentlemen, the efficiency of His Majesty's navy so largely depends. His function was a responsible one; at once

onerous and thankless and his fidelity in it the greater
because of his strong patriotic impulse. In this instance as
in so many other instances in these days, the character of
this unfortunate man signally refutes, if refutation were
needed, that peevish saying attributed to the late Dr. John-
son, that patriotism is the last refuge of a scoundrel.

"The criminal paid the penalty of his crime. The promptitude of the punishment has proved salutary. Nothing
amiss is now apprehended aboard H.M.S. *Indomitable*."

The above appearing in a publication now long ago
superannuated and forgotten is all that hitherto has stood
in human record to attest what manner of men respectively
were John Claggart and Billy Budd.

31

Everything is for a term remarkable in navies. Any tangi-
ble object associated with some striking incident of the
service is converted into a monument. The spar from
which the Foretopman was suspended, was for some few
years kept trace of by the blue-jackets. Their knowledge
followed it from ship to dock-yard and again from dock-
yard to ship, still pursuing it even when at last reduced
to a mere dock-yard boom. To them a chip of it was as a
piece of the Cross. Ignorant though they were of the secret
facts of the tragedy, and not thinking but that the penalty
was somehow unavoidably inflicted from the naval point
of view, for all that they instinctively felt that Billy was a
sort of man as incapable of mutiny as of wilful murder.
They recalled the fresh young image of the Handsome
Sailor, that face never deformed by a sneer or subtler vile
freak of the heart within. Their impression of him was
doubtless deepened by the fact that he was gone, and in a
measure mysteriously gone. On the gun-decks of the *Indomitable* the general estimate of his nature and its unconscious simplicity eventually found rude utterance from

another foretopman one of his own watch gifted, as some sailors are, with an artless poetic temperament. The tarry hands made some lines which after circulating among the shipboard crew for a while, finally got rudely printed at Portsmouth as a ballad. The title given to it was the sailor's.

BILLY IN THE DARBIES

Good of the Chaplain to enter Lone Bay
And down on his marrow-bones here and pray
For the likes just o' me, Billy Budd.—But look:
Through the port comes the moon-shine astray!
It tips the guard's cutlas and silvers this nook;
But 'twill die in the dawning of Billy's last day.
A jewel-block they'll make of me tomorrow,
Pendant pearl from the yard-arm-end
Like the ear-drop I gave to Bristol Molly—
O, 'tis me, not the sentence they'll suspend.
Ay, Ay, all is up; and I must up too
Early in the morning, aloft from alow.
On an empty stomach, now, never it would do.
They'll give me a nibble—bit o' biscuit ere I go.
Sure, a messmate will reach me the last parting cup;
But, turning heads away from the hoist and the belay,
Heaven knows who will have the running of me up!
No pipe to those halyards.—But aren't it all sham?
A blur's in my eyes; it is dreaming that I am.
A hatchet to my hawser? all adrift to go?
The drum roll to grog, and Billy never know?
But Donald he has promised to stand by the plank;
So I'll shake a friendly hand ere I sink.
But—no! It is dead then I'll be, come to think.—
I remember Taff the Welshman when he sank.
And his cheek it was like the budding pink.

But me they'll lash me in hammock, drop me deep.
Fathoms down, fathoms down, how I'll dream fast asleep.
I feel it stealing now. Sentry, are you there?
Just ease this darbies at the wrist,
And roll me over fair,
I am sleepy, and the oozy weeds about me twist.

END OF BOOK

April 19th
1891

NOON WINE

Katherine Anne Porter

Katherine Anne Porter

. . . .

Katherine Anne Porter was born in Indian Creek, Texas, in 1894. She has worked on a newspaper, she has taught, and she has traveled extensively in America, Mexico, and Europe. Her considerable reputation as a first-rate writer is based on a comparatively small number of books and some fragments of others; but this reputation is richly deserved. Her first volume, *Flowering Judas and Other Stories*, was published in 1930. When it appeared Miss Porter seemed, as a writer, to have sprung full grown out of the head of Zeus, so superb was the work. This assumption discounted the care and the patience involved in the writing of and the decision to publish each story. *Pale Horse, Pale Rider*, a volume of three short novels, appeared as a book in 1939; *The Leaning Tower and Other Stories* was published in 1944; and *The Days Before*, a collection of essays and critical writing, appeared in 1953. All of these books are published by Harcourt, Brace & Company, New York; *Flowering Judas* and *Pale Horse, Pale Rider* are available in the Modern Library. Miss Porter can be heard on records reading *Pale Horse, Pale Rider* and "*The Downward Path to Wisdom.*"

NOON WINE

Time: 1896-1905
Place: Small South Texas Farm

THE TWO grubby small boys with tow-colored hair
who were digging among the ragweed in the front yard
sat back on their heels and said, "Hello," when the tall
bony man with straw-colored hair turned in at their gate.
He did not pause at the gate; it had swung back, con-
veniently half open, long ago, and was now sunk so firmly
on its broken hinges no one thought of trying to close it.
He did not even glance at the small boys, much less give
them good-day. He just clumped down his big square
dusty shoes one after the other steadily, like a man following a plow, as if he knew the place well and knew where
he was going and what he would find there. Rounding the
right-hand corner of the house under the row of chinaberry
trees, he walked up to the side porch where Mr. Thompson was pushing a big swing churn back and forth.

Mr. Thompson was a tough weather-beaten man with
stiff black hair and a week's growth of black whiskers. He
was a noisy proud man who held his neck so straight his
whole face stood level with his Adam's apple, and the
whiskers continued down his neck and disappeared into a
black thatch under his open collar. The churn rumbled
and swished like the belly of a trotting horse, and Mr.
Thompson seemed somehow to be driving a horse with one
hand, reining it in and urging it forward; and every now
and then he turned halfway around and squirted a tremendous spit of tobacco juice out over the steps. The door
stones were brown and gleaming with fresh tobacco juice.
Mr. Thompson had been churning quite a while and he

was tired of it. He was just fetching a mouthful of juice to squirt again when the stranger came around the corner and stopped. Mr. Thompson saw a narrow-chested man with blue eyes so pale they were almost white, looking and not looking at him from a long gaunt face, under white eyebrows. Mr. Thompson judged him to be another of these Irishmen, by his long upper lip.

"Howdy do, sir," said Mr. Thompson politely, swinging his churn.

"I need work," said the man, clearly enough but with some kind of foreign accent Mr. Thompson couldn't place. It wasn't Cajun and it wasn't Nigger and it wasn't Dutch, so it had him stumped. "You need a man here?"

Mr. Thompson gave the churn a great shove and it swung back and forth several times on its own momentum. He sat on the steps, shot his quid into the grass, and said, "Set down. Maybe we can make a deal. I been kinda lookin' round for somebody. I had two niggers but they got into a cutting scrape up the creek last week, one of 'em dead now and the other in the hoosegow at Cold Springs. Neither one of 'em worth killing, come right down to it. So it looks like I'd better get somebody. Where'd you work last?"

"North Dakota," said the man, folding himself down on the other end of the steps, but not as if he were tired. He folded up and settled down as if it would be a long time before he got up again. He never had looked at Mr. Thompson, but there wasn't anything sneaking in his eye, either. He didn't seem to be looking anywhere else. His eyes sat in his head and let things pass by them. They didn't seem to be expecting to see anything worth looking at. Mr. Thompson waited a long time for the man to say something more, but he had gone into a brown study.

"North Dakota," said Mr. Thompson, trying to remember where that was. "That's a right smart distance off, seems to me."

"I can do everything on farm," said the man; "cheap. I need work."

Mr. Thompson settled himself to get down to business. "My name's Thompson, Mr. Royal Earle Thompson," he said.

"I'm Mr. Helton," said the man, "Mr. Olaf Helton." He did not move.

"Well, now," said Mr. Thompson in his most carrying voice, "I guess we'd better talk turkey."

When Mr. Thompson expected to drive a bargain he always grew very hearty and jovial. There was nothing wrong with him except that he hated like the devil to pay wages. He said so himself. "You furnish grub and a shack," he said, "and then you got to pay 'em besides. It ain't right. Besides the wear and tear on your implements," he said, "they just let everything go to rack and ruin." So he began to laugh and shout his way through the deal.

"Now, what I want to know is, how much you fixing to gouge outa me?" he brayed, slapping his knee. After he had kept it up as long as he could, he quieted down, feeling a little sheepish, and cut himself a chew. Mr. Helton was staring out somewhere between the barn and the orchard, and seemed to be sleeping with his eyes open.

"I'm good worker," said Mr. Helton as from the tomb. "I get dollar a day."

Mr. Thompson was so shocked he forgot to start laughing again at the top of his voice until it was nearly too late to do any good. "Haw, haw," he bawled. "Why, for a dollar a day I'd hire out myself. What kinda work is it where they pay you a dollar a day?"

"Wheatfields, North Dakota," said Mr. Helton, not even smiling.

Mr. Thompson stopped laughing. "Well, this ain't any wheatfield by a long shot. This is more of a dairy farm," he said, feeling apologetic. "My wife, she was set on a dairy, she seemed to like working around with cows and calves, so I humored her. But it was a mistake," he said. "I got nearly everything to do, anyhow. My wife ain't very strong. She's sick today, that's a fact. She's been porely for the last few days. We plant a little feed, and a corn patch, and there's the orchard, and a few pigs and chickens, but our main hold is the cows. Now just speakin' as one man to another, there ain't any money in it. Now I can't give you no dollar a day because ackshally I don't make that much out of it. No, sir, we get along on a lot less than a dollar a day, I'd say, if we figger up everything in the long run. Now, I paid seven dollars a month to the two niggers, three-fifty each, and grub, but what I say is, one middlin'-good white man ekals a whole passel of niggers any day in the week, so I'll give you seven dollars and you eat at the table with us, and you'll be treated like a white man, as the feller says—"

"That's all right," said Mr. Helton. "I take it."

"Well, now I guess we'll call it a deal, hey?" Mr. Thompson jumped up as if he had remembered important business. "Now, you just take hold of that churn and give it a few swings, will you, while I ride to town on a coupla little errands. I ain't been able to leave the place all week. I guess you know what to do with butter after you get it, don't you?"

"I know," said Mr. Helton without turning his head. "I know butter business." He had a strange drawling voice, and even when he spoke only two words his voice waved slowly up and down and the emphasis was in the wrong place. Mr. Thompson wondered what kind of foreigner Mr. Helton could be.

"Now just where did you say you worked last?" he asked, as if he expected Mr. Helton to contradict himself.

"North Dakota," said Mr. Helton.

"Well, one place is good as another once you get used to it," said Mr. Thompson, amply. "You're a forriner, ain't you?"

"I'm a Swede," said Mr. Helton, beginning to swing the churn.

Mr. Thompson let forth a booming laugh, as if this was the best joke on somebody he'd ever heard. "Well, I'll be damned," he said at the top of his voice. "A Swede: well, now, I'm afraid you'll get pretty lonesome around here. I never seen any Swedes in this neck of the woods."

"That's all right," said Mr. Helton. He went on swinging the churn as if he had been working on the place for years.

"In fact, I might as well tell you, you're practically the first Swede I ever laid eyes on."

"That's all right," said Mr. Helton.

Mr. Thompson went into the front room where Mrs. Thompson was lying down, with the green shades drawn. She had a bowl of water by her on the table and a wet cloth over her eyes. She took the cloth off at the sound of Mr. Thompson's boots and said, "What's all the noise out there? Who is it?"

"Got a feller out there says he's a Swede, Ellie," said Mr. Thompson; "says he knows how to make butter."

"I hope it turns out to be the truth," said Mrs. Thompson. "Looks like my head never will get any better."

"Don't you worry," said Mr. Thompson. "You fret too much. Now I'm gointa ride into town and get a little order of groceries."

"Don't you linger, now, Mr. Thompson," said Mrs. Thompson. "Don't go to the hotel." She meant the saloon; the proprietor also had rooms for rent upstairs.

"Just a coupla little toddies," said Mr. Thompson, laughing loudly, "never hurt anybody."

"I never took a dram in my life," said Mrs. Thompson, "and what's more I never will."

"I wasn't talking about the womenfolks," said Mr. Thompson.

The sound of the swinging churn rocked Mrs. Thompson first into a gentle doze, then a deep drowse from which she waked suddenly knowing that the swinging had stopped a good while ago. She sat up shading her weak eyes from the flat strips of late summer sunlight between

the sill and the lowered shades. There she was, thank
God, still alive, with supper to cook but no churning on
hand, and her head still bewildered, but easy. Slowly she
realized she had been hearing a new sound even in her
sleep. Somebody was playing a tune on the harmonica,
not merely shrilling up and down making a sickening
noise, but really playing a pretty tune, merry and sad.

She went out through the kitchen, stepped off the porch,
and stood facing the east, shading her eyes. When her
vision cleared and settled, she saw a long, pale-haired man
in blue jeans sitting in the doorway of the hired man's
shack, tilted back in a kitchen chair, blowing away at the
harmonica with his eyes shut. Mrs. Thompson's heart flut-
tered and sank. Heavens, he looked lazy and worthless, he
did, now. First a lot of no-count fiddling darkies and then
a no-count white man. It was just like Mr. Thompson to
take on that kind. She did wish he would be more considerate, and take a little trouble with his business. She
wanted to believe in her husband, and there were too
many times when she couldn't. She wanted to believe that
tomorrow, or at least the day after, life, such a battle at
best, was going to be better.

She walked past the shack without glancing aside, stepping carefully, bent at the waist because of the nagging
pain in her side, and went to the springhouse, trying to
harden her mind to speak very plainly to that new hired
man if he had not done his work.

The milk house was only another shack of weather-
beaten boards nailed together hastily years before because
they needed a milk house; it was meant to be temporary,
and it was; already shapeless, leaning this way and that
over a perpetual cool trickle of water that fell from a little
grot, almost choked with pallid ferns. No one else in the
whole countryside had such a spring on his land. Mr. and
Mrs. Thompson felt they had a fortune in that spring, if
ever they got around to doing anything with it.

Rickety wooden shelves clung at hazard in the square

around the small pool where the larger pails of milk and butter stood, fresh and sweet in the cold water. One hand supporting her flat, pained side, the other shading her eyes, Mrs. Thompson leaned over and peered into the pails. The cream had been skimmed and set aside, there was a rich roll of butter, the wooden molds and shallow pans had been scrubbed and scalded for the first time in who knows when, the barrel was full of buttermilk ready for the pigs and the weanling calves, the hard packed-dirt floor had been swept smooth. Mrs. Thompson straightened up again, smiling tenderly. She had been ready to scold him, a poor man who needed a job, who had just come there and who might not have been expected to do things properly at first. There was nothing she could do to make up for the injustice she had done him in her thoughts but to tell him how she appreciated his good clean work, finished already, in no time at all. She ventured near the door of the shack with her careful steps; Mr. Helton opened his eyes, stopped playing, and brought his chair down straight, but did not look at her, or get up. She was a little frail woman with long thick brown hair in a braid, a suffering patient mouth and diseased eyes which cried easily. She wove her fingers into an eyeshade, thumbs on temples, and, winking her tearful lids, said with a polite little manner, "Howdy do, sir. I'm Miz Thompson, and I wanted to tell you I think you did real well in the milk house. It's always been a hard place to keep."

He said, "That's all right," in a slow voice, without moving.

Mrs. Thompson waited a moment. "That's a pretty tune you're playing. Most folks don't seem to get much music out of a harmonica."

Mr. Helton sat humped over, long legs sprawling, his spine in a bow, running his thumb over the square mouth-stops; except for his moving hand he might have been asleep. The harmonica was a big shiny new one, and Mrs. Thompson, her gaze wandering about, counted five others, all good and expensive, standing in a row on the shelf beside his cot. "He must carry them around in his jumper pocket," she thought, and noted there was not a sign of any other possession lying about. "I see you're mighty fond of music," she said. "We used to have an old accordion, and Mr. Thompson could play it right smart, but the little boys broke it up."

Mr. Helton stood up rather suddenly, the chair clattered under him, his knees straightened though his shoulders did not, and he looked at the floor as if he were listening carefully. "You know how little boys are," said Mrs. Thompson. "You'd better set them harmonicas on a high shelf or they'll be after them. They're great hands for getting into things. I try to learn 'em, but it don't do much good."

Mr. Helton, in one wide gesture of his long arms, swept his harmonicas up against his chest, and from there transferred them in a row to the ledge where the roof joined to the wall. He pushed them back almost out of sight.

"That'll do, maybe," said Mrs. Thompson. "Now I wonder," she said, turning and closing her eyes helplessly against the stronger western light, "I wonder what became of them little tads. I can't keep up with them." She had a way of speaking about her children as if they were rather troublesome nephews on a prolonged visit.

"Down by the creek," said Mr. Helton, in his hollow voice. Mrs. Thompson, pausing confusedly, decided he had answered her question. He stood in silent patience, not exactly waiting for her to go, perhaps, but pretty plainly not waiting for anything else. Mrs. Thompson was perfectly accustomed to all kinds of men full of all kinds of cranky ways. The point was, to find out just how Mr. Helton's crankiness was different from any other man's, and then get used to it, and let him feel at home. Her father had been cranky, her brothers and uncles had all been set in their ways and none of them alike; and every hired man she'd ever seen had quirks and crotchets of his own. Now here was Mr. Helton, who was a Swede, who wouldn't talk, and who played the harmonica besides.

"They'll be needing something to eat," said Mrs. Thompson in a vague friendly way, "pretty soon. Now I wonder what I ought to be thinking about for supper? Now what do you like to eat, Mr. Helton? We always have plenty of good butter and milk and cream, that's a blessing. Mr. Thompson says we ought to sell all of it, but I say my family comes first." Her little face went all out of shape in a pained blind smile.

"I eat anything," said Mr. Helton, his words wandering up and down.

He *can't* talk, for one thing, thought Mrs. Thompson, it's a shame to keep at him when he don't know the language good. She took a slow step away from the shack, looking back over her shoulder. "We usually have corn-bread except on Sundays," she told him. "I suppose in your part of the country you don't get much good corn-bread."

Not a word from Mr. Helton. She saw from her eye-corner that he had sat down again, looking at his harmonica, chair tilted. She hoped he would remember it was getting near milking time. As she moved away, he started playing again, the same tune.

Milking time came and went. Mrs. Thompson saw Mr. Helton going back and forth between the cow barn and the milk house. He swung along in an easy lope, shoulders bent, head hanging, the big buckets balancing like a pair of scales at the ends of his bony arms. Mr. Thompson rode in from town sitting straighter than usual, chin in, a tow-sack full of supplies swung behind the saddle. After a trip to the barn, he came into the kitchen full of good will, and gave Mrs. Thompson a hearty smack on the cheek after dusting her face off with his tough whiskers. He had been to the hotel, that was plain. "Took a look around the premises, Ellie," he shouted. "That Swede sure is grinding out the labor. But he is the closest mouthed feller I ever met up with in all my days. Looks like he's scared he'll crack his jaw if he opens his front teeth."

Mrs. Thompson was stirring up a big bowl of buttermilk cornbread. "You smell like a toper, Mr. Thompson," she said with perfect dignity. "I wish you'd get one of the little boys to bring me in an extra load of firewood. I'm thinking about baking a batch of cookies tomorrow."

Mr. Thompson, all at once smelling the liquor on his own breath, sneaked out, justly rebuked, and brought in the firewood himself. Arthur and Herbert, grubby from thatched head to toes, from skin to shirt, came stamping in yelling for supper. "Go wash your faces and comb your hair," said Mrs. Thompson, automatically. They retired to the porch. Each one put his hand under the pump and wet his forelock, combed it down with his fingers, and returned at once to the kitchen, where all the fair prospects of life were centered. Mrs. Thompson set an extra plate and commanded Arthur, the eldest, eight years old, to call Mr. Helton for supper.

Arthur, without moving from the spot, bawled like a bull calf, "Saaaaaay, Hellllllton, suuuuuupper's ready!" and added in a lower voice, "You big Swede!"

"Listen to me," said Mrs. Thompson, "that's no way to act. Now you go out there and ask him decent, or I'll get your daddy to give you a good licking."

Mr. Helton loomed, long and gloomy, in the doorway. "Sit right there," boomed Mr. Thompson, waving his arm. Mr. Helton swung his square shoes across the kitchen in two steps, slumped onto the bench and sat. Mr. Thompson occupied his chair at the head of the table, the two boys scrambled into place opposite Mr. Helton, and Mrs. Thompson sat at the end nearest the stove. Mrs. Thompson clasped her hands, bowed her head and said aloud hastily, "Lord, for all these and Thy other blessings we thank Thee in Jesus' name, amen," trying to finish before Herbert's rusty little paw reached the nearest dish. Otherwise she would be duty-bound to send him away from the table, and growing children need their meals. Mr. Thompson and Arthur always waited, but Herbert, aged six, was too young to take training yet.

Mr. and Mrs. Thompson tried to engage Mr. Helton in conversation, but it was a failure. They tried first the weather, and then the crops, and then the cows, but Mr. Helton simply did not reply. Mr. Thompson then told something funny he had seen in town. It was about some of the other old grangers at the hotel, friends of his, giving beer to a goat, and the goat's subsequent behavior. Mr. Helton did not seem to hear. Mrs. Thompson laughed dutifully, but she didn't think it was very funny. She had heard it often before, though Mr. Thompson, each time he told it, pretended it had happened that self-same day. It must have happened years ago if it ever happened at all, and it had never been a story that Mrs. Thompson thought suitable for mixed company. The whole thing came of Mr. Thompson's weakness for a dram too much now and then, though he voted for local option at every election. She passed the food to Mr. Helton, who took a helping of everything, but not much, not enough to keep him up to his full powers if he expected to go on working the way he had started.

At last, he took a fair-sized piece of cornbread, wiped his plate up as clean as if it had been licked by a hound dog, stuffed his mouth full, and, still chewing, slid off the bench and started for the door.

"Good night, Mr. Helton," said Mrs. Thompson, and the other Thompsons took it up in a scattered chorus. "Good night, Mr. Helton!"

"Good night," said Mr. Helton's wavering voice grudgingly from the darkness.

"Gude not," said Arthur, imitating Mr. Helton.

"Gude not," said Herbert, the copy-cat.

"You don't do it right," said Arthur. "Now listen to me. Guuuuuude naht," and he ran a hollow scale in a luxury

of successful impersonation. Herbert almost went into a
fit with joy.

"Now you *stop* that," said Mrs. Thompson. "He can't
help the way he talks. You ought to be ashamed of yourselves, both of you, making fun of a poor stranger like
that. How'd you like to be a stranger in a strange land?"

"I'd like it," said Arthur. "I think it would be fun."

"They're both regular heathens, Ellie," said Mr.
Thompson. "Just plain ignoramuses." He turned the face
of awful fatherhood upon his young. "You're both going
to get sent to school next year, and that'll knock some
sense into you."

"I'm going to git sent to the 'formatory when I'm old
enough," piped up Herbert. "That's where I'm goin'."

"Oh, you are, are you?" asked Mr. Thompson. "Who
says so?"

"The Sunday School Supintendant," said Herbert, a
bright boy showing off.

"You see?" said Mr. Thompson, staring at his wife.
"What did I tell you?" He became a hurricane of wrath.
"Get to bed, you two," he roared until his Adam's apple
shuddered. "Get now before I take the hide off you!" They
got, and shortly from their attic bedroom the sounds of
scuffling and snorting and giggling and growling filled
the house and shook the kitchen ceiling.

Mrs. Thompson held her head and said in a small uncertain voice, "It's no use picking on them when they're
so young and tender. I can't stand it."

"My goodness, Ellie," said Mr. Thompson, "we've got
to raise 'em. We can't just let 'em grow up hog wild."

She went on in another tone. "That Mr. Helton seems
all right, even if he can't be made to talk. Wonder how
he comes to be so far from home."

"Like I said, he isn't no whamper-jaw," said Mr.
Thompson, "but he sure knows how to lay out the work.
I guess that's the main thing around here. Country's full
of fellers trampin' round looking for work."

Mrs. Thompson was gathering up the dishes. She now gathered up Mr. Thompson's plate from under his chin. "To tell you the honest truth," she remarked, "I think it's a mighty good change to have a man round the place who knows how to work and keep his mouth shut. Means he'll keep out of our business. Not that we've got anything to hide, but it's convenient."

"That's a fact," said Mr. Thompson. "Haw, haw," he shouted suddenly. "Means you can do all the talking, huh?"

"The only thing," went on Mrs. Thompson, "is this: he don't eat hearty enough to suit me. I like to see a man set down and relish a good meal. My granma used to say it was no use putting dependence on a man who won't set down and make out his dinner. I hope it won't be that way this time."

"Tell *you* the truth, Ellie," said Mr. Thompson, picking his teeth with a fork and leaning back in the best of good humors, "I always thought your granma was a ter'ble ole fool. She'd just say the first thing that popped into her head and call it God's wisdom."

"My granma wasn't anybody's fool. Nine times out of ten she knew what she was talking about. I always say, the first thing you think is the best thing you can say."

"Well," said Mr. Thompson, going into another shout, "you're so reefined about that goat story, you just try speaking out in mixed comp'ny sometime! You just try it. S'pose you happened to be thinking about a hen and a rooster, hey? I reckon you'd shock the Babtist preacher!" He gave her a good pinch on her thin little rump. "No more meat on you than a rabbit," he said, fondly. "Now I like 'em cornfed."

Mrs. Thompson looked at him open-eyed and blushed. She could see better by lamplight. "Why, Mr. Thompson, sometimes I think you're the evilest-minded man that ever lived." She took a handful of hair on the crown of his head and gave it a good, slow pull. "That's to show you how it feels, pinching so hard when you're supposed to be playing," she said, gently.

In spite of his situation in life, Mr. Thompson had never been able to outgrow his deep conviction that running a dairy and chasing after chickens was woman's work. He was fond of saying that he could plow a furrow, cut sorghum, shuck corn, handle a team, build a corn crib, as well as any man. Buying and selling, too, were man's work. Twice a week he drove the spring wagon to market with the fresh butter, a few eggs, fruits in their proper season, sold them, pocketed the change, and spent it as seemed best, being careful not to dig into Mrs. Thompson's pin money.

But from the first the cows worried him, coming up regularly twice a day to be milked, standing there reproaching him with their smug female faces. Calves worried him, fighting the rope and strangling themselves until their eyes bulged, trying to get at the teat. Wrestling with a calf unmanned him, like having to change a baby's diaper. Milk worried him, coming bitter sometimes, drying up, turning sour. Hens worried him, cackling, clucking, hatching out when you least expected it and leading their broods into the barnyard where the horses could step on them; dying of roup and wryneck and getting plagues of chicken lice; laying eggs all over God's creation so that half of them were spoiled before a man could find them, in spite of a rack of nests Mrs. Thompson had set out for them in the feed room. Hens were a blasted nuisance.

Slopping hogs was hired man's work, in Mr. Thompson's opinion. Killing hogs was a job for the boss, but scraping them and cutting them up was for the hired man again; and again woman's proper work was dressing meat, smoking, pickling, and making lard and sausage. All his carefully limited fields of activity were related somehow to Mr. Thompson's feeling for the appearance of things, his own appearance in the sight of God and man. "It don't *look* right," was his final reason for not doing anything he did not wish to do.

It was his dignity and his reputation that he cared about, and there were only a few kinds of work manly enough for Mr. Thompson to undertake with his own hands. Mrs. Thompson, to whom so many forms of work would have been becoming, had simply gone down on him early. He saw, after a while, how short-sighted it had been of him to expect much from Mrs. Thompson; he had fallen in love with her delicate waist and lace-trimmed petticoats and big blue eyes, and, though all those charms had disappeared, she had in the meantime become Ellie to him, not at all the same person as Miss Ellen Bridges, popular Sunday School teacher in the Mountain City First Baptist Church, but his dear wife, Ellie, who was not strong. Deprived as he was, however, of the main support in life which a man might expect in marriage, he had almost without knowing it resigned himself to failure. Head erect, a prompt payer of taxes, yearly subscriber to the preacher's salary, land owner and father of a family, employer, a hearty good fellow among men, Mr. Thompson knew, without putting it into words, that he had been going steadily down hill. God amighty, it did look like somebody around the place might take a rake in hand now and then and clear up the clutter around the barn and the kitchen steps. The wagon shed was so full of broken-down machinery and ragged harness and old wagon wheels and battered milk pails and rotting lumber you could hardly drive in there any more. Not a soul on the place would raise a hand to it, and as for him, he had all he could do with his regular work. He would sometimes in the slack season sit for hours worrying about it, squirting tobacco on the ragweeds growing in a thicket against the wood pile, wondering what a fellow could do, handicapped as he was. He looked forward to the boys growing up soon; he was going to put them through the mill just as his own father had done with him when he was a boy; they were

going to learn how to take hold and run the place right.
He wasn't going to overdo it, but those two boys were going to earn their salt, or he'd know why. Great big lubbers
sitting around whittling! Mr. Thompson sometimes grew
quite enraged with them, when imagining their possible
future, big lubbers sitting around whittling or thinking
about fishing trips. Well, he'd put a stop to that, mighty
damn quick.

As the seasons passed, and Mr. Helton took hold more
and more, Mr. Thompson began to relax in his mind a
little. There seemed to be nothing the fellow couldn't do,
all in the day's work and as a matter of course. He got up
at five o'clock in the morning, boiled his own coffee and
fried his own bacon and was out in the cow lot before Mr.
Thompson had even begun to yawn, stretch, groan, roar
and thump around looking for his jeans. He milked the
cows, kept the milk house, and churned the butter;
rounded the hens up and somehow persuaded them to lay
in the nests, not under the house and behind the hay-
stacks; he fed them regularly and they hatched out until
you couldn't set a foot down for them. Little by little the
piles of trash around the barns and house disappeared.
He carried buttermilk and corn to the hogs, and curried
cockleburs out of the horses' manes. He was gentle with
the calves, if a little grim with the cows and hens; judging
by his conduct, Mr. Helton had never heard of the difference between man's and woman's work on a farm.

In the second year, he showed Mr. Thompson the picture of a cheese press in a mail order catalogue, and said,
"This is a good thing. You buy this, I make cheese." The
press was bought and Mr. Helton did make cheese, and
it was sold, along with the increased butter and the crates
of eggs. Sometimes Mr. Thompson felt a little contemp-
tuous of Mr. Helton's ways. It did seem kind of picayune
for a man to go around picking up half a dozen ears of
corn that had fallen off the wagon on the way from the
field, gathering up fallen fruit to feed to the pigs, storing

up old nails and stray parts of machinery, spending good time stamping a fancy pattern on the butter before it went to market. Mr. Thompson, sitting up high on the spring-wagon seat, with the decorated butter in a five-gallon lard can wrapped in wet towsack, driving to town, chirruping to the horses and snapping the reins over their backs, sometimes thought that Mr. Helton was a pretty meeching sort of fellow; but he never gave way to these feelings, he knew a good thing when he had it. It was a fact the hogs were in better shape and sold for more money. It was a fact that Mr. Thompson stopped buying feed, Mr. Helton managed the crops so well. When beef- and hog-slaughtering time came, Mr. Helton knew how to save the scraps that Mr. Thompson had thrown away, and wasn't above scraping guts and filling them with sausages that he made by his own methods. In all, Mr. Thompson had no grounds for complaint. In the third year, he raised Mr. Helton's wages, though Mr. Helton had not asked for a raise. The fourth year, when Mr. Thompson was not only out of debt but had a little cash in the bank, he raised Mr. Helton's wages again, two dollars and a half a month each time.

"The man's worth it, Ellie," said Mr. Thompson, in a glow of self-justification for his extravagance. "He's made this place pay, and I want him to know I appreciate it."

Mr. Helton's silence, the pallor of his eyebrows and hair, his long, glum jaw and eyes that refused to see anything, even the work under his hands, had grown perfectly familiar to the Thompsons. At first, Mrs. Thompson complained a little. "It's like sitting down at the table with a disembodied spirit," she said. "You'd think he'd find something to say, sooner or later."

"Let him alone," said Mr. Thompson. "When he gets ready to talk, he'll talk."

The years passed, and Mr. Helton never got ready to talk. After his work was finished for the day, he would come up from the barn or the milk house or the chicken house, swinging his lantern, his big shoes clumping like pony hoofs on the hard path. They, sitting in the kitchen in the winter, or on the back porch in summer, would hear him drag out his wooden chair, hear the creak of it tilted back, and then for a little while he would play his single tune on one or another of his harmonicas. The harmonicas were in different keys, some lower and sweeter than the others, but the same changeless tune went on, a strange tune, with sudden turns in it, night after night, and some-times even in the afternoons when Mr. Helton sat down to catch his breath. At first the Thompsons liked it very much, and always stopped to listen. Later there came a time when they were fairly sick of it, and began to wish to each other that he would learn a new one. At last they did not hear it any more, it was as natural as the sound of the wind rising in the evenings, or the cows lowing, or their own voices.

Mrs. Thompson pondered now and then over Mr. Helton's soul. He didn't seem to be a church-goer, and worked straight through Sunday as if it were any common day of the week. "I think we ought to invite him to go to hear Dr. Martin," she told Mr. Thompson. "It isn't very Christian of us not to ask him. He's not a forward kind of man. He'd wait to be asked."

"Let him alone," said Mr. Thompson. "The way I look at it, his religion is every man's own business. Besides, he ain't got any Sunday clothes. He wouldn't want to go to church in them jeans and jumpers of his. I don't know what he does with his money. He certainly don't spend it foolishly."

Still, once the notion got into her head, Mrs. Thompson could not rest until she invited Mr. Helton to go to church with the family next Sunday. He was pitching hay into neat little piles in the field back of the orchard. Mrs. Thompson put on smoked glasses and a sunbonnet and walked all the way down there to speak to him. He stopped and leaned on his pitchfork, listening, and for a moment Mrs. Thompson was almost frightened at his face.

The pale eyes seemed to glare past her, the eyebrows frowned, the long jaw hardened. "I got work," he said bluntly, and lifting his pitchfork he turned from her and began to toss the hay. Mrs. Thompson, her feelings hurt, walked back thinking that by now she should be used to Mr. Helton's ways, but it did seem like a man, even a foreigner, could be just a little polite when you gave him a Christian invitation. "He's not polite, that's the only thing I've got against him," she said to Mr. Thompson. "He just can't seem to behave like other people. You'd think he had a grudge against the world," she said. "I sometimes don't know what to make of it."

In the second year something had happened that made Mrs. Thompson uneasy, the kind of thing she could not put into words, hardly into thoughts, and if she had tried to explain to Mr. Thompson it would have sounded worse than it was, or not bad enough. It was that kind of queer thing that seems to be giving a warning, and yet, nearly always nothing comes of it. It was on a hot, still spring day, and Mrs. Thompson had been down to the garden patch to pull some new carrots and green onions and string beans for dinner. As she worked, sunbonnet low over her eyes, putting each kind of vegetable in a pile by itself in her basket, she noticed how neatly Mr. Helton weeded, and how rich the soil was. He had spread it all over with manure from the barns, and worked it in, in the fall, and the vegetables were coming up fine and full. She walked back under the nubbly little fig trees where the unpruned branches leaned almost to the ground, and the thick leaves made a cool screen. Mrs. Thompson was always looking for shade to save her eyes. So she, looking idly about, saw through the screen a sight that struck her as very strange. If it had been a noisy spectacle, it would have been quite natural. It was the silence that struck her. Mr. Helton was shaking Arthur by the shoulders, ferociously, his face most terribly fixed and pale. Arthur's head snapped back and forth and he had not stiffened in

resistance, as he did when Mrs. Thompson tried to shake
him. His eyes were rather frightened, but surprised, too,
probably more surprised than anything else. Herbert stood
by meekly, watching. Mr. Helton dropped Arthur, and
seized Herbert, and shook him with the same methodical
ferocity, the same face of hatred. Herbert's mouth crumpled as if he would cry, but he made no sound. Mr. Helton
let him go, turned and strode into the shack, and the little
boys ran, as if for their lives, without a word. They disappeared around the corner to the front of the house.

Mrs. Thompson took time to set her basket on the
kitchen table, to push her sunbonnet back on her head
and draw it forward again, to look in the stove and make
certain the fire was going, before she followed the boys.
They were sitting huddled together under a clump of
chinaberry trees in plain sight of her bedroom window, as
if it were a safe place they had discovered.

"What are you doing?" asked Mrs. Thompson.

They looked hang-dog from under their foreheads and
Arthur mumbled, "Nothin'."

"Nothing *now*, you mean," said Mrs. Thompson, severely. "Well, I have plenty for you to do. Come right in here
this minute and help me fix vegetables. This minute."

They scrambled up very eagerly and followed her close.
Mrs. Thompson tried to imagine what they had been up
to; she did not like the notion of Mr. Helton taking it on
himself to correct her little boys, but she was afraid to
ask them for reasons. They might tell her a lie, and she
would have to overtake them in it, and whip them. Or she
would have to pretend to believe them, and they would
get in the habit of lying. Or they might tell her the truth,
and it would be something she would have to whip them
for. The very thought of it gave her a headache. She supposed she might ask Mr. Helton, but it was not her place
to ask. She would wait and tell Mr. Thompson, and let
him get at the bottom of it. While her mind ran on, she
kept the little boys hopping. "Cut those carrot tops closer,

Herbert, you're just being careless. Arthur, stop breaking up the beans so little. They're little enough already. Herbert, you go get an armload of wood. Arthur, you take these onions and wash them under the pump. Herbert, as soon as you're done here, you get a broom and sweep out this kitchen. Arthur, you get a shovel and take up the ashes. Stop picking your nose, Herbert. How often must I tell you? Arthur, you go look in the top drawer of my bureau, left-hand side, and bring me the vaseline for Herbert's nose. Herbert, come here to me. . . ."

They galloped through their chores, their animal spirits rose with activity, and shortly they were out in the front yard again, engaged in a wrestling match. They sprawled and fought, scrambled, clutched, rose and fell shouting, as aimlessly, noisily, montonously as two puppies. They imitated various animals, not a human sound from them, and their dirty faces were streaked with sweat. Mrs. Thompson, sitting at her window, watched them with baffled pride and tenderness, they were so sturdy and healthy and growing so fast; but uneasily, too, with her pained little smile and the tears rolling from her eyelids that clinched themselves against the sunlight. They were so idle and careless, as if they had no future in this world, and no immortal souls to save, and oh, what had they been up to that Mr. Helton had shaken them, with his face positively dangerous?

In the evening before supper, without a word to Mr. Thompson of the curious fear the sight had caused her, she told him that Mr. Helton had shaken the little boys for some reason. He stepped out to the shack and spoke to Mr. Helton. In five minutes he was back, glaring at his young. "He says them brats been fooling with his harmonicas, Ellie, blowing in them and getting them all dirty and full of spit and they don't play good."

"Did he say all that?" asked Mrs. Thompson. "It doesn't seem possible."

"Well, that's what he meant, anyhow," said Mr. Thompson. "He didn't say it just that way. But he acted pretty worked up about it."

"That's a shame," said Mrs. Thompson, "a perfect shame. Now we've got to do something so they'll remember they mustn't go into Mr. Helton's things."

"I'll tan their hides for them," said Mr. Thompson. "I'll take a calf rope to them if they don't look out."

"Maybe you'd better leave the whipping to me," said Mrs. Thompson. "You haven't got a light enough hand for children."

"That's just what's the matter with them now," shouted Mr. Thompson, "rotten spoiled and they'll wind up in the penitentiary. You don't half whip 'em. Just little love taps. My pa used to knock me down with a stick of stove wood or anything else that came handy."

"Well, that's not saying it's right," said Mrs. Thompson. "I don't hold with that way of raising children. It makes them run away from home. I've seen too much of it."

"I'll break every bone in 'em," said Mr. Thompson, simmering down, "if they don't mind you better and stop being so bull-headed."

"Leave the table and wash your face and hands," Mrs. Thompson commanded the boys, suddenly. They slunk out and dabbled at the pump and slunk in again, trying to make themselves small. They had learned long ago that their mother always made them wash when there was trouble ahead. They looked at their plates. Mr. Thompson opened up on them.

"Well, now, what you got to say for yourselves about going into Mr. Helton's shack and ruining his harmonicas?"

The two little boys wilted, their faces drooped into the grieved hopeless lines of children's faces when they are brought to the terrible bar of blind adult justice; their eyes telegraphed each other in panic, "Now we're really going to catch a licking"; in despair, they dropped their buttered cornbread on their plates, their hands lagged on the edge of the table.

"I ought to break your ribs," said Mr. Thompson, "and I'm a good mind to do it."

"Yes, sir," whispered Arthur, faintly.

"Yes, sir," said Herbert, his lip trembling.

"Now, papa," said Mrs. Thompson in a warning tone. The children did not glance at her. They had no faith in her good will. She had betrayed them in the first place. There was no trusting her. Now she might save them and she might not. No use depending on her.

"Well, you ought to get a good thrashing. You deserve it, don't you, Arthur?"

Arthur hung his head. "Yes, sir."

"And the next time I catch either of you hanging around Mr. Helton's shack, I'm going to take the hide off *both* of you, you hear me, Herbert?"

Herbert mumbled and choked, scattering his cornbread. "Yes, sir."

"Well, now sit up and eat your supper and not another word out of you," said Mr. Thompson, beginning on his own food. The little boys perked up somewhat and started chewing, but every time they looked around they met their parents' eyes, regarding them steadily. There was no telling when they would think of something new. The boys ate warily, trying not to be seen or heard, the corn-bread sticking, the buttermilk gurgling, as it went down their gullets.

"And something else, Mr. Thompson," said Mrs. Thompson after a pause. "Tell Mr. Helton he's to come straight to us when they bother him, and not to trouble shaking them himself. Tell him we'll look after that."

"They're so mean," answered Mr. Thompson, staring at them. "It's a wonder he don't just kill 'em off and be done with it." But there was something in the tone that told Arthur and Herbert that nothing more worth worrying about was going to happen this time. Heaving deep sighs, they sat up, reaching for the food nearest them.

"Listen," said Mrs. Thompson, suddenly. The little boys stopped eating. "Mr. Helton hasn't come for his supper. Arthur, go and tell Mr. Helton he's late for supper. Tell him nice, now."

Arthur, miserably depressed, slid out of his place and made for the door, without a word.

There were no miracles of fortune to be brought to pass on a small dairy farm. The Thompsons did not grow rich, but they kept out of the poor house, as Mr. Thompson was fond of saying, meaning he had got a little foothold in spite of Ellie's poor health, and unexpected weather, and strange declines in market prices, and his own mysterious handicaps which weighed him down. Mr. Helton was the hope and the prop of the family, and all the Thompsons became fond of him, or at any rate they ceased to regard him as in any way peculiar, and looked upon him, from a distance they did not know how to bridge, as a good man and a good friend. Mr. Helton went his way, worked, played his tune. Nine years passed. The boys grew up and learned to work. They could not remember the time when Ole Helton hadn't been there: a grouchy cuss, Brother Bones; Mr. Helton, the dairymaid; that Big Swede. If he had heard them, he might have been annoyed at some of the names they called him. But he did not hear them, and besides they meant no harm—or at least such harm as existed was all there, in the names; the boys referred to their father as the Old Man, or the Old Geezer, but not to his face. They lived through by main strength all the grimy, secret, oblique phases of growing up and got past the crisis safely if anyone does. Their parents could see they were good solid boys with hearts of gold in spite of their rough ways. Mr. Thompson was relieved to find that, without knowing how he had done it, he had succeeded in raising a set of boys who were not trifling whittlers. They were such good boys Mr. Thompson began to believe they were born that way, and that he had never spoken a harsh word to them in their lives, much less thrashed them. Herbert and Arthur never disputed his word.

Mr. Helton, his hair wet with sweat, plastered to his dripping forehead, his jumper streaked dark and light blue and clinging to his ribs, was chopping a little firewood. He chopped slowly, struck the ax into the end of the chopping log, and piled the wood up neatly. He then disappeared round the house into his shack, which shared with the wood pile a good shade from a row of mulberry trees. Mr. Thompson was lolling in a swing chair on the front porch, a place he had never liked. The chair was new, and Mrs. Thompson had wanted it on the front porch, though the side porch was the place for it, being cooler; and Mr. Thompson wanted to sit in the chair, so there he was. As soon as the new wore off of it, and Ellie's pride in it was exhausted, he would move it round to the side porch. Meantime the August heat was almost unbearable, the air so thick you could poke a hole in it. The dust was inches thick on everything, though Mr. Helton sprinkled the whole yard regularly every night. He even shot the hose upward and washed the tree tops and the roof of the house. They had laid waterpipes to the kitchen and an outside faucet. Mr. Thompson must have dozed, for he opened his eyes and shut his mouth just in time to save his face before a stranger who had driven up to the front gate. Mr. Thompson stood up, put on his hat, pulled up his jeans, and watched while the stranger tied his team, attached to a light spring wagon, to the hitching post. Mr. Thompson recognized the team and wagon. They were from a livery stable in Buda. While the stranger was opening the gate, a strong gate that Mr. Helton had built and set firmly on its hinges several years back, Mr. Thompson strolled down the path to greet him and find out what in God's world a man's business might be that would bring him out at this time of day, in all this dust and welter.

He wasn't exactly a fat man. He was more like a man who had been fat recently. His skin was baggy and his clothes were too big for him, and he somehow looked like a man who should be fat, ordinarily, but who might have just got over a spell of sickness. Mr. Thompson didn't take to his looks at all, he couldn't say why.

The stranger took off his hat. He said in a loud hearty voice, "Is this Mr. Thompson, Mr. Royal Earle Thompson?"

"That's my name," said Mr. Thompson, almost quietly, he was so taken aback by the free manner of the stranger.

"My name is Hatch," said the stranger, "Mr. Homer T. Hatch, and I've come to see you about buying a horse."

"I reckon you've been misdirected," said Mr. Thompson. "I haven't got a horse for sale. Usually if I've got anything like that to sell," he said, "I tell the neighbors and tack up a little sign on the gate."

The fat man opened his mouth and roared with joy, showing rabbit teeth brown as shoeleather. Mr. Thompson saw nothing to laugh at, for once. The stranger shouted, "That's just an old joke of mine." He caught one of his hands in the other and shook hands with himself heartily. "I always say something like that when I'm calling on a stranger, because I've noticed that when a feller says he's come to buy something nobody takes him for a suspicious character. You see? Haw, haw, haw."

His joviality made Mr. Thompson nervous, because the expression in the man's eyes didn't match the sounds he was making. "Haw, haw," laughed Mr. Thompson obligingly, still not seeing the joke. "Well, that's all wasted on me because I never take any man for a suspicious character 'til he shows hisself to be one. Says or does something," he explained. "Until that happens, one man's as good as another, so far's *I'm* concerned."

"Well," said the stranger, suddenly very sober and sensible, "I ain't come neither to buy nor sell. Fact is, I want to see you about something that's of interest to us both.

Yes, sir, I'd like to have a little talk with you, and it won't cost you a cent."

"I guess that's fair enough," said Mr. Thompson, reluctantly. "Come on around the house where there's a little shade."

They went round and seated themselves on two stumps under a chinaberry tree.

"Yes, sir, Homer T. Hatch is my name and America is my nation," said the stranger. "I reckon you must know the name? I used to have a cousin named Jameson Hatch lived up the country a ways."

"Don't think I know the name," said Mr. Thompson. "There's some Hatchers settled somewhere around Mountain City."

"Don't know the old Hatch family," cried the man in deep concern. He seemed to be pitying Mr. Thompson's ignorance. "Why, we came over from Georgia fifty years ago. Been here long yourself?"

"Just all my whole life," said Mr. Thompson, beginning to feel peevish. "And my pa and my grampap before me. Yes, sir, we've been right here all along. Anybody wants to find a Thompson knows where to look for him. My grampap immigrated in 1836."

"From Ireland, I reckon?" said the stranger.

"From Pennsylvania," said Mr. Thompson. "Now what makes you think we came from Ireland?"

The stranger opened his mouth and began to shout with merriment, and he shook hands with himself as if he hadn't met himself for a long time. "Well, what I always says is, a feller's got to come from *somewhere*, ain't he?"

While they were talking, Mr. Thompson kept glancing at the face near him. He certainly did remind Mr. Thompson of somebody, or maybe he really had seen the man himself somewhere. He couldn't just place the features. Mr. Thompson finally decided it was just that all rabbit-teethed men looked alike.

"That's right," acknowledged Mr. Thompson, rather

sourly, "but what I always say is, Thompsons have been settled here for so long it don't make much difference any more *where* they come from. Now a course, this is the slack season, and we're all just laying round a little, but nevertheless we've all got our chores to do, and I don't want to hurry you, and so if you've come to see me on business maybe we'd better get down to it."

"As I said, it's not in a way, and again in a way it is," said the fat man. "Now I'm looking for a man named Helton, Mr. Olaf Eric Helton, from North Dakota, and I was told up around the country a ways that I might find him here, and I wouldn't mind having a little talk with him. No, siree, I sure wouldn't mind, if it's all the same to you."

"I never knew his middle name," said Mr. Thompson, "but Mr. Helton is right here, and been here now for going on nine years. He's a mighty steady man, and you can tell anybody I said so."

"I'm glad to hear that," said Mr. Homer T. Hatch. "I like to hear of a feller mending his ways and settling down. Now when I knew Mr. Helton he was pretty wild, yes, sir, wild is what he was, he didn't know his own mind atall. Well, now, it's going to be a great pleasure to me to meet up with an old friend and find him all settled down and doing well by hisself."

"We've all got to be young once," said Mr. Thompson. "It's like the measles, it breaks out all over you, and you're a nuisance to yourself and everybody else, but it don't last, and it usually don't leave no ill effects." He was so pleased with this notion he forgot and broke into a guffaw. The stranger folded his arms over his stomach and went into a kind of fit, roaring until he had tears in his eyes. Mr. Thompson stopped shouting and eyed the stranger uneasily. Now he liked a good laugh as well as any man, but there ought to be a little moderation. Now this feller laughed like a perfect lunatic, that was a fact. And he wasn't laughing because he really thought things were funny, either. He was laughing for reasons of his own. Mr. Thompson fell into a moody silence, and waited until Mr. Hatch settled down a little.

Mr. Hatch got out a very dirty blue cotton bandanna and wiped his eyes. "That joke just about caught me where I live," he said, almost apologetically. "Now I wish I could think up things as funny as that to say. It's a gift. It's . . ."

"If you want to speak to Mr. Helton, I'll go and round him up," said Mr. Thompson, making motions as if he might get up. "He may be in the milk house and he may be setting in his shack this time of day." It was drawing towards five o'clock. "It's right around the corner," he said.

"Oh, well, there ain't no special hurry," said Mr. Hatch. "I've been wanting to speak to him for a good long spell now and I guess a few minutes more won't make no difference. I just more wanted to locate him, like. That's all."

Mr. Thompson stopped beginning to stand up, and unbuttoned one more button of his shirt, and said, "Well, he's here, and he's this kind of man, that if he had any business with you he'd like to get it over. He don't dawdle, that's one thing you can say for him."

Mr. Hatch appeared to sulk a little at these words. He wiped his face with the bandanna and opened his mouth to speak, when round the house there came the music of Mr. Helton's harmonica. Mr. Thompson raised a finger. "There he is," said Mr. Thompson. "Now's your time."

Mr. Hatch cocked an ear towards the east side of the house and listened for a few seconds, a very strange expression on his face.

"I know that tune like I know the palm of my own hand," said Mr. Thompson, "but I never heard Mr. Helton say what it was."

"That's a kind of Scandahoovian song," said Mr. Hatch. "Where I come from they sing it a lot. In North Dakota, they sing it. It says something about starting out in the morning feeling so good you can't hardly stand it, so you

drink up all your likker before noon. All the likker, y'
understand, that you was saving for the noon lay-off. The
words ain't much, but it's a pretty tune. It's a kind of
drinking song." He sat there drooping a little, and Mr.
Thompson didn't like his expression. It was a satisfied
expression, but it was more like the cat that et the canary.

"So far as I know," said Mr. Thompson, "he ain't
touched a drop since he's been on the place, and that's
nine years this coming September. Yes, sir, nine years, so
far as I know, he ain't wetted his whistle once. And that's
more than I can say for myself," he said, meekly proud.

"Yes, that's a drinking song," said Mr. Hatch. "I used
to play 'Little Brown Jug' on the fiddle when I was younger
than I am now," he went on, "but this Helton, he just
keeps it up. He just sits and plays it by himself."

"He's been playing it off and on for nine years right
here on the place," said Mr. Thompson, feeling a little
proprietary.

"And he was certainly singing it as well, fifteen years
before that, in North Dakota," said Mr. Hatch. "He used
to sit up in a straitjacket, practically, when he was in the
asylum—"

"What's that you say?" said Mr. Thompson. "What's
that?"

"Shucks, I didn't mean to tell you," said Mr. Hatch, a
faint leer of regret in his drooping eyelids. "Shucks, that
just slipped out. Funny, now I'd made up my mind I
wouldn' say a word, because it would just make a lot of
excitement, and what I say is, if a man has lived harmless
and quiet for nine years it don't matter if he *is* loony, does
it? So long's he keeps quiet and don't do nobody harm."

"You mean they had him in a straitjacket?" asked Mr.
Thompson, uneasily. "In a lunatic asylum?"

"They sure did," said Mr. Hatch. "That's right where
they had him, from time to time."

"They put my Aunt Ida in one of them things in the
State asylum," said Mr. Thompson. "She got vi'lent, and

they put her in one of these jackets with long sleeves and tied her to an iron ring in the wall, and Aunt Ida got so wild she broke a blood vessel and when they went to look after her she was dead. I'd think one of them things was dangerous."

"Mr. Helton used to sing his drinking song when he was in a straitjacket," said Mr. Hatch. "Nothing ever bothered him, except if you tried to make him talk. That bothered him, and he'd get vi'lent, like your Aunt Ida. He'd get vi'lent and then they'd put him in the jacket and go off and leave him, and he'd lay there perfickly contented, so far's you could see, singing his song. Then one night he just disappeared. Left, you might say, just went, and nobody ever saw hide or hair of him again. And then I come along and find him here," said Mr. Hatch, "all settled down and playing the same song."

"He never acted crazy to me," said Mr. Thompson. "He always acted like a sensible man, to me. He never got married, for one thing, and he works like a horse, and I bet he's got the first cent I paid him when he landed here, and he don't drink, and he never says a word, much less swear, and he don't waste time runnin' around Saturday nights, and if he's crazy," said Mr. Thompson, "why, I think I'll go crazy myself for a change."

"Haw, ha," said Mr. Hatch, "heh, he, that's good! Ha, ha, ha, I hadn't thought of it jes like that. Yeah, that's right! Let's all go crazy and get rid of our wives and save our money, hey?" He smiled unpleasantly, showing his little rabbit teeth.

Mr. Thompson felt he was being misunderstood. He turned around and motioned toward the open window back of the honeysuckle trellis. "Let's move off down here a little," he said. "I oughta thought of that before." His visitor bothered Mr. Thompson. He had a way of taking the words out of Mr. Thompson's mouth, turning them around and mixing them up until Mr. Thompson didn't know himself what he had said. "My wife's not very strong," said Mr. Thompson. "She's been kind of invalid now goin' on fourteen years. It's mighty tough on a poor man, havin' sickness in the family. She had four operations," he said proudly, "one right after the other, but they didn't do any good. For five years handrunnin', I just turned every nickel I made over to the doctors. Upshot is, she's a mighty delicate woman."

"My old woman," said Mr. Homer T. Hatch, "had a back like a mule, yes, sir. That woman could have moved the barn with her bare hands if she'd ever took the notion. I used to say, it was a good thing she didn't know her own stren'th. She's dead now, though. That kind wear out quicker than the puny ones. I never had much use for a woman always complainin'. I'd get rid of her mighty quick, yes, sir, mighty quick. It's just as you say: a dead loss, keepin' one of 'em up."

This was not at all what Mr. Thompson had heard himself say; he had been trying to explain that a wife as expensive as his was a credit to a man. "She's a mighty reasonable woman," said Mr. Thompson, feeling baffled, "but I wouldn't answer for what she'd say or do if she found out we'd had a lunatic on the place all this time." They had moved away from the window; Mr. Thompson took Mr. Hatch the front way, because if he went the back way they would have to pass Mr. Helton's shack. For some reason he didn't want the stranger to see or talk to Mr. Helton. It was strange, but that was the way Mr. Thompson felt.

Mr. Thompson sat down again, on the chopping log, offering his guest another tree stump. "Now, I mighta got upset myself at such a thing, once," said Mr. Thompson, "but now I *deefy* anything to get me lathered up." He cut himself an enormous plug of tobacco with his horn-handled pocketknife, and offered it to Mr. Hatch, who then produced his own plug and, opening a huge bowie knife with a long blade sharply whetted, cut off a large wad and put it in his mouth. They then compared plugs and both of them were astonished to see how different men's ideas of good chewing tobacco were.

"Now, for instance," said Mr. Hatch, "mine is lighter colored. That's because, for one thing, there ain't any sweetenin' in this plug. I like it dry, natural leaf, medium strong."

"A little sweetenin' don't do no harm so far as I'm concerned," said Mr. Thompson, "but it's got to be mighty little. But with me, now, I want a strong leaf, I want it heavy-cured, as the feller says. There's a man near here, named Williams, Mr. John Morgan Williams, who chews a plug—well, sir, it's black as your hat and soft as melted tar. It fairly drips with molasses, jus' plain molasses, and it chews like licorice. Now, I don't call that a good chew."

"One man's meat," said Mr. Hatch, "is another man's poison. Now, such a chew would simply gag me. I couldn't begin to put it in my mouth."

"Well," said Mr. Thompson, a tinge of apology in his voice, "I jus' barely tasted it myself, you might say. Just took a little piece in my mouth and spit it out again."

"I'm dead sure I couldn't even get that far," said Mr. Hatch. "I like a dry natural chew without any artificial flavorin' of any kind."

Mr. Thompson began to feel that Mr. Hatch was trying to make out he had the best judgment in tobacco, and was going to keep up the argument until he proved it. He began to feel seriously annoyed with the fat man. After all, who was he and where did he come from? Who was he to go around telling other people what kind of tobacco to chew?

"Artificial flavorin'," Mr. Hatch went on, doggedly, "is jes put in to cover up a cheap leaf and make a man think he's gettin' somethin' more than he *is* gettin'. Even a little sweetenin' is a sign of a cheap leaf, you can mark my words."

"I've always paid a fair price for my plug," said Mr. Thompson, stiffly. "I'm not a rich man and I don't go round settin' myself up for one, but I'll say this, when it comes to such things as tobacco, I buy the best on the market."

"Sweetenin', even a little," began Mr. Hatch, shifting his plug and squirting tobacco juice at a dry-looking little rose bush that was having a hard enough time as it was, standing all day in the blazing sun, its roots clenched in the baked earth, "is the sign of—"

"About this Mr. Helton, now," said Mr. Thompson, determinedly, "I don't see no reason to hold it against a man because he went loony once or twice in his lifetime and so I don't expect to take no steps about it. Not a step. I've got nothin' against the man, he's always treated me fair. They's things and people," he went on, " 'nough to drive any man loony. The wonder to me is, more men don't wind up in straitjackets, the way things are going these days and times."

"That's right," said Mr. Hatch, promptly, entirely too promptly, as if he were turning Mr. Thompson's meaning back on him. "You took the words right out of my mouth. There ain't every man in a straitjacket that ought to be there. Ha, ha, you're right all right. You got the idea."

Mr. Thompson sat silent and chewed steadily and stared at a spot on the ground about six feet away and felt a slow muffled resentment climbing from somewhere deep down in him, climbing and spreading all through him. What was this fellow driving at? What was he trying to say? It wasn't so much his words, but his looks and his way of talking: that droopy look in the eye, that tone of voice, as if he was trying to mortify Mr. Thompson about something. Mr. Thompson didn't like it, but he couldn't get hold of it either. He wanted to turn around and shove the fellow off the stump, but it wouldn't look reasonable. Suppose something happened to the fellow when he fell off the stump, just for instance, if he fell on the ax and cut himself, and then someone should ask Mr. Thompson why he shoved him, and what could a man say? It would look mighty funny, it would sound mighty strange to say, Well, him and me fell out over a plug of tobacco. He might just shove him anyhow and then tell people he was a fat man not used to the heat and while he was talking he got dizzy and fell off by himself, or something like that, and it wouldn't be the truth either, because it wasn't the heat and it wasn't the tobacco. Mr. Thompson made up his mind to get the fellow off the place pretty quick, without seeming to be anxious, and watch him sharp till he was out of sight. It doesn't pay to be friendly with strangers from another part of the country. They're always up to something, or they'd stay at home where they belong.

"And they's some people," said Mr. Hatch, "would jus' as soon have a loonatic around their house as not, they can't see no difference between them and anybody else. I always say, if that's the way a man feels, don't care who he associates with, why, why, that's his business, not mine. I don't wanta have a thing to do with it. Now back home in North Dakota, we don't feel that way. I'd like to a seen anybody hiring a loonatic there, aspecially after what he done."

"I didn't understand your home was North Dakota," said Mr. Thompson. "I thought you said Georgia."

"I've got a married sister in North Dakota," said Mr. Hatch, "married a Swede, but a white man if ever I saw one. So I say we because we got into a little business together out that way. And it seems like home, kind of."

"What did he do?" asked Mr. Thompson, feeling very uneasy again.

"Oh, nothin' to speak of," said Mr. Hatch, jovially, "jus' went loony one day in the hayfield and shoved a pitchfork right square through his brother, when they was makin' hay. They was goin' to execute him, but they found out he had went crazy with the heat, as the feller says, and so they put him in the asylum. That's all he done. Nothin' to get lathered up about, ha, ha, ha!" he said, and taking out his sharp knife he began to slice off a chew as carefully as if he were cutting cake.

"Well," said Mr. Thompson, "I don't deny that's news. Yes, sir, news. But I still say somethin' must have drove him to it. Some men make you feel like giving 'em a good killing just by lookin' at you. His brother may a been a mean ornery cuss."

"Brother was going to get married," said Mr. Hatch; "used to go courtin' his girl nights. Borrowed Mr. Helton's harmonica to give her a serenade one evenin', and lost it. Brand new harmonica."

"He thinks a heap of his harmonicas," said Mr. Thompson. "Only money he ever spends, now and then he buys hisself a new one. Must have a dozen in that shack, all kinds and sizes."

"Brother wouldn't buy him a new one," said Mr. Hatch, "so Mr. Helton just ups, as I says, and runs his pitchfork through his brother. Now you know he musta been crazy to get all worked up over a little thing like that."

"Sounds like it," said Mr. Thompson, reluctant to agree in anything with this intrusive and disagreeable fellow. He kept thinking he couldn't remember when he had taken such a dislike to a man on first sight.

"Seems to me you'd get pretty sick of hearin' the same tune year in, year out," said Mr. Hatch.

"Well, sometimes I think it wouldn't do no harm if he learned a new one," said Mr. Thompson, "but he don't, so there's nothin' to be done about it. It's a pretty good tune, though."

"One of the Scandahoovians told me what it meant, that's how I come to know," said Mr. Hatch. "Especially that part about getting so gay you jus' go ahead and drink up all the likker you got on hand before noon. It seems like up in them Swede countries a man carries a bottle of wine around with him as a matter of course, at least that's the way I understood it. Those fellers will tell you anything, though—" He broke off and spat.

The idea of drinking any kind of liquor in this heat

made Mr. Thompson dizzy. The idea of anybody feeling good on a day like this, for instance, made him tired. He felt he was really suffering from the heat. The fat man looked as if he had grown to the stump; he slumped there in his damp, dark clothes too big for him, his belly slack in his pants, his wide black felt hat pushed off his narrow forehead red with prickly heat. A bottle of good cold beer, now, would be a help, thought Mr. Thompson, remembering the four bottles sitting deep in the pool at the springhouse, and his dry tongue squirmed in his mouth. He wasn't going to offer this man anything, though, not even a drop of water. He wasn't even going to chew any more tobacco with him. He shot out his quid suddenly, and wiped his mouth on the back of his hand, and studied the head near him attentively. The man was no good, and he was there for no good, but what was he up to? Mr. Thompson made up his mind he'd give him a little more time to get his business, whatever it was, with Mr. Helton over, and then if he didn't get off the place he'd kick him off.

Mr. Hatch, as if he suspected Mr. Thompson's thoughts, turned his eyes, wicked and pig-like, on Mr. Thompson. "Fact is," he said, as if he had made up his mind about something, "I might need your help in the little matter I've got on hand, but it won't cost you any trouble. Now, this Mr. Helton here, like I tell you, he's a dangerous escaped loonatic, you might say. Now fact is, in the last twelve years or so I musta rounded up twenty-odd escaped loonatics, besides a couple of escaped convicts that I just run into by accident, like. I don't make a business of it, but if there's a reward, and there usually is a reward, of course, I get it. It amounts to a tidy little sum in the long run, but that ain't the main question. Fact is, I'm for law and order, I don't like to see lawbreakers and loonatics at large. It ain't the place for them. Now I reckon you're bound to agree with me on that, aren't you?"

Mr. Thompson said, "Well, circumstances alters cases,

as the feller says. Now, what I know of Mr. Helton, he ain't dangerous, as I told you." Something serious was going to happen, Mr. Thompson could see that. He stopped thinking about it. He'd just let this fellow shoot off his head and then see what could be done about it. Without thinking he got out his knife and plug and started to cut a chew, then remembered himself and put them back in his pocket.

"The law," said Mr. Hatch, "is solidly behind me. Now this Mr. Helton, he's been one of my toughest cases. He's kept my record from being practically one hundred per cent. I knew him before he went loony, and I know the fam'ly, so I undertook to help out rounding him up. Well, sir, he was gone slick as a whistle, for all we knew the man was as good as dead long while ago. Now we never might have caught up with him, but do you know what he did? Well, sir, about two weeks ago his old mother gets a letter from him, and in that letter, what do you reckon she found? Well, it was a check on that little bank in town for eight hundred and fifty dollars, just like that; the letter wasn't nothing much, just said he was sending her a few little savings, she might need something, but there it was, name, postmark, date, everything. The old woman practically lost her mind with joy. She's gettin' childish, and it looked like she kinda forgot that her only living son killed his brother and went loony. Mr. Helton said he was getting along all right, and for her not to tell nobody. Well, natchally, she couldn't keep it to herself, with that check to cash and everything. So that's how I come to know." His feelings got the better of him. "You coulda knocked me down with a feather." He shook hands with himself and rocked, wagging his head, going "Heh, heh," in his throat. Mr. Thompson felt the corners of his mouth turning down. Why, the dirty low-down hound, sneaking around spying into other people's business like that. Collecting blood money, that's what it was! Let him talk!

"Yea, well, that musta been a surprise all right," he said,

trying to hold his voice even. "I'd say a surprise."

"Well, siree," said Mr. Hatch, "the more I got to thinking about it, the more I just come to the conclusion that I'd better look into the matter a little, and so I talked to the old woman. She's pretty decrepit, now, half blind and all, but she was all for taking the first train out and going to see her son. I put it up to her square—how she was too feeble for the trip, and all. So, just as a favor to her, I told her for my expenses I'd come down and see Mr. Helton and bring her back all the news about him. She gave me a new shirt she made herself by hand, and a big Swedish kind of cake to bring to him, but I musta mislaid them along the road somewhere. It don't reely matter, though, he prob'ly ain't in any state of mind to appreciate 'em."

Mr. Thompson sat up and turning round on the log looked at Mr. Hatch and asked as quietly as he could, "And now what are you aiming to do? That's the question."

Mr. Hatch slouched up to his feet and shook himself. "Well, I come all prepared for a little scuffle," he said. "I got the handcuffs," he said, "but I don't want no violence if I can help it. I didn't want to say nothing around the countryside, making an uproar. I figured the two of us could overpower him." He reached into his big inside pocket and pulled them out. Handcuffs, for God's sake, thought Mr. Thompson. Coming round on a peaceable afternoon worrying a man, and making trouble, and fishing handcuffs out of his pocket on a decent family homestead, as if it was all in the day's work.

Mr. Thompson, his head buzzing, got up too. "Well," he said, roundly, "I want to tell you I think you've got a mighty sorry job on hand, you sure must be hard up for something to do, and now I want to give you a good piece of advice. You just drop the idea that you're going to come here and make trouble for Mr. Helton, and the quicker you drive that hired rig away from my front gate the better I'll be satisfied."

Mr. Hatch put one handcuff in his outside pocket, the

other dangling down. He pulled his hat down over his eyes, and reminded Mr. Thompson of a sheriff, somehow. He didn't seem in the least nervous, and didn't take up Mr. Thompson's words. He said, "Now listen just a minute, it ain't reasonable to suppose that a man like yourself is going to stand in the way of getting an escaped loonatic back to the asylum where he belongs. Now I know it's enough to throw you off, coming sudden like this, but fact is I counted on your being a respectable man and helping me out to see that justice is done. Now a course, if you won't help, I'll have to look around for help somewheres else. It won't look very good to your neighbors that you was harboring an escaped loonatic who killed his own brother, and then you refused to give him up. It will look mighty funny."

Mr. Thompson knew almost before he heard the words that it would look funny. It would put him in a mighty awkward position. He said, "But I've been trying to tell you all along that the man ain't loony now. He's been perfectly harmless for nine years. He's—he's—"

Mr. Thompson couldn't think how to describe how it was with Mr. Helton. "Why, he's been like one of the family," he said, "the best standby a man ever had." Mr. Thompson tried to see his way out. It was a fact Mr. Helton might go loony again any minute, and now this fellow talking around the country would put Mr. Thompson in a fix. It was a terrible position. He couldn't think of any way out. "You're crazy," Mr. Thompson roared suddenly, "you're the crazy one around here, you're crazier than he ever was! You get off this place or I'll handcuff you and turn you over to the law. You're trespassing," shouted Mr. Thompson. "Get out of here before I knock you down!"

He took a step towards the fat man, who backed off, shrinking, "Try it, try it, go ahead!" and then something happened that Mr. Thompson tried hard afterwards to piece together in his mind, and in fact it never did come straight. He saw the fat man with his long bowie knife in his hand, he saw Mr. Helton come round the corner on the run, his long jaw dropped, his arms swinging, his eyes wild. Mr. Helton came in between them, fists doubled up, then stopped short, glaring at the fat man, his big frame seemed to collapse, he trembled like a shied horse; and then the fat man drove at him, knife in one hand, handcuffs in the other. Mr. Thompson saw it coming, he saw the blade going into Mr. Helton's stomach, he knew he had the ax out of the log in his own hands, felt his arms go up over his head and bring the ax down on Mr. Hatch's head as if he were stunning a beef.

Mrs. Thompson had been listening uneasily for some time to the voices going on, one of them strange to her, but she was too tired at first to get up and come out to see what was going on. The confused shouting that rose so suddenly brought her up to her feet and out across the front porch without her slippers, hair half-braided. Shading her eyes, she saw first Mr. Helton, running all stooped over through the orchard, running like a man with dogs after him; and Mr. Thompson supporting himself on the ax handle was leaning over shaking by the shoulder a man Mrs. Thompson had never seen, who lay doubled up with the top of his head smashed and the blood running away in a greasy-looking puddle. Mr. Thompson without taking his hand from the man's shoulder, said in a thick voice, "He killed Mr. Helton, he killed him, I saw him do it. I had to knock him out," he called loudly, "but he won't come to."

Mrs. Thompson said in a faint scream, "Why, yonder goes Mr. Helton," and she pointed. Mr. Thompson pulled himself up and looked where she pointed. Mrs. Thompson sat down slowly against the side of the house and began to slide forward on her face; she felt as if she were drowning, she couldn't rise to the top somehow, and her only thought was she was glad the boys were not there, they were out, fishing at Halifax, oh, God, she was glad the boys were not there.

Mr. and Mrs. Thompson drove up to their barn about sunset. Mr. Thompson handed the reins to his wife, got out to open the big door, and Mrs. Thompson guided old Jim in under the roof. The buggy was gray with dust and age, Mrs. Thompson's face was gray with dust and weariness, and Mr. Thompson's face, as he stood at the horse's head and began unhitching, was gray except for the dark blue of his freshly shaven jaws and chin, gray and blue and caved in, but patient, like a dead man's face.

Mrs. Thompson stepped down to the hard packed manure of the barn floor, and shook out her light flower-sprigged dress. She wore her smoked glasses, and her wide shady leghorn hat with the wreath of exhausted pink and blue forget-me-nots hid her forehead, fixed in a knot of distress.

The horse hung his head, raised a huge sigh and flexed his stiffened legs. Mr. Thompson's words came up muffled and hollow. "Poor ole Jim," he said, clearing his throat, "he looks pretty sunk in the ribs. I guess he's had a hard week." He lifted the harness up in one piece, slid it off and Jim walked out of the shafts halting a little. "Well, this is the last time," Mr. Thompson said, still talking to Jim. "Now you can get a good rest."

Mrs. Thompson closed her eyes behind her smoked glasses. The last time, and high time, and they should never have gone at all. She did not need her glasses any more, now the good darkness was coming down again, but her eyes ran full of tears steadily, though she was not crying, and she felt better with the glasses, safer, hidden away behind them. She took out her handkerchief with her hands shaking as they had been shaking ever since *that day,* and blew her nose. She said, "I see the boys have lighted the lamps. I hope they've started the stove going."

She stepped along the rough path holding her thin dress

and starched petticoats around her, feeling her way between the sharp small stones, leaving the barn because she could hardly bear to be near Mr. Thompson, advancing slowly towards the house because she dreaded going there. Life was all one dread, the faces of her neighbors, of her boys, of her husband, the face of the whole world, the shape of her own house in the darkness, the very smell of the grass and the trees were horrible to her. There was no place to go, only one thing to do, bear it somehow—but how? She asked herself that question often. How was she going to keep on living now? Why had she lived at all? She wished now she had died one of those times when she had been so sick, instead of living on for this.

The boys were in the kitchen; Herbert was looking at the funny pictures from last Sunday's newspapers, the Katzenjammer Kids and Happy Hooligan. His chin was in his hands and his elbows on the table, and he was really reading and looking at the pictures, but his face was unhappy. Arthur was building the fire, adding kindling a stick at a time, watching it catch and blaze. His face was heavier and darker than Herbert's, but he was a little sullen by nature; Mrs. Thompson thought, he takes things harder, too. Arthur said, "Hello, Momma," and went on with his work. Herbert swept the papers together and moved over on the bench. They were big boys—fifteen and seventeen, and Arthur as tall as his father. Mrs. Thompson sat down beside Herbert, taking off her hat. She said, "I guess you're hungry. We were late today. We went the Log Hollow road, it's rougher than ever." Her pale mouth drooped with a sad fold on either side.

"I guess you saw the Mannings, then," said Herbert.

"Yes, and the Fergusons, and the Allbrights, and that new family McClellan."

"Anybody say anything?" asked Herbert.

"Nothing much, you know how it's been all along, some of them keeps saying, yes, they know it was a clear case and a fair trial and they say how glad they are your papa came out so well, and all that, some of 'em do, anyhow, but it looks like they don't really take sides with him. I'm about wore out," she said, the tears rolling again from under her dark glasses. "I don't know what good it does, but your papa can't seem to rest unless he's telling how it happened. I don't know."

"I don't think it does any good, not a speck," said Arthur, moving away from the stove. "It just keeps the whole question stirred up in people's minds. Everybody will go round telling what he heard, and the whole thing is going to get worse mixed up than ever. It just makes matters worse. I wish you could get Papa to stop driving round the country talking like that."

"Your papa knows best," said Mrs. Thompson. "You oughtn't to criticize him. He's got enough to put up with without that."

Arthur said nothing, his jaw stubborn. Mr. Thompson came in, his eyes hollowed out and dead-looking, his thick hands gray white and seamed from washing them clean every day before he started out to see the neighbors to tell them his side of the story. He was wearing his Sunday clothes, a thick pepper-and-salt-colored suit with a black string tie.

Mrs. Thompson stood up, her head swimming. "Now you-all get out of the kitchen, it's too hot in here and I need room. I'll get us a little bite of supper, if you'll just get out and give me some room."

They went as if they were glad to go, the boys outside, Mr. Thompson into his bedroom. She heard him groaning to himself as he took off his shoes, and heard the bed creak as he lay down. Mrs. Thompson opened the icebox and felt the sweet coldness flow out of it; she had never expected to have an icebox, much less did she hope to afford to keep it filled with ice. It still seemed like a miracle, after two or three years. There was the food, cold and clean, all ready to be warmed over. She would never have had that icebox if Mr. Helton hadn't happened along one day, just by the strangest luck; so saving, and so managing, so good, thought Mrs. Thompson, her heart swelling until she feared she would faint again, standing there with the door open and leaning her head upon it. She simply could not bear to remember Mr. Helton, with his long sad face and silent ways, who had always been so quiet and harmless, who had worked so hard and helped Mr. Thompson so much, running through the hot fields and woods, being hunted like a mad dog, everybody turning out with ropes and guns and sticks to catch and tie him. Oh, God, said Mrs. Thompson in a long dry moan, kneeling before the icebox and fumbling inside for the dishes, even if they did pile mattresses all over the jail floor and against the walls, and five men there to hold him to keep him from hurting himself any more, he was already hurt too badly, he couldn't have lived anyway. Mr. Barbee, the sheriff, told her about it. He said, well, they didn't aim to harm him but they had to catch him, he was crazy as a loon; he picked up rocks and tried to brain every man that got near him. He had two harmonicas in his jumper pocket, said the sheriff, but they fell out in the scuffle, and Mr. Helton tried to pick 'em up again, and that's when they finally got him. "They *had* to be rough, Miz Thompson, he fought like a wildcat." Yes, thought Mrs. Thompson again with the same bitterness, of course, they had to be rough. They always have to be rough. Mr. Thompson can't argue with a man and get him off the place peaceably; no, she thought, standing up and shutting the icebox, he has to kill somebody, he has to be a murderer and ruin his boys' lives and cause Mr. Helton to be killed like a mad dog.

Her thoughts stopped with a little soundless explosion, cleared and began again. The rest of Mr. Helton's harmonicas were still in the shack, his tune ran in Mrs. Thompson's head at certain times of the day. She missed it in the evenings. It seemed so strange she had never known the name of that song, nor what it meant, until after Mr. Helton was gone. Mrs. Thompson, trembling in

the knees, took a drink of water at the sink and poured
the red beans into the baking dish, and began to roll the
pieces of chicken in flour to fry them. There was a time,
she said to herself, when I thought I had neighbors and
friends, there was a time when we could hold up our heads,
there was a time when my husband hadn't killed a man
and I could tell the truth to anybody about anything.

Mr. Thompson, turning on his bed, figured that he had
done all he could, he'd just try to let the matter rest from
now on. His lawyer, Mr. Burleigh, had told him right at
the beginning, "Now you keep calm and collected. You've
got a fine case, even if you haven't got witnesses. Your wife
must sit in court, she'll be a powerful argument with the
jury. You just plead not guilty and I'll do the rest.
The trial is going to be a mere formality, you haven't
got a thing to worry about. You'll be clean out of this before you know it." And to make talk Mr. Burleigh had
got to telling about all the men he knew around the country who for one reason or another had been forced to kill
somebody, always in self-defense, and there just wasn't
anything to it at all. He even told about how his own
father in the old days had shot and killed a man just for
setting foot inside his gate when he told him not to. "Sure,
I shot the scoundrel," said Mr. Burleigh's father, "in self-
defense; I *told* him I'd shoot him if he set his foot in my
yard, and he did, and I did." There had been bad blood
between them for years, Mr. Burleigh said, and his father
had waited a long time to catch the other fellow in the
wrong, and when he did he certainly made the most of his
opportunity.

"But Mr. Hatch, as I told you," Mr. Thompson had
said, "made a pass at Mr. Helton with his bowie knife.
That's why I took a hand."

"All the better," said Mr. Burleigh. "That stranger
hadn't any right coming to your house on such an errand.
Why, hell," said Mr. Burleigh, "that wasn't even man-

slaughter you committed. So now you just hold your horses and keep your shirt on. And don't say one word without I tell you."

Wasn't even manslaughter. Mr. Thompson had to cover Mr. Hatch with a piece of wagon canvas and ride to town to tell the sheriff. It had been hard on Ellie. When they got back, the sheriff and the coroner and two deputies, they found her sitting beside the road, on a low bridge over a gulley, about half a mile from the place. He had taken her up behind his saddle and got her back to the house. He had already told the sheriff that his wife had witnessed the whole business, and now he had time, getting her to her room and in bed, to tell her what to say if they asked anything. He had left out the part about Mr. Helton being crazy all along, but it came out at the trial. By Mr. Burleigh's advice Mr. Thompson had pretended to be perfectly ignorant; Mr. Hatch hadn't said a word about that. Mr. Thompson pretended to believe that Mr. Hatch had just come looking for Mr. Helton to settle old scores, and the two members of Mr. Hatch's family who had come down to try to get Mr. Thompson convicted didn't get anywhere at all. It hadn't been much of a trial, Mr. Burleigh saw to that. He had charged a reasonable fee, and Mr. Thompson had paid him and felt grateful, but after it was over Mr. Burleigh didn't seem pleased to see him when he got to dropping into the office to talk it over, telling him things that had slipped his mind at first: trying to explain what an ornery low hound Mr. Hatch had been, anyhow. Mr. Burleigh seemed to have lost his interest; he looked sour and upset when he saw Mr. Thompson at the door. Mr. Thompson kept saying to himself that he'd got off, all right, just as Mr. Burleigh had predicted, but, but— and it was right there that Mr. Thompson's mind stuck, squirming like an angleworm on a fishhook: he had killed Mr. Hatch, and he was a murderer. That was the truth about himself that Mr. Thompson couldn't grasp, even when he said the word to himself. Why, he had not even once *thought* of killing anybody, much less Mr. Hatch, and if Mr. Helton hadn't come out so unexpectedly, hearing the row, why, then—but then, Mr. Helton had come on the run that way to help him. What he couldn't understand was what happened next. He had seen Mr. Hatch go after Mr. Helton with the knife, he had seen the point, blade up, go into Mr. Helton's stomach and slice up like you slice a hog, but when they finally caught Mr. Helton there wasn't a knife scratch on him. Mr. Thompson knew he had the ax in his own hands and felt himself lifting it, but he couldn't remember hitting Mr. Hatch. He couldn't remember it. He couldn't. He remembered only that he had been determined to stop Mr. Hatch from cutting Mr. Helton. If he was given a chance he could explain the whole matter. At the trial they hadn't let him talk. They just asked questions and he answered yes or no, and they never did get to the core of the matter. Since the trial, now, every day for a week he had washed and shaved and put on his best clothes and had taken Ellie with him to tell every neighbor he had that he never killed Mr. Hatch on purpose, and what good did it do? Nobody believed him. Even when he turned to Ellie and said, "You was there, you saw it, didn't you?" and Ellie spoke up, saying, "Yes, that's the truth. Mr. Thompson was trying to save Mr. Helton's life," and he added, "If you don't believe me, you can believe my wife. She won't lie," Mr. Thompson saw something in all their faces that disheartened him, made him feel empty and tired out. They didn't believe he was not a murderer.

Even Ellie never said anything to comfort him. He hoped she would say finally, "I remember now, Mr. Thompson, I really did come round the corner in time to see everything. It's not a lie, Mr. Thompson. Don't you worry." But as they drove together in silence, with the days still hot and dry, shortening for fall, day after day, the buggy jolting in the ruts, she said nothing; they grew to dread the sight of another house, and the people in it:

all houses looked alike now, and the people—old neighbors or new—had the same expression when Mr. Thompson told them why he had come and began his story. Their eyes looked as if someone had pinched the eyeball at the back; they shriveled and the light went out of them. Some of them sat with fixed tight smiles trying to be friendly. "Yes, Mr. Thompson, we know how you must feel. It must be terrible for you, Mrs. Thompson. Yes, you know, I've about come to the point where I believe in such a thing as killing in self-defense. Why, certainly, we believe you, Mr. Thompson, why shouldn't we believe you? Didn't you have a perfectly fair and above-board trial? Well, now, natchally, Mr. Thompson, we think you done right."

Mr. Thompson was satisfied they didn't think so. Sometimes the air around him was so thick with their blame he fought and pushed with his fists, and the sweat broke out all over him, he shouted his story in a dust-choked voice. he would fairly bellow at last: "My wife, here, you know her, she was there, she saw and heard it all, if you don't believe me, ask her, she won't lie!" and Mrs. Thompson, with her hands knotted together, aching, her chin trembling, would never fail to say: "Yes, that's right, that's the truth—"

The last straw had been laid on today, Mr. Thompson decided. Tom Allbright, an old beau of Ellie's, why, he had squired Ellie around a whole summer, had come out to meet them when they drove up, and standing there bareheaded had stopped them from getting out. He had looked past them with an embarrassed frown on his face, telling them his wife's sister was there with a raft of young ones, and the house was pretty full and everything upset, or he'd ask them to come in. "We've been thinking of trying to get up to your place one of these days," said Mr. Allbright, moving away trying to look busy, "we've been mighty occupied up here of late." So they had to say, "Well, we just happened to be driving this way," and go on. "The Allbrights," said Mrs. Thompson, "always was fair-weather friends." "They look out for number one, that's a fact," said Mr. Thompson. But it was cold comfort to them both.

Finally Mrs. Thompson had given up. "Let's go home," she said. "Old Jim's tired and thirsty, and we've gone far enough."

Mr. Thompson said, "Well, while we're out this way, we might as well stop at the McClellans'." They drove in, and asked a little cotton-haired boy if his mamma and papa were at home. Mr. Thompson wanted to see them. The little boy stood gazing with his mouth open, then galloped into the house shouting, "Mommer, Popper, come out hyah. That man that kilt Mr. Hatch has come ter see yer!"

The man came out in his sock feet, with one gallus up, the other broken and dangling, and said, "Light down, Mr. Thompson, and come in. The ole woman's washing, but she'll git here." Mrs. Thompson, feeling her way, stepped down and sat in a broken rocking-chair on the porch that sagged under her feet. The woman of the house, barefooted, in a calico wrapper, sat on the edge of the porch, her fat sallow face full of curiosity. Mr. Thompson began, "Well, as I reckon you happen to know, I've had some strange troubles lately, and, as the feller says, it's not the kind of trouble that happens to a man every day in the year, and there's some things I don't want no misunderstanding about in the neighbors' minds, so—" He halted and stumbled forward, and the two listening faces took on a mean look, a greedy, despising look, a look that said plain as day, "My, you must be a purty sorry feller to come round worrying about what *we* think, *we* know you wouldn't be here if you had anybody else to turn to—my, I wouldn't lower myself that much, myself." Mr. Thompson was ashamed of himself, he was suddenly in a rage, he'd like to knock their dirty skunk heads together, the low-down white trash—but he held himself down and went on to the end. "My wife will tell you," he said, and this was the hardest place, because Ellie always without moving a muscle seemed to stiffen as if somebody had threatened to hit her; "ask my wife, she won't lie."

"It's true, I saw it—"

"Well, now," said the man, drily, scratching his ribs inside his shirt, "that sholy is too bad. Well, now, I kaint see what we've got to do with all this here, however. I kaint see no good reason for us to git mixed up in these murder matters, I shore kaint. Whichever way you look at it, it ain't none of my business. However, it's mighty nice of you-all to come around and give us the straight of it, fur we've heerd some mighty queer yarns about it, mighty queer, I golly you couldn't hardly make head ner tail of it."

"Evvybody goin' round shootin' they heads off," said the woman. "Now we don't hold with killin'; the Bible says—"

"Shet yer trap," said the man, "and keep it shet 'r I'll shet it fer yer. Now it shore looks like to me—"

"We mustn't linger," said Mrs. Thompson, unclasping her hands. "We've lingered too long now. It's getting late, and we've far to go." Mr. Thompson took the hint and followed her. The man and the woman lolled against their rickety porch poles and watched them go.

Now lying on his bed, Mr. Thompson knew the end had come. Now, this minute, lying in the bed where he had slept with Ellie for eighteen years; under this roof where he had laid the shingles when he was waiting to get married; there as he was with his whiskers already sprouting since his shave that morning; with his fingers feeling his bony chin, Mr. Thompson felt he was a dead man. He was dead to his other life, he had got to the end of something without knowing why, and he had to make a fresh start, he did not know how. Something different was going to begin, he didn't know what. It was in some way not his business. He didn't feel he was going to have much to do with it. He got up, aching, hollow, and went out to the kitchen where Mrs. Thompson was just taking up the supper.

"Call the boys," said Mrs. Thompson. They had been down to the barn, and Arthur put out the lantern before hanging it on a nail near the door. Mr. Thompson didn't like their silence. They had hardly said a word about anything to him since that day. They seemed to avoid him, they ran the place together as if he wasn't there, and attended to everything without asking him for any advice. "What you boys been up to?" he asked, trying to be hearty. "Finishing your chores?"

"No, sir," said Arthur, "there ain't much to do. Just greasing some axles." Herbert said nothing. Mrs. Thompson bowed her head: "For these and all Thy blessings. . . . Amen," she whispered weakly, and the Thompsons sat there with their eyes down and their faces sorrowful, as if they were at a funeral.

Every time he shut his eyes, trying to sleep, Mr. Thompson's mind started up and began to run like a rabbit. It jumped from one thing to another, trying to pick up a trail here or there that would straighten out what had happened that day he killed Mr. Hatch. Try as he might, Mr. Thompson's mind would not go anywhere that it had not already been, he could not see anything but what he had seen once, and he knew that was not right. If he had not seen straight that first time, then everything about his killing Mr. Hatch was wrong from start to finish, and there was nothing more to be done about it, he might just as well give up. It still seemed to him that he had done, maybe not the right thing, but the only thing he could do, that day, but had he? *Did he have to kill Mr. Hatch?* He had never seen a man he hated more, the minute he laid eyes on him. He knew in his bones the fellow was there for trouble. What seemed so funny now was this: Why hadn't he just told Mr. Hatch to get out before he ever even got in?

Mrs. Thompson, her arms crossed on her breast, was lying beside him, perfectly still, but she seemed awake, somehow. "Asleep, Ellie?"

After all, he might have got rid of him peaceably, or maybe he might have had to overpower him and put those handcuffs on him and turn him over to the sheriff for disturbing the peace. The most they could have done was to lock Mr. Hatch up while he cooled off for a few days, or fine him a little something. He would try to think of things he might have said to Mr. Hatch. Why, let's see, I could just have said, Now look here, Mr. Hatch, I want to talk to you as man to man. But his brain would go empty. What could he have said or done? But if he *could* have done anything else almost except kill Mr. Hatch, then nothing would have happened to Mr. Helton. Mr. Thompson hardly ever thought of Mr. Helton. His mind just skipped over him and went on. If he stopped to think about Mr. Helton he'd never in God's world get anywhere. He tried to imagine how it might all have been, this very night even, if Mr. Helton were still safe and sound out in his shack playing his tune about feeling so good in the morning, drinking up all the wine so you'd feel even better; and Mr. Hatch safe in jail somewhere, mad as hops, maybe, but out of harm's way and ready to listen to reason and to repent of his meanness, the dirty, yellow-livered hound coming around persecuting an innocent man and ruining a whole family that never harmed him! Mr. Thompson felt the veins of his forehead start up, his fists clutched as if they seized an ax handle, the sweat broke out on him, he bounded up from the bed with a yell smothered in his throat, and Ellie started up after him, crying out, "Oh, oh, don't! Don't! Don't!" as if she were having a nightmare. He stood shaking until his bones rattled in him, crying hoarsely, "Light the lamp, light the lamp, Ellie."

Instead, Mrs. Thompson gave a shrill weak scream, almost the same scream he had heard on that day she came around the house when he was standing there with the ax in his hand. He could not see her in the dark, but she was on the bed, rolling violently. He felt for her in horror, and his groping hands found her arms, up, and her own hands pulling her hair straight out from her head, her neck strained back, and the tight screams strangling her. He shouted out for Arthur, for Herbert. "Your mother!" he bawled, his voice cracking. As he held Mrs. Thompson's arms, the boys came tumbling in, Arthur with the lamp above his head. By this light Mr. Thompson saw Mrs. Thompson's eyes, wide open, staring dreadfully at him, the tears pouring. She sat up at sight of the boys, and held out one arm towards them, the hand wagging in a crazy circle, then dropped on her back again, and suddenly went limp. Arthur set the lamp on the table and turned on Mr. Thompson. "She's scared," he said, "she's scared to death." His face was in a knot of rage, his fists were doubled up, he faced his father as if he meant to strike him. Mr. Thompson's jaw fell, he was so surprised he stepped back from the bed. Herbert went to the other side. They stood on each side of Mrs. Thompson and watched Mr. Thompson as if he were a dangerous wild beast. "What did you do to her?" shouted Arthur, in a grown man's voice. "You touch her again and I'll blow your heart out!" Herbert was pale and his cheek twitched, but he was on Arthur's side; he would do what he could to help Arthur.

Mr. Thompson had no fight left in him. His knees bent as he stood, his chest collapsed. "Why, Arthur," he said, his words crumbling and his breath coming short. "She's fainted again. Get the ammonia." Arthur did not move. Herbert brought the bottle, and handed it, shrinking, to his father.

Mr. Thompson held it under Mrs. Thompson's nose. He poured a little in the palm of his hand and rubbed it on her forehead. She gasped and opened her eyes and turned her head away from him. Herbert began a doleful hopeless sniffling. "Mamma," he kept saying, "Mamma, don't die."

"I'm all right," Mrs. Thompson said. "Now don't you worry around. Now Herbert, you mustn't do that. I'm all right." She closed her eyes. Mr. Thompson began pulling on his best pants; he put on his socks and shoes. The boys sat on each side of the bed, watching Mrs. Thompson's face. Mr. Thompson put on his shirt and coat. He said, "I reckon I'll ride over and get the doctor. Don't look like all this fainting is a good sign. Now you just keep watch until I get back." They listened, but said nothing. He said, "Don't you get any notions in your head. I never did your mother any harm in my life, on purpose." He went out, and, looking back, saw Herbert staring at him from under his brows, like a stranger. "You'll know how to look after her," said Mr. Thompson.

Mr. Thompson went through the kitchen. There he lighted the lantern, took a thin pad of scratch paper and a stub pencil from the shelf where the boys kept their schoolbooks. He swung the lantern on his arm and reached into the cupboard where he kept the guns. The shotgun was there to his hand, primed and ready, a man never knows when he may need a shotgun. He went out of the house without looking around, or looking back when he had left it, passed his barn without seeing it, and struck out to the farthest end of his fields, which ran for half a mile to the east. So many blows had been struck at Mr. Thompson and from so many directions he couldn't stop any more to find out where he was hit. He walked on, over plowed ground and over meadow, going through barbed wire fences cautiously, putting his gun through first; he could almost see in the dark, now his eyes were used to it. Finally he came to the last fence; here he sat down, back against a post, lantern at his side, and, with the pad on his knee, moistened the stub pencil and began to write:

"Before Almighty God, the great judge of all before who I am about to appear, I do hereby solemnly swear that I did not take the life of Mr. Homer T. Hatch on purpose. It was done in defense of Mr. Helton. I did not aim to hit him with the ax but only to keep him off Mr. Helton. He aimed a blow at Mr. Helton who was not looking for it. It was my belief at the time that Mr. Hatch would of taken the life of Mr. Helton if I did not interfere. I have told all this to the judge and the jury and they let me off but nobody believes it. This is the only way I can prove I am not a cold blooded murderer like everybody seems to think. If I had been in Mr. Helton's place he would of done the same for me. I still think I done the only thing there was to do. My wife—"

Mr. Thompson stopped here to think a while. He wet the pencil point with the tip of his tongue and marked out the last two words. He sat a while blacking out the words until he had made a neat oblong patch where they had been, and started again:

"It was Mr. Homer T. Hatch who came to do wrong to a harmless man. He caused all this trouble and he deserved to die but I am sorry it was me who had to kill him."

He licked the point of his pencil again, and signed his full name carefully, folded the paper and put it in his outside pocket. Taking off his right shoe and sock, he set the butt of the shotgun along the ground with the twin barrels pointed towards his head. It was very awkward. He thought about this a little, leaning his head against the gun mouth. He was trembling and his head was drumming until he was deaf and blind, but he lay down flat on the earth on his side, drew the barrel under his chin and fumbled for the trigger with his great toe. That way he could work it.

THE OVERCOAT

· ·

Nikolay Gogol

Nikolay Gogol

. . . .

Nikolay Gogol, born in 1809, not only wrote at least one of the masterpieces of Russian literature but helped to influence that literature—so much so that Dostoievsky once remarked that all Russian writers were descended from Gogol's Overcoat. Gogol's two other most famous works are *The Inspector General*, a hilarious play lampooning bureaucracy; and *Dead Souls*, a classic novel presenting a penetrating insight into life in the Russian provinces. In these works humor and symbol and message are combined into superb stories. They are the imaginative works of a genius. But it was "message" that Gogol tragically mistook to be his most important task. And he died, finally, with his faith in his imagination destroyed, in 1852.

THE OVERCOAT

IN THE department of . . . but I had better not mention in what department. There is nothing in the world more readily moved to wrath than a department, a regiment, a government office, and in fact any sort of official body. Nowadays every private individual considers all society insulted in his person. I have been told that very lately a petition was handed in from a police-captain of what town I don't recollect, and that in this petition he set forth clearly that the institutions of the State were in danger and that its sacred name was being taken in vain; and, in proof thereof, he appended to his petition an enormously long volume of some work of romance in which a police-captain appeared on every tenth page, occasionally, indeed, in an intoxicated condition. And so, to avoid any unpleasantness, we had better call the department of which we are speaking a certain department.

And so, in a certain department there was a government clerk; a clerk of whom it cannot be said that he was very remarkable; he was short, somewhat pock-marked, with rather reddish hair and rather dim, bleary eyes, with a small bald patch on the top of his head, with wrinkles on both sides of his cheeks and the sort of complexion which is usually associated with hæmorrhoids . . . no help for that, it is the Petersburg climate. As for his grade in the service (for among us the grade is what must be put first), he was what is called a perpetual titular councillor, a class at which, as we all know, various writers who indulge in the praiseworthy habit of attacking those who cannot defend themselves jeer and jibe to their hearts' content. This clerk's surname was Bashmatchkin. From the very name it is clear that it must have been derived from a shoe *(bashmak)*; but when and under what circumstances it was derived from a shoe, it is impossible to say. Both his father and his grandfather and even his brother-in-law, and all the Bashmatchkins without exception wore boots, which they simply re-soled two or three times a year. His name was Akaky Akakyevitch. Perhaps it may strike the reader as a rather strange and far-fetched name, but I can assure him that it was not far-fetched at all, that the circumstances were such that it was quite out of the question to give him any other name. Akaky Akakyevitch was born towards nightfall, if my memory does not deceive me, on the twenty-third of March. His mother, the wife of a government clerk, a very good woman, made arrangements in due course to christen the child. She was still lying in bed, facing the door, while on her right hand stood the godfather, an excellent man called Ivan Ivanovitch Yeroshkin, one of the head clerks in the Senate, and the godmother, the wife of a police official, and a woman of rare qualities, Arina Semyonovna Byelobryushkov. Three names were offered to the happy mother for selection—Moky, Sossy, or the name of the martyr Hozdazat. "No," thought the poor lady, "they are all such names!" To satisfy her, they opened the calendar at another place, and the names which turned up were: Trifily, Dula, Varahasy. "What an infliction!" said the mother. "What names they all are! I really never heard such names. Varadat or Varuh would be bad enough, but Trifily and Varahasy!" They turned over another page and the names were: Pavsikahy and Vahtisy. "Well, I see," said the mother, "it is clear that it is his fate. Since that is how it is, he had better be called after his father, his father is Akaky, let the son be Akaky, too." This was how he came to be Akaky Akakyevitch. The baby was christened and cried and made wry faces during the ceremony, as though he foresaw that he would be a titular councillor. So that was how it all came to pass. We have recalled it here so that the reader may see for himself that it happened quite inevitably and that

to give him any other name was out of the question. No one has been able to remember when and how long ago he entered the department, nor who gave him the job. However many directors and higher officials of all sorts came and went, he was always seen in the same place, in the same position, at the very same duty, precisely the same copying clerk, so that they used to declare that he must have been born a copying clerk in uniform all complete and with a bald patch on his head. No respect at all was shown him in the department. The porters, far from getting up from their seats when he came in, took no more notice of him than if a simple fly had flown across the vestibule. His superiors treated him with a sort of domineering chilliness. The head clerk's assistant used to throw papers under his nose without even saying: "Copy this" or "Here is an interesting, nice little case" or some agreeable remark of the sort, as is usually done in well-behaved offices. And he would take it, gazing only at the paper without looking to see who had put it there and whether he had the right to do so; he would take it and at once set to work to copy it. The young clerks jeered and made jokes at him to the best of their clerkly wit, and told before his face all sorts of stories of their own invention about him; they would say of his landlady, an old woman of seventy, that she beat him, would enquire when the wedding was to take place, and would scatter bits of paper on his head, calling them snow. Akaky Akakyevitch never answered a word, however, but behaved as though there were no one there. It had no influence on his work even; in the midst of all this teasing, he never made a single mistake in his copying. Only when the jokes were too unbearable, when they jolted his arm and prevented him from going on with his work, he would bring out: "Leave me alone! Why do you insult me?" and there was something strange in the words and in the voice in which they were uttered. There was a note in it of something that aroused compassion, so that one young man, new to the office, who, following the example of the rest, had allowed himself to mock at him, suddenly stopped as though cut to the heart, and from that time forth, everything was, as it were, changed and appeared in a different light to him. Some unnatural force seemed to thrust him away from the companions with whom he had become acquainted, accepting them as well-bred, polished people. And long afterwards, at moments of the greatest gaiety, the figure of the humble little clerk with a bald patch on his head rose before him with his heart-rending words: "Leave me alone! Why do you insult me?" and in those heart-rending words he heard others: "I am your brother." And the poor young man hid his face in his hands, and many times afterwards in his life he shuddered, seeing how much inhumanity there is in man, how much savage brutality lies hidden under refined, cultured politeness, and, my God! even in a man whom the world accepts as a gentleman and a man of honor. . . .

It would be hard to find a man who lived in his work as did Akaky Akakyevitch. To say that he was zealous in his work is not enough; no, he loved his work. In it, in that copying, he found a varied and agreeable world of his own. There was a look of enjoyment on his face; certain letters were favorites with him, and when he came to them he was delighted; he chuckled to himself and winked and moved his lips, so that it seemed as though every letter his pen was forming could be read in his face. If rewards had been given according to the measure of zeal in the service, he might to his amazement have even found himself a civil councillor; but all he gained in the service, as the wits, his fellow-clerks expressed it, was a buckle in his button-hole and a pain in his back. It cannot be said, however, that no notice had ever been taken of him. One director, being a good-natured man and anxious to reward him for his long service, sent him something a little more important than his ordinary copying; he was instructed from a finished document to make some sort of report for another office; the work consisted only of altering the headings and in places changing the first person into the third. This cost him such an effort that it threw him into a regular perspiration: he mopped his brow and said at last, "No, better let me copy something."

From that time forth they left him to go on copying for ever. It seemed as though nothing in the world existed for him outside his copying. He gave no thought at all to his clothes; his uniform was—well, not green but some sort of rusty, muddy color. His collar was very short and narrow, so that, although his neck was not particularly long, yet, standing out of the collar, it looked as immensely long as those of the plaster kittens that wag their heads and are carried about on trays on the heads of dozens of foreigners living in Russia. And there were always things sticking to his uniform, either bits of hay or threads; moreover, he had a special art of passing under a window at the very moment when various rubbish was being flung out into the street, and so was continually carrying off bits of melon rind and similar litter on his hat. He had never once in his life noticed what was being done and going on in the street, all those things at which, as we all know, his colleagues, the young clerks, always stare, carrying their sharp sight so far even as to notice anyone on the other side of the pavement with a trouser strap hanging loose—a detail which always calls forth a sly grin. Whatever Akaky Akakyevitch looked at, he saw nothing anywhere but his clear, evenly written lines, and only perhaps when a horse's head suddenly appeared from nowhere just on his shoulder, and its nostrils blew a perfect gale upon his cheek, did he notice that he was not in the middle of his writing, but rather in the middle of the street.

On reaching home, he would sit down at once to the table, hurriedly sup his soup and eat a piece of beef with an onion; he did not notice the taste at all, but ate it all up together with the flies and anything else that Providence chanced to send him. When he felt that his stomach was beginning to be full, he would rise up from the table, get out a bottle of ink and set to copying the papers he had brought home with him. When he had none to do, he would make a copy expressly for his own pleasure, particularly if the document were remarkable not for the beauty of its style but for the fact of its being addressed to some new or important personage.

Even at those hours when the grey Petersburg sky is completely overcast and the whole population of clerks have dined and eaten their fill, each as best he can, according to the salary he receives and his personal tastes; when they are all resting after the scratching of pens and bustle of the office, their own necessary work and other people's, and all the tasks that an over-zealous man voluntarily sets himself even beyond what is necessary; when the clerks are hastening to devote what is left of their time to pleasure; some more enterprising are flying to the theatre, others to the street to spend their leisure, staring at women's hats, some to spend the evening paying compliments to some attractive girl, the star of a little official circle, while some—and this is the most frequent of all—go simply to a fellow-clerk's flat on the third or fourth storey, two little rooms with an entry or a kitchen, with some pretentions to style, with a lamp or some such article that has cost many sacrifices of dinners and excursions—at the time when all the clerks are scattered about the little flats of their friends, playing a tempestuous game of whist, sipping tea out of glasses to the accompaniment of farthing rusks, sucking in smoke from long pipes, telling, as the cards are dealt, some scandal that has floated down from higher circles, a pleasure which the Russian can never by any possibility deny himself, or, when there is nothing better to talk about, repeating the everlasting anecdote of the commanding officer who was told that the tail had been cut off his horse on the Falconet monument—in short, even when every one was eagerly seeking entertainment, Akaky Akakyevitch did not give himself up to any amusement. No one could say that they had ever seen him at an evening party. After working to his heart's content, he would go to bed, smiling at the thought of the next day and wondering what God would send him to copy. So flowed on the peaceful life of a man who knew how to be content with his fate on a salary of four hundred roubles, and so perhaps it would have flowed on to extreme old age, had it not been for the various calamities that bestrew the path through life, not only of titular, but even of privy, actual court and all other councillors, even those who neither give counsel to others nor accept it themselves.

There is in Petersburg a mighty foe of all who receive a salary of four hundred roubles or about that sum. That foe is none other than our northern frost, although it is said to be very good for the health. Between eight and nine in the morning, precisely at the hour when the streets are full of clerks going to their departments, the frost begins giving such sharp and stinging flips at all their noses indiscriminately that the poor fellows don't know what to do with them. At that time, when even those in the higher grade have a pain in their brows and tears in their eyes from the frost, the poor titular councillors are sometimes almost defenceless. Their only protection lies in running as fast as they can through five or six streets in a wretched, thin little overcoat and then warming their feet thoroughly in the porter's room, till all their faculties and qualifications for their various duties thaw again after being frozen on the way. Akaky Akakyevitch had for some time been feeling that his back and shoulders were particularly nipped by the cold, although he did try to run the regular distance as fast as he could. He wondered at last whether there were any defects in his overcoat. After examining it thoroughly in the privacy of his home, he discovered that in two or three places, to wit on the back and the shoulders, it had become a regular sieve; the cloth was so worn that you could see through it and the lining was coming out. I must observe that Akaky Akakyevitch's overcoat had also served as a butt for the jibes of the clerks.

It had even been deprived of the honorable name of overcoat and had been referred to as the "dressing jacket." It
was indeed of rather a strange make. Its collar had been
growing smaller year by year as it served to patch the other
parts. The patches were not good specimens of the tailor's
art, and they certainly looked clumsy and ugly. On seeing
what was wrong, Akaky Akakyevitch decided that he
would have to take the overcoat to Petrovitch, a tailor who
lived on a fourth storey up a back staircase, and, in spite
of having only one eye and being pock-marked all over his
face, was rather successful in repairing the trousers and
coats of clerks and others—that is, when he was sober, be
it understood, and had no other enterprise in his mind.
Of this tailor I ought not, of course, to say much, but since
it is now the rule that the character of every person in a
novel must be completely drawn, well, there is no help
for it, here is Petrovitch too. At first he was called simply
Grigory, and was a serf belonging to some gentleman or
other. He began to be called Petrovitch from the time that
he got his freedom and began to drink rather heavily on
every holiday, at first only on the chief holidays, but afterwards on all church holidays indiscriminately, wherever
there is a cross in the calendar. On that side he was true
to the customs of his forefathers, and when he quarrelled
with his wife used to call her "a worldly woman and a German." Since we have now mentioned the wife, it will be
necessary to say a few words about her too, but unfortunately not much is known about her, except indeed that
Petrovitch had a wife and that she wore a cap and not a
kerchief, but apparently she could not boast of beauty;
anyway, none but soldiers of the Guards peeped under
her cap when they met her, and they twitched their moustaches and gave vent to a rather peculiar sound.

As he climbed the stairs, leading to Petrovitch's—which,
to do them justice, were all soaked with water and slops
and saturated through and through with that smell of
spirits which makes the eyes smart, and is, as we all know,

inseparable from the backstairs of Petersburg houses—
Akaky Akakyevitch was already wondering how much
Petrovitch would ask for the job, and inwardly resolving
not to give more than two roubles. The door was open, for
Petrovitch's wife was frying some fish and had so filled the
kitchen with smoke that you could not even see the black-
beetles. Akaky Akakyevitch crossed the kitchen unnoticed
by the good woman, and walked at last into a room where
he saw Petrovitch sitting on a big, wooden, unpainted
table with his legs tucked under him like a Turkish Pasha.
The feet, as is usual with tailors when they sit at work,
were bare; and the first object that caught Akaky Akakyevitch's eye was the big toe, with which he was already familiar, with a misshapen nail as thick and strong as the
shell of a tortoise. Round Petrovitch's neck hung a skein
of silk and another of thread and on his knees was a rag
of some sort. He had for the last three minutes been trying
to thread his needle, but could not get the thread into the
eye and so was very angry with the darkness and indeed
with the thread itself, muttering in an undertone: "It
won't go in, the savage! You wear me out, you rascal."
Akaky Akakyevitch was vexed that he had come just at
the minute when Petrovitch was in a bad humor; he liked
to give him an order when he was a little "elevated," or,
as his wife expressed it, "had fortified himself with fizz, the
one-eyed devil." In such circumstances Petrovitch was as
a rule very ready to give way and agree, and invariably
bowed and thanked him, indeed. Afterwards, it is true,
his wife would come wailing that her husband had been
drunk and so had asked too little, but adding a single ten-
kopeck piece would settle that. But on this occasion Petrovitch was apparently sober and consequently curt, unwill-
ing to bargain, and the devil knows what price he would
be ready to lay on. Akaky Akakyevitch perceived this, and
was, as the saying is, beating a retreat, but things had gone
too far, for Petrovitch was screwing up his solitary eye
very attentively at him and Akaky Akakyevitch involun-

tarily brought out: "Good day, Petrovitch!" "I wish you a good day, sir," said Petrovitch, and squinted at Akaky Akakyevitch's hands, trying to discover what sort of goods he had brought.

"Here I have come to you, Petrovitch, do you see . . . !"

It must be noticed that Akaky Akakyevitch for the most part explained himself by apologies, vague phrases, and particles which have absolutely no significance whatever. If the subject were a very difficult one, it was his habit indeed to leave his sentences quite unfinished, so that very often after a sentence had begun with the words, "It really is, don't you know . . ." nothing at all would follow and he himself would be quite oblivious, supposing he had said all that was necessary.

"What is it?" said Petrovitch, and at the same time with his solitary eye he scrutinized his whole uniform from the collar to the sleeves, the back, the skirts, the button-holes—with all of which he was very familiar, they were all his own work. Such scrutiny is habitual with tailors, it is the first thing they do on meeting one.

"It's like this, Petrovitch . . . the overcoat, the cloth . . . you see everywhere else it is quite strong; it's a little dusty and looks as though it were old, but it is new and it is only in one place just a little . . . on the back, and just a little worn on one shoulder and on this shoulder, too, a little . . . do you see? that's all, and it's not much work. . . ."

Petrovitch took the "dressing jacket," first spread it out over the table, examined it for a long time, shook his head and put his hand out to the window for a round snuff-box with a portrait on the lid of some general—which precisely I can't say, for a finger had been thrust through the spot where a face should have been, and the hole had been pasted up with a square bit of paper. After taking a pinch of snuff, Petrovitch held the "dressing jacket" up in his hands and looked at it against the light, and again he shook his head; then he turned it with the lining upwards and once more shook his head; again he took off the lid with the general pasted up with paper and stuffed a pinch into his nose, shut the box, put it away and at last said: "No, it can't be repaired; a wretched garment!" Akaky Akakyevitch's heart sank at those words.

"Why can't it, Petrovitch?" he said, almost in the imploring voice of a child. "Why, the only thing is it is a bit worn on the shoulders; why, you have got some little pieces. . . ."

"Yes, the pieces will be found all right," said Petrovitch, "but it can't be patched, the stuff is quite rotten; if you put a needle in it, it would give way."

"Let it give way, but you just put a patch on it."

"There is nothing to put a patch on. There is nothing for it to hold on to; there is a great strain on it, it is not worth calling cloth, it would fly away at a breath of wind."

"Well, then, strengthen it with something—upon my word, really, this is . . . !"

"No," said Petrovitch resolutely, "there is nothing to be done, the thing is no good at all. You had far better, when the cold winter weather comes, make yourself leg wrappings out of it, for there is no warmth in stockings, the Germans invented them just to make money." (Petrovitch was fond of a dig at the Germans occasionally.) "And as for the overcoat, it is clear that you will have to have a new one."

At the word "new" there was a mist before Akaky Akakyevitch's eyes, and everything in the room seemed blurred. He could see nothing clearly but the general with the piece of paper over his face on the lid of Petrovitch's snuff-box.

"A new one?" he said, still feeling as though he were in a dream; "why, I haven't the money for it."

"Yes, a new one," Petrovitch repeated with barbarous composure.

"Well, and if I did have a new one, how much would it . . . ?"

"You mean what will it cost?"

"Yes."

"Well, three fifty-rouble notes or more," sad Petrovitch, and he compressed his lips significantly. He was very fond of making an effect, he was fond of suddenly disconcerting a man completely and then squinting sideways to see what sort of a face he made.

"A hundred and fifty roubles for an overcoat," screamed poor Akaky Akakyevitch—it was perhaps the first time he had screamed in his life, for he was always distinguished by the softness of his voice.

"Yes," said Petrovitch, "and even then it's according to the coat. If I were to put marten on the collar, and add a hood with silk linings, it would come to two hundred."

"Petrovitch, please," said Akaky Akakyevitch in an imploring voice, not hearing and not trying to hear what Petrovitch said, and missing all his effects, "do repair it somehow, so that it will serve a little longer."

"No, that would be wasting work and spending money for nothing," said Petrovitch, and after that Akaky Akakyevitch went away completely crushed, and when he had gone Petrovitch remained standing for a long time with his lips pursed up significantly before he took up his work again, feeling pleased that he had not demeaned himself nor lowered the dignity of the tailor's art.

When he got into the street, Akaky Akakyevitch was as though in a dream. "So that is how it is," he said to himself. "I really did not think it would be so . . ." and then after a pause he added, "So there it is! so that's how it is at last! and I really could never have supposed it would have been so. And there . . ." There followed another long silence, after which he brought out: "So there it is! well, it really is so utterly unexpected . . . who would have thought . . . what a circumstance. . . ." Saying this, instead of going home he walked off in quite the opposite direction without suspecting what he was doing. On the way a clumsy sweep brushed the whole of his sooty side against him and blackened all his shoulder; a regular hatful of plaster scattered upon him from the top of a house that was being built. He noticed nothing of this, and only after he had jostled against a sentry who had set his halberd down beside him and was shaking some snuff out of his horn into his rough fist, he came to himself a little and then only because the sentry said: "Why are you poking yourself right in one's face, haven't you the pavement to yourself?" This made him look round and turn homeward; only there he began to collect his thoughts, to see his position in a clear and true light and began talking to himself no longer incoherently but reasonably and openly as with a sensible friend with whom one can discuss the most intimate and vital matters. "No, indeed," said Akaky Akakyevitch, "it is no use talking to Petrovitch now; just now he really is . . . his wife must have been giving it to him. I had better go to him on Sunday morning; after the Saturday evening he will be squinting and sleepy, so he'll want a little drink to carry it off and his wife won't give him a penny. I'll slip ten kopecks into his hand and then he will be more accommodating and maybe take the overcoat. . . ."

So reasoning with himself, Akaky Akakyevitch cheered up and waited until the next Sunday; then, seeing from a distance Petrovitch's wife leaving the house, he went straight in. Petrovitch certainly was very tipsy after the Saturday. He could hardly hold his head up and was very drowsy: but, for all that, as soon as he heard what he was speaking about, it seemed as though the devil had nudged him. "I can't," he said, "you must kindly order a new one." Akaky Akakyevitch at once slipped a ten-kopeck piece into his hand. "I thank you, sir, I will have just a drop to your health, but don't trouble yourself about the overcoat; it is not a bit of good for anything. I'll make you a fine new coat, you can trust me for that."

Akaky Akakyevitch would have said more about repairs, but Petrovitch, without listening, said: "A new one now I'll make you without fail; you can rely upon that, I'll do my best. It could even be like the fashion that has come in with the collar to button with silver claws under appliqué."

Then Akaky Akakyevitch saw that there was no escape from a new overcoat and he was utterly depressed. How indeed, for what, with what money could he get it? Of course he could to some extent rely on the bonus for the coming holiday, but that money had long ago been appropriated and its use determined beforehand. It was needed for new trousers and to pay the cobbler an old debt for putting some new tops to some old boot-legs, and he had to order three shirts from a seamstress as well as two specimens of an under-garment which it is improper to mention in print; in short, all that money absolutely must be spent, and even if the director were to be so gracious as to assign him a gratuity of forty-five or even fifty, instead of forty roubles, there would be still left a mere trifle, which would be but as a drop in the ocean beside the fortune needed for an overcoat. Though, of course, he knew that Petrovitch had a strange craze for suddenly putting on the devil knows what enormous price, so that at times his own wife could not help crying out: "Why, you are out of your wits, you idiot! Another time he'll undertake a job for nothing, and here the devil has bewitched him to ask more than he is worth himself." Though, of course, he knew that Petrovitch would undertake to make it for eighty roubles, still where would he get those eighty roubles? He might manage half of that sum; half of it could be found, perhaps even a little more; but where could he get the other half? . . . But, first of all, the reader ought to know where that first half was to be found. Akaky Akakyevitch had the habit every time he spent a rouble of putting aside two kopecks in a little locked-up box with a slit in the lid for slipping the money in. At the end of every half-year he would inspect the pile of coppers there and change them for small silver. He had done this for a long time, and in the course of many years the sum had mounted up to forty roubles and so he had half the money in his hands, but where was he to get the other half, where was he to get another forty roubles? Akaky Akakyevitch pondered and pondered and decided at last that he would have to diminish his ordinary expenses, at least for a year; give up burning candles in the evening, and if he had to do anything he must go into the landlady's room and work by her candle; that as he walked along the streets he must walk as lightly and carefully as possible, almost on tiptoe, on the cobbles and flagstones, so that his soles might last a little longer than usual; that he must send his linen to the wash less frequently, and that, to preserve it from being worn, he must take it off every day when he came home and sit in a thin cotton-shoddy dressing-gown, a very ancient garment which Time itself had spared. To tell the truth, he found it at first rather hard to get used to these privations, but after a while it became a habit and went smoothly enough—he even became quite accustomed to being hungry in the evening; on the other hand, he had spiritual nourishment, for he carried ever in his thoughts the idea of his future overcoat. His whole existence had in a sense become fuller, as though he had married, as though some other person were present with him, as though he were no longer alone, but an agreeable companion had consented to walk the path of life hand in hand with him, and that companion was no other than the new overcoat with its thick wadding and its strong, durable lining. He became, as it were, more alive, even more strong-willed, like a man who has set before himself a definite aim. Uncertainty, indecision, in fact all the hesitating and vague characteristics vanished from his face and his manners. At times there was a gleam in his eyes, indeed, the most bold and audacious ideas flashed through his mind. Why not really have marten on the collar? Meditation on the subject always made him absent-minded. On one occasion when he was copying a document, he very nearly made a mistake, so that he almost cried out "ough" aloud and crossed himself. At least once every month he went to

Petrovitch to talk about the overcoat, where it would be best to buy the cloth, and what color it should be, and what price, and, though he returned home a little anxious, he was always pleased at the thought that at last the time was at hand when everything would be bought and the overcoat would be made. Things moved even faster than he had anticipated. Contrary to all expectations, the director bestowed on Akaky Akakyevitch a gratuity of no less than sixty roubles. Whether it was that he had an inkling that Akaky Akakyevitch needed a greatcoat, or whether it happened so by chance, owing to this he found he had twenty roubles extra. This circumstance hastened the course of affairs. Another two or three months of partial fasting and Akaky Akakyevitch had actually saved up nearly eighty roubles. His heart, as a rule very tranquil, began to throb. The very first day he set off in company with Petrovitch to the shops. They bought some very good cloth, and no wonder, since they had been thinking of it for more than six months before, and scarcely a month had passed without their going to the shop to compare prices; now Petrovitch himself declared that there was no better cloth to be had. For the lining they chose calico, but of a stout quality, which in Petrovitch's words was even better than silk, and actually as strong and handsome to look at. Marten they did not buy, because it certainly was dear, but instead they chose cat fur, the best to be found in the shop—cat which in the distance might almost be taken for marten. Petrovitch was busy over the coat for a whole fortnight, because there were a great many buttonholes, otherwise it would have been ready sooner. Petrovitch asked twelve roubles for the work; less than that it hardly could have been, everything was sewn with silk, with fine double seams, and Petrovitch went over every seam afterwards with his own teeth imprinting various figures with them. It was . . . it is hard to say precisely on what day, but probably on the most triumphant day of the life of Akaky Akakyevitch that Petrovitch at last

brought the overcoat. He brought it in the morning, just
before it was time to set off for the department. The overcoat could not have arrived more in the nick of time, for
rather sharp frosts were just beginning and seemed threatening to be even more severe. Petrovitch brought the
greatcoat himself as a good tailor should. There was an
expression of importance on his face, such as Akaky
Akakyevitch had never seen there before. He seemed fully
conscious of having completed a work of no little moment
and of having shown in his own person the gulf that sep-
arates tailors who only put in linings and do repairs from
those who make up new materials. He took the greatcoat
out of the pocket-handkerchief in which he had brought
it (the pocket-handkerchief had just come home from the
wash), he then folded it up and put it in his pocket for
future use. After taking out the overcoat, he looked at it
with much pride and, holding it in both hands, threw it
very deftly over Akaky Akakyevitch's shoulders, then
pulled it down and smoothed it out behind with his hands;
then draped it about Akaky Akakyevitch with somewhat
jaunty carelessness. The latter, as a man advanced in years,
wished to try it with his arms in the sleeves. Petrovitch
helped him to put it on, and it appeared that it looked
splendid too with his arms in the sleeves. In fact it turned
out that the overcoat was completely and entirely successful. Petrovitch did not let slip the occasion for observing
that it was only because he lived in a small street and had
no signboard, and because he had known Akaky Akakyevitch so long, that he had done it so cheaply, but on the
Nevsky Prospect they would have asked him seventy-five
roubles for the work alone. Akaky Akakyevitch had no
inclination to discuss this with Petrovitch, besides he was
frightened of the big sums that Petrovitch was fond of
flinging airily about in conversation. He paid him, thanked
him, and went off on the spot, with his new overcoat on,
to the department. Petrovitch followed him out and
stopped in the street, staring for a good time at the coat

from a distance and then purposely turned off and, taking a short cut by a side street, came back into the street and got another view of the coat from the other side, that is, from the front.

Meanwhile Akaky Akakyevich walked along with every emotion in its most holiday mood. He felt every second that he had a new overcoat on his shoulders, and several times he actually laughed from inward satisfaction. Indeed, it had two advantages, one that it was warm and the other that it was good. He did not notice the way at all and found himself all at once at the department; in the porter's room he took off the overcoat, looked it over and put it in the porter's special care. I cannot tell how it happened, but all at once every one in the department learned that Akaky Akakyevitch had a new overcoat and that the "dressing jacket" no longer existed. They all ran out at once into the porter's room to look at Akaky Akakyevitch's new overcoat, they began welcoming him and congratulating him so that at first he could do nothing but smile and afterwards felt positively abashed. When, coming up to him, they all began saying that he must "sprinkle" the new overcoat and that he ought at least to stand them all a supper, Akaky Akakyevitch lost his head completely and did not know what to do, how to get out of it, nor what to answer. A few minutes later, flushing crimson, he even began assuring them with great simplicity that it was not a new overcoat at all, that it was just nothing, that it was an old overcoat. At last one of the clerks, indeed the assistant of the head clerk of the room, probably in order to show that he was not proud and was able to get on with those beneath him, said: "So be it, I'll give a party instead of Akaky Akakyevitch and invite you all to tea with me this evening; as luck would have it, it is my nameday." The clerks naturally congratulated the assistant head clerk and eagerly accepted the invitation. Akaky Akakyevitch was beginning to make excuses, but they all declared that it was uncivil of him, that it was simply a shame and a disgrace and that he could not possibly refuse. However, he felt pleased about it afterwards when he remembered that through this he would have the opportunity of going out in the evening, too, in his new overcoat. That whole day was for Akaky Akakyevitch the most triumphant and festive day in his life. He returned home in the happiest frame of mind, took off the overcoat and hung it carefully on the wall, admiring the cloth and lining once more, and then pulled out his old "dressing jacket," now completely coming to pieces, on purpose to compare them. He glanced at it and positively laughed, the difference was so immense! And long afterwards he went on laughing at dinner, as the position in which the "dressing jacket" was placed recurred to his mind. He dined in excellent spirits and after dinner wrote nothing, no papers at all, but just took his ease for a little while on his bed, till it got dark, then, without putting things off, he dressed, put on his overcoat, and went out into the street. Where precisely the clerk who had invited him lived we regret to say that we cannot tell; our memory is beginning to fail sadly, and everything there is in Petersburg, all the streets and houses, are so blurred and muddled in our head that it is a very difficult business to put anything in orderly fashion. However that may have been, there is no doubt that the clerk lived in the better part of the town and consequently a very long distance from Akaky Akakyevitch. At first the latter had to walk through deserted streets, scantily lighted, but as he approached his destination the streets became more lively, more full of people, and more brightly lighted; passers-by began to be more frequent, ladies began to appear, here and there, beautifully dressed, beaver collars were to be seen on the men. Cabmen with wooden trellis-work sledges, studded with gilt nails, were less frequently to be met; on the other hand, jaunty drivers in raspberry colored velvet caps with varnished sledges and bearskin rugs appeared, and carriages with decorated boxes dashed along the streets, their wheels crunching through the snow.

Akaky Akakyevitch looked at all this as a novelty; for several years he had not gone out into the streets in the evening. He stopped with curiosity before a lighted shop-window to look at a picture in which a beautiful woman was represented in the act of taking off her shoe and displaying as she did so the whole of a very shapely leg, while behind her back a gentleman with whiskers and a handsome imperial on his chin was putting his head in at the door. Akaky Akakyevitch shook his head and smiled and then went on his way. Why did he smile? Was it because he had come across something quite unfamiliar to him, though every man retains some instinctive feeling on the subject, or was it that he reflected, like many other clerks, as follows: "Well, upon my soul, those Frenchmen! it's beyond anything! if they try on anything of the sort, it really is . . . !" Though possibly he did not even think that; there is no creeping into a man's soul and finding out all that he thinks. At last he reached the house in which the assistant head clerk lived in fine style; there was a lamp burning on the stairs, and the flat was on the second floor. As he went into the entry Akaky Akakyevitch saw whole rows of goloshes. Amongst them in the middle of the room stood a samovar hissing and letting off clouds of steam. On the walls hung coats and cloaks, among which some actually had beaver collars or velvet revers. The other side of the wall there was noise and talk, which suddenly became clear and loud when the door opened and the footman came out with a tray full of empty glasses, a jug of cream, and a basket of biscuits. It was evident that the clerks had arrived long before and had already drunk their first glass of tea. Akaky Akakyevitch, after hanging up his coat with his own hands, went into the room, and at the same moment there flashed before his eyes a vision of candles, clerks, pipes, and card tables, together with the confused sounds of conversation rising up on all sides and the noise of moving chairs. He stopped very awkwardly in the middle of the room, looking about and trying to think what to do, but he was observed and received with a shout and they all went at once into the entry and again took a look at his overcoat. Though Akaky Akakyevitch was somewhat embarrassed, yet, being a simple-hearted man, he could not help being pleased at seeing how they all admired his coat. Then of course they all abandoned him and his coat, and turned their attention as usual to the tables set for whist. All this—the noise, the talk, and the crowd of people—was strange and wonderful to Akaky Akakyevitch. He simply did not know how to behave, what to do with his arms and legs and his whole figure; at last he sat down beside the players, looked at the cards, stared first at one and then at another of the faces, and in a little while began to yawn and felt that he was bored—especially as it was long past the time at which he usually went to bed. He tried to take leave of his hosts, but they would not let him go, saying that he absolutely must have a glass of champagne in honor of the new coat. An hour later supper was served, consisting of salad, cold veal, a pasty, pies, and tarts from the confectioner's, and champagne. They made Akaky Akakyevitch drink two glasses, after which he felt that things were much more cheerful, though he could not forget that it was twelve o'clock and that he ought to have been home long ago. That his host might not take it into his head to detain him, he slipped out of the room, hunted in the entry for his greatcoat, which he found, not without regret, lying on the floor, shook it, removed some fluff from it, put it on, and went down the stairs into the street. It was still light in the streets. Some little general shops, those perpetual clubs for house-serfs and all sorts of people, were open; others which were closed showed, however, a long streak of light at every crack of the door, proving that they were not yet deserted, and probably maids and men-servants were still finishing their conversation and discussion, driving their masters to utter perplexity as to their whereabouts. Akaky Akakye-vitch walked along in a cheerful state of mind; he was even

on the point of running, goodness knows why, after a lady
of some sort who passed by like lightning with every part
of her frame in violent motion. He checked himself at
once, however, and again walked along very gently, feeling
positively surprised himself at the inexplicable impulse
that had seized him. Soon the deserted streets, which are
not particularly cheerful by day and even less so in the
evening, stretched before him. Now they were still more
dead and deserted; the light of street lamps was scantier,
the oil was evidently running low; then came wooden
houses and fences; not a soul anywhere; only the snow
gleamed on the streets and the low-pitched slumbering
hovels looked black and gloomy with their closed shutters.
He approached the spot where the street was intersected
by an endless square, which looked like a fearful desert
with its houses scarcely visible on the further side.

In the distance, goodness knows where, there was a gleam
of light from some sentry-box which seemed to be standing at the end of the world. Akaky Akakyevitch's lightheartedness grew somehow sensibly less at this place. He
stepped into the square, not without an involuntary uneasiness, as though his heart had a foreboding of evil. He
looked behind him and to both sides—it was as though the
sea were all round him. "No, better not look," he thought,
and walked on, shutting his eyes, and when he opened
them to see whether the end of the square were near, he
suddenly saw standing before him, almost under his very
nose, some men with moustaches; just what they were like
he could not even distinguish. There was a mist before
his eyes and a throbbing in his chest. "I say the overcoat
is mine!" said one of them in a voice like a clap of thunder,
seizing him by the collar. Akaky Akakyevitch was on the
point of shouting "Help" when another put a fist the size
of a clerk's head against his very lips, saying: "You just
shout now." Akaky Akakyevitch felt only that they took
the overcoat off, and gave him a kick with their knees, and
he fell on his face in the snow and was conscious of noth-

ing more. A few minutes later he came to himself and got on to his feet, but there was no one there. He felt that it was cold on the ground and that he had no overcoat, and began screaming, but it seemed as though his voice could not carry to the end of the square. Overwhelmed with despair and continuing to scream, he ran across the square straight to the sentry-box, beside which stood a sentry leaning on his halberd and, so it seemed, looking with curiosity to see who the devil the man was who was screaming and running towards him from the distance. As Akaky Akakyevitch reached him, he began breathlessly shouting that he was asleep and not looking after his duty not to see that a man was being robbed. The sentry answered that he had seen nothing, that he had only seen him stopped in the middle of the square by two men, and supposed that they were his friends, and that, instead of abusing him for nothing, he had better go the next day to the superintendent and that he would find out who had taken the overcoat. Akaky Akakyevitch ran home in a terrible state: his hair, which was still comparatively abundant on his temples and the back of his head, was completely dishevelled; his sides and chest and his trousers were all covered with snow. When his old landlady heard a fearful knock at the door she jumped hurriedly out of bed and, with only one slipper on, ran to open it, modestly holding her shift across her bosom; but when she opened it she stepped back, seeing what a state Akaky Akakyevitch was in. When he told her what had happened, she clasped her hands in horror and said that he must go straight to the superintendent, that the police constable of the quarter would deceive him, make promises and lead him a dance; that it would be best of all to go to the superintendent, and that she knew him indeed, because Anna the Finnish girl who was once her cook was now in service as a nurse at the superintendent's; and that she often saw him himself when he passed by their house, and that he used to be every Sunday at church too, saying his prayers and at the same time looking goodhumoredly at every one, and that therefore by every token he must be a kind-hearted man. After listening to this advice, Akaky Akakyevitch made his way very gloomily to his room, and how he spent that night I leave to the imagination of those who are in the least able to picture the position of others. Early in the morning he set off to the police superintendent's, but was told that he was asleep. He came at ten o'clock, he was told again that he was asleep; he came at eleven and was told that the superintendent was not at home; he came at dinner-time, but the clerks in the ante-room would not let him in, and insisted on knowing what was the matter and what business had brought him and exactly what had happened; so that at last Akaky Akakyevitch for the first time in his life tried to show the strength of his character and said curtly that he must see the superintendent himself, that they dare not refuse to admit him, that he had come from the department on government business, and that if he made complaint of them they would see. The clerks dared say nothing to this, and one of them went to summon the superintendent. The latter received his story of being robbed of his overcoat in an extremely strange way. Instead of attending to the main point, he began asking Akaky Akakyevitch questions, why had he been coming home so late? wasn't he going, or hadn't he been, to some house of ill-fame? so that Akaky Akakyevitch was overwhelmed with confusion, and went away without knowing whether or not the proper measures would be taken in regard to his overcoat. He was absent from the office all that day (the only time that it had happened in his life). Next day he appeared with a pale face, wearing his old "dressing jacket" which had become a still more pitiful sight. The tidings of the theft of the overcoat— though there were clerks who did not let even this chance slip of jeering at Akaky Akakyevitch—touched many of them. They decided on the spot to get up a subscription for him, but collected only a very trifling sum, because the clerks had already spent a good deal on subscribing to the director's portrait and on the purchase of a book, at the suggestion of the head of their department, who was a friend of the author, and so the total realized was very insignificant. One of the clerks, moved by compassion, ventured at any rate to assist Akaky Akakyevitch with good advice, telling him not to go to the district police inspector, because, though it might happen that the latter might be sufficiently zealous of gaining the approval of his superiors to succeed in finding the overcoat, it would remain in the possession of the police unless he presented legal proofs that it belonged to him; he urged that far the best thing would be to appeal to a Person of Consequence; that the Person of Consequence, by writing and getting into communication with the proper authorities, could push the matter through more successfully. There was nothing else for it. Akaky Akakyevitch made up his mind to go to the Person of Consequence. What precisely was the nature of the functions of the Person of Consequence has remained a matter of uncertainty. It must be noted that this Person of Consequence had only lately become a person of consequence, and until recently had been a person of no consequence. Though, indeed, his position even now was not reckoned of consequence in comparison with others of still greater consequence. But there is always to be found a circle of persons to whom a person of little consequence in the eyes of others is a person of consequence. It is true that he did his utmost to increase the consequence of his position in various ways, for instance by insisting that his subordinates should come out on to the stairs to meet him when he arrived at his office; that no one should venture to approach him directly but all proceedings should be by the strictest order of precedence, that a collegiate registration clerk should report the matter to the provincial secretary, and the provincial secretary to the titular councillor or whomsoever it might be, and that business should only reach him by this channel.

Every one in Holy Russia has a craze for imitation, every one apes and mimics his superiors. I have actually been told that a titular councillor who was put in charge of a small separate office, immediately partitioned off a special room for himself, calling it the head office, and set special porters at the door with red collars and gold lace, who took hold of the handle of the door and opened it for every one who went in, though the "head office" was so tiny that it was with difficulty that an ordinary writing table could be put into it. The manners and habits of the Person of Consequence were dignified and majestic, but not complex. The chief foundation of his system was strictness, "strictness, strictness, and—strictness!" he used to say, and at the last word he would look very significantly at the person he was addressing, though, indeed, he had no reason to do so, for the dozen clerks who made up the whole administrative mechanism of his office stood in befitting awe of him; any clerk who saw him in the distance would leave his work and remain standing at attention till his superior had left the room. His conversation with his subordinates was usually marked by severity and almost confined to three phrases: "How dare you? Do you know to whom you are speaking? Do you understand who I am?" He was, however, at heart a good-natured man, pleasant and obliging with his colleagues; but the grade of general had completely turned his head. When he received it, he was perplexed, thrown off his balance, and quite at a loss how to behave. If he chanced to be with his equals, he was still quite a decent man, a very gentlemanly man, in fact, and in many ways even an intelligent man, but as soon as he was in company with men who were even one grade below him, there was simply no doing anything with him: he sat silent and his position excited compassion, the more so as he himself felt that he might have been spending his time to incomparably more advantage. At times there could be seen in his eyes an intense desire to join in some interesting conversation, but he was restrained by the doubt whether it would not be too much on his part, whether it would not be too great a familiarity and lowering of his dignity, and in consequence of these reflections he remained everlastingly in the same mute condition, only uttering from time to time mono-syllabic sounds, and in this way he gained the reputation of being a very tiresome man.

So this was the Person of Consequence to whom our friend Akaky Akakyevitch appealed, and he appealed to him at a most unpropitious moment, very unfortunate for himself, though fortunate, indeed, for the Person of Con-sequence. The latter happened to be in his study, talking in the very best of spirits with an old friend of his child-hood who had only just arrived and whom he had not seen for several years. It was at this moment that he was in-formed that a man called Bashmatchkin was asking to see him. He asked abruptly, "What sort of man is he?" and received the answer, "A government clerk." "Ah! he can wait, I haven't time now," said the Person of Consequence. Here I must observe that this was a complete lie on the part of the Person of Consequence: he had time; his friend and he had long ago said all they had to say to each other and their conversation had begun to be broken by very long pauses during which they merely slapped each other on the knee, saying, "So that's how things are, Ivan Abramovitch!"—"There it is, Stepan Varlamovitch!" but, for all that, he told the clerk to wait in order to show his friend, who had left the service years before and was living at home in the country how long clerks had to wait in his ante-room. At last after they had talked, or rather been silent to their heart's content and had smoked a cigar in very comfortable arm-chairs with sloping backs, he seemed suddenly to recollect, and said to the secretary, who was standing at the door with papers for his signature: "Oh, by the way, there is a clerk waiting, isn't there? tell him he can come in." When he saw Akaky Akakyevitch's meek appearance and old uniform, he turned to him at once and said: "What do you want?" in a firm and abrupt voice, which he had purposely practiced in his own room in solitude before the looking-glass for a week before receiving his present post and the grade of a general. Akaky Akakyevitch, who was overwhelmed with befitting awe beforehand, was somewhat confused and, as far as his tongue would allow him, explained to the best of his powers, with even more frequent "ers" than usual, that he had had a perfectly new overcoat and now he had been robbed of it in the most inhuman way, and that now he had come to beg him by his intervention either to correspond with his honor the head policemaster or anybody else, and find the overcoat. This mode of proceeding struck the general for some reason as taking a great liberty. "What next sir," he went on as abruptly, "don't you know the way to proceed? To whom are you addressing yourself? Don't you know how things are done? You ought first to have handed in a petition to the office; it would have gone to the head clerk of the room, and to the head clerk of the section, then it would have been handed to the secretary and the secretary would have brought it to me. . . ."

"But, your Excellency," said Akaky Akakyevitch, trying to collect all the small allowance of presence of mind he possessed and feeling at the same time that he was getting into a terrible perspiration, "I ventured, your Excellency, to trouble you because secretaries . . . er . . . are people you can't depend on. . . ."

"What? what? what?" said the Person of Consequence, "where did you get hold of that spirit? where did you pick up such ideas? What insubordination is spreading among young men against their superiors and betters." The Person of Consequence did not apparently observe that Akaky Akakyevitch was well over fifty, and therefore if he could have been called a young man it would only have been in comparison with a man of seventy. "Do you know to whom you are speaking? do you understand who I am? do you understand that, I ask you?" At this point he stamped, and raised his voice to such a powerful note that Akaky Akakyevitch was not the only one to be terrified. Akaky Akakyevitch was positively petrified; he staggered, trembling all over, and could not stand; if the porters had not run up to support him, he would have flopped upon the floor; he was led out almost unconscious. The Person of Consequence, pleased that the effect had surpassed his expectations and enchanted at the idea that his words could even deprive a man of consciousness, stole a sideway glance at his friend to see how he was taking it, and perceived not without satisfaction that his friend was feeling very uncertain and even beginning to be a little terrified himself.

How he got downstairs, how he went out into the street —of all that Akaky Akakyevitch remembered nothing, he had no feeling in his arms or his legs. In all his life he had never been so severely reprimanded by a general, and this was by one of another department, too. He went out into the snowstorm, that was whistling through the streets, with his mouth open, and as he went he stumbled off the pavement; the wind, as its way is in Petersburg, blew upon him from all points of the compass and from every side street. In an instant it had blown a quinsy into his throat, and when he got home he was not able to utter a word; with a swollen face and throat he went to bed. So violent is sometimes the effect of a suitable reprimand!

Next day he was in a high fever. Thanks to the gracious assistance of the Petersburg climate, the disease made more rapid progress than could have been expected, and when the doctor came, after feeling his pulse he could find nothing to do but prescribe a fomentation, and that simply that the patient might not be left without the benefit of medical assistance; however, two days later he informed him that his end was at hand, after which he turned to his landlady and said: "And you had better lose no time, my good woman, but order him now a deal coffin, for an oak one will be too dear for him." Whether Akaky Akakyevitch heard these fateful words or not, whether they produced a shattering effect upon him, and whether he regretted his pitiful life, no one can tell, for he was all the time in delirium and fever. Apparitions, each stranger than the one before, were continually haunting him: first, he saw Petrovitch and was ordering him to make a greatcoat trimmed with some sort of traps for robbers, who were, he fancied, continually under the bed, and he was calling his landlady every minute to pull out a thief who had even got under the quilt; then he kept asking why his old "dressing jacket" was hanging before him when he had a new overcoat, then he fancied he was standing before the general listening to the appropriate reprimand and saying "I am sorry, your Excellency," then finally he became abusive, uttering the most awful language, so that his old landlady positively crossed herself, having never heard anything of the kind from him before, and the more horrified because these dreadful words followed immediately upon the phrase "your Excellency." Later on, his talk was a mere medley of nonsense, so that it was quite unintelligible; all that could be seen was that his incoherent words and thoughts were concerned with nothing but the overcoat. At last poor Akaky Akakyevitch gave up the ghost. No seal was put upon his room nor upon his things, because, in the first place, he had no heirs and, in the second, the property left was very small, to wit, a bundle of goose-feathers, a quire of white government paper, three pairs of socks, two or three buttons that had come off his trousers, and the "dressing jacket" with which the reader is already familiar. Who came into all this wealth God only knows, even I who tell the tale must own that I have not troubled to enquire. And Petersburg remained without Akaky Akakyevitch, as though, indeed, he had never been in the city. A creature had vanished and departed whose cause no one had championed, who was dear to no one, of interest to no one, who never even attracted the attention of the student of natural history, though the latter does not disdain to fix a common fly upon a pin and look at him under the microscope—a creature who bore patiently the jeers of the office and for no particular reason went to his grave, though even he at the very end of his life was visited by a gleam of brightness in the form of an overcoat that for one instant brought color into his poor life—a creature on whom calamity broke as insufferably as it breaks upon the heads of the mighty ones of this world . . . !

Several days after his death, the porter from the department was sent to his lodgings with instructions that he should go at once to the office, for his chief was asking for him; but the porter was obliged to return without him, explaining that he could not come, and to the enquiry, "Why?" he added, "Well, you see: the fact is he is dead, he was buried three days ago." This was how they learned at the office of the death of Akaky Akakyevitch, and the next day there was sitting in his seat a new clerk who was very much taller and who wrote not in the same upright hand but made his letters more slanting and crooked.

But who could have imagined that this was not all there was to tell about Akaky Akakyevitch, that he was destined for a few days to make a noise in the world after his death, as though to make up for his life having been unnoticed by anyone? But so it happened, and our poor story unexpectedly finishes with a fantastic ending. Rumors were suddenly floating about Petersburg that in the neighborhood of the Kalinkin Bridge and for a little distance beyond, a corpse had taken to appearing at night in the form of a clerk looking for a stolen overcoat, and stripping from the shoulders of all passers-by, regardless of grade and calling, overcoats of all descriptions—trimmed with cat fur, or beaver or wadded, lined with raccoon, fox and bear—made, in fact, of all sorts of skin which men have adapted for the covering of their own. One of the clerks of the department saw the corpse with his own eyes and at once recognized it as Akaky Akakyevitch; but it excited in him such terror, however, that he ran away as fast as his legs could carry him and so could not get a very clear view of him, and only saw him hold up his finger threateningly in the distance.

From all sides complaints were continually coming that backs and shoulders, not of mere titular councillors, but even of upper court councillors, had been exposed to taking chills, owing to being stripped of their greatcoats. Orders were given to the police to catch the corpse regardless of trouble or expense, alive or dead, and to punish him in the cruellest way, as an example to others, and, indeed, they very nearly succeeded in doing so. The sentry of one district police station in Kiryushkin Place snatched a corpse by the collar on the spot of the crime in the very act of attempting to snatch a frieze overcoat from a retired musician, who used in his day to play the flute. Having caught him by the collar, he shouted until he had brought two other comrades, whom he charged to hold him while he felt just a minute in his boot to get out a snuff-box in order to revive his nose which had six times in his life been frost-bitten, but the snuff was probably so strong that not even a dead man could stand it. The sentry had hardly had time to put his finger over his right nostril and draw up some snuff in the left when the corpse sneezed violently right into the eyes of all three. While they were putting their fists up to wipe them, the corpse completely vanished, so that they were not even sure whether he had actually been in their hands. From that time forward, the sentries conceived such a horror of the dead that they were even afraid to seize the living and confined themselves to shouting from the distance: "Hi, you there, be off!" and the dead clerk began to appear even on the other side of the Kalinkin Bridge, rousing no little terror in all timid people.

We have, however, quite deserted the Person of Consequence, who may in reality almost be said to be the cause of the fantastic ending of this perfectly true story. To begin with, my duty requires me to do justice to the Person of Consequence by recording that soon after poor Akaky Akakyevitch had gone away crushed to powder, he felt something not unlike regret. Sympathy was a feeling not unknown to him; his heart was open to many kindly impulses, although his exalted grade very often prevented them from being shown. As soon as his friend had gone out of his study, he even began brooding over poor Akaky Akakyevitch, and from that time forward, he was almost every day haunted by the image of the poor clerk who had succumbed so completely to the befitting reprimand. The thought of the man so worried him that a week later he actually decided to send a clerk to find out how he was and whether he really could help him in any way. And when they brought him word that Akaky Akakyevitch had died suddenly in delirium and fever, it made a great impression on him, his conscience reproached him and he was depressed all day. Anxious to distract his mind and to forget the unpleasant impression, he went to spend the evening with one of his friends, where he found a genteel company and, what was best of all, almost everyone was of the same grade so that he was able to be quite free from restraint. This had a wonderful effect on his spirits, he expanded, became affable and genial—in short, spent a very agreeable evening. At supper he drank a couple of glasses of champagne—a proceeding which we all know has a happy effect in inducing good humor. The champagne made him inclined to do something unusual, and he decided not to go home yet but to visit a lady of his acquaintance, one Karolina Ivanovna—a lady apparently of German extraction, for whom he entertained extremely friendly feelings. It must be noted that the Person of Consequence was a man no longer young, an excellent husband, and the respectable father of a family. He had two sons, one already serving in his office, and a nice-looking daughter of sixteen with a rather turned-up, pretty little nose, who used to come every morning to kiss his hand, saying: *"Bon jour, Papa."* His wife, who was still bloom-

ing and decidedly good-looking, indeed, used first to give
him her hand to kiss and then would kiss his hand, turning it the other side upwards. But though the Person of
Consequence was perfectly satisfied with the kind ameni-
ties of his domestic life, he thought it proper to have a
lady friend in another quarter of the town. This lady
friend was not a bit better looking nor younger than his
wife, but these mysterious facts exist in the world and it
is not our business to criticize them. And so the Person of
Consequence went downstairs, got into his sledge, and
said to his coachman, "To Karolina Ivanovna," while
luxuriously wrapped in his warm fur coat he remained
in that agreeable frame of mind sweeter to a Russian than
anything that could be invented, that is, when one thinks
of nothing while thoughts come into the mind of themselves, one pleasanter than the other, without the labor
of following them or looking for them. Full of satisfaction,
he recalled all the amusing moments of the evening he
had spent, all the phrases that had set the little circle
laughing; many of them he repeated in an undertone and
found them as amusing as before, and so, very naturally,
laughed very heartily at them again. From time to time,
however, he was disturbed by a gust of wind which, blowing suddenly, God knows whence and wherefore, cut him
in the face, pelting him with flakes of snow, puffing out
his coat-collar like a sack, or suddenly flinging it with unnatural force over his head and giving him endless trouble to extricate himself from it. All at once, the Person of
Consequence felt that some one had clutched him very
tightly by the collar. Turning round he saw a short man
in a shabby old uniform, and not without horror recognized him as Akaky Akakyevitch. The clerk's face was
white as snow and looked like that of a corpse, but the
horror of the Person of Consequence was beyond all
bounds when he saw the mouth of the corpse distorted
into speech and, breathing upon him the chill of the
grave, it uttered the following words: "Ah, so here you

are at last! At last I've . . . er . . . caught you by the collar. It's your overcoat I want, you refused to help me and abused me into the bargain! So now give me yours!" The poor Person of Consequence very nearly died. Resolute and determined as he was in his office and before subordinates in general, and though any one looking at his manly air and figure would have said: "Oh, what a man of character!" yet in this plight he felt, like very many persons of athletic appearance, such terror that not without reason he began to be afraid he would have some sort of fit. He actually flung his overcoat off his shoulders as fast as he could and shouted to his coachman in a voice unlike his own: "Drive home and make haste!" The coachman, hearing the tone which he had only heard in critical moments and then accompanied by something even more rousing, hunched his shoulders up to his ears in case of worse following, swung his whip and flew on like an arrow. In a little over six minutes the Person of Consequence was at the entrance of his own house. Pale, panic-stricken, and without his overcoat, he arrived home instead of at Karolina Ivanovna's, dragged himself to his own room and spent the night in great perturbation, so that next morning his daughter said to him at breakfast, "You look quite pale today, Papa": but her papa remained mute and said not a word to anyone of what had happened to him, where he had been, and where he had been going. The incident made a great impression upon him. Indeed, it happened far more rarely that he said to his subordinates, "How dare you? do you understand who I am?" and he never uttered those words at all until he had first heard all the rights of the case.

What was even more remarkable is that from that time the apparition of the dead clerk ceased entirely: apparently the general's overcoat had fitted him perfectly, anyway nothing more was heard of overcoats being snatched from anyone. Many restless and anxious people refused, however, to be pacified, and still maintained that in remote

parts of the town the ghost of the dead clerk went on appearing. One sentry in Kolomna, for instance, saw with
his own eyes a ghost appear from behind a house; but, being by natural constitution somewhat feeble—so much so
that on one occasion an ordinary, well-grown pig, making
a sudden dash out of some building, knocked him off his
feet to the vast entertainment of the cabmen standing
round, from whom he exacted two kopecks each for snuff
for such rudeness—he did not dare to stop it, and so followed it in the dark until the ghost suddenly looked round
and, stopping, asked him: "What do you want?" displaying a fist such as you never see among the living. The
sentry said: "Nothing," and turned back on the spot. This
ghost, however, was considerably taller and adorned with
immense moustaches, and, directing its steps apparently
towards Obuhov Bridge, vanished into the darkness of
the night.

(Translated by Constance Garnett)

THE PILGRIM HAWK

* *

Glenway Wescott

Glenway Wescott

. . . .

Glenway Wescott was born in Wisconsin in 1901 and, like so many mid-westerners, like so many Americans, like so many writers of his and the following generation, bid a final good-bye to his home, in his case in 1928, with the publication of *Good-Bye, Wisconsin*, one year after his fine novel *The Grandmothers* won the Harper Prize. Wescott spent a decade or so in France and was associated with many "little magazines," particularly *The Dial*; in this country he is Vice-President of the National Institute of Arts and Letters. He has published but two novels since *Good-Bye, Wisconsin*: they are *Apartment in Athens*, a popular novel of the resistance in Greece; and *The Pilgrim Hawk*. Highly praised as a "stylist," Wescott has much more than impeccable style to offer. *The Pilgrim Hawk* is a masterful fusion of reality and symbol, knowledge of human beings, and sensitive story-telling.

THE PILGRIM HAWK

THE CULLENS were Irish; but it was in France that I met them and was able to form an impression of their love and their trouble. They were on their way to a property they had rented in Hungary; and one afternoon they came to Chancellet to see my great friend Alexandra Henry. That was in May of 1928 or 1929, before we all returned to America, and she met my brother and married him.

Needless to say, the twenties were very different from the thirties, and now the forties have begun. In the twenties it was not unusual to meet foreigners in some country as foreign to them as to you, your peregrination just crossing theirs; and you did your best to know them in an afternoon or so; and perhaps you called that little lightning knowledge, friendship. There was a kind of idealistic or optimistic curiosity in the air. And vagaries of character, and the various war and peace that goes on in the psyche, seemed of the greatest interest and even importance.

Chancellet must be a painful place in the forties, although one of the least changed in France, I suppose, because it is unimportant. As I remember, there was a school of what is now romantically called celestial navigation, with a modest flying field and a few hangars, two or three kilometers away, at Pelors; but if that is in use now the foreigners must have it. In our day, day in and day out, the old Duchesse de Challot and her poor relations and friends in tight coats on windbroken mounts used to hunt in the forest of Pelors. We could hear their hunting horns which sounded like a picnic of boy sopranos, lost. Meanwhile perhaps there have been anti-aircraft guns for the

defense of Paris embedded all amid the earths of foxes:
angry radio stammering in the well-kept branches. Now
at least the foxes and the thrushes can come back. The old
ex-cabinet-minister whose château and little park adjoined
Alex's garden is dead.

Her house was just a section of the village street: two
small dwellings and a large horse-stable combined and
rebuilt and expensively furnished in the plain modern
style. She or her architect made a mistake in the planning
of the ground floor. The dining room and the chief guest-
room were on the street, which is also the highway to
Orléans and the tourist country of the Loire; so that the
reckless French traffic practically brushed the walls, and
heavy trucks alarmed one all night. Not only Alex's bedroom but the kitchen and pantry opened into the spacious
and quiet garden. This delighted the new servants whom
Alex had brought up from Morocco, a romantic pair
named Jean and Eva. They promptly took a far corner of
it under some plane trees for their own use; and all spring
they passed every spare moment there, quarreling and occasionally weeping during the day, but like clockwork
making peace and sealing it with kisses in the twilight or
moonlight. . . . I mention this odd location of the servants'
quarters because, that afternoon of the Cullens' visit, I
went to speak to Jean and happened to look out the kitch-
en window and saw Cullen in the garden, futilely giving
way to his awful jealousy, emancipated from love for a
few minutes.

There had been no mention of their coming, or perhaps
I had forgotten it. I heard the doorbell ring, then ring
again. Jean and Eva must have been outdoors or napping.
Alex had put through a telephone call to London upon
some little annoying matter of business, and wished not
to be disturbed. So I went to the door; and there was the
long dark Daimler entirely occupying the cobbled space
between the house and the highway, and there stood the
Irishman about to ring a third time. "Oh, how d'ya do, is

this Miss Henry's house, my name's Cullen," he said; and turned to help Mrs. Cullen out of the car, which was a delicate operation, for she bore a full-grown hooded falcon on her wrist. A dapper young chauffeur also helped. She was dressed with extreme elegance and she wore the highest heels I ever saw, on which, with one solicitous male at each elbow, she stumbled across the ancient cobblestones, the bird swaying a little and hunching its wings to steady itself.

I told them my name, and they repeated it after me and shook hands with a somewhat grand and vague affability. "I brought my hawk," Mrs. Cullen unnecessarily announced. "She's new. I thought Alex wouldn't mind. And I hope you too," she added and paused a moment, with bright eyes to flatter me just in case I felt entitled to authority of some sort in Alex's house, "I hope you won't mind." She had no way of knowing who or what I was: casual caller or one of Alex's kinsmen or perhaps a sweetheart.

Her eyes were a crystal blue, unmistakably Irish; and she was unmistakable in other ways too, in spite of her brisk London voice and fine French dress. Her make-up was better than you would have expected of a lady falconer; still you could see that her skin was naturally downy and her snub nose tended to be pink. There was also a crookedness, particularly in the alignment of her nostrils and her voluble little lips. How rare pulchritude is among the Irish, I said to myself; therefore what a trouble is made when it does appear: Emer and Deirdre, Mrs. O'Shea and Mrs. McBride. Then my glance fell upon Mrs. Cullen's snowy dimpled fingers, with a considerable diamond on one, a star sapphire on another. Between her sleeve and the rough gauntlet to which the falcon clung, her wrist showed like a bit of Easter lily; and her ankle was a match for it, perfectly straight in a mere glimmer of stocking. No doubt these fine points were enough to entitle her to a certain enchantment and disturbance of the opposite sex:

her husband for one.

Meanwhile Jean had come running in a fine embarrassment, buttoning his white jacket; and I sent him to inform his mistress of the arrival of her guests and to guide their chauffeur to the garage, while I tried to usher them into the living room. But Mrs. Cullen went on explaining the hawk. "Her name's Lucy. Don't you think she's sweet? She's Scottish; I've only had her five or six weeks. A gamekeeper near Inverness trapped her, but she's all right, only one toe bent in the trap. D'you, see, this toe?" She paused on the threshold and held up the gloved hand and wrist on which Lucy perched, and I saw: gripping the rugged and stained leather, one sharp talon that did not grip straight. The stain on the leather was dried blood.

"I call her Lucy because my old father used to make me read Scott to him in the winter whenever the weather got too beastly to hunt. I thought Alex would like to see her."

"We had to bring her anyway," her husband loudly chimed in. "The most awful things happen if we leave her in the hotel. She frightens the chambermaids, and they scream and weep. I have to give immense tips."

He was a large man, not really fat but with bulk and softness irregularly here and there, not so much in the middle as up and down his back, all around his head, in his hands. His British complexion suggested eating and drinking rather than hunting and shooting; certainly nothing about him suggested hawking. His hazel eyes were a little bloodshot, wavering golden now and then; and he had a way of opening and shutting his lips, like an unsympathetic pout, or a dispirited kiss, under the tufts of his mustache.

We were about to sit down in the living room when they both noticed it, and evidently felt obliged to comment. "What a splendid room, splendid," they said; "most unusual and modern and comfortable." It was not splendid, but it was very large: the entire former stable with the hayloft removed so that the roof constituted the ceiling,

with old chestnut rafters gothically pointing up twenty-
five or thirty feet; the woodwork darkly waxed and the
walls painted white. It reminded me of a village church.
At regular intervals all around hung certain modern pictures with only blunt rudimentary drawing and overflowing color, like stained glass. But on as fine a day as this,
modern art was dimmed and dwarfed by the view of the
garden and the park beyond it, Alex's architect having removed almost a third of the wall on that side and put in
two great panes of plate glass.

Mrs. Cullen tripped over to this great window and
courteously exclaimed once more: "Splendid garden. What
luck to have a pond!" It was what the French call an
English garden; no formal flower beds—a few blossoms
amid the grass, paths along the water, and shrubs flourishing, in the muffled brilliance of late May. The characteristic Seine-et-Oise sky, foamy cloud and weak blue, lay
at our feet also, daubed in a soft copy on the surface of the
pond. In the background every tree was draped in a slightly different shade of the same ecstatic color.

But as Mrs. Cullen stood facing all this, I had an impression of indifference and mere courtesy; her look did not
take in much. A little narrow frown, an efficient survey,
only to discover if there was anything in it for her personally; and there was not. In a moment the light eyelashes
began to flutter again, and the blue pupils loosened, merely sparkling. Her prolonged and expressive looks were all
for her husband or her hawk.

Now, what seeing the garden chiefly reminded her of,
was that the hawk could not see: its entire head except
the beak encased in its plumed Dutch hood. "Poor Lucy,
blind as a bat," she murmured; and very deftly, taking one
drawstring in her teeth and the other between thumb and
forefinger of her right hand, she unhooded it. It also
frowned, and stared circularly at the room and blinked at
the window. Then it opened out and rearranged the whit-
ish and bluish feathers around its throat; combed its head

between its tethered legs; smoothed its cheek against its powerful shoulder.

Mrs. Cullen paced up and down, evidently trying to decide which armchair would suit her and Lucy best. Then Alex came in from her long-distance business, with apologies for not welcoming them at once. They replied with another round of compliments upon the house and garden, and there was a new introduction of the falcon. "Lucy, for Lucy Ashton, Lucy of Lammermoor," Mrs. Cullen explained. "Don't you remember her song? *Easy live and quiet die, Vacant hand and heart and eye.*"

To my amusement Cullen hummed a few notes of the Mad Scene from "Lucia" in a manly Irish treble. His wife hushed him by murmuring his name, which was Larry; and went on informing Alex that they were at the Plaza-Honoré, busy shopping in Paris, eager to leave for Hungary via Strasbourg on the morrow. I was impatient for them to cease this small talk and be seated, because I wanted to sit down and admire the falcon comfortably, and to ask certain questions. At last Mrs. Cullen requested a straight chair, which I brought from the dining room.

I was much impressed by Alex's enthusiasm during this first part of the Cullens' visit. It reminded me that she must be lonely here in France with only myself and my cousin and a few other friends rather like us. She had spent a number of years in Scotland with her father, and in Morocco, and journeying around the Orient; and in London also the acquaintances of her girlhood had been outdoor people like these two, self-centered but without any introspection, strenuous but emotionally idle. It was a type of humanity that she no longer quite respected or trusted, but evidently still enjoyed.

Their enthusiasm about themselves and all that exactly appertained to them, always overflowing, coolly playing and bubbling over in mild agitation like a fountain, held your attention and mirrored itself in your mind; little by little you began to bubble with it. One of Alex's obvious

characteristics was lack of curiosity; and I think that was
chiefly fear of arousing or authorizing others' inquiry
about herself. Perhaps selfishness reassured her and made
her less shy. In any case, that afternoon she eagerly asked
questions, including some that I had in mind; and Mrs.
Cullen was charmed to answer; and Cullen was charmed
to listen and give back his approximate echoes. Thus an
odd kind of compatibility was established, in which I too
gradually let myself be included, somewhat to my surprise.

For one thing, the bird charmed me so that nothing else
mattered much. And it served as an embodiment or em-
blem for me of all the truly interesting subjects of conversation that these very sociable, traveling, sporting people
leave out as a rule: illness, poverty, sex, religion, art.
Whenever I began to be bored, a solemn glance of its
maniacal eyes helped me to stop listening and to think
concentratedly of myself instead, or for myself.

Furthermore the Cullens began to puzzle me, to charm
me in that sense. Whether or not I finally arrive at a proper
understanding of people, I often begin in the way of a
vexed, intense superficiality. And indeed they were mere
male and female of that species of well-to-do British which
haunts the entire world with excess of energy and sedate
manner. They were self-absorbed, coldly gregarious, mere
passers of time. But nothing about them was authentically
sedate or even peaceful. There Cullen plumply sat in
Alex's softest armchair, his legs more widely spread or
loosely crossed than you would expect of a conventional
gentleman; licking his lips under his fringy mustache;
evidently thinking of his dinner; interrupting his wife's
conversation at regular intervals as if that were his life
work. Yet he seemed to be constantly fighting against some
strange feeling, and to be somehow outwitted by it. Whenever he spoke, his wife smiled or at least tilted her head
toward him. This, I felt, was chiefly good breeding on her
part; many of his remarks, and especially his tone of voice,
seemed unpleasant. But between remarks, in her glances

at him, there was affection as bright as tears. And during the loving fuss she made over the great bird on her arm, she kept shifting her eyes in his direction, imploring him to try to like it too. It might have been a baby, and he a lover; or was it the other way around?

Alex expressed surprise that they should willingly leave Ireland at this lovely time of year. Mrs. Cullen answered that, in season or out, there was nothing much to do in Ireland except hunt. "And our terrible sons pinch our hunters when they come home. We can't afford to keep enough for them. I can't bear a horse that others have been riding."

She also alluded mildly to the diminishment of the old quiet kind of fortune like theirs. The banshee in the draughty corridor or the weedy hedge crying not the deaths of relatives, but increase of taxes, decrease of rents and investments . . . Indeed they still appeared rich, in hand-woven silk with diamonds, in tweed as soft as silk, stopping at the Plaza-Honoré, en route to Budapest in a Daimler. But all that in fact is cheaper than an old country house full of guests, and the requisite stable and kennel and larder and cellar, and servants enough. Having closed Cullen Hall, Mrs. Cullen pointed out, they were in a position to accept invitations half the year; and the continent was cheap.

Evidently her telling us this vexed Cullen. He warmly informed us that one of his neighbors, a drunken idiot anyway, had sold everything that the entail permitted, and two of his cousins were obliged to rent; and so it went all over the British Isles. Their own circumstances were neither discreditable nor hopeless. There were still certain inheritances due them, on his side, not Mrs. Cullen's. His sons might be considered grown men, except by their mother; but they were still engaged in that great postponement, education, which is expensive. His brother and sister were happy to have them during their long vacations; but as a rule they preferred to loiter at Cullen Hall with two or three servants who were too old to dismiss anyway; and they hunted with the neighbors. It is easy for youngsters to get on with new people, even such as the latest in their county, a manufacturing peer named Bild, a Jew; not at all easy for him.

Mrs. Cullen said a word in defense of Lord Bild. Thank heaven it was he who had bought the estate adjoining Cullen Hall, on their youngsters' account especially. Although of common Germanic origin he was very strict about manners and sportsmanship and keeping fit; more so than they were. Neighborly influence is like education; the best teachers belong to the races and classes which have been learning themselves just lately.

Now Cullen had risen and was standing at his wife's elbow, shaking his finger at the falcon teasingly. I thought that the bird's great eyes showed only a slight natural bewilderment; whereas a slow sneer came over his face and he turned pale. It was the first revelation I had of the interesting fact that he hated Lucy. He would willingly have sacrificed a finger tip in order to have an excuse to retaliate, I thought; and I imagined him picking up a chair or a coffee table and going at her with smashing blows. What a difference there is between animals and humans! Lucy no doubt would be disgustingly fierce when her time came; but meanwhile sat pleasantly and idly, in abeyance. Whereas humanity is histrionic, and must prepare and practice every stroke of passion; so half our life is a vague and stormy make-believe.

Mrs. Cullen merely looked up at her husband and said in a velvety tone, "The trouble with Ireland, from my point of view, is that they don't like our having a falcon. Naturally Lord Bild disapproves; but I don't mind him. He's so unsure of himself; he's a Jew furthermore; you can scarcely expect him to live and let live. But our other neighbors and the family are almost as tiresome."

Cullen thrust the teasing hand in his pocket and returned to his armchair. Her eyes sparkled fast, perhaps with that form of contrition which pretends to be joking. Or perhaps it pleased her to break off the subject of their Irish circumstance and worldly situation and to resume the dear theme of hawk, which meant all the world to her.

The summer before, she told us, an old Hungarian had sold her a trained tiercel. "I took him with me last winter when we stayed with some pleasant Americans in Scotland. There's a bad ailment called croaks, and he caught that and died. They had installed their American heating, which I think makes an old house damp; don't you? Then their gamekeeper trapped Lucy and gave her to me. Wasn't that lucky? I've always wanted a real falcon, a haggard, to man and train myself."

In strict terminology of the sport, she explained, only a female is called a falcon; and a haggard is one that has already hunted on her own account, that is, at least a year old when caught.

Except for that one deformed bit of one foot, Lucy was a perfect example of her species, *Falco peregrinus,* pilgrim hawk. Her body was as long as her mistress's arm; the wing feathers in repose a little too long, slung across her back like a folded tent. Her back was an indefinable hue of iron; only a slight patina of the ruddiness of youth still shone on it. Her luxurious breast was white, with little tabs or tassels of chestnut. Out of tasseled pantaloons her legs came down straight to the perch with no apparent flesh on them, enameled a greenish yellow.

But her chief beauty was that of expression. It was like a little flame; it caught and compelled your attention like that, although it did not flicker and there was nothing bright about it nor any warmth in it. It is a look that men sometimes have; men of great energy, whose appetite or vocation has kept them absorbed every instant all their lives. They may be good men but they are often mistaken for evil men, and vice versa. In Lucy's case it appeared chiefly in her eyes, not black but funereally brown, and extravagantly large, set deep in her flattened head.

On each side of the upper beak there was a little tooth or tusk. Mrs. Cullen explained that the able bird in the prime of life uses this to snap the spinal cord of its quarry, which is the most merciful death in nature. It reminded me of the hooked gloves which our farmers wear to husk corn; and so in fact, I thought, it must work: the falcon in the sky like a large angelic hand, stripping the meat of pigeon or partridge out of its feathers, the soul out of its throat.

I think Mrs. Cullen was the most talkative woman I ever met; and it was hawk, hawk, all afternoon. A good many inhabitants of the British Isles are hell-bent all their lives upon killing some wild animal somehow, and naturally are keen about the domestic animals which assist them. Others, who know all about human nature, nevertheless prefer to converse about animals, perhaps because it is the better part of conversational valor. Mrs. Cullen's enthusiasm was nothing like that, and it probably would have annoyed or alarmed the majority of her compatriots. As it seemed to me after listening a while, she felt welling up in her mind some peculiar imagination, or some trouble impossible to ignore, which she tried to relieve by talking, with a kind of continuous double meaning. I think she would never have admitted the duplicity, and perhaps could not have expressed herself in plain terms. People as a rule do mean much more than they understand.

She informed us, for example, that in a state of nature hawks rarely die of disease; they starve to death. Their eyesight fails; some of their flight feathers break off or fall out; and their talons get dull or broken. They cease to be able to judge what quarry is worth flying at; or their flight slows up so that even the likely quarry gets away. Or, because they have lost weight, the victim is not stunned by their swooping down on it. Or when they have clutched it, they cannot hang on long enough to kill. Day after day they make fools of themselves. Then they have to depend upon very young birds or sick birds, or little animals on the ground, which are the hardest of all to see; and in any case there are not enough of these easy conquests to keep them in flesh. The hungrier they get, the more wearily and weakly they hunt. And the weaker they get, the more often they go hungry, in a miserable confusion of cause and effect. Finally what appears to be shame and morbid discouragement overcomes them. They simply sit on the rocks or in a tree somewhere waiting to die, as you might say philosophically, letting themselves die.

"I met a man on the staff of our great madhouse in Dublin last year," Mrs. Cullen added. "I was curious to see what it was like; so he took me with him one afternoon on a tour of inspection. Some of the mad people reminded me of hawks, exactly." The lethargically mad, sitting with their hands in their laps, imaginarily exhausted, unable to speak above a whisper, with burning but unfocusable eyes, unable to concentrate. . . .

Cullen cleared his throat boisterously, perhaps to protest against the curiosity of women or against this folly of reading meaning into the ways of mere birds.

Falconers believe that hunger must be worse for falcons than for other birds and animals, Mrs. Cullen said. It maddens them, with a soreness in every feather; an unrelievable itching in their awful feet; a bloody lump in their throats, with the light plumage wrapped loose around like a bandage. This painful greed, sick single-mindedness, makes it possible to tame them and to perfect the extraordinary technique of falconry, which is more than any other bird can learn. You hear it in their cry—*aik, aik*—as Mrs. Cullen then imitated it for us, ache, ache—a small flat scream with a bubbling or gargling undertone, as if their mouths were full of scalding water. "I suppose human beings never feel anything like it."

"But Madeleine, Madeleine, we're never hungry," her husband protested with a chuckle in which there was great satisfaction. "How can we tell?"

She begged him not to be silly. She had known people

who had starved, Irish republicans hiding from the Black and Tans, Germans in 1922, and had inquired of them; and they had described it as rather a soft cool drowsy feeling.

I wondered about this. Although I had been a poor boy, on a Wisconsin farm and in a slum in Chicago and in Germany in 1922, I could not recollect any exact sensation of hunger, that is to say, hunger of the stomach. And I thought—as the relatively well-fed do think—of the other human hungers, mental and sentimental and so on. For example, my own undertaking in early manhood to be a literary artist. No one warned me that I really did not have talent enough. Therefore my hope of becoming a very good artist turned bitter, hot and nerve-racking; and it would get worse as I grew older. The unsuccessful artist also ends in an apathy, too proud and vexed to fly again, waiting upon withheld inspiration, bored to death. . . . Naturally I did not speak of this to Alex and the Cullens. It seemed rude and somehow abnormal even to be thinking of it, while they sat exchanging information about real life, really starving nations and greedy species of bird.

Whereupon our present bird mantled, that is, stood a moment on one leg, shook the other leg and wing downward, and spread that half of her plumage in a long fan, gazing at me, blinking or winking at me. But because my writing had gone badly all spring I could not bear to give her more than a passing thought with reference to that. I began to think of her as an image of amorous desire instead. That is the great relief of weariness of work in any case; the natural consolation for its not going well. Or perhaps the Cullens' feeling about each other suggested it to me. No doubt art is too exceptional to be worth talking about; but sex is not. At least in good countries such as France and the United States during prosperous periods like the twenties, it must be the keenest of all appetites for a majority of men most of their lives.

And highly sexed men, unless they give in and get mar-

ried and stay married, more or less starve to death. I myself
was still young then and I had been lucky in love. But
little early quarrels and failures warn one; and in the con-
fidences of friends and in gossip about other men, one
discovers the vague beastly shape of what to expect. Life
goes on and on after one's luck has run out. Youthfulness
persists, alas, long after one has ceased to be young. Love-
life goes on indefinitely, with less and less likelihood of
being loved, less and less ability to love, and the stomach-
ache of love still as sharp as ever. The old bachelor is like
an old hawk.

Civilized human beings have learned how to avoid lit-
eral starvation and the fear of death and real enslavement;
so at least it seemed in the twenties. They have this kind
of thing instead: fear of old age, loss of charm, lack of love.
Therefore I caught myself gazing at my young unmarried
Alex anxiously, sentimentally, and at her Irish guests with
idle envy. But the Irish wife's uneasiness and the husband's captivated but uncomfortable look reminded me
that I was making a false distinction. There is not as much
sweet safety in marriage as one hopes. Hunger and its
twin, disgust, are in it too; need and greed; and passage
of time, the punishment. Of course true love and lust are
not the same, neither are they inseparable, nor indistinguishable. Only they reflect and imitate and elucidate each
other.

Looking back upon that afternoon's talk and thought,
I am inclined to hold Mrs. Cullen responsible for this
daydreaming of mine, personal worry and exhilaration,
which made me inattentive to what she said now and then.
In a woman as energetic and attractive as that, the hint of
hidden emotion and the sense of double meaning naturally
are exciting; and the excitement leads in one's own private
direction. But as it were in a mirror, looking at myself, I
could see something of her character and plight before the
circumstances of the afternoon betrayed her. I think that
was what she instinctively wanted.

Meanwhile she had gone on answering Alex's questions: something about the craftsmen who outfit falcons, generation after generation of avian haberdashers especially in India, and which bell resounds the clearest through the grass and bushes and breezes, and what hood is least likely to ulcerate the waxen lids and lips; and something about an ancient Persian text with a thrice-hyphenated title which is still the best handbook of falconry. I wanted to know all this, yet I failed to pay attention.

Then Lucy bated, that is, threw herself headlong off the fist. The leather jesses around her legs and the leash looped through Mrs. Cullen's fingers held her ignominiously, upside down. It was a painful sight, like an epileptic fit or an insane fit. There was no possibility of the thongs breaking; I half-expected her lean bright legs to snap instead. I expected her to scream, aik! But the only sound was the jingling of her bell and the convulsion of her plumage, air panting through her plumage. The tail feathers and the flight feathers, shooting out rigidly, threshed against herself and against her mistress from head to foot. Mrs. Cullen, not the least disconcerted, raised her left arm straight up over her head, and stood up and stood quite still, only turning her face away from the flapping and whipping. Her equanimity impressed me as much as her strength.

In a minute Lucy gave up little by little. It was extraordinary: you could see her self-control returning, recurring in one feather after another. Then she hung peacefully like a mere turkey or goose hooked up in a butchershop; only for an instant. The long wings began again, but in a different exertion: hugging the air, bracing against the air, until her talons got a grip on the gauntlet and she succeeded in pulling herself up again where she belonged. There she stared or glared at us, blinking the rush of blood back out of her embarrassed eyes and pulling her plumage together.

With a sigh and a half-smile Mrs. Cullen brought her burdened and shaken arm down, and seated herself again

in the straight chair. Some such hopeless attempt to escape, crazy fit of freedom, comes over all domesticated
falcons at fairly regular intervals, she explained, especially
in their first year or two; all their lives if they have not
been well manned. "They never get over being wild. It's
like malaria or that other intermittent fever, the one you
have to be so careful about in the Orient."

Lucy happened to be an unusually frank, active bird,
so that you could often tell when her trouble was to be
expected; by a soft repeated tinkle of her bells or a steady
pull at one of her jesses. The leather might of course be
loose or worn out. "And instead it pinches her, which
makes her angry, and everything seems hopeless," Mrs.
Cullen concluded. "She can't help it, can't bear it. It's like
committing suicide."

"Give me liberty or give me death, ha, ha," cried Cullen,
seeming to expect special applause from us because we
were Americans, or perhaps because Alex's name was Henry like the American who first expressed that sentiment.
His wife gave him that look of hers which was the opposite of applause; and he took it as usual. His hazel eyes
stood out like jewels, the tip of his tongue brightened his
lips.

Meanwhile she was slowly caressing Lucy's lower plumage and tired feet. She might have been a trained nurse
and Lucy her patient, after a bout of illness or craziness.
Or she might have been in love and Lucy her beloved,
pleasure absent-mindedly ebbing . . . And every word she
uttered added a little to the confused significance. "Sometimes I can prevent her independent fits. The way a governess gets to know a child, and can see its tantrums beginning and distract it somehow. . . . Being stroked like
this often does the trick. At first I used a dried pigeon's
wing as you're supposed to, but this suits Lucy as well."

Idly she went on with it: two dimpled fingers with long
tinted nails and heavy rings just brushing the spent feathers. "Or if I notice it in time, I lift her over my head for a

moment. She likes to perch as high as possible, so she can look down upon everything around her. I think it must frighten her to see things higher than she is. We're like that sometimes ourselves, aren't we?" she added, smiling gently.

Time after time her transitions like this—from hawk to human, objective to subjective—startled me. To be sure, any woman greatly in love must know how a flattery in time saves trouble, how the illusion of superiority counteracts the illusion of inferiority, as well as any governess. But it had not occurred to me that her love for Cullen was great in that sense: cunning, instructive, curative.

Falcons, she informed us, do not breed in captivity. Various attempts have been made to induce them to, but with no success. Thus, the entire sport has to start again from scratch for each falconer, whenever he trains a new playmate. Little by little the perfectly wild creature surrenders, individually, in the awful difficulty of hunger. But surrender is all, domestication is all; they never feel at home. You can carry male and female side by side in the same cage year in and year out; nothing happens. They will cease to fight but they stay solitary. Scorn of each other for giving in, or self-scorn, seems to break their hearts. They never build a nest or lay an egg. Not one chick or eyas is ever reared in bondage. There is no real acceptance or inheritance of the state of surrender.

Mrs. Cullen mentioned, as a kind of exception, the make-hawks: old good-natured birds which some professionals use in the training of the young wild ones. But even their influence must be in the way of a rationalization of necessary evil, inculcation of vice, making the best of a bad bargain. For they too are born in the vacant rocks or uncomfortable trees; and they too keep sterile.

"Like schoolmasters," crowed Cullen. That appealed to my sense of humor. But Cullen's smile was a leer if I ever saw one, and evidently embarrassed his wife and Alex; so I kept from smiling.

Mrs. Cullen then quoted Buffon's famous sentence

about falcons: *"L'individu seul est esclave; l'espèce est libre."* Buffon had been her father's second-best author, after Scott. Her French accent was incorrect but very pretty. Only the individual hawk is a slave; the species is free. . . .

Then Alex spoke up, in what was a loud voice for her: "Oh, dear, it is the opposite of human beings. We are slaves in the mass, aren't we? Only one man can hope to free himself; one at a time, then another, and another."

"Oh, I dare say," Mrs. Cullen assented. "Yes, perhaps." But she smiled patronizingly. I think she was congratulating herself upon knowing a freer and stronger type of humanity than our pampered, subtle, self-questioning American type; and perhaps she did: Irish republicans, wild Hungarians with hawks, Germans during their defeat.

"But it is true, isn't it?" Alex insisted. "The man who really loves freedom is the exception."

"Oh, quite. How right you are," our lady falconer dubiously murmured.

But her husband disagreed. "No, Alex! What a disgusting idea! Love of liberty is the deepest instinct we have— if you will excuse my saying so."

We silently considered this for a moment; the three of us, it seemed, regretfully. Alex wanted freedom more than anything; and if others as a rule did not, she might have a lonely life. In any case it would take a better man than Cullen to dispel her young misanthropy. I myself regretted never having been able to decide what to think: how much liberty is a true human motive, and how much is wasteful and foolish? And for the first time that afternoon Mrs. Cullen gazed at her husband sadly, that is, weakly. She agreed with him, I felt sure. But there are circumstances in which it may be obvious that at least one human being requires freedom; and you bitterly regret that it is so: because you need to keep that one captive.

"Why, hang it all," Cullen still sputtered, "why, independence is the only thing that is human about hawks. Don't you agree, Madeleine?"

She slightly turned her back to him and contemplated Alex and me rather unkindly. It was the careful absence of expression, absence of frown, that you see on a clever lecturer's face when the irrelevant questioning or heckling begins. There was also a sadness about it which, if I read it aright, I have often felt myself. She did not want us to take her hawk, her dear subject-matter, her hobby and symbol—whatever it meant to her—and turn it this way and that to mean what we liked. It was hers and we were spoiling it. Around her eyes and mouth there were lines of that caricatural weariness which is peculiar to those who talk too much.

Indeed our sociability as a whole had gone off; something a little sour and dark had developed in it. We had been sitting there too long. Alex, I fancied, was counting the minutes until they departed. But suddenly she grew hospitable. "You'll stay to dinner, Madeleine, won't you? Please, Larry, do. I can promise you a good dinner," she added with an indulgent smile.

I wondered whether she had mentioned this invitation to Jean and Eva, and whether the short notice would exasperate or inspire them. Mrs. Cullen also thought of that. "Servants are devils, don't you know. Mine used to behave madly, when extra people turned up at Cullen Hall."

Poor Alex was accustomed to the madness of servants; but, as she explained, this new couple did not mind surprises. She had found them in Tangier, where the secretary of the pig-sticking club had engaged them to cook in camp for several tentfuls of unmarried members. With only primitive utensils, a few iron kettles and a spit over an outdoor fire, and unpredictable guests at all hours, it evidently was child's play for them, and a welcome opportunity to show off. One afternoon a French general and a party of eight had motored out from the town, and some thoughtless fellow had asked them to stay. Jean had taken

a boar killed that morning, and by slicing it thin, rubbing
it with certain herbs which grew there underfoot amid the
tents, and marinating it in four bottles of brandy, rendered
it quite edible by nightfall. Alex was inclined to think of
her entire lifetime as an emergency of that sort. So she had
hired the proud pair and secured passports for them and
embarked them for France and Chancellet. And this, she
told Mrs. Cullen, was what she had hired them for.

"If we do stay," Mrs. Cullen said, "my bird will have to
be fed, toward six o'clock." Alex in any case intended to
suggest to Jean a dish of pigeons baked with white currants. He would procure them from a neighbor who had
an immense old dovecot; and one could be brought back
alive for Lucy. The reminiscence of the brandied wild
pig, the prospect of *pigeons aux groseilles*, charmed Cullen; you could see the gourmandise shining on his rosy
lips.

Alex went to the kitchen, and by her comfortable air
when she came back I judged that Jean was well disposed.
Then she suggested our taking a walk until dinner-time,
which also charmed Cullen, though his appetite did not
need whetting. "By Jove," he said, "I do look forward to
those squabs."

They were disappointed to learn that the park was not
Alex's property. It belonged to the nation, along with the
little château de Chancellet in the midst of it. Bidou, the
illustrious aged ex-minister, was permitted to live there.
But he kept the gates open in the daytime, and the entire
village strolled in and out. Meeting all classes when he
took his daily exercise perhaps made him think proudly
how democratic a statesman he had been all his life. He
gave everyone a *bon jour*. He especially liked meeting Alex
because she was an American and he vaguely remembered
having advocated the payment of the war debts.

"Oh, aren't politicians a bore?" Cullen exclaimed with
an odd proud laugh. "Worse than poets."

"Larry, please," his wife said in haste, "please let's not

talk about that." I wondered what that meant.

Alex unlocked the little gate on the far side of the pond, and we strolled along an *allée* of ancient beeches. She warned us that if Bidou should appear in the distance, she would have to turn back. He had a way of inviting her to dine, and Mme. Bidou had asked her not to accept on account of the failing of his health, the folly of his old manhood.

We all felt happier now that we were outdoors. It was beautiful in the park. The trees had been so lovingly tended ever since a pupil of Lenôtre's set them out, that each had developed its maximum character. The way they stood in informal groups, or in line, or alone at a little distance, seemed not only to conform to the art of parks but to express their feelings about each other: idiosyncrasies of affection or obedience, pride or pain. And unlike human characters in such an assembly, they promised or threatened nothing more; no episodes or developments.

Cullen walked up ahead with Alex. Now in the open air he not only laughed but shouted; so that I could hear him telling her a yarn about an old English politician who had attached himself to a young married woman. And one day he and the husband had gone out alone together on the moor for a bit of rough shooting; and he had shot the husband by accident, so to speak. Then he had married her. But he had worried about it all the rest of his life, which was not long; and he had impoverished her in his will. It was ancient gossip: I had heard it before; and at the time I did not see any oddity in Cullen's telling it, except that it seemed funny to him and not to me. When love is diabolic, I thought, a triangle is the simplest form it can take; and a convenient form, if it cannot be endured. The lovers to be pitied perhaps are those who have no one to hate—what they long to kill, and what the killing would be for, incorporated in one and the same person, the one they love—whose rough shooting therefore can take place only in imagination, and never ends.

Presently we came to a crossroads; and there we did see
the short silhouette of old Bidou headed in our direction:
his peculiar march or trudge, and the shrugging of his
shoulders inside a great cape. All his life he had gone
booted like a common soldier and blackly wrapped up,
which had been a boon to caricaturists and a kind of elec-
toral trade mark; which now made it easy to avoid him.
Mrs. Cullen asked if they might go on ahead and have a
look at the famous old fellow.

Alex and I turned back alone toward her house, by a
short cut through a dense plantation of young trees, with
vernal branches of old trees rounded overhead. It was
like walking inside a great recumbent telescope, pointed
at the château half a kilometer away. In the nineteenth
century, under the personal supervision of Viollet-le-Duc
and his friend the author of *Carmen,* Chancellet had been
entirely and fussily restored. In the round bit of sunshine
afar off, the lens of our telescope, it looked too good to be
true, amid the patchy flower beds and the moat, where a
few ducks were splashing and lovemaking.

I was in as foolish a good humor as Cullen; everything
seemed mysterious and sentimental. The rounded frame
of branches in which we strolled, looking ahead into pink-
ish sunlight; the tidy little architecture enframed, with
its associations literary as well as historical; the dying, absent-minded, erotic statesman exercising daily in an immutable circle around it; our odd guests walking to meet
him, woman with hawk and greedy man, whose eyes turned
golden when he looked at her, whose spit ran at the mere
mention of his dinner—all were gathered around me, I
vainly fancied, to make one great vague thing very simple
and clear to me. What more could I ask? But it is always
foolish to expect simplicity. All one can do is to substitute
little facts for great speculations, little performances for
immense desire, and call this, simplification.

The return by ourselves gave me a chance to question
Alex about the Cullens. They had come to Tangier two

or three years before for the pig-sticking. Madeleine rode ideally, but the rule of the club forbade women to carry a spear. Cullen had shown a definite lack of enthusiasm and indeed a lack of talent; however, he had gone out every day and not done badly. When one of the vile brave beasts appeared in the distance—flickering along the shrub, suddenly fleeing out across open ground like the shadow of a flying bird—the Irish woman would gallop out with the very first riders; her husband following hard, looking as if he might fall any minute but not falling. At the last minute, when the spears began to point down along the shoulders of the horses, she would rein up short or turn aside. Suddenly she would not be there any longer, and Cullen still would be. Her ambition for him and his poor horsemanship—so it appeared to the others—betrayed him into prowess. Alex heard a club member say that once or twice at the kill his audacity and ferocity had been rather too much of a good thing; shocking. One morning his horse stepped into a hole and threw him right down beside the boar, a big wicked one already wounded; and he behaved with great sense and courage, and kept his horse away from its tushes, although he was not quite sober. His not being quite sober was the trouble in general.

One afternoon Mrs. Cullen had said as much to Alex. "Poor Larry, when we're in Ireland or in London with nothing to do, is inclined to overeat, and furthermore to drink far too much." Alex must have been impressed by this confession, for she quoted some of it word for word. "Most things are a beastly bore for him, you know; that's his real weakness. But you can't say anything to a grown man about drinking, after all, can you? It's such a horrid little unimportant thing. They're proud, and they resent having to think of it. I had an aunt who talked about it, and it made my uncle worse." As discreetly as she could therefore, she told Alex, she tried to keep him distracted; busy doing things, in good company which inspired him to do well; abroad, and outdoors as much as possible. He often complained that it was no way to live; but it had kept him fit and good-natured.

She was younger than he, Alex pointed out; and she had money of her own; and she was a clever, unconventional, and rather self-indulgent woman. Yet she devoted herself entirely to him, every instant, year in and year out. He on the other hand was not perfectly faithful, in spite of his devotion to her. When they were in Tangier a pretty young American named Baroness Levene came across from Malaga, and flirted with Cullen; and he obviously responded to it. One of the Tangier residents asked them all to dine, and while the men stayed in the dining room, Madeleine had been very rude to the little interloper. A day or two later she spoke of it apologetically. It was disgraceful of her, she assured Alex, to mind her husband's virile frivolity. She never doubted for an instant that he loved her, and no other woman. His response to the others was all make-believe or in fun. She alluded again to his deadly tedium; his need of some novelty to pass the time somehow, every day of his life, every hour; and his other weaknesses in direct consequence. A little philandering, like eating and drinking, gave him something to think about.

Whereas marriage was infinitely simple for her, she said; she never needed the attention of other men. She supposed this to be so settled and so apparent in her character that it bored men and they let her alone. Alex had observed a number of acceptable men not letting her alone in the least; rather smitten. Yet there seemed to be no affectation or insincerity in Mrs. Cullen's account of herself. Women who have been spoiled by the many, tormented by one, often have an air of innocence.

Alex had seen a great deal of them the following winter in London; and there they were engaged in a very odd sport indeed: underground activity of Irish rebellion. Cullen was perfectly and anciently Irish, and one of his brothers had been a friend of Casement's. Whereas Madeleine was not a Catholic; and she had Ulster blood and English blood; and as a child she had lived in Canada. Yet she was the rebel, or she ardently played the part of one; Larry followed. Alex heard him speak very angrily of the British, disgustedly of de Valera. But he loved joining in others' opinion, no matter what, and embellishing his repetition of it, as best he could—how could one tell what he thought? Perhaps it was hard for him to tell himself.

All that winter they were at home informally almost every evening to the oddest patriots. At first glance it looked like a literary salon. The ringleader was the poet McVoy: a young man of great conversation, with a half-rapacious, half-religious face. Alex also met a man who had done a little bombing, another with a bit of his cheek shot away, and certain bereaved and cruel women, and a bizarre priest. Their political opinion was all tinged with piety, even puritanism. They would have been ashamed to eat or drink or be merry in any way, with so much to be done for Eire. Cullen yielded to the general austerity. Furthermore, he told Alex, they could not afford to live well that winter, because of their contributions to the cause. Alex had never seen him in better form, lean and youthful and if not exactly cheerful, amiable. Rebellion evidently served as an excellent exercise and diet. There was also amorous anxiety: he thought McVoy in love with Madeleine. Alex indeed thought so too. But all Madeleine appeared to want of the poet was to keep on his political high horse, in his fascinating conspiratorial vein, for Larry's amusement. Rioting and sabotage and perhaps even assassination—as it were sticking of the Ulster pig, mort of the English stag—with poor Larry in the thick of it, because it would be good for him. . . . Suddenly all that ceased, Alex never heard why. They sublet their house and spent the summer in Vienna and Budapest. That was the summer Mrs. Cullen bought her first hawk, the tiercel that died of the croaks.

This little information Alex gave me as we sauntered slowly through the ex-minister's park. Now we were back near our gate, under the great beeches. Alex had been a little anxious lest the Cullens get lost. But there in the broken light, pallid shade, there they came at a brisk pace, engaged in a vivacious discussion of some sort, which they ceased as soon as they saw us. "He's a dear, your old politician," Mrs. Cullen said. "He spoke to us, and then what do you suppose he did? He did bird imitations for Lucy; I mean to say, he whistled at her."

Evidently Cullen preferred French politicians to Irish. "A good old boy! He did a nightingale and a lark and some bird I didn't know. He told us what it was, but it was French. Quite good."

"And Larry, wasn't he cheerful and civil? Perhaps he thought that if he kept whistling long enough, Lucy would answer. Wasn't it funny?"

I thought it touching as well as funny: that old man had been whistling to his compatriots like that for half a century, and as a rule a majority had answered; but, alas, nothing much had come of it, for France.

Now Mrs. Cullen was ready to feed Lucy. But her chauffeur and Jean who had gone to the neighbor's dovecot, had not returned. Foolish Eva felt sure they were in a ditch somewhere, or quarreling, or lost. So we sat down again; and I like a fool inquired what they thought of French and English and German politics. Cullen was out of breath but he sniffed wonderfully and cleared his throat, preliminary to an opinion. "Please, Larry, no politics," his wife requested, smiling at me to make it less impolite.

She was fondling Lucy, gazing at her eye to eye, slowly shaking her head at her; and the wicked beak moved in exact obedience to the tip of her nose as if it were magnetized. "Lucy's hungry," she said solemnly.

"Feel her breast." She took my hand and held it against the tasseled plumage; and indeed there was a humming and stiffening in it, like a little voltage of electricity. Her eyes were moist and explosive; and the instant her mistress's eyes released them, down they went to the gauntlet, as if expecting a feathery form in agony to materialize out of the leather.

"Feel her feet," Mrs. Cullen added; and I did, while she explained that birds always have a higher temperature than animals. Fever heat; and yet they were slick and dry like a serpent. I could feel what they wanted to do, what they wanted to have, swelling in them and ticking the dull minutes meanwhile with little throbs. My pleasure in touching them was half embarrassment; and it set my mind running back to the thought I had left off an hour ago; that this hawk's hunger was like amorous appetite. I call it thought—and it is thought now, as I remember and try to tell it—but at the time it was only a vague flashing daydream. It all came together like one large composite phrase: old bachelor hungry bird, aging-hungry-man-bird, and how I hate desire, how I need pleasure, how I adore love, how difficult middle age must be!

Then, I lamented to myself, if your judgment is poor you fall in love with those who could not possibly love you. If romance of the past has done you any harm, you will not be able to hold on to love when you do attain it; your grasp of it will be out of alignment. Or pity or self-pity may have blunted your hand so that it makes no mark. Back you fly to your perch, ashamed as well as frustrated. Life is almost all perch. There is no nest; and no one is with you, on exactly the same rock or out on the same limb. The circumstances of passion are all too petty to be companionable. So there you sit, and you try to sit still, and doze and dream to save trouble. It is the kind of thing you have to keep quiet about for others' sake, politeness's sake: itching palm and ugly tongue and unsighted eye and empty flatulent physiology as a whole; and your cry of desire, ache, ache, ringing in your own ears. No one else hears it; and you get so tired of it yourself that you can't wait to grow old. . . .

Thus in an instant I foolishly imagined myself growing old; and meanwhile Mrs. Cullen had not ceased speaking with that single-minded vivacity of hers, but a little somber. "Since we caught Lucy," she said, "she's never had a mouthful to eat except out of my hand, and I've always worn the same glove. Think what it must mean to her!"

It was an impressive unpleasant object, that glove, stiffened and discolored by a hundred little sanguinary banquets. It resembled things you see in cases in anthropological museums; fetishes of awful religion, sacrificial utensils, witch-doctors' kits. And the feet with crescent toenails trod it so passionately that you wondered how the wrist inside endured it.

"You know, she's not really attached to me personally," Mrs. Cullen said. "If I gave you the glove she'd be yours instead of mine. It's as simple as that, I think. It's what's called behaviorism, isn't it? Would you like to try it? Try taking her a moment."

She turned around and held Lucy some five or six inches below the chair-back, and after a moment's hesitation Lucy hopped up there. Mrs. Cullen's hand was large and mine is not; so that I was able to squeeze into the gauntlet. It surprised me to see that she wore another large diamond on that hand, which under the pressure of the leather had bruised her finger a little. . . Then I held my wrist five or six inches above the chair-back; and Lucy, with her belief in food-stained leather added to her belief in the highest possible perch, hopped again.

"That's what they call an inferiority complex, don't they?" Cullen proudly demanded, not to be outdone by his wife's use of that other catchword. "Madeleine can't understand one thing about psychology."

"Very well, Larry. I tell you she's hungry," his wife answered. And by the tone of her voice you would have thought her the hungry one.

I drew a deep breath, in which I got the hawk odor, slightly bloody, slightly peppery. I had noticed it before, but without distinguishing it from Mrs. Cullen's French scent. The body, well balanced on its hot feet, weighed less than I had supposed. At the least move her talons pricked the leather and pulled it a bit—as fashionable women's fingernails do on certain fabrics—though evidently she held them as loose and harmless as she could. Only her grip as a whole was hard, like a pair of tight, heated iron bracelets.

Alex offered her congratulations upon Lucy's evident peace of mind with me; I would make a good falconer. That reminded me of my father and his magic with animals which filled me with envy and antipathy when I was a boy. He could force a crazy colt to its knees, or castrate a young boar, or chloroform a desperate trapped owl; and their wretched muscles relaxed and surrendered, their eyes blinked in perfect gentleness in alignment with his eyes. His eyes, or perhaps it was his hands, seemed able to promise them something. Half my life, I said to myself, has been discovering that my character is not the antithesis or the contradiction of his; here was a new kinship. Perhaps I could cope with horse or hog or doomed bird too, if I had to; perhaps even with a wild antipathetic son, disinclined to live—who knows? This was a gratifying thought but not altogether happy: vast vague potentiality of things I did not wish to do in any case.

I happen to be a trifle long-sighted; and now Lucy was so close that I could not quite see her in focus; and I have always had a fear of going blind. One good flutter, one simple thrust, and she could have slit an eyelid or ruptured an eyeball in an instant. She did not shuffle much on the borrowed gauntlet. But the vague dilated dark of her eye, the naked ring around it, the inner eyelids opening and closing as instantly as bubbles, seemed worse than restlessness. I was ashamed to tell her mistress that I was afraid. No doubt the chances of her actually hurting me were negligible. Mrs. Cullen's half-supercilious glance at us was reassuring. Still, I felt rather as if I had a great

thought of death concentrated and embodied and perched
on me. Whatever had possessed me, I wondered, to think
of this Lucy—bloodthirsty brute with a face like a gouge,
feet like two sets of dirty scalpels—as significant of love?
Perhaps those two things, imaginary death and hopeless
desire, always lie close together in one's mind, foolishly
interchangeable.

Mrs. Cullen meanwhile, with vacated wrist, seemed the
most restless woman in the world. She kept crossing and
uncrossing her perfect stilted feet; leaning this way and
that in the soft armchair; clasping and unclasping her
jeweled fingers. It suggested one more explanation of her
attachment to Lucy; falconry made her sit still. Perhaps
too she was slightly jealous of my successful deputyship.
"The real reason Lucy likes you so much," she murmured,
"is that it's getting on toward mealtime. She fancies you
may have a little steak or half a pigeon in your pocket.
You look promising to her. What do you suppose has become of your cook? I do hope he and Ricketts haven't gone
off to get drunk together."

She rose and tripped across to the great window. She
tripped back and paused beside us and teased Lucy as
Cullen had done, but in the opposite spirit. The star sapphire slid a little from one teasing finger to the next,
which Lucy observed with interest. It looked like an un-
socketed eye, I thought.

"Oh, Alex," Mrs. Cullen said, "you're so intelligent.
I'm afraid you think me very sentimental. I'm not really.
I do not want a falcon to be attached to me personally.
When animals get that sort of feeling, it's too awful. Knowing the sound of your voice, liking the way you smell, wanting to be touched, all that. I hate it. It's such a parody of
us, it's worse than we are. A bird like Lucy is so simple
and straight. You make a promise and she expects you to
keep it, that's all. She knows what she wants, and who
gives it to her, and that's that."

Cullen grunted, and assured us that his wife didn't mean

a word of this cynical stuff. But he did agree about one thing: "Birds are selfish as the devil. That's why I can't care for them. I'd rather have a dog, I tell you."

"Do you hear, Lucy? He'd rather have a dog." She said this in the way of wicked affectation, perhaps toying with the idea of being hated by him for it.

Then she turned briskly to me: "I'll take her back now, Mr. Tower, if you please. I think she'll bate in a minute."

Once more we exchanged the glove. Once more Lucy considered, on the rough leather, the stain of yesterdays' meals and the hope of today's and tomorrow's, and leaped up with alacrity. Her mistress carefully fondled her to prevent her bating, but she bated nevertheless.

After that, Mrs. Cullen heaved a greater sigh than before, not because it had been a harder struggle, but because her own light but significant remarks had hurt her at last, I fancied. And now she added that, simple though hawks all were, you could never really trust one. "Oh, I shall have to be so careful, never to fly Lucy at things she cannot catch and kill. The least failure makes her hopeless. My man in Hungary says that if she misses her quarry twice, I must call it a day and keep her hooded; otherwise it's risky. Because if she should miss a third time she might leave me; fly off and never return. They're all alike: the haggard you've hunted with for years; even the eyas you have taken from the nest and babied all its life. . . ."

"Damned ungrateful, I say," Cullen jeered.

"No, Larry. Lucy gives up her freedom and stays with me because it's a better life, more food and more fun. If it doesn't work, after all, what's the use? If my falconry isn't good enough. . . ."

Cullen giggled. I didn't. For it is the way religious faith goes, in the sense of God's failure; and it is the way true love ends: missing the third time. That much of life I already knew; I had missed twice. I glanced at Alex, wondering if the mysterious turn this small talk was taking troubled her too. But her face had its pretty well-bred passivity; I could not tell. The light in the Irish woman's eyes was fantastic, focused like glass on her great weak husband, then on me for just a moment with something like embarrassing affection. She and I understood each other.

She seemed to me a very passionate woman, but it was a kind of plural passion, all confused or crossed: work and play and sense of beauty, the maternal and the conjugal and the misanthropic, mixed. Perhaps that is a peculiarity of childless women. Female character has a great many secondary traits and minor talents; the wear and tear of motherhood may weaken them or stamp them out. It is anarchy if they all flourish.

"Tower," she said, "you would make a good falconer. Why don't you take it up, in the States? And you too, Alex. Everyone should have some hobby, some pet, I think. And all the other pets really are too awful.

"Ugh, how I despise dogs!" she then exclaimed in a dull disgusted tone of voice. "Do you know what dogs remind me of? It's not a nice thing to say but I do mean it. Prostitutes; all things to all men, and all that. And all shapes and sizes, from adapting themselves to everything and everybody for centuries, with no integrity. Men love them for that; it's flattering.

"Falcons have never changed. Forty centuries of falconry, think of it! And still wild; every feather as it was, and the same everywhere. I tell you, there's nothing like it in nature. Cats have more character than dogs, if they only weren't so damned amorous. Kittens to be drowned every few months, isn't it awful!"

My well-bred Alex in spite of herself made a little shocked face. It startled me too, because just then like a fool I had been thinking of Mrs. Cullen as a childless woman. What about those wild Irish sons of hers, shifting for themselves at Cullen Hall, riding and spoiling her favorite hunters, hunting with Lord Bild? I said a kind of prayer for them. That is, I hoped that they really were wild. Cullen had spoken of them as practically mature men; but perhaps he himself was not mature enough to judge of it. I hoped that they did not love their mother much. If they were at all backward or sensitive it was good of her, wise of her, to keep out of Ireland.

At this point wild Lucy flung up her wings and let her mute drop to the floor. Mrs. Cullen cheerfully apologized, and also proudly called our attention to its whiteness. It meant that Lucy was in excellent health. A healthy falcon's mute is the cleanest wastage in nature, and by no stretch of imagination could Alex or I have been offended by it. Cullen offendedly stirred his great body about in the great soft armchair; his face got redder; his light eyes protruded. But they protruded at us rather than it. Perhaps he feared, or perhaps hoped, that we would somehow express disapprobation or disgust. Alex rang for Eva, and of course that simple creature did not mind; it rather amused her. She fetched a towel and some wax, and knelt beautifully, and gave the parquet a very good restoration.

During which, Jean came rushing in, sweaty and pleased with himself. When he saw his dear beauty there on her knees he made a gleeful sound and gave her a tap as he passed, which made her blush. He and Ricketts in the Daimler had had a blowout on the back road. But dinner would not be much delayed; for while Ricketts had changed the tire, he had seated himself by the roadside and dressed the pigeons with his jackknife.

Mrs. Cullen asked him how large Lucy's pigeon was; and he sent Eva after it: a rumpled thing in a basket with warm damned eyes. She instructed them to wring its neck and chop it in half and bring it back, with its feathers and half the giblets. Meanwhile she asked me to move the straight chair into a dusky corner under the staircase. Though the least shy hawk in the world, Lucy would not feed properly outdoors or with a light in her eyes. Next Mrs. Cullen requested a number of towels to protect her dress, and Eva brought a worn-out tablecloth; and Alex helped tie this

under her chin like a bib and spread it out over her lap.
She sat with her pretty legs far apart, no longer a fashionable woman but rather like a gypsy or a priestess; or as if
this were to be some surgical operation or painful travail.

Whereupon Jean returned with the portion of pigeon.
He let two or three drops of blood and a bit of gizzard fall
on the waxed floor; and again Eva cheerfully mopped up.
Mrs. Cullen took the half-bird in the hand on which Lucy
perched, pinching it between gloved forefinger and thumb,
at Lucy's feet; turning it temptingly. At first Lucy stared
at Alex and me so insolently that we drew a few steps away
from the staircase. Jean and Eva also wanted to watch, but
Alex reminded them that we too were hungry.

I had been hearing so much and thinking so romantically of hawk-hunger, that I expected a lunge and a grab, like
a wolf or a cat; it was not so at all. It took two or three
minutes for Lucy's appetite to develop, to accumulate. In
a state of nature, no doubt it depends upon the fun of pursuit, voluptuous air in her wings, and the hovering and
teasing; and there would not be any real spasm of Lucy's
love of food until the instant she felt food in her beak.
Now there had to be time for some equivalent of all that
to take place in her narrow mind; time at least to regret it.
The tedium of this conjugal kind of repast had to be overcome somehow, so she doubted and deliberated and imagined.

"Damn your pride, Lucy," Mrs. Cullen muttered; then
murmured to us in her schoolgirl French, because Lucy
did not understand French, *"l'appétit vient en mangeant."*
Upon which I reminded myself that on the whole, throughout life as a whole, the appetites which do not arise until
we have resolved to eat, which we cannot comprehend
until we have eaten, are the noblest—marital, aesthetic,
religious. . . .

At last Lucy's curly breast did throb; a few feathers
bristled up; her wings stood out a few inches; her greenish
fists clenched on the glove; then her whole body began to

point down beak first like a water-diviner's stick. She set
her feet a little farther apart on her mistress's wrist. Then
she stooped straight between them and thrust into the
piece of pigeon. Mrs. Cullen held it tight. Lucy braced her
legs and pulled and straightened back up with a morsel,
which after a moment she shifted away into her throat and
with a sinuous motion or a toss, swallowed.

Until the end, until there was no more pigeon, Mrs.
Cullen had to encourage her to keep her mind on what
she was doing. "The important thing," she said, "is to get
her to take feathers enough. Her digestion depends a good
deal on that."

When Lucy paused and raised her weird face between
mouthfuls, it seemed spiritual rather than sensual; a bigoted face. There was no histrionic angry temper, no showing off. Thoroughly and slowly it went on to the end, with
meditation upon every feather, every crumb of meat, every
sip of blood—sacramental. Once or twice, because she did
not like the way some wisp of plumage or tiny tendon felt
—or because she liked it extremely—she shook her head
hard; and a spot of blood appeared on Mrs. Cullen's bib,
a feather drifted to the floor. Perhaps you could not have
watched it if you were squeamish; neither Alex nor I were.
But after the fourth or fifth beakful Lucy had a bad moment, modesty or imaginary repletion, and Mrs. Cullen
asked us to move still farther away; and we were glad to
go. We sat down beside Cullen in front of the big window.

It interested me to observe, or to guess at, his feeling
about this. When his wife first called for Lucy's banquet
he had pulled a long face. I think that may have been only
fond anxiety, lest in her serving of it she appear to Alex
and me coarse, or comical. He kept his eyes averted, but it
was not disgust, surely, for it put him in mind of his own
eating. He talked to us of that with enthusiasm and in
great detail. In Paris the past week someone had sent them
away out on the Avenue Jean Jaurès for a steak: year after
year they always telephoned a certain small unsuccessful

restaurant to prepare a supreme *cassoulet* which took two days; and so forth. Which brought him finally to the present, the great casserole of pigeons which Jean was preparing. At that point, I think, Alex regarded him almost with detestation.

The half-pigeon out of the way, Mrs. Cullen decided to put Lucy outdoors to weather, as it is called. We followed her into the garden where she selected the back of a rustic bench as a suitable perch. But there had been signs of more than usual nervousness during the feeding: it seemed best to leave her hooded. Because of the unaccustomed warmth of the afternoon, after Scotland, Mrs. Cullen said, she had a slight headache; and she retired with Alex to the bedroom for some aspirin and a moment's repose.

Then I offered Cullen a cocktail. He rose with enthusiasm and followed me to what I called the choir loft, that is, the balcony, where Alex's decorator had seen fit to install a bar, in the fashion of the twenties: all chromium and copper with a fine hierarchy of glasses and remarkable liquors in odd bottles. My Irishman had never seen the like of it. There was a magnum of prewar vodka; and I suggested a kind of modified Alexander with that in it instead of gin. Missing a syllable, he thought it charming of me, and so American, to serve a drink named after our hostess. I tried to set him right on that point but he was too charmed to care. The drink itself also suited him and for a while he concentrated on it, without a word.

The ladies did not return, so presently I mixed a second shakerful; and Alex's silver shaker was large. It was indiscreet, perhaps a little perverse, and in a way characteristic of me. As a rule I dislike being with people who have had too much to drink. It often brings on in me a kind of misanthropic fit; pity verging upon repugnance, and a mean sense of humor which they sometimes notice. But just because I am aware of the old-maidishness and even injustice of this, whenever the hospitality of the bottle is up to me I am inclined to overdo it.

Cullen in fact had been a little tight all afternoon, and I had not realized it. Now as he got tighter I saw that it was the same thing. They had arrived at Chancellet about two-thirty; so probably it had happened at luncheon, perhaps at breakfast. That explained his wife's anxious and resentful air, and her rude motherly snubs to keep him in order. He must have been in misery the last few hours, while we failed to offer him anything: thoughtlessness on my part, perhaps prudence or dislike on Alex's. She of course knew him well and must have noticed.

Perhaps the unnoticeable sort of heavy daytime drinker has the worst trouble; certainly they are more troublesome to others than they think. And others—sobersides like myself—are often more unjust to them than to their reeling, roaring, festive confreres. Half the time they themselves are only half aware of any incapacity or lack of charm. Or perhaps they know, and they think that you do not, and you do, and of course it is not manners to tell them so. They make an effort, often a heroic effort; and you feel that you have to respect and applaud that, whether or not it is fun for you.

But the worst injustice must be when you scarcely know them, and you judge them without reference to their habit, as in my case with Cullen that afternoon. He had simply seemed to me mediocre; old for his age, and weak for his size, dull, vain, and rather cross. No one had warned me that I was not seeing him at his best. It was his character, for all I knew, the nature of the creature; take it or leave it. That is to say, I had left it. So now I felt a slight embarrassment and grudging contrition.

Perhaps at other times, I reminded myself, his character was ideal; his mind vigorous; his great physique fresh and energetic. That would explain the love his wife bore him. Suppose you have learned to like or to love such a man when he was sober; and you happen to dislike him when he is not; and he doesn't know the difference or can't help it. The temptation to interfere, the fond hope of reforma-

tion, must be very great. Thus I began to think indulgent-
ly of Mrs. Cullen's selfish nervousness and sharp tongue.
Although, if what I had seen that afternoon was the worst
of it, certainly she exaggerated and overemphasized the
plight she was in with him. An ordinary boring conceited
uneasy childish man! Yet out of his petty instability she
seemed to expect something odious or dangerous to develop any minute—as if she felt the ground underfoot
move a bit, like a landslide starting, and caught glimpses
of little creeping sickening things close to the surface,
coming up! Love itself is an exaggeration, and very likely
to lead to others.

After the first pouring of the second round, suddenly
Cullen began a long complaint of the merry chase she led
him year in and year out: her Mediterranean cruises, her
falcons, her Irish republicans. No home to speak of, no
creature comforts; nothing like the good time Alex and I
had here in Chancellet, this pretty bar for example. Nothing but wild men, wild birds, and two silly maids to mop
up after the birds instead of a good cook: hotel food all
the year round, never a leg of boar soaked in brandy nor
squab with currants.

At first, I think his outburst embarrassed him as well as
me. For he explained that if I were an Englishman he
would not be talking to me in this way; nor, for that matter, if he were an Englishman! But the Irish are like Americans in this respect. He had been in the States three or
four years when he was a young fellow; therefore he felt
the likeness. "The English never talk freely, as we're talking now. They're sly; they simply rule, and have their own
way about everything. Britannia rules the waves and so on.
You know, Tower, my wife's English. . . ."

These little distinctions of nationality were what reminded him of their winter in London with the Irish republicans. He not only disliked that type of Irish; their
political principle seemed suspect to him. "They're not
really republicans, that's just talk. They're anarchists. It

was beastly for me. I'm a fool, I'd do anything in the world for my wife, and she does whatever strikes her fancy. She kept asking those patriots to the house. It cost me a pretty penny too, I can tell you. I had to pay for a lot of pamphlets, I had to support two widows, I had to hire halls for their meetings. Then, if you please, some of 'em said they needed some guns and bombs. Can you believe it? Only I don't think they got any bombs. Nothing happened. It would serve the English right if they did blow things up, you know. I suppose my wife's little friends just pocketed the money; or they bought a poor make of bomb that wouldn't do. Nothing happened."

He also complained that they were comic little characters, not gentlemen. And all their women appeared halfcrazed with loving them, weeping in the corridor, losing their tempers with each other; some of them occult, some religious, and all of course talking Ireland, Ireland. Not a class of women that a man of a sensual nature would look twice at, not if he had any self-respect; nothing soft or sweet or tidy about them. "But I must say I enjoyed it for a while," he admitted, "seeing how that class of people get on and hearing their stories. I could always shut them up when I felt like it, or chuck them all altogether, you understand, because I had the money."

Of course I had begun to feel my misanthropy; but still his monologue amused me, especially the vulgar touches like this last. No doubt he was a quite good county aristocrat of that modest rank which as a rule is less mixed than any other. But not even aristocracy can be expected to give good examples of itself all the time. It seems rather to secrete commonness little by little, and to keep it in reserve, along with those odds and ends of mere human nature which aristocratic manners are intended to hide. And every generation or two it purges itself, in the form of some odd son or daughter, perfect little shopkeeper or predestined courtesan, upon whom manners wear thin.

Cullen silently ruminated two or three minutes; and

when he began again it was in the middle of a new bit of subject matter. Probably it seemed to him that he had told me something which he had been saying to himself, something about his wife. "Make no mistake, Tower, I respect my wife." And he went on to assure me, or to warn me, that anyone who doubted it or slighted her in the least was quite likely to be knocked down by him; in fact he had done it once. She was like a swan in his opinion; pure as snow, with never a harmful thought all her life. "Only she's thoughtless," he added. "She never thinks of anything except what she happens to want. She's spoiled. When I met her she was the prettiest girl in Dublin. Lovely breasts for one thing. And ankles; you saw her ankles! Her family wasn't well off either. I took her without a penny; and I've spoiled her."

Aristocracy had nothing to do with it. It was my own fault; the vodka and cream had done it. Alcohol is the great leveler. Given a stiff drink, the true descendant of princes boasts of it as if it were not true, the multimillionaire feels poor, and Tristan talks to you about Isolde like a pimp, I said to myself. My malice was beginning to keep pace with my companion's folly.

"I spoiled her myself," he continued. "That's why she's so restless. Damn it, Tower, for years now she's kept me on the go like a gypsy. We've done everything." He held up one large moist freckled hand and counted on its unsteady fingers the things they had done: salmon fishing and photography and pig-sticking and now hawking. They had also been everywhere, and he counted places too, with a boastful as well as pathetic intonation: Norway and America and Java and Morocco and Africa—to say nothing of that winter when she had insisted on Irish rebellion, the most expensive thing on earth.

"I've let her have all my money," he said proudly. "She isn't as pretty as she was; but you know, I let her go to London for all her dresses, or Paris; and she has two maids. Before I married her I had a man to look after me; I gave him up. Now we need this chauffeur, Ricketts, because we're always on the go. I have to keep an eye on him too, because he has an eye for a pretty woman. Funny thing, one day when we were shooting in Scotland with those Americans, I thought Ricketts was insolent about Mrs. Cullen, and I'd have killed him. But she said I imagined it."

All alcoholism in a nutshell, I foolishly mused. And while he, poor man, counted his sports and his travels on his fingers, I meanly ticked off the drunkard's faults and pitfalls of drink as it were on my fingers—indiscretion and boastfulness and snobbism; and sentimentality so nervous that it may switch any minute to the exact opposite; and the sexual note and the sadistic note, undesirable desire, improbable murder. All of it of course a bit unreal and unrealizable in fact. . . .

What exaggeration I had drifted into! Cullen really was not in very bad shape; I have spent afternoons with a hundred drunker men. The point is that I exaggerated at the time, item by item as he talked along; and I think he sensed it and played up to it: a fatalist and a play-actor. The presence of my fastidious Alex and his over-wrought wife downstairs—my wishing they would hurry up and join us, and my dreading it at the same time—made his loose talk more exciting than it would have been in ordinary circumstances. I had been too happy all afternoon, thinking meanwhile of unhappiness; which is a heady combination. Sometimes I am as sensitive as a woman to others' temper or temperament; and it is a kind of sensitivity which may turn, almost by chance, for them or against them. Perhaps at the end of our tête-à-tête I was not much soberer than my companion.

I began to wonder whether, after all, he was not going to tell me the little tale of anxiety or jealousy that winter in London which Alex had half told me in the park. And then he did.

"That winter in London one of our patriots," he began,

"had the insolence to fall in love with my wife. A brute of a young fellow named McVoy who was a poet. It got very sticky then. I made up my mind to show them the door, the lot of them. But the more I worried about it, the easier it was for my wife to get around me and have her own way. I didn't want to be unjust to her; and if I'd made a scene before I knew what was up, you see, I might never have known. Terrible, the power a woman has over a man of my nature. You see that side of it, don't you?"

He told it tranquilly enough, though with some breathing between words. He reached out and grasped the cocktail shaker; and having helped himself, kept a tight hold on it. Once or twice he slipped off the tall stool and took steps up and down, carrying the shaker with him instead of his glass, to gesture with; coming back to drink and refill. I had not poured any of this second shakerful for myself; it was almost empty. The whites of his eyes grew more and more untidy, the hazel pupils a harder color; sense of humor and self-knowledge dying down in them. The strong though puffy fingers fixed on the large silver vessel, melting the frostiness off it in patches. I thought of wresting it away from him; emptying it slyly down the little chromium sink; perhaps pretending to be getting drunk myself, and jollying and bullying him along downstairs. . . . Naturally I did nothing; I looked and listened; I nodded. I wiped the copper top of the bar more than it needed, like a bartender. Probably even bartenders feel a little ignominious curiosity amid their professional boredom.

"One fine day there had to be an end of it, McVoy and all that. Especially one night. The police misunderstood something about him, and were waiting for him at his lodgings; so we had to put him up for the night. I couldn't sleep a wink. I kept hearing him sneaking around in the dark after my wife, I thought. All imagination; I've too much imagination anyway. My wife and I shared a bedroom; we always do; and he'd never have had the courage to come in there.

"Then I had a disgusting dream. I woke up standing beside my wife's bed. There was a moon, and I could see her, and she was sleeping. But I couldn't sleep. So about three o'clock I got up and took a knife from the butler's pantry. I thought I'd tackle McVoy with it. But my wife woke up and came and followed me, across the hall. When she saw the knife naturally it frightened her terribly. And the funny thing was, she frightened me too: there on the landing in her white nightgown. She made me give her the knife and go back to our bedroom. The wonder is we didn't wake McVoy. If we had, there'd have been an awful fuss, I expect. But he slept through it all. Or perhaps he was listening and hiding, scared, under his bed.

"After that I think my wife saw my point of view about it, and was sorry for me. She wept, and it wasn't like her to weep. In a way I was sorry for her too. Think of it, Tower! Think of a common little fellow like that coming to your house, whinnying like a horse around a respectable married woman. He'd have had only himself to blame if I had knifed him. After that Mrs. Cullen sent them all packing, believe me. All the rebels."

He picked up the shaker and shook it hopefully. Now there was only the clunk of small ice in diluted cream, to which I was deaf: a poor host at last, now that it was too late. My feeling about it all really was an absurd mixture. I felt a certain compassion; all the world loves a lover, and especially I do. I also longed to laugh aloud and to tease him. I also itched to tell him the miserable truth about himself, and rather vengefully than for the good it might do. There are a number of circumstances in which the truth does no good; and oh, this was one. I began to feel a mixture of sadness with my malice; a fellow feeling in spite of myself.

Drunkenness does superimpose a certain peculiarity and opaqueness of its own—monotonous complexion, odd aroma, pitch of voice, and nervous twitch—on the rest of a man's humanity; over the personality that you have known sober. But worse still is the transparency and the revelation, as it were sudden little windows uncurtained, or little holes cut, into common recesses of character. It is an anatomy lesson: behold the ducts and sinuses and bladders of the soul, common to every soul ever born! Drunken tricks are nothing but basic human traits. Ordinary frame of mind is never altogether unlike this babble of morbid Irishman. I felt the sickish embarrassment of being mere human clay myself. It seems to me that only art has the right to make one feel that. I am inclined to detest anyone who makes me feel it, as you might say, socially.

"God, Tower, it's tragic," my man sighed. "There's always something. Now I have to keep an eye on our damned Ricketts." He kept it on me for a while then, flashing it or rolling it; sometimes as simply as Othello, sometimes with the imagination and abstraction of a eunuch.

"You know, Tower, it's very interesting. My wife and I are the ideal married couple, so to speak. It's real love. She wouldn't look at another man. I'm as good a man as ever in spite of my age; it runs in the family; and I understand women. Oh, it's not all roses; it never was all roses. There were times when I thought I'd leave her, after some of the mistreatment she's given me. At least I could pretend to, and she might learn to treat me better. All it would need to summon her back would be a wink and a beckoning. She'd do it; she'd stoop her proud neck, I tell you; she'd come on her hands and knees. But I'd never humiliate her, Tower; I never have. To me she's still the proud ignorant girl as I married her; the prettiest in all Dublin.

"The worst mistreatment I've had to bear, you know, is this hawk. There are things only a common fellow could bear peaceably, and a hawk is one of 'em. Funny about hawks, you know, they can't learn to control themselves. They make their messes when they feel the need. Oh, well, you saw it with your own eyes; I sympathized with you.

It happens in the hotel, the maids mop up after it, and I can't tell you how ashamed I am. I can't look the man at the desk in the face; he might make a joke of it. Madeleine has to tell him what we want; I won't go near him. . . . Funny about women, isn't it? They haven't the same natural shame about things that men have. Let's face it: that's why the church has to keep them in their place, they can't help it. I suppose if they had finer feelings, we men would get left out in the cold, wouldn't we? They'd have none of our kisses. So there you are.

"My wife's a fine trainer of hawks; her crooked old Hungarian admits it himself. But that is one way she can't subdue 'em; it's their nature. She can't teach me much either. She's got to get rid of that hawk, pretty quick; I won't stand for it. You see, I love her, Tower; that's the trouble. Suppose I want to put my arm around her, and she has that hawk on her arm. Can I? No, Larry, no, dear, you'll break a feather, a very important flight feather! Day after day now on the way to Hungary I'll have to sit there pushed over in the corner of the back seat out of Lucy's way; and I tell you, it makes me sick.

"She's been keeping it in our bedroom, because it doesn't like the bathroom. She's sorry for it. I lie awake all night hearing it stir on the perch, and I never forget it for a minute. When I'm beginning to fall asleep I think it's coming to attack me with its nasty beak. You can't imagine what it means to me. I dream of it. I dream sometimes it's an obscene thing; and that wakes me and I reach my arm over to my wife's bed; but she's asleep and takes no notice of me. I tell you, it's not healthy. I dream sometimes it's death. You know, I had an old uncle who saw ghosts, in a big house we had in Galway. I inherited that kind of feeling, you see, and Lucy brings it on. I'll tell you another dream. When I was a boy my old nurse taught me to weave osier baskets; and the other night I dreamed Lucy was a basket. Her feathers weren't right for it because they were sticky, but I wove her; and I gave her to my wife. But this is the end! No more Lucy!"

That was a lovely moment, to my way of thinking. My animosity toward this fool husband suddenly wafted away. It is a manner of self-revelation that I especially delight in: by means of loose imagery, and dreams, and careless connection of odd bits of memory as they come. Even as he spoke I hoped that I should be able to remember every word.

For alcohol is a god, as the Greeks decided when it was first introduced from the East, although a god of vengeance. The drinker becomes the drunkard. Everyone is to blame. The soberest man or woman in the world at some time or another has helped the sad process along in some poor dear drinker's case. For example, I think someone must have looked at Cullen in his youth when drunkenness became him, and so loved or admired him in it that he began to regard that as the secret of love and admiration. There are men who master the trick of drink, and practically never take a drop without being made admirable by it. I have known one or two; they were extraordinary men in other ways as well.

But even for the average man, even in the poorest booze-fight—between the vanity of the beginning and the sickness at last—there is a fine moment. It is the mark of its oriental origin and the proof of the Greek belief in it. The fumes seem suddenly mixed with more light and air than usual, and it is the right mixture. The silly self-consciousness clears up; the chip falls from the shoulder. Your friend is drinking, and you are not, or not much; so naturally there is an undercurrent of quarrel between you; now suddenly it ceases, peaceful. His tipsy mind is as it were sitting quiet, like an oracle on a tripod, under the influence not of alcohol simply, but of himself, his very nature, his fatality, his childhood. Whatever has been kept secret, damped in ashes, smothered and contemptible, begins to come out; and for the average man there is no harm in it. The murderous man may murder then, the madman talk nonsense; who cares? For most of us the ashes are bad, the secrecy mistaken, the contempt and self-contempt contemptible—and the raking of the ashes is good. For a moment, drunk as a lord, instead of coarseness and looseness you have the intuition of a child or an old woman. . . .

Of course it does not last long. Ordinarily when it has occurred, befuddlement and some bodily incompetence are in the offing. Too much delight in it may cause one to keep the worst company in the world all one's life. But certainly it is one of the main things in human nature, worth experiencing and worth watching. Cullen did not quite reach it that afternoon, on vodka and cream in Alex's silly de luxe bar. But I thought he was about to, when we were interrupted. As I really did not like him anyway I did not care much.

It was Alex who interrupted us, coming into the big room under the balcony and calling to me. She wanted me to visit Jean and Eva in the kitchen, and encourage them about the impromptu dinner and hurry them up. She had been hearing strange tones of voice out there; and she was afraid that if she went herself, Jean might make speeches and Eva might weep.

It was a large, unmistakably French kitchen: the stove in a deep niche of brick; dim walls and array of copper; the open doorway and windows full of little landscape with afternoon sunlight slanting across it. The Cullens' chauffeur was there with our two servants, and somehow it seemed to me dramatic as well as picturesque. Jean was the classic manservant, a type that you find more or less the same all around the Mediterranean: doubtless very good-looking and amorous as a boy; forty now and the worse for wear, with a bald spot and dark jowls and several teeth missing; a man broken to harness but still apt to show off his emotions, and still amorous. He had acquired Eva in Morocco; and she certainly had Moorish blood though she called herself Italian. She was half his age and lovely, although of an increasing billowy fatness; pale in

the way that seems sallow at times, silvery at other times.
Ricketts was a fine Cockney, bright-eyed and sharp-nosed.
He sat at the table in the middle of the room in a spoiled
young male attitude, with a bottle of wine half empty and
half a plate of Eva's little Moorish cakes.

Dinner was flourishing; that I could tell by the smell of
it. Along with which I breathed the early summer wafting
in: a tart exhalation of the sod, a scent of some shrub that
was like a dark candy. In spite of the open door, the stove
going full tilt for the squabs and the strawberry tart made
the room hot, which brought out the men's untidy healthy
body odor. Eva had one of those cheap North African per-
fumes in a little cake like a rubber eraser, and had put that
on to excess, which, alas, I fancied, was for the young Englishman's benefit. And the mood of the room, the morality
or psychology of the three together, was as confusing as
this fragrant air in it. Eva stood and stared at Ricketts. Her
great eyes were a little reddened; probably she had been
weeping; at the moment she was smiling vaguely. Ricketts
poured the sour red wine down his throat half a glass at a
time; and between throatfuls looked up at her with a becoming brightness. Jean pretended to be busy beside the
stove with his back to them. But he agitated the pots and
pans, and flashed glances over his shoulder, and replied
to my questions about the tart and the cheese with a little
more obscurity and more assurance than I liked.

Then I happened to look outdoors. It pleased me to be
able to see, in a little interval between two shrubs, the
dreamy hawk hunched up on the rustic bench. And then,
to my amazement, I saw Cullen on the left coming across
the lawn. Very slowly, with a kind of noticeable alcoholic
endeavor not to be noticed; on tiptoe, and as if the grass
were a loud and slippery surface like a ballroom floor. . . .
Instantly I sensed that it was abnormal and scandalous.
But I could not run out to see what he was up to, without
making a little scandal myself. Jean and Eva and Ricketts
would follow or at least watch. So there I stood, acting

absent-minded, murmuring about the Camembert and the iced hock.

Cullen vanished for a moment behind one of those two shrubs near Lucy's perch. When he reappeared he was crouching, and hitching along on the balls of his feet, and steadying himself with one hand, closer and closer to her. The grotesque furtive approach indicated for one thing that he had no rational plan, no serious intention. For Lucy was hooded as well as leashed; she could not see him. He kept stretching out one hand, very tense; but he could scarcely have reached her from that quadruped position. I began to think it funny. But from the bedroom window Alex and Mrs. Cullen could have seen him as well as I: that was a pity.. . . .

Perhaps it occurred to him. He scrambled to his feet, and somewhat assumed an attitude of knowing what he was about, and leaned over the bench with his back to me. Perhaps he was undoing the knot or knots of the leash. Evidently he was not alarming Lucy much; she opened her wings a few inches, as if expecting to be picked up. But he drew back, and to my dismay, my disgust, thrust his hand in his pocket and brought out a large pocketknife and opened it. Murder at last, I thought. It was Lucy's turn; no more Lucy!

Before I even got started to run out and stop him, he simply pushed her hard off the back of the bench, recoiling away from her at the same time. It was obvious how afraid of her he was. With a large indignant flutter she landed on the grass. He had cut the leash; he had not cut her throat. Also he had unhooded her. On the grass for a moment she took a rapid confused look in every direction. Then with a great lift of her legs and two or three strokes of her wings, she climbed up on top of the air, and above the lawn, and across the pond. It was lovely. Her searching looks still, this way and that—to discover why she had been loosed, what quarry there was for her—made her appear to be shaking her head, saying no, no.

I lost sight of her when she passed behind a tree; again, when she rose beyond the scope of the kitchen window. Down she came then, with neck and wing and tail and legs all out—in the shape of a sixpointed star, big and dim, collapsing. She rested her weight on the air again for an instant, and alighted on a post in the far corner of the garden. It was one of two posts from which Eva hung Alex's lingerie to dry early in the morning. The gesture of alighting was lovely: her rigid hands clutching the top of the post like a living victim. It might have been a little angel seizing a tall man by the hair. Then there she sat, still wondering what in the world—what, in terms of a hawk's simple murderous instinct—this liberation meant.

Meanwhile, of course Cullen too had gazed up at her, gazed across the pond at her. Now like a ninny he waved good-bye, good-bye. Then he turned and ambled back through the bushes. Jean and Eva and Ricketts, in their matrimonial or adulterous absorption, had not seen a thing. I was thankful for that; I also felt a childish optimism because of it. I waited a bit, to give Cullen time to get settled in the living room. Then I dashed out of the kitchen, and knocked at Alex's bedroom door, and shouted through it to Mrs. Cullen. I simply said that Lucy was no longer on her perch. Then I hastened away to see what state of mind Cullen was in. There he sat in the living room, one leg over the arm of his easy chair, stoutly puffing; sorrowful and also smug, I thought, and somewhat sobered by his exploit; that at least was a blessing.

"The hawk has got loose. It's not on the bench. I've called Mrs. Cullen. She's coming to look for it. It must have untied the leash itself." I said this as emphatically as I could, to suggest to him the line he should take.

"But what about the hood?" he asked in an infuriating little tone. "I cut the leash myself, damn it all."

Whereupon I groaned or I cursed; I can't remember which. I didn't want him to confess; I should have spoken to him before I called his wife; now it was too late. She came rushing from the bedroom; and it was as if the news had instantly disheveled her from head to foot. She shuffled, her fine shoes half unlaced. Her perfect dress hung or clung around her one-sidedly. She was pulling on the blood-stained gauntlet; and as she crossed the room she impatiently ran her other hand up through her hair, which fell down on that side over her cheek. She did not close her mouth between her voluble exclamations. "Damn, damn. Oh, I am so unhappy. I must get her back, I can't bear to lose her."

At the sight of her, Cullen pulled himself up out of the easy chair and stood at a kind of attention: but badly, not a bit brave. She must have seen him; she took no notice. I had a sense of her knowing what had happened, who had done it. She looked like the type of old Irishwoman who has second sight: countrified, frumpy, and frightened. And in spite of her outcries and panicky movements, it seemed to me that she had an air of experience and familiarity; familiarity with fright.

"Oh, Mr. Tower, can you get me the other half of that pigeon?" she begged. "The pigeon I fed her. She hasn't, I hope she hasn't, gone far away."

Upon which her husband behind us chimed in as usual, worse than usual: "Madeleine, Madeleine, surely they've cooked it. That's the dinner, you know, pigeons with white currants."

She took notice of that. She swung around and answered in a devilish voice, "Of course they have not cooked it." For one second I thought she might strike him; perhaps he did too. He wrinkled his nose and flung up his hands.

I started toward the kitchen and she followed, explaining, "I'll never catch her without a lure. Thank heaven it was a small pigeon, she'll still be hungry." She gave me a perhaps affectionate pat on the shoulder which amounted to a push.

Then she ran back to the window and there gave a wonderful small shriek. It should have been hawklike, I

said to myself; what it really made me think of was a valkyrie, a very small valkyrie. For in spite of my admiration
of Lucy and sympathy for the other two, I was enjoying
all this.

I met Alex at the kitchen door, and she had the half-
pigeon. Mrs. Cullen called to us, "What in God's name did
I do with my bag? My extra leash is in it. She must have
broken hers."

Alex ran for the bag, handing me the pigeon. I dropped
it, and it smudged the parquet. Jean and Eva were there
beside me, but they were too thrilled to do any mopping
now. Then Mrs. Cullen lost one shoe and stumbled into
an armchair; and her husband knelt and tried to put it
back on, fumbling around her silky ankle with those
freckled fingers which could so easily have snapped it in
two like a twig—until she lost patience and kicked the
other shoe off, over his shoulder, and rose to go in her
stocking-feet.

"Stay here, all of you," she ordered. "Please, please, let
me go alone." She paused a moment on the threshold
staring across the pond at heedless Lucy. She held her
gloved fingers up to her mouth as you do when you blow
a kiss. Then she swung around toward us, demanding,
with a kind of loud lump in her throat, "Where in God's
name is her hood? How wicked! Who did it? One of you,
how wicked!"

It was poor Eva who answered, with her primitive sensi-
bility, primitive expectation of blame: "Oh, Madame,
Madame, Jean and I never left the kitchen," and began to
cry.

Alex told her to hush, which she did, more or less. As I
watched our angry birdcatcher, I still kept one eye on these
other watchers, so assorted and attractive, there inside
the house in a row close to the plate-glass window in the
last murky sunshine. I thought that Alex glanced oddly
back at me; perhaps my eyewitnessing and slight com-
plicity had given me an odd expression. Certainly she

hated their disorder: obscure common blundering around her house, and general self-betrayal, with the servants goggle-eyed. On the other hand catching a great runaway bird was the sort of problem she loved. Her mild brown eyes lit up, and she breathed like a happy child. Ricketts came tip-toeing in and stood behind us as close to Eva as he dared. Whereupon Jean began whispering to her in Italian, *prestissimo,* until Alex hushed him too. Eva dabbed her eyes with the corner of the towel, another corner of which had pigeon's blood on it. As for Cullen, his face was quite mottled with his mixed emotions; heaven knows what they were.

As Mrs. Cullen left us, across the lawn, along the left side of the pond, I was struck by the change this emergency had made in her appearance and carriage. Perhaps it was chiefly her going in stocking-feet. When she first descended from the Daimler, how delicately she had stumbled on the cobblestones; then foolishly tripped back and forth on the waxed parquet, and weakly strolled in the park! That French or Italian footwear of hers with three-inch heels not only incapacitated her but flattered her, and disguised her. Now her breasts seemed lower on her torso, out of the way of her nervous arms. Her hips were wide and her back powerful, with that curve from the shoulder blades to the head which you see in the nudes of Ingres. She walked with her legs well apart, one padding footfall after another, as impossible to trip up as a cat.

Suddenly she must have remembered that she had brought an extra leash but no extra hood. She hurried back along the water and across to the rustic bench, where she picked up the one Cullen had removed and let fall; then set out again, by the right bank, more slow and cat-like as she approached her quarry. What followed took only a few moments. We heard the falconer's cry: *hai, hai,* a desolate sound, which probably has not varied much in the three or four thousand years of falconry, for it is based on eternal acoustics, agreeable to the changeless ears of hawks. I loved to hear it. Lucy's head stirred swiftly around in response to it. I wanted her to cry back, *aik,* which she did not. They were too far away for us to see much. We saw the swing of Mrs. Cullen's arm as she tossed the piece of the pigeon over the hedge, toward the foot of the post; and after a breathless instant, we saw Lucy's descent upon it, down in one smooth rush, like a large, dusky, finished flower off its stem. Instantly the birdcatcher bent over, lurked along the hedge, and squattingly slipped around behind it. Then we had to wait, wait—until she briskly stood up and started back toward us with Lucy hooded on her wrist, where she belonged. Before hooding her, I suppose, she let her have a few good beakfuls of the unscheduled pigeon so that even this mishap or misdemeanor should be a lesson to her, as it was to us all in a sense.

Inside the house, before the great window, we were smiling from ear to ear, and murmuring or exclaiming each in his or her way. Only Cullen was deathly still, not even puffing. I moved far enough away from him to see his face, and found there, added to the bibulous pink, a pale light of wild relief, reprieve, even rapture, as if that horrid bird on his wife's arm returning to haunt him again had been his heart's desire. It was too much of a good thing; he was sober perhaps, but tormentedly sentimental; I should not have trusted him an instant.

Mrs. Cullen came down the left side of the pond, the long way. The sun, muffled all afternoon, was setting brightly. Some of its beams turned back up from the water, broken into a sparkle, through which we could not see her well. There were vague irises and something else up to her ankles; and branches of lilac occasionally hung between us and her. Her face looked to me calm, careless. Her hair still absurdly fell down one cheek; now and then she blew it out of her eyes. Dress disarranged and petticoat showing and stocking-feet and all, she walked back proudly, taking her time; a springy walk that reminded me of

Isadora Duncan.

The five of us happy onlookers trooped out on the lawn to meet her. "Isn't it wonderful?" she rejoiced. "You see, she's perfectly manned. She understands. Otherwise I could never have caught her. I'll be hunting with her in no time. Larry, go and find the other leash; which I left on the bench." And she decidedly emphasized the I. She too wished him not to admit what he had done.

He went meekly for the leash. The servants returned to the kitchen. Mrs. Cullen asked permission to retire and put herself to rights, declining Alex's offer of company and assistance. "No more weathering for you, my haggard Lucy," I heard her mutter as she left us.

I had not dared hope that Lucy—haggard that she was, with only two months of the least comfortable phase of captivity to look back upon, and none of the pleasure of the chase so far, and one toe still sore from the trap—would allow herself to be caught. That had made the little spectacle of her capture or surrender the more exciting for me. On the other hand I had not wanted her to escape. I had not pictured her setting out lonelily over Normandy toward Scotland, or whatever resort in the summer she might instinctively choose. Given my sentimental imagination, it was an odd lapse. And it made me aware of my really not wanting Larry Cullen to escape from Mrs. Cullen either, or vice versa. Perhaps I do not believe in liberty, or I regard it as only episodic in life; a circumstance that one must be able to bear and profit by when it occurs; a kind of necessary evil. When love itself is at stake, love of liberty as a rule is only fear of captivity.

Alex thought a drink would help at this juncture, and started to the balcony; but with one glance in Cullen's direction and another in mine, she returned and sat down. Cullen slumped in his armchair, gazing at apparently nothing, in that calm which is only the entire expenditure of energy; the coming down of a dull curtain upon the drama in head or heart. But probably it was only

entr'acte. There was something turgid if not turbulent
throughout his aging bulky frame; his jaws stirred a bit
in his double chin; his bloodshot eyes kept lighting up.

Then we heard a persistent ringing of the bell in Alex's
room, and Alex went anxiously to see what it meant, and
came back and informed us that Mrs. Cullen had decided
to return to town at once, before dinner. She had a brother
in Paris, and she had telephoned him; something had
gone wrong in Paris, and he needed her. I did not believe
a word of this, and Alex's expression confirmed my disbelief. Evidently it did not surprise Cullen. He sighed
hard, which perhaps referred to *pigeons aux groseilles;*
but he said nothing even about that.

Alex left it to me to inform Jean and Eva of the super-
fluity of their dinner. I could scarcely tell how Eva took
it, not well in any case: she gaped at me and fled to her
bedroom. Jean on the other hand chose to be superior and
calm. Something always went wrong, he observed, when
the English upper classes came to see poor Mademoiselle,
in their automobiles as big as busses driven by idiotic
little boys. In his opinion also the boy Ricketts had something to do with the escape of Madame Cullen's eagle. At
that moment the idiot was paying a visit to the *bistrot* or
bar at the corner. I let Jean go after him. The announcement of the Cullens' change of plan might somewhat relieve his evident personal desire to put him out of the
house.

Meanwhile with a certain simplicity our unhappy guests
gathered up their belongings here and there: severed leash
and mislaid lipstick and cigarette case with a diamond
button. As we waited in the hallway for the Daimler to be
brought around Mrs. Cullen quietly asked, "Dear Alex,
you don't need a new chauffeur, do you?"

As it happened Alex did need one. "What luck! I wish
you'd take Ricketts," Mrs. Cullen quietly continued. "I'll
be giving him notice when we get to Budapest. And I know
he hates Ireland, and he speaks quite decent French. He's

very good, very fast, and a mechanic and all that." And she recommended him in other particulars as well, including semi-genteel birth.

Cullen beside me was shuffling and loudly hemming, and at last could not hold his peace. "But Madeleine, really, my dear woman, you're fantastic. We've never had anybody as good as Ricketts. What in the world!"

Slightly embarrassed, Alex said that indeed they might have difficulty in finding a chauffeur in Hungary in summer; it should not be decided in haste on her account. Perhaps she sensed what was coming; I did.

"Oh, I shall easily find another," Mrs. Cullen said, "or I can do without. You see, Ricketts doesn't like Lucy. He laughs at me up his sleeve. I doubtless am an old fool, but I cannot have people around me who think so." She said this in a great sad false way; and it was unmistakably intended for her husband.

Again I could not see his banal but significant face when I wished, to read the emotion in it; we stood shoulder to shoulder facing our dear women. There was still some of that fine pre-bolshevik distillation on his somewhat accelerated and audible breath; but its troublesome effects must have passed. We all kept silent for a moment.

Mrs. Cullen was quite willing to look either of us in the eye; but her sparkle was all extinguished. It would have seemed healthier, more rational, if her eyes had looked angry; they looked nothing at all, nullified. Lucy was hooded now; under her mistress's chin the frivolous topknot on the stitched leather nodded very slightly; and Mrs. Cullen's crooked Irish face as a whole was not much more expressive than that. Her serenity, her stoical wit, her obscurity, were a sort of mental or moral craftsmanship; ornamentation. Inside all that, I suspected, her spirit was as bland as Lucy's. The point of not allowing a hawk to see is to keep it from being frightened; and I hoped that Mrs. Cullen's grand, mean manner served that purpose as well. I was afraid it did not.

Along the cobblestones under the plane trees I heard the Daimler come purring, not a moment too soon. By that time I also felt—as it seemed, aching in my bones and running in my veins and tempering my nerves—something like the mixture of hot and cold, good and bad, which troubled the difficult hearts of this odd couple.

Unrequited passion; romance put asunder by circumstances or mistakes; sexually pretending to be love—all that is a matter of little consequence, a mere voluntary temporary uneasiness, compared with the long course of true love, especially marriage. In marriage, insult arises again and again and again; and pain has to be not only endured, but consented to; and the amount of forgiveness that it necessitates is incredible and exhausting. When love has given satisfaction, then you discover how large a part of the rest of life is only payment for it, installment after installment . . . That was the one definite lesson which these petty scenes of the Cullens illustrated. Early in life I had learned it for myself well enough. It was on Alex's account that I minded. To see the cost of love before one has felt what it is worth, is a pity; one may never have the courage to begin.

There stood the Daimler; and Cullen and I helped Mrs. Cullen and Lucy up into it, while Ricketts, cap in hand, held the door. I observed that in fact Ricketts was laughing, in a silent subaltern way; but surely it was not at his mistress or her bird. Thin lips very red, rough eyelashes very shadowy: the effect of a Moorish-Italian kiss behind the kitchen door, I fancied. Or perhaps—for Cockneys are a malicious breed—the mere discomfiture of Jean amused him. He glanced over my shoulder, then up at a likely window, and so did I; but I did not discover the Mediterranean couple peeping out anywhere.

Neither the Cullens nor Alex and I had the heart for much repetition of farewell. Cullen had tears in his eyes. We turned back to the house and shut the door before Ricketts could get the long car out onto the highway, amid cars coming toward him from Paris.

There had been just time for us to reach the living room and sit down and light cigarettes, when we heard a fearful grinding of brakes; then several cars honking as in panic; and a Frenchman shouting the usual insults. A moment after, a car drove in under our plane trees. I got up and looked out a small window on that side: it was the Daimler.

Alex and I hastened back through the hall to see what had happened. There we heard Mrs. Cullen's voice, very loud and exclamatory but incomprehensible; and she was pushing the doorbell, rattling the doorknob, and calling, "Alex, Alex!" As I opened the door she stepped back, turning away from us, gesticulating and exclaiming, "No, Ricketts, stay where you are. Larry, please! Now wait for me, Ricketts. Oh, dear, you fool, you fool!"

She stumbled on the cobblestones; Lucy was having a hard time. Then she returned to us and grasped Alex's arm and motioned us back inside the house. "Don't get out of the car, Larry, I'll attend to it," she cried, over her shoulder.

"Alex, dear, I'm sorry, I've forgotten something. Poor damned fool," she repeated. By the heart-broken tone of her voice I judged that the fool was not Ricketts.

That young man was not laughing now, nor smacking his lips upon any recollection of pleasure or rivalry. His lips were white; he was badly frightened. The Daimler stood at a very odd angle between two trees; he must have made a U-turn on the highway. A little further along on the verge of a ditch stood an old Renault, with which, I supposed, they had narrowly escaped a collision. Its French driver stood beside it, still vehemently expressing himself, shaking his fist. But, oddly, neither the Cullens nor Ricketts even glanced in that Frenchman's direction. Something else must have happened; just before, just after, or at the same time. Inside the Daimler, Cullen had his great hand pressed over his mouth as if he were gnawing it, and

he too was pale: the worst pallor in the world, like cooked
veal. During the little drama of recapturing Lucy he had
ceased to be drunk, I thought. But now I was afraid that
he was going to be sick.

Alex and I followed Mrs. Cullen inside the house. She
too was in a worse emotion and looked worse than before.
Not only a portion of her lovely hair but her hat as well
this time, hung over one ear. There were beads of sweat
on her brow and her upper lip. "Oh, Alex, do forgive us,"
she kept saying, "I'm so ashamed, so ashamed;" and hurried past us into the living room.

Shame, I must say, was one thing which all this did not
suggest. Across that great expanse of waxed parquet toward the garden door she sped ahead of us—her pretty feet
on her too high heels wide apart, lest she skid and fall
headlong—saying to Alex over her shoulder, "Excuse me.
Please, dear. Don't mind me. Let me go into the garden
alone a minute."

On her wrist of course Lucy still perched, that is, rode,
with some difficulty: her green-gold feet also wide apart,
ducking or dipping to keep her balance, with characteristic
indignation of her shoulders and that nervous puffing of
breast-feathers which, as Mrs. Cullen had informed us, is
a good sign in a hunting hawk. Hawks are not really tree-
birds; and if in a state of nature Lucy had ever found
herself on a perch as agitated as this female arm, blown by
any such passionate wind as this, whatever this was—she
would have left it instantly and sought out a rock. It was
absurd. Even her little blind headgear with parrot feathers seemed to me absurd; it matched the French hat which
her mistress was wearing at so Irish an angle, except that
it was provided with secure drawstrings. In spite of my bewilderment and alarm, I began to laugh. It struck me as a
completion of the cycle of the afternoon, an end of the
sequence of meanings I had been reading into everything,
especially Lucy. The all-embracing symbolic bird; primitive image with iron wings and rusty tassels and enameled

feet; airy murderess like an angel; young predatory sanguinary de luxe hen—now she was funny; she had not
seemed funny before. Perhaps all pets, all domesticated
animals, no matter how ancient or beautiful or strange,
show a comic aspect sooner or later; a part of the shame
of our humanity that we gradually convey to them.

Just then I saw what Mrs. Cullen had in her right hand,
half concealed against her breast and behind Lucy's wing:
a large revolver. Alex must have seen it before I did. She
was clinging to my elbow and whispering, "Stay back.
Don't laugh, don't follow her."

I am not a judge of firearms, but this was a grim important object, glimmering, apparently brand-new and
in working order. "Shall I try to take it away from her?"
I asked Alex in a whisper.

"Heavens, no. She'll be all right. Don't worry her."
Women, even some young girls, have this ability to guess
at degrees of trouble; this equanimity of a trained nurse.
And, with or without much affection, they sometimes suddenly know each other as if they were twins.

There was more to it than that. Looking back on that
moment I have wondered just how her friend's passion
appeared to Alex. How could she tell, as the disheveled
creature fled ahead of us into the garden, that she was not
going to kill herself? Then it occurred to me that in my
friend's character and way of life in those days there was
a certain passivity; at least abstention from other's lives.
Whatever she did not understand about them might, she
felt, be more awful than anything she could imagine. If
others said that things were unbearable, she could well
believe it. If the Irishwoman's life had reached that point,
the point of suicide, I think she might not have cared to
interfere or prevent it.

Outside on the terrace Mrs. Cullen stopped; and grasping the gun by the barrel, brought it back over her shoulder and hurled it high above the shrubs, far across the
lawn, so that it splashed into the pond.

This important gesture was too much for Lucy. Off the dear wrist she went, hung in a paroxysm once more. But this time it was not bating, not mystical dread or symbolical love of liberty; it was just ordinary loss of balance. Symbol or no symbol, I said to myself, if I were busy getting rid of a suicidal or murderous weapon I should hate to have a heavy hysterical bird tied to me, yanking my wrist, flapping in my face. Mrs. Cullen, the good sportswoman, did not mind. Perhaps because of her own hysteria —the real meaning of this episode pulling at her heartstrings and beating upon her intellect—she merely did the thing to do, as usual. Up went her embattled left arm over her head; stock-still she stood, until terrible Lucy grew tired, and recovered her self-control, and resumed her domestication.

From our viewpoint, behind her, seeing her through the sunset-streaked window, against the background of the old park and the shrubs and the gray pond with ripples unclosing away from the place where the gun had gone down, Mrs. Cullen was beautiful. Throughout her somewhat bulky body—motherly torso and panting breasts and round neck—there was wonderful strength; and between her absurd high heels and her fist in the rough glove, there was exact perpendicularity: the yard-wind wings now settling back on top. And the fact that she looked a bit ridiculous, disheveled and second-rate and past her prime, made it all the finer, I thought, as she turned and came slowly back indoors.

There were tears in her eyes, but she chuckled, or pretended to, or tried to. "Darling Alex," she said hoarsely, "did you ever have guests who behaved so madly? Don't, please, don't ever ask me what this was all about."

Then in her way, in a series of little dull, prosaic, but shameless statements, she told us what it was about. "You see, dear, why we can't live in Ireland. It's such a bad example for my silly sons."

My presence did not make her shy. For a moment that

flattered me; upon second thought it seemed to me to have the opposite implication. Quite early in the afternoon, I suppose, she had perceived that Alex was not in love with me; therefore, in her view of life, I did not count, I was a supernumerary. What harm could I do with her secrets? Women are fantastic.

Holding her left arm and Lucy well out of the way, she threw her right arm somewhat around Alex and kissed her. "Dear, dear friend," she murmured. "You're so clever, you'll marry well when the time comes. Thank you so much for your patience with us." Alex shrank a little as she always did from female affection, but the odd compliment seemed to please her.

"Larry's been threatening to leave me for weeks," Mrs. Cullen added. "Oh, I'm so afraid he will one day. I don't know what would become of him by himself, the fool, the old darling."

Poor Larry, I sighed; poor supernumerary me! Women are no respecters of men. I also felt a little indignation on Lucy's account. Trapped out of the real wind and rock, and perverted rather than domesticated, kept blind and childish, at the mercy of every human absurdity, vodka and automobiles, guns and kisses: poor Lucy! She no doubt personified for Mrs. Cullen the deep problems of life; certainly. Mrs. Cullen now devoted a large part of her life to her. Yet again and again, splendid *falco's* position in fact, her proprietress's handling of her, was in the way of a handkerchief or a muff or a hat. Absorbed in her narration of what had just occurred on the highway in the Daimler, Mrs. Cullen forgot about her and gestured a little with her left hand as well as her right. Lucy had to embrace the air desperately to stabilize herself; her plumage all thickened up and homely, sick-looking. It afforded me an instant's characteristic grim amusement to think how often the great issues which I had taken this bird to augur, come down in fact to undignified appearance, petty neurasthenic anecdote; bring one in fact at last to a poor domestication like Lucy's. It also reminded me of the absurd position of the artist in the midst of the disorders of those who honor and support him, but who can scarcely be expected to keep quiet around him for art's sake.

"I don't even know which of us Larry thought of shooting," Mrs. Cullen said. "Wife or chauffeur or haggard. I dare say I never shall know, unless some day he does it. The minute you closed your door, he began saying things at the top of his voice about Lucy and Ricketts. It upset Ricketts, and there was a car coming toward us, and for a moment I really thought we would crash. I told Ricketts to stop at the side of the road, and instead he turned back here, with two other cars speeding around the corner. That was what made the little Frenchman in the Renault angry. In the midst of which poor Larry began to threaten us with the revolver. It was in the side pocket of the car. I can't imagine when he put it there, or where he got it. You know, I think the Frenchman saw it. Lucky for us he didn't call the police."

She began to have an almost cheerful expression. If you have been lonelily excited a long while, expecting the worst to happen, with no validation for your fear in fact, no excuse that others would understand—perhaps the trouble in question must always come as a slight relief. At least you know then that you have not morbidly made it all up out of whole cloth.

"I'll tell you an odd thing about myself," she said, with her vaguest smile. "I happen to be a very good shot; and d'you know, all the while I was trying to take that beastly gun away from Larry—with Ricketts driving like a fool, and poor Lucy on my arm so awfully in the way—I kept calculating every instant just where the bullet would go if he pulled the trigger. The trajectory and all that. I suppose I'm a born sportswoman; how childish it is! At the last moment I simply can't take things quite seriously. I suppose that's what made me good at lions in Kenya years ago."

She frowned and sighed then, as if ashamed of her coldness or lightheartedness. "Now Ricketts of course is quite out of patience with Larry. I suppose I shall have to give him notice; what a pity! If Larry wasn't quiet after I got out of the car, I expect Ricketts knocked him out. He did once before. There's nothing I can do; Larry is as strong as an ox. But I'd have gone mad, I'd have killed Ricketts— if I had waited to see what happened. Ricketts is so damned English; the instant he clenches his fist he makes a smug face, like a governess. But I say it's time to go back now; I've been cowardly long enough; perhaps at this point I can be of some comfort to my man."

She intended to give Alex another kiss, but Alex avoided it. "Oh, Alex, I do," she lamented, "do love that great fool desperately. Whatever shall I do with him? Oh, well, we'll see. Do you think I must get rid of Lucy? It was astonishing, you know, how well Larry hawked, last summer in Hungary. I thought he'd enjoy it so."

Then she laughed, and all afternoon I think she had not laughed; rather a bad sound, two loud liquid feverish notes. "Ho, ho, perhaps this may have done him good. He has bated, don't you know."

So she took her second departure. "Good-bye, Mr. Tower. Good-bye, Alex, dear child. I shall miss you. Larry will be ashamed to see you after all this, I'm afraid. Don't come out to the car; it would embarrass them." She slipped across the hall and out the door, opening it only a little and immediately slamming it.

"Well!" exclaimed Alex, as we returned to the living room, and her delivery of that syllable made me laugh: ooo-ell; the soft bark of a very small dog.

After so much disorder we thought it would be indiscreet to seem impatient for our dinner. We wandered into the garden, sighing, tired. "I hope Jean and Eva did not see this last bit of melodrama," Alex said. "It's not the kind of idea I should like him to get into his head and develop. He's no Cullen; he's an imitative Italian, and he might not muff it."

"That great comfortable greedy easy old boy," I mumbled, meaning Cullen. "Did you dream he had murder in him? Vodka or no vodka."

"But it was suicide surely, not murder," said Alex. "Madeleine Cullen has no imagination."

"I wonder. It overlaps in any case. People do kill themselves just because they want to murder someone," I replied in my quibbling way. "Someone they love."

Alex made a little face, expressive of skepticism of everything and practically universal disapproval. "You know, he wasn't really very drunk."

"Two shakerfuls of prewar vodka," I reminded her.

"No matter. That's not much for those immense Irishmen. I've seen him drunk and it wasn't anything like this. Or perhaps he pretended to be drunk for your benefit; and to have an excuse for what was happening anyway, what was bound to happen. You're such a sober creature, my dear; you naturally overestimate other people's intoxication."

Her saying that made me suddenly unhappy. I thought of the wicked way I had watched him as he drank, the grandiose theories of drunkenness I had spun for myself meanwhile; and I blushed. Half the time, I am afraid, my opinion of people is just guessing; cartooning. Again and again I give way to a kind of inexact and vengeful lyricism; I cannot tell what right I have to be avenged, and I am ashamed of it. Sometimes I entirely doubt my judgment in moral matters; and so long as I propose to be a storyteller, that is the whisper of the devil for me.

But my dear Alex then sensed, as a good young woman should, my doubt and weak self-criticism; and she smiled. "You must tell me what he said to you, before you forget it. I gathered from your expression that he'd been weeping on your shoulder."

Then Eva, with even less etiquette than usual, came out of the kitchen waving a napkin, huskily imploring us to hurry in to dinner, half-spoiled in any case, she thought. As if to point the moral of the changes of the day from a cook's angle, Jean sent in to us eight pigeons, a veritable sheaf of asparagus, and two good-sized tarts. It was perfect; and melodrama all afternoon evidently gave us appetite. Eva shed a sequence of tears as she served, mutely and prettily, with a wan smile whenever I looked at her, like a seventeenth-century Magdalen. Jean brought the tart himself and thanked us for our overeating, as if it had been a special effort to console him.

After he had served our coffee in the living room, I told Alex what I had seen from the kitchen window. I was surprised to learn that she too had seen it, from her bedroom window, while Mrs. Cullen lay stretched on the bed with her eyes shut. But she had missed the jackknife. Then I tried to remember and report to her Cullen's confession to me, man to man over our vodka, which entertained her, although I think it shocked her.

Then she went to write a note and send a telegram, and she did not return for three-quarters of an hour. I sat there by myself, not even trying to read. I was still excited; and I fell into a form of fatigued stupidity which, while it lasts, often seems to me an important intellectual effort. It was an effort to compress the excessive details of the afternoon into an abstraction or two, a formula of a moral; in order to store that away in my head for future use, and yet leave room for something new, for the next thing. Morally speaking, those Cullens had crowded me out of myself. I also hoped to distinguish a little more clearly between what the Cullens meant to me and certain fine points of my own meaning to myself which had fascinated me in the midst of their afternoon's performance. Of course it was not possible.

I have learned—but again and again I forget—that abstraction is a bad thing, innumerable and infinitesimal and tiresome; worse than any amount of petty fact. The emotion that comes blurring my retrospect is warmer and weaker than the excitement of whatever happened, good or bad. It is like a useless, fruitless vegetation, spreading and twining and fading and corrupting; even the ego disappears under it. . . . Therefore I scarcely noticed how long my dear friend stayed away in her bedroom; and therefore I was glad when she came back. For me, putting a stop to so-called thought is one of the functions of friendship.

It was not writing or telegraphing which had kept her; it was Eva weeping and denouncing Jean, laughing and worshiping Jean. They had quarreled about Ricketts, and after that he had gone to the village to get drunk. He would kill her, he had said, and sooner or later he might well, Eva thought; certainly he would beat her the minute he returned. He was the most jealous man alive, in her opinion, and she worshiped him.

In any case she was much to blame. She had a way of obviously reveling in the sense of her own beauty whenever a new man appeared in the kitchen; a look of being at the mercy of circumstances, or perhaps at the man's mercy. Neighbor or workman or tradesman would appear; and casually Eva would come up, and stand close by, with a sleepy stare, letting her eyes drop sideways in their wide sockets amid African eyelashes, giving off her sweetness like a flower bed—while Jean watched her, admiring and suffering, until his storm broke.

Alex had asked what made her behave so; why she flirted with men like Ricketts if she loved Jean and wanted to be at peace with him. Seriously she had explained that, when she flirted, it gave him a chance to come between her and the rival, which made her feel his love, and to that of course she promptly yielded; and her yielding also gave him assurance that she loved him. "And if you please, terrible female that she is," said Alex, "she laughed as she explained it, deep in her fat throat.

"But she would not go on laughing. This time, she thinks, it has gone too far. He will beat her, and he may kill her, and *tutti quanti*. Therefore she began to cry again, and she wanted to tell me their story again, from the beginning. I pretended to lose my temper and sent her to bed.

"I shall have to dismiss them, you know, if they go on like this," Alex added. "The lower classes have a way of making one ashamed of one's sex."

She always had trouble with servants. The trouble really was that her kind interest in them, if aroused at all, soon went too far. Shrinking from them, but pinned down by them at last, she gave a great deal of the warmth that lay in her. But between their demands upon her, she fancied that she had no sympathy for them at all. She often said that she wished she could be served by machinery.

The door stood open; but amid the breath of the garden, it seemed to me that I could detect, at least I could strongly remember, Lucy's little body odor of blood and honey. The talk of Jean and Eva and Ricketts had carried my imagination again to the Cullen triangle: the virtuous passionate hard-hearted woman, the sad man, and the bird; and I had a new notion. It was that Mrs. Cullen now loved Cullen less than she intended; and lived with him, lived for him, perhaps only to fulfil a dear bootless contract with herself. In any case she loved Lucy, and I hoped she would refuse to give her up.

In the garden, over by the kitchen door, we heard a few notes of mellow laughter. Jean had returned and it had not gone according to Eva's expectation. Laughter, and a rustle and scuffle—the make-believe fighting that when all goes well, relaxes and relieves the true struggle of love—and footsteps diminishing toward the far corner of the garden hidden by the plane trees. The moon that night was not a fine carved shape. It hung under a little loose cloud; only a piece of pallor, a bit of anti-darkness. The air was as warm as Tangier but one could not lie outdoors, I thought, for the grass would be splashed with dew.

"You'll never marry, dear," I said, to tease Alex. "Your

friend Mrs. Cullen thinks you will, but she has no imagination. You'll be afraid to, after this fantastic bad luck."

"What bad luck, if you please?" she inquired, smiling
to show that my mockery was welcome.

"Fantastic bad object lessons."

"You're no novelist," she said, to tease me. "I envy the
Cullens, didn't you know?" And I concluded from the
look on her face that she herself did not quite know
whether she meant it.

THE BEAR

. . . .

William Faulkner

William Faulkner

· ·

William Faulkner received the 1949 Nobel Prize for Literature. This award gave public recognition to work that he has produced steadily and with increasing mastery since 1924 when the *Marble Faun* was published. Born in 1897 in New Albany, Mississippi, Faulkner has spent much of his life in Oxford, Mississippi, a town and state he has helped make world-famous. Most of Faulkner's novels are available in Random House editions, in Modern Library and paper-cover reprints.

So much has recently been written explaining and explicating Faulkner's work that it seems pertinent to quote here the simple and exalting speech he made on receiving the Nobel Prize:

"I feel that this award was not made to me as a man, but to my work—a life's work in the agony and sweat of the human spirit, not for glory and least of all for profit, but to create out of the materials of the human spirit something which did not exist before. So this award is only mine in trust. It will not be difficult to find a dedication for the money part of it commensurate with the purpose and significance of its origin. But I would like to do the same with the acclaim too, by using this moment as a pinnacle from which I might be listened to by the young men and women already dedicated to the same anguish and travail, among whom is already that one who will some day stand here where I am standing.

"Our tragedy today is a general and universal physical fear so long sustained by now that we can even bear it. There are no longer problems of the spirit. There is only the question: When will I be blown up? Because of this, the young man or woman writing today has forgotten the problems of the human heart in conflict with itself which alone can make good writing because only that is worth writing about, worth the agony and the sweat.

"He must learn them again. He must teach himself that the basest of all things is to be afraid; and, teaching himself that, forget it forever, leaving no room in his workshop for anything but the old verities and truths of the heart, the old universal truths lacking which any story is ephemeral and doomed—love and honor and pity and pride and compassion and sacrifice. Until he does so, he labors under a curse. He writes not of love but of lust, of defeats in which nobody loses anything of value, of victories without hope and, worst of all, without pity or compassion. His griefs grieve on no universal bones, leaving no scars. He writes not of the heart but of the glands.

"Until he relearns these things, he will write as though he stood among and watched the end of man. I decline to accept the end of man. It is easy enough to say that man is immortal simply because he will endure: that when the last ding-dong of doom has clanged and faded from the last worthless rock hanging tideless in the last red and dying evening, that even then there will still be one more sound: that of his puny inexhaustible voice, still talking. I refuse to accept this. I believe that man will not merely endure: he will prevail. He is immortal, not because he alone among creatures has an inexhaustible voice, but because he has a soul, a spirit capable of compassion and sacrifice and endurance. The poet's, the writer's, duty is to write about these things. It is his privilege to help man endure by lifting his heart, by reminding him of the courage and honor and hope and pride and compassion and pity and sacrifice which have been the glory of his past. The poet's voice need not merely be the record of man, it can be one of the props, the pillars to help him endure and prevail."

10 December 1950

THE BEAR

THERE WAS a man and a dog too this time. Two beasts, counting Old Ben, the bear, and two men, counting Boon Hogganbeck, in whom some of the same blood ran which ran in Sam Fathers, even though Boon's was a plebeian strain of it and only Sam and Old Ben and the mongrel Lion were taintless and incorruptible.

He was sixteen. For six years now he had been a man's hunter. For six years now he had heard the best of all talking. It was of the wilderness, the big woods, bigger and older than any recorded document:—of white man fatuous enough to believe he had bought any fragment of it, of Indian ruthless enough to pretend that any fragment of it had been his to convey; bigger than Major de Spain and the scrap he pretended to, knowing better; older than old Thomas Sutpen of whom Major de Spain had had it and who knew better; older even than old Ikkemotubbe, the Chickasaw chief, of whom old Sutpen had had it and who knew better in his turn. It was of the men, not white nor black nor red but men, hunters, with the will and hardihood to endure and the humility and skill to survive, and the dogs and the bear and deer juxtaposed and reliefed against it, ordered and compelled by and within the wilderness in the ancient and unremitting contest according to the ancient and immitigable rules which voided all regrets and brooked no quarter;—the best game of all, the best of all breathing and forever the best of all listening, the voices quiet and weighty and deliberate for retrospection and recollection and exactitude among the concrete trophies—the racked guns and the heads and skins—in the libraries of town houses or the offices of plantation houses or (and best of all) in the camps themselves where the intact and still-warm meat yet hung, the men who had slain it sitting before the burning logs on hearths when there were houses and hearths or about the smoky blazing of piled wood in front of stretched tarpaulins when there were not. There was always a bottle present, so that it would seem to him that those fine fierce instants of heart and brain and courage and wiliness and speed were concentrated and distilled into that brown liquor which not women, not boys and children, but only hunters drank, drinking not of the blood they spilled but some condensation of the wild immortal spirit, drinking it moderately, humbly even, not with the pagan's base and baseless hope of acquiring thereby the virtues of cunning and strength and speed but in salute to them. Thus it seemed to him on this December morning not only natural but actually fitting that this should have begun with whisky.

He realised later that it had begun long before that. It had already begun on that day when he first wrote his age in two ciphers and his cousin McCaslin brought him for the first time to the camp, the big woods, to earn for himself from the wilderness the name and state of hunter provided he in his turn were humble and enduring enough. He had already inherited then, without ever having seen it, the big old bear with one trap-ruined foot that in an area almost a hundred miles square had earned for himself a name, a definite designation like a living man:—the long legend of corncribs broken down and rifled, of shoats and grown pigs and even calves carried bodily into the woods and devoured and traps and deadfalls overthrown and dogs mangled and slain and shotgun and even rifle shots delivered at point-blank range yet with no more effect than so many peas blown through a tube by a child—a corridor of wreckage and destruction beginning back before the boy was born, through which sped, not fast but rather with the ruthless and irresistible deliberation of a locomotive, the shaggy tremendous shape. It ran in his knowledge before he ever saw it. It loomed and towered in his dreams before he even saw the unaxed woods where it left its crooked print, shaggy, tremendous, red-eyed, not malevolent but just big, too big for the dogs which tried to bay it, for the horses which tried to ride it down, for the men and the bullets they fired into it; too big for the very country which was its constricting scope. It was as if the boy had already divined what his senses and intellect had not encompassed yet: that doomed wilderness whose edges were being constantly and punily gnawed at by men with plows and axes who feared it because it was wilderness, men myriad and nameless even to one another in the land where the old bear had earned a name, and through which ran not even a mortal beast but an anachronism indomitable and invincible out of an old dead time, a phantom, epitome and apotheosis of the old wild life which the little puny humans swarmed and hacked at in a fury of abhorrence and fear like pygmies about the ankles of a drowsing elephant;—the old bear, solitary, indomitable, and alone; widowered childless and absolved of mortality—old Priam reft of his old wife and outlived all his sons.

Still a child, with three years then two years then one year yet before he too could make one of them, each November he would watch the wagon containing the dogs and the bedding and food and guns and his cousin Mc-Caslin and Tennie's Jim and Sam Fathers too until Sam moved to the camp to live, depart for the Big Bottom, the big woods. To him, they were going not to hunt bear and deer but to keep yearly rendezvous with the bear which they did not even intend to kill. Two weeks later they would return, with no trophy, no skin. He had not expected it. He had not even feared that it might be in the wagon this time with the other skins and heads. He did not even tell himself that in three years or two years or one year more he would be present and that it might even be his gun. He believed that only after he had served his apprenticeship in the woods which would prove him worthy to be a hunter, would he even be permitted to dis-

tinguish the crooked print, and that even then for two
November weeks he would merely make another minor
one, along with his cousin and Major de Spain and General Compson and Walter Ewell and Boon and the dogs
which feared to bay it and the shotguns and rifles which
failed even to bleed it, in the yearly pageant-rite of the old
bear's furious immortality.

His day came at last. In the surrey with his cousin and
Major de Spain and General Compson he saw the wilderness through a slow drizzle of November rain just above
the ice point as it seemed to him later he always saw it or
at least always remembered it—the tall and endless wall
of dense November woods under the dissolving afternoon
and the year's death, sombre, impenetrable (he could not
even discern yet how, at what point they could possibly
hope to enter it even though he knew that Sam Fathers
was waiting there with the wagon), the surrey moving
through the skeleton stalks of cotton and corn in the last
of open country, the last trace of man's puny gnawing at
the immemorial flank, until, dwarfed by that perspective
into an almost ridiculous diminishment, the surrey itself
seemed to have ceased to move (this too to be completed
later, years later, after he had grown to a man and had
seen the sea) as a solitary small boat hangs in lonely immobility, merely tossing up and down, in the infinite waste
of the ocean while the water and then the apparently impenetrable land which it nears without appreciable progress, swings slowly and opens the widening inlet which is
the anchorage. He entered it. Sam was waiting, wrapped
in a quilt on the wagon seat behind the patient and steaming mules. He entered his novitiate to the true wilderness
with Sam beside him as he had begun his apprenticeship
in miniature to manhood after the rabbits and such with
Sam beside him, the two of them wrapped in the damp,
warm Negro-rank quilt while the wilderness closed behind
his entrance as it had opened momentarily to accept him,
opening before his advancement as it closed behind his

progress, no fixed path the wagon followed but a channel nonexistent ten yards ahead of it and ceasing to exist ten yards after it had passed, the wagon progressing not by its own volition but by attrition of their intact yet fluid circumambience, drowsing, earless, almost lightless.

It seemed to him that at the age of ten he was witnessing his own birth. It was not even strange to him. He had experienced it all before, and not merely in dreams. He saw the camp—a paintless six-room bungalow set on piles above the spring high-water—and he knew already how it was going to look. He helped in the rapid orderly disorder of their establishment in it and even his motions were familiar to him, foreknown. Then for two weeks he ate the coarse, rapid food—the shapeless sour bread, the wild strange meat, venison and bear and turkey and coon which he had never tasted before—which men ate, cooked by men who were hunters first and cooks afterward; he slept in harsh sheetless blankets as hunters slept. Each morning the gray of dawn found him and Sam Fathers on the stand, the crossing, which had been allotted him. It was the poorest one, the most barren. He had expected that; he had not dared yet to hope even to himself that he would even hear the running dogs this first time. But he did hear them. It was on the third morning—a murmur, sourceless, almost indistinguishable, yet he knew what it was although he had never before heard that many dogs running at once, the murmur swelling into separate and distinct voices until he could call the five dogs which his cousin owned from among the others. "Now," Sam said, "slant your gun up a little and draw back the hammers and then stand still."

But it was not for him, not yet. The humility was there; he had learned that. And he could learn the patience. He was only ten, only one week. The instant had passed. It seemed to him that he could actually see the deer, the buck, smoke-colored, elongated with speed, vanished, the woods, the gray solitude still ringing even when the voices of the dogs had died away; from far away across the sombre woods

and the gray half-liquid morning there came two shots.
"Now let your hammers down," Sam said.

He did so. "You knew it too," he said.

"Yes," Sam said. "I want you to learn how to do when
you didn't shoot. It's after the chance for the bear or the
deer has done already come and gone that men and dogs
get killed."

"Anyway, it wasn't him," the boy said. "It wasn't even
a bear. It was just a deer."

"Yes," Sam said, "it was just a deer."

Then one morning, it was in the second week, he heard
the dogs again. This time before Sam even spoke he
readied the too-long, too-heavy, man-size gun as Sam had
taught him, even though this time he knew the dogs and
the deer were coming less close than ever, hardly within
hearing even. They didn't sound like any running dogs
he had ever heard before even. Then he found that Sam,
who had taught him first of all to cock the gun and take
position where he could see best in all directions and then
never to move again, had himself moved up beside him.
"There," he said. "Listen." The boy listened, to no ringing chorus strong and fast on a free scent but a moiling
yapping an octave too high and with something more
than indecision and even abjectness in it which he could
not yet recognise, reluctant, not even moving very fast,
taking a long time to pass out of hearing, leaving even
then in the air that echo of thin and almost human hysteria, abject, almost humanly grieving, with this time nothing ahead of it, no sense of a fleeing unseen smoke-colored
shape. He could hear Sam breathing at his shoulder. He
saw the arched curve of the old man's inhaling nostrils.

"It's Old Ben!" he cried, whispering.

Sam didn't move save for the slow gradual turning of
his head as the voices faded on and the faint steady rapid
arch and collapse of his nostrils. "Hah," he said. "Not even
running. Walking."

"But up here!" the boy cried. "Way up here!"

"He do it every year," Sam said. "Once. Ash and Boon say he comes up here to run the other little bears away. Tell them to get to hell out of here and stay out until the hunters are gone. Maybe." The boy no longer heard anything at all, yet still Sam's head continued to turn gradually and steadily until the back of it was toward him. Then it turned back and looked down at him—the same face, grave, familiar, expressionless until it smiled, the same old man's eyes from which as he watched there faded slowly a quality darkly and fiercely lambent, passionate and proud. "He dont care no more for bears than he does for dogs or men neither. He come to see who's here, who's new in camp this year, whether he can shoot or not, can stay or not. Whether we got the dog yet that can bay and hold him until a man gets there with a gun. Because he's the head bear. He's the man." It faded, was gone; again they were the eyes as he had known them all his life. "He'll let them follow him to the river. Then he'll send them home. We might as well go too; see how they look when they get back to camp."

The dogs were there first, ten of them huddled back under the kitchen, himself and Sam squatting to peer back into the obscurity where they crouched, quiet, the eyes rolling and luminous, vanishing, and no sound, only that effluvium which the boy could not quite place yet, of something more than dog, stronger than dog and not just animal, just beast even. Because there had been nothing in front of the abject and painful yapping except the solitude, the wilderness, so that when the eleventh hound got back about midafternoon and he and Tennie's Jim held the passive and still trembling bitch while Sam daubed her tattered ear and raked shoulder with turpentine and axle-grease, it was still no living creature but only the wilderness which, leaning for a moment, had patted lightly once her temerity. "Just like a man," Sam said. "Just like folks. Put off as long as she could having to be brave, knowing all the time that sooner or later she would have to be brave once so she could keep on calling herself a dog, and knowing beforehand what was going to happen when she done it.''

He did not know just when Sam left. He only knew that he was gone. For the next three mornings he rose and ate breakfast and Sam was not waiting for him. He went to his stand alone; he found it without help now and stood on it as Sam had taught him. On the third morning he heard the dogs again, running strong and free on a true scent again, and he readied the gun as he had learned to do and heard the hunt sweep past on since he was not ready yet, had not deserved other yet in just one short period of two weeks as compared to all the long life which he had already dedicated to the wilderness with patience and humility; he heard the shot again, one shot, the single clapping report of Walter Ewell's rifle. By now he could not only find his stand and then return to camp without guidance, by using the compass his cousin had given him he reached Walter waiting beside the buck and the moiling of dogs over the cast entrails before any of the others except Major de Spain and Tennie's Jim on the horses, even before Uncle Ash arrived with the one-eyed wagon-mule which did not mind the smell of blood or even, so they said, of bear.

It was not Uncle Ash on the mule. It was Sam, returned. And Sam was waiting when he finished his dinner and, himself on the one-eyed mule and Sam on the other one of the wagon team, they rode for more than three hours through the rapid shortening sunless afternoon, following no path, no trail even that he could discern, into a section of country he had never seen before. Then he understood why Sam had made him ride the one-eyed mule which would not spook at the smell of blood, of wild animals. The other one, the sound one, stopped short and tried to whirl and bolt even as Sam got down, jerking and wrenching at the rein while Sam held it, coaxing it forward with his voice since he did not dare risk hitching it, drawing it forward while the boy dismounted from the marred one which would stand. Then, standing beside Sam in the thick great gloom of ancient woods and the winter's dying afternoon, he looked quietly down at the rotted log scored and gutted with claw-marks and, in the wet earth beside it, the print of the enormous warped two-toed foot. Now he knew what he had heard in the hounds' voices in the woods that morning and what he had smelled when he peered under the kitchen where they huddled. It was in him too, a little different because they were brute beasts and he was not, but only a little different—an eagerness, passive; an abjectness, a sense of his own fragility and impotence against the timeless woods, yet without doubt or dread; a flavor like brass in the sudden run of saliva in his mouth, a hard sharp constriction either in his brain or his stomach, he could not tell which and it did not matter; he knew only that for the first time he realised that the bear which had run in his listening and loomed in his dreams since before he could remember and which therefore must have existed in the listening and the dreams of his cousin and Major de Spain and even old General Compson before they began to remember in their turn, was a mortal animal and that they had departed for the camp each November with no actual intention of slaying it, not because it could not be slain but because so far they had no actual hope of being able to. "It will be tomorrow," he said.

"You mean we will try tomorrow," Sam said. "We aint got the dog yet."

"We've got eleven," he said. "They ran him Monday."

"And you heard them," Sam said. "Saw them too. We aint got the dog yet. It wont take but one. But he aint there. Maybe he aint nowhere. The only other way will be for him to run by accident over somebody that had a gun and knowed how to shoot it."

"That wouldn't be me," the boy said. "It would be Walter or Major or—"

"It might," Sam said. "You watch close tomorrow. Be-

cause he's smart. That's how come he has lived this long.
If he gets hemmed up and has got to pick out somebody
to run over, he will pick out you."

"How?" he said. "How will he know. . . ." He ceased.
"You mean he already knows me, that I aint never been
to the big bottom before, aint had time to find out yet
whether I . . ." He ceased again, staring at Sam; he said
humbly, not even amazed: "It was me he was watching. I
dont reckon he did need to come but once."

"You watch tomorrow," Sam said. "I reckon we better
start back. It'll be long after dark now before we get to
camp."

The next morning they started three hours earlier than
they had ever done. Even Uncle Ash went, the cook, who
called himself by profession a camp cook and who did
little else save cook for Major de Spain's hunting and
camping parties, yet who had been marked by the wilderness from simple juxtaposition to it until he responded as
they all did, even the boy who until two weeks ago had
never even seen the wilderness, to a hound's ripped ear
and shoulder and the print of a crooked foot in a patch of
wet earth. They rode. It was too far to walk: the boy and
Sam and Uncle Ash in the wagon with the dogs, his cousin
and Major de Spain and General Compson and Boon and
Walter and Tennie's Jim riding double on the horses;
again the first gray light found him, as on that first morning two weeks ago, on the stand where Sam had placed and
left him. With the gun which was too big for him, the
breech-loader which did not even belong to him but to
Major de Spain and which he had fired only once, at a
stump on the first day to learn the recoil and how to reload
it with the paper shells, he stood against a big gum tree
beside a little bayou whose black still water crept without
motion out of a cane-brake, across a small clearing and
into the cane again, where, invisible, a bird, the big woodpecker called Lord-to-God by Negroes, clattered at a dead
trunk. It was a stand like any other stand, dissimilar only

in incidentals to the one where he had stood each morning for two weeks; a territory new to him yet no less familiar than that other one which after two weeks he had come to believe he knew a little—the same solitude, the same loneliness through which frail and timorous man had merely passed without altering it, leaving no mark nor scar, which looked exactly as it must have looked when the first ancestor of Sam Fathers' Chickasaw predecessors crept into it and looked about him, club or stone axe or bone arrow drawn and ready, different only because, squatting at the edge of the kitchen, he had smelled the dogs huddled and cringing beneath it and saw the raked ear and side of the bitch that, as Sam had said, had to be brave once in order to keep on calling herself a dog, and saw yesterday in the earth beside the gutted log, the print of the living foot. He heard no dogs at all. He never did certainly hear them. He only heard the drumming of the woodpecker stop short off, and knew that the bear was looking at him. He never saw it. He did not know whether it was facing him from the cane or behind him. He did not move, holding the useless gun which he knew now he would never fire at it, now or ever, tasting in his saliva that taint of brass which he had smelled in the huddled dogs when he peered under the kitchen.

Then it was gone. As abruptly as it had stopped, the woodpecker's dry hammering set up again, and after a while he believed he even heard the dogs—a murmur, scarce a sound even, which he had probably been hearing for a time, perhaps a minute or two, before he remarked it, drifting into hearing and then out again, dying away. They came nowhere near him. If it was dogs he heard, he could not have sworn to it; if it was a bear they ran, it was another bear. It was Sam himself who emerged from the cane and crossed the bayou, the injured bitch following at heel as a bird dog is taught to walk. She came and crouched against his leg, trembling. "I didn't see him," he said. "I didn't, Sam."

"I know it," Sam said. "He done the looking. You didn't
hear him neither, did you?"

"No," the boy said. "I—"

"He's smart," Sam said. "Too smart." Again the boy saw
in his eyes that quality of dark and brooding lambence as
Sam looked down at the bitch trembling faintly and steadily against the boy's leg. From her raked shoulder a few
drops of fresh blood clung like bright berries. "Too big.
We aint got the dog yet. But maybe some day."

Because there would be a next time, after and after. He
was only ten. It seemed to him that he could see them, the
two of them, shadowy in the limbo from which time
emerged and became time: the old bear absolved of mortality and himself who shared a little of it. Because he
recognised now what he had smelled in the huddled dogs
and tasted in his own saliva, recognised fear as a boy, a
youth, recognises the existence of love and passion and
experience which is his heritage but not yet his patrimony,
from entering by chance the presence or perhaps even
merely the bedroom of a woman who has loved and been
loved by many men. *So I will have to see him,* he thought,
without dread or even hope. *I will have to look at him.* So
it was in June of the next summer. They were at the camp
again, celebrating Major de Spain's and General Compson's birthdays. Although the one had been born in September and the other in the depth of winter and almost
thirty years earlier, each June the two of them and McCaslin and Boon and Walter Ewell (and the boy too from
now on) spent two weeks at the camp, fishing and shooting
squirrels and turkey and running coons and wildcats with
the dogs at night. That is, Boon and the Negroes (and the
boy too now) fished and shot squirrels and ran the coons
and cats, because the proven hunters, not only Major de
Spain and old General Compson (who spent those two
weeks sitting in a rocking chair before a tremendous iron
pot of Brunswick stew, stirring and tasting, with Uncle
Ash to quarrel with about how he was making it and

Tennie's Jim to pour whisky into the tin dipper from which he drank it) but even McCaslin and Walter Ewell who were still young enough, scorned such other than shooting the wild gobblers with pistols for wagers or to test their marksmanship.

That is, his cousin McCaslin and the others thought he was hunting squirrels. Until the third evening he believed that Sam Fathers thought so too. Each morning he would leave the camp right after breakfast. He had his own gun now, a new breech-loader, a Christmas gift; he would own and shoot it for almost seventy years, through two new pairs of barrels and locks and one new stock, until all that remained of the original gun was the silver-inlaid trigger-guard with his and McCaslin's engraved names and the date in 1878. He found the tree beside the little bayou where he had stood that morning. Using the compass he ranged from that point; he was teaching himself to be better than a fair woodsman without even knowing he was doing it. On the third day he even found the gutted log where he had first seen the print. It was almost completely crumbled now, healing with unbelievable speed, a passionate and almost visible relinquishment, back into the earth from which the tree had grown. He ranged the summer woods now, green with gloom, if anything actually dimmer than they had been in November's gray dissolution, where even at noon the sun fell only in windless dappling upon the earth which never completely dried and which crawled with snakes—moccasins and watersnakes and rattlers, themselves the color of the dappled gloom so that he would not always see them until they moved; returning to camp later and later and later, first day, second day, passing in the twilight of the third evening the little log pen enclosing the log barn where Sam was putting up the stock for the night. "You aint looked right yet," Sam said.

He stopped. For a moment he didn't answer. Then he said peacefully, in a peaceful rushing burst, as when a boy's miniature dam in a little brook gives way: "All right. Yes. But how? I went to the bayou. I even found that log again. I—"

"I reckon that was all right. Likely he's been watching you. You never saw his foot?"

"I . . ." the boy said. "I didn't . . . I never thought . . ."

"It's the gun," Sam said. He stood beside the fence, motionless, the old man, son of a Negro slave and a Chickasaw chief, in the battered and faded overalls and the frayed five-cent straw hat which had been the badge of the Negro's slavery and was now the regalia of his freedom. The camp—the clearing, the house, the barn and its tiny lot with which Major de Spain in his turn had scratched punily and evanescently at the wilderness—faded in the dusk, back into the immemorial darkness of the woods. *The gun*, the boy thought. *The gun*. "You will have to choose," Sam said.

He left the next morning before light, without breakfast, long before Uncle Ash would wake in his quilts on the kitchen floor and start the fire. He had only the compass and a stick for the snakes. He could go almost a mile before he would need to see the compass. He sat on a log, the invisible compass in his hand, while the secret night-sounds which had ceased at his movements, scurried again and then fell still for good and the owls ceased and gave over to the waking day birds and there was light in the gray wet woods and he could see the compass. He went fast yet still quietly, becoming steadily better and better as a woodsman without yet having time to realise it; he jumped a doe and a fawn, walked them out of the bed, close enough to see them—the crash of undergrowth, the white scut, the fawn scudding along behind her, faster than he had known it could have run. He was hunting right, upwind, as Sam had taught him, but that didn't matter now. He had left the gun; by his own will and relinquishment he had accepted not a gambit, not a choice, but a condition in which not only the bear's heretofore inviolable anonymity but all the ancient rules and balances of hunter and hunted had been abrogated. He would not even be afraid, not even in the moment when the fear would take him completely: blood, skin, bowels, bones, memory from the long time before it even became his memory—all save that thin clear quenchless lucidity which alone differed him from this bear and from all the other bears and bucks he would follow during almost seventy years, to which Sam had said: "Be scared. You cant help that. But dont be afraid. Aint nothing in the woods going to hurt you if you dont corner it or it dont smell that you are afraid. A bear or a deer has got to be scared of a coward the same as a brave man has got to be."

By noon he was far beyond the crossing on the little bayou, farther into the new and alien country than he had ever been, traveling now not only by the compass but by the old, heavy, biscuit-thick silver watch which had been his father's. He had left the camp nine hours ago; nine hours from now, dark would already have been an hour old. He stopped, for the first time since he had risen from the log when he could see the compass face at last, and looked about, mopping his sweating face on his sleeve. He had already relinquished, of his will, because of his need, in humility and peace and without regret, yet apparently that had not been enough, the leaving of the gun was not enough. He stood for a moment—a child, alien and lost in the green and soaring gloom of the markless wilderness. Then he relinquished completely to it. It was the watch and the compass. He was still tainted. He removed the linked chain of the one and the looped thong of the other from his overalls and hung them on a bush and leaned the stick beside them and entered it.

When he realised he was lost, he did as Sam had coached and drilled him: made a cast to cross his backtrack. He had not been going very fast for the last two or three hours, and he had gone even less fast since he left the compass and watch on the bush. So he went slower still now, since the tree could not be very far; in fact, he found it before he really expected to and turned and went to it. But there was no bush beneath it, no compass nor watch, so he did next as Sam had coached and drilled him: made this next circle in the opposite direction and much larger, so that the pattern of the two of them would bisect his track somewhere, but crossing no trace nor mark anywhere of his feet or any feet, and now he was going faster though still not panicked, his heart beating a little more rapidly but strong and steady enough, and this time it was not even the tree because there was a down log beside it which he had never seen before and beyond the log a little swamp, a seepage of moisture somewhere between earth and water, and he did what Sam had coached and drilled him as the next and the last, seeing as he sat down on the log the crooked print, the warped indentation in the wet ground which while he looked at it continued to fill with water until it was level full and the water began to overflow and the sides of the print began to dissolve away. Even as he looked up he saw the next one, and, moving, the one beyond it; moving, not hurrying, running, but merely keeping pace with them as they appeared before him as though they were being shaped out of thin air just one constant pace short of where he would lose them forever and be lost forever himself, tireless, eager, without doubt or dread, panting a little above the strong rapid little hammer of his heart, emerging suddenly into a little glade and the wilderness coalesced. It rushed, soundless, and solidified—the tree, the bush, the compass and the watch glinting where a ray of sunlight touched them. Then he saw the bear. It did not emerge, appear: it was just there, immobile, fixed in the green and windless noon's hot dappling, not as big as he had dreamed it but as big as he had expected, bigger, dimensionless against the dappled obscurity, looking at him. Then it moved. It crossed the glade without haste, walking for an instant into the sun's full glare and out of it, and stopped again and looked back at him across one shoulder. Then it was gone. It didn't walk into the woods. It faded, sank back into the wilderness without motion as he had watched a fish, a huge old bass, sink back into the dark depths of its pool and vanish without even any movement of its fins.

—2—

So he should have hated and feared Lion. He was thirteen then. He had killed his buck and Sam Fathers had marked his face with the hot blood, and in the next November he killed a bear. But before that accolade he had become as competent in the woods as many grown men with the same experience. By now he was a better woodsman than most grown men with more. There was no territory within twenty-five miles of the camp that he did not know—bayou, ridge, landmark trees and path; he could have led anyone direct to any spot in it and brought him back. He knew game trails that even Sam Fathers had never seen; in the third fall he found a buck's bedding-place by himself and unbeknown to his cousin he borrowed Walter Ewell's rifle and lay in wait for the buck at dawn and killed it when it walked back to the bed as Sam had told him how the old Chickasaw fathers did.

By now he knew the old bear's footprint better than he did his own, and not only the crooked one. He could see any one of the three sound prints and distinguish it at once from any other, and not only because of its size. There were other bears within that fifty miles which left tracks almost as large, or at least so near that the one would have appeared larger only by juxtaposition. It was more than that. If Sam Fathers had been his mentor and the backyard rabbits and squirrels his kindergarten, then the wilderness the old bear ran was his college and the old male bear itself, so long unwifed and childless as to have become its own ungendered progenitor, was his alma mater.

He could find the crooked print now whenever he

wished, ten miles or five miles or sometimes closer than that, to the camp. Twice while on stand during the next three years he heard the dogs strike its trail and once even jump it by chance, the voices high, abject, almost human in their hysteria. Once, still-hunting with Walter Ewell's rifle, he saw it cross a long corridor of down timber where a tornado had passed. It rushed through rather than across the tangle of trunks and branches as a locomotive would, faster than he had ever believed it could have moved, almost as fast as a deer even because the deer would have spent most of that distance in the air; he realised then why it would take a dog not only of abnormal courage but size and speed too ever to bring it to bay. He had a little dog at home, a mongrel, of the sort called fyce by Negroes, a ratter, itself not much bigger than a rat and possessing that sort of courage which had long since stopped being bravery and had become foolhardiness. He brought it with him one June and, timing them as if they were meeting an appointment with another human being, himself carrying the fyce with a sack over its head and Sam Fathers with a brace of the hounds on a rope leash, they lay downwind of the trail and actually ambushed the bear. They were so close that it turned at bay although he realised later this might have been from surprise and amazement at the shrill and frantic uproar of the fyce. It turned at bay against the trunk of a big cypress, on its hind feet; it seemed to the boy that it would never stop rising, taller and taller, and even the two hounds seemed to have taken a kind of desperate and despairing courage from the fyce. Then he realised that the fyce was actually not going to stop. He flung the gun down and ran. When he overtook and grasped the shrill, frantically pinwheeling little dog, it seemed to him that he was directly under the bear. He could smell it, strong and hot and rank. Sprawling, he looked up where it loomed and towered over him like a thunderclap. It was quite familiar, until he remembered: this was the way he had used to dream about it.

Then it was gone. He didn't see it go. He knelt, holding the frantic fyce with both hands, hearing the abased wailing of the two hounds drawing further and further away, until Sam came up, carrying the gun. He laid it quietly down beside the boy and stood looking down at him. "You've done seed him twice now, with a gun in your hands," he said. "This time you couldn't have missed him."

The boy rose. He still held the fyce. Even in his arms it continued to yap frantically, surging and straining toward the fading sound of the hounds like a collection of live-wire springs. The boy was panting a little. "Neither could you," he said. "You had the gun. Why didn't you shoot him?"

Sam didn't seem to have heard. He put out his hand and touched the little dog in the boy's arms which still yapped and strained even though the two hounds were out of hearing now. "He's done gone," Sam said. "You can slack off and rest now, until next time." He stroked the little dog until it began to grow quiet under his hand. "You's almost the one we wants," he said. "You just aint big enough. We aint got that one yet. He will need to be just a little bigger than smart, and a little braver than either." He withdrew his hand from the fyce's head and stood looking into the woods where the bear and the hounds had vanished. "Somebody is going to, some day."

"I know it," the boy said. "That's why it must be one of us. So it wont be until the last day. When even he dont want it to last any longer."

So he should have hated and feared Lion. It was in the fourth summer, the fourth time he had made one in the celebration of Major de Spain's and General Compson's birthday. In the early spring Major de Spain's mare had foaled a horse colt. One evening when Sam brought the horses and mules up to stable them for the night, the colt was missing and it was all he could do to get the frantic mare into the lot. He had thought at first to let the mare lead him back to where she had become separated from the foal. But she would not do it. She would not even feint toward any particular part of the woods or even in any particular direction. She merely ran, as if she couldn't see, still frantic with terror. She whirled and ran at Sam once, as if to attack him in some ultimate desperation, as if she could not for the moment realise that he was a man and a long-familiar one. He got her into the lot at last. It was too dark by that time to back-track her, to unravel the erratic course she had doubtless pursued.

He came to the house and told Major de Spain. It was an animal, of course, a big one, and the colt was dead now, wherever it was. They all knew that. "It's a panther," General Compson said at once. "The same one. That doe and fawn last March." Sam had sent Major de Spain word of it when Boon Hogganbeck came to the camp on a routine visit to see how the stock had wintered—the doe's throat torn out, and the beast had run down the helpless fawn and killed it too.

"Sam never did say that was a panther," Major de Spain said. Sam said nothing now, standing behind Major de Spain where they sat at supper, inscrutable, as if he were just waiting for them to stop talking so he could go home. He didn't even seem to be looking at anything. "A panther might jump a doe, and he wouldn't have much trouble catching the fawn afterward. But no panther would have jumped that colt with the dam right there with it. It was Old Ben," Major de Spain said. "I'm disappointed in him. He has broken the rules. I didn't think he would have done that. He has killed mine and McCaslin's dogs, but that was all right. We gambled the dogs against him; we gave each other warning. But now he has come into my house and destroyed my property, out of season too. He broke the rules. It was Old Ben, Sam." Still Sam said nothing, standing there until Major de Spain should stop talking. "We'll back-track her tomorrow and see," Major de Spain said.

Sam departed. He would not live in the camp; he had built himself a little hut something like Joe Baker's, only stouter, tighter, on the bayou a quarter-mile away, and a stout log crib where he stored a little corn for the shoat he raised each year. The next morning he was waiting when they waked. He had already found the colt. They did not even wait for breakfast. It was not far, not five hundred yards from the stable—the three-months' colt lying on its side, its throat torn out and the entrails and one ham partly eaten. It lay not as if it had been dropped but as if it had been struck and hurled, and no cat-mark, no claw-mark where a panther would have gripped it while finding its throat. They read the tracks where the frantic mare had circled and at last rushed in with that same ultimate desperation with which she had whirled on Sam Fathers yesterday evening, and the long tracks of dead and terrified running and those of the beast which had not even rushed at her when she advanced but had merely walked three or four paces toward her until she broke, and General Compson said, "Good God, what a wolf!"

Still Sam said nothing. The boy watched him while the men knelt, measuring the tracks. There was something in Sam's face now. It was neither exultation nor joy nor hope. Later, a man, the boy realised what it had been, and that Sam had known all the time what had made the tracks and what had torn the throat out of the doe in the spring and killed the fawn. It had been foreknowledge in Sam's face that morning. *And he was glad,* he told himself. *He was old. He had no children, no people, none of his blood anywhere above earth that he would ever meet again. And even if he were to, he could not have touched it, spoken to it, because for seventy years now he had had to be a Negro. It was almost over now and he was glad.*

They returned to camp and had breakfast and came back with guns and the hounds. Afterward the boy realised that they also should have known then what killed the colt as well as Sam Fathers did. But that was neither the first nor the last time he had seen men rationalise from and even act upon their misconceptions. After Boon, standing astride the colt, had whipped the dogs away from it with his belt, they snuffed at the tracks. One of them, a young dog hound without judgment yet, bayed once, and they ran for a few feet on what seemed to be a trail. Then they stopped, looking back at the men, eager enough, not baffled, merely questioning, as if they were asking "Now what?" Then they rushed back to the colt, where Boon, still astride it, slashed at them with the belt.

"I never knew a trail to get cold that quick," General Compson said.

"Maybe a single wolf big enough to kill a colt with the dam right there beside it dont leave scent," Major de Spain said.

"Maybe it was a hant," Walter Ewell said. He looked at Tennie's Jim. "Hah, Jim?"

Because the hounds would not run it, Major de Spain had Sam hunt out and find the tracks a hundred yards farther on and they put the dogs on it again and again the young one bayed and not one of them realised then that the hound was not baying like a dog striking game but was merely bellowing like a country dog whose yard has been invaded. General Compson spoke to the boy and Boon and Tennie's Jim: to the squirrel hunters. "You boys keep the dogs with you this morning. He's probably hanging around somewhere, waiting to get his breakfast off the colt. You might strike him."

But they did not. The boy remembered how Sam stood watching them as they went into the woods with the leashed hounds—the Indian face in which he had never seen anything until it smiled, except that faint arching of the nostrils on that first morning when the hounds had found Old Ben. They took the hounds with them on the next day, though when they reached the place where they hoped to strike a fresh trail, the carcass of the colt was gone. Then on the third morning Sam was waiting again, this time until they had finished breakfast. He said, "Come." He led them to his house, his little hut, to the corn-crib beyond it. He had removed the corn and had made a deadfall of the door, baiting it with the colt's carcass; peering between the logs, they saw an animal almost the color of a gun or pistol barrel, what little time they had to examine its color or shape. It was not crouched nor even standing. It was in motion, in the air, coming toward them—a heavy body crashing with tremendous force against the door so that the thick door jumped and clattered in its frame, the animal, whatever it was, hurling itself against the door again seemingly before it could have touched the floor and got a new purchase to spring from. "Come away," Sam said, "fore he break his neck." Even when they retreated the heavy and measured crashes continued, the stout door jumping and clattering each time, and still no sound from the beast itself—no snarl, no cry.

"What in hell's name is it?" Major de Spain said.

"It's a dog," Sam said, his nostrils arching and collapsing faintly and steadily and that faint, fierce milkiness in his eyes again as on that first morning when the hounds had struck the old bear. "It's the dog."

"*The* dog?" Major de Spain said.

"That's gonter hold Old Ben."

"Dog the devil," Major de Spain said. "I'd rather have Old Ben himself in my pack than that brute. Shoot him."

"No," Sam said.

"You'll never tame him. How do you ever expect to make an animal like that afraid of you?"

"I don't want him tame," Sam said; again the boy watched his nostrils and the fierce milky light in his eyes. "But I almost rather he be tame than scared, of me or any man or any thing. But he wont be neither, of nothing."

"Then what are you going to do with it?"

"You can watch," Sam said.

Each morning through the second week they would go

to Sam's crib. He had removed a few shingles from the roof and had put a rope on the colt's carcass and had drawn it out when the trap fell. Each morning they would watch him lower a pail of water into the crib while the dog hurled itself tirelessly against the door and dropped back and leaped again. It never made any sound and there was nothing frenzied in the act but only a cold and grim indomitable determination. Toward the end of the week it stopped jumping at the door. Yet it had not weakened appreciably and it was not as if it had rationalised the fact that the door was not going to give. It was as if for that time it simply disdained to jump any longer. It was not down. None of them had ever seen it down. It stood, and they could see it now—part mastiff, something of Airedale and something of a dozen other strains probably, better than thirty inches at the shoulders and weighing as they guessed almost ninety pounds, with cold yellow eyes and a tremendous chest and over all that strange color like a blued gun-barrel.

Then the two weeks were up. They prepared to break camp. The boy begged to remain and his cousin let him. He moved into the little hut with Sam Fathers. Each morning he watched Sam lower the pail of water into the crib. By the end of that week the dog was down. It would rise and half stagger, half crawl to the water and drink and collapse again. One morning it could not even reach the water, could not raise its forequarters even from the floor. Sam took a short stick and prepared to enter the crib. "Wait," the boy said. "Let me get the gun—"

"No," Sam said. "He cant move now." Nor could it. It lay on its side while Sam touched it, its head and the gaunted body, the dog lying motionless, the yellow eyes open. They were not fierce and there was nothing of petty malevolence in them, but a cold and almost impersonal malignance like some natural force. It was not even looking at Sam nor at the boy peering at it between the logs.

Sam began to feed it again. The first time he had to raise

its head so it could lap the broth. That night he left a bowl of broth containing lumps of meat where the dog could reach it. The next morning the bowl was empty and the dog was lying on its belly, its head up, the cold yellow eyes watching the door as Sam entered, no change whatever in the cold yellow eyes and still no sound from it even when it sprang, its aim and co-ordination still bad from weakness so that Sam had time to strike it down with the stick and leap from the crib and slam the door as the dog, still without having had time to get its feet under it to jump again seemingly, hurled itself against the door as if the two weeks of starving had never been.

At noon that day someone came whooping through the woods from the direction of the camp. It was Boon. He came and looked for a while between the logs, at the tremendous dog lying again on its belly, its head up, the yellow eyes blinking sleepily at nothing: the indomitable and unbroken spirit. "What we better do," Boon said, "is to let that son of a bitch go and catch Old Ben and run him on the dog." He turned to the boy his weather-reddened and beetling face. "Get your traps together. Cass says for you to come on home. You been in here fooling with that horse-eating varmint long enough."

Boon had a borrowed mule at the camp; the buggy was waiting at the edge of the bottom. He was at home that night. He told McCaslin about it. "Sam's going to starve him again until he can go in and touch him. Then he will feed him again. Then he will starve him again, if he has to."

"But why?" McCaslin said. "What for? Even Sam will never tame that brute."

"We dont want him tame. We want him like he is. We just want him to find out at last that the only way he can get out of that crib and stay out of it is to do what Sam or somebody tells him to do. He's the dog that's going to stop Old Ben and hold him. We've already named him. His name is Lion."

Then November came at last. They returned to the
camp. With General Compson and Major de Spain and
his cousin and Walter and Boon he stood in the yard
among the guns and bedding and boxes of food and
watched Sam Fathers and Lion come up the lane from the
lot—the Indian, the old man in battered overalls and rubber boots and a worn sheepskin coat and a hat which had
belonged to the boy's father; the tremendous dog pacing
gravely beside him. The hounds rushed out to meet them
and stopped, except the young one which still had but
little of judgment. It ran up to Lion, fawning. Lion didn't
snap at it. He didn't even pause. He struck it rolling and
yelping for five or six feet with a blow of one paw as a bear
would have done and came on into the yard and stood,
blinking sleepily at nothing, looking at no one, while
Boon said, "Jesus. Jesus.—Will he let me touch him?"

"You can touch him," Sam said. "He dont care. He dont
care about nothing or nobody."

The boy watched that too. He watched it for the next
two years from that moment when Boon touched Lion's
head and then knelt beside him, feeling the bones and
muscles, the power. It was as if Lion were a woman—or
perhaps Boon was the woman. That was more like it—the
big, brave, sleepy-seeming dog which, as Sam Fathers said,
cared about no man and no thing; and the violent, insensi-
tive, hard-faced man with his touch of remote Indian
blood and the mind almost of a child. He watched Boon
take over Lion's feeding from Sam and Uncle Ash both.
He would see Boon squatting in the cold rain beside the
kitchen while Lion ate. Because Lion neither slept nor
ate with the other dogs though none of them knew where
he did sleep until in the second November, thinking until
then that Lion slept in his kennel beside Sam Fathers'
hut, when the boy's cousin McCaslin said something about
it to Sam by sheer chance and Sam told him. And that
night the boy and Major de Spain and McCaslin with a
lamp entered the back room where Boon slept—the little,

tight, airless room rank with the smell of Boon's unwashed body and his wet hunting-clothes—where Boon, snoring on his back, choked and waked and Lion raised his head beside him and looked back at them from his cold, slumbrous yellow eyes.

"Damn it, Boon," McCaslin said. "Get that dog out of here. He's got to run Old Ben tomorrow morning. How in hell do you expect him to smell anything fainter than a skunk after breathing you all night?"

"The way I smell aint hurt my nose none that I ever noticed," Boon said.

"It wouldn't matter if it had," Major de Spain said. "We're not depending on you to trail a bear. Put him outside. Put him under the house with the other dogs."

Boon began to get up. "He'll kill the first one that happens to yawn or sneeze in his face or touches him."

"I reckon not," Major de Spain said. "None of them are going to risk yawning in his face or touching him either, even asleep. Put him outside. I want his nose right tomorrow. Old Ben fooled him last year. I dont think he will do it again."

Boon put on his shoes without lacing them; in his long soiled underwear, his hair still tousled from sleep, he and Lion went out. The others returned to the front room and the poker game where McCaslin's and Major de Spain's hands waited for them on the table. After a while McCaslin said, "Do you want me to go back and look again?"

"No," Major de Spain said. "I call," he said to Walter Ewell. He spoke to McCaslin again. "If you do, dont tell me. I am beginning to see the first sign of my increasing age: I dont like to know that my orders have been disobeyed, even when I knew when I gave them that they would be.—A small pair," he said to Walter Ewell.

"How small?" Walter said.

"Very small," Major de Spain said.

And the boy, lying beneath his piled quilts and blankets waiting for sleep, knew likewise that Lion was already

back in Boon's bed, for the rest of that night and the next
one and during all the nights of the next November and
the next one. He thought then: *I wonder what Sam thinks.
He could have Lion with him, even if Boon is a white
man. He could ask Major or McCaslin either. And more
than that. It was Sam's hand that touched Lion first and
Lion knows it.* Then he became a man and he knew that
too. It had been all right. That was the way it should have
been. Sam was the chief, the prince; Boon, the plebeian,
was his huntsman. Boon should have nursed the dogs.

On the first morning that Lion led the pack after Old
Ben, seven strangers appeared in the camp. They were
swampers: gaunt, malaria-ridden men appearing from nowhere, who ran trap-lines for coons or perhaps farmed
little patches of cotton and corn along the edge of the bottom, in clothes but little better than Sam Fathers' and
nowhere near as good as Tennie's Jim's, with worn shotguns and rifles, already squatting patiently in the cold
drizzle in the side yard when day broke. They had a spokesman; afterward Sam Fathers told Major de Spain how all
during the past summer and fall they had drifted into the
camp singly or in pairs and threes, to look quietly at Lion
for a while and then go away: "Mawnin, Major. We heerd
you was aimin to put that ere blue dawg on that old two-
toed bear this mawnin. We figgered we'd come up and
watch, if you dont mind. We wont do no shooting, lessen
he runs over us."

"You are welcome," Major de Spain said. "You are welcome to shoot. He's more your bear than ours."

"I reckon that aint no lie. I done fed him enough cawn
to have a sheer in him. Not to mention a shoat three years
ago."

"I reckon I got a sheer too," another said. "Only it aint
in the bear." Major de Spain looked at him. He was chewing tobacco. He spat. "Hit was a heifer calf. Nice un too.
Last year. When I finally found her, I reckon she looked
about like that colt of yourn looked last June."

"Oh," Major de Spain said. "Be welcome. If you see game in front of my dogs, shoot it."

Nobody shot Old Ben that day. No man saw him. The dogs jumped him within a hundred yards of the glade where the boy had seen him that day in the summer of his eleventh year. The boy was less than a quarter-mile away. He heard the jump but he could distinguish no voice among the dogs that he did not know and therefore would be Lion's, and he thought, believed, that Lion was not among them. Even the fact that they were going much faster than he had ever heard them run behind Old Ben before and that the high thin note of hysteria was missing now from their voices was not enough to disabuse him. He didn't comprehend until that night, when Sam told him that Lion would never cry on a trail. "He gonter growl when he catches Old Ben's throat," Sam said. "But he aint gonter never holler, no more than he ever done when he was jumping at that two-inch door. It's that blue dog in him. What you call it?"

"Airedale," the boy said.

Lion was there; the jump was just too close to the river. When Boon returned with Lion about eleven that night, he swore that Lion had stopped Old Ben once but that the hounds would not go in and Old Ben broke away and took to the river and swam for miles down it and he and Lion went down one bank for about ten miles and crossed and came up the other but it had begun to get dark before they struck any trail where Old Ben had come up out of the water, unless he was still in the water when he passed the ford where they crossed. Then he fell to cursing the hounds and ate the supper Uncle Ash had saved for him and went off to bed and after a while the boy opened the door of the little stale room thunderous with snoring and the great grave dog raised its head from Boon's pillow and blinked at him for a moment and lowered its head again.

When the next November came and the last day, the

day on which it was now becoming traditional to save for
Old Ben, there were more than a dozen strangers waiting.
They were not all swampers this time. Some of them were
townsmen, from other county seats like Jefferson, who had
heard about Lion and Old Ben and had come to watch
the great blue dog keep his yearly rendezvous with the
old two-toed bear. Some of them didn't even have guns
and the hunting-clothes and boots they wore had been on
a store shelf yesterday.

This time Lion jumped Old Ben more than five miles
from the river and bayed and held him and this time the
hounds went in, in a sort of desperate emulation. The
boy heard them; he was that near. He heard Boon whooping; he heard the two shots when General Compson delivered both barrels, one containing five buckshot, the
other a single ball, into the bear from as close as he could
force his almost unmanageable horse. He heard the dogs
when the bear broke free again. He was running now;
panting, stumbling, his lungs bursting, he reached the
place where General Compson had fired and where Old
Ben had killed two of the hounds. He saw the blood from
General Compson's shots, but he could go no further. He
stopped, leaning against a tree for his breathing to ease
and his heart to slow, hearing the sound of the dogs as it
faded on and died away.

In camp that night—they had as guests five of the still
terrified strangers in new hunting coats and boots who
had been lost all day until Sam Fathers went out and got
them—he heard the rest of it: how Lion had stopped and
held the bear again but only the one-eyed mule which did
not mind the smell of wild blood would approach and
Boon was riding the mule and Boon had never been
known to hit anything. He shot at the bear five times with
his pump gun, touching nothing, and Old Ben killed another hound and broke free once more and reached the
river and was gone. Again Boon and Lion hunted as far
down one bank as they dared. Too far; they crossed in the

first of dusk and dark overtook them within a mile. And this time Lion found the broken trail, the blood perhaps, in the darkness where Old Ben had come up out of the water, but Boon had him on a rope, luckily, and he got down from the mule and fought Lion hand-to-hand until he got him back to camp. This time Boon didn't even curse. He stood in the door, muddy, spent, his huge gargoyle's face tragic and still amazed. "I missed him," he said. "I was in twenty-five feet of him and I missed him five times."

"But we have drawn blood," Major de Spain said. "General Compson drew blood. We have never done that before."

"But I missed him," Boon said. "I missed him five times. With Lion looking right at me."

"Never mind," Major de Spain said. "It was a damned fine race. And we drew blood. Next year we'll let General Compson or Walter ride Katie, and we'll get him."

Then McCaslin said, "Where is Lion, Boon?"

"I left him at Sam's," Boon said. He was already turning away. "I aint fit to sleep with him."

So he should have hated and feared Lion. Yet he did not. It seemed to him that there was a fatality in it. It seemed to him that something, he didn't know what, was beginning; had already begun. It was like the last act on a set stage. It was the beginning of the end of something, he didn't know what except that he would not grieve. He would be humble and proud that he had been found worthy to be a part of it too or even just to see it too.

—3—

It was December. It was the coldest December he had ever remembered. They had been in camp four days over two weeks, waiting for the weather to soften so that Lion and Old Ben could run their yearly race. Then they would break camp and go home. Because of these unforeseen additional days which they had had to pass waiting on the weather, with nothing to do but play poker, the whisky had given out and he and Boon were being sent to Memphis with a suitcase and a note from Major de Spain to Mr. Semmes, the distiller, to get more. That is, Major de Spain and McCaslin were sending Boon to get the whisky and sending him to see that Boon got back with it or most of it or at least some of it.

Tennie's Jim waked him at three. He dressed rapidly, shivering, not so much from the cold because a fresh fire already boomed and roared on the hearth, but in that dead winter hour when the blood and the heart are slow and sleep is incomplete. He crossed the gap between house and kitchen, the gap of iron earth beneath the brilliant and rigid night where dawn would not begin for three hours yet, tasting, tongue palate and to the very bottom of his lungs the searing dark, and entered the kitchen, the lamp-lit warmth where the stove glowed, fogging the windows, and where Boon already sat at the table at breakfast, hunched over his plate, almost in his plate, his working jaws blue with stubble and his face innocent of water and his coarse, horse-mane hair innocent of comb—the quarter Indian, grandson of a Chickasaw squaw, who on occasion resented with his hard and furious fists the intimation of one single drop of alien blood and on others, usually after whisky, affirmed with the same fists and the same fury that his father had been the full-blood Chickasaw and even a chief and that even his mother had been only half white. He was four inches over six feet; he had the mind of a child, the heart of a horse, and little hard shoe-button eyes without depth or meanness or generosity or viciousness or gentleness or anything else, in the ugliest face the boy had ever seen. It looked like somebody had found a walnut a little larger than a football and with a machinist's hammer had shaped features into it and then painted it, mostly red; not Indian red but a fine bright ruddy color which whisky might have had something to do with but which was mostly just happy and violent out-of-doors, the wrinkles in it not the residue of the forty years it had survived but from squinting into the sun or into the gloom of cane-brakes where game had run, baked into it by the camp fires before which he had lain trying to sleep on the cold November or December ground while waiting for daylight so he could rise and hunt again, as though time were merely something he walked through as he did through air, aging him no more than air did. He was brave, faithful, improvident and unreliable; he had neither profession job nor trade and owned one vice and one virtue: whisky, and that absolute and unquestioning fidelity to Major de Spain and the boy's cousin McCaslin. "Sometimes I'd call them both virtues," Major de Spain said once. "Or both vices," McCaslin said.

He ate his breakfast, hearing the dogs under the kitchen, wakened by the smell of frying meat or perhaps by the feet overhead. He heard Lion once, short and peremptory, as the best hunter in any camp has only to speak once to all save the fools, and none other of Major de Spain's and McCaslin's dogs were Lion's equal in size and strength and perhaps even in courage, but they were not fools; Old Ben had killed the last fool among them last year.

Tennie's Jim came in as they finished. The wagon was outside. Ash decided he would drive them over to the logline where they would flag the outbound log-train and let Tennie's Jim wash the dishes. The boy knew why. It would not be the first time he had listened to old Ash badgering Boon.

It was cold. The wagon wheels banged and clattered on the frozen ground; the sky was fixed and brilliant. He was not shivering, he was shaking, slow and steady and hard, the food he had just eaten still warm and solid inside him while his outside shook slow and steady around it as though his stomach floated loose. "They wont run this morning," he said. "No dog will have any nose today."

"Cep Lion," Ash said. "Lion dont need no nose. All he need is a bear." He had wrapped his feet in towsacks and he had a quilt from his pallet bed on the kitchen floor drawn over his head and wrapped around him until in the thin brilliant starlight he looked like nothing at all that the boy had ever seen before. "He run a bear through a thousand-acre ice-house. Catch him too. Them other dogs dont matter because they aint going to keep up with Lion nohow, long as he got a bear in front of him."

"What's wrong with the other dogs?" Boon said. "What the hell do you know about it anyway? This is the first time you've had your tail out of that kitchen since we got here except to chop a little wood."

"Aint nothing wrong with them," Ash said. "And long as it's left up to them, aint nothing going to be. I just wish I had knowed all my life how to take care of my health good as them hounds knows."

"Well, they aint going to run this morning," Boon said. His voice was harsh and positive. "Major promised they wouldn't until me and Ike get back."

"Weather gonter break today. Gonter soft up. Rain by night." Then Ash laughed, chuckled, somewhere inside the quilt which concealed even his face. "Hum up here, mules!" he said, jerking the reins so that the mules leaped forward and snatched the lurching and banging wagon for several feet before they slowed again into their quick, short-paced, rapid plodding. "Sides, I like to know why Major need to wait on you. It's Lion he aiming to use. I aint never heard tell of you bringing no bear nor no other kind of meat into this camp."

Now Boon's going to curse Ash or maybe even hit him, the boy thought. But Boon never did, never had; the boy knew he never would even though four years ago Boon had shot five times with a borrowed pistol at a Negro on the street in Jefferson, with the same result as when he had shot five times at Old Ben last fall. "By God," Boon said, "he aint going to put Lion or no other dog on nothing until I get back tonight. Because he promised me. Whip up them mules and keep them whipped up. Do you want me to freeze to death?"

They reached the log-line and built a fire. After a while the log-train came up out of the woods under the paling east and Boon flagged it. Then in the warm caboose the boy slept again while Boon and the conductor and brakeman talked about Lion and Old Ben as people later would talk about Sullivan and Kilrain and, later still, about Dempsey and Tunney. Dozing, swaying as the springless caboose lurched and clattered, he would hear them still talking, about the shoats and calves Old Ben had killed and the cribs he had rifled and the traps and deadfalls he had wrecked and the lead he probably carried under his hide—Old Ben, the two-toed bear in a land where bears with trap-ruined feet had been called Two-Toe or Three-Toe or Cripple-Foot for fifty years, only Old Ben was an extra bear (the head bear, General Compson called him) and so had earned a name such as a human man could have worn and not been sorry.

They reached Hoke's at sunup. They emerged from the warm caboose in their hunting clothes, the muddy boots and stained khaki and Boon's blue unshaven jowls. But that was all right. Hoke's was a sawmill and commissary and two stores and a loading-chute on a sidetrack from the main line, and all the men in it wore boots and khaki too. Presently the Memphis train came. Boon bought three packages of popcorn-and-molasses and a bottle of beer from the news butch and the boy went to sleep again to the sound of his chewing.

But in Memphis it was not all right. It was as if the high buildings and the hard pavements, the fine carriages and the horse cars and the men in starched collars and neckties made their boots and khaki look a little rougher and a little muddier and made Boon's beard look worse and more unshaven and his face look more and more like he

should never have brought it out of the woods at all or at
least out of reach of Major de Spain or McCaslin or someone who knew it and could have said, "Dont be afraid. He
wont hurt you." He walked through the station, on the
slick floor, his face moving as he worked the popcorn out
of his teeth with his tongue, his legs spraddled and stiff
in the hips as if he were walking on buttered glass, and
that blue stubble on his face like the filings from a new
gun-barrel. They passed the first saloon. Even through the
closed doors the boy could seem to smell the sawdust and
the reek of old drink. Boon began to cough. He coughed
for something less than a minute. "Damn this cold," he
said. "I'd sure like to know where I got it."

"Back there in the station," the boy said.

Boon had started to cough again. He stopped. He looked
at the boy. "What?" he said.

"You never had it when we left camp nor on the train
either." Boon looked at him, blinking. Then he stopped
blinking. He didn't cough again. He said quietly:

"Lend me a dollar. Come on. You've got it. If you ever
had one, you've still got it. I dont mean you are tight with
your money because you aint. You just dont never seem
to ever think of nothing you want. When I was sixteen a
dollar bill melted off of me before I even had time to read
the name of the bank that issued it." He said quietly:
"Let me have a dollar, Ike."

"You promised Major. You promised McCaslin. Not till
we get back to camp."

"All right," Boon said in that quiet and patient voice.
"What can I do on just one dollar? You aint going to lend
me another."

"You're damn right I aint," the boy said, his voice quiet
too, cold with rage which was not at Boon, remembering:
Boon snoring in a hard chair in the kitchen so he could
watch the clock and wake him and McCaslin and drive
them the seventeen miles in to Jefferson to catch the train
to Memphis; the wild, never-bridled Texas paint pony

which he had persuaded McCaslin to let him buy and which he and Boon had bought at auction for four dollars and seventy-five cents and fetched home wired between two gentle old mares with pieces of barbed wire and which had never even seen shelled corn before and didn't even know what it was unless the grains were bugs maybe and at last (he was ten and Boon had been ten all his life) Boon said the pony was gentled and with a towsack over its head and four Negroes to hold it they backed it into an old two-wheeled cart and hooked up the gear and he and Boon got up and Boon said, "All right, boys. Let him go" and one of the Negroes—it was Tennie's Jim—snatched the towsack off and leaped for his life and they lost the first wheel against a post of the open gate only at that moment Boon caught him by the scruff of the neck and flung him into the roadside ditch so he only saw the rest of it in fragments: the other wheel as it slammed through the side gate and crossed the back yard and leaped up onto the gallery and scraps of the cart here and there along the road and Boon vanishing rapidly on his stomach in the leaping and spurting dust and still holding the reins until they broke too and two days later they finally caught the pony seven miles away still wearing the hames and the headstall of the bridle around its neck like a duchess with two necklaces at one time. He gave Boon the dollar.

"All right," Boon said. "Come on in out of the cold."

"I aint cold," he said.

"You can have some lemonade."

"I dont want any lemonade."

The door closed behind him. The sun was well up now. It was a brilliant day, though Ash had said it would rain before night. Already it was warmer; they could run tomorrow. He felt the old lift of the heart, as pristine as ever, as on the first day; he would never lose it, no matter how old in hunting and pursuit: the best, the best of all breathing, the humility and the pride. He must stop thinking about it. Already it seemed to him that he was running, back to the station, to the tracks themselves: the first train going south; he must stop thinking about it. The street was busy. He watched the big Norman draft horses, the Percherons; the trim carriages from which the men in the fine overcoats and the ladies rosy in furs descended and entered the station. (They were still next door to it but one.) Twenty years ago his father had ridden into Memphis as a member of Colonel Sartoris' horse in Forrest's command, up Main street and (the tale told) into the lobby of the Gayoso Hotel where the Yankee officers sat in the leather chairs spitting into the tall bright cuspidors and then out again, scot-free—

The door opened behind him. Boon was wiping his mouth on the back of his hand. "All right," he said. "Let's go tend to it and get the hell out of here."

They went and had the suitcase packed. He never knew where or when Boon got the other bottle. Doubtless Mr. Semmes gave it to him. When they reached Hoke's again at sundown, it was empty. They could get a return train to Hoke's in two hours; they went straight back to the station as Major de Spain and then McCaslin had told Boon to do and then ordered him to do and had sent the boy along to see that he did. Boon took the first drink from his bottle in the washroom. A man in a uniform cap came to tell him he couldn't drink there and looked at Boon's face once and said nothing. The next time he was pouring into his water glass beneath the edge of a table in the restaurant when the manager (she was a woman) did tell him he couldn't drink there and he went back to the washroom. He had been telling the Negro waiter and all the other people in the restaurant who couldn't help but hear him and who had never heard of Lion and didn't want to, about Lion and Old Ben. Then he happened to think of the zoo. He had found out that there was another train to Hoke's at three oclock and so they would spend the time at the zoo and take the three oclock train until he came back from the washroom for the third time. Then they would take the first train back to camp, get Lion and come back to the zoo where, he said, the bears were fed on ice cream and lady fingers and he would match Lion against them all.

So they missed the first train, the one they were supposed to take, but he got Boon onto the three oclock train and they were all right again, with Boon not even going to the washroom now but drinking in the aisle and talking about Lion and the men he buttonholed no more daring to tell Boon he couldn't drink there than the man in the station had dared.

When they reached Hoke's at sundown, Boon was asleep. The boy waked him at last and got him and the suitcase off the train and he even persuaded him to eat some supper at the sawmill commissary. So he was all right when they got in the caboose of the log-train to go back into the woods, with the sun going down red and the sky already overcast and the ground would not freeze tonight. It was the boy who slept now, sitting behind the ruby stove while the springless caboose jumped and clattered and Boon and the brakeman and the conductor talked about Lion and Old Ben because they knew what Boon was talking about because this was home. "Overcast and already thawing," Boon said. "Lion will get him tomorrow."

It would have to be Lion, or somebody. It would not be Boon. He had never hit anything bigger than a squirrel that anybody ever knew, except the Negro woman that day when he was shooting at the Negro man. He was a big Negro and not ten feet away but Boon shot five times with the pistol he had borrowed from Major de Spain's Negro coachman and the Negro he was shooting at outed with a dollar-and-a-half mail-order pistol and would have burned Boon down with it only it never went off, it just went snicksnicksnicksnicksnick five times and Boon still blasting away and he broke a plate-glass window that cost Mc-Caslin forty-five dollars and hit a Negro woman who happened to be passing in the leg only Major de Spain paid for that; he and McCaslin cut cards, the plate-glass window against the Negro woman's leg. And the first day on stand this year, the first morning in camp, the buck ran right over Boon; he heard Boon's old pump gun go whow. whow. whow. whow. whow. and then his voice: "God damn, here he comes! Head him! Head him!" and when he got there the buck's tracks and the five exploded shells were not twenty paces apart.

There were five guests in camp that night, from Jefferson: Mr. Bayard Sartoris and his son and General Compson's son and two others. And the next morning he looked out the window, into the gray thin drizzle of daybreak which Ash had predicted, and there they were, standing and squatting beneath the thin rain, almost two dozen of them who had fed Old Ben corn and shoats and even calves for ten years, in their worn hats and hunting coats and overalls which any town Negro would have thrown away or burned and only the rubber boots strong and sound, and the worn and blueless guns and some even without guns. While they ate breakfast a dozen more arrived, mounted and on foot: loggers from the camp thirteen miles below and sawmill men from Hoke's and the only gun among them that one which the log-train conductor carried: so that when they went into the woods this morning Major de Spain led a party almost as strong, excepting that some of them were not armed, as some he had led in the last darkening days of '64 and '65. The little yard would not hold them. They overflowed it, into the lane where Major de Spain sat his mare while Ash in his dirty apron thrust the greasy cartridges into his carbine and passed it up to him and the great grave blue dog stood at his stirrup not as a dog stands but as a horse stands, blinking his sleepy topaz eyes at nothing, deaf even to the yelling of the hounds which Boon and Tennie's Jim held on leash.

"We'll put General Compson on Katie this morning,"

Major de Spain said. "He drew blood last year; if he'd had a mule then that would have stood, he would have—"

"No," General Compson said. "I'm too old to go helling through the woods on a mule or a horse or anything else any more. Besides, I had my chance last year and missed it. I'm going on a stand this morning. I'm going to let that boy ride Katie."

"No, wait," McCaslin said. "Ike's got the rest of his life to hunt bears in. Let somebody else—"

"No," General Compson said. "I want Ike to ride Katie. He's already a better woodsman than you or me either and in another ten years he'll be as good as Walter."

At first he couldn't believe it, not until Major de Spain spoke to him. Then he was up, on the one-eyed mule which would not spook at wild blood, looking down at the dog motionless at Major de Spain's stirrup, looking in the gray streaming light bigger than a calf, bigger than he knew it actually was—the big head, the chest almost as big as his own, the blue hide beneath which the muscles flinched or quivered to no touch since the heart which drove blood to them loved no man and no thing, standing as a horse stands yet different from a horse which infers only weight and speed while Lion inferred not only courage and all else that went to make up the will and desire to pursue and kill, but endurance, the will and desire to endure beyond all imaginable limits of flesh in order to overtake and slay. Then the dog looked at him. It moved its head and looked at him across the trivial uproar of the hounds, out of the yellow eyes as depthless as Boon's, as free as Boon's of meanness or generosity or gentleness or viciousness. They were just cold and sleepy. Then it blinked, and he knew it was not looking at him and never had been, without even bothering to turn its head away.

That morning he heard the first cry. Lion had already vanished while Sam and Tennie's Jim were putting saddles on the mule and horse which had drawn the wagon and he watched the hounds as they crossed and cast, snuffing

and whimpering, until they too disappeared. Then he
and Major de Spain and Sam and Tennie's Jim rode after
them and heard the first cry out of the wet and thawing
woods not two hundred yards ahead, high, with that abject, almost human quality he had come to know, and the
other hounds joining in until the gloomed woods rang
and clamored. They rode then. It seemed to him that he
could actually see the big blue dog boring on, silent, and
the bear too: the thick, locomotive-like shape which he
had seen that day four years ago crossing the blow-down,
crashing on ahead of the dogs faster than he had believed
it could have moved, drawing away even from the running
mules. He heard a shotgun, once. The woods had opened,
they were going fast, the clamor faint and fading on ahead;
they passed the man who had fired—a swamper, a pointing
arm, a gaunt face, the small black orifice of his yelling
studded with rotten teeth.

He heard the changed note in the hounds' uproar and
two hundred yards ahead he saw them. The bear had
turned. He saw Lion drive in without pausing and saw
the bear strike him aside and lunge into the yelling hounds
and kill one of them almost in its tracks and whirl and
run again. Then they were in a streaming tide of dogs. He
heard Major de Spain and Tennie's Jim shouting and the
pistol sound of Tennie's Jim's leather thong as he tried to
turn them. Then he and Sam Fathers were riding alone.
One of the hounds had kept on with Lion though. He
recognised its voice. It was the young hound which even a
year ago had had no judgment and which, by the lights of
the other hounds anyway, still had none. *Maybe that's
what courage is,* he thought. "Right," Sam said behind
him. "Right. We got to turn him from the river if we can."

Now they were in cane: a brake. He knew the path
through it as well as Sam did. They came out of the undergrowth and struck the entrance almost exactly. It would
traverse the brake and come out onto a high open ridge
above the river. He heard the flat clap of Walter Ewell's

rifle, then two more. "No," Sam said. "I can hear the hound. Go on."

They emerged from the narrow roofless tunnel of snapping and hissing cane, still galloping, onto the open ridge below which the thick yellow river, reflectionless in the gray and streaming light, seemed not to move. Now he could hear the hound too. It was not running. The cry was a high frantic yapping and Boon was running along the edge of the bluff, his old gun leaping and jouncing against his back on its sling made of a piece of cotton plowline. He whirled and ran up to them, wild-faced, and flung himself onto the mule behind the boy. "That damn boat!" he cried. "It's on the other side! He went straight across! Lion was too close to him! That little hound too! Lion was so close I couldn't shoot! Go on!" he cried, beating his heels into the mule's flanks. "Go on!"

They plunged down the bank, slipping and sliding in the thawed earth, crashing through the willows and into the water. He felt no shock, no cold, he on one side of the swimming mule, grasping the pommel with one hand and holding his gun above the water with the other, Boon opposite him. Sam was behind them somewhere, and then the river, the water about them, was full of dogs. They swam faster than the mules; they were scrabbling up the bank before the mules touched bottom. Major de Spain was whooping from the bank they had just left and, looking back, he saw Tennie's Jim and the horse as they went into the water.

Now the woods ahead of them and the rain-heavy air were one uproar. It rang and clamored; it echoed and broke against the bank behind them and reformed and clamored and rang until it seemed to the boy that all the hounds which had ever bayed game in this land were yelling down at him. He got his leg over the mule as it came up out of the water. Boon didn't try to mount again. He grasped one stirrup as they went up the bank and crashed through the undergrowth which fringed the bluff

and saw the bear, on its hind feet, its back against a tree
while the bellowing hounds swirled around it and once
more Lion drove in, leaping clear of the ground.

This time the bear didn't strike him down. It caught
the dog in both arms, almost loverlike, and they both
went down. He was off the mule now. He drew back both
hammers of the gun but he could see nothing but moiling
spotted houndbodies until the bear surged up again. Boon
was yelling something, he could not tell what; he could
see Lion still clinging to the bear's throat and he saw the
bear, half erect, strike one of the hounds with one paw
and hurl it five or six feet and then, rising and rising as
though it would never stop, stand erect again and begin
to rake at Lion's belly with its forepaws. Then Boon was
running. The boy saw the gleam of the blade in his hand
and watched him leap among the hounds, hurdling them,
kicking them aside as he ran, and fling himself astride the
bear as he had hurled himself onto the mule, his legs locked
around the bear's belly, his left arm under the bear's throat
where Lion clung, and the glint of the knife as it rose and
fell.

It fell just once. For an instant they almost resembled a
piece of statuary: the clinging dog, the bear, the man
astride its back, working and probing the buried blade.
Then they went down, pulled over backward by Boon's
weight, Boon underneath. It was the bear's back which
reappeared first but at once Boon was astride it again. He
had never released the knife and again the boy saw the
almost infinitesimal movement of his arm and shoulder
as he probed and sought; then the bear surged erect, raising with it the man and the dog too, and turned and still
carrying the man and the dog it took two or three steps
toward the woods on its hind feet as a man would have
walked and crashed down. It didn't collapse, crumple. It
fell all of a piece, as a tree falls, so that all three of them,
man dog and bear, seemed to bounce once.

He and Tennie's Jim ran forward. Boon was kneeling

t the bear's head. His left ear was shredded, his left coat
leeve was completely gone, his right boot had been ripped
rom knee to instep; the bright blood thinned in the thin
ain down his leg and hand and arm and down the side of
his face which was no longer wild but was quite calm. To-
;ether they prized Lion's jaws from the bear's throat.
"Easy, goddamn it," Boon said. "Cant you see his guts are
ill out of him?" He began to remove his coat. He spoke
o Tennie's Jim in that calm voice: "Bring the boat up.
t's about a hundred yards down the bank there. I saw it."
Tennie's Jim rose and went away. Then, and he could not
emember if it had been a call or an exclamation from
Tennie's Jim or if he had glanced up by chance, he saw
Tennie's Jim stooping and saw Sam Fathers lying motion-
ess on his face in the trampled mud.

The mule had not thrown him. He remembered that
Sam was down too even before Boon began to run. There
was no mark on him whatever and when he and Boon
urned him over, his eyes were open and he said something
n that tongue which he and Joe Baker had used to speak
ogether. But he couldn't move. Tennie's Jim brought the
kiff up; they could hear him shouting to Major de Spain
across the river. Boon wrapped Lion in his hunting coat
and carried him down to the skiff and they carried Sam
lown and returned and hitched the bear to the one-eyed
mule's saddle-bow with Tennie's Jim's leash-thong and
dragged him down to the skiff and got him into it and left
Tennie's Jim to swim the horse and the two mules back
across. Major de Spain caught the bow of the skiff as Boon
umped out and past him before it touched the bank. He
ooked at Old Ben and said quietly: "Well." Then he
walked into the water and leaned down and touched Sam
and Sam looked up at him and said something in that old
ongue he and Joe Baker spoke. "You dont know what
happened?" Major de Spain said.

"No, sir," the boy said. "It wasn't the mule. It wasn't
anything. He was off the mule when Boon ran in on the

bear. Then we looked up and he was lying on the ground."
Boon was shouting at Tennie's Jim, still in the middle of
the river.

"Come on, goddamn it!" he said. "Bring me that mule!"

"What do you want with a mule?" Major de Spain said.

Boon didn't even look at him. "I'm going to Hoke's to
get the doctor," he said in that calm voice, his face quite
calm beneath the steady thinning of the bright blood.

"You need a doctor yourself," Major de Spain said.
"Tennie's Jim—"

"Damn that," Boon said. He turned on Major de Spain.
His face was still calm, only his voice was a pitch higher.
"Cant you see his goddamn guts are all out of him?"

"Boon!" Major de Spain said. They looked at one another. Boon was a good head taller than Major de Spain;
even the boy was taller now than Major de Spain.

"I've got to get the doctor," Boon said. "His goddamn
guts—"

"All right," Major de Spain said. Tennie's Jim came up
out of the water. The horse and the sound mule had already scented Old Ben; they surged and plunged all the
way up to the top of the bluff, dragging Tennie's Jim with
them, before he could stop them and tie them and come
back. Major de Spain unlooped the leather thong of his
compass from his buttonhole and gave it to Tennie's Jim.
"Go straight to Hoke's," he said. "Bring Doctor Crawford
back with you. Tell him there are two men to be looked
at. Take my mare. Can you find the road from here?"

"Yes, sir," Tennie's Jim said.

"All right," Major de Spain said. "Go on." He turned
to the boy. "Take the mules and the horse and go back
and get the wagon. We'll go on down the river in the boat
to Coon bridge. Meet us there. Can you find it again?"

"Yes, sir," the boy said.

"All right. Get started."

He went back to the wagon. He realised then how far
they had run. It was already afternoon when he put the

mules into the traces and tied the horse's lead-rope to the tail-gate. He reached Coon bridge at dusk. The skiff was already there. Before he could see it and almost before he could see the water he had to leap from the tilting wagon, still holding the reins, and work around to where he could grasp the bit and then the ear of the plunging sound mule and dig his heels and hold it until Boon came up the bank. The rope of the led horse had already snapped and it had already disappeared up the road toward camp. They turned the wagon around and took the mules out and he led the sound mule a hundred yards up the road and tied it. Boon had already brought Lion up to the wagon and Sam was sitting up in the skiff now and when they raised him he tried to walk, up the bank and to the wagon and he tried to climb into the wagon but Boon did not wait; he picked Sam up bodily and set him on the seat. Then they hitched Old Ben to the one-eyed mule's saddle again and dragged him up the bank and set two skid-poles into the open tail-gate and got him into the wagon and he went and got the sound mule and Boon fought it into the traces, striking it across its hard hollow-sounding face until it came into position and stood trembling. Then the rain came down, as though it had held off all day waiting on them.

They returned to camp through it, through the streaming and sightless dark, hearing long before they saw any light the horn and the spaced shots to guide them. When they came to Sam's dark little hut he tried to stand up. He spoke again in the tongue of the old fathers; then he said clearly: "Let me out. Let me out."

"He hasn't got any fire," Major said. "Go on!" he said sharply.

But Sam was struggling now, trying to stand up. "Let me out, master," he said. "Let me go home."

So he stopped the wagon and Boon got down and lifted Sam out. He did not wait to let Sam try to walk this time. He carried him into the hut and Major de Spain got light on a paper spill from the buried embers on the hearth and lit the lamp and Boon put Sam on his bunk and drew off his boots and Major de Spain covered him and the boy was not there, he was holding the mules, the sound one which was trying again to bolt since when the wagon stopped Old Ben's scent drifted forward again along the streaming blackness of air, but Sam's eyes were probably open again on that profound look which saw further than them or the hut, further than the death of a bear and the dying of a dog. Then they went on, toward the long wailing of the horn and the shots which seemed each to linger intact somewhere in the thick streaming air until the next spaced report joined and blended with it, to the lighted house, the bright streaming windows, the quiet faces as Boon entered, bloody and quite calm, carrying the bundled coat. He laid Lion, blood coat and all, on his stale sheetless pallet bed which not even Ash, as deft in the house as a woman, could ever make smooth.

The sawmill doctor from Hoke's was already there. Boon would not let the doctor touch him until he had seen to Lion. He wouldn't risk giving Lion chloroform. He put the entrails back and sewed him up without it while Major de Spain held his head and Boon his feet. But he never tried to move. He lay there, the yellow eyes open upon nothing while the quiet men in the new hunting clothes and in the old ones crowded into the little airless room rank with the smell of Boon's body and garments, and watched. Then the doctor cleaned and disinfected Boon's face and arm and leg and bandaged them and, the boy in front with a lantern and the doctor and McCaslin and Major de Spain and General Compson following, they went to Sam Fathers' hut. Tennie's Jim had built up the fire; he squatted before it, dozing. Sam had not moved since Boon had put him in the bunk and Major de Spain had covered him with the blankets, yet he opened his eyes and looked from one to another of the faces and when McCaslin touched his shoulder and said, "Sam. The doctor wants to look at you," he even drew his hands out of the blanket and began to fumble at his shirt buttons until McCaslin said, "Wait. We'll do it." They undressed him. He lay there—the copper-brown, almost hairless body, the old man's body, the old man, the wild man not even one generation from the woods, childless, kinless, peopleless—motionless, his eyes open but no longer looking at any of them, while the doctor examined him and drew the blankets up and put the stethoscope back into his bag and snapped the bag and only the boy knew that Sam too was going to die.

"Exhaustion," the doctor said. "Shock maybe. A man his age swimming rivers in December. He'll be all right. Just make him stay in bed for a day or two. Will there be somebody here with him?"

"There will be somebody here," Major de Spain said.

They went back to the house, to the rank little room where Boon still sat on the pallet bed with Lion's head under his hand while the men, the ones who had hunted behind Lion and the ones who had never seen him before today, came quietly in to look at him and went away. Then it was dawn and they all went out into the yard to look at Old Ben, with his eyes open too and his lips snarled back from his worn teeth and his mutilated foot and the little hard lumps under his skin which were the old bullets (there were fifty-two of them, buckshot rifle and ball) and the single almost invisible slit under his left shoulder where Boon's blade had finally found his life. Then Ash began to beat on the bottom of the dishpan with a heavy spoon to call them to breakfast and it was the first time he could remember hearing no sound from the dogs under the kitchen while they were eating. It was as if the old bear, even dead there in the yard, was a more potent terror still than they could face without Lion between them.

The rain had stopped during the night. By midmorning the thin sun appeared, rapidly burning away mist and cloud, warming the air and the earth; it would be one of those windless Mississippi December days which are a sort of Indian summer's Indian summer. They moved Lion out to the front gallery, into the sun. It was Boon's idea. "Goddamn it," he said, "he never did want to stay in the house until I made him. You know that." He took a crowbar and loosened the floor boards under his pallet bed so it could be raised, mattress and all, without disturbing Lion's position, and they carried him out to the gallery and put him down facing the woods.

Then he and the doctor and McCaslin and Major de Spain went to Sam's hut. This time Sam didn't open his eyes and his breathing was so quiet, so peaceful that they could hardly see that he breathed. The doctor didn't even take out his stethoscope nor even touch him. "He's all right," the doctor said. "He didn't even catch cold. He just quit."

"Quit?" McCaslin said.

"Yes. Old people do that sometimes. Then they get a good night's sleep or maybe it's just a drink of whisky, and they change their minds."

They returned to the house. And then they began to arrive—the swamp-dwellers, the gaunt men who ran trap-lines and lived on quinine and coons and river water, the farmers of little corn- and cotton-patches along the bottom's edge whose fields and cribs and pig-pens the old bear had rifled, the loggers from the camp and the sawmill men from Hoke's and the town men from further away than that, whose hounds the old bear had slain and traps and deadfalls he had wrecked and whose lead he carried. They came up mounted and on foot and in wagons, to enter the yard and look at him and then go on to the front where Lion lay, filling the little yard and overflowing it until there were almost a hundred of them squatting and standing in the warm and drowsing sunlight, talking quietly of hunting, of the game and the dogs which ran it, of hounds and bear and deer and men of yesterday vanished from the earth, while from time to time the great blue dog would open his eyes, not as if he were listening to them but as though to look at the woods for a moment before closing his eyes again, to remember the woods or to see that they were still there. He died at sundown.

Major de Spain broke camp that night. They carried Lion into the woods, or Boon carried him that is, wrapped in a quilt from his bed, just as he had refused to let anyone else touch Lion yesterday until the doctor got there; Boon carrying Lion, and the boy and General Compson and Walter and still almost fifty of them following with lanterns and lighted pine-knots—men from Hoke's and even further, who would have to ride out of the bottom in the dark, and swampers and trappers who would have to walk even, scattering toward the little hidden huts where they lived. And Boon would let nobody else dig the grave either and lay Lion in it and cover him and then General Compson stood at the head of it while the blaze and smoke of the pine-knots streamed away among the winter branches and spoke as he would have spoken over a man. Then they returned to camp. Major de Spain and McCaslin and Ash had rolled and tied all the bedding. The mules were hitched to the wagon and pointed out of the bottom and the wagon was already loaded and the stove in the kitchen was cold and the table was set with scraps of cold food and bread and only the coffee was hot when the boy ran into the kitchen where Major de Spain and McCaslin had already eaten. "What?" he cried. "What? I'm not going."

"Yes," McCaslin said, "we're going out tonight. Major wants to get on back home."

"No!" he said. "I'm going to stay."

"You've got to be back in school Monday. You've already missed a week more than I intended. It will take you from now until Monday to catch up. Sam's all right. You heard Doctor Crawford. I'm going to leave Boon and Tennie's Jim both to stay with him until he feels like getting up."

He was panting. The others had come in. He looked rapidly and almost frantically around at the other faces.

Boon had a fresh bottle. He upended it and started the cork by striking the bottom of the bottle with the heel of his hand and drew the cork with his teeth and spat it out and drank. "You're damn right you're going back to school," Boon said. "Or I'll burn the tail off of you myself if Cass dont, whether you are sixteen or sixty. Where in hell do you expect to get without education? Where would Cass be? Where in hell would I be if I hadn't never went to school?"

He looked at McCaslin again. He could feel his breath coming shorter and shorter and shallower and shallower, as if there were not enough air in the kitchen for that many to breathe. "This is just Thursday. I'll come home Sunday night on one of the horses. I'll come home Sunday, then. I'll make up the time I lost studying Sunday night. McCaslin," he said, without even despair.

"No, I tell you," McCaslin said. "Sit down here and eat your supper. We're going out to—"

"Hold up, Cass," General Compson said. The boy did not know General Compson had moved until he put his hand on his shoulder. "What is it, bud?" he said.

"I've got to stay," he said. "I've got to."

"All right," General Compson said. "You can stay. If missing an extra week of school is going to throw you so far behind you'll have to sweat to find out what some hired pedagogue put between the covers of a book, you better quit altogether.—And you shut up, Cass," he said, though McCaslin had not spoken. "You've got one foot straddled into a farm and the other foot straddled into a bank; you aint even got a good hand-hold where this boy was already an old man long before you damned Sartorises and Edmondses invented farms and banks to keep yourselves from having to find out what this boy was born knowing and fearing too maybe but without being afraid, that could go ten miles on a compass because he wanted to look at a bear none of us had ever got near enough to put a bullet in and looked at the bear and came the ten miles back on the compass in the dark; maybe by God that's the why and the wherefore of farms and banks.—I reckon you still aint going to tell what it is?"

But still he could not. "I've got to stay," he said.

"All right," General Compson said. "There's plenty of grub left. And you'll come home Sunday, like you promised McCaslin? Not Sunday night: Sunday."

"Yes, sir," he said.

"All right," General Compson said. "Sit down and eat, boys," he said. "Let's get started. It's going to be cold before we get home."

They ate. The wagon was already loaded and ready to depart; all they had to do was to get into it. Boon would drive them out to the road, to the farmer's stable where the surrey had been left. He stood beside the wagon, in silhouette on the sky, turbaned like a Paythan and taller than any there, the bottle tilted. Then he flung the bottle from his lips without even lowering it, spinning and glinting in the faint starlight, empty. "Them that's going," he said, "get in the goddamn wagon. Them that aint, get out of the goddamn way." The others got in. Boon mounted to the seat beside General Compson and the wagon moved, on into the obscurity until the boy could no longer see it, even the moving density of it amid the greater night. But he could still hear it, for a long while: the slow, deliberate banging of the wooden frame as it lurched from rut to rut. And he could hear Boon even when he could no longer hear the wagon. He was singing, harsh, tuneless, loud.

That was Thursday. On Saturday morning Tennie's Jim left on McCaslin's woods-horse which had not been out of the bottom one time now in six years, and late that afternoon rode through the gate on the spent horse and on to the commissary where McCaslin was rationing the tenants and the wage-hands for the coming week, and this time McCaslin forestalled any necessity or risk of having to wait while Major de Spain's surrey was being horsed and harnessed. He took their own, and with Tennie's Jim already asleep in the back seat he drove in to Jefferson and waited while Major de Spain changed to boots and put on his overcoat, and they drove the thirty miles in the dark of that night and at daybreak on Sunday morning they swapped to the waiting mare and mule and as the sun rose they rode out of the jungle and onto the low ridge where they had buried Lion: the low mound of unannealed earth where Boon's spade-marks still showed and beyond the grave the platform of freshly cut saplings bound between four posts and the blanket-wrapped bundle upon the platform and Boon and the boy squatting between the platform and the grave until Boon, the bandage removed, ripped, from his head so that the long scoriations of Old Ben's claws resembled crusted tar in the sunlight, sprang up and threw down upon them with the old gun with which he had never been known to hit anything although McCaslin was already off the mule, kicked both feet free of the irons and vaulted down before the mule had stopped, walking toward Boon.

"Stand back," Boon said. "By God, you wont touch him. Stand back, McCaslin." Still McCaslin came on, fast yet without haste.

"Cass!" Major de Spain said. Then he said "Boon! You, Boon!" and he was down too and the boy rose too, quickly, and still McCaslin came on not fast but steady and walked up to the grave and reached his hand steadily out, quickly yet still not fast, and took hold the gun by the middle so that he and Boon faced one another across Lion's grave, both holding the gun, Boon's spent indomitable amazed and frantic face almost a head higher than McCaslin's beneath the black scoriations of beast's claws and then Boon's chest began to heave as though there were not enough air in all the woods, in all the wilderness, for all of them, for him and anyone else, even for him alone.

"Turn it loose, Boon," McCaslin said.

"You damn little spindling—" Boon said. "Dont you know I can take it away from you? Dont you know I can tie it around your neck like a damn cravat?"

"Yes," McCaslin said. "Turn it loose, Boon."

"This is the way he wanted it. He told us. He told us exactly how to do it. And by God you aint going to move him. So we did it like he said, and I been sitting here ever since to keep the damn wildcats and varmints away from him and by God—" Then McCaslin had the gun, down-slanted while he pumped the slide, the five shells snicking out of it so fast that the last one was almost out before the first one touched the ground and McCaslin dropped the gun behind him without once having taken his eyes from Boon's.

"Did you kill him, Boon?" he said. Then Boon moved. He turned, he moved like he was still drunk and then for a moment blind too, one hand out as he blundered toward the big tree and seemed to stop walking before he reached the tree so that he plunged, fell toward it, flinging up both hands and catching himself against the tree and turning until his back was against it, backing with the tree's trunk his wild spent scoriated face and the tremendous heave and collapse of his chest, McCaslin following, facing him again, never once having moved his eyes from Boon's eyes. "Did you kill him, Boon?"

"No!" Boon said. "No!"

"Tell the truth," McCaslin said. "I would have done it if he had asked me to." Then the boy moved. He was between them, facing McCaslin; the water felt as if it had burst and sprung not from his eyes alone but from his whole face, like sweat.

"Leave him alone!" he cried. "Goddamn it! Leave him alone!"

—4—

Then he was twenty-one. He could say it, himself and his cousin juxtaposed not against the wilderness but against the tamed land which was to have been his herit-

age, the land which old Carothers McCaslin his grandfather had bought with white man's money from the wild
men whose grandfathers without guns hunted it, and
tamed and ordered or believed he had tamed and ordered
it for the reason that the human beings he held in bondage
and in the power of life and death had removed the forest
from it and in their sweat scratched the surface of it to a
depth of perhaps fourteen inches in order to grow something out of it which had not been there before and which
could be translated back into the money he who believed
he had bought it had had to pay to get it and hold it and
a reasonable profit too: and for which reason old Carothers
McCaslin, knowing better, could raise his children, his
descendants and heirs, to believe the land was his to hold
and bequeath since the strong and ruthless man has a cynical foreknowledge of his own vanity and pride and
strength and a contempt for all his get: just as, knowing
better, Major de Spain and his fragment of that wilderness
which was bigger and older than any recorded deed: just
as, knowing better, old Thomas Sutpen, from whom
Major de Spain had had his fragment for money: just as
Ikkemotubbe, the Chickasaw chief, from whom Thomas
Sutpen had had the fragment for money or rum or whatever it was, knew in his turn that not even a fragment of
it had been his to relinquish or sell

not against the wilderness but against the land, not in
pursuit and lust but in relinquishment, and in the commissary as it should have been, not the heart perhaps but certainly the solar-plexus of the repudiated and relinquished:
the square, galleried, wooden building squatting like a
portent above the fields whose laborers it still held in
thrall '65 or no and placarded over with advertisements
for snuff and cures for chills and salves and potions manufactured and sold by white men to bleach the pigment and
straighten the hair of Negroes that they might resemble
the very race which for two hundred years had held them
in bondage and from which for another hundred years not

even a bloody civil war would have set them completely free

himself and his cousin amid the old smells of cheese and salt meat and kerosene and harness, the ranked shelves of tobacco and overalls and bottled medicine and thread and plow-bolts, the barrels and kegs of flour and meal and molasses and nails, the wall pegs dependant with plowlines and plow-collars and hames and trace-chains, and the desk and the shelf above it on which rested the ledgers in which McCaslin recorded the slow outward trickle of food and supplies and equipment which returned each fall as cotton made and ginned and sold (two threads frail as truth and impalpable as equators yet cable-strong to bind for life them who made the cotton to the land their sweat fell on) , and the older ledgers clumsy and archaic in size and shape, on the yellowed pages of which were recorded in the faded hand of his father Theophilus and his uncle Amodeus during the two decades before the Civil War, the manumission in title at least of Carothers McCaslin's slaves:

'Relinquish,' McCaslin said. 'Relinquish. You, the direct male descendant of him who saw the opportunity and took it, bought the land, took the land, got the land no matter how, held it to bequeath, no matter how, out of the old grant, the first patent, when it was a wilderness of wild beasts and wilder men, and cleared it, translated it into something to bequeath to his children, worthy of bequeathment for his descendants' ease and security and pride and to perpetuate his name and accomplishments. Not only the male descendant but the only and last descendant in the male line and in the third generation, while I am not only four generations from old Carothers, I derived through a woman and the very McCaslin in my name is mine only by sufferance and courtesy and my grandmother's pride in what that man accomplished whose legacy and monument you think you can repudiate.' and he

'I cant repudiate it. It was never mine to repudiate. It

was never Father's and Uncle Buddy's to bequeath me to repudiate because it was never Grandfather's to bequeath them to bequeath me to repudiate because it was never old Ikkemotubbe's to sell to Grandfather for bequeathment and repudiation. Because it was never Ikkemotubbe's fathers' fathers' to bequeath Ikkemotubbe to sell to Grandfather or any man because on the instant when Ikkemotubbe discovered, realised, that he could sell it for money, on that instant it ceased ever to have been his forever, father to father to father, and the man who bought it bought nothing.'

'Bought nothing?' and he

'Bought nothing. Because He told in the Book how He created the earth, made it and looked at it and said it was all right, and then He made man. He made the earth first and peopled it with dumb creatures, and then He created man to be His overseer on the earth and to hold suzerainty over the earth and the animals on it in His name, not to hold for himself and his descendants inviolable title forever, generation after generation, to the oblongs and squares of the earth, but to hold the earth mutual and intact in the communal anonymity of brotherhood, and all the fee He asked was pity and humility and sufferance and endurance and the sweat of his face for bread. And I know what you are going to say,' he said: 'That nevertheless Grandfather—' and McCaslin

'—did own it. And not the first. Not alone and not the first since, as your Authority states, man was dispossessed of Eden. Nor yet the second and still not alone, on down through the tedious and shabby chronicle of His chosen sprung from Abraham, and of the sons of them who dispossessed Abraham, and of the five hundred years during which half the known world and all it contained was chattel to one city as this plantation and all the life it contained was chattel and revokeless thrall to this commissary store and those ledgers yonder during your grandfather's life, and the next thousand years while men fought over the

fragments of that collapse until at last even the fragments
were exhausted and men snarled over the gnawed bones of
the old world's worthless evening until an accidental egg
discovered to them a new hemisphere. So let me say it:
That nevertheless and notwithstanding old Carothers did
own it. Bought it, got it, no matter; kept it, held it, no
matter; bequeathed it: else why do you stand here relinquishing and repudiating? Held it, kept it for fifty years
until you could repudiate it, while He—this Arbiter, this
Architect, this Umpire—condoned—or did He? looked
down and saw—or did He? Or at least did nothing: saw,
and could not, or did not see; saw, and would not, or perhaps He would not see—perverse, impotent, or blind:
which?' and he

   'Dispossessed.' and McCaslin

   'What?' and he

   'Dispossessed. Not impotent: He didn't condone; not
blind, because He watched it. And let me say it. Dispossessed of Eden. Dispossessed of Canaan, and those who
dispossessed him dispossessed him dispossessed, and the five
hundred years of absentee landlords in the Roman bagn-
ios, and the thousand years of wild men from the northern woods who dispossessed them and devoured their
ravished substance ravished in turn again and then snarled
in what you call the old world's worthless twilight over
the old world's gnawed bones, blasphemous in His name
until He used a simple egg to discover to them a new
world where a nation of people could be founded in humility and pity and sufferance and pride of one to another.
And Grandfather did own the land nevertheless and notwithstanding because He permitted it, not impotent and
not condoning and not blind because He ordered and
watched it. He saw the land already accursed even as
Ikkemotubbe and Ikkemotubbe's father old Issetibbeha
and old Issetibbeha's fathers too held it, already tainted
even before any white man owned it by what Grandfather
and his kind, his fathers, had brought into the new land

which He had vouchsafed them out of pity and sufferance, on condition of pity and humility and sufferance and endurance, from that old world's corrupt and worthless twilight as though in the sailfuls of the old world's tainted wind which drove the ships—' and McCaslin

'Ah.'

'—and no hope for the land anywhere so long as Ikkemotubbe and Ikkemotubbe's descendants held it in unbroken succession. Maybe He saw that only by voiding the land for a time of Ikkemotubbe's blood and substituting for it another blood, could He accomplish His purpose. Maybe He knew already what that other blood would be, maybe it was more than justice that only the white man's blood was available and capable to raise the white man's curse, more than vengeance when—' and McCaslin

'Ah.'

'—when He used the blood which had brought in the evil to destroy the evil as doctors use fever to burn up fever, poison to slay poison. Maybe He chose Grandfather out of all of them He might have picked. Maybe He knew that Grandfather himself would not serve His purpose because Grandfather was born too soon too, but that Grandfather would have descendants, the right descendants; maybe He had foreseen already the descendants Grandfather would have, maybe He saw already in Grandfather the seed progenitive of the three generations He saw it would take to set at least some of His lowly people free—' and McCaslin

'The sons of Ham. You who quote the Book: the sons of Ham.' and he

'There are some things He said in the Book, and some things reported of Him that He did not say. And I know what you will say now: That if truth is one thing to me and another thing to you, how will we choose which is truth? You dont need to choose. The heart already knows. He didn't have His Book written to be read by what must elect and choose, but by the heart, not by the wise of the earth because maybe they dont need it or maybe the wise no longer have any heart, but by the doomed and lowly of the earth who have nothing else to read with but the heart. Because the men who wrote His Book for Him were writing about truth and there is only one truth and it covers all things that touch the heart.' and McCaslin

'So these men who transcribed His Book for Him were sometime liars.' and he

'Yes. Because they were human men. They were trying to write down the heart's truth out of the heart's driving complexity, for all the complex and troubled hearts which would beat after them. What they were trying to tell, what He wanted said, was too simple. Those for whom they transcribed His words could not have believed them. It had to be expounded in the everyday terms which they were familiar with and could comprehend, not only those who listened but those who told it too, because if they who were that near to Him as to have been elected from among all who breathed and spoke language to transcribe and relay His words, could comprehend truth only through the complexity of passion and lust and hate and fear which drives the heart, what distance back to truth must they traverse whom truth could only reach by word-of-mouth?' and McCaslin

'I might answer that, since you have taken to proving your points and disproving mine by the same text, I dont know. But I dont say that, because you have answered yourself: No time at all if, as you say, the heart knows truth, the infallible and unerring heart. And perhaps you are right, since although you admitted three generations from old Carothers to you, there were not three. There were not even completely two. Uncle Buck and Uncle Buddy. And they not the first and not alone. A thousand other Bucks and Buddies in less than two generations and sometimes less than one in this land which so you claim God created and man himself cursed and tainted. Not to mention 1865.' and he

'Yes. More men than Father and Uncle Buddy,' not even glancing toward the shelf above the desk, nor did McCaslin. They did not need to. To him it was as though the ledgers in their scarred cracked leather bindings were being lifted down one by one in their fading sequence and spread open on the desk or perhaps upon some apocryphal Bench or even Altar or perhaps before the Throne Itself for a last perusal and contemplation and refreshment of the Allknowledgeable before the yellowed pages and the brown thin ink in which was recorded the injustice and a little at least of its amelioration and restitution faded back forever into the anonymous communal original dust

the yellowed pages scrawled in fading ink by the hand first of his grandfather and then of his father and uncle, bachelors up to and past fifty and then sixty, the one who ran the plantation and the farming of it and the other who did the housework and the cooking and continued to do it even after his twin married and the boy himself was born

the two brothers who as soon as their father was buried moved out of the tremendously-conceived, the almost barn-like edifice which he had not even completed, into a one-room log cabin which the two of them built themselves and added other rooms to while they lived in it, refusing to allow any slave to touch any timber of it other than the actual raising into place the logs which two men alone could not handle, and domiciled all the slaves in the big house some of the windows of which were still merely boarded up with odds and ends of plank or with the skins of bear and deer nailed over the empty frames: each sundown the brother who superintended the farming would parade the Negroes as a first sergeant dismisses a company, and herd them willynilly, man woman and child, without question protest or recourse, into the tremendous abortive edifice scarcely yet out of embryo, as if even old Carothers McCaslin had paused aghast at the concrete indication of his own vanity's boundless conceiving: he would call his mental roll and herd them in and with a hand-wrought nail as long as a flenching-knife and suspended from a short deer-hide thong attached to the door-jamb for that purpose, he would nail to the door of that house which lacked half its windows and had no hinged back door at all, so that presently and for fifty years afterward, when the boy himself was big to hear and remember it, there was in the land a sort of folk-tale: of the countryside all night long full of skulking McCaslin slaves dodging the moonlit roads and the Patrol-riders to visit other plantations, and of the unspoken gentlemen's agreement between the two white men and the two dozen black ones that, after the white man had counted them and driven the home-made nail into the front door at sundown, neither of the white men would go around behind the house and look at the back door, provided that all the Negroes were behind the front one when the brother who drove it drew out the nail again at daybreak

the twins who were identical even in their handwriting, unless you had specimens side by side to compare, and even when both hands appeared on the same page (as often happened, as if, long since past any oral intercourse, they had used the diurnally advancing pages to conduct the unavoidable business of the compulsion which had traversed all the waste wilderness of North Mississippi in 1830 and '40 and singled them out to drive) they both looked as though they had been written by the same perfectly normal ten-year-old boy, even to the spelling, except that the spelling did not improve as one by one the slaves which Carothers McCaslin had inherited and purchased— Roscius and Phoebe and Thucydides and Eunice and their descendants, and Sam Fathers and his mother for both of whom he had swapped an underbred trotting gelding to old Ikkemotubbe, the Chickasaw chief from whom he had likewise bought the land, and Tennie Beauchamp whom the twin Amodeus had won from a neighbor in a poker-game, and the anomaly calling itself Percival Brownlee which the twin Theophilus had purchased, neither he nor his brother ever knew why apparently, from Bedford Forrest while he was still only a slave-dealer and not yet a general (It was a single page, not long and covering less than a year, not seven months in fact, begun in the hand which the boy had learned to distinguish as that of his father:

> Percavil Brownly 26yr Old. cleark @ Bookepper. bought from N.B.Forest at Cold Water 3 Mar 1856 $265. dolars

and beneath that, in the same hand:

> 5 mar 1856 No bookepper any way Cant read. Can write his Name but I already put that down My self Says he can Plough but dont look like it to Me. sent to Feild to day Mar 5 1856

and the same hand:

> 6 Mar 1856 Cant plough either Says he aims to be a Precher so may be he can lead live stock to Crick to Drink

and this time it was the other, the hand which he now recognised as his uncle's when he could see them both on the same page:

> Mar 23th 1856 Cant do that either Except one at a Time Get shut of him

then the first again:

> 24 Mar 1856 Who in hell would buy him

then the second:

> 19th of Apr 1856 Nobody You put yourself out of Market at Cold Water two months ago I never said sell him Free him

the first:

22 Apr 1856 Ill get it out of him

the second:

Jun 13th 1856 How $1 per yr 265$ 265 yrs Wholl sign his Free paper

then the first again:

1 Oct 1856 Mule josephine Broke Leg @ shot Wrong stall wrong niger wrong everything $100. dolars

and the same:

2 Oct 1856 Freed Debit McCaslin @ McCaslin $265. dolars

then the second again:

Oct 3th Debit Theophilus McCaslin Niger 265$ Mule 100$ 365$ He hasnt gone yet Father should be here

then the first:

3 Oct 1856 Son of a bitch wont leave What would father done

the second:

29th of Oct 1856 Renamed him

the first:

31 Oct 1856 Renamed him what

the second:

Chrstms 1856 Spintrius

) took substance and even a sort of shadowy life with their passions and complexities too as page followed page and year year; all there, not only the general and condoned injustice and its slow amortization but the specific tragedy which had not been condoned and could never be amortized, the new page and the new ledger, the hand which he could now recognise at first glance as his father's:

> Father dide Lucius Quintus Carothers McCaslin, Cal-
> lina 1772 Missippy 1837. Dide and burid 27 June
> 1837
> Roskus. rased by Granfather in Callina Dont know
> how old. Freed 27 June 1837 Dont want to leave. Dide
> and Burid 12 Jan 1841
> Fibby Roskus Wife. bought by granfather in Callina
> says Fifty Freed 27 June 1837 Dont want to leave.
> Dide and burd 1 Aug 1849
> Thucydus Roskus @ Fibby Son born in Callina 1779.
> Refused 10acre peace fathers Will 28 June 1837 Re-
> fused Cash offer $200. dolars from A.@ T. McCaslin
> 28 Jun 1837 Wants to stay and work it out

and beneath this and covering the next five pages and almost that many years, the slow, day-by-day accruement of
the wages allowed him and the food and clothing—the
molasses and meat and meal, the cheap durable shirts and
jeans and shoes and now and then a coat against rain and
cold—charged against the slowly yet steadily mounting sum
of balance (and it would seem to the boy that he could
actually see the black man, the slave whom his white owner had forever manumitted by the very act from which the
black man could never be free so long as memory lasted,
entering the commissary, asking permission perhaps of
the white man's son to see the ledger-page which he could
not even read, not even asking for the white man's word,
which he would have had to accept for the reason that
there was absolutely no way under the sun for him to test
it, as to how the account stood, how much longer before
he could go and never return, even if only as far as Jefferson seventeen miles away) on to the double pen-stroke
closing the final entry:

> 3 Nov 1841 By Cash to Thucydus McCaslin $200.
> dolars Set Up blaksmith in J. Dec 1841 Dide and

burid in J. 17 feb 1854
Eunice Bought by Father in New Orleans 1807 $650.
dolars. Marrid to Thucydus 1809 Drownd in Crick
Cristmas Day 1832

and then the other hand appeared, the first time he had
seen it in the ledger to distinguish it as his uncle's, the
cook and housekeeper whom even McCaslin, who had
known him and the boy's father for sixteen years before
the boy was born, remembered as sitting all day long in
the rocking chair from which he cooked the food, before
the kitchen fire on which he cooked it:

June 21th 1833 Drownd herself

and the first:

23 Jun 1833 Who in hell ever heard of a niger
drownding him self

and the second, unhurried, with a complete finality; the
two identical entries might have been made with a rubber
stamp save for the date:

Aug 13 1833 Drownd herself

and he thought *But why? But why?* He was sixteen then.
It was neither the first time he had been alone in the commissary nor the first time he had taken down the old ledgers
familiar on their shelf above the desk ever since he could
remember. As a child and even after nine and ten and
eleven, when he had learned to read, he would look up at
the scarred and cracked backs and ends but with no particular desire to open them, and though he intended to
examine them someday because he realised that they probably contained a chronological and much more comprehensive though doubtless tedious record than he would
ever get from any other source, not alone of his own flesh
and blood but of all his people, not only the whites but
the black one too, who were as much a part of his ancestry

as his white progenitors, and of the land which they had
all held and used in common and fed from and on and
would continue to use in common without regard to color
or titular ownership, it would only be on some idle day
when he was old and perhaps even bored a little since what
the old books contained would be after all these years
fixed immutably, finished, unalterable, harmless. Then
he was sixteen. He knew what he was going to find before
he found it. He got the commissary key from McCaslin's
room after midnight while McCaslin was asleep and with
the commissary door shut and locked behind him and the
forgotten lantern stinking anew the rank dead icy air, he
leaned above the yellowed page and thought not Why
drowned herself, but thinking what he believed his father
had thought when he found his brother's first comment:
Why did Uncle Buddy think she had drowned herself:
finding, beginning to find on the next succeeding page
what he knew he would find, only this was still not it because he already knew this:

> Tomasina called Tomy Daughter of Thucydus @
> Eunice Born 1810 dide in Child bed June 1833 and
> Burd. Yr stars fell

nor the next:

> Turl Son of Thucydus @ Eunice Tomy born Jun
> 1833 yr stars fell Fathers will

and nothing more, no tedious recording filling this page
of wages day by day and food and clothing charged against
them, no entry of his death and burial because he had
outlived his white half-brothers and the books which Mc-
Caslin kept did not include obituaries: just Fathers will
and he had seen that too: old Carothers' bold cramped
hand far less legible than his sons' even and not much
better in spelling, who while capitalising almost every
noun and verb, made no effort to punctuate or construct
whatever, just as he made no effort either to explain or

obfuscate the thousand-dollar legacy to the son of an un-married slave-girl, to be paid only at the child's coming-of-age, bearing the consequence of the act of which there was still no definite incontrovertible proof that he ac-knowledged, not out of his own substance but penalising his sons with it, charging them a cash forfeit on the acci-dent of their own paternity; not even a bribe for silence toward his own fame since his fame would suffer only after he was no longer present to defend it, flinging almost contemptuously, as he might a cast-off hat or pair of shoes, the thousand dollars which could have had no more reality to him under those conditions than it would have to the Negro, the slave who would not even see it until he came of age, twenty-one years too late to begin to learn what money was. *So I reckon that was cheaper than saying My son to a nigger* he thought. *Even if My son wasn't but just two words. But there must have been love* he thought. *Some sort of love. Even what he would have called love: not just an afternoon's or a night's spittoon.* There was the old man, old, within five years of his life's end, long a wid-ower and, since his sons were not only bachelors but were approaching middleage, lonely in the house and doubtless even bored since his plantation was established now and functioning and there was enough money now, too much of it probably for a man whose vices even apparently re-mained below his means; there was the girl, husbandless and young, only twenty-three when the child was born: perhaps he had sent for her at first out of loneliness, to have a young voice and movement in the house, summoned her, bade her mother send her each morning to sweep the floors and make the beds and the mother acquiescing since that was probably already understood, already planned: the only child of a couple who were not field hands and who held themselves something above the other slaves not alone for that reason but because the husband and his father and mother too had been inherited by the white man from his father, and the white man himself had trav-

elled three hundred miles and better to New Orleans in
day when men travelled by horseback or steamboat, and
bought the girl's mother as a wife for

and that was all. The old frail pages seemed to turn o
their own accord even while he thought *His own daughte*
His own daughter. No No Not even him back to that on
where the white man (not even a widower then) wh
never went anywhere any more than his sons in their tim
ever did and who did not need another slave, had gone al
the way to New Orleans and bought one. And Tomey'
Terrel was still alive when the boy was ten years old and
he knew from his own observation and memory that ther
had already been some white in Tomey's Terrel's bloo
before his father gave him the rest of it; and looking dow
at the yellowed page spread beneath the yellow glow o
the lantern smoking and stinking in that rank chill mid
night room fifty years later, he seemed to see her actuall
walking into the icy creek on that Christmas day six month
before her daughter's and her lover's *(Her first lover's h*
thought. *Her first)* child was born, solitary, inflexible
griefless, ceremonial, in formal and succinct repudiatio
of grief and despair who had already had to repudiate be
lief and hope

that was all. He would never need look at the ledger
again nor did he; the yellowed pages in their fading and
implacable succession were as much a part of his conscious
ness and would remain so forever, as the fact of his ow
nativity:

> *Tennie Beauchamp 21yrs Won by Amodeus McCaslir*
> *from Hubert Beauchamp Esqre Possible Strait agains*
> *three Treys in sigt Not called 1851 Marrid to Tomy*
> *Turl 1859*

and no date of freedom because her freedom, as well as tha
of her first surviving child, derived not from Buck and
Buddy McCaslin in the commissary but from a stranger ir
Washington and no date of death and burial, not onl

because McCaslin kept no obituaries in his books, but because in this year 1883 she was still alive and would remain
so to see a grandson by her last surviving child:

> *Amodeus McCaslin Beauchamp Son of tomys Turl @*
> *Tennie Beauchamp 1859 dide 1859*

then his uncle's hand entire, because his father was now
a member of the cavalry command of that man whose
name as a slave-dealer he could not even spell: and not
even a page and not even a full line:

> *Dauter Tomes Turl and tenny 1862*

and not even a line and not even a sex and no cause given
though the boy could guess it because McCaslin was thirteen then and he remembered how there was not always
enough to eat in more places than Vicksburg:

> *Child of tomes Turl and Tenny 1863*

and the same hand again and this one lived, as though
Tennie's perseverance and the fading and diluted ghost of
old Carothers' ruthlessness had at last conquered even
starvation: and clearer, fuller, more carefully written and
spelled than the boy had yet seen it, as if the old man, who
should have been a woman to begin with, trying to run
what was left of the plantation in his brother's absence in
the intervals of cooking and caring for himself and the
fourteen-year-old orphan, had taken as an omen for renewed hope the fact that this nameless inheritor of slaves
was at least remaining alive long enough to receive a name:

> *James Thucydus Beauchamp Son of Tomes Turl and*
> *Tenny Beauchamp Born 29th december 1864 and*
> *both Well Wanted to call him Theophilus but Tride*
> *Amodeus McCaslin and Callina McCaslin and both*
> *dide so Disswaded Them Born at Two clock A,m,*
> *both Well*

but no more, nothing; it would be another two years yet

before the boy, almost a man now, would return from th
abortive trip into Tennessee with the still-intact third o
old Carothers' legacy to his Negro son and his descendants
which as the three surviving children established at las
one by one their apparent intention of surviving, thei
white half-uncles had increased to a thousand dollars each
conditions permitting, as they came of age, and complete
the page himself as far as it would even be completed whe
that day was long passed beyond which a man born i
1864 (or 1867 either, when he himself saw light) coul
have expected or himself hoped or even wanted to be stil
alive; his own hand now, queerly enough resembling nei
ther his father's nor his uncle's nor even McCaslin's, bu
like that of his grandfather's save for the spelling:

> *Vanished sometime on night of his twenty-first birth*
> *day Dec 29 1885. Traced by Isaac McCaslin to Jackso*
> *Tenn. and there lost. His third of legacy $1000.0*
> *returned to McCaslin Edmonds Trustee this day Ja*
> *12 1886*

but not yet: that would be two years yet, and now his fa
ther's again, whose old commander was now quit of sol
diering and slave-trading both; once more in the ledge
and then not again and more illegible than ever, almos
indecipherable at all from the rheumatism which now
crippled him and almost completely innocent now ever
of any sort of spelling as well as punctuation, as if the fou
years during which he had followed the sword of the onl
man ever breathing who ever sold him a Negro, let alon
beat him in a trade, had convinced him not only of th
vanity of faith and hope but of orthography too:

> *Miss sophonsiba b dtr t t @ t 1869*

but not of belief and will because it was there, written, a
McCaslin had told him, with the left hand, but there in
the ledger one time more and than not again, for the bo
himself was a year old, and when Lucas was born six year

later, his father and uncle had been dead inside the same twelve-months almost five years; his own hand again, who was there and saw it, 1886, she was just seventeen, two years younger than himself, and he was in the commissary when McCaslin entered out of the first of dusk and said, He wants to marry Fonsiba,' like that: and he looked past McCaslin and saw the man, the stranger, taller than McCaslin and wearing better clothes than McCaslin and most of the other white men the boy knew habitually wore, who entered the room like a white man and stood in it like a white man, as though he had let McCaslin precede him into it not because McCaslin's skin was white but simply because McCaslin lived there and knew the way, and who talked like a white man too, looking at him past McCaslin's shoulder rapidly and keenly once and then no more, without further interest, as a mature and contained white man not impatient but just pressed for time might have looked. Marry Fonsiba?' he cried. 'Marry Fonsiba?' and then no more either, just watching and listening while McCaslin and the Negro talked:

'To live in Arkansas, I believe you said.'

'Yes. I have property there. A farm.'

'Property? A farm? You own it?'

'Yes.'

'You dont say Sir, do you?'

'To my elders, yes.'

'I see. You are from the North.'

'Yes. Since a child.'

'Then your father was a slave.'

'Yes. Once.'

'Then how do you own a farm in Arkansas?'

'I have a grant. It was my father's. From the United States. For military service.'

'I see,' McCaslin said. 'The Yankee army.'

'The United States army,' the stranger said; and then himself again, crying it at McCaslin's back:

'Call aunt Tennie! I'll go get her! I'll—' But McCaslin

was not even including him; the stranger did not even
glance back toward his voice, the two of them speaking to
one another again as if he were not even there:

'Since you seem to have it all settled,' McCaslin said,
'why have you bothered to consult my authority at all?'

'I dont,' the stranger said. 'I acknowledge your authority
only so far as you admit your responsibility toward her as
a female member of the family of which you are the head.
I dont ask your permission. I—'

'That will do!' McCaslin said. But the stranger did not
falter. It was neither as if he were ignoring McCaslin nor
as if he had failed to hear him. It was as though he were
making, not at all an excuse and not exactly a justification,
but simply a statement which the situation absolutely re-
quired and demanded should be made in McCaslin's hearing whether McCaslin listened to it or not. It was as if he
were talking to himself, for himself to hear the words
spoken aloud. They faced one another, not close yet at
slightly less than foils' distance, erect, their voices not
raised, not impactive, just succinct:

'—I inform you, notify you in advance as chief of her
family. No man of honor could do less. Besides, you have,
in your way, according to your lights and upbringing—'

'That's enough, I said,' McCaslin said. 'Be off this place
by full dark. Go.' But for another moment the other did
not move, contemplating McCaslin with that detached
and heatless look, as if he were watching reflected in Mc
Caslin's pupils the tiny image of the figure he was sustain-
ing.

'Yes,' he said. 'After all, this is your house. And in your
fashion you have. . . . But no matter. You are right. This
is enough.' He turned back toward the door; he paused
again but only for a second, already moving while he
spoke: 'Be easy. I will be good to her.' Then he was gone.

'But how did she ever know him?' the boy cried. 'I never
even heard of him before! And Fonsiba, that's never been
off this place except to go to church since she was born—

'Ha,' McCaslin said. 'Even their parents dont know until too late how seventeen-year-old girls ever met the men who marry them too, if they are lucky.' And the next morning they were both gone, Fonsiba too. McCaslin never saw her again, nor did he, because the woman he found at last five months later was no one he had ever known. He carried a third of the three-thousand-dollar fund in gold in a money-belt, as when he had vainly traced Tennie's Jim into Tennessee a year ago. They—the man—had left an address of some sort with Tennie, and three months later a letter came, written by the man although McCaslin's wife Alice had taught Fonsiba to read and write too a little. But it bore a different postmark from the address the man had left with Tennie, and he travelled by rail as far as he could and then by contracted stage and then by a hired livery rig and then by rail again for a distance: an experienced traveller by now and an experienced bloodhound too and a successful one this time because he would have to be; as the slow interminable empty muddy December miles crawled and crawled and night followed night in hotels, in roadside taverns of rough logs and containing little else but a bar, and in the cabins of strangers and the hay of lonely barns, in none of which he dared undress because of his secret golden girdle like that of a disguised one of the Magi travelling incognito and not even hope to draw him but only determination and desperation, he would tell himself: *I will have to find her. I will have to. We have already lost one of them. I will have to find her this time.* He did. Hunched in the slow and icy rain, on a spent hired horse splashed to the chest and higher, he saw it—a single log edifice with a clay chimney which seemed in process of being flattened by the rain to a nameless and valueless rubble of dissolution in that roadless and even pathless waste of unfenced fallow and wilderness jungle— no barn, no stable, not so much as a hen-coop: just a log cabin built by hand and no clever hand either, a meagre pile of clumsily-cut firewood sufficient for about one day and not even a gaunt hound to come bellowing out from under the house when he rode up—a farm only in embryo, perhaps a good farm, maybe even a plantation someday, but not now, not for years yet and only then with labor, hard and enduring and unflagging work and sacrifice; he shoved open the crazy kitchen door in its awry frame and entered an icy gloom where not even a fire for cooking burned and after another moment saw, crouched into the wall's angle behind a crude table, the coffee-colored face which he had known all his life but knew no more, the body which had been born within a hundred yards of the room that he was born in and in which some of his own blood ran but which was now completely inheritor of generation after generation to whom an unannounced white man on a horse was a white man's hired Patroller wearing a pistol sometimes and a blacksnake whip always; he entered the next room, the only other room the cabin owned, and found, sitting in a rocking chair before the hearth, the man himself, reading—sitting there in the only chair in the house, before that miserable fire for which there was not wood sufficient to last twenty-four hours, in the same ministerial clothing in which he had entered the commissary five months ago and a pair of gold-framed spectacles which, when he looked up and then rose to his feet, the boy saw did not even contain lenses, reading a book in the midst of that desolation, that muddy waste fenceless and even pathless and without even a walled shed for stock to stand beneath: and over all, permeant, clinging to the man's very clothing and exuding from his skin itself, that rank stink of baseless and imbecile delusion, that boundless rapacity and folly, of the carpet-bagger followers of victorious armies.

'Dont you see?' he cried. 'Dont you see? This whole land, the whole South, is cursed, and all of us who derive from it, whom it ever suckled, white and black both, lie under the curse? Granted that my people brought the curse onto the land: maybe for that reason their descendants alone can—not resist it, not combat it—maybe just endure and outlast it until the curse is lifted. Then your peoples' turn will come because we have forfeited ours. But not now. Not yet. Dont you see?'

The other stood now, the unfrayed garments still ministerial even if not quite so fine, the book closed upon one finger to keep the place, the lensless spectacles held like a music master's wand in the other workless hand while the owner of it spoke his measured and sonorous imbecility of the boundless folly and the baseless hope: 'You're wrong. The curse you whites brought into this land has been lifted. It has been voided and discharged. We are seeing a new era, an era dedicated, as our founders intended it, to freedom, liberty and equality for all, to which this country will be the new Canaan—'

'Freedom from what? From work? Canaan?' He jerked his arm, comprehensive, almost violent: whereupon it all seemed to stand there about them, intact and complete and visible in the drafty, damp, heatless, Negro-stale Negro-rank sorry room—the empty fields without plow or seed to work them, fenceless against the stock which did not exist within or without the walled stable which likewise was not there. 'What corner of Canaan is this?'

'You are seeing it at a bad time. This is winter. No man farms this time of year.'

'I see. And of course her need for food and clothing will stand still while the land lies fallow.'

'I have a pension,' the other said. He said it as a man might say *I have grace* or *I own a gold mine*. 'I have my father's pension too. It will arrive on the first of the month. What day is this?'

'The eleventh,' he said. 'Twenty days more. And until then?'

'I have a few groceries in the house from my credit account with the merchant in Midnight who banks my pension check for me. I have executed to him a power of attorney to handle it for me as a matter of mutual—'

'I see. And if the groceries dont last the twenty days?''
'I still have one more hog.'
'Where?'
'Outside,' the other said. 'It is customary in this country to allow stock to range free during the winter for food. It comes up from time to time. But no matter if it doesn't; I can probably trace its footprints when the need—'
'Yes!' he cried. 'Because no matter: you still have the pension check. And the man in Midnight will cash it and pay himself out of it for what you have already eaten and if there is any left over, it is yours. And the hog will be eaten by then or you still cant catch it, and then what will you do?'
'It will be almost spring then,' the other said. 'I am planning in the spring—'
'It will be January,' he said. 'And then February. And then more than half of March—' and when he stopped again in the kitchen she had not moved, she did not even seem to breathe or to be alive except her eyes watching him; when he took a step toward her it was still not movement because she could have retreated no further: only the tremendous fathomless ink-colored eyes in the narrow, thin, too thin coffee-colored face watching him without alarm, without recognition, without hope. 'Fonsiba,' he said. 'Fonsiba. Are you all right?'
'I'm free,' she said. Midnight was a tavern, a livery stable, a big store (that would be where the pension check banked itself as a matter of mutual elimination of bother and fret, he thought) and a little one, a saloon and a blacksmith shop. But there was a bank there too. The president (the owner, for all practical purposes) of it was a translated Mississippian who had been one of Forrest's men too: and his body lightened of the golden belt for the first time since he left home eight days ago, with pencil and paper he multiplied three dollars by twelve months and divided it into one thousand dollars; it would stretch that way over almost twenty-eight years and for twenty-eight

years at least she would not starve, the banker promising
to send the three dollars himself by a trusty messenger on
the fifteenth of each month and put it into her actual
hand, and he returned home and that was all because in
1874 his father and his uncle were both dead and the old
ledgers never again came down from the shelf above the
desk to which his father had returned them for the last
time that day in 1869. But he could have completed it:

> *Lucas Quintus Carothers McCaslin Beauchamp. Last
> surviving son and child of Tomey's Terrel and Ten-
> nie Beauchamp. March 17, 1874*

except that there was no need: not *Lucius Quintus @c
@c @c,* but *Lucas Quintus,* not refusing to be called Lucius, because he simply eliminated that word from the
name; not denying, declining the name itself, because he
used three quarters of it; but simply taking the name and
changing, altering it, making it no longer the white man's
but his own, by himself composed, himself selfprogenitive
and nominate, by himself ancestored, as, for all the old
ledgers recorded to the contrary, old Carothers himself was
   and that was all: 1874 the boy; 1888 the man, repudiated
denied and free; 1895 and husband but no father, unwid-
owered but without a wife, and found long since that no
man is ever free and probably could not bear it if he were;
married then and living in Jefferson in the little new jerry-
built bungalow which his wife's father had given them:
and one morning Lucas stood suddenly in the doorway
of the room where he was reading the Memphis paper and
he looked at the paper's dateline and thought *It's his
birthday. He's twenty-one today* and Lucas said: 'Whar's
the rest of that money old Carothers left? I wants it. All
of it.'
   that was all: and McCaslin
   'More men than that one Buck and Buddy to fumble-
heed that truth so mazed for them that spoke it and so confused for them that heard yet still there was 1865:' and he

'But not enough. Not enough of even Father and Uncle Buddy to fumble-heed in even three generations not even three generations fathered by Grandfather not even if there had been nowhere beneath His sight any but Grandfather and so He would not even have needed to elect and choose. But He tried and I know what you will say. That having Himself created them He could have known no more of hope than He could have pride and grief but He didn't hope He just waited because He had made them: not just because He had set them alive and in motion but because He had already worried with them so long: worried with them so long because He had seen how in individual cases they were capable of anything any height or depth remembered in mazed incomprehension out of heaven where hell was created too and so He must admit them or else admit His equal somewhere and so be no longer God and therefore must accept responsibility for what He Himself had done in order to live with Himself in His lonely and paramount heaven. And He probably knew it was vain but He had created them and knew them capable of all things because He had shaped them out of the primal Absolute which contained all and had watched them since in their individual exaltation and baseness and they themselves not knowing why nor how nor even when: until at last He saw that they were all Grandfather all of them and that even from them the elected and chosen the best the very best He could expect (not hope mind: not hope) would be Bucks and Buddies and not even enough of them and in the third generation not even Bucks and Buddies but—' and McCaslin

'Ah:' and he

'Yes. If He could see Father and Uncle Buddy in Grandfather He must have seen me too. —an Isaac born into a later life than Abraham's and repudiating immolation: fatherless and therefore safe declining the altar because maybe this time the exasperated Hand might not supply the kid—' and McCaslin

'Escape:' and he

'All right. Escape.—Until one day He said what you told Fonsiba's husband that afternoon here in this room: *This will do. This is enough:* not in exasperation or rage or even just sick to death as you were sick that day: just *This is enough* and looked about for one last time, for one time more since He had created them, upon this land this South for which He had done so much with woods for game and streams for fish and deep rich soil for seed and lush springs to sprout it and long summers to mature it and serene falls to harvest it and short mild winters for men and animals and saw no hope anywhere and looked beyond it where hope should have been, where to East North and West lay illimitable that whole hopeful continent dedicated as a refuge and sanctuary of liberty and freedom from what you called the old world's worthless evening and saw the rich descendants of slavers, females of both sexes, to whom the black they shrieked of was another specimen another example like the Brazilian macaw brought home in a cage by a traveller, passing resolutions about horror and outrage in warm and air-proof halls: and the thundering cannonade of politicians earning votes and the medicine-shows of pulpiteers earning Chautauqua fees, to whom the outrage and the injustice were as much abstractions as Tariff or Silver or Immortality and who employed the very shackles of its servitude and the sorry rags of its regalia as they did the other beer and banners and mottoes redfire and brimstone and sleight-of-hand and musical handsaws: and the whirling wheels which manufactured for a profit the pristine replacements of the shackles and shoddy garments as they wore out and spun the cotton and made the gins which ginned it and the cars and ships which hauled it, and the men who ran the wheels for that profit and established and collected the taxes it was taxed with and the rates for hauling it and the commissions for selling it: and He could have repudiated them since they were his creation

now and forever more throughout all their generations
until not only that old world from which He had rescued
them but this new one too which He had revealed and
led them to as a sanctuary and refuge were become the
same worthless tideless rock cooling in the last crimson
evening except that out of all that empty sound and bootless fury one silence, among that loud and moiling all of
them just one simple enough to believe that horror and
outrage were first and last simply horror and outrage and
was crude enough to act upon that, illiterate and had no
words for talking or perhaps was just busy and had no
time to, one out of them all who did not bother Him
with cajolery and adjuration then pleading then threat
and had not even bothered to inform Him in advance
what he was about so that a lesser than He might have
even missed the simple act of lifting the long ancestral
musket down from the deerhorns above the door, whereupon He said *My name is Brown too* and the other *So is
mine* and He *Then mine or yours cant be because I am
against it* and the other *So am I* and He triumphantly
Then where are you going with that gun? and the other
told him in one sentence one word and He: amazed: Who
knew neither hope nor pride nor grief *But your Associa-
tion, your Committee, your Officers. Where are your Minutes, your Motions, your Parliamentary Procedures?* and
the other *I aint against them. They are all right I reckon
for them that have the time. I am just against the weak because they are niggers being held in bondage by the strong
just because they are white.* So He turned once more to
this land which He still intended to save because He had
done so much for it—' and McCaslin

'What?' and he

'—to these people He was still committed to because
they were his creations—' and McCaslin

'Turned back to us? His face to us?' and he

'—whose wives and daughters at least made soups and
jellies for them when they were sick and carried the trays

through the mud and the winter too into the stinking cabins and sat in the stinking cabins and kept fires going until crises came and passed but that was not enough: and when they were very sick had them carried into the big house itself into the company room itself maybe and nursed them there which the white man would have done too for any other of his cattle that was sick but at least the man who hired one from a livery wouldn't have and still that was not enough: so that He said and not in grief either Who had made them and so could know no more of grief than He could of pride or hope: *Apparently they can learn nothing save through suffering, remember nothing save when underlined in blood—*' and McCaslin

'Ashby on an afternoon's ride, to call on some remote maiden cousins of his mother or maybe just acquaintances of hers, comes by chance upon a minor engagement of outposts and dismounts and with his crimson-lined cloak for target leads a handful of troops he never saw before against an entrenched position of backwoods-trained riflemen. Lee's battle-order, wrapped maybe about a handful of cigars and doubtless thrown away when the last cigar was smoked, found by a Yankee Intelligence officer on the floor of a saloon behind the Yankee lines after Lee had already divided his forces before Sharpsburg. Jackson on the Plank Road, already rolled up the flank which Hooker believed could not be turned and, waiting only for night to pass to continue the brutal and incessant slogging which would fling that whole wing back into Hooker's lap where he sat on a front gallery in Chancellorsville drinking rum toddies and telegraphing Lincoln that he had defeated Lee, is shot from among a whole covey of minor officers and in the blind night by one of his own patrols, leaving as next by seniority Stuart that gallant man born apparently already horsed and sabred and already knowing all there was to know about war except the slogging and brutal stupidity of it: and that same Stuart off raiding Pennsylvania hen-roosts when

Lee should have known of all of Meade just where Hancock was on Cemetery Ridge: and Longstreet too at Gettysburg and that same Longstreet shot out of saddle by his own men in the dark by mistake just as Jackson was. His face to us? His face to us?' and he

'How else have made them fight? Who else but Jacksons and Stuarts and Ashbys and Morgans and Forrests?—the farmers of the central and middle-west, holding land by the acre instead of the tens or maybe even the hundreds, farming it themselves and to no single crop of cotton or tobacco or cane, owning no slaves and needing and wanting none and already looking toward the Pacific coast, not always as long as two generations there and having stopped where they did stop only through the fortuitous mischance that an ox died or a wagon-axle broke. And the New England mechanics who didn't even own land and measured all things by the weight of water and the cost of turning wheels and the narrow fringe of traders and ship-owners still looking backward across the Atlantic and attached to the continent only by their counting-houses. And those who should have had the alertness to see: the wildcat manipulators of mythical wilderness townsites; and the astuteness to rationalise: the bankers who held the mortgages on the land which the first were only waiting to abandon and on the railroads and steamboats to carry them still further west, and on the factories and the wheels and the rented tenements those who ran them lived in; and the leisure and scope to comprehend and fear in time and even anticipate: the Boston-bred (even when not born in Boston) spinster descendants of long lines of similarly-bred and likewise spinster aunts and uncles whose hands knew no callus except that of the indicting pen, to whom the wilderness itself began at the top of tide and who looked, if at anything other than Beacon Hill, only toward heaven—not to mention all the loud rabble of the camp-followers of pioneers: the bellowing of politicians, the mellifluous choiring of self-styled men of God, the—' and

McCaslin

'Here, here. Wait a minute:' and he

'Let me talk now. I'm trying to explain to the head of my family something which I have got to do which I dont quite understand myself, not in justification of it but to explain it if I can. I could say I dont know why I must do it but that I do know I have got to because I have got myself to have to live with for the rest of my life and all I want is peace to do it in. But you are the head of my family. More. I knew a long time ago that I would never have to miss my father, even if you are just finding out that you have missed your son.—the drawers of bills and the shavers of notes and the schoolmasters and the self-ordained to teach and lead and all that horde of the semi-literate with a white shirt but no change for it, with one eye on themselves and watching each other with the other one. Who else could have made them fight: could have struck them so aghast with fear and dread as to turn shoulder to shoulder and face one way and even stop talking for a while and even after two years of it keep them still so wrung with terror that some among them would seriously propose moving their very capital into a foreign country lest it be ravaged and pillaged by a people whose entire white male population would have little more than filled any one of their larger cities: except Jackson in the Valley and three separate armies trying to catch him and none of them ever knowing whether they were just retreating from a battle or just running into one and Stuart riding his whole command entirely around the biggest single armed force this continent ever saw in order to see what it looked like from behind and Morgan leading a cavalry charge against a stranded man-of-war. Who else could have declared a war against a power with ten times the area and a hundred times the men and a thousand times the resources, except men who could believe that all necessary to conduct a successful war was not acumen nor shrewdness nor politics nor diplomacy nor money nor even integrity and simple arithmetic but just love of land and courage—'

'And an unblemished and gallant ancestry and the ability to ride a horse,' McCaslin said. 'Dont leave that out.' It was evening now, the tranquil sunset of October mazy with windless woodsmoke. The cotton was long since picked and ginned, and all day now the wagons loaded with gathered corn moved between field and crib, processional across the enduring land. 'Well, maybe that's what He wanted. At least, that's what He got.' This time there was no yellowed procession of fading and harmless ledgerpages. This was chronicled in a harsher book and McCaslin, fourteen and fifteen and sixteen, had seen it and the boy himself had inherited it as Noah's grandchildren had inherited the Flood although they had not been there to see the deluge: that dark corrupt and bloody time while three separate peoples had tried to adjust not only to one another but to the new land which they had created and inherited too and must live in for the reason that those who had lost it were no less free to quit it than those who had gained it were:—those upon whom freedom and equality had been dumped overnight and without warning or preparation or any training in how to employ it or even just endure it and who misused it not as children would nor yet because they had been so long in bondage and then so suddenly freed, but misused it as human beings always misuse freedom, so that he thought *Apparently there is a wisdom beyond even that learned through suffering necessary for a man to distinguish between liberty and license;* those who had fought for four years and lost to preserve a condition under which that franchisement was anomaly and paradox, not because they were opposed to freedom as freedom but for the old reasons for which man (not the generals and politicians but man) has always fought and died in wars: to preserve a status quo or to establish a better future one to endure for his children; and lastly, as if that were not enough for bitterness and hatred and fear, that third race even more alien to the people

whom they resembled in pigment and in whom even the
same blood ran, than to the people whom they did not,—
that race three-fold in one and alien even among themselves save for a single fierce will for rapine and pillage,
composed of the sons of middleaged Quartermaster lieutenants and Army sutlers and contractors in military blankets and shoes and transport mules, who followed the battles they themselves had not fought and inherited the
conquest they themselves had not helped to gain, sanctioned and protected even if not blessed, and left their
bones and in another generation would be engaged in a
fierce economic competition of small sloven farms with
the black men they were supposed to have freed and the
white descendants of fathers who had owned no slaves anyway whom they were supposed to have disinherited and
in the third generation would be back once more in the
little lost county seats as barbers and garage mechanics
and deputy sheriffs and mill- and gin-hands and power-
plant firemen, leading, first in mufti then later in an actual
formalised regalia of hooded sheets and passwords and
fiery christian symbols, lynching mobs against the race
their ancestors had come to save: and of all that other
nameless horde of speculators in human misery, manipulators of money and politics and land, who follow catastrophe and are their own protection as grasshoppers are
and need no blessing and sweat no plow or axe-helve and
batten and vanish and leave no bones, just as they derived
apparently from no ancestry, no mortal flesh, no aet even
of passion or even of lust: and the Jew who came without
protection too since after two thousand years he had got
out of the habit of being or needing it, and solitary, without even the solidarity of the locusts and in this a sort of
courage since he had come thinking not in terms of simple
pillage but in terms of his great-grandchildren, seeking
yet some place to establish them to endure even though
forever alien: and unblessed: a pariah about the face of
the Western earth which twenty centuries later was still

taking revenge on him for the fairy tale with which he had conquered it. McCaslin had actually seen it, and the boy even at almost eighty would never be able to distinguish certainly between what he had seen and what had been told him: a lightless and gutted and empty land where women crouched with the huddled children behind locked doors and men armed in sheets and masks rode the silent roads and the bodies of white and black both, victims not so much of hate as of desperation and despair, swung from lonely limbs: and men shot dead in polling-booths with the still wet pen in one hand and the unblotted ballot in the other: and a United States marshal in Jefferson who signed his official papers with a crude cross, an ex-slave called Sickymo, not at all because his ex-owner was a doctor and apothecary but because, still a slave, he would steal his master's grain alcohol and dilute it with water and peddle it in pint bottles from a cache beneath the roots of a big sycamore tree behind the drug store, who had attained his high office because his half-white sister was the concubine of the Federal A.P.M.: and this time McCaslin did not even say Look but merely lifted one hand, not even pointing, not even specifically toward the shelf of ledgers but toward the desk, toward the corner where it sat beside the scuffed patch on the floor where two decades of heavy shoes had stood while the white man at the desk added and multiplied and subtracted. And again he did not need to look because he had seen this himself and, twenty-three years after the Surrender and twenty-four after the Proclamation, was still watching it: the ledgers, new ones now and filled rapidly, succeeding one another rapidly and containing more names than old Carothers or even his father and Uncle Buddy had ever dreamed of; new names and new faces to go with them, among which the old names and faces that even his father and uncle would have recognised, were lost, vanished—Tomey's Terrel dead, and even the tragic and miscast Percival Brownlee, who couldn't keep books and couldn't farm either,

found his true niche at last, reappeared in 1862 during the
boy's father's absence and had apparently been living on
the plantation for at least a month before his uncle found
out about it, conducting impromptu revival meetings
among Negroes, preaching and leading the singing also
in his high sweet true soprano voice and disappeared
again on foot and at top speed, not behind but ahead of a
body of raiding Federal horse and reappeared for the
third and last time in the entourage of a travelling Army
paymaster, the two of them passing through Jefferson in
a surrey at the exact moment when the boy's father (it
was 1866) also happened to be crossing the Square, the
surrey and its occupants traversing rapidly that quiet and
bucolic scene and even in that fleeting moment and to
others beside the boy's father giving an illusion of flight
and illicit holiday like a man on an excursion during his
wife's absence with his wife's personal maid, until Brownlee glanced up and saw his late co-master and gave him
one defiant female glance and then broke again, leaped
from the surrey and disappeared this time for good and
it was only by chance that McCaslin, twenty years later,
heard of him again, an old man now and quite fat, as the
well-to-do proprietor of a select New Orleans brothel;
and Tennie's Jim gone, nobody knew where, and Fonsiba
in Arkansas with her three dollars each month and the
scholar-husband with his lensless spectacles and frock coat
and his plans for the spring; and only Lucas was left, the
baby, the last save himself of old Carothers' doomed and
fatal blood which in the male derivation seemed to destroy all it touched, and even he was repudiating and at
least hoping to escape it;—Lucas, the boy of fourteen whose
name would not even appear for six years yet among those
rapid pages in the bindings new and dustless too since
McCaslin lifted them down daily now to write into them
the continuation of that record which two hundred years
had not been enough to complete and another hundred
would not be enough to discharge; that chronicle which

was a whole land in miniature, which multiplied and compounded was the entire South, twenty-three years after surrender and twenty-four from emancipation—that slow trickle of molasses and meal and meat, of shoes and straw hats and overalls, of plowlines and collars and heel-bolts and buckheads and clevises, which returned each fall as cotton—the two threads frail as truth and impalpable as equators yet cable-strong to bind for life them who made the cotton to the land their sweat fell on: and he

'Yes. Binding them for a while yet, a little while yet. Through and beyond that life and maybe through and beyond the life of that life's sons and maybe even through and beyond that of the sons of those sons. But not always, because they will endure. They will outlast us because they are—' it was not a pause, barely a falter even, possibly appreciable only to himself, as if he couldn't speak even to McCaslin, even to explain his repudiation, that which to him too, even in the act of escaping (and maybe this was the reality and the truth of his need to escape) was heresy: so that even in escaping he was taking with him more of that evil and unregenerate old man who could summon, because she was his property, a human being because she was old enough and female, to his widower's house and get a child on her and then dismiss her because she was of an inferior race, and then bequeath a thousand dollars to the infant because he would be dead then and wouldn't have to pay it, than even he had feared. 'Yes. He didn't want to. He had to. Because they will endure. They are better than we are. Stronger than we are. Their vices are vices aped from white men or that white men and bondage have taught them: improvidence and intemperance and evasion—not laziness: evasion: of what white men had set them to, not for their aggrandisement or even comfort but his own—' and McCaslin

'All right. Go on: Promiscuity. Violence. Instability and lack of control. Inability to distinguish between mine and thine—' and he

'How distinguish, when for two hundred years mine did not even exist for them?' and McCaslin

'All right. Go on. And their virtues—' and he

'Yes. Their own. Endurance—' and McCaslin

'So have mules:' and he

'—and pity and tolerance and forbearance and fidelity and love of children—' and McCaslin

'So have dogs:' and he

'—whether their own or not or black or not. And more: what they got not only not from white people but not even despite white people because they had it already from the old free fathers a longer time free than us because we have never been free—' and it was in McCaslin's eyes too, he had only to look at McCaslin's eyes and it was there, that summer twilight seven years ago, almost a week after they had returned from the camp before he discovered that Sam Fathers had told McCaslin: an old bear, fierce and ruthless not just to stay alive but ruthless with the fierce pride of liberty and freedom, jealous and proud enough of liberty and freedom to see it threatened not with fear nor even alarm but almost with joy, seeming deliberately to put it into jeopardy in order to savor it and keep his old strong bones and flesh supple and quick to defend and preserve it; an old man, son of a Negro slave and an Indian king, inheritor on the one hand of the long chronicle of a people who had learned humility through suffering and learned pride through the endurance which survived the suffering, and on the other side the chronicle of a people even longer in the land than the first, yet who now existed there only in the solitary brotherhood of an old and childless Negro's alien blood and the wild and invincible spirit of an old bear; a boy who wished to learn humility and pride in order to become skillful and worthy in the woods but found himself becoming so skillful so fast that he feared he would never become worthy because he had not learned humility and pride though he had tried, until one day an old man who could not have de-

fined either led him as though by the hand to where an
old bear and a little mongrel dog showed him that, by possessing one thing other, he would possess them both; and
a little dog, nameless and mongrel and many-fathered,
grown yet weighing less than six pounds, who couldn't be
dangerous because there was nothing anywhere much
smaller, not fierce because that would have been called
just noise, not humble because it was already too near the
ground to genuflect, and not proud because it would not
have been close enough for anyone to discern what was
casting that shadow and which didn't even know it was
not going to heaven since they had already decided it had
no immortal soul, so that all it could be was brave even
though they would probably call that too just noise. *'And
you didn't shoot,'* McCaslin said. *'How close were you?'*

'I dont know,' he said. *'There was a big wood tick just
inside his off hind leg. I saw that. But I didn't have the
gun then.'*

'But you didn't shoot when you had the gun,' McCaslin
said. *'Why?'* But McCaslin didn't wait, rising and crossing
the room, across the pelt of the bear he had killed two
years ago and the bigger one McCaslin had killed before
he was born, to the bookcase beneath the mounted head
of his first buck, and returned with the book and sat down
again and opened it. *'Listen,'* he said. He read the five
stanzas aloud and closed the book on his finger and looked
up. *'All right,'* he said. *'Listen,'* and read again, but only
one stanza this time and closed the book and laid it on the
table. *'She cannot fade, though thou hast not thy bliss,'*
McCaslin said: *'Forever wilt thou love, and she be fair.'*

'He's talking about a girl,' he said.

'He had to talk about something,' McCaslin said. Then
he said, *'He was talking about truth. Truth is one. It
doesn't change. It covers all things which touch the heart—
honor and pride and pity and justice and courage and love.
Do you see now?'* He didn't know. Somehow it had seemed
simpler than that, simpler than somebody talking in a

*book about a young man and a girl he would never need
to grieve over because he could never approach any nearer
and would never have to get any further away. He had
heard about an old bear and finally got big enough to
hunt it and he hunted it four years and at last met it with
a gun in his hands and he didn't shoot. Because a little
dog—But he could have shot long before the fyce covered
the twenty yards to where the bear waited, and Sam Fathers could have shot at any time during the interminable
minute while Old Ben stood on his hind legs over them.
. . . He ceased. McCaslin watched him, still speaking, the
voice, the words as quiet as the twilight itself was: 'Courage and honor and pride, and pity and love of justice and
of liberty. They all touch the heart, and what the heart
holds to becomes truth, as far as we know truth. Do you
see now?'* and he could still hear them, intact in this twilight as in that one seven years ago, no louder still because
they did not need to be because they would endure: and
he had only to look at McCaslin's eyes beyond the thin
and bitter smiling, the faint lip-lift which would have
had to be called smiling;—his kinsman, his father almost,
who had been born too late into the old time and too
soon for the new, the two of them juxtaposed and alien
now to each other against their ravaged patrimony, the
dark and ravaged fatherland still prone and panting from
its etherless operation:

'Habet then.—So this land is, indubitably, of and by itself cursed:' and he

'Cursed:' and again McCaslin merely lifted one hand,
not even speaking and not even toward the ledgers: so
that, as the stereopticon condenses into one instantaneous
field the myriad minutia of its scope, so did that slight
and rapid gesture establish in the small cramped and clut-
tered twilit room not only the ledgers but the whole plantation in its mazed and intricate entirety—the land, the
fields and what they represented in terms of cotton ginned
and sold, the men and women whom they fed and clothed

and even paid a little cash money at Christmas-time in
return for the labor which planted and raised and picked
and ginned the cotton, the machinery and mules and
gear with which they raised it and their cost and upkeep
and replacement—that whole edifice intricate and complex and founded upon injustice and erected by ruthless
rapacity and carried on even yet with at times downright
savagery not only to the human beings but the valuable
animals too, yet solvent and efficient and, more than that:
not only still intact but enlarged, increased; brought still
intact by McCaslin, himself little more than a child then,
through and out of the debacle and chaos of twenty years
ago where hardly one in ten survived, and enlarged and
increased and would continue so, solvent and efficient and
intact and still increasing so long as McCaslin and his
McCaslin successors lasted, even though their surnames
might not even be Edmonds then: then he: 'Habet too.
Because that's it: not the land, but us. Not only the blood,
but the name too; not only its color but its designation:
Edmonds, white, but, a female line, could have no other
but the name his father bore; Beauchamp, the elder line
and the male one, but, black, could have had any name
he liked and no man would have cared, except the name
his father bore who had no name—' and McCaslin

'And since I know too what you know I will say now,
once more let me say it: And one other, and in the third
generation too, and the male, the eldest, the direct and
sole and white and still McCaslin even, father to son to
son—' and he

'I am free:' and this time McCaslin did not even gesture,
no inference of fading pages, no postulation of the stere-
optic whole, but the frail and iron thread strong as truth
and impervious as evil and longer than life itself and
reaching beyond record and patrimony both to join him
with the lusts and passions, the hopes and dreams and
griefs, of bones whose names while still fleshed and capable
even old Carothers' grandfather had never heard: and he:

'And of that too:' and McCaslin

'Chosen, I suppose (I will concede it) out of all your time by Him as you say Buck and Buddy were from theirs. And it took Him a bear and an old man and four years just for you. And it took you fourteen years to reach that point and about that many, maybe more, for Old Ben, and more than seventy for Sam Fathers. And you are just one. How long then? How long?' and he

'It will be long. I have never said otherwise. But it will be all right because they will endure—' and McCaslin

'And anyway, you will be free.—No, not now nor ever, we from them nor they from us. So I repudiate too. I would deny even if I knew it were true. I would have to. Even you can see that I could do no else. I am what I am; I will be always what I was born and have always been. And more than me. More than me, just as there were more than Buck and Buddy in what you called His first plan which failed:' and he

'And more than me:' and McCaslin

'No. Not even you. Because mark. You said how on that instant when Ikkemotubbe realised that he could sell the land to Grandfather, it ceased forever to have been his. All right; go on: Then it belonged to Sam Fathers, old Ikkemotubbe's son. And who inherited from Sam Fathers, if not you? co-heir perhaps with Boon, if not of his life maybe, at least of his quitting it?' and he

'Yes. Sam Fathers set me free.' And Isaac McCaslin, not yet Uncle Ike, a long time yet before he would be uncle to half a county and still father to none, living in one small cramped fireless rented room in a Jefferson boardinghouse where petit juries were domiciled during court terms and itinerant horse- and mule-traders stayed, with his kit of brand-new carpenter's tools and the shotgun McCaslin had given him with his name engraved in silver and old General Compson's compass (and, when the General died, his silver-mounted horn too) and the iron cot and mattress and the blankets which he would take each fall into the woods for more than sixty years and the bright tin coffee-pot

there had been a legacy, from his Uncle Hubert Beauchamp, his godfather, that bluff burly roaring childlike man from whom Uncle Buddy had won Tomey's Terrel's wife Tennie in the poker-game in 1859—'possible strait against three Treys in sigt Not called'—; no pale sentence or paragraph scrawled in cringing fear of death by a weak and trembling hand as a last desperate sop flung backward at retribution, but a Legacy, a Thing, possessing weight to the hand and bulk to the eye and even audible: a silver cup filled with gold pieces and wrapped in burlap and sealed with his godfather's ring in the hot wax, which (intact still) even before his Uncle Hubert's death and long before his own majority, when it would be his, had become not only a legend but one of the family lares. After his father's and his Uncle Hubert's sister's marriage they moved back into the big house, the tremendous cavern which old Carothers had started and never finished, cleared the remaining Negroes out of it and with his mother's dowry completed it, at least the rest of the windows and doors and moved into it, all of them save Uncle Buddy who declined to leave the cabin he and his twin had built, the move being the bride's notion and more than just a notion and none ever to know if she really wanted to live in the big house or if she knew before hand that Uncle Buddy would refuse to move: and two weeks after his birth in 1867, the first time he and his mother came down stairs, one night and the silver cup sitting on the cleared dining-room table beneath the bright lamp and while his mother and his father and McCaslin and Tennie (his nurse: carrying him) —all of them again but Uncle Buddy—watched, his Uncle Hubert rang one by one into the cup the bright and glinting mintage and wrapped it into the burlap envelope and heated the wax and sealed it and carried it back home with him where he lived alone now without even his sister either to hold him down as McCaslin said or to try to raise him up as Uncle Buddy said, and (dark times then in Mississippi) Uncle Buddy said most of the niggers gone and the ones that didn't go even Hub Beauchamp could not have wanted: but the dogs remained and Uncle Buddy said Beauchamp fiddled while Nero fox-hunted

they would go and see it there; at last his mother would prevail and they would depart in the surrey, once more all save Uncle Buddy and McCaslin to keep Uncle Buddy company until one winter Uncle Buddy began to fail and from then on it was himself, beginning to remember now, and his mother and Tennie and Tomey's Terrel to drive: the twenty-two miles into the next county, the twin gate-posts on one of which McCaslin could remember the half-grown boy blowing a fox-horn at breakfast dinner and supper-time and jumping down to open to any passer who happened to hear it but where there were no gates at all now, the shabby and overgrown entrance to what his mother still insisted that people call Warwick because her brother was if truth but triumphed and justice but prevailed the rightful earl of it, the paintless house which outwardly did not change but which on the inside seemed each time larger because he was too little to realise then that there was less and less in it of the fine furnishings, the rosewood and mahogany and walnut which for him had never existed anywhere anyway save in his mother's tearful lamentations and the occasional piece small enough to be roped somehow onto the rear or the top of the carriage on their return (And he remembered this, he had seen it: an instant, a flash, his mother's soprano 'Even my dress! Even my dress!' loud and outraged in the barren unswept hall; a face young and female and even lighter in color than Tomey's Terrel's for an instant in a closing door; a swirl, a glimpse of the silk gown and the flick and glint of an ear-ring: an apparition rapid and tawdry and illicit yet somehow even to the child, the infant still almost, breathless and exciting and evocative: as though, like

two limpid and pellucid streams meeting, the child which
he still was had made serene and absolute and perfect
rapport and contact through that glimpsed nameless illicit
hybrid female flesh with the boy which had existed at that
stage of inviolable and immortal adolescence in his uncle
for almost sixty years; the dress, the face, the ear-rings
gone in that same aghast flash and his uncle's voice: 'She's
my cook! She's my new cook! I had to have a cook, didn't
I?' then the uncle himself, the face alarmed and aghast
too yet still innocently and somehow even indomitably of
a boy, they retreating in their turn now, back to the front
gallery, and his uncle again, pained and still amazed, in a
sort of desperate resurgence if not of courage at least of
self-assertion: 'They're free now! They're folks too just
like we are!' and his mother: 'That's why! That's why! My
mother's house! Defiled! Defiled!' and his uncle: 'Damn
it, Sibbey, at least give her time to pack her grip:' then
over, finished, the loud uproar and all, himself and Tennie
and he remembered Tennie's inscrutable face at the
broken shutterless window of the bare room which had
once been the parlor while they watched, hurrying down
the lane at a stumbling trot, the routed compounder of
his uncle's uxory: the back, the nameless face which he
had seen only for a moment, the once-hooped dress bal-
looning and flapping below a man's overcoat, the worn
heavy carpet-bag jouncing and banging against her knee,
routed and in retreat true enough and in the empty lane
solitary young-looking and forlorn yet withal still exciting
and evocative and wearing still the silken banner captured
inside the very citadel of respectability, and unforgettable.)

the cup, the sealed inscrutable burlap, sitting on the
shelf in the locked closet, Uncle Hubert unlocking the
door and lifting it down and passing it from hand to hand:
his mother, his father, McCaslin and even Tennie, insisting that each take it in turn and heft it for weight and
shake it again to prove the sound, Uncle Hubert himself

standing spraddled before the cold unswept hearth in which the very bricks themselves were crumbling into a litter of soot and dust and mortar and the droppings of chimney-sweeps, still roaring and still innocent and still indomitable: and for a long time he believed nobody but himself had noticed that his uncle now put the cup only into his hands, unlocked the door and lifted it down and put it into his hands and stood over him until he had shaken it obediently until it sounded then took it from him and locked it back into the closet before anyone else could have offered to touch it, and even later, when competent not only to remember but to rationalise, he could not say what it was or even if it had been anything because the parcel was still heavy and still rattled, not even when, Uncle Buddy dead and his father, at last and after almost seventy-five years in bed after the sun rose, said: 'Go get that damn cup. Bring that damn Hub Beauchamp too if you have to:' because it still rattled though his uncle no longer put it even into his hands now but carried it himself from one to the other, his mother, McCaslin, Tennie, shaking it before each in turn, saying: 'Hear it? Hear it?' his face still innocent, not quite baffled but only amazed and not very amazed and still indomitable: and, his father and Uncle Buddy both gone now, one day without reason or any warning the almost completely empty house in which his uncle and Tennie's ancient and quarrelsome great-grandfather (who claimed to have seen Lafayette and McCaslin said in another ten years would be remembering God) lived, cooked and slept in one single room, burst into peaceful conflagration, a tranquil instantaneous sourceless unanimity of combustion, walls floors and roof: at sunup it stood where his uncle's father had built it sixty years ago, at sundown the four blackened and smokeless chimneys rose from a light white powder of ashes and a few charred ends of planks which did not even appear to have been very hot: and out of the last of evening, the last one of the twenty-two miles, on the old white mare which

was the last of that stable which McCaslin remembered, the
two old men riding double up to the sister's door, the one
wearing his fox-horn on its braided deerhide thong and
the other carrying the burlap parcel wrapped in a shirt,
the tawny wax-daubed shapeless lump sitting again and
on an almost identical shelf and his uncle holding the
half-opened door now, his hand not only on the knob but
one foot against it and the key waiting in the other hand,
the face urgent and still not baffled but still and even in
domitably not very amazed and himself standing in the
half-opened door looking quietly up at the burlap shape
become almost three times its original height and a good
half less than its original thickness and turning away and
he would remember not his mother's look this time no:
yet Tennie's inscrutable expression but McCaslin's dark
and aquiline face grave insufferable and bemused: then
one night they waked him and fetched him still half-asleep
into the lamp light, the smell of medicine which was fa
miliar by now in that room and the smell of something
else which he had not smelled before and knew at once
and would never forget, the pillow, the worn and ravaged
face from which looked out still the boy innocent and
immortal and amazed and urgent, looking at him and
trying to tell him until McCaslin moved and leaned over
the bed and drew from the top of the nightshirt the big
iron key on the greasy cord which suspended it, the eyes
saying Yes Yes Yes now, and cut the cord and unlocked
the closet and brought the parcel to the bed, the eyes still
trying to tell him even when he took the parcel so that
was still not it, the hands still clinging to the parcel even
while relinquishing it, the eyes more urgent than ever try
ing to tell him but they never did; and he was ten and his
mother was dead too and McCaslin said, 'You are almost
halfway now. You might as well open it:' and he: 'No. He
said twenty-one:' and he was twenty-one and McCaslin
shifted the bright lamp to the center of the cleared dining
room table and set the parcel beside it and laid his open

knife beside the parcel and stood back with that expression of old grave intolerant and repudiating and he lifted it, the burlap lump which fifteen years ago had changed its shape completely overnight, which shaken gave forth a thin weightless not-quite-musical curiously muffled clatter, the bright knife-blade hunting amid the mazed intricacy of string, the knobby gouts of wax bearing his uncle's Beauchamp seal rattling onto the table's polished top and, standing amid the collapse of burlap folds, the unstained tin coffee-pot still brand new, the handful of copper coins and now he knew what had given them the muffled sound: a collection of minutely-folded scraps of paper sufficient almost for a rat's nest, of good linen bond, of the crude ruled paper such as Negroes use, of raggedly-torn ledger-pages and the margins of newspapers and once the paper label from a new pair of overalls, all dated and all signed, beginning with the first one not six months after they had watched him seal the silver cup into the burlap on this same table in this same room by the light even of this same lamp almost twenty-one years ago:

> *I owe my Nephew Isaac Beauchamp McCaslin five (5) pieces Gold which I.O.U. constitutes My note of hand with Interest at 5 percent.*
>   *Hubert Fitz-Hubert Beauchamp*
> *at Warwick 27 Nov 1867*

and he: 'Anyway he called it Warwick:' once at least, even if no more. But there was more:

> *Isaac 24 Dec 1867 I.O.U. 2 pieces Gold H.Fh.B. I.O.U. Isaac 1 piece Gold 1 Jan 1868 H.Fh.B.*

then five again then three then one then one then a long time and what dream, what dreamed splendid recoup, not of any injury or betrayal of trust because it had been merely a loan: nay, a partnership:

> *I.O.U. Beauchamp McCaslin or his heirs twenty-five*

    (25) pieces Gold This & All preceeding constituting
My notes of hand at twenty (20) percentum com
pounded annually. This date of 19th January 187:
                                   Beauchamp

no location save that in time and signed by the single no
name but word as the old proud earl himself might have
scrawled Nevile: and that made forty-three and he could
not remember himself of course but the legend had it a
fifty, which balanced: one: then one: then one: then one
and then the last three and then the last chit, dated after
he came to live in the house with them and written in the
shaky hand not of a beaten old man because he had never
been beaten to know it but of a tired old man maybe and
even at that tired only on the outside and still indomitable
the simplicity of the last one the simplicity not of resigna
tion but merely of amazement, like a simple comment or
remark, and not very much of that:

    One silver cup. Hubert Beauchamp

and McCaslin: 'So you have plenty of coppers anyway
But they are still not old enough yet to be either raritie
or heirlooms. So you will have to take the money:' except
that he didn't hear McCaslin, standing quietly beside the
table and looking peacefully at the coffee-pot and the po
sitting one night later on the mantel above what was no
even a fireplace in the little cramped icelike room in
Jefferson as McCaslin tossed the folded banknotes onto
the bed and, still standing (there was nowhere to sit save
on the bed) did not even remove his hat and overcoat
and he
    'As a loan. From you. This one:' and McCaslin
    'You cant. I have no money that I can lend to you. And
you will have to go to the bank and get it next month be
cause I wont bring it to you:' and he could not hear Mc
Caslin now either, looking peacefully at McCaslin, hi
kinsman, his father almost yet no kin now as, at the last

even fathers and sons are no kin: and he

'It's seventeen miles, horseback and in the cold. We could both sleep here:' and McCaslin

'Why should I sleep here in my house when you wont sleep yonder in yours?' and gone, and he looking at the bright rustless unstained tin and thinking and not for the first time how much it takes to compound a man (Isaac McCaslin for instance) and of the devious intricate choosing yet unerring path that man's (Isaac McCaslin's for instance) spirit takes among all that mass to make him at last what he is to be, not only to the astonishment of them (the ones who sired the McCaslin who sired his father and Uncle Buddy and their sister, and the ones who sired the Beauchamp who sired his Uncle Hubert and his Uncle Hubert's sister) who believed they had shaped him, but to Isaac McCaslin too

as a loan and used it though he would not have had to: Major de Spain offered him a room in his house as long as he wanted it and asked nor would ever ask any question, and old General Compson more than that, to take him into his own room, to sleep in half of his own bed and more than Major de Spain because he told him baldly why: 'You sleep with me and before this winter is out, I'll know the reason. You'll tell me. Because I dont believe you just quit. It looks like you just quit but I have watched you in the woods too much and I dont believe you just quit even if it does look damn like it:' using it as a loan, paid his board and rent for a month and bought the tools, not simply because he was good with his hands because he had intended to use his hands and it could have been with horses, and not in mere static and hopeful emulation of the Nazarene as the young gambler buys a spotted shirt because the old gambler won in one yesterday, but (without the arrogance of false humility and without the false humbleness of pride, who intended to earn his bread, didn't especially want to earn it but had to earn it and for more than just bread) because if the Nazarene had found

carpentering good for the life and ends He had assumed
and elected to serve, it would be all right too for Isaac
McCaslin even though Isaac McCaslin's ends, although
simple enough in their apparent motivation, were and
would be always incomprehensible to him, and his life,
invincible enough in its needs, if he could have helped
himself, not being the Nazarene, he would not have chosen
it: and paid it back. He had forgotten the thirty dollars
which McCaslin would put into the bank in his name
each month, fetched it in to him and flung it onto the bed
that first one time but no more; he had a partner now or
rather he was the partner: a blasphemous profane clever
old dipsomaniac who had built blockade-runners in
Charleston in '62 and '3 and had been a ship's carpenter
since and appeared in Jefferson two years ago nobody
knew from where nor why and spent a good part of his
time since recovering from delirium tremens in the jail;
they had put a new roof on the stable of the bank's president and (the old man in jail again still celebrating that
job) he went to the bank to collect for it and the president
said, 'I should borrow from you instead of paying you:'
and it had been seven months now and he remembered
for the first time, two-hundred-and-ten dollars, and this
was the first job of any size and when he left the bank the
account stood at two-twenty, two-forty to balance, only
twenty dollars more to go, then it did balance though by
then the total had increased to three hundred and thirty
and he said, 'I will transfer it now:' and the president said,
'I cant do that. McCaslin told me not to. Haven't you got
another initial you could use and open another account?
but that was all right, the coins the silver and the bills as
they accumulated knotted into a handkerchief and the
coffee-pot wrapped in an old shirt as when Tennie's great-
grandfather had fetched it from Warwick eighteen years
ago, in the bottom of the iron-bound trunk which old
Carothers had brought from Carolina and his landlady
said, 'Not even a lock! And you dont even lock your door

not even when you leave!' and himself looking at her as
peacefully as he had looked at McCaslin that first night
in this same room, no kin to him at all yet more than kin
as those who serve you even for pay are your kin and those
who injure you are more than brother or wife

and had the wife now, got the old man out of jail and
fetched him to the rented room and sobered him by superior strength, did not even remove his own shoes for
twenty-four hours, got him up and got food into him and
they built the barn this time from the ground up and he
married her: an only child, a small girl yet curiously bigger
than she seemed at first, solider perhaps, with dark eyes
and a passionate heart-shaped face, who had time even on
that farm to watch most of the day while he sawed timbers
to the old man's measurements: and she: 'Papa told me
about you. That farm is really yours, isn't it?' and he

'And McCaslin's:' and she

'Was there a will leaving half of it to him?' and he

'There didn't need to be a will. His grandmother was
my father's sister. We were the same as brothers:' and she

'You are the same as second cousins and that's all you
ever will be. But I dont suppose it matters:' and they were
married, they were married and it was the new country,
his heritage too as it was the heritage of all, out of the
earth, beyond the earth yet of the earth because his too
was of the earth's long chronicle, his too because each
must share with another in order to come into it and in
the sharing they become one: for that while, one: for that
little while at least, one: indivisible, that while at least
irrevocable and unrecoverable, living in a rented room
still but for just a little while and that room wall-less and
topless and floorless in glory for him to leave each morning
and return to at night; her father already owned the lot in
town and furnished the material and he and his partner
would build it, her dowry from one: her wedding-present
from three, she not to know it until the bungalow was
finished and ready to be moved into and he never know

who told her, not her father and not his partner and not even in drink though for a while he believed that, himself coming home from work and just time to wash and rest a moment before going down to supper, entering no rented cubicle since it would still partake of glory even after they would have grown old and lost it: and he saw her face then, just before she spoke: 'Sit down:' the two of them sitting on the bed's edge, not even touching yet, her face strained and terrible, her voice a passionate and expiring whisper of immeasurable promise: 'I love you. You know I love you. When are we going to move?' and he

'I didn't—I didn't know—Who told you—' the hot fierce palm clapped over his mouth, crushing his lips into his teeth, the fierce curve of fingers digging into his cheek and only the palm slacked off enough for him to answer:

'The farm. Our farm. Your farm:' and he

'I—' then the hand again, finger and palm, the whole enveloping weight of her although she still was not touching him save the hand, the voice: 'No! No!' and the fingers themselves seeming to follow through the cheek the impulse to speech as it died in his mouth, then the whisper the breath again, of love and of incredible promise, the palm slackening again to let him answer:

'When?' and he

'I—' then she was gone, the hand too, standing, her back to him and her head bent, the voice so calm now that for an instant it seemed no voice of hers that he ever remembered: 'Stand up and turn your back and shut your eyes:' and repeated before he understood and stood himself with his eyes shut and heard the bell ring for supper below stairs and the calm voice again: 'Lock the door:' and he did so and leaned his forehead against the cold wood, his eyes closed, hearing his heart and the sound he had begun to hear before he moved until it ceased and the bell rang again below stairs and he knew it was for them this time and he heard the bed and turned and he had never seen her naked before, he had asked her to once, and why: that he wanted to see her naked because he loved her and he wanted to see her looking at him naked because he loved her but after that he never mentioned it again, even turning his face when she put the nightgown on over her dress to undress at night and putting the dress on over the gown to remove it in the morning and she would not let him get into bed beside her until the lamp was out and even in the heat of summer she would draw the sheet up over them both before she would let him turn to her: and the landlady came up the stairs up the hall and rapped on the door and then called their names but she didn't move, lying still on the bed outside the covers, her face turned away on the pillow, listening to nothing, thinking of nothing, not of him anyway he thought then the landlady went away and she said, "Take off your clothes:' her head still turned away, looking at nothing, thinking of nothing, waiting for nothing, not even him, her hand moving as though with volition and vision of its own, catching his wrist at the exact moment when he paused beside the bed so that he never paused but merely changed the direction of moving, downward now, the hand drawing him and she moved at last, shifted, a movement one single complete inherent not practiced and one time older than man, looking at him now, drawing him still downward with the one hand down and down and he neither saw nor felt it shift, palm flat against his chest now and holding him away with the same apparent lack of any effort or any need for strength, and not looking at him now, she didn't need to, the chaste woman, the wife, already looked upon all the men who ever rutted and now her whole body had changed, altered, he had never seen it but once and now it was not even the one he had seen but composite of all woman-flesh since man that ever of its own will reclined on its back and opened, and out of it somewhere, without any movement of lips even, the dying and invincible whisper: 'Promise:' and he

'Promise?'

'The farm.' He moved. He had moved, the hand shift
ing from his chest once more to his wrist, grasping it, the
arm still lax and only the light increasing pressure of the
fingers as though arm and hand were a piece of wire cable
with one looped end, only the hand tightening as he pulled
against it. 'No,' he said. 'No:' and she was not looking a
him still but not like the other but still the hand: 'No,
tell you. I wont. I cant. Never:' and still the hand and he
said, for the last time, he tried to speak clearly and he
knew it was still gently and he thought, *She already know*
more than I with all the man-listening in camps where
there was nothing to read ever even heard of. They ar
born already bored with what a boy approaches only a
fourteen and fifteen with blundering and aghast trem
bling: 'I cant. Not ever. Remember:' and still the stead
and invincible hand and he said Yes and he thought, *Sh*
is lost. She was born lost. We were all born lost then he
stopped thinking and even saying Yes, it was like nothing
he had ever dreamed, let alone heard in mere man-talking
until after a no-time he returned and lay spent on the
insatiate immemorial beach and again with a movemen
one time more older than man she turned and freed hersel
and on their wedding night she had cried and he though
she was crying now at first, into the tossed and wadded
pillow, the voice coming from somewhere between the
pillow and the cachinnation: 'And that's all. That's al
from me. If this dont get you that son you talk about, i
wont be mine:' lying on her side, her back to the empt
rented room, laughing and laughing

—5—

He went back to the camp one more time before the
lumber company moved in and began to cut the timber
Major de Spain himself never saw it again. But he mad
them welcome to use the house and hunt the land when
ever they liked, and in the winter following the last hun

when Sam Fathers and Lion died, General Compson and Walter Ewell invented a plan to corporate themselves, the old group, into a club and lease the camp and the hunting privileges of the woods—an invention doubtless of the somewhat childish old General but actually worthy of Boon Hogganbeck himself. Even the boy, listening, recognised it for the subterfuge it was: to change the leopard's spots when they could not alter the leopard, a baseless and illusory hope to which even McCaslin seemed to subscribe for a while, that once they had persuaded Major de Spain to return to the camp he might revoke himself, which even the boy knew he would not do. And he did not. The boy never knew what occurred when Major de Spain declined. He was not present when the subject was broached and McCaslin never told him. But when June came and the time for the double birthday celebration there was no mention of it and when November came no one spoke of using Major de Spain's house and he never knew whether or not Major de Spain knew they were going on the hunt though without doubt old Ash probably told him: he and McCaslin and General Compson (and that one was the General's last hunt too) and Walter and Boon and Tennie's Jim and old Ash loaded two wagons and drove two days and almost forty miles beyond any country the boy had ever seen before and lived in tents for the two weeks. And the next spring they heard (not from Major de Spain) that he had sold the timber-rights to a Memphis lumber company and in June the boy came to town with McCaslin one Saturday and went to Major de Spain's office—the big, airy, book-lined second-storey room with windows at one end opening upon the shabby hinder purlieus of stores and at the other a door giving onto the railed balcony above the Square, with its curtained alcove where sat a cedar water-bucket and a sugar-bowl and spoon and tumbler and a wicker-covered demijohn of whisky, and the bamboo-and-paper punkah swinging back and forth above the desk while old Ash in a tilted chair beside the entrance pulled the cord.

"Of course," Major de Spain said. "Ash will probably like to get off in the woods himself for a while, where he wont have to eat Daisy's cooking. Complain about it, anyway. Are you going to take anybody with you?"

"No sir," he said. "I thought that maybe Boon—" For six months now Boon had been town-marshal at Hoke's. Major de Spain had compounded with the lumber company—or perhaps compromised was closer, since it was the lumber company who had decided that Boon might be better as a town-marshal than head of a logging gang.

"Yes," Major de Spain said. "I'll wire him today. He can meet you at Hoke's. I'll send Ash on by the train and they can take some food in and all you will have to do will be to mount your horse and ride over."

"Yes sir," he said. "Thank you." And he heard his voice again. He didn't know he was going to say it yet he did know, he had known it all the time: "Maybe if you . . ." His voice died. It was stopped, he never knew how because Major de Spain did not speak and it was not until his voice ceased that Major de Spain moved, turned back to the desk and the papers spread on it and even that without moving because he was sitting at the desk with a paper in his hand when the boy entered, the boy standing there looking down at the short plumpish gray-haired man in sober fine broadcloth and an immaculate glazed shirt whom he was used to seeing in boots and muddy corduroy, unshaven, sitting the shaggy powerful long-hocked mare with the worn Winchester carbine across the saddlebow and the great blue dog standing motionless as bronze at the stirrup, the two of them in that last year and to the boy anyway coming to resemble one another somehow as two people competent for love or for business who have been in love or in business together for a long time sometimes do. Major de Spain did not look up again.

"No. I will be too busy. But good luck to you. If you have it, you might bring me a young squirrel."

"Yes sir," he said. "I will."

He rode his mare, the three-year-old filly he had bred and raised and broken himself. He left home a little after midnight and six hours later, without even having sweated her, he rode into Hoke's, the tiny long-line junction which he had always thought of as Major de Spain's property too although Major de Spain had merely sold the company (and that many years ago) the land on which the side-tracks and loading-platforms and the commissary store stood, and looked about in shocked and grieved amazement even though he had had forewarning and had believed himself prepared: a new planing-mill already half completed which would cover two or three acres and what looked like miles and miles of stacked steel rails red with the light bright rust of newness and of piled crossties sharp with creosote, and wire corrals and feeding-troughs for two hundred mules at least and the tents for the men who drove them; so that he arranged for the care and stabling of his mare as rapidly as he could and did not look any more, mounted into the log-train caboose with his gun and climbed into the cupola and looked no more save toward the wall of wilderness ahead within which he would be able to hide himself from it once more anyway.

Then the little locomotive shrieked and began to move: a rapid churning of exhaust, a lethargic deliberate clashing of slack couplings traveling backward along the train, the exhaust changing to the deep slow clapping bites of power as the caboose too began to move and from the cupola he watched the train's head complete the first and only curve in the entire line's length and vanish into the wilderness, dragging its length of train behind it so that it resembled a small dingy harmless snake vanishing into weeds, drawing him with it too until soon it ran once more at its maximum clattering speed between the twin walls of unaxed wilderness as of old. It had been harmless once. Not five years ago Walter Ewell had shot a six-point buck from this same moving caboose, and there was the

story of the half-grown bear: the train's first trip in to the
cutting thirty miles away, the bear between the rails, its
rear end elevated like that of a playing puppy while it
dug to see what sort of ants or bugs they might contain or
perhaps just to examine the curious symmetrical squared
barkless logs which had appeared apparently from nowhere
in one endless mathematical line overnight, still digging
until the driver on the braked engine not fifty feet away
blew the whistle at it, whereupon it broke frantically and
took the first tree it came to: an ash sapling not much bigger than a man's thigh and climbed as high as it could and
clung there, its head ducked between its arms as a man
(a woman perhaps) might have done while the brakeman
threw chunks of ballast at it, and when the engine returned
three hours later with the first load of outbound logs the
bear was halfway down the tree and once more scrambled
back up as high as it could and clung again while the train
passed and was still there when the engine went in again
in the afternoon and still there when it came back out at
dusk; and Boon had been in Hoke's with the wagon after
a barrel of flour that noon when the train-crew told about
it and Boon and Ash, both twenty years younger then, sat
under the tree all that night to keep anybody from shooting it and the next morning Major de Spain had the log-
train held at Hoke's and just before sundown on the second
day, with not only Boon and Ash but Major de Spain and
General Compson and Walter and McCaslin, twelve then
watching, it came down the tree after almost thirty-six
hours without even water and McCaslin told him how for
a minute they thought it was going to stop right there at
the barrow-pit where they were standing and drink, how
it looked at the water and paused and looked at them and
at the water again, but did not, gone, running, as bears
run, the two sets of feet, front and back, tracking two
separate though parallel courses.

It had been harmless then. They would hear the passing
log-train sometimes from the camp; sometimes, because

nobody bothered to listen for it or not. They would hear it going in, running light and fast, the light clatter of the trucks, the exhaust of the diminutive locomotive and its shrill peanut-parcher whistle flung for one petty moment and absorbed by the brooding and inattentive wilderness without even an echo. They would hear it going out, loaded, not quite so fast now yet giving its frantic and toylike illusion of crawling speed, not whistling now to conserve steam, flinging its bitten laboring miniature puffing into the immemorial woodsface with frantic and bootless vainglory, empty and noisy and puerile, carrying to no destination or purpose sticks which left nowhere any scar or stump as the child's toy loads and transports and unloads its dead sand and rushes back for more, tireless and unceasing and rapid yet never quite so fast as the Hand which plays with it moves the toy burden back to load the toy again. But it was different now. It was the same train, engine cars and caboose, even the same enginemen brakeman and conductor to whom Boon, drunk then sober then drunk again then fairly sober once more all in the space of fourteen hours, had bragged that day two years ago about what they were going to do to Old Ben tomorrow, running with its same illusion of frantic rapidity between the same twin walls of impenetrable and impervious woods, passing the old landmarks, the old game crossings over which he had trailed bucks wounded and not wounded and more than once seen them, anything but wounded, break out of the woods, up and across the embankment which bore the rails and ties then down and into the woods again as the earth-bound supposedly move but crossing as arrows travel, groundless, elongated, three times its actual length and even paler, different in color, as if there were a point between immobility and absolute motion where even mass chemically altered, changing without pain or agony not only in bulk and shape but in color too, approaching the color of wind, yet this time it was as though the train (and not only the train but himself, not only his vision which had seen it and his memory which remembered it but his clothes too, as garments carry back into the clean edgeless blowing of air the lingering effluvium of a sick-room or of death) had brought with it into the doomed wilderness even before the actual axe the shadow and portent of the new mill not even finished yet and the rails and ties which were not even laid; and he knew now what he had known as soon as he saw Hoke's this morning but had not yet thought into words, why Major de Spain had not come back, and that after this time he himself, who had had to see it one time other, would return no more.

Now they were near. He knew it before the engine driver whistled to warn him. Then he saw Ash and the wagon, the reins without doubt wrapped once more about the brake-lever as within the boy's own memory Major de Spain had been forbidding him for eight years to do, the train slowing, the slackened couplings jolting and clashing again from car to car, the caboose slowing past the wagon as he swung down with his gun, the conductor leaning out above him to signal the engine, the caboose still slowing, creeping, although the engine's exhaust was already slatting in mounting tempo against the unechoing wilderness, the crashing of draw-bars once more travelling backward along the train, the caboose picking up speed at last. Then it was gone. It had not been. He could no longer hear it. The wilderness soared, musing, inattentive, myriad, eternal, green; older than any mill-shed, longer than any spurline. "Mr Boon here yet?" he said.

"He beat me in," Ash said. "Had the wagon loaded and ready for me at Hoke's yistiddy when I got there and setting on the front steps at camp last night when I got in. He already been in the woods since fo daylight this morning. Said he gwine up to the Gum Tree and for you to hunt up that way and meet him." He knew where that was: a single big sweet-gum just outside the woods, in an old clearing; if you crept up to it very quietly this time of year and then ran suddenly into the clearing, sometimes you caught as many as a dozen squirrels in it, trapped, since there was no other tree near they could jump to. So he didn't get into the wagon at all.

"I will," he said.

"I figured you would," Ash said, "I fotch you a box of shells." He passed the shells down and began to unwrap the lines from the brake-pole.

"How many times up to now do you reckon Major has told you not to do that?" the boy said.

"Do which?" Ash said. Then he said: "And tell Boon Hogganbeck dinner gonter be on the table in a hour and if yawl want any to come on and eat it."

"In an hour?" he said. "It aint nine oclock yet." He drew out his watch and extended it face-toward Ash. "Look." Ash didn't even look at the watch.

"That's town time. You aint in town now. You in the woods."

"Look at the sun then."

"Nemmine the sun too," Ash said. "If you and Boon Hogganbeck want any dinner, you better come on in and get it when I tole you. I aim to get done in that kitchen because I got my wood to chop. And watch your feet. They're crawling."

"I will," he said.

Then he was in the woods, not alone but solitary; the solitude closed about him, green with summer. They did not change, and, timeless, would not, anymore than would the green of summer and the fire and rain of fall and the iron cold and sometimes even snow

the day, the morning when he killed the buck and Sam marked his face with its hot blood, they returned to camp and he remembered old Ash's blinking and disgruntled and even outraged disbelief until at last McCaslin had had to affirm the fact that he had really killed it: and that night Ash sat snarling and unapproachable behind the stove so that Tennie's Jim had to serve the supper and waked them with breakfast already on the table the next morning and it was only half-past one oclock and at last out of Major de Spain's angry cursing and Ash's snarling and sullen rejoinders the fact emerged that Ash not only wanted to go into the woods and shoot a deer also but he intended to and Major de Spain said, 'By God, if we dont let him we will probably have to do the cooking from now on:' and Walter Ewell said, 'Or get up at midnight to eat what Ash cooks:' and since he had already killed his buck for this hunt and was not to shoot again unless they needed meat, he offered his gun to Ash until Major de Spain took command and allotted that gun to Boon for the day and gave Boon's unpredictable pump gun to Ash, with two buckshot shells but Ash said, 'I got shells:' and showed them, four: one buck, one of number three shot for rabbits, two of bird-shot and told one by one their history and their origin and he remembered not Ash's face alone but Major de Spain's and Walter's and General Compson's too, and Ash's voice: 'Shoot? In course they'll shoot! Genl Cawmpson guv me this un'—the buckshot—'right outen the same gun he kilt that big buck with eight years ago. And this un'—it was the rabbit shell: triumphantly—'is oldern thisyer boy!' And that morning he loaded the gun himself, reversing the order: the bird-shot, the rabbit, then the buck so that the buckshot would feed first into the chamber, and himself without a gun, he and Ash walked beside Major de Spain's and Tennie's Jim's horses and the dogs (that was the snow) until they cast and struck, the sweet strong cries ringing away into the muffled falling air and gone almost immediately, as if the constant and unmurmuring flakes had already buried even the unformed echoes beneath their myriad and weightless falling, Major de Spain and Tennie's Jim gone too, whooping on into the woods; and then it was all right, he knew as plainly as if Ash had told him that Ash had now hunted his deer and that even his tender years had been forgiven for having killed one, and they turned back toward home

*through the falling snow—that is, Ash said, 'Now whut?'
and he said, 'This way'—himself in front because, although
they were less than a mile from camp, he knew that Ash,
who had spent two weeks of his life in the camp each year
for the last twenty, had no idea whatever where they were,
until quite soon the manner in which Ash carried Boon's
gun was making him a good deal more than just nervous
and he made Ash walk in front, striding on, talking now,
an old man's garrulous monologue beginning with where
he was at the moment then of the woods and of camping
in the woods and of eating in camps then of eating then
of cooking it and of his wife's cooking then briefly of his
old wife and almost at once and at length of a new light-
colored woman who nursed next door to Major de Spain's
and if she didn't watch out who she was switching her tail
at he would show her how old was an old man or not if
his wife just didn't watch him all the time, the two of them
in a game trail through a dense brake of cane and brier
which would bring them out within a quarter-mile of
camp, approaching a big fallen tree-trunk lying athwart
the path and just as Ash, still talking, was about to step
over it the bear, the yearling, rose suddenly beyond the
log, sitting up, its forearms against its chest and its wrists
limply arrested as if it had been surprised in the act of covering its face to pray: and after a certain time Ash's gun
yawed jerkily up and he said, 'You haven't got a shell in
the barrel yet. Pump it:' but the gun already snicked and
he said, 'Pump it. You haven't got a shell in the barrel
yet:' and Ash pumped the action and in a certain time the
gun steadied again and snicked and he said, 'Pump it:'
and watched the buckshot shell jerk, spinning heavily,
into the cane. This is the rabbit shot: he thought and the
gun snicked and he thought: The next is bird-shot: and
he didn't have to say Pump it; he cried, 'Dont shoot! Dont
shoot!' but that was already too late too, the light dry
vicious snick! before he could speak and the bear turned
and dropped to all-fours and then was gone and there was*

*only the log, the cane, the velvet and constant snow and
Ash said, 'Now whut?' and he said, 'This way. Come on:'
and began to back away down the path and Ash said, 'I got
to find my shells:' and he said, 'Goddamn it, goddamn it,
come on:' but Ash leaned the gun against the log and returned and stooped and fumbled among the cane roots
until he came back and stooped and found the shells and
they rose and at that moment the gun, untouched, leaning
against the log six feet away and for that while even forgotten by both of them, roared, bellowed and flamed, and
ceased: and he carried it now, pumped out the last mum-
mified shell and gave that one also to Ash and, the action
still open, himself carried the gun until he stood it in the
corner behind Boon's bed at the camp*
—; summer, and fall, and snow, and wet and saprife
spring in their ordered immortal sequence, the deathless
and immemorial phases of the mother who had shaped
him if any had toward the man he almost was, mother and
father both to the old man born of a Negro slave and a
Chickasaw chief who had been his spirit's father if any
had, whom he had revered and harkened to and loved and
lost and grieved: and he would marry someday and they
too would own for their brief while that brief unsub-
stanced glory which inherently of itself cannot last and
hence why glory: and they would, might, carry even the
remembrance of it into the time when flesh no longer talks
to flesh because memory at least does last: but still the
woods would be his mistress and his wife.

He was not going toward the Gum Tree. Actually he
was getting farther from it. Time was and not so long ago
either when he would not have been allowed here without
someone with him, and a little later, when he had begun
to learn how much he did not know, he would not have
dared be here without someone with him, and later still,
beginning to ascertain, even if only dimly, the limits of
what he did not know, he could have attempted and carried it through with a compass, not because of any in-

creased belief in himself but because McCaslin and Major de Spain and Walter and General Compson too had taught him at last to believe the compass regardless of what it seemed to state. Now he did not even use the compass but merely the sun and that only subconsciously, yet he could have taken a scaled map and plotted at any time to within a hundred feet of where he actually was; and sure enough, at almost the exact moment when he expected it, the earth began to rise faintly, he passed one of the four concrete markers set down by the lumber company's surveyor to establish the four corners of the plot which Major de Spain had reserved out of the sale, then he stood on the crest of the knoll itself, the four corner-markers all visible now, blanched still even beneath the winter's weathering, lifeless and shockingly alien in that place where dissolution itself was a seething turmoil of ejaculation tumescence conception and birth, and death did not even exist. After two winters' blanketings of leaves and the flood-waters of two springs, there was no trace of the two graves anymore at all. But those who would have come this far to find them would not need headstones but would have found them as Sam Fathers himself had taught him to find such: by bearings on trees: and did, almost the first thrust of the hunting knife finding (but only to see if it was still there) the round tin box manufactured for axle-grease and containing now Old Ben's dried mutilated paw, resting above Lion's bones.

He didn't disturb it. He didn't even look for the other grave where he and McCaslin and Major de Spain and Boon had laid Sam's body, along with his hunting horn and his knife and his tobacco-pipe, that Sunday morning two years ago; he didn't have to. He had stepped over it, perhaps on it. But that was all right. *He probably knew I was in the woods this morning long before I got here,* he thought, going on to the tree which had supported one end of the platform where Sam lay when McCaslin and Major de Spain found them—the tree, the other axle-grease tin nailed to the trunk, but weathered, rusted, alien too yet healed already into the wilderness' concordant generality, raising no tuneless note, and empty, long since empty of the food and tobacco he had put into it that day, as empty of that as it would presently be of this which he drew from his pocket—the twist of tobacco, the new bandanna handkerchief, the small paper sack of the peppermint candy which Sam had used to love; that gone too, almost before he had turned his back, not vanished but merely translated into the myriad life which printed the dark mold of these secret and sunless places with delicate fairy tracks, which, breathing and biding and immobile, watched him from beyond every twig and leaf until he moved, moving again, walking on; he had not stopped, he had only paused, quitting the knoll which was no abode of the dead because there was no death, not Lion and not Sam: not held fast in earth but free in earth and not in earth but of earth, myriad yet undiffused of every myriad part, leaf and twig and particle, air and sun and rain and dew and night, acorn oak and leaf and acorn again, dark and dawn and dark and dawn again in their immutable progression and, being myriad, one: and Old Ben too, Old Ben too; they would give him his paw back even, certainly they would give him his paw back: then the long challenge and the long chase, no heart to be driven and outraged, no flesh to be mauled and bled—Even as he froze himself, he seemed to hear Ash's parting admonition. He could even hear the voice as he froze, immobile, one foot just taking his weight, the toe of the other just lifted behind him, not breathing, feeling again and as always the sharp shocking inrush from when Isaac McCaslin long yet was not, and so it was fear all right but not fright as he looked down at it. It had not coiled yet and the buzzer had not sounded either, only one thick rapid contraction, one loop cast sideways as though merely for purchase from which the raised head might start slightly backward, not in fright either, not in threat quite yet, more than six feet of it, the head raised higher than his knee and less than his knee's length away, and old, the once-bright markings of its youth dulled now to a monotone concordant too with the wilderness it crawled and lurked: the old one, the ancient and accursed about the earth, fatal and solitary and he could smell it now: the thin sick smell of rotting cucumbers and something else which had no name, evocative of all knowledge and an old weariness and of pariahhood and of death. At last it moved. Not the head. The elevation of the head did not change as it began to glide away from him, moving erect yet off the perpendicular as if the head and that elevated third were complete and all: an entity walking on two feet and free of all laws of mass and balance and should have been because even now he could not quite believe that all that shift and flow of shadow behind that walking head could have been one snake: going and then gone; he put the other foot down at last and didn't know it, standing with one hand raised as Sam had stood that afternoon six years ago when Sam led him into the wilderness and showed him and he ceased to be a child, speaking the old tongue which Sam had spoken that day without premeditation either: "Chief," he said: "Grandfather."

He couldn't tell when he first began to hear the sound, because when he became aware of it, it seemed to him that he had been already hearing it for several seconds—a sound as though someone were hammering a gun-barrel against a piece of railroad iron, a sound loud and heavy and not rapid yet with something frenzied about it, as the hammerer were not only a strong man and an earnest one but a little hysterical too. Yet it couldn't be on the log-line because, although the track lay in that direction, it was at least two miles from him and this sound was not three hundred yards away. But even as he thought that, he realised where the sound must be coming from: whoever the man was and whatever he was doing, he was somewhere near the edge of the clearing where the Gum Tree was and

where he was to meet Boon. So far, he had been hunting
as he advanced, moving slowly and quietly and watching
the ground and the trees both. Now he went on, his gun
unloaded and the barrel slanted up and back to facilitate
its passage through brier and undergrowth, approaching
as it grew louder and louder that steady savage somehow
queerly hysterical beating of metal on metal, emerging
from the woods, into the old clearing, with the solitary
gum tree directly before him. At first glance the tree
seemed to be alive with frantic squirrels. There appeared
to be forty or fifty of them leaping and darting from
branch to branch until the whole tree had become one
green maelstrom of mad leaves, while from time to time,
singly or in twos and threes, squirrels would dart down
the trunk then whirl without stopping and rush back up
again as though sucked violently back by the vacuum of
their fellows' frenzied vortex. Then he saw Boon, sitting,
his back against the trunk, his head bent, hammering furiously at something on his lap. What he hammered with
was the barrel of his dismembered gun, what he hammered at was the breech of it. The rest of the gun lay
scattered about him in a half-dozen pieces while he bent
over the piece on his lap his scarlet and streaming walnut
face, hammering the disjointed barrel against the gun
breech with the frantic abandon of a madman. He didn't
even look up to see who it was. Still hammering, he merely
shouted back at the boy in a hoarse strangled voice:

"Get out of here! Dont touch them! Dont touch a one
of them! They're mine!"

Daughtry had married a man she'd never met...

In the foggy uncertainty of sleep, Daughtry struggled to open her eyes. A part of her wanted to go on sleeping so that she could enjoy the dream, but another part of her was being beckoned. She could almost hear someone calling her name.

Daughtry tried to concentrate on the voice but it faded and, as it did, she became more awake, until she suddenly realized that she wasn't alone. Opening her eyes wide, Daughtry stared into the amused dark eyes of Nicholas Dawson.

For a moment all Daughtry could do was stare. Was she dreaming or was this real? The shocked look on her face caused the man beside her to chuckle.

"I—I—" Daughtry couldn't speak a coherent word to save herself. Shyly, she pulled her arms from the man's neck and tried to ease away from him, as if he wouldn't notice.

Nicholas sat up and Daughtry could see he was fully clothed and sitting atop the covers she so carefully clutched to her neck. With a grin he spoke. "I sure hope you're my wife."

Tracie J. Peterson is a popular inspirational writer and a regular columnist for a Christian newspaper in Topeka, Kansas. Tracie has also written eight successful **Heartsong Presents** titles under the name of Janelle Jamison.

HEARTSONG PRESENTS

Books by Janelle Jamison

HP19—A Place to Belong
HP40—Perfect Love
HP47—Tender Journeys
HP56—A Light in the Window
HP63—The Willing Heart
HP71—Destiny's Road
HP88—Beyond Today
HP93—Iditarod Dream

Books by Tracie J. Peterson

HP102—If Given a Choice
HP111—A Kingdom Divided

Don't miss out on any of our super romances. Write to us at the following address for information on our newest releases and club information.

Heartsong Presents Readers' Service
P.O. Box 719
Uhrichsville, OH 44683

Forever Yours

Tracie J. Peterson

A sequel to *A Place to Belong*
and *The Willing Heart*
by Janelle Jamison.

Heartsong Presents

Dedicated to all the would-be writers out there, with
three supportive suggestions that were once offered to
me, and one extra that I would like to add.
1. Write what you know.
2. Learn what you don't know.
3. Never give up on the dream.
4. Colossians 3:23

A note from the Author:
*I love to hear from my readers! You may correspond
with me by writing:*

Tracie J. Peterson
Author Relations
P.O. Box 719
Uhrichsville, OH 44683

ISBN 1-55748-710-3

FOREVER YOURS

Cover illustration by Kathy Arbuckle.

PRINTED IN THE U.S.A.

prologue

Riotous changes, for which the young country was already famous, ushered in the turn of the century in America. As the 1900s quickly added years and headed into their teens, a fascination grew for things mechanical and complicated. America was hungry for change and innovation, and her people were only too happy to comply.

Among those changes were some that would drastically alter the course of history. Skeptical crowds viewed automobiles and airplanes, never believing the contraptions would retire the horse and buggy. Meanwhile, the warm wonder of electric lighting spread like a fire out of control and soon engulfed the young nation. New carbonated drinks, rising hemlines, and a variety of contraptions and conveniences that baffled the mind were part of the flood that swept the country into young adulthood.

The world was, of course, not without its problems. Racial hatred ran rampant, especially in larger cities in the East. Leonardo da Vinci's "Mona Lisa" was stolen in August of 1911 and not recovered until two years later. And in 1912 the nation mourned in stunned dismay the sinking of the Titanic.

In an almost frantic frenzy, Americans pressed forward at such an alarming rate that old-timers questioned the sanity of those younger. Where would it all lead? And how could it possibly be good?

In the unspoiled innocence of the recently admitted state

of New Mexico, things were no different from the rest of
the country. A hunger was growing for the wealth and
wonder of all that their sister states enjoyed. Perhaps the
old-timers weren't panting for change like the younger
citizens, and maybe the natives looked with contempt on
the destruction that always accompanied progress. But in
the growing town of Bandelero, New Mexico, the children of its founders were now coming of age, and with
this came bold ideals for the years to come.

one

"Daughtry!"

The voice sounded loud and clear from outside the adobe stable.

"In here, Daddy!" a young, auburn-haired woman called. She finished cleaning the hoof she held between her slender, jean-clad legs before making any move to greet her father.

Garrett Lucas bounded into the stable with a look of determined frustration on his face. Now in his mid-fifties, Garrett was still lean and muscular from his years of ranch work. His hair was a salt and pepper brown that he fondly told his children was growing whiter by the minute due to their antics.

"Where have you been?" he asked.

Daughtry patted the back of her horse Poco and moved to put away her grooming equipment. "Dad, you know very well that I ride before breakfast every single morning. Then I come back here and see to Poco, just like you taught me."

Relief crossed Garrett's face before he nodded to his daughter. "I think you ought to have one of the hands ride out with you," he advised. "Or at least you could ask one of your brothers."

"Daddy! I'm twenty-three years old. When are you going to realize that I'm fully capable of taking care of myself?" Daughtry's voice betrayed the frustration she felt with her father's constant overshadowing protection.

Garrett pushed back his black Stetson and sighed. He knew she was right, but he had a hard time seeing her as the woman she'd grown into, instead of the five-year-old who flitted about in his memories.

"Just because you're grown doesn't mean I stop worrying about you," Garrett offered by way of apology.

Daughtry sighed and brushed the dirt from her pants. "I know and I'm glad you love me, but I have to have some room to breathe. You have one of the largest ranches in New Mexico to run, so why not concentrate on that and let me go my own way?" Daughtry paused and looked at her father seriously. "Sometimes you and the boys are just more than I care to deal with. I don't know how Mother stands it."

Garrett grinned. "I keep your mother too busy to worry about it. Besides, she likes my keepin' an eye on her."

"Well," Daughtry said coming forward to place a quick kiss on her father's cheek, "I'm not Mother."

She walked past her father and kept moving toward the adobe-styled ranch house. For all her life Piñon Canyon Ranch had been her home, and all her memories, both good and bad, were enclosed by its boundaries. Now, it seemed more like a prison. The world was changing out there, but here time seemed to stand still. Her family didn't have electricity, telephones, or automobiles, and often Daughtry had the dreadful feeling that life was passing her by.

"I wish you wouldn't wear your brother's clothes," Garrett said from behind her.

Daughtry stopped in her tracks and turned, and her father quickly covered the distance between them. The look on his daughter's face told him that although they'd had this argument before, she was ready, willing, and able to address the issue once again. Garrett, however, really didn't want to argue on such a beautiful summer morning. He shrugged his shoulders and raised his hands in the air.

"Okay, I give up. Wear jeans when you work around the ranch. But I better never catch you wearing them into town. They're too revealing and I won't have every guy there drooling and following you around."

Daughtry laughed. "Oh, Daddy. You are impossible. No man is ever going to drool over me, because you're always two steps behind or in front of me. No gentleman can get close enough to ask my name, much less ogle me."

"Good," Garrett said, putting his arm around his daughter. "Let's keep it that way." He meant it in jest, and he missed the frown that marred his daughter's otherwise pretty face.

Inside the ranch house, a flurry of activity was managing to create absolute chaos. This was typical of breakfast at the Lucas table, and Maggie Lucas took it all in stride. Still a fine looking woman, with a shapely figure and dark auburn hair, Maggie so closely resembled her daughter Daughtry that people often mistook them at a quick glance.

When her husband and daughter came into the dining room, arm and arm, Maggie couldn't help but smile. Then, just as quickly, a frown crossed her face as she caught sight of her daughter's grim expression. Garrett was obviously making himself a pest again.

Maggie knew why, but it didn't help matters any. Her own heartfelt grief at the loss of their daughter Julie, almost four years earlier, caused her to sympathize with her husband. When Julie had ridden out on a cold December morning, no one thought that only hours later she would lie dead at the bottom of an icy ravine. Her horse had lost its footing, and Garrett had never forgiven himself for letting Julie ride out alone. Truth be told, Garrett had never stopped blaming himself for the tragedy and had become incessantly more preoccupied with Daughtry's safety. Indeed, his concern had rapidly approached a level of grief all its own, for he knew his inability to protect Daughtry from all of life's many dangers. His grief and frustration threatened to drive Daughtry away from her father and their home.

Daughtry's brothers swarmed around the room. Dolan and Don were arguing, as was typical for the seventeen-year-old twins. Joseph, sixteen, was trying to snag pieces of food off the plates as Anna Maria and Pepita hurried around the table to avoid his reach, and fifteen-year-old Jordan, Jordy to everyone except when he was in trouble, was reading as he walked. No doubt another western. Jordy loved to read them and point out the inaccuracies. There was only one author he held any esteem for and that was Zane Grey.

Finally, Gavin, the oldest of the boys at twenty-one, entered, gave his mother a peck on the cheek, whirled her in a circle, more to clear her out of his way than anything, and took his seat at the table.

"I'm starved!" Gavin fairly roared, then grinned up at his mother who was shaking her head at him.

"Well, if we can get everyone to take a seat," Maggie said, "we'll have breakfast." Nearly in unison, four boys took their seat, leaving Garrett and Daughtry standing.

"Well, come on Sis, Dad," Gavin said, reaching out to take hold of his mother's hand. "Let's pray and eat."

Garrett took his place at the head of the table, while Daughtry went to sit across from her mother. Everyone joined hands, while Garrett blessed the food. When his brief prayer ended, the chaos which had existed earlier died away to civility and calm. Maggie Lucas would tolerate no rowdiness at her table.

Daughtry picked at her food, while all around her, her brothers ate as though they were starving. She was hungry, or at least had been until that morning's episode with her father. How could she ever get him to stop worrying that she was going to die tragically like her sister?

"Aren't you hungry?" Maggie asked her softly.

Six pairs of eyes followed their mother's gaze to see what Daughtry's response would be. Sometimes, she felt as though she held the entire ranch hostage, awaiting her answers. But most of the time, Daughtry felt like she was the hostage.

"I'm fine," she muttered under her breath and continued to pick at the biscuits and gravy on her plate.

"We've got a heap of work cut out for us today," Garrett was telling his sons, and Daughtry let her mind wander, knowing that this would keep everyone occupied for a spell.

Why can't I just get away from here? Her mind reeled at the unspoken question. What she wouldn't give to leave Piñon Canyon. At least for a little while. *I've never even been out of New Mexico,* she thought. *There's a whole world out there that I only know from magazines and books. Will I ever see it? Will I ever be able to enjoy the things other people do?* She was twenty-three years old.

An old maid by some standards, not that her father cared. If he had his way about it, she'd stay unmarried and lonely, until her dying day.

The boys all seemed to be talking at once, and Daughtry nearly laughed out loud at the thought of being lonely. *How could anyone claim such a feat in this house?* she wondered. But she was. She was lonely and bored and unhappy with her life. She prayed about it often. She read her Bible. She even sought the advice of their long-time family friend, Pastor David Monroe, but nothing seemed to help.

David had suggested she mingle more with people her own age, but every time she tried to do just that, her father would come looking for her. She'd hoped that after a little time had passed and the pain of Julie's death had dimmed, her father and brothers wouldn't be quite so possessive of her. But, if anything, it was more of a problem than ever.

What made matters even worse was that Daughtry and Julie had never been that close—and now Daughtry felt as though her sister was to blame for all her misery. That only managed to add guilt to the loneliness and frustration that already smothered Daughtry.

I miss her too, Daughtry thought. *Even if we didn't see things eye to eye, she was my sister and I loved her.* Daughtry looked around her at the family she cared for more than anything or anyone. *I love them all,* she argued with her heart. *But they're killing me!*

"What are you going to do today, Daughtry?"

"Huh?" Daughtry's mind fumbled to recall the question.

Garrett seemed undaunted. "I was just asking what you

had planned to do today?"

"Oh," Daughtry said and glanced at Maggie. "I guess Mother and I are going to finish sewing our dresses for the fair."

Garrett nodded. "Sounds like a good idea. The fair's in two days and I wouldn't want my favorite ladies to show up looking shoddy."

Maggie rolled her eyes. "You wouldn't care if we wore potato sacks, as long as you had one of us on either side of you."

The boys snickered, but Daughtry didn't. Her mother spoke the truth. Except maybe dressing in potato sacks was pushing the boundaries a bit.

"I guess you're right," Garrett said with a smile and leaned over to place a kiss on his wife's temple. "I'd go anywhere with you, Mrs. Lucas, and you could indeed be wearing potato sacks and still outshine everybody else." His eyes betrayed his pride and passion for the woman at his side.

Maggie blushed ever so lightly. Even after all these years of marriage, Garrett never failed to stir the fires in her heart.

"Well, I for one will not be wearing potato sacks," Maggie replied. "Nor will Daughtry. We have some very special dresses planned. You just wait. There won't be an eligible bachelor in town who won't sit up and take notice of our daughter."

"Not that it would do any good," Daughtry said before she could check the thought.

"What's that supposed to mean?" Garrett questioned. All eyes turned once more to her for an answer.

Daughtry pushed back her chair and got to her feet. "It

means just what you think it means. No one is going to
look at me twice because my daddy might take offense at
their forwardness and put them in their place. And if not
him, then one of the mighty Lucas brothers. I'm so tired
of being treated like I'm five years old. Did it ever once
dawn on any of you that I'd like to meet a nice young
man, fall in love, and move away from here?"

Everyone stared at Daughtry in surprise. She had never
before given such an outburst of criticism for what they
perceived as their dutiful love for her.

"Daughtry!" her mother gasped. "You apologize to your
father and brothers, this minute."

Daughtry leaned against her chair and considered the
situation for a moment. Her eyes betrayed her sadness,
and the futility of her circumstances became clearly evident.

"Sorry," she muttered and turned to leave. Stalking down
the hall, she added in a whisper for her ears alone, "Sorry
that I live in this house and will probably die in this house,
too!"

When the boys had finished with breakfast, leaving their
parents alone, Maggie couldn't help but try to ease the
tension between her husband and daughter.

"Daughtry does have a small point," Maggie began.
She tenderly ran her fingers across the back of Garrett's
hand. "She is grown up and does deserve to settle down
with her own husband and family."

Garrett's eyes flashed anger, as though Maggie's declaration was one of betrayal. "I just want to see her with the
kind of man who's going to respect her and love her. He
needs to know what's going on with this world and how
to make a living that will support her. You've never taken

her side over mine before. Why now?"

Maggie sighed. "I'm not taking sides, Garrett. It's just that I see something in Daughtry these last few months that worries me. I'm afraid if you don't find a way to work it out, Daughtry will put a permanent wall between the two of you. You don't want that, Garrett. You've already lost one daughter."

Garrett stormed from the table without another word. He wasn't about to argue his right to protect what was his. Maggie stared after him for a moment, tears brimming in her eyes. "Help him, Father," she prayed. "Help Garrett to heal before it's too late."

two

Daughtry remained silent on the ride into town. The growing community of Bandelero was overflowing with people due to the fair, and Daughtry tried to put her feelings behind her and smile. At least she was away from the ranch and she was wearing something pretty.

She glanced down at the lavender dress she'd helped to make. It had a pleated bodice with hand embroidery and lace to edge the scooped neckline. At the waist a darker lavender ribbon trimmed the gown and tied in the back to show off her very feminine form. Outlandishly gaudy hats were the rage these days, but Maggie and Daughtry had found little use for them on the ranch. Instead, they had ordered less complicated arrangements from Sears and Roebuck. Her mother predicted the simplicity would do more to turn heads, and, when it did, Daughtry could only hope that her father wouldn't be anywhere nearby.

As Garrett brought the carriage to a halt outside of a two-story adobe house, a sudden ruckus caused the horses to rear and prance. Everybody waited for the smelly, noisy automobile to pass by before even trying to dismount.

"Useless things!" Garrett declared, finally settling the horses. "You won't ever see me in one. I'll stick with horses."

"I think they look like fun," Dolan said from the back of his horse. "I hear they actually have races with those things. They go for days and days, and people even get

16

killed."

"How awful!" Maggie exclaimed, taking her husband's hand as she exited the carriage.

Daughtry stared past her brothers to the street where the car was rapidly disappearing. She silently wished that she could be one of the happy passengers.

"Daughtry, you day dreamin' up there?"

Daughtry looked down at her father and smiled. *If he only knew,* she thought. As she stepped from the carriage, however, they were bombarded with friends, and she was distracted from her thoughts.

"Garrett! Maggie! I'm so glad to see you all," Lillie Monroe called from behind a swirl of people.

"Where's Dan?" Garrett asked, while Maggie embraced her life-long friend.

"Had to set a broken arm," Lillie said with a shrug. "That's all part of being married to the town doctor. You always have to share him. I'll be glad when he takes a partner."

Lillie's sons John and James joined them and soon were catching up the Lucas boys on all the news. Sixteen-year-old Angeline Monroe was nowhere to be seen, much to Daughtry's relief. Angeline only reminded Daughtry how old and outdated she'd rapidly become under Garrett's overprotective hand. Angeline was young and just beginning to live, while Daughtry felt her life was over.

"The fair is going to be a great deal of fun," Lillie was saying, while Garrett and Maggie kept stride with her. Daughtry took advantage of the moment to slip out of sight and wander around town alone. Heaving a great sigh, she rounded the corner and ran smack into the broad chest of a stranger.

"Excuse me," she said, looking upward into soft brown eyes.

"I'm afraid the fault is mine," the man returned. "I just came to town for the fair and I don't know my way around."

Daughtry laughed. "It's not all that difficult, believe me."

The man smiled appreciatively. "Maybe you could show me."

"I'm not sure that would be proper," Daughtry said, glancing around for her father or brothers. "I don't even know you."

"Bill," he replied and extended his hand. "Bill Davis."

"Daughtry Lucas," she replied and extended her small gloved hand to take his.

"There," he said confidently, "now we're no longer strangers. Would you do me the honor of introducing me to your fair city?"

Daughtry laughed, glad to be free for once. "Of course."

The rest of the day passed much too quickly for Daughtry. She ran into Jordy once, but he seemed unconcerned that his sister was on the arm of some stranger. Later, Daughtry narrowly avoided a confrontation with Gavin, when she and Bill happened into a knot of people who stood laughing and talking, blocking the street. As the crowd thinned a bit for them to pass by, Daughtry found Angeline Monroe to be the focal point of the group. Laughing and enjoying the attention, Angeline didn't so much as nod when she caught Daughtry's eye.

"Do you know her?" Bill questioned after they'd managed to slip past the gathering.

"Yes," Daughtry replied, hoping Bill wasn't going to

ask to be introduced.

"She seems awfully young to be flirting with so many men. You ought to have a talk with her folks," Bill said, surprising Daughtry with his words.

"People have been trying to tell her folks for years," Daughtry laughed. "But she's very spoiled."

"Unlike you," Bill said, his sincerity clear in his voice. Daughtry blushed furiously but said nothing as she kept walking.

With Angeline just a memory, Daughtry cast sly upward glances at the sandy-haired man who walked beside her. He was as tall as her father, and the width of his shoulders was also nearly the same. He was dressed in jeans and a light brown shirt, but it all seemed rather regal to Daughtry. Perhaps Bill was her Prince Charming, and he would whisk her away from the stifling life she'd known.

"So how come a pretty thing like you hasn't up and married?" Bill asked her while they walked the festive avenue of carnival games.

"Truth? Or would you rather some fabulously devised story?" Daughtry asked, completely serious.

Bill studied her for a moment and laughed. "Truth."

"It won't appeal to you," she said, glancing around her for the millionth time.

"You looking for someone?" Bill asked her softly. "I mean, ever since this morning, you've been looking over your shoulder and down the street. What's the problem?"

Daughtry sighed. "The same reason I've never married. I have a very possessive father—and five brothers who feel it's their duty to fill in for him when he can't be there to do the job."

"I see," Bill said, and Daughtry thought he sounded a little nervous. "Are they the killing kind or just the wounding and maiming type?"

Daughtry laughed out loud, catching the attention of several people around them. Stifling her amusement, she waited until they'd walked away from the listening crowd. "I've only known them to be the ranting and raving kind, actually."

Bill grinned. "Ah, that won't bother me then. My ears can tolerate the hollering."

"Don't be so sure." Daughtry glanced at the railroad depot clock and sighed. "I'd better get back. I've been gone way too long."

"I'll walk you," Bill said and tucked her arm around his.

Daughtry wanted to tell him no, but the truth was, she was enjoying herself too much. Maybe God had decided to smile down on her and allow her to meet a respectable young man after all.

"Daughtry, I've been looking for you." Her father blocked their path, and behind him stood three of her brothers.

Garrett was frowning fiercely at Bill, and the scowl was so intimidating that the younger man immediately dropped his hold on Daughtry.

"I've just been seeing the sights and enjoying the fair," Daughtry said, trying to control her temper. Then, hoping she could smooth matters, Daughtry turned to introduce her friend. "This is Bill Davis. Bill, this is my father, Garrett Lucas, and my brothers, Gavin, Dolan, and Joseph."

Garrett was barely controlling his temper as he reached

out and yanked Daughtry by the arm. "Evening, Mr. Davis. You'll have to excuse us now."

Daughtry was livid. Garrett continued pulling her down the street, while her brothers firmly discouraged Bill from trying to interfere.

When they were back in the solitude of the Monroe backyard, Daughtry dug her heels in and stopped.

"How dare you!" she exclaimed and the hurt in her eyes changed quickly into rage. "I can't believe you would embarrass me like that."

Garrett looked at her for a moment. A part of him realized he'd acted out of place, while another part was incensed at the scene he'd come across. His only daughter on the arm of a stranger, laughing and looking up at him with a look like—well, he didn't like to think about it.

"Daughtry, I was only looking out for your best interest. You don't know that man and he had no right to be handling you."

Daughtry shook her head. "Enough is enough. I've had all I'm going to take. You may be my father, but I'm of age and old enough to make my own choices. Good night!"

Garrett called after her, but Daughtry ran into the house without so much as a glance over her shoulder. She knew they were spending the night with the Monroes, but she had no idea where she was to sleep. Gratefully, she ran into her mother.

Tears were blinding her eyes, but Daughtry didn't want to talk about it. "Mother, where am I supposed to sleep?"

Maggie noted her daughter's state of mind. "Daughtry, what's wrong?"

"The same old thing. Now, I just want to go to bed. Where am I sleeping?"

Maggie led her daughter to the small room she was to share with Angeline. "I'm sorry, Daughtry. I don't know what has happened, but I hate the fact that it's hurt you so much." She reached out and hugged her daughter close.

Daughtry wrapped her arms around her mother and sobbed. "I can't stand it anymore, Mother. I love you all so much, but I have to be allowed to grow up." She abruptly released Maggie and turned away. "I just want to go to sleep now, please."

Daughtry knew that she hurt her mother when she shut her out, but she could see no sense in discussing the matter any further. Silently, she undressed and slipped into bed for a good cry before going to sleep.

❧

Morning light dawned, and Daughtry woke with a new determination and outlook on her life. During the night, after hours of praying and pleading with God, she'd decided to run away from home. At least that's what she called it, though she doubted that someone could actually run away at her age.

Angeline still slept peacefully, and, because Daughtry knew the girl had come to bed quite late, she tiptoed around the room collecting her things. After dressing and pinning up her hair, Daughtry made her way downstairs.

"Morning, Daughtry," Lillie called to her from the kitchen. "Did you sleep well?"

"Yes, thank you." Daughtry struggled to sound pleasant.

"Are you hungry? I've fixed enough food for a small army. Of course with your brothers and James and John, it very nearly resembles just that."

Daughtry smiled. "Are Pastor David and Jenny coming

over this morning?" Daughtry questioned, referring to Dr. Monroe's brother and his wife. "I was hoping to talk to them before we left for home."

"I think they plan to stop by," Lillie responded. "Did you not get a chance to see them last night?"

"No," Daughtry replied. "I didn't."

"Did you need to talk to them about anything in particular?"

"Yes," Daughtry murmured, "but it's rather, well, personal." She thought maybe David or Jenny could offer some help or suggestions on where she could go.

Lillie smiled and nodded. "That's quite all right, I understand."

Within moments, the quiet talk was forgotten as the room filled with the bodies of young men all rivaling the other for the center of discussion.

Daughtry managed to slip outside with her plate of food. She ate with a ravenous appetite, suddenly remembering that she hadn't had any supper the night before.

"I brought you a peace offering," Garrett said, coming up behind her. Daughtry looked up but said nothing. Garrett held out a newspaper. "I knew you'd want to catch up on what was happening around the world. I managed to latch onto this copy of the *Denver Post*."

Daughtry took the newspaper from her father. He was trying so hard to make up for his behavior, and even though she had no intention of changing her mind about leaving, Daughtry couldn't treat him badly.

"Thank you, Daddy," she said softly and glanced briefly at the headlines.

"I really am sorry," Garrett said.

"I know," Daughtry replied and thought to herself, *You*

always are.

Seeing that she wasn't in a mood to talk, Garrett left Daughtry to finish her breakfast alone. Daughtry knew that he wanted her to laugh and think nothing more about the events of the previous night, but that wasn't possible for her.

Flipping through the pages of the paper, Daughtry came across an advertisement. It was like no other she'd ever seen. This was an advertisement for a wife. Quickly scanning the lines, Daughtry read:

> *Wife wanted to share the dream of building a ranching empire. Looking for a hard-working woman who isn't afraid to love and live with a man who will provide a home and remain forever yours in the eyes of God and man.*

It was signed N. Dawson, with an address in care of the post office in a small town in eastern New Mexico.

How romantic, Daughtry thought as she reread the ad. The days of mail-order brides were a thing of the past but, from time to time, people did still seek a mate through that unconventional manner.

Daughtry began to get an idea. A very serious idea about answering the advertisement. She folded the paper and stared at it for several minutes. *It could work,* she thought to herself. It could be everything she'd prayed for.

Back at Piñon Canyon, Daughtry penned a response to the man she could only address as Mr. Dawson. She wondered as she wrote what his first name might be. She imagined Nicodemus or Nathaniel—maybe even Navin or Ned, although those names didn't appeal to her sense of romance.

She stared at the blank paper for several minutes and then began to pour out her thoughts.

> *Dear Mr. Dawson,*
> *I am responding to your advertisement and would very much like to receive more information about the marriage and dream you propose. I have grown up on a ranch and thus have spent my entire life working at the same dream you seem to have. I would be happy to correspond with you regarding the matter. Please address your reply in care of the Bandelero, New Mexico, Post Office.*
>
> *Daughtry Lucas*

Almost as an afterthought, Daughtry picked up her pen again and added a postscript indicating that she had enclosed a picture of herself. Then, scouting through her desk drawer, she managed to find one that had been taken recently at a church picnic. She thought the photo did her justice.

Slipping the letter and picture into an envelope, Daughtry addressed it and made plans for how she would get away the next morning to mail it. This was a great adventure, she thought to herself, and, for once, she looked forward to the next day with less dread.

N. Dawson, she thought with a smile. *Maybe, just maybe, he will be my answer to prayer.*

three

Daughtry had nearly given up hearing anything from N. Dawson when, much to her surprise, she found a letter awaiting her at the post office. Giddy with excitement and grateful that she'd ridden in alone for the mail, Daughtry tore open the envelope.

She wasn't prepared for the many pieces of paper that accompanied the letter. Reviewing the items, Daughtry was shocked to find legal documentation for a marriage by proxy, a train ticket, and photograph. The picture was face down and Daughtry decided to leave it that way until after reading the letter. *This way,* she thought, *I won't be influenced by looks alone.*

Carefully opening the letter, Daughtry eagerly read the contents.

> *Dear Miss Lucas,*
> *I was enchanted by your photograph and letter. I would like to say that I believe you are a Godsend. My faith being firmly rooted in Him, I can say without a doubt that you are the woman I am to marry.*

Daughtry reread that line several times before continuing. A strange feeling was coursing through her, and it made her hand shake ever so slightly as she read on.

*Enclosed you will find a train ticket to
bring you to me and a legal document
which will allow you to marry me before
you make the journey. It is most imperative
that you marry by proxy by the twenty-fifth
of September, otherwise the documents will
be null and void.*

*I hope this answers your questions and I
hope the enclosed photograph will put your
mind at ease regarding my appearance and
age.*

Forever yours,
Nicholas Dawson

"Nicholas!" Daughtry breathed. "His name is Nicholas." Gingerly, she refolded the letter and turned the photograph over. Her breath caught in her throat. He was clearly the handsomest man she'd ever seen. She studied the man who casually sat for the photograph. He was dressed in a smart suit, with dark hair and even darker eyes staring back at her. His eyes seemed to twinkle, if that were possible, and his lips were curled upward.

"Oh my," she said breathlessly. "He's wonderful."

She lost track of time, studying the picture as though trying to memorize each and every feature of the man. Finally, when a train whistle blew and broke her concentration, Daughtry realized she would have to be heading back to the ranch.

After another quick examination of the document and train ticket, Daughtry replaced the papers in the envelope and tucked the letter into the deep pocket of her split skirt. Without much thought, she tossed the rest of the mail into her saddle bag and mounted Poco.

"What have I done?" she questioned aloud. All around her the rich cobalt blue sky stretched out to the purple haze of mountains. The noise of Bandelero faded, leaving Daughtry with only one pounding question in her mind. *What do I do now?*

She felt the side of her skirt to reassure herself that the letter hadn't been dreamed. "This man is serious, Poco," she said, as though the horse might offer her some insight. "He's sent me a train ticket and the means by which to marry him before coming to his place." The horse kept a steady trot, mindless of its owner's ramblings.

"Dear God," Daughtry finally prayed, looking upward to the cloudless sky. "I didn't mean to cause trouble, but maybe this is the direction You're leading me. The man says I have to make up my mind before September twenty-fifth." Daughtry paused in her prayers. "Father, that's only ten days from now."

A trembling started anew in Daughtry. Ten days! That's all the time she had to make a lifelong decision. She argued and reasoned with herself all the way back to Piñon Canyon. How could she leave her home and marry a stranger? Even if he were a very nice looking stranger? On the other hand, Daughtry knew she was going to leave this place, one way or another. She had no idea how she would care for herself alone, and marriage to anyone would be better than dying an old maid, she thought.

❧

Three days later, Daughtry was still mulling over her proposal. She'd reread the letter until it was well-worn and she knew every word by heart. Always, she came back to the picture and lost her heart a little more. "Forever yours,

Nicholas Dawson," she sighed and stared at the dark eyes of the man who wished to marry her. Only seven days were left.

Daughtry had never been a person given over to moments of spontaneous decision. She always thought things out and, inevitably, reasoned away any urge to do something foolish. This was no exception, and as time passed, Daughtry recognized too many good arguments against accepting Nicholas's proposal.

"I can't hurt Mother that way," Daughtry thought aloud. She had taken Poco out for her routine morning ride, grateful to escape the escort her father thought necessary. Pulling back on the reins, Daughtry slipped down from Poco's back and walked alongside the gelding for a while. "I can't just walk away from my responsibilities," she continued. Poco seemed more interested in the patches of fading green grass than in this mistress's declarations.

"I've always been a good girl," Daughtry said firmly. "I've always been dependable and reasonable. I'll just have to make it clear to Daddy that I need to be allowed to court and marry and eventually leave Piñon Canyon to make my own home. He'll come around in time."

Daughtry studied the landscape for a moment. The rocky western slopes of their property headed upward into the Sangre de Cristo mountain range. Soon snow would cover the magnificent crests and Piñon Canyon would be blanketed in white.

Another winter, Daughtry thought to herself. *And in January, I'll be twenty-four.*

Daughtry walked on in silence. She had to do the right thing, she reasoned. She had to trust God and endure the situation as best she could. When she got back to the house,

she would simply write to Nicholas—no, Mr. Dawson—
and tell him that she couldn't marry him.

She was about to remount Poco when a cloud of dust in
the distance caught her attention. Riding hard and fast
across the open plain was her father. Daughtry remained
on the ground until a worried-looking Garrett reined up
beside her.

"You're on foot," he said, looking Daughtry over from
head to toe. "Is something wrong?"

"No, Daddy," Daughtry said, taking a defensive tone.
"I'm just enjoying the morning."

Garrett frowned. "Why didn't you bring someone with
you?"

"Because I'm a grown woman and I don't need an escort. I like to spend time on my own and I don't want to
have someone following me around all the time. It's bad
enough that you won't leave me alone."

Garrett's eyes revealed his hurt but Daughtry was rapidly growing angry, and her father's pain was furthest
from her mind.

"Daddy, you and I have to talk about this," Daughtry
said firmly. "Why don't you walk with me a spell."

Garrett quickly complied and joined his daughter on
the ground. He started to speak, but Daughtry held up her
hand. "Please let me say what I need to say," she began.
"Then you can tell me what you think and we'll go from
there."

"All right."

Daughtry swallowed hard and took a deep breath. She
prayed that God would give her the right words to say.
"Daddy, I know how much losing Julie hurts you. I hurt
too. I miss her and I wish that she would never have gone

out riding that morning. But the truth is, she did, and I can't change that and neither can you. You can't change it by smothering me or watching my every step. You can't do God's job, Dad."

Daughtry stopped and looked at her father for a moment. He was still a young man, vital and strong, and Daughtry knew he was perfectly capable of providing for his family. He'd helped her with so many things in life. He was the one who had helped her find Christ as her Savior. He was also the one who had taught her to ride and shoot and a hundred other things that pertained to her life on the ranch.

"I love you, Daddy," Daughtry said, looking deep into his eyes. "But I want to get married and have a family. I want a life of my own and I want you to let me go."

Garrett looked at her blankly for a moment. His heart was heavy with the words his daughter had just spoken. He knew they were valid, but he was incapable of letting her go.

"Have you found someone?" Garrett asked softly.

Daughtry smiled ever so slightly at the thought of Nicholas. "I thought I had, but now I'm not sure. I do know, however, that it's what I want for my life, and I believe it's what God wants for me too. I don't want to go to school or hold a job or make a great splash in society. I just want to be a wife and mother. I don't want to grow old taking care of you and Mother. You're supposed to care for each other, and we children are supposed to leave the nest." Garrett nodded and Daughtry thought he finally understood. Feeling a bit of relief, she offered him a smile.

For a moment, Garrett was taken back to the first time

he'd met Daughtry's mother. Maggie had been angry. Perhaps just as angry as Daughtry was when he tried to interfere with her life. Daughtry looked just like her mother, and he couldn't help but remember the way Maggie had nearly gotten herself killed when she'd run away from him, rather than accompany him to New Mexico where her father waited for her. Young women, he knew from experience, made decisions based on their feelings. Daughtry was feeling angry at him, maybe justifiably, maybe not. But now she was telling him that she'd actually considered marriage with someone. Someone he knew nothing about.

"Who is it?" Garrett asked without thinking.

"Who is who?"

"Who were you thinking about marrying?" Garrett questioned, and Daughtry could see the determination in his eyes.

"It isn't important," Daughtry said in exasperation.

"Well, why don't you let me be the judge of that."

"Because I'm a grown woman and you aren't the judge of my life," Daughtry stated in anger. "I'm the one who will decide whom I marry and when. This isn't the Middle Ages, Daddy, and I'm not going to be like Momma and let my father decide for me." Daughtry stormed past him and remounted Poco with a fury in her eyes that Garrett had never before seen.

"You're still under my authority, Daughtry," Garrett said, swinging up into his own saddle. "That gives me a say in what you do."

Daughtry gripped the reins tightly. She tried to steady her voice before she spoke. "Dad, you're making this very difficult. Will you allow me to make some choices for myself? Will you stop shadowing everything I do in the fear that I will end up dead, like my sister?"

Garrett looked at her for a moment before silently shaking his head. "I can't, Daughtry. God made you my responsibility."

Daughtry refused to answer. Instead she dug her heels into Poco's sides, something she rarely did, and flew out across the ground for home. By the time she'd headed into the stable yard, Daughtry had made up her mind. No matter what else happened, she was going to marry Nicholas Dawson! She would have the last word on this and no one, especially not her father, would stand in her way.

four

At a few minutes before three o'clock in the morning, Daughtry led Poco from his stall. She walked him out past the stables and corrals and moved silently toward the open range. She prayed that she was doing the right thing by leaving, and a part of her sincerely thought she was. She remembered her mother saying on more than one occasion that God often expected a person to step out in faith. Mounting Poco in the New Mexican darkness, Daughtry figured this was as big a step of faith as she could possibly make.

The ride into town was uneventful, and when Daughtry arrived, she quickly tied Poco up outside of the church, knowing that Pastor David would recognize the horse and get him back to Piñon Canyon. She wished she could take Poco with her. At least then she'd have something to comfort herself with at the end of her trip. But arranging to take Poco would require her making her presence known to the freight agent, and he would no doubt remember where she had gone when her father came looking.

Knowing the church would be open, Daughtry took her two heavy bags and slipped inside the dark protection of the sanctuary. Quickly, she pulled on clothes she'd borrowed from Pepita in order to board the train and not be recognized. She pulled a heavy shawl over her head and secured it under her chin. Then, taking her bags in hand, Daughtry made her way to the train depot.

Only a handful of people waited for the five-thirty eastbound. Gratefully, Daughtry didn't recognize any of them. She waited in the shadows, however, just in case one of them recognized her. When the train whistle blasted through the early morning silence, though, Bandelero was just coming awake, and no one Daughtry knew was anywhere to be seen.

Daughtry grew fidgety waiting for her turn to board, but as soon as she took her place on the nearly empty train car, she began to relax. Freedom, she thought to herself, came at a high price, but she was sure it would be worth it.

Looking out the soot-smudged window, she nearly ducked down at the sight of Dr. Monroe, or Dr. Dan as she affectionately called him. He was hurrying down the street, however, black bag tucked under his arm and a look of determination on his face, and he never glanced at the train. No doubt another medical emergency, Daughtry thought.

Soon the train began its journey, and Daughtry breathed a sigh of relief. When they reached the town of Springer, the conductor announced an hour wait while they took on several carloads of cattle. Daughtry realized this would be the perfect opportunity to find a minister and have the proxy marriage ceremony performed.

Hurrying through the town, she wondered to herself what minister in his right mind would marry two strangers together. *What if I can't find someone willing to do the job?* Worry flooded her soul. What if she had to turn back, or worse, meet Mr. Dawson without the marriage in place as he'd requested?

Daughtry's worries were for naught, however. The first

minister she approached was more than happy to take her offering of five dollars to perform the proxy service. Armed with marriage papers in hand, Daughtry made her way back to the train, ten minutes before it pulled out and headed east to her new home.

Staring out the window, Daughtry felt something akin to excitement and foolish regret, both at the same time. She was a married woman! She was no longer Daughtry Ann Lucas. Now, she was Daughtry Dawson, wife of Nicholas.

Taking out the photograph of her husband, Daughtry tried to imagine what type of man he was. He looked tall and she could see that he was broad-shouldered. He looked strong and healthy, maybe even older than she. She realized with a start that she had no idea how old her husband was. Nor did she know whether he'd ever been married before or if he had children.

"What have I done?" she questioned softly, then glanced around quickly to make certain no one else had heard her.

When the train finally arrived at Daughtry's destination, she panicked. Nicholas wouldn't know she was coming. She hadn't sent a telegram or tried to telephone or anything else that would let him know of her arrival. She'd brought a small amount of money with her, enough to rent a room for the night, but fear gnawed at her like a hungry animal. Daughtry had never been on her own before.

She stepped from the train and immediately signaled a man to assist her. "Do you know where the Nicholas Dawson ranch is located?" she asked the man.

"No, ma'am. I can't rightly say I've ever heard of the man."

Daughtry's face fell. Just as she was about to ask the man who might know, another voice sounded from behind her.

"Did I hear you say you were lookin' for the Dawson place?"

Daughtry turned and met the eyes of a dust-laden stranger. The man was older than her father, but his shoulders and chest were massive.

"Yes," she managed to say. "I need to get to Nicholas Dawson's ranch."

"Well, you're in luck," the man said in a noncommittal way. "I'm on my way out there with this load of freight. I just have to finish picking up the rest of it and we can be on our way."

Daughtry sighed aloud. "You, sir, are an answer to prayer."

The man snorted at her declaration and pointed to his wagon. "You just wait over there and I'll be with you directly. These your bags?" he questioned, glancing at the luggage beside Daughtry.

"Yes."

"That all you brought?"

"Yes," Daughtry replied and ignored his look of curiosity.

Without another word, the man took the bags, threw them up into the freight wagon, and went off in the direction of the train. Daughtry hurriedly planted herself by the wagon and was relieved when the man returned fifteen minutes later to finish stacking the cargo.

The afternoon was late when Daughtry and the freighter finally arrived at the Dawson ranch. The man had offered her no name, and, in return, Daughtry hadn't explained who she was. Now, as the man unloaded his wagon and stacked lumber and supplies inside a rather rundown barn, Daughtry glanced around nervously for her husband. When the freighter finished and Nicholas had still not appeared, Daughtry grew frightened.

"Are you certain this property belongs to Nicholas Dawson?"

"Sure as I am of anything," the man replied. "I've been bringing supplies out here for weeks now. He's gone a lot, which would explain why he isn't out here to greet us now. I notice his horse is gone, so there's no telling where he is or when he'll be back. Did he expect you?"

"No. Well, yes." Daughtry tried to answer reasonably. "He didn't know what day I would get here. Tell me, what else do you know about Mr. Dawson?"

The man eyed her suspiciously for a moment. "Don't know much. He's new to these parts. Took this old place off the hands of Widow Cummings and declared he wanted to turn it into a fine ranch again. Other than that, I don't guess I know anything else."

"You have met him though?"

"Sure," the man said and scratched his head. "I take it you haven't?"

Daughtry shook her head. "No, I haven't met him yet. I have his picture and a letter, but that's all."

"You kin of his?"

"No," Daughtry replied and smiled weakly. "I'm his wife." The man burst out laughing, and Daughtry felt foolish for having mentioned the matter.

"Well, I'll be. I heard he was after gettin' himself hitched. Didn't find any prospects in our little town though, and I heard tell he advertised in the papers for one. Is that how you came to marry him?"

Daughtry felt completely stupid. "Yes," she managed to whisper, "that's how it happened."

"Well, I wish you the best, Mrs. Dawson," the man said, climbing up into the wagon. "Here." He turned to rummage under the seat of his buckboard and handed her something down. "You might want to order something and then I'll have a reason to come back out this way."

Daughtry stared down at the Sears and Roebuck catalog the freighter had just handed her. Daughtry greatly needed his gesture of kindness. "Thank you," she said softly. "You have been so very kind. What do I owe you for the ride out?"

"Not a thing, pretty lady. Not a thing." He retrieved his hat, tipped it to her, and moved his horses back out to the road. Within minutes the dust of his wagon faded into the distance, leaving Daughtry all alone in the middle of nowhere.

"I've brought this on myself," Daughtry said, squaring her shoulders with a look of determination. "I've just got to make the best of it."

She took her bags in hand and headed toward the rundown house. Staring at it in the soft glow of early evening light, Daughtry realized it was sorely neglected. No wonder Nicholas needed a woman who was willing to work hard. *Well,* Daughtry thought to herself, *this will be a challenge and I will meet it head on and with a light heart.*

Her resolve lasted as long as it took to get through the back mud porch and into the kitchen. She could see well enough to realize that the place was hopelessly filthy and in need of more than just a little attention.

Setting her mind to the work at hand, Daughtry decided to do as much as she could to put the place in order before her husband returned. She quickly lighted several lamps and explored the rest of the house in order to determine what should be done first.

Through the kitchen, Daughtry found a small but promising dining room. This connected to a small parlor, and this in turn came out onto a short hall that blended into a vestibule of sorts that ended at the front door. Crossing the hall, Daughtry found a larger sitting room filled with an assortment of odd looking crates, furniture, and a wood stove that had been used recently but not cleaned in a long time. Finding more lamps here, Daughtry lit another and left it to radiate a cheery glow in the room, while she continued to explore.

Back in the hall, she turned and opened the door to a small closet. Further down, she noticed two more doors and opened cne onto a small room that looked as though it had been a sewing room at one time. Hadn't the freighter said the ranch belonged to a widow before Nicholas bought it?

The other door opened onto the bedroom, and Daughtry became suddenly aware of Nicholas's masculine presence. Several articles of clothing lay around the room in disarray. Putting the lamp on the nightstand beside the four poster bed, Daughtry picked up a black suit coat and held it in front of her. The shoulders were broader than she'd even imagined. Nicholas must be quite a large man, Daughtry surmised, by the look of his coat.

She picked up other items and stared at them, as if hoping they would answer her unspoken questions. Picking up a pair of discarded jeans, Daughtry held them against her, trying to get an idea of how Nicholas' size might contrast to her own. She'd worn her brothers' clothes on many occasions, but they'd always been old clothes they had long outgrown. These were the clothes of a man, not a boy, and Daughtry knew there was no comparison.

Realizing that the sky was getting darker and feeling the need to relieve herself, Daughtry went back down the hall and made her way outside. She instantly spotted the outhouse and started across the yard.

For a moment she paused to take in the beauty of the sunset. The sun looked like a ball of molten scarlet against the fading colors of the sky. Lavender, so dusty and dark that it was nearly purple, blended into streaks of blue and amber. Daughtry hugged her arms against her body and thanked God for the wonder of it.

"Only God can paint the sky like that," she sighed.

Back in the house, Daughtry realized she could do little about the house's untidiness so late in the day. She found a can of peaches and a tin of crackers and made her supper on these. Morning would surely prove to offer her more understanding of her new home.

When she'd finished with the meager provisions, Daughtry extinguished all the lamps but the one she carried with her. She took her bags and made her way to the bedroom. Her only thought was to get a good night's sleep, but when she was actually in the room once again, Daughtry grew uncomfortable. Should she sleep in his bed? What if he came home in the night?

She was about to make a pallet on the floor, when a mouse scurried across the room and out the door. With a shriek of fright, Daughtry's mind was made up. Nicholas or no Nicholas, she was sleeping in the bed!

five

Daughtry tried to ignore her concern for the absent husband she'd never met. Three days had passed since she'd arrived at the ranch and Nicholas had still not come back. Trying to sooth her worry, Daughtry set up Nicholas's picture on the small table in the kitchen and, as she worked, she talked to him as though he were there.

"I'm going to have to start bringing up wood," she said absent-mindedly. "It's getting considerably colder and pretty soon it's bound to snow. I used the last of the coal, or at least what I could find, so I guess I'll just have to go down to that grove of trees and see what I can find there."

Daughtry had worked wonders with the place and, in spite of her nervous state of mind, she was pleased with the way things were shaping up. She'd inventoried the supplies and managed to find a pantry just off the kitchen that she'd not seen in her first day of exploring. Nicholas had laid up quite a store of canned goods and smoked meats, as well as plenty of flour, sugar, soda, and salt. Daughtry nearly cried in joy at the sight of so much food.

Her first project had been to clean the kitchen. She reasoned that if she could have this one room in perfect order, she could easily work with the others at her leisure. Going around the room, she noted what was worth keeping and what was plain and simple trash. The curtains were still in good shape but needed to be washed, so Daughtry removed them and began heating water in the biggest pot she could find.

Piece by piece, she emptied the room, until nothing remained but the dirty black stove and the empty ice-box. She found soap in the supplies that the freighter had left in the barn, as well as brushes and a well-made broom. Taking these, she scrubbed the grime from the walls, floors, counters, and cabinets, until everything was spotless. After this, she tackled the stove, washing it thoroughly until she was satisfied that she could cook food without fear of catching something from the filth.

Bit by bit, the room took shape, and Daughtry continued to talk to Nicholas as though he were there, relating her plans as she continued.

She went to work cleaning the small table and chairs that had set in the kitchen, as well as the pie saver and jelly cabinet that she'd taken outside. She was just about to move them indoors, when she remembered something in the barn.

Setting out across the yard, Daughtry opened the barn door and went inside. After several minutes of searching, she returned to the house with a bucket of white paint and a brush. Maybe Nicholas hadn't planned on the house being painted inside, but Daughtry thought a fresh coat of whitewash would help matters a great deal. If he were mad at her, then she'd just have to apologize and try to fix the matter. That was, if he ever showed up.

More nosing around revealed a wealth of useful household goods, and Daughtry began to take courage from the way the house shaped up. The kitchen was actually attractive now with its freshly painted walls and cabinets. The shelves were lined with sparkling dishes from sets that Daughtry had found in crates in the large sitting room and the pots gleamed from her hours of scrubbing.

Every night, Daughtry went to bed more exhausted than the night before. After the second day, she'd made notable progress with the bedroom, feeling that this was the next place to be put in order. After wrestling the mattress outside and beating it until the entire yard looked like the middle of a dust storm, Daughtry scrubbed down the room and furniture. Finally, she washed every article of clothing and all of the linens before deeming the bedroom acceptable.

She didn't have long to wonder what she'd need to turn her attention to next. When it rained on the second night, Daughtry learned quickly that the roof was leaky. Steady drips fell from the ceiling in more than one place, and Daughtry knew that her job in the morning would consist of trying to repair and reshingle her roof.

She barely had time to worry about her husband. For all she knew, he didn't even exist, except that she had papers that told her otherwise. Every day, she tried to make ready for his return. She wanted very much to prove herself worthy in his eyes. And oh, what eyes, she thought as she drifted into sleep. Dark, dark eyes that seemed to laugh at some private joke. Dark eyes that Daughtry prayed would behold her with love and devotion.

Daughtry rose early, thankful that the storm had passed early in the night. She pulled on the set of boy's clothes she'd brought with her from home, finding them much easier to work in, and planned her day.

She set bread out to rise and made herself some breakfast before considering the roof. The kitchen was chilly and Daughtry was grateful for the warmth of the stove. She reminded herself that leaky roofs could be lived with as long as she could keep a fire warming the house. With that in mind, she decided to bring more wood up to the house before worrying herself with anything else.

The day was rapidly getting away from her and the sky was clouding up again. Daughtry knew she should at least try to check the roof out and see if she could do anything about the leaks, just in case it rained again that night.

Making her way to the barn, Daughtry found an old wooden ladder and took it with her to the house. She climbed up on top, noting several very soft spots, and began picking away at the tattered shingles. She was used to adobe houses, but this clapboard house she now called home was very similar to some of the other buildings at Piñon Canyon. Daughtry had helped her father and brothers on more than one occasion with roofing, repairing, and building. She had loved working alongside her family and learning every aspect of how to make the ranch run prosperously.

This was the first time Daughtry had allowed herself to remember her family and tears came to her eyes. Were they worried about her? Of course they were, she chided herself. Her father would be frantic, even though she'd left them a long letter explaining her need to get out on her own. Would they ever forgive her for stealing away in the night? Would she ever be welcomed back?

Exhaustion overwhelmed Daughtry as she climbed into bed that night. How she longed for a bath in a tub of hot water. But for now, she had to settle for washing out of the kitchen sink, where she poured pans of heated water. Perhaps she could talk Nicholas into purchasing a tub— if he ever showed up.

She drifted immediately into sleep, succumbing to the strain of the days that had passed in heavy, never-ending work. Daughtry dreamed of dark eyes and a handsome face, wondering where her husband was and why he'd not returned. The picture of Nicholas faded into that of her father's angry image, and Daughtry tossed restlessly as she sought to escape his rage.

Then the dream took another path, one that Daughtry had never before envisioned. She was being held safe and warm in muscular arms. Snuggling closer, Daughtry felt a hand run through her long hair. Sighing, she relished the dream. This would be what it was like to be held by Nicholas, she decided.

Then, to her surprise, Daughtry felt warm lips against her cheek. They trailed down to capture her lips, and Daughtry returned the kiss.

In the foggy uncertainty of sleep, Daughtry struggled to open her eyes. A part of her wanted to go on sleeping so that she could enjoy the dream, but another part of her was being beckoned. She could almost hear someone calling her name.

Daughtry tried to concentrate on the voice but it faded and, as it did, she became more awake, until she suddenly realized that she wasn't alone. Opening her eyes wide, Daughtry stared into the amused dark eyes of Nicholas Dawson.

For a moment all Daughtry could do was stare. Was she dreaming or was this real? The shocked look on her face caused the man beside her to chuckle.

"I—I—" Daughtry couldn't speak a coherent word to save herself. Shyly, she pulled her arms from the man's neck and tried to ease away from him, as if he wouldn't notice.

Nicholas sat up and Daughtry could see he was fully clothed and sitting atop the covers she so carefully clutched to her neck. With a grin he spoke. "I sure hope you're my wife."

Daughtry saw nothing amusing about the situation. She was trembling from head to toe, and whether it was from the shock of finding Nicholas in her bed or from the passion he'd awoke in her, Daughtry wasn't sure.

In a flash, Daughtry leaped from the bed and ran for the door. She knew her long flannel nightgown wouldn't offer her much coverage, but she wasn't about to stop and retrieve her robe on the way out the door. She reached for the handle and had just turned it, when Nicholas was beside her.

"Don't go. I'm sorry I scared you. It wasn't very nice of me, but I couldn't help myself." His voice was rich and warm, just as Daughtry knew it would be. Daughtry let her hand slip from the handle, but she couldn't bring herself to face her husband.

Slowly, as if dealing with a terrified child, Nicholas turned her to face him. "I'm Nicholas Dawson, although I'm sure you've already figured that out. You look just like your picture."

Daughtry lifted her face to meet his. "You too," she whispered.

Nicholas smiled and his eyes lit up. "I never figured on getting out of a newspaper such a beauty for a wife. I wasn't even sure you'd agree, what with me in such a hurry and all. I'm sorry I wasn't here when you arrived. I had to be away on business and I just got back this morning."

Daughtry nodded and looked away. Her senses were suddenly raging with all that she was seeing, hearing, and feeling. As if realizing she needed the space, Nicholas stepped back and waited for her to speak.

"I'm Daughtry Lucas, I mean, Dawson," she said nervously. She took a deep breath to steady her nerves. "I didn't know when you'd be back. I took some liberty with the house. I'm sorry if I overstepped my rights, I mean, I didn't know what you'd expect of a wife, and I, well..." Daughtry stopped as she realized she was rambling and twisting her nightgown.

Nicholas just grinned at her, making the whole situation even more uncomfortable. Daughtry glanced at the bed and her face flushed crimson.

Noting where her gaze ended, Nicholas reached out and touched Daughtry's cheek. "I really am sorry for startling you. I should have waited until you woke up good and proper, but I haven't always used the sense the good Lord gave me. What say you get dressed and come on out to the kitchen and we'll talk?"

Daughtry was mesmerized by the way his thumb was rubbing her jawline. His fingers were on her neck, and the warmth of their contact against her bare skin sent tremors through Daughtry that she couldn't control.

Surprising them both, Daughtry jumped from the door and moved back to the end of the bed. "I've got my things in here," she said motioning to the wardrobe. "If you'll wait in the other room, I'll get dressed."

Nicholas nodded, the smile never leaving his face. When he had gone from the room, closing the door firmly behind him, Daughtry's knees gave out and she crumpled to the floor.

"Dear God," she prayed in a whisper, "I've really done it this time. Please help me to know what to do and say, and please don't let Nicholas be mad about the paint. Amen."

Getting dressed as quickly as she could, Daughtry laughed to herself. *Paint? I'm worried about paint?*

six

Daughtry hurried into the kitchen to find her husband sitting comfortably at the small table. She pulled her apron from a hook near the door and tied it around her trim waist. Nicholas watched all of this in complete silence, surprised at the control Daughtry seemed to have managed to regain in her few minutes alone.

He watched her as she put wood in the stove and got the fire going. He was more than a little impressed at what he'd found upon his return. Truth be told, he nearly walked back out the door, fearing that he'd entered the wrong house. A double take confirmed that he was indeed in the right house but that a transformation of tremendous proportions had taken place. Now looking at the petite and delicate woman he'd married, Nicholas was even more surprised.

Daughtry knew that he was watching her every move. His gaze made her nervous, but she consoled herself with the reminder that this was a situation that would test the endurance of anyone. She put a pot of coffee on the stove and turned to question her husband.

"What would you like for breakfast?"

Nicholas smiled to himself. He hadn't had someone to wait on him since leaving home and that seemed a million years ago. "Whatever you're having," he replied and leaned back against the chair.

Daughtry looked thoughtful for a moment. "Well, I have

fresh bread and of course there are the canned foods. I wasn't able to locate any eggs or potatoes, so I can't really do you justice with anything grand. I could make tortillas and heat up some of the meat from the pantry." She fell silent and shrugged her shoulders. "I was just going to have toasted bread and jam."

"Sounds fine for me as well."

Daughtry nodded and went back to work, while Nicholas continued his silent study. He figured she was about five feet, four inches tall. Surely no taller, and she couldn't weigh more than 100 pounds. She had pulled her hair up into a loose bun of rich copper. He liked the shade, never even imagining from her photograph what color her hair might be. She had a sweet face. Almost angelic, he thought. In fact, she looked so childlike that Nicholas suddenly sat up with a start.

"How old are you?"

His question surprised Daughtry. Maybe he thought she looked a lot older than she really was. Maybe he didn't like the idea of having married an old maid. Feeling self-conscious, Daughtry decided to make sport of it.

"A lady should never reveal her age, Mr. Dawson." Her smile was brief and Nicholas caught her teasing tone. "However, because you are my husband and entitled to know full well what you've saddled yourself with, I will admit that I'm quite old."

Nicholas laughed at this, and the amusement lingered in his eyes. "How old?"

"I'm twenty-three. I'll be twenty-four in January," Daughtry said with something akin to regret in her voice.

"A mere baby," he chided and was rewarded with a look of sincere appreciation in his wife's eyes. Had someone honestly told this slip of girl that she was old?

Daughtry brought the toast and coffee to the table, then retrieved two mugs, a knife, and the jam before sitting opposite Nicholas.

"Would you ask the blessing?" she asked rather timidly.

"Certainly," he said without a second thought and bowed his head. "Father, thank You for this food and the hard labors of this industrious young woman. I ask that You would bless this house and this union between Daughtry and me and let us live our days devoted to You, Amen."

Daughtry looked up filled with wonder. "That was a beautiful prayer. Especially asking God to bless our marriage." She paused for a moment, then jumped right into the matter. "We do have a rather strange arrangement here, don't we?"

Amused, Nicholas reached out and took several pieces of toast. He liberally slathered jam across each piece and handed two to Daughtry before replying. "Strange doesn't half seem to explain it."

Daughtry poured the coffee and began to feel at ease. "I've always been a very straightforward kind of woman, Mr. Dawson."

"Please don't call me Mr. Dawson. Call me Nicholas or Nick, but not that."

Daughtry smiled. "All right. As I was saying, I like to be honest about things and I don't like to play games, at least not people games. Do you know what I mean?"

"I think so," he said with a gentleness in his expression that further dispelled Daughtry's anxieties.

"I've never been the kind of person to jump into things without real regard to the consequences, but this time seems to be an exception. I'm not sure I did the right thing in marrying you, but it is done and I don't believe in divorce or annulments. I just wanted you to know that I take our marriage very seriously." Nicholas stared at her soberly while she continued. "I intend to make you a good wife. I will work hard and I know a great deal about ranching. I'm not weak or fragile and I've spent most all of my life working outdoors alongside..." Daughtry stopped abruptly. "Well," she continued hesitantly, "I've spent a lot of time working at the kind of things that will build this place into a respectable and profitable ranch."

A smile played at the corners of Nicholas's lips. "Anything else?"

Daughtry put her coffee down and took a deep breath. "I suppose I should say that I'm a Christian. I believe in walking close with the Lord and reading the Word every day. I like to go to church and fellowship with other believers, and I will never do anything willingly that goes against the laws of God."

"I see."

Daughtry pressed on lest she lose her nerve. "I'm a very devoted person to those I love and care for. I will endeavor to be whatever you need me to be." She was blushing profusely at this point. "And, while I know very little about you, I am very teachable and happy to learn."

Nicholas reached out and put his hand over hers. "What about children?"

Daughtry's eyes flashed up to meet his. For a moment she lost herself in the heated stare. "I love children."

Nicholas patted her hand and smiled. "Good, because I do too and hope that we can fill this house with a dozen or more."

Daughtry's eyes widened at his boldness. "Well, I don't know if I love them that much." Her teasing was clearly evident and Nicholas laughed.

"I think I'm going to enjoy being married to you, Daughtry. I, too, have had my misgivings about marrying a person of which I knew nothing more about than the fact that she had beautiful penmanship and took a lovely picture."

Daughtry started to thank him for the compliment, but he continued to speak. "I did, however, pray about this matter and felt that God's answer was found in your letter. I worried that perhaps my desire to rush the marriage would put you off, but again I prayed and asked God to intercede and bring the event about. And, well, here you are and I must say that I am more than a little bit impressed with the answer God's given. Not only are you the loveliest woman I've had the pleasure of knowing, but you're intelligent, witty, and very charming. Not to mention that you've accomplished in a few short days what I believe would have taken most men weeks to do."

Daughtry remembered the paint and grimaced. "I used your paint," she said, still not sure why it upset her so much. "I saw it with the supplies in the barn and, while I was cleaning the kitchen, I thought it looked like it could use a good coat. I hope you aren't upset with me. I didn't mean to use something without permission."

Nicholas stared at her rather sternly for a moment before replying. "What I have is yours, Daughtry. How could I possibly fault you for benefiting us both? That's just another thing I like about you. You're willing to just get in there and do what needs to be done. That's to your credit. You aren't one of those sad little women who sit around all lost and doe-eyed, waiting for their husband to instruct them in what they should do next. I like what you've done here, so stop fretting." Daughtry relaxed, realizing he was completely sincere.

"I do have some questions, though," Nick said, surprising her. Daughtry nodded to show her willingness to answer, but was even more surprised with the topic of his question. "Have you ever been in love?"

Daughtry thought back through her life, especially the years before Julie had died. She'd found more than one cowboy fascinating company, but only on friendly terms. She couldn't honestly remember feeling anything akin to what she was feeling for Nicholas, however, and that gave her reason to believe that she'd actually fallen in love with her husband.

"No," she answered softly.

"Me neither," he offered. "I just wondered if there were any ghosts that needed to be laid to rest. You know, broken hearts, lost loves, that kind of thing."

Daughtry shook her head. "I can honestly say there was no one."

"Why were you inclined to answer my advertisement?" he continued, and Daughtry now grew uncomfortable.

How could she explain to this no-nonsense kind of man that she'd run away from home? How could she explain that taking a vow of marriage had come about through the rebellious actions of a woman desperate to get away from her father?

"I guess," she began, "that your advertisement intrigued me. I thought the whole notion sounded, well, rather," she hesitated and looked away, "romantic."

"I've never been called romantic before."

"I find that hard to believe," Daughtry replied without thinking.

"Why's that?" Nicholas questioned, honestly wanting to know what was going through his young wife's mind.

Daughtry shifted uncomfortably. "Do I have to answer

that?"

Nick laughed. "I'd sure like it if you did."

"Very well," she murmured and tried to reason out her words before speaking. "You strike me as a very considerate man," she began, "a man who would be most sought after by the ladies of his community. You are very...." She swallowed several times, then took a drink of coffee. The lump in her throat refused to leave.

"I am very what?" He sensed her discomfort, but was completely captivated with what she had to say.

"You are very handsome," she said, rationalizing that he'd already complimented her looks. "I was very taken with your photograph and the way you signed your letter."

"The way I signed my letter?"

Daughtry nodded and wished that the ground would open and swallow her whole. How could she explain to this man, this stranger, that she'd fallen in love with his picture and letter? Or had she truly fallen in love with *him*, the person who now sat in front of her?

Nicholas leaned back in his chair and waited for her to explain. If she took all day, he wanted to hear exactly what she had to say.

Daughtry blushed and confusion filled her mind. "Forever yours," she whispered. "You signed your letter, 'Forever yours.'"

Nicholas smiled. He'd purposefully chosen that very ending after remembering it from one of his father's letters to his mother. His mother had told Nicholas once that the phrase was more than mere words, it was a pledge of sorts, and she had cherished it greatly. Now his own wife seemed to savor the words for the exact same reason.

"Something I learned from my father," he explained.

Daughtry used that introduction to Nick's past to question him further. "Tell me about yourself."

Nicholas shrugged. "Not much to tell. Nobody ever baked me bread as good as this, that's for sure."

"I'm serious," Daughtry said, pouring more coffee into her empty cup. "What about your family?"

"What about yours?"

"I'm alone," Daughtry replied. She told herself she wasn't really speaking a lie, because she didn't want to go against God and tell a falsehood, but she still could not bring herself to explain to him about her father.

"Me too," her husband replied and furthered her frustration.

"How am I to get to know you, if you won't tell me about yourself?" questioned Daughtry softly.

Nicholas leaned forward and smiled, revealing gleaming white teeth and eyes that fairly danced. "We have a lifetime to get to know one another," he answered. "I just don't think we need to do it all at one time. I'm going to enjoy getting to know you, little by little."

His words were pleasant enough, but Daughtry got the feeling he'd just as soon forget his past. *Well*, she thought to herself, *I feel the same way, so how can I fault him?* Without another word, Daughtry got to her feet, left the room for a moment, and returned with papers in hand.

"These are the marriage documents," she said, handing them to Nicholas.

Nicholas read them over and cast a glance upward to meet Daughtry's eyes. "Our wedding day was the twenty-first of September?"

Daughtry nodded.

"Wish I could have been there. I'll bet you were something to behold." Daughtry laughed at this, and Nicholas smiled broadly at her. "Did I say something wrong?"

"No, it's just that I look a whole sight better now than I did that day. Later, I'll show you what I was wearing."

Nick got up and went to the front sitting room where he retrieved a lock box, which he promptly brought back with him to the table. Taking a key from his vest pocket, he unlocked the box and carefully put the papers inside. Daughtry noticed when he did that her picture and letter were also inside the box, along with a large amount of money.

"They should be safe here," he announced and held up the key. "If you need anything, money or such, or you want to put something in here, just holler."

Daughtry nodded, then remembered the money she'd brought with her from home. "Just a minute, please," she said and went to the bedroom to get her cash. Fearfully, she wondered if she were doing the right thing, then a sense of peace washed over her and stilled her concerns.

When she walked back into the kitchen, she hoped that Nicholas would see her gesture for the trust she felt in their new marriage. "I'd like to add this to your savings," she whispered and thrust the money into Nick's hands. "It's all I had left after the trip."

Nicholas took the money and met Daughtry's eyes. He knew what she was doing and felt what she was trying to say without even hearing the words. He nodded, placed the money with his own, and shut the box. "Our savings," he said, locking the box and handing Daughtry the key. It was his way of meeting her trust with his own.

Daughtry felt her heart skip a beat. She reached up, but instead of taking the key, simply closed her hand around Nicholas's and smiled. "I'm content for you to have control."

seven

Daughtry felt as though she lived a lifetime within a single day. Nicholas asked her to share with him all that she'd done in his absence and Daughtry happily complied. He seemed especially impressed with the large stack of wood she'd positioned near the back of the house.

"I couldn't find any more coal," she explained, "so I did the next best thing."

"Those must be some arms you have," he teased and reached out to gently caress her upper arm. "Hmmm, you don't feel like a lumberjack."

Daughtry giggled and looked at him shyly. "I felt like one and I think I probably got as dirty as one. I went down to that grove of trees by the creek," she said and pointed. "There was quite a bit of dead wood there and I just made good use of it."

"I have a load of coal coming," Nicholas said, reluctantly removing his hand from her arm. "It ought to get here tomorrow or the next day at the latest. I also arranged for the ice man to deliver here until the creek freezes. I figure I can manage to keep us supplied through the winter."

Daughtry felt her skin tingle long after Nicholas had stopped touching her. She barely heard his words as he continued to speak of his arrangements for the ranch.

"I thought we might go into town tomorrow. We could purchase some of the things we'll need for the winter and also get some staples that I didn't have on hand. Milk and eggs ought to be readily available."

"A milk cow and chickens would suit us better," Daughtry said without thinking.

"I suppose that's true enough," Nicholas said thoughtfully, "but with winter coming on and us not having the ranch really prepared for livestock, I thought maybe we'd just rely on store bought."

"I guess that makes sense," Daughtry replied, walking with slow even strides beside her husband.

They paused at the broken down corral, and Nicholas leaned against a piece of fencing. The wind had picked up a bit and blew wisps of Daughtry's hair across her face. Nick smiled, wanting to reach out and touch the silky waves, but something held him back.

Daughtry noticed the look of hesitancy in her husband's eyes, and she couldn't help but wonder if he were hiding something from her. How could she know what type of man he'd been before or what type he'd be now? Mother had once said that people always proved their true nature by their actions. Well, so far Nicholas's actions had given Daughtry little to fear.

"What do you suppose we should do first?" he asked her seriously.

Daughtry's introspection was released as she shrugged. "It all depends on your plans."

"What would you suggest?"

Daughtry smiled. "Well, being a woman, I suggest the house be put in order first. When I was trying to repair the roof the other day..."

"What? You were up on the roof?" Nicholas interrupted.

Daughtry felt her face flush. "Not exactly ladylike,

was it?"

Nick laughed. "Ladylike or not, I'm amazed at your abilities. Did you actually get up there to fix the roof?"

Daughtry nodded, feeling rather proud. "I was inspired. The second night here it rained so hard that I had puddles all through the house. I can't say I accomplished much, but it was a healthy start."

"I guess that's what I'll do first then," Nick said with a thoughtful glance back at the house. "What else?"

Daughtry smiled. He genuinely wanted her to have a say in the matter. "Well, I'd like to cart everything out of the house and clean it good before winter sets in," Daughtry admitted. "As you could see, I only managed to set the kitchen and bedroom to rights before your return."

"Two very important rooms, if I do say so myself," Nicholas remarked.

"I figured it that way, too," Daughtry said and, without thinking of the implications, added, "after all, I figured most of my time would be spent in one place or the other." The words were no sooner out than Daughtry realized how they sounded. She clapped her hand over her mouth.

Nicholas laughed until he doubled over, and Daughtry turned crimson, knowing he must think her terribly forward.

"I didn't mean," she started to justify herself, then realized she would only make matters worse by continuing.

Nicholas straightened up and tried to control his mirth. "That's quite all right, honey," he said with tears of laughter gleaming in his eyes. "I pretty well figured what you meant."

Daughtry had to turn away to hide her embarrassment at her own statement. *Sometimes,* she thought, *I say the stupidest things.*

Nicholas sobered as he noticed her discomfort. "So we empty the house," he said matter-of-factly, struggling to keep the amusement from his tone, "and we wash it all down. Then what?"

"We put it all back inside," she answered softly. "Of course, if we don't want something back in the house, we can store it in the barn. I don't really know where you want things, so it might be nice if you had a part in the sorting through."

"I'm not sure what's even in there," Nicholas admitted. He stared at Daughtry's back for a moment before continuing. "I bought the place as is from a widow woman who wanted to move back East to live with her daughter. She'd let the place run down to this state and was barely able to feed herself. I heard from the sheriff in town that they were considering trying to force her out for her own good, so I came out here and we made a deal. She left a lot behind, but I have no idea whether it's useful stuff or just junk."

Daughtry nodded and finally turned to meet Nicholas's gaze. "I uncrated the dishes," she said, "but I didn't go through much else. I guess we can do that together, if you like."

"It would be my pleasure. Now, why don't you tell me about our grove of trees. Did you see anything of value there?"

"There were several apple trees and I think I recognized a plum or two. Would you like to walk down there?"

"Yes," Nicholas replied. "I'd like that."

Daughtry began to walk at a fairly good pace. She was disturbed for some reason by the feelings Nicholas brought about. She thought back to the days she'd spent with nothing more than his picture and realized how much she'd lost her heart to him. *He can't possibly feel the same way,* she scolded herself. *Men are much more level-headed about such matters.* Nicholas obviously needed a hardworking wife, and he probably hadn't wanted to waste his time with romantic notions and courting.

Daughtry was so lost in these thoughts that she didn't pay any attention to the ground she was covering. Before she could tell what was happening, she lost her footing on a large rock and fell forward.

Nicholas's arm shot out in a flash and encircled her waist protectively. He pulled her upright and then, as though he were doing the most natural thing in the world, he pulled her close against him.

Daughtry stared up into his face, knowing he would kiss her. She saw the questioning look in his eyes, as though he were asking permission. Without thought, she reached her hand up to the back of his head and pulled his face down to meet hers.

Nicholas needed no more encouragement. He quickly captured her lips with his own and kissed her so ardently that Daughtry forgot for a moment who and where she was. When he pulled away, Daughtry uttered the first thing that came to mind.

"I love you, Nicholas! I have ever since seeing your picture." Daughtry no longer cared that the declaration sounded like that of an infatuated teenager. She meant the words with all her heart. She really did love this man.

Nicholas held her at arm's length for a moment. The troubled look on his face brought Daughtry back to reality. Somehow, she had offended him.

"I'm sorry," she whispered and walked backwards a step. "That must sound insincere. After all, we've known each other for such a short time." She turned to go back to the house, wanting to run away and hide from her feelings and the man she'd so clearly startled.

Nicholas crossed the distance between them and halted Daughtry from going any farther. "I don't believe you could be insincere if you tried," he whispered.

Daughtry lifted her face, revealing all the emotion and misgivings she felt. "Please don't be angry with me. It's just that I haven't had much practice at things like this. Maybe it's because I've never felt this way before." She shrugged her shoulders before continuing. "My mouth gets a little ahead of itself sometimes, as you've witnessed before."

Nick shook his head. "I'm not angry. Surprised, yes, but not angry."

Daughtry nodded and tried to think of something she could say to negate her declaration of love. Short of lying, however, she didn't know what she could say. She meant her words of love. As crazy and untimely as it seemed, Daughtry knew they were truer than anything else she'd said to Nicholas.

As if reading her mind, Nick took hold of her hand and squeezed it gently. "Just answer me this. Now that we're not in the middle of a kiss, did you mean it?"

Daughtry knew exactly what he was asking of her. "I meant it," she barely whispered. "I know it sounds impossible, but it's true. I never would have married you otherwise."

Nick felt a twinge of guilt in his heart. This young, beautiful girl was baring her soul to him, and he knew he wasn't worthy of her trust. Nicholas kissed her hand, then let it fall back to her side. What could he possibly say to her?

They walked back to the house in silence, but Daughtry felt the awkwardness between them. She knew Nicholas was taken aback by her statement, but she sensed that something more than just that was troubling him.

Without a word, they sat down at the table and stared at each other. When Nicholas finally did speak, Daughtry felt her heart skip a beat.

"Tell me about your family, Daughtry."

The soft request shouldn't have caused her such fear, but Daughtry felt confident that Nicholas would never allow her to stay if he knew the truth. And more than ever now, Daughtry didn't want to lose her husband and new life. She didn't want Nicholas to send her back home.

"I grew up on a ranch," she said carefully. "I learned just about everything there is to know. I can ride, shoot, rope, brand, mend fence, whatever. I've nursed sick calves back to health, assisted with birthings, medicatings, and even helped to drive the herds to market. Ranching isn't just something I learned," she admitted. "It's something that's in my blood."

"But that doesn't answer my question. I want to know about your family. You said that you were alone, but there must have someone with you at one time or another. What became of your father and mother? Do you have brothers or sisters?"

"I had a sister," Daughtry said, feeling it safe to speak of Julie. "She died several years ago when her horse slipped on an icy trail and went over the side of a ravine."

"I'm sorry. That must have been terribly hard on your

folks."

"Yes, it was," Daughtry admitted before realizing that Nick had led her where she didn't want to go.

He was looking at her intensely now, expecting her to continue, but Daughtry knew she couldn't. "I don't want to talk about it anymore," she whispered and quickly left the room.

Nick stared at her chair for several minutes. What was she hiding and why did she look so fearful whenever he mentioned her past? Frustration began to build into anger at her distrust, but then Nicholas caught himself and realized that he had no room to express such thoughts. He was just as guilty of hiding from the past as she. Maybe it was what had brought them together. Maybe it was what God expected them both to deal with.

eight

The weeks that passed were the happiest Daughtry had ever known. She worked at Nicholas's side, laughing, teasing, and falling into a comfortable routine of being Mrs. Dawson. At night, they snuggled down under handmade quilts to share each other's warmth. Beneath the covers, they talked and dreamed about the future.

Daughtry loved it all. Not a single part of her new life caused her regret, except that she had to avoid her past. She started having nightmares about her father coming to tear her away from Nicholas's strong arms, but she choked back her fears and refused to let them surface. She couldn't risk losing all that had come to mean so much to her.

But, try as she might, Daughtry couldn't forget her family, nor could she dispel the building anxieties that haunted her every waking moment. All she could do was pray and ask God to forgive her and guide her steps, convincing herself that nothing else needed to be done.

Sundays were always a joy to Daughtry. She prepared for church with great enthusiasm, though today the sniffles from a passing bout with a head cold caused her some discomfort.

Nicholas popped his head through the bedroom door with a grin as broad as the barn door opening. "You need help with the buttons, Mrs. Dawson?"

Daughtry looked up and shook her head. "You can't

appreciate what we women have to go through in order to look just right for our men."

Nicholas rolled his eyes. "You always look just right to me, even when you're wearing those boy's jeans you seem to favor." Nicholas could still remember the first time he'd caught her wearing the form-fitting articles.

"Sometime I wish I could wear jeans to church," Daughtry said with a giggle. "Especially when the wind whips up and comes blasting across the open range."

"Well, I'd better never find you wearing those things off the property. It wouldn't be decent to have all the townsmen following you around with their tongues hanging out."

"You sound just like my dad," she replied without thinking. The words were no sooner out than she realized her mistake and paled.

Nick was rapidly coming to realize that Daughtry's biggest fears in life seemed to center around her parents. Especially her father. He'd seen her walk the edge of the roof, watched as she came face to face with a coil of snakes in the barn, even watched her deal with his bloody finger after he'd cut himself, and never had she shown the kind of fear in her eyes that she did at the mention of her father.

Coming to her, Nicholas pulled Daughtry into his arms. "Why are you so afraid to tell me about him? Did he hurt you?"

Daughtry shook her head, but Nicholas could still imagine her father as one of those overbearing types that beat his children. A frown crossed Nick's face. Maybe it was something even worse than him hitting her. Nicholas didn't like to think about it.

"I promise to understand. Whatever it is—whatever he did to you...." His words trailed into silence.

"He was a wonderful father," Daughtry said, still trembling beneath Nicholas's touch. She would say nothing more, though, and in frustration Nicholas released her.

"I'll get the wagon," he said and stalked out of the room.

Daughtry knew she'd hurt him by refusing to deal honestly with him. She comforted herself by remembering that Nicholas refused to share any real details of his own past with her. They were both hurting and hiding, she decided. They might as well do it together.

Daughtry was glad that Nicholas wasn't a man given to holding a grudge. By the time they headed into town he was laughing and joking about first one thing and then another.

After church they enjoyed a leisurely ride home and Nick shared his plans to buy Daughtry a horse. Good horse flesh was something to get excited about, and Daughtry squealed her delight at the news and threw her arms around Nicholas's neck.

"You really mean it?" she asked, hugging him so tight that he had to stop the horses in order to control her.

"Yes. Yes," he said, laughing at her enthusiasm. "Who would've thought that a little ol' horse would have gotten me so much attention?"

"It's just that I've really missed riding," Daughtry said happily. "Back home, I used to ride every day. I had the most wonderful gelding named Poco. He was about fifteen hands high and had the most beautiful gray coat." She stopped talking because Nicholas was looking at her strangely.

Daughtry jumped back and hung her head. She'd done

it again. She couldn't keep from bringing up her family and the home life she'd once loved. "He was a good horse," she finally said, when Nicholas wouldn't speak.

Nicholas remained silent and, when Daughtry said nothing more, he snapped the reins and sent the horse down the path to home. One way or another, he was determined to find out what she was hiding.

Daughtry tried not to think about her family that night as she curled into her husband's arms. The day had brought on too many memories, and more than once she'd nearly told Nicholas everything just to be rid of the burden.

"Nicholas?" she whispered against his ear.

"Yeah?"

"I love you." Her voice sounded like a child's trying to get on the good side of an adult.

For a minute, Nicholas said nothing. He tightened his grip on her and sighed. "I don't think you can love me and not trust me," he finally replied.

Daughtry stiffened in his arms. "What would you know about it? You don't love me. At least you've never said that you do."

Nick chuckled at her little girllike voice. "Never said I didn't, either."

Daughtry tried to ease away, but Nicholas would have no part of it. "Daughtry," he whispered her name and it sounded like a song. "Don't leave me."

Daughtry wanted to cry out that she'd never leave, but in the back of her mind that one thing spread panic through her like no other. She might not ever leave of her own accord, but what if her father forced her to leave?

"Never!" she declared in a whisper and settled down into his arms again.

Daughtry faded into a deep sleep, but soon she found herself in the middle of a most realistic nightmare. Her father had learned of her marriage to Nicholas and now he had come to face him in some sort of showdown, straight out of the frontier days she'd heard so much about.

Tossing from side to side, Daughtry fought with the images, pleading with her father to leave things as they were. He was furious and unyielding, promising to take Daughtry back home where she belonged and to hurt Nick if he dared to interfere.

He quoted the Bible to her, as Daughtry fell to her knees at his feet. "Children are to obey their parents," she heard him say. Turning in her dream to face her husband, Daughtry cried out at the betrayal and pain she saw in his eyes.

"You can't be my wife, Daughtry. You are his daughter," Nicholas told her through the misty fog.

"No," Daughtry moaned softly in her sleep. "No."

Something woke Nicholas but he wasn't sure what it was. Lying there, he quickly realized that it was Daughtry and she was sobbing. He lit the lamp at their bedside and had just reached out to pull her close when Daughtry sat straight up and screamed.

"Daughtry!" Nick exclaimed and gently shook her shoulders.

"Oh, Nick," she cried and fell limp against him as though all of her strength had been drained away.

Gently, he eased back against the pillows, taking her with him. "Why don't you stop all of this and tell me what's wrong. Tell me what you're keeping from me that causes you to have such fitful nights."

Daughtry looked up at him in surprise. Nicholas just

shook his head. "This isn't the first time, you know. You nearly flail me to death night after night. It's only getting worse, so you might as well deal with it here and now."

Daughtry knew he was right, but the fear in her heart caused her to hesitate. "You won't like it," she whispered.

"Why not let me be the judge of that?"

"Because I can already tell," Daughtry replied. "You're so serious about everything and you handle things in such a mature way that I'm afraid this will make you very angry with me."

"Daughtry," Nick said, reaching out to touch her cheek, "I could never be angry with you. Tell me."

Daughtry wiped at her tears with the back of her sleeve, took a deep breath, and got up on her knees. "I ran away from home to marry you."

"What?" Nick's eyes widened in surprise. "Don't tell me you're really sixteen or something."

Daughtry laughed. "No, I'm honestly as old as I said. A woman wouldn't joke about a thing like that."

"Then why do you say you ran away?"

Daughtry folded her hands. "My father was devastated after my sister died. It will be four years this November—but he only gets worse with each year that passes. Julie's death caused him to become overprotective of me. Everywhere I went, either he or one of my five brothers was there to shadow my every step. He wouldn't let me meet anyone or court. That's why I never fell in love with anyone else. You have to understand, I love my father and brothers, but they were smothering me to death. Even my mother understood how I felt, but she couldn't seem to reason any sense into my dad."

Daughtry could not bring herself to look at Nick's face

as she continued. "We had a terrible argument the night before I learned of your advertisement. When I saw your ad in the paper, I thought it just might be my way out. I decided to write to you and at least learn more about you, but then you wrote back with the proxy and the train ticket." She paused. "And your picture."

She looked up to see that Nicholas had put his hands behind his head and was studying her intently. Fearing what he might say, she hurried on. "I was going to write to you and refuse the proposal. I thought I could reason with my father, but when I tried to ask him nicely to give me more space—to let me grow up and fall in love—he refused. I was so angry, that I wrote them a long letter and slipped out in the middle of the night to come to you. I didn't let them know I was marrying you and I didn't say where I was going, only that I would be taken care of and safe."

She sighed. "I'm really sorry, Nicholas. I thought I was doing the right thing, or at least I thought it would work out to be the right thing. I saw it as an opportunity and I took it. Now, I keep having these horrible dreams that my dad and brothers come to take me back. They're always so angry and ugly, and I never have a chance to save you."

By now she was crying and Nick could no longer remain aloof. "Five brothers?" he asked, his forehead wrinkling up in disbelief.

Daughtry only cried all the more and nodded her head. "I don't want to leave you. I don't want them to take me away." She nearly wailed the words, and Nicholas began to chuckle.

"No one is going to take you away from me, Daughtry. Especially not now, not after all this time has passed between us. You're a grown woman and you made your choice. You're a married woman and you belong with me." His words forcefully placed the boundaries for Daughtry to see.

"What's done is done," he added. "You can't let them worry about you, though. And you can't go on having nightmares every night. I have to believe that this father of yours must be someone pretty special. Otherwise, it wouldn't upset you so much. Tomorrow we'll go to town and you can telephone them, or we'll send a telegram. Either way, you have to let them know what you've done and that you're all right."

"You aren't mad at me?" she asked through her tears.

Nicholas opened his arms to her with a smile, and Daughtry nestled down eagerly. "How could I be mad at you?" he whispered and reached over to turn down the lamp. "I love you."

nine

Daughtry felt November's chill air breathe down her damp back. She was working to pull out the last of the brush that had once surrounded her house. Rising up and stretching, Daughtry relished the sun, mild as it was, and put her face upward to catch every single ray. Winter was soon to be upon them and, by all the signs, Daughtry feared it might be a difficult one.

Nicholas watched his wife from his vantage point in the barn loft. She grew more beautiful every day, and every day he knew he loved her more. How good of God to throw them together. He observed her as she went back to work, thinking back to the day they'd gone to the post office and mailed the letter to her father and mother.

"I don't think I can do this, Nicholas," she had said in a pleading tone that begged him to let her forget the whole thing.

"You have to," he'd insisted firmly. "Nothing bad will come of it, Daughtry. If your folks come here, they'll see how happy you are and they won't even want you to leave."

At least Nick hoped things would work out that way. He continued to watch Daughtry, but he was thinking now of his own parents. They'd be livid if he'd pulled such a stunt, but then they were always critical of the choices he'd made in life. If it weren't for them, however, he might never have met and married Daughtry and that would have been a pity.

Turning his attention back to the work at hand, Nick was surprised when Daughtry called up to him in a frantic voice.

"Nicholas! Someone's coming!"

Like he'd done as a child, Nicholas jumped from the loft to the stacked bales of hay and then to the floor of the barn. He bounded out quickly to note the three horseback riders approaching from the west.

"Oh, Nick," Daughtry whimpered. "I just know it's my father and brothers."

"At least he only brought two," Nick said with a smile. "Go on in the house. You wait there for me and I'll talk to them first. You'll see, Daughtry. It's going to be all right."

Daughtry did as she was told, not because she felt overly obedient, but because she was a coward. She had no desire to hear the things her father would no doubt have to say to her husband. "Why, God?" she prayed aloud. "Why couldn't I have just done things the right way?"

In only a matter of minutes, angry voices rang loud and clear. Daughtry tried to cover her ears, not wanting to know what was said. What if her father said something really ugly? What if Nicholas refused to let them see her?

Daughtry started to pace. A part of her was certain that she should go outside and try to smooth over the situation. Maybe once her father saw how happy she had become and how wonderful Nicholas truly was, he'd let things be and go back home.

She reached for the door, just as things quieted considerably. A horse whinnied nervously, and Daughtry pulled back. Nicholas had told her to wait inside. She at least had to show him that she could follow his instructions. She might have misled him regarding her family, but that was all behind her now and she wanted to be a good wife.

Just as she'd convinced herself that everything was going to be all right, shots rang out, and Daughtry felt her knees turn to jelly.

"They've killed each other!" she gasped and ran to the window.

Outside, two men lay on the ground holding their bleeding arms, while one man remained on his horse with his hands raised high in the air. Daughtry didn't recognize any of them. She breathed a sigh of relief and turned her attention to her husband.

Nicholas stood with his feet fixed and a rifle leveled at the third man. The rage in his face was terrifying, and Daughtry saw blind hatred in his eyes. She stared at her husband's face and thought, *Who is this man?* He certainly didn't resemble the gentle one she'd married. Daughtry clutched her apron to her mouth to keep from screaming.

Her mind whirled. Who were these men and why had Nicholas shot them? Furthermore, where had he gotten the rifle to do the deed? She'd never seen a gun of any kind on the grounds, although she wouldn't have been surprised had there been one.

Staring at the scene outside her house, Daughtry couldn't hear a word that was being said. She watched the third man dismount from his horse and stare down the barrel of Nick's rifle. She couldn't watch anymore.

Daughtry moved to the far end of the house and cowered in the corner. She was wavering between tears and out-and-out hysteria. The more she thought about the scene, the more frightened she felt. A nervous laugh escaped her as she shook her head. Had Nicholas killed the two men? She sobbed and drew a ragged breath. Suddenly, she felt more terrified than she'd ever been in her life. She would have gladly welcomed the sight of her father and brothers at that moment, but she knew she could hope for no such reprieve.

The kitchen door banged, and Daughtry knew someone had come into the house. Trembling, she backed into the corner even tighter.

"Daughtry!" Nicholas called out to her as he moved from room to room. "Daughtry, where are you?" His voice sounded worried, almost panicked.

When he came into the front room, he sighed when he saw her. "Why didn't you answer me? Are you okay?"

Daughtry couldn't say a word. She stared at him, trying to force herself to calm down. It was an impossible task.

Nick knew immediately that she was frightened, but he didn't know he had anything to do with it. "Daughtry, come here, honey. It's all right now."

Daughtry shook her head, not really seeing him. She saw instead the man who'd held the rifle in black rage. She saw a killer in her mind and felt her breath quicken.

Nick stepped forward with his arms extended. He wanted to comfort her and let her know that she was safe. When he came to her, Nicholas reached out his hands to pull her into his arms. Daughtry went wild.

"No!" she screamed and fought his grasp. "Don't touch me!"

Nicholas looked at her with such shock on his face that for a moment he didn't realize she was slapping at him. He tried to still her hands, but this only frightened her more. She doubled up her fists and flailed them in the air at his face and chest.

With stunned realization, Nicholas understood that Daughtry was terrified of him, not the men he'd tied up in the barn.

As gently as he could, Nicholas pinned her arms to her

side and physically carried her to the sofa. Daughtry was crying and yelling incoherently, begging him not to hurt her. Nick thought he'd die inside.

"It's all right, Daughtry. Honey, don't do this," he whispered. Holding her against him with one arm, he began to stroke her face with his other hand. "Daughtry!" He nearly yelled the name, and she immediately settled.

Raising her blue eyes to meet his dark, almost black ones, Daughtry couldn't hide the fear she felt. All of her foolishness in running away, marrying, and hiding here with a stranger had suddenly come home to her. Gasping for breath, she strained against his touch, while at the same time she heard his gentle words.

"Daughtry, those men are outlaws—a part of my past catching up with me. They meant to hurt us. I only did what I had to do in order to protect us." He felt her calm a bit and pressed on. "I was only defending myself."

Daughtry let the words sink in. Reason drove out the fear, and she began to relax in his hold. "Who—who—" she stammered, "are they?"

"It's not important. They're wanted by the law and later I'll take them into the sheriff. I have them tied up in the barn and they can't hurt you." He softened his expression and loosened his hold ever so slightly. "But then, you aren't really worried about them hurting you, are you?"

Daughtry couldn't answer him. She felt so foolish for her behavior.

"Daughtry, have I ever given you reason to fear me?"

"No," she managed to whisper.

"I'm not a bad man, Daughtry. I know there's things I can't tell you just yet, but trust me. I understood about your secrets, now I'm asking you to understand about mine."

She felt her fears give way to sympathy and then relief. He had only defended himself, she thought. Slumping against him, completely spent, Daughtry clung to his shirt. "I'm sorry," she said softly.

Nicholas brushed back her hair with his hand. "It's all right. I can honestly understand your misgivings."

"Why can't you tell me about your past?" she questioned. "I told you about mine."

Nicholas sighed. "It's a long story, but for now I'm just begging you to trust me and to trust God to work it all out. I love you, Daughtry. Please, don't doubt me on that."

"I don't," she replied and sat up. She studied the worry in his eyes. It went beyond concern and seemed like something that bordered fear. Was he afraid she'd stopped loving him?

"Oh, Nicholas," she said and kissed his face several times, "I was so afraid you'd be killed. Then when I saw you with that gun and you were so angry—well, I just didn't know what to think."

"I know, honey, and believe me, I would have saved you from having to go through it if I could have."

Daughtry nodded. It was all right, she told herself. Whatever his past consisted of, she no longer cared. She only knew that she loved him and that she would stand by him no matter what.

Leaning down to put her face on his shoulder, Daughtry spoke. "We'll just trust God to get us through this," she pledged.

"That's my girl," Nicholas said and leaned back against the sofa. A frown crossed his face as he thought of the men in the barn, but the young woman in his arms helped him to forget the incident. There'd be time to face the truth soon enough.

ten

Days later, Daughtry had nearly forgotten the unpleasant incident. "Are we really going to get the horse today?" she asked eagerly. Securing her bonnet, she waited for Nick's reply.

"Yes, for the millionth time," he said laughing. "I've never seen you so excited about anything in our two months of marriage."

"Well, there was the time that rat got in the house," Daughtry said with a grimace. "Or wait, what about the bathtub? I got pretty excited about the bathtub."

Nicholas's eyes twinkled. "Yes, yes, you did. I seem to recall having some very fine apple cake that evening. Wonder if I'll get another one for buying the horse?"

"We'll see," Daughtry said with a smug look of satisfaction. "Depends on how good the horse is."

"Now, while we're in town," Nicholas said, bringing the wagon to a halt, "I want you to get whatever you think we might need. We've got to make sure we're stocked up for the winter, just in case we have trouble getting into town."

Daughtry nodded and pulled out a small list. "I wrote down things for the kitchen." She glanced up and down the street which was already teaming with people. Several suffragists stood at one end of the street expounding on the necessity of women having the vote. At the opposite end of town there seemed to be an unusual amount of traffic at the railroad depot. "We seem to have come on a busy day."

"Looks that way." Nicholas helped her from the wagon and put a finger under her chin. "Get yourself some warm clothes while you're at it. I was looking through the things you brought into this marriage and you aren't at all well supplied." His mouth curled into a grin and Daughtry returned his smile.

"Do you need anything?" she asked. "I can sew, you know, and we still have Mrs. Cummings's old sewing machine. I'm sure I could get it in working shape."

"I could use some heavy shirts for winter," he said, then placed a light kiss on her forehead. "But don't worry about me. I want you to make sure you have everything you need. Everything, understood? Even if you worry that I might think it frivolous. I've never had a wife before, so I wouldn't be knowing what one might need."

Daughtry was touched by his generosity. "I'll try to be thorough. Where will you be?"

"Oh, here and there. I have to get the horse and there's a few other things I need to attend to. I'll pick up the mail, so you don't have to worry about it. Now, here's some money and if that's not enough, tell them to hold whatever it is you want and I'll pay them before we head home."

Daughtry watched as Nicholas took off down the street. He was so kind and loving. Gone were the images of the hateful man with the rifle. All Daughtry could see was the man who touched her heart.

She was headed across the street to the general store when she happened to glance once more at her husband's retreating form. Surprised, she noticed he'd headed to the sheriff's office. Watching him go into the small building,

Daughtry quickly made her way down the street to follow him. She wanted very much to know if her husband were in some kind of trouble.

"But why would he come here if he was an outlaw?" Daughtry wondered aloud. Biting her lip, she looked around quickly and was grateful to find herself alone on the boardwalk.

The town was much too small to have a very grand affair for a jail. Daughtry knew from what folks had told her on the train coming here that this was a one saloon, one cell kind of town. She would have been just as happy had they told her it had no saloon, but then, the world wasn't perfect.

Leaning close to the window, Daughtry could see her husband in deep discussion with a man she could only guess was the sheriff. She couldn't hear anything from this vantage point, however. Quietly, she made her way around the building and up the alley. She came to the window nearest the two men and paused. This one had the shade pulled down on the inside. She could see nothing, but she pressed her ear to the glass after a cautious glance down the alleyway.

"You go far enough back with these men to be related," she heard the sheriff saying. He said something more, but his words were garbled and Daughtry couldn't begin to understand.

Then Nicholas bellowed in voice so loud Daughtry had no trouble distinguishing every word, "I didn't ask them to look me up. They rode in looking for trouble and I gave it to them."

The sheriff, equally enraged, ranted back. "Well, you made your bed this time for sure. You brought it all on yourself!"

Daughtry wondered silently what Nick had brought on himself, but she was unable to continue listening at the window because someone was coming down the alley. She made her way down the street, crossing to avoid the suffragists and their battle cries.

She quickly entered the general store and furiously began her shopping. Her mind was filled with ugly images and worrisome thoughts. What if Nicholas had once been an outlaw? Maybe he was once partners with the men who sat in the jail cell. She shuddered at the thought. That just couldn't be possible. Or could it?

She toyed with several bolts of flannel material and finally settled on a dark blue plaid and a solid brown. She ordered the yardage and sought out buttons to match, planning in her mind to make Nicholas two good shirts before winter set in. Remembering his instructions to her, Daughtry went through the material a second time and chose several colors of wool to make herself some simple skirts. She finished by securing some plain white cotton and two calico prints for blouses, before turning her attention to colorful skeins of knitting yarn.

She paid for the goods, certain that she'd overspent what Nicholas had given her, but found to her surprise that she had plenty of cash left over. Seeing that she still had enough money, Daughtry quickly instructed the store owner to throw in several pairs of long underwear for her husband.

"What size?" the man asked her as he went to retrieve the goods.

"Oh, my," she said in surprise. "I don't know."

"Well," the man said looking at the blushing woman, "is he bigger than me?"

Daughtry sized the man up for a moment. "Yes," she

determined quickly. "He's at least this much taller than me and about this much wider," she said, holding her hands out to indicate the size. Just then, Nicholas came into the store and Daughtry motioned to the storekeeper. "That's him."

The man behind the counter smiled and nodded. "Morning, Mr. Dawson. I didn't know this little lady was your wife."

"We're newlyweds," Nicholas said, coming up behind Daughtry. "Now what did you mean 'That's him'?"

"I was just buying you some..." Daughtry blushed again, unable to talk about underwear in the presence of her husband.

The storekeeper quickly brought the requested product to the counter and added it to the stack of things Daughtry had already paid for. "Will these do?" he asked, looking at Nicholas and not Daughtry.

Nicholas had to hold himself in check to keep from laughing out loud at Daughtry's sudden embarrassment. "She thinks of everything," he said with a wink over Daughtry's shoulder to the storekeeper. "They're fine."

Daughtry handed the storekeeper the remaining amount due, while Nicholas put his arm around her lovingly. "Did you get everything you needed?"

"Yes and then some. I certainly can't complain about your generosity, Mr. Dawson."

Nicholas picked up their supplies and led Daughtry to the door. "Would you like to get something to eat while we're in town?"

"That might be fun," Daughtry replied, looping her arm through Nick's. "But it's also a bit frivolous. We're going to have a great many expenses come spring and...."

"Madam," a deep, but clearly female voice called out,

"you are a victim of our society."

Daughtry and Nicholas both stopped directly in front of a sour-faced woman who was dressed in black with a white sash that clearly identified her suffrage cause. The woman continued before either Nick or Daughtry could comment.

"This man seeks to enslave you! You needn't be chained to him like a dog. The men of America seek to make women their possessions. They want to control them. He," the woman said, sticking a bony finger in the middle of Nick's face, "wants to control you. He wants to dominate your every living moment."

Daughtry stared up at Nick as if contemplating the woman's words. Nick just shrugged and raised a questioning brow.

"That's right," the woman continued. "This man would just as soon see you bound to him—fit only to serve his pleasures and bear his children!"

Daughtry smiled broadly at the woman. "I know. Isn't it great?"

At this, the woman sputtered and stepped back in horror, while Nicholas threw back his head and roared with laughter.

"You, young woman, are the very reason women are oppressed. You are the reason we can't voice our opinions and vote for our own representation," the woman called to Nicholas and Daughtry as they made their way down the boardwalk.

"You certainly made a spectacle of yourself, Mrs. Dawson. Probably set back women's rights a hundred years," Nick said, helping her down from the boardwalk.

"Oh, dear," Daughtry said in feigned concern. "I suppose that means I'll be bound to you even longer now."

"Only forever," Nick said with a gentleness in his voice that warmed Daughtry's heart.

Daughtry stared up at her husband, all the love she felt for him shining clear in her eyes.

"Well, are you going to just stand there or are you going to tell me what you think of your new horse?" he questioned.

Daughtry's eyes widened and she quickly looked around. Standing there, tied to the back of the wagon, was a beautiful chestnut mare, complete with western saddle. "I thought you might like to ride her home," Nicholas whispered against her ear.

"Oh, she's beautiful! Of course I want to ride her home. Oh, Nicholas, thank you!" She threw her arms around her husband, nearly causing him to drop their packages.

Helping to set things back in place, Daughtry composed herself a bit, but the delight was evident in her eyes.

"You're welcome," he said and happily deposited the packages in the back of the wagon before turning to lend Daughtry some help in mounting.

"Does she have a name?" Daughtry questioned, running her hand along the mare's sleek neck.

"She does. The owner called her Nutmeg."

Daughtry cooed and talked to the mare, whispering the name several times. "I think we'll be good friends, you and I," she said to the horse.

Nicholas helped her up into the saddle, then took his place on the wagon. "You sure you want to ride her home?"

"Of course I'm sure," Daughtry replied indignantly. "I could ride before I could walk, at least that's what my father used to say." She frowned only briefly at the reference before moving Nutmeg forward.

Nicholas pulled up alongside her once they were on the

road out of town. "It's going to be all right, Daughtry. You can't be worrying all the time about what might or might not happen."

"I know, but it's been a while since we sent the letter. I figure it won't be long before...." She couldn't finish the sentence, but Nicholas understood and conveyed his sympathy with his eyes. Taking a deep breath, Daughtry reminded herself that she had Nicholas's love and that he would protect her. Then an earlier scene crossed her mind and Daughtry grimaced. *But who's going to protect Nicholas?* she wondered silently. Who would protect him when his past caught up with him again?

With the sheriff's words still reverberating through her head and her own imagination running wild, Daughtry couldn't help but fear the truth. She worked almost mindlessly around the kitchen that evening, putting the finishing touches on supper, waiting for Nicholas to reappear after seeing to the horses. She pulled a peach cobbler from the oven and smiled. At least she could offer him a good home-cooked meal. Cooking was one thing her mother had insisted Daughtry learn.

"Ummm, smells mighty fine in here," Nicholas said, coming through the mud porch into the kitchen. "And it's warmer in here, too."

Daughtry came to him and helped him off with his coat. "It does feel a lot colder," she replied, feeling the chilled night air as it followed him through the open door.

"No sign of snow just yet," Nicholas added, giving his hat a toss to a hook beside the door. "It might just go around us."

Daughtry nodded. "Supper's ready."

"I can see that," he said, staring appreciatively at the table. "You're going to make me fat," he laughed but eagerly took a seat.

"I baked you a cobbler," Daughtry said proudly. She brought the bubbling concoction to the table in order to show it off. "It ought to taste even better with the fresh cream we brought home."

"I'm going to have to keep buying you presents, I see."

"Maybe you could just share secrets with me instead," she replied soberly.

"What do you mean?" he asked, knowing full well what she wanted.

"I just think it would be nice to know more about you. Like those men the other day. I can't just forget about them. Who were they and why did they want to hurt you?" Daughtry sat down to the table and waited for Nick to speak.

"It's nothing," Nick snapped and began putting food on his plate. Softening his tone, he looked at her with pleading eyes and added, "Nothing that needs to concern you."

"But I heard the sheriff yell at you," Daughtry said without thinking. She bowed her head, ashamed to admit she'd spied on her husband.

"Don't nose into this, Daughtry," he replied sternly, the first time he'd ever sounded angry with her.

"I have a right to know," she protested, lifting her face to meet his.

Nicholas's eyes narrowed slightly. "Stay out of it. I mean it!" He slammed his fist down on the table, causing all the dishes to rattle. Daughtry stared at him for a heartbeat, then got up and ran from the table.

She was out the back door and running past the barn before she realized he was calling after her. Pride wouldn't let her slow down, however, and Daughtry continued until she came to her favorite place. The little grove of trees by the creek offered her a safe haven, but not much warmth. Shivering uncontrollably under the full moon, Daughtry began to cry. Why had he been so mean?

She knew he'd follow her, but when he wrapped his arms around her and pulled her close, Daughtry jumped back in fear.

"Don't," she said between chattering teeth.

She could see the pain in his face. Pain of rejection and fear of loss. "I'm sorry, Daughtry. I didn't mean to lose my temper."

She said nothing, wondering at the strained apology. Did he think that was enough? Just an "I'm sorry?" *What do you want him to say?* Daughtry asked herself and could think of no answer.

Nicholas reached out to her again and this time Daughtry didn't push away. "I really am sorry," he whispered against her ear. "It's just that the whole episode with those men unnerved me. I can't help but worry that we aren't safe here anymore. I can't help but worry that I've exposed you to something harmful and ugly. Before, when it was just me, I didn't have to worry about things like that. I prayed and asked God to ride with me, watch over me, and take me home when the time came. But now, there's so much more. There's you and...." He fell silent. What was the use? He couldn't explain it.

Daughtry's heart softened toward him. His worry for their safety concerned her more than she wanted to admit but, right now, all she wanted to do was comfort him.

"It's all right, Nicholas. I'm sorry to have pressed the matter and I'm sorry that I spied on you. I do love you and I trust you, so from now on, I'll leave the matter be."

eleven

Thanksgiving drew near and with it the haunting reminder of Julie's death. Daughtry found herself thinking about her sister, even when she didn't want to. Julie would have been eighteen. Thoughts of her naturally turned Daughtry's mind to her father. She was both worried and relieved that he'd done nothing to interfere in her life. Was he so angry that he no longer cared?

"It's a beautiful day out here, Daughtry!" Nicholas called from just outside the back door.

Daughtry made her way outside, wearing only her dark green wool skirt and long-sleeved calico blouse. "Yes," she murmured, relishing the reminder of summer. "I think I'll do the wash outside today."

Nick mounted his horse and gave her an admonishing look. "Don't overdo it and don't stay outside if it turns cold. I don't want you getting sick."

Daughtry grinned at his fatherly words. "I'm surprised you're willing to leave me here alone."

"I'm not very happy about the idea," Nicholas said, "but you're insistent on having fresh turkey for Thanksgiving and since the Shaunasseys offered to sell me one of their birds, I guess I'll just have to overlook my discomfort."

"Oh, go on with you, now," Daughtry said and reached out to smack the horse on the rump. Instead, Nicholas caught her hand and lowered his lips to her fingers.

"Please stay out of trouble," he whispered. "I've grown

very fond of you, Mrs. Dawson."

Daughtry's heart warmed to his words. "And I, you, Mr. Dawson."

With nothing more said, Nicholas took off for his five-mile ride to the Shaunasseys, while Daughtry went back inside to ready her laundry.

With most of the wash done by noon, Daughtry was just putting away her wash tub and scrub board when the unmistakable sound of a wagon caught her attention. Peering around the house, Daughtry was pleased to see the freighter, Tom O'Toole, making his way up the long Dawson drive.

She quickly hurried inside to put on coffee and arrange a plate of cookies, while Tom completed the trip to the barn. He was bringing in the last of their ordered supplies for winter, and Daughtry was hopeful that he might have thought to bring the mail as well.

"Afternoon, Mrs. Dawson," the man said, jumping to the ground.

"Afternoon, Tom," Daughtry replied. "When you finish there, I've got hot coffee and cinnamon cookies for you."

"That ought to make my work pass quicklike," he announced. Pulling down a heavy crate, Tom motioned. "This here is a bunch of them canned goods you asked for last time. It just came in from Denver."

"Oh, good," Daughtry replied. "You can bring that on up to the house and I'll get to work putting it away."

Tom nodded and followed Daughtry into the house, where he deposited the crate, requested a hammer, and pulled the nailed lid off. Daughtry immediately went to work, while Tom made his way back outside.

Humming to herself, Daughtry felt good about their filled pantry. There was more than enough food to tide them over for a great many months, if necessary. Nicholas, however, seemed to think that even if heavy snows buried them, a good strong prairie wind would most likely clear a path to town. With that in mind, Daughtry didn't worry much about the distance.

She was nearly finished when Tom gave a heavy knock on the door and bounded into the room. "All done out there," he said and Daughtry poured him a mug of coffee and pointed him to the chair.

"You just rest a while and help yourself to those cookies. Nicholas has gone over to the Shaunasseys' to get our Thanksgiving turkey."

"Me and the missus are planning on heading up to Raton for Thanksgiving. She's got a sister there and nieces and nephews and since it wasn't that far by train, we thought it might make a nice trip before the snows set in."

"It does sound like fun," Daughtry said half-heartedly, for, in truth, she loved her little hideaway home and didn't desire to travel away from it, even to visit her family.

"You got kin nearby?" Tom asked, draining his coffee and reaching for a third cookie. Daughtry started to refill his cup but he waved her off. "I still have two more deliveries to make, so I'd best be on my way." He got to his feet and Daughtry followed him out of the house.

"This weather is sure enough pleasant," Tom said, making his way to the wagon. "I could do without the snow for a while."

"Me too," Daughtry replied. "Well, take care, Tom." She waited while he climbed up into the worn wooden seat of his freight wagon.

"Oh, I plum forgot," he said, reaching under the seat. "I brought the mail for you."

Daughtry's face lit up, hoping that maybe a newspaper or magazine might be included in his delivery. Nicholas had ordered several magazines for her when they were last in town and Daughtry was beginning to think they'd never arrive. To her disappointment, though, Tom handed down only a single envelope.

"This one's for you," he said and picked up the reins. "I'll be seeing you, Mrs. Dawson." He snapped the reins and took off on his route while Daughtry stared at the unmistakable handwriting of her father.

With shaking hands, Daughtry forced herself to open the letter. She waited until she made it back to the kitchen table, however, to read it. She was feeling weak in the knees and almost green with anxiety by the time she unfolded the single page.

Daughtry stared down at the words in disbelief. Her father was coming! She read the brief statement of when he planned to arrive and found that the date in his letter matched the one on the calendar. Her father planned to arrive today!

Daughtry dropped the letter on the table. If her father showed up and Nicholas were not there to prevent him from taking her back, what would she do? Feeling sick inside, Daughtry got up from the table and began to pace.

"Dear Lord," she whispered, "I know that sinful nature got me here. I know that I was out and out disobedient, but, Father, I love Nicholas and I don't want my dad to take me back to Piñon Canyon. I want to stay here and be Nicholas's wife." She paused and realized her prayer was more the uncontrollable babblings of a rebellious child.

She folded her hands together and took a deep breath.

"Show me what I need to do, Father. Show me how to make this right. Please forgive me for going against my father's wishes, and help my father to understand why I did what I did and to forgive me for hurting him. Amen."

Daughtry felt only marginally better. She knew that God was in charge and would take care of everything. She even knew that He'd already forgiven her for her willful disobedience. Daughtry couldn't wash away the feelings of helplessness, however.

A quick glance at the clock on the wall started Daughtry panicking again. *He plans to arrive today,* she thought, *but when?* Finally, Daughtry decided she'd ride over to the Shaunasseys' and get Nicholas. She could face anything with Nick at her side.

Despite the nice weather, she put on heavy wool stockings and a wool, split skirt. She pulled on her riding boots and grabbed a warm, fitted jacket to throw in her saddle bag in case the weather turned cool. Then suddenly, without really knowing that she was packing, Daughtry found herself throwing together gloves, a bonnet, her jeans, and one of Nicholas's thick flannel shirts. When she'd gathered these things, Daughtry took two wool blankets and rolled all of it together into a pack that would fit behind her saddle.

Somewhere in the midst of her worry, Daughtry knew she was running away again, but her mind wouldn't let her reason out the truth.

"I can't go to Nicholas," she said aloud, "or I might pass Daddy on the way." The thought of being already en route when her father caught up with her made Daughtry believe he'd have just that much easier of a time forcing her home.

Running with the pack into the kitchen, Daughtry laid out provisions for herself, including matches, a small pot, and a generous amount of food. She stuffed as much as she could into her saddle bags, then leaving the kitchen in complete disarray, she grabbed her things and ran for the barn.

❧

Nicholas was in a good mood as he made his way home that afternoon. He had a nice fat turkey confined in a crate on the back of his rather skeptical horse and two warm loaves of pumpkin bread in the saddle bags behind him. His mood was founded on more than the food, however. He was going home to her. Home to his wife. Daughtry!

He hadn't realized how much he'd come to love her until he spent time away from her. This was the first time since she'd arrived that he'd spent nearly an entire day without her by his side. Even the time he'd had to take the outlaws into the sheriff hadn't amounted to more than a couple of hours.

Anxious to hold her in his arms and see her pleasure at the turkey, Nick urged his horse into a gallop and hurried for home.

Nicholas approached the house without giving much thought to the cloud of dust that rose to his right. He was preoccupied with his thoughts and didn't even see the riders until he was bringing his horse to a stop just outside the barn.

Nicholas thought to dismount but sat instead with his eyes fixed on the riders. Without being told, he knew they were Daughtry's father and three of her brothers.

"Well, Lord," he whispered against the silence, "I guess

this is it. I'm about to answer for what I've done with this man's daughter. I could sure use some direction in how to come under my father-in-law's good graces."

The riders approached, slowing to a slow walk until they were directly in front of Nicholas. The older of the three pressed his horse forward until he was nearly nose to nose with Nick.

"You Nicholas Dawson?" Garrett Lucas asked from between clenched teeth.

"I am," Nick replied softly. "You must be..." He never got the words out, because Garrett flew across the saddle and knocked Nicholas off of his horse and to the ground.

twelve

After two well-placed blows against Nick's face, Garrett's sons managed to pull their father off the stunned man. Nicholas refused to fight back and got to his feet slowly. Knocking the dust from his backside, he moved away a step, while Garrett strained at the resistance of his sons.

"You have to answer for what you've done!" Garrett declared. His face was reddened with anger.

Nicholas rubbed his jaw and a hint of a smile played at his bloodied lip. "I think I just did."

Garrett was livid and refused to be humored. "Where's my daughter? Where's Daughtry?"

"I would imagine in the house. As you can see for yourself, I just got back," Nicholas replied gingerly. He didn't believe his jaw was broken, but it hurt nevertheless.

"Dad, you promised to be levelheaded about this," one of the boys was saying. Nicholas watched as the other two nodded in agreement. Maybe Daughtry's brothers were able to see that their sister had a right to make her own choices.

"Don't tell me what I said, Joseph!"

"He's right, Dad. Daughtry told us in the letter that she's happy. Why don't we let her tell us otherwise."

Garrett seemed to relax a bit, and Nick took the opportunity to speak. "I'm sorry, I truly am. Not for having married your daughter, but for the way we went about it. I know what Daughtry put in her letter, so I know that you realize I was completely unaware of your existence when she married me. It's a poor excuse, I know, but I hope in time you will forgive me."

Garrett recognized the peaceful apology and knew in his heart that further violence was uncalled for. His sons instantly sensed the change in their father and let go of him.

Garrett stared at Nicholas for several minutes without saying a word. He was angry, but more than that he was humbled by the younger man's willingness to seek his forgiveness.

"I'm Garrett Lucas," he finally said. "These are my sons, Gavin, Dolan, and Joseph."

"Pleased to meet all of you," Nicholas responded. He didn't offer his hand, feeling if he did he might be forcing the issue a bit. Instead, he motioned to the horses. "What say we tie these fellows up and you let me put my turkey in the barn, and we'll go inside and talk this out with Daughtry."

The other men nodded. Nicholas could see the boys speaking in low whispers to Garrett, while they tied the horses to the corral fence and waited for their host. They seemed like good men, he thought to himself, and he smiled. Of course they were good men; they were Daughtry's family.

Making his way to where they awaited him, Nicholas took the lead. "Come on inside."

Nicholas immediately sensed that all was not right when he entered the kitchen. Things were strewn about in a haphazard way that was not indicative of his wife's normal sense of order. For a minute he stood in the silence, while Garrett and the boys glanced around the room.

"Daughtry!" he called out, but in his heart, Nicholas knew she wouldn't answer.

He rushed from one room to the next, and when he saw the same disarray in the bedroom that had greeted him in the kitchen, Nicholas knew that she was gone. Panic filled his soul. Had friends of the men he'd jailed come for him and taken her instead?

The fear was clear in Nick's eyes as he returned to the kitchen. "She's not here. I'm going to check the barn and see if her horse is gone. You wait here," he instructed and ran out the back door.

Nick began to pray as he'd never done before. "Dear God, keep her safe. Please don't let any harm come to her. Oh, God, please help me find her."

When Nicholas realized the horse was indeed missing, he made his way back to the house with a heavy heart. Where was she? The light was fading and the wind was picking up, causing a chill to fill the air. Where was Daughtry?

The defeat on his face made it clear to Garrett that Nicholas was more than a little upset at finding Daughtry gone. "Where do you suppose she got off to?" Garrett asked, trying to keep his voice even.

Just then, Nicholas spied the letter on the table. He picked it up, praying that it might be some note of explanation from Daughtry.

"She's run away again," Nicholas muttered and handed the letter to Garrett. "She found out you were due to be here and, what with me gone, she was afraid."

"Afraid? Of me?" Garrett nearly growled in disbelief.

Nicholas nodded his head. "She's been in a real stew since we married. Always looking over her shoulder, wondering when you were going to come and take her by force."

"She was afraid of me," Garrett stated sadly as if all the wind had gone out from him. "I don't know why she thought I would try to make her unhappy."

"It's not important now. What is important is that we find her," Gavin offered and Nick nodded.

"I just wanted her to make good choices," Garrett said, trying to explain himself.

"She's a good woman," Nick responded without hesitancy. "She makes good choices."

"Ha," Garrett sounded. "She doesn't seem to have made a very good one this time. She's out there somewhere, only God knows where, and she's alone. It's getting colder and...."

"I'm going after her," Nicholas said and turned to leave. "You make yourselves comfortable here, in case she comes back."

"No," Garrett replied, "I'm going after her. She's my daughter and if I caused this like you said, then I'll find her."

"She's my responsibility now," Nicholas said a bit more forcefully than he'd intended.

"And I say she's still under my authority and protection," Garrett replied, coming to stand only inches from Nicholas. "I was there when she came into this world and God gave me charge over her."

"But I married her and that authority now falls to me," Nicholas replied softly. "I love her as much as you do."

Gavin, Dolan, and Joseph stared in silence at their father and new brother-in-law. They knew arguing was a waste of precious time, but they also saw the futility of trying to interfere.

"You may love her," Garrett answered, "but she's still my daughter. Flesh of my flesh and blood of my blood."

He stood his ground with the same tenacious determination that was clear on Nicholas's face. They were two of a kind, Gavin thought to himself, but he said nothing.

Nicholas nodded. "I know. But she's my wife and she's carrying our child."

Garrett's mouth dropped open at this sudden declaration. A part of him wanted to fight Nicholas all over again, while another part of him stood in awed amazement.

"A baby?" he questioned in disbelief.

"Yes," Nicholas replied, his dark eyes losing all trace of anger.

"Why don't we stop this nonsense," Gavin finally spoke up. "We should go together. With all of us looking, we're bound to find her sooner."

Garrett and Nicholas's eyes were still locked. Garrett remembered another time, long ago, maybe even a lifetime ago. He'd met the eyes of Maggie's dying father and knew in a glance that he was being given the care of Jason Intissar's most precious possession, his only child.

Something in Garrett softened even as another part of him died; aching with loss, another part rejoiced at the creation of life from God's hand to his daughter's body.

"He's right," Nicholas said, seeing the change in Garrett. "Let's all go. I've a feeling she won't be all that far."

"Yeah, but we're talking about my sister," Dolan joked. "She's very stubborn and who knows where that'll take her."

Nicholas grinned. "She's had good training, though. I know Daughtry can take care of herself." Grabbing his coat, he added, "I'll tell you about her fixing the roof while we ride."

⋆

Daughtry had found the perfect place to make camp for the night. She had ridden for several hours before coming to a rocky wall barrier. As she paralleled it for a short time, the sky began to grow dark, and Daughtry realized she'd have to stop and take shelter. She also noticed that the air was getting cold.

At the first sound of water, Daughtry felt a bit of contentment wash over her. She'd have a good camp for both Nutmeg and herself. Bringing the horse to a stop by the stream, Daughtry quickly went to work, and before the last few glimmers of late autumn sun had faded behind the mountain peaks, she had a nice fire going.

She thought how beautiful the night was and how the tiny pinpricks of light that were millions of stars in the sky seemed to keep her company through the loneliness of her vigil. "I know I've brought this on myself, Father," she prayed. "But I just didn't know what else to do. I wanted to trust You to work it out. I wanted to have faith that everything would be all right, but I was so frightened."

The wind picked up a bit and Daughtry hugged a blanket close to her. Foolish or not, she was out here alone and had to make the most of it. Garrett Lucas had raised his children to be capable of caring for themselves outdoors, and Daughtry was certainly no exception to that rule. As the fire began to die down, she tossed several large logs on the coals and settled down for the night.

"Oh, Nicholas," she sighed against the haunting sounds of the canyon winds. "I need you."

thirteen

Daughtry tried to sleep but couldn't. Perhaps the hour was just not late enough, she reasoned; after all the sun had only been down for an hour, maybe two. In frustration, she sat up and leaned back against the rock to contemplate her actions.

In the distant night she could make out little noises but nothing that offered either comfort or fear. She thought of her life and all that she'd known.

This region of New Mexico was still very rustic. They didn't have electricity to the outlying houses, and while most of the towns sported not only electricity but running water, telephones, and automobiles, Daughtry's world hadn't consisted of any of these things. She felt as though she stood between the past and the future, not really taking hold of either one.

She smiled to herself as she thought of Nicholas building the small addition off the kitchen to house the bathtub. He'd seemed so happy when he realized how much pleasure it gave Daughtry.

They were a strange couple, Daughtry thought. "How could two people who had never before met be so perfect for each other?" she questioned the air. Clearly, the hand of God had been working in spite of human rebellion and disobedience.

Daughtry frowned. Her father was no doubt at her house right this very minute. What a coward she was to leave

103

Nicholas to face him alone. She hugged her knees to her chest. *Oh, God,* she thought, *please help him. Help Nicholas to deal evenhandedly with my father and help my father to keep his temper under control.*

She must have dozed, or so she figured, because suddenly the sound of horses clipping at a slow, even pace caused her to jerk upright. Getting to her feet, Daughtry was further stunned to see her husband, father, and three of her brothers ride casually into camp as though they were there for supper.

Standing with her mouth open and her eyes wide, Daughtry was speechless. Nick jumped down from his horse, throwing the reins to Joseph, while Garrett dismounted and handed his to Gavin. Before she could utter a single protest, Nicholas had her in his arms and was turning her around as if to inspect every single inch of her.

"She looks to be in one piece," she heard her husband mutter.

Still Daughtry could say nothing, and not until Nicholas completely shocked her by handing her over to her father to continue the examination, did Daughtry finally voice her protest.

"Stop this at once!" she exclaimed and pushed away from her father. "I'm not a helpless child, you know. I'm perfectly fine—or at least I was until you all got here."

She looked from the two men at her side to her brothers. "How dare you interfere in my life this way! I'm old enough to know my own mind. You can't just waltz in here and think to control me!"

Garrett glanced at Nicholas and received one of his lazy, I-told-you-so grins. "I think you should spank her," Garrett said with a slow drawl.

"Sp—sp—spank me?" Daughtry sputtered, completely enraged. "You think he should spank me?"

"That's right," Garrett replied.

"If he doesn't want to do the job, I'll do it," Gavin called down from his mount.

"You're all insufferable." Daughtry put hands on her hips and struck a defiant pose. "I'm a grown woman and...."

"You may be a grown woman, but you haven't got a lick of sense," Garrett replied.

"I have plenty of sense."

"Then what are you doing out here when you have a perfectly fine home, not five miles away?" Garrett questioned.

Daughtry looked to her husband for help, but Nicholas looked away to keep from laughing. He was so relieved to find her safe that he wasn't about to interfere with his father-in-law's tender comeuppance.

Daughtry crossed her arms. "I wouldn't be out here at all if it hadn't been for the way you treated me. I may have run off, but you forced me to make that decision."

Garrett knew she was talking about more than her escape that evening. "I know," he said in a dejected tone that immediately softened Daughtry's heart.

Garrett pushed his black Stetson back and drew a deep breath. "I know I've been unfair to you, Daughtry. It's just that ever since Julie died, I guess I felt like I had to keep a better eye on you. I couldn't get past feeling that if I'd only watched her closer, made her take someone with her when she rode, that maybe she'd be alive today. You'll feel different when you have your child. You'll know just how much a child means to a parent."

Daughtry reached out to touch her father's cheek. "I know. I miss her too. And I also feel guilty."

"Guilty for what?" Garrett asked in complete surprise.

"For being angry with her. Angry that she died. Angry that because of the way she died, I had to bear the consequences." Garrett grimaced at the latter, but Daughtry continued. "We all miss her, but overprotecting me won't change the fact that she's gone to heaven and we're still here."

"You're right, of course," Garrett answered and opened his arms. "Will you forgive me?"

Daughtry melted into her father's embrace. "Of course," she sighed. "I forgave you a long time ago. If it hadn't been for our confrontation, I might never have met Nicholas—and, Daddy, I do love him. I didn't just marry him to get away from home. He's a good man and he loves God."

Garrett glanced over her shoulder at Nicholas. He seemed to be everything Daughtry declared him to be. Maybe he was a little older than he'd have chosen for his daughter but, nevertheless, he did appear to be a good man.

"I'm glad you love him, Daughtry," Garrett managed and felt tears come to his eyes. He was having a hard time accepting that the little girl he'd cared for so long now belonged to another.

As if reading her father's feelings, Daughtry pulled back. "I'll always love you too, Daddy. It's all just a part of life, though. You and Momma brought me into the world and raised me up to love God and my fellow man—and now it's time for me to go on and live my life with Nicholas."

Garrett nodded. "I know. Just as Julie's death isn't the end, I know that your marriage is just the beginning of many wonderful things. Nicholas helped me to see that.

He helped me to realize that life and death are just a part of the circle that makes us who we are. Julie may be gone, but now there's your baby and life starts a new."

Daughtry dropped her hold on Garrett and stepped back a pace. Her face paled and even in the shadowy light from her campfire, the shock was clearly written in her eyes. "My *what*?" Her mouth dropped open in stunned silence.

Garrett looked at Nicholas, feeling rather helpless for a moment. Nicholas stepped forward with a sheepish grin.

"I think Daughtry's been a bit preoccupied these last few weeks even to realize that she's expecting," he offered by way of explanation. "But I feel very confident that she is."

Daughtry felt her face flush. She calculated the days of their marriage, her monthly cycles, and felt a strange knowledge settle over her. "A baby!" She looked up at Nick who seemed quite pleased to have known before even she did.

Without warning, she felt her knees buckle and she fell forward into her father. Garrett managed to take hold of her under the arms, and, looking at Nicholas with a telling smile, he unceremoniously handed the unconscious Daughtry over to him.

"Good luck," Garrett said with a laugh. "You're going to need it."

Quite a while later, Daughtry and Nick made their way to bed. Garrett and the boys had taken up residency in the front sitting room, refusing to let Daughtry and Nick even think of giving up their room.

Daughtry brushed her long coppery hair and thought of the news that she was to be a mother. How could she have been so caught up in her guilt and fears that she hadn't realized she was with child? She was almost humiliated that her husband had to be the one to point the news out to her.

Just then Nicholas came in, deposited his boots, and got ready for bed. Daughtry turned and stared at him for a moment. He was so very handsome with his dark hair and broad shoulders. She liked the way he moved with catlike grace and confidence.

Realizing that she was watching him, Nicholas turned and smiled. Daughtry's hand automatically went to her stomach in wonder. How could it be that they were to become parents? Why had God chosen to bless their union so early on, with such a miracle?

"How?" Daughtry questioned, getting up and slipping into bed. "How did you know?"

Nicholas shrugged and eased into the covers. "I'm not stupid. I know all about women. I have a mother after all. Not to mention my sisters."

"Imagine that," Daughtry said rather sarcastically. "You have sisters."

"Yes, I have two sisters and a brother," Nicholas replied. "I am the oldest."

"I see."

"Lance is twenty-eight," Nicholas continued, knowing her unspoken questions. "Natalie is twenty-five and Joelle is nineteen. So, you see, I am more than a little familiar with things that pertain to the female species."

Daughtry blushed and shook her head. "I can't believe that I didn't realize what was happening."

"I thought maybe you did," Nicholas replied. "But when we went to town and I told you to get anything you thought you might need, and you only worried about my underwear—well, then I knew that you didn't know."

Daughtry laughed. "You must think me pathetic."

Nicholas opened his arms to her and Daughtry slid into them eagerly. "I would never think you pathetic," Nicholas answered softly. "You are most precious to me."

Daughtry leaned her head against his chest. "You aren't angry, are you? About the baby, I mean."

"Why would I be angry?"

"Well, it certainly happened a lot quicker than I anticipated, so I figure it must be just as shocking for you."

"It did surprise me," Nicholas admitted, "but once I realized that it was most likely true, I kind of liked the idea."

"It's just so amazing and wondrous," Daughtry said, her hand going again to her abdomen. "But, I couldn't bear it if you were unhappy." She lifted her face to his, her eyes huge pools of blue.

"I couldn't be more happy about it," Nicholas replied and kissed her forehead. "If you'll recall, I was the one who planned for a dozen or so."

Daughtry laughed. "Well, one down and eleven to go."

Nicholas joined her laughter with his own, then suddenly grew sober. "Daughtry, you have to promise me that you'll be more careful. I nearly died when I came home and found you gone. I know you were scared, but so many things could have happened to you out there. Not to mention that I'm still not all that sure we're safe from my past."

His words both startled and frustrated her. Why wouldn't he tell her what past it was that he was running from?

Daughtry eased up on one elbow to study him for a moment. She was about to protest his silence when she saw something in his eyes that made her want to comfort him. She placed her hand on his chest and smiled. "Whatever you decide is fine by me. If you need to leave this place, you'll do so with me by your side."

"No questions asked?" Nicholas whispered, staring hard at his wife.

"No questions asked."

Morning light brought the blended family together at breakfast. For the first time, Daughtry used her dining room table and chairs and enjoyed preparing a feast fit for an army. Nicholas spoke about the ranch with her father and brothers, while Daughtry made sure that all the cups were filled with steaming coffee and that no one went away hungry.

"I've got a great deal to learn," Nicholas confessed. "But Daughtry's been a tremendous help."

"She ought to be. She's grown up ranching all her life. Piñon Canyon is probably the largest ranch in New Mexico, although I've never concerned myself with such things. We do a good business in beef and horses," Garrett said between forkfuls of food. "There's certainly enough business there, and I always presumed it would pass equally to all of my children." As he spoke, an idea came to Garrett and he put down his fork.

"What say you and Daughtry come live at Piñon Canyon for the winter? I could teach you firsthand all that you'd need to know to get this place running, and, come spring, I would send you off with a starter herd of the best cattle this side of the Mississippi."

Garrett had his own private motives for making the offer, but he said nothing of them. This would allow him to really get to know his son-in-law and to insure that Daughtry was married happily. But even as he made his offer, Garrett realized that if Daughtry had made a mistake by marrying Nicholas Dawson, he could do little about it now.

Daughtry looked at her father in surprise and then to Nicholas. What would he think of the offer, she wondered? She didn't have long to contemplate as Nick raised his eyes to hers. They both thought back to the day of the shootout, and Daughtry nodded as if in answer to Nick's unspoken question.

"I think we'd both like that," Nicholas replied, and Daughtry nodded and continued seeing to her brothers' plates.

Garrett couldn't have been more surprised or grateful. "Good," he answered, feeling the first real peace since Daughtry left home. "I don't think you'll be sorry."

"I'm sure we won't be," Nicholas replied. "We won't need to do much here, maybe just board up the windows so that no harm comes to them. We'll take our horses with us and there's no other livestock or obligation to contend with."

"What about our turkey?" Daughtry asked with a grin. "I can hear him out there even now." Everybody laughed, having heard the turkey's protests through much of the night.

"We'll take him with us," Garrett announced. "We ought to be home in time for Thanksgiving and he'll make a great main course."

"It's settled then," Nick said and caught Daughtry's expression of acceptance. No questions asked, he thought, but he realized that one day soon her trust in him wouldn't be enough. One day, he'd have to answer even unspoken questions or risk losing the woman he loved.

fourteen

Nicholas stared down at the mammoth ranch that spread across the endless valley. Nestled between the mountains was Piñon Canyon, the home where Daughtry had grown up. He looked in awe from the empire below, to the man who owned it all, and finally to his wife.

"Like it?" she questioned with a grin. "You should see it in the springtime when all the grass is newly green and the wild flowers are blooming."

Nicholas nodded. "I can only imagine. It's easy to see why you love it." Daughtry smiled. She'd only recently told Nicholas of her fondness for her childhood home.

Her father and brothers moved ahead on the trail, leaving Nicholas and Daughtry to themselves. "When I left," Daughtry said, remembering her escape, "I thought I was leaving a terrible place. A prison. Now I can see that it was more the way I perceived things inside and not at all the way it really was."

"Can you be happy here again?" Nick questioned, reaching out to touch her arm.

Daughtry gave him a radiant smile, and, in spite of the blustery cold winds that came down from the mountain, she was warm and content. "I can be happy anywhere that you are."

Maggie Lucas fussed and pampered her daughter from the moment she got down from her horse. Arm and arm, they walked off toward the house, while the men saw to the horses and gear.

"He's very nice looking, this Nicholas Dawson," Maggie said, bringing Daughtry a steaming cup of hot chocolate.

"Yes, he is. He's also very kind and considerate, and he's a Christian, Momma."

"That's good," Maggie said, and Daughtry heard the unmistakable sound of relief in her voice.

"I'm truly sorry for the way I acted." Daughtry put the cup down and looked up at her mother. "I know I must have just about broke your heart in two, and I can't live with myself any longer. Will you please forgive me for running off and hurting you like I did?"

Maggie put her arms around Daughtry and hugged her close. "I could see how bad things were. I only wanted you to be happy, but I knew how miserable you were. I tried to talk to your father and he only snapped at me. There's nothing to forgive. I knew in my heart, after learning that you'd left, that God was with you and that He'd guide you safely. It gave me a great deal of peace, even when I didn't know where you were."

"Why did it take Daddy so long to show up?" Daughtry suddenly asked.

"He was mad and real hurt. Mostly because he knew he was responsible for your actions. At first he refused to even deal with it but, as time passed, I could see the anger burning inside him like a spark just waiting for kindling to feed its flame. One day, he marched in here, told Gavin and Dolan to saddle up, and announced he was going to find you and this man who'd stolen you from him."

Daughtry smiled and pulled away from her mother. "I take it Joey went along to keep the peace."

Maggie nodded. "You know Joseph." This time

Daughtry nodded, while Maggie continued. "That's what happened here. How about what happened at your end?"

"I got Daddy's letter and it spooked me. I'm sorry to say I ran away again, because Nicholas was at a neighbor's house and wasn't due home for a while. I had no idea how soon Dad would arrive, so I packed a horse and left. I figured I'd rather camp out in the cold than face his wrath alone. Besides, I was so scared he'd take me away and I'd never see Nicholas again."

"What happened then?"

Daughtry laughed. "They all came riding into my camp as big as you please. Nick was sporting a bruised face and Dad was wearing skinned knuckles. I heard later that Nick wouldn't even defend himself. Just let Dad have at him, then asked him to forgive him for marrying me."

"He is quite a man," Maggie said in surprised awe.

"You don't know the half of it," Daughtry said with a mischievous twinkle in her eye. "I have a surprise for you."

"What?" Maggie cocked her head to one side as if trying to figure out what her daughter would say next.

"Daddy asked us to live here for the winter, so that he could teach Nicholas all about ranching."

"And your husband agreed?"

"He did," Daughtry said with great happiness. "But we're going home in the spring and Daddy promised to send us with some prime stock to start our own herd."

"Well, I am impressed," Maggie said, taking a seat beside her daughter.

"And," Daughtry added, reaching out to take hold of her mother's hand, "I have one more surprise. I'm going to have a baby."

"A baby!"

Her mother looked as though she might faint, and

Daughtry squeezed her hand. "I was so worried about Daddy coming to take me away that I didn't even know it myself, until Nicholas pointed out the obvious things."

"A baby," Maggie said again, this time more steadily. "I'm going to be a grandmother. Wait until Lillie hears this one."

Daughtry laughed. "You'll no doubt have me knee-deep in sewing projects and before the winter is over, I'll have enough clothes for triplets."

The women were still laughing when the men came in the room. Maggie got up and received a heartfelt kiss from her husband, while Nicholas went to Daughtry's side and waited to be introduced.

"Momma, this is Nicholas, my husband," Daughtry said proudly.

Maggie surprised Nicholas by brushing aside his extended hand as she threw her arms around him in a motherly hug. "Welcome home, Nicholas," she said with love. "I'm so glad to have acquired another son."

≈

Nicholas spent most of his waking hours with Garrett and Daughtry's brothers. He worked harder than he'd ever worked in his life and knew that he was in many ways facing up to whatever tests Garrett could put him through. At night he collapsed into a tub of hot water, which Daughtry always saw was ready for him, and then he would crawl into bed, more asleep than awake.

More than one night, Daughtry would lie beside her husband and watch him. His dark black hair would curl just at the collar and beg her touch, but Daughtry was always careful not to disturb him. She knew her father was working him too hard, but she reasoned that both men had something to prove and, for now, she'd not interfere.

Daughtry settled into the routine with misgivings. She missed the days when Nicholas had belonged just to her. Their ranch hadn't been so demanding, and Nicholas could take plenty of time to stop and talk or hold her. Now, however, she rarely saw him until dinner time, and by then he was so tired he didn't care whether he was married or not.

At dinner one night the family finally began to feel comfortable enough to ask Nicholas questions and one of the first was about his family.

"My mother and father are both still living. They live near Kansas City, where my father handles investments."

Daughtry hung onto every word, but tried to appear as though this was all old news to her. She wasn't about to inform her family that Nicholas hadn't seen fit to confide in her.

"And do you have brothers and sisters, Nick?" Maggie questioned and Daughtry jumped in to reply.

"He has a brother and two sisters," she said confidently before Nicholas could get a word in edgewise. She looked over at her husband, daring him to say more, but Nick just grinned and went on eating.

"I guess I still don't understand how you could just up and marry a fellow after you read about him in the paper," Jordy said and turned to Nick. "No offense, I think you're as good a man for a brother-in-law as any, but my sister's always been rather picky."

Everyone laughed at this but Daughtry. "I'm not picky, just cautious."

"So cautious you answered a stranger's letter out of the _Denver Post_ and sneaked away in the night to marry him? He could have been three times your age and given to fits of rage for all you knew," Gavin said.

"He is given to small fits," Daughtry laughed.

"So what made you do it?" Jordy pressed his luck. "I mean, other than getting away from here?"

Daughtry put her fork down and stared at Nicholas for a moment. "I fell in love with his picture."

Garrett and the boys thought this hysterical and started laughing and slapping the table. Nicholas looked across the table at Daughtry and winked at her blushing face, while Maggie cleared her throat loud enough that the others quieted down.

"That's a silly reason to get married," Jordy replied.

"Sure is," Garrett seconded. "Imagine, marrying someone just because you've fallen in love with their picture. Why, for all you knew, he hadn't even sent you a picture of himself. It could have been anyone's picture."

"I seem to recall," Maggie began slowly, concentrating on moving the food around her plate, "a certain love-sick cowboy who fell in love with a 'spitfire of a girl' as he called her. This man had never met this girl," Maggie continued, "but her father had a portrait of her hanging in his house and that cowboy fell in love with her after staring many hours at it."

Everyone fell into silence as all eyes were drawn to Garrett. Garrett looked across the table at his wife and smiled. Their romance had begun very nearly as she said, and now his daughter had gone and fallen for her mate in much the same way.

"Is it true, Daddy?" Daughtry asked with a hint of laughter in her voice.

"No," Garrett said, surprising Maggie. Her eyes narrowed questioningly, but he quickly continued. "I fell in love with her the first time I saw the portrait, not after hours of studying it." Maggie's smile broadened and the boys broke into laughter.

"What about you, Nick?" Don suddenly asked.

All heads turned and waited for Nicholas to reply. Even Daughtry couldn't imagine what he might say, and her hand froze in mid-air, her water glass clutched in her fingers, as she waited for his answer.

"I prayed a lot about a wife," Nicholas finally answered. "I was never much the courting type and even though I had plenty of women giving me the chase, I just wasn't interested in settling down. But I guess I started to see the benefits of having a partner and so I prayed and then put the advertisement in the paper." His eyes never left Daughtry as he spoke. "Then your sister answered and sent her picture—and while I thought her a remarkably good-looking woman, I can't say that I fell head-over-heels just then."

"What was it then?" Jordy piped up to ask.

"I guess I was intrigued by her letter," Nicholas responded, seeing the disappointment that flickered across Daughtry's face as she lowered her head to drink. "Of course, once I met her I knew she was exactly what I needed. She's everything a man could want in a wife."

Jordy thought the answer reasonable and continued the conversation by telling of a letter he'd received from some girl in town. The laughter around her did little to revive Daughtry's spirits. Something in Nicholas's response troubled her, and while she couldn't quite figure out what it was, it remained between them nevertheless.

fifteen

Daughtry let her frustration boil until morning when she had no other recourse but to vent her emotions at Nicholas. She'd had too much time to think about things and her imagination was running wild.

"Why did you marry me?" she questioned while Nicholas was dressing.

"What?"

"You heard me. Why did you marry me? Why did you push for a quick wedding by proxy? Why didn't you just come here if you wanted a fast wedding?"

Nicholas stopped buttoning his shirt and stared at Daughtry for a moment. He recognized the barely controlled anger in her eyes. "What happened to no questions asked?"

"What happened to sharing your life with me?" Daughtry asked simply.

"What's this all about?"

"It's about us," Daughtry replied rather indignantly. "It's about who you are and why you wanted me to marry you. It's about you being intrigued by my letter, but not in love with me."

"But I love you now," Nicholas offered.

"I want to know the truth, Nicholas. I want to know what you are hiding and why you refuse to trust me."

Nicholas winced at her words. He stared blankly at the wall behind Daughtry for a moment, then in a sad voice said, "Proverbs 19:13 says, 'A foolish son is the calamity of his father; and the contentions of a wife are a continual dropping.'"

"Are you calling me contentious? Just because I ask for the truth?" Daughtry appeared truly hurt, and Nicholas wished to ease her pain.

"No," he shook his head and replied. "I use that verse in reference to myself." Then he grinned and tried to ease the tension between them. "However, if you're feeling guilty...."

Daughtry put her hands on her hips and started to say something but held her tongue. Nick saw the softening in her eyes. "Why do call yourself a foolish son?" she finally asked.

Nicholas ran his hands back through his hair and sighed loudly. "You'd better sit down," he said, coming around to her and pulling out a chair from a nearby desk. Daughtry did as he told her, her eyes never leaving his face.

"I did my share of wild oat sowing when I was young. My folks, good people, saw that I was headed into trouble and began working on me, but I already knew it all, or thought I did, and sought my own way instead. Around the turn of the century, I struck out on my own and hooked up with the wrong crowd. I never really did anything myself, but I was always with one of them when they did something. My name started getting just naturally linked to the kind of bad men that could cause me some major entanglements with the law."

"Are you a criminal?" Daughtry asked hesitantly.

"No," Nicholas said and sat down on the edge of the bed directly in front of her. "No, I always managed to stay just inside the law. I was finally taken aside by an older friend of the family and given a good talking to. As a result I ended up getting myself deputized and began working with the law. Unfortunately, my old friends saw it as a means of advantage for their schemes. They figured their old buddy Nick wasn't about to hand them a prison cell in exchange for the good times they'd showed me."

"Were you a Christian when all of this was going on?"

"I thought I was. Thought I knew about the Gospel and how to live. But I was just as lost as those outlaws when it came to salvation for my soul. Anyway, years like this went on and my folks were getting more and more worried about me. My brother had married and so had my sister Natalie, and here I was outrunning bullets and breaking up outlaw gangs." He paused for a moment to see how she was taking the news.

"Those three men," Daughtry whispered, "the three you had to turn over to the sheriff, were they...?"

"Part of the old Chancellor Gang."

Daughtry gasped, and Nicholas realized that she knew full well who and what that notorious group represented.

"A couple of the gang died in prison, but most of them were paroled just months before you and I married. Everybody was afraid if I stuck around Missouri, they'd locate me and kill me like they promised. Guess nobody gave them much credit for tracking me down out here."

"Kill you?" Daughtry hadn't heard a word past those two.

Nicholas reached out and took her shaking hands into his own. "God helped me to see that I needed more than a casual relationship with Him. When I started thinking about my own mortality and how one of the outlaws I'd helped to put away could just as easily get out and come gunning for me, I knew I wasn't ready to die.

"My father and mother were beside themselves, however, even before the Chancellors got out of prison. My father cornered me when I turned twenty-eight and told me that he was through giving me free rein to do as I wished. He offered to take me into his investment house, but I knew that wasn't for me and I refused. So he told me I had until I was thirty to settle down—or else."

"Or else what?"

Nick smiled a little sadly. "He said he'd disinherit me for my own good."

Daughtry looked at him rather puzzled. "Your own father would do that to you?"

"He knew what he was doing," Nick replied. "He knew that it would shame me into obedience even at twenty-eight. I didn't want to lose out on the money but, more than that, I didn't want to alienate myself from the family. I knew there would be a full-scale war between him and my mother, not to mention my sisters and brother if they thought Dad were picking on me."

"So what did you have to do to meet his demands?" Daughtry said, suddenly feeling fearful of the response. "What constituted settling down?"

"I had to get a reliable profession, a home in one place, and...." He paused, unable to finish the sentence.

"And a wife?" Daughtry asked, her eyes wide.

"Yes."

"And you had to do all of this before you turned thirty?"

"Yes."

"And when did you turn thirty?"

"September twenty-fifth," Nicholas replied softly.

Daughtry stared at him in shock for several minutes.

"That was the day the proxy would no longer be any good. That's why you pressed me to hurry and marry you before coming to the ranch."

"Yes," Nicholas said and held her hand tightly. "I had to fulfill my father's requirements. It was important to me. Not just for the inheritance, but because his approval meant a lot to me. I wanted to make him proud of me. I bought the ranch and went about looking into how to be a rancher and then, before I knew it, time had slipped up on me and it was almost too late to get a wife."

"You used me," Daughtry said, suddenly feeling ill. The look in her eyes reflected the betrayal she felt.

"Now, wait just a minute," Nick said and took hold of her shoulders firmly. "Isn't that a bit like the pot calling the kettle black? Did you or did you not answer my advertisement in order to escape your overprotective father?"

"That's not why I married you!" Daughtry exclaimed. But even as she said it, she remembered only too well having decided not to marry Nicholas. Not until her father had refused to listen to reason did she change her mind, and she knew that was one truth she couldn't escape.

"And why did you marry me, Daughtry? Surely not because you were head over heels in love with me from all the courting and flowery words I'd spoken. Maybe it was the hours of evening walks by the river or the cards and flowers." His tone was much too sarcastic for her to bear.

Daughtry jumped to her feet. "I loved you when I married you. I'd fallen in love with your picture and your letter. I thought you'd fallen in love with me as well."

Nick stood and spoke calmly. "I did fall in love with you. I told you the truth when I said that. I can't help it that I didn't fall in love with your photograph or letter. I can't help it that I felt desperate to meet a deadline and didn't give the matter as much consideration as I should have. I did pray about it, though. I had a good peace about it too. Daughtry, I know without a doubt that God intended us to be together."

Daughtry tried to grasp all that he said. "Just when did you fall in love with me?"

Nicholas smiled, hoping that her question meant they were making headway. "I'm still falling in love with you," he answered softly, "but I think I first knew it when I came into the bedroom that morning and found an angel asleep in my bed. You know, we've never talked about that."

"Yes, I know," Daughtry said, suddenly feeling a bit uncomfortable at the memory. Everything had happened so quickly. Her marriage, getting to know Nicholas, finding herself with child—it had all come on so fast.

Nicholas pulled her to sit with him on the bed. "I came back to the ranch and all I could think about was that you might or might not be there. I knew I wouldn't have much hope of finding another wife, even though I had two other replies."

"You had other replies?" Daughtry asked, sounding like a little girl.

Nick grinned. "Yes, I did. But yours was the only one I answered."

"Oh."

Nicholas continued, "You can't imagine what I thought when I'd seen all the work you'd done. I figured at first maybe you'd lied about yourself and sent me someone else's picture, because there was no way that I figured a little thing like you could accomplish so much in so little time. Then when I walked into the bedroom...." He fell silent, closing his eyes to revisit the memory. "When I walked in and found you asleep in my bed, it was like Christmas morning. I knew then that you'd married me by proxy and that my obligations to my father were fulfilled. But," he said, putting a finger to her lips as she started to protest, "I was completely captivated to know that you belonged to me."

He pulled her close to him and breathed in the sweet scent of roses and lavender. "You were so beautiful, just lying there asleep." His words were warm, and Daughtry felt them relaxing her against her will. "Your hair was spilled out across my pillow and when I reached out to touch it, I just naturally found myself climbing onto the bed. I couldn't believe how God had blessed me, Daughtry. I still can't. I love you with all my heart and I am forever yours. I want to be a good husband to you. I've told you everything and I hope you'll find it in your heart to forgive me."

Daughtry looked at him, his dark eyes revealing a conflict of emotions from within. "I can forgive you," Daughtry finally said, "but I don't know if I can forget." She pulled away from him and got to her feet. A shadow of hurt still lingered in her eyes.

Nicholas came to her, but Daughtry held her hand out. "Please don't touch me. I need to think."

"Daughtry, even God forgets the past when we ask Him to. I'm not only asking, I'm pleading with you. This isn't a matter between just you and me now—we have a child to consider as well."

"I know."

"If you can forgive me, then please forget what I've done to hurt you. Just put it behind you. It's insignificant and unimportant."

Daughtry's eyes flashed anger for just a moment. "It's important to me," she said and stormed from the room to contemplate what her husband had revealed.

"Lord," Nicholas prayed even as Daughtry's footsteps echoed down the hall, "help her to see that I love her. Forgive me for the deception and help her to forgive me. I love her, Father, and I know that You've brought us together for a purpose. I don't know what the future will hold in store for us, but You do, and I'm asking You to direct me so that I don't mess things up again. Amen."

sixteen

Daughtry pulled on her coat and made her way to the barn. She had to get away from the house and Nicholas in order to sort through her feelings. Grabbing a bridle, Daughtry went to the corral, intent on singling out Nutmeg for a ride.

Nutmeg saw Daughtry and whinnied softly, but Poco, after months of neglect and an absent owner, was the one that came to Daughtry. The horse snorted once, then pushed its muzzle against Daughtry's neck, almost pleading.

"So you want to go for a run, do you, boy?" Daughtry asked softly while stroking the velvety nose. She looked across the corral at Nutmeg, then secured the bridle on Poco and led the horse to the stable to be saddled.

Several of the ranch hands immediately offered to assist her. She started to refuse, but because of her condition and her own uncertainty as to what she should or shouldn't do, she finally relented and accepted their help.

Once on Poco's back, she headed out for a trail she'd ridden most of her life. The air was cold and snow had fallen on the high mountains the night before. The open valley in which the ranch was situated had received only a dusting of snow, though, nothing that Daughtry concerned herself with. Instead, she took the opportunity to pray and think about what Nicholas had said.

"Dear God," she whispered with a glance heavenward,

"I think I need to talk about this. You're the only One I can explain it all to, because You're the only One who truly knows what I did and why."

Poco was used to years of such prayers and kept plodding along as though this were perfectly normal.

"I realize," Daughtry continued, "that I did wrong in marrying Nicholas the way I did. I wronged him, I wronged my folks, and I wronged You. I made pledges that I shouldn't have—but now that they're made, there is certainly no turning back."

The words of Ecclesiastes five, verse two came to mind. "Be not rash with thy mouth, and let not thine heart be hasty to utter any thing before God: for God is in heaven, and thou upon earth: therefore let thy words be few."

Daughtry pondered the Scripture for a moment before resuming her prayer. "I did speak rashly and without any real thought of the consequences," she admitted. "But I'm not trying to take back my pledge in marriage and my vows to You. I just need to understand them. I need to know what my marriage really and truly means."

Not that I can do anything to change the past, Daughtry thought to herself. She noted that Poco had followed their old trail high into the rocks, so she slowed the steed down, still contemplating her life before God.

"I love Nicholas," she told God, "but I'm afraid we both married each other for all the wrong reasons. He needed a wife to please his father and keep his inheritance, and I needed to escape my father's ever-watchful eye." She laughed at her choice of words and glanced heavenward again. "I suppose You know all about children who try to escape Your watchfulness."

&

Back at the ranch, Nicholas began to worry about Daughtry. He searched through the house and when he found her gone, he tore out, barely grabbing his coat, and headed for the barn.

"Daughtry?" he called as he entered the empty stable. There was no answer.

"Daughtry!" Nicholas called again, coming from the stable. Just then Garrett rounded the corner.

"What's wrong?" he questioned, seeing the concern on Nick's face.

Nicholas gave a sigh. "Daughtry is upset with me. She stormed out of the house and I haven't seen her for about an hour. I thought maybe she went for a ride, but Nutmeg is right there in the corral."

Garrett quickly surveyed the horses and shook his head. "But Poco's not."

"Poco?"

"Her horse and favorite traveling companion before she left home. Nobody else would be inclined to ride it." Nicholas saw the apprehension in Garrett's eyes.

"I'd better go find her," Nick replied and went to saddle his horse.

"I'm coming too," Garrett stated, his mind filled with images of Julie. What if Daughtry had met a similar fate?

The men were saddled and ready to ride within minutes, and, without telling anyone else where they were headed, Garrett and Nicholas rode out side by side.

∗

Daughtry felt renewed by her prayers. She could see now that though both she and Nicholas had made mistakes, the focus needed to be taken from the past and placed on the future. They had both been wrong in their actions, but they could easily put those things behind them and start anew. Of this, Daughtry was confident.

Realizing she'd been gone for a considerable amount of time, Daughtry turned Poco around and headed for home. Nicholas had asked her to forget the past and forgive him, and Daughtry intended to do just that. Somehow, together, they would put aside the circumstances under which they married and build a marriage that would be strong and faithful. A marriage that would bind them together, forever.

Daughtry smiled and began to hum to herself. She let Poco pick its way through the narrow canyon path and thought absentmindedly about what she would say to Nicholas. She was so deep in thought that the first few bits of rock falling from the steep canyon wall didn't even attract her attention. They did, however, cause Poco to stop and prance back a step or two.

Poco's actions caused Daughtry to snap to attention just as a huge rock slide covered the path directly in front of them. The loose rock combined with small amounts of snow gained momentum and rushed downward to block the passage through the canyon.

"Easy, Poco," Daughtry whispered and stroked the animal's neck to offer comfort. "We're okay." Daughtry glanced around behind her and knew that she would need to dismount in order to get Poco turned around.

Daughtry slid to the ground and reached out to take Poco's reins just as another slide captured the horse's attention and caused him to rear up and whinny nervously. Daughtry barely managed to avoid the pounding hooves. While backing away from Poco, she lost control of him and thes scared horse seized its freedom and ran.

For a moment, all Daughtry could do was stare after Poco's retreating form. "Great!" she muttered. "Now, I'll have to walk home."

Daughtry picked her way through the rubble and moved past the slide area. She knew she would need at least two hours to make the trek home, but what else could she do except begin walking? No one knew where she was, and only Nicholas knew that she was upset. He might even presume that she needed the extra time to sort through her feelings about him. Walking with determined steps, Daughtry would have laughed at herself had the whole situation not been so infuriating.

❧

"Do you have any idea where she might have ridden?" Nicholas asked his father-in-law.

"She has her favorite places. One path in particular," Garrett responded and pointed to the west. "There's a secluded path that winds up into the rocky foothills. She always liked to take that route."

"Let's check there first," Nicholas replied.

"Look!" Garrett pointed to the ground. "Tracks! I'd stake my ranch that those belong to Poco."

The two men followed the tracks that led them in the same direction Garrett had suggested. With a smile, Garrett turned to Nicholas. "Daughtry can be pretty predictable."

"So far, I haven't been privileged to see that side of her."

Garrett laughed. "I think you have. Isn't this about the third or fourth time you've been involved in her running away?"

Nicholas grinned. "I guess I hadn't thought of it that

way. She does seem to favor running rather than dealing with issues head on."

"She can be quite stubborn," Garrett agreed. "So can her mother."

The men had progressed along the path for nearly half an hour when they heard the unmistakable sound of horse hooves pounding through the canyon.

Garrett gave Nicholas a fearful look. "She wouldn't be riding like that unless something were wrong."

Just then Poco cleared the canyon and came into view. Nicholas felt his heart in his throat and Garrett turned ashen at the sight of the riderless horse.

"Dear God," Garrett whispered, "let her be all right."

Nicholas pressed forward to halt Poco while Garrett watched in stunned silence. The horse whinnied and snorted at Nicholas, rearing back twice before finally settling down to allow the man access to the reins.

"What do you think?" Nicholas questioned, turning to Garrett.

"In truth, I don't know what to think. I don't like to think about it at all. It reminds me of Julie."

Nicholas nodded. "But the horse is unhurt. Maybe he just got spooked and threw Daughtry."

"That girl would have to be unconscious to be thrown from this horse. They're too comfortable with each other. Most likely something happened to cause Daughtry to dismount."

Nicholas looked hard at his father-in-law. "Have there been any strangers around lately?"

"None that I know of. Why?"

Nicholas shook his head. "It's nothing. I just wondered if someone could have made her dismount."

"I doubt there's anyone around these parts that would want to do harm to Daughtry. Years ago we had banditos to worry about, but they moved off to the south as Bandelero grew. Most likely she got off Poco to see to nature's call—or some other perfectly logical explanation." Garrett was trying hard to sound convincing, but in truth he was desperately frightened for his child.

"You're probably right," Nicholas admitted, but the words did nothing to comfort him.

Nick tied Poco to his saddle and urged his own mount forward. Before he could go very far, however, Garrett called out to him, "Nick, would you pray with me?"

Nicholas turned to the man who had once wanted to beat him for stealing his daughter. The minute his eyes met Garrett's, a silent bond was formed. Each man acknowledged, without regret, the position the other held in the life of Daughtry.

With a slow nod, Nicholas waited until Garrett came even, then bowed his head and prayed for his wife.

seventeen

Nicholas and Garrett proceeded together, each praying silently and fervently hoping that Daughtry would be found unharmed. In the back of Garrett's mind was the lifeless body of his fourteen-year-old Julie, only four years earlier. Meanwhile, Nicholas was envisioning the remaining members of the Chancellor gang trying to force his hand, using Daughtry as bait.

Neither man was of a mind to talk. Garrett watched his son-in-law out of the corner of his eye and had to admit that he was a fine young man. He never seemed to lose his temper with Daughtry and always treated her with the utmost respect. What more could any father want for his child?

As the canyon narrowed and they could no longer ride side by side, Garrett edged his horse forward. "I'd better lead," he told Nicholas, "since I know the lay of the land." Nicholas nodded and brought up the rear, with Poco trailing behind.

At least in the canyon they were more secluded from the December wind, which was blowing hard and cold across the open valley. High mountain snows capped their surroundings in white, while the red-orange and sandy brown of the rock walls bore only minuscule traces of winter's impending touch.

Nicholas thought of their own ranch to the east. There they had no mountains to contend with—but no barriers against the harsh snows either. He wondered if they'd made the right decision in coming to Piñon Canyon. While he'd learned a great deal more in the few weeks since they'd arrived than he'd hoped to learn all winter, Nicholas was troubled.

Where was she? Where was Daughtry?

Nicholas' mind was so absorbed in thoughts of his wife that he had to glance up to see why his horse had suddenly stopped. Directly in front of Garrett were two men, both with guns leveled at his head.

"What's the meaning of this?" Garrett called out.

"Ain't none of your affair, mister," a man dressed completely in black called out.

"Well, then, just whose affair is it?" Garrett asked, the irritation evident in his voice.

The other man, a short, squatty character, spit out a stream of tobacco juice and wiped his mouth with the back of his coat. "Well, Nick, it's been a while, but I guess fate just throwed us together again. You ain't looking too bad for a man about to die."

Nick's eyes narrowed, and the scowl on his face was enough to make the man rethink his words. Garrett glanced back at his son-in-law and wondered about the connection between him and the men.

"Jeb, for a man who just spent the last years of his life in prison, I wouldn't think you'd want to throw yourself right back into a cell again," Nick replied, never taking his eyes from the man.

The man in black cursed Nick's smugness, but Jeb was the one who addressed the issue. "I don't care if I do get throwed back in. It'll be worth it just to say I had the honor of stringin' up your miserable hide."

"So you intend to hang me? I figured that'd be too much work. Why not just put a bullet in me here and now and be done with it?" Nicholas took a gamble with his words, knowing that Jeb answered to his older brother, the ringleader of the gang, Aaron Chancellor. With Aaron nowhere in sight, Nick hoped he could buy himself some time.

Jeb spit again before answering. His voice was full of anger and frustration. "I ain't going to do nothin' with you just yet. But when the time comes, I intend to see you suffer good and long."

"Still taking your orders from Aaron, eh?" Both outlaws scowled at the reference, but neither one said a word.

Garrett finally broke the silence and drew the attention of the men. "I demand to know what's going on and why you're even on my land." The men exchanged glances and Nicholas knew immediately that they were up to no good.

"You own this here land?" Jeb questioned.

"I do," Garrett stated without hesitation.

Nicholas hoped to intercede and take Jeb's mind off of whatever he was plotting. "This man is nothing to you. Your war is with me."

"You've got that right, but I'll just bet there's some money to be made. This here landowner might be our ticket to Mexico."

"You can head on over to Mexico any time you want. It's not that far," Nicholas replied dryly.

"Shut up, Dawson," Jeb demanded. "Gus, what say we take the both of 'em and give Aaron a call. He can make the decision then as to what we do next."

"Doesn't he always?" Nicholas said, hoping to goad

either one of them into immediate action.

"Tie 'em up, Gus," Jeb said, keeping his pistol leveled at the middle of Garrett's chest. With a smirk he added, "And gag Dawson if he so much as utters another word."

⋆

Daughtry had worked up quite a sweat on her hike back to Piñon Canyon. She knew she was still a couple of miles away when she heard the unmistakable sound of voices. Hoping that Nicholas or even her father and brothers had come searching for her, Daughtry climbed up on a rocky ledge to get a better look.

Easing into position, Daughtry gasped and flattened herself against the ground when she saw the men who threatened to shoot her husband and father. Immediately, her mind went back to the day when Nicholas had faced three outlaws alone. Were these men part of the Chancellor gang?

She struggled to make out what was being said but could only hear pieces of words. Try as she might, she was simply too far away to make any sense out of them. She lifted her head just enough to watch the scene below her. A man dressed in black handed his pistol to his partner, dismounted his horse, and took a length of rope from the horn of his saddle.

Helpless, Daughtry watched as the man first tied up Nicholas and then her father. In a matter of minutes the entire matter was completed, and the man remounted, claiming his gun and turning it once again on her husband.

"I have to get help," Daughtry whispered to herself. She watched as the men led Nicholas and her father off in the opposite direction from the ranch. Perhaps she could get back and tell her brothers before the men got too far.

Slipping noiselessly from her perch, Daughtry began to run as fast as she could move. She was panting heavily, unused to the activity, before she'd even crossed half the distance to home. She sucked in lungfulls of cold air, praying for strength to continue, and just when she felt her legs giving out, she caught sight of the corral fences and the orange adobe ranch house.

Dear God, she prayed, *please don't let them hurt Nicholas or Daddy.* The prayer continued, the same words, the same plea, over and over until Daughtry collapsed against the corral in order to catch her breath.

Gavin walked out of the barn in time to see his sister fall against the fence. Without hesitation, he ran as fast as his legs would carry him and scooped Daughtry into his arms.

"Are you all right?" he asked fearfully.

"No," Daughtry gasped, still breathless. "I...I have to...."

"Just be quiet," Gavin said, carrying her to the house. "You can tell me later."

"No," Daughtry said, putting her hand to Gavin's shoulder. "They have Nicholas and Dad."

Gavin stopped dead and looked down at his sister. "Who has Nicholas and Dad?"

"I don't know, I think they might be part of the old Chancellor gang." Daughtry clutched her brother's neck tightly, the fear evident in her eyes.

"Why would you imagine such a thing?"

"Nicholas used to be a lawman. He was primarily responsible for putting the gang away." Daughtry drew a deeper breath. "You can put me down, Gavin. I'm okay."

Gavin shook his head. "No, we'd best get on in the

house and let everybody hear the rest of this." He started walking again and spied Mack, his father's longtime ranch foreman. "Mack, something's happened, you'd best join us in the house." The dark-headed man nodded and followed Gavin inside.

"Mom!" Gavin yelled loudly. He put Daughtry down on a chair and yelled again, this time even louder.

"What is it?" Maggie questioned, coming into the living room. "I'm not deaf, you know."

"We've got trouble," Gavin explained. Maggie looked at Daughtry for a moment, noticing the redness of her face, as well as the dirt and disarray of her clothes.

"What trouble?" Maggie asked slowly and looked from Daughtry to Gavin and finally to Mack.

Just then, as if sensing that something weren't right, Daughtry's other brothers bounded into the room.

"What's going on?" Joey asked. The question was echoed by each of the others before Daughtry stood up to explain.

"Two men have taken Nicholas and Daddy. I went out riding this morning and a rockslide blocked my route home. I dismounted and Poco got away from me. I guess I took too long getting back, because Nick and Dad came looking for me. I heard voices and came up over a rock just above where the canyon narrows. There were two men with guns and they tied up Daddy and Nick and headed off in the opposite direction from the ranch."

"Who were they?" asked Dolan.

"Daughtry thinks they're part of the Chancellor gang," Gavin piped up. "Seems Nicholas used to be some kind of lawman and they bear him a grudge."

"Daughtry, are you sure?" Maggie asked, trembling.

"I can't be positive. I couldn't hear what they were saying, but something happened a while back, when Nicholas and I were on our ranch. Nick told me then that there was a good chance more of the Chancellors would come gunning for him."

"We'd better round up as many hands as we can," Gavin said to Mack. "Make sure everybody is armed and has what they need in the way of ammunition. Jordy, go get the guns from the cabinet in Dad's office. Don, Dolan, go saddle our horses and Joseph, get provisions for all of us. We don't know how long it's going to take or how far we'll have to ride." Without a word of protest, the brothers flew into action with Mack fast on their heels.

"I'm going too!" Daughtry exclaimed.

"Oh no, you're not," Gavin said and the way he looked at her was so much like his father that Maggie had to laugh.

"But I can't just sit here," Daughtry protested. "I want to go."

Maggie came and put an arm around her daughter. "You're expecting a child, Daughtry. You have to think of more than just what you want."

"I suppose you're right," Daughtry replied sadly. The defeat in her voice caused Gavin to give her shoulder a reassuring squeeze.

"We'll get them back," he said, looking into both Daughtry and Maggie's eyes. "I promise you, we'll bring them back safe."

The women watched as their men mounted up and headed out. Daughtry felt hot tears slide down her cheeks. Would she ever get a chance to tell Nicholas that she was sorry and that she understood why he'd married her the way he had?

&

Jeb Chancellor led the way to the range shack, while Gus brought up the rear with Nicholas and Garrett sandwiched in between. Garrett immediately recognized the place as one they used only on occasion. It was well secluded and far enough away from the rest of civilization that no one would have any idea they were even there.

"This place belong to you, too?" Jeb asked Garrett.

"Yeah."

"How much land you own, anyway?"

"Enough." Garrett was quickly realizing their game. "If it's money you're after, why don't you just name your price?"

"Just like that?" Jeb laughed. "What then? You gonna ride back to the house and write out a draft?"

"Is that what you want?"

"I don't know what I want yet," Jeb replied.

"Of course you don't," Nicholas sneered, "you haven't talked to Aaron yet. Big brother has to tell him what to think."

"I'm warning you, Dawson," Jeb said in a menacing tone. "Keep your mouth shut and you just might live to see tomorrow."

"He'd better live to see a whole lot more than tomorrow if you want any of my money," Garrett declared.

"What's he to you?" Jeb asked, halting his horse in front of the shack.

"He's family." Garrett's eyes met Nicholas's for a brief moment.

"Well, family or no, whether he lives or dies is up to Aaron. There ain't no amount of money what can buy back a man's years wasted behind bars." Jeb dismounted and slapped his reins around the hitching post. "Get 'em down, Gus, and bring 'em inside."

In spite of the way their hands were tied, both Garrett and Nicholas swung their legs over the necks of their mounts and jumped down unassisted. Gus poked Nicholas forward with the barrel of his gun pressed firmly in the small of Nick's back. In turn, Jeb motioned Garrett inside.

"Tie them to the chairs." Jeb took a defensive position with the gun leveled directly at Garrett, while Gus did as he was told. Once Nicholas and Garrett were securely tied, Jeb motioned Gus outside for a talk.

"Can you work the ropes loose?" Nicholas asked Garrett. Although they sat nearly side by side, Nick had to strain to get a look at the way Gus had tied Garrett's ropes.

"I don't know," Garrett whispered back. He strained against the hemp, feeling it chafe and bite at his wrists.

"I think, with any luck at all, I can work through mine," Nick replied.

"I think we'd best count on more than luck."

Nicholas grinned. "You do have a point there. I've been praying since we left to look for Daughtry." The smile quickly faded from his face. "Daughtry! I'd nearly forgotten." The agitation he felt was quickly mirrored in Garrett's eyes.

"It's in God's hands," Garrett replied. "I guess it always has been, except for the times I yank it back out." He smiled weakly at his son-in-law.

"I know what you mean. I guess I've pretty much messed up my share of living. I can't say that I've always done things to make my folks proud of me, nor can I stand on

the memory of always trusting God to see me through."
Nick paused for a minute, wondering if he should continue.

"Who are these men to you?" Garrett finally asked.

"Part of the Chancellor gang. I hung out with some of them before I became a lawman. They figured I'd overlook their shenanigans, for old times, sake, I suppose."

"But you didn't?"

"No," Nicholas replied. "I couldn't. Like I told Daughtry, I grew up in a Christian home and even though I felt the urge to spread my wings and buck up against the wind, I never broke the law. Bad thing was, I constantly kept company with those who did. Finally, a friend took me in hand and I became involved with working for the law instead of against it."

"Were you the one to put them away? Is that why they want to kill you?"

Nicholas took a deep breath and looked his father-in-law in the eye. "Yes. They tried once before back at my ranch. Daughtry unfortunately witnessed the whole thing. I hope you'll forgive me for bringing this on you and your family. I figured when you offered us a home for the winter that they'd lose track of me and give up the search. I guess they won't quit until they're all back in prison or dead."

"Don't be so hard on yourself," Garrett replied with genuine affection. "You've proven yourself to me more than once. I happen to think Daughtry made a good choice for a husband."

Nicholas's smile didn't reach the look of worry in his eyes. "If I only knew that she was safe."

"God's watching over her, Nick. We have to count on

that. I guess I'm just now starting to see things more clearly. When Julie died, I figured I'd failed somewhere along the way. Now, I know better and my heart is cleared of the guilt. God's timing isn't always something we mortals can understand."

"I admire your faith, Garrett," Nicholas said honestly. "I hope some of it rubs off."

Garrett grinned. "I have a feeling your faith is greater than you know. Now, how are we going to get out of this mess?"

eighteen

After several hours, Daughtry had had her fill of waiting. As soon as she saw that her mother was amply occupied in the kitchen, Daughtry pled a headache and went to her room.

At first she didn't know what she'd do. All she really knew was that somehow, some way, she had to help. Without another thought, Daughtry began to discard her dirty riding outfit. Standing in nothing more than her heavy knit chemise and black wool stockings, she glanced into the mirror and smiled as a plan formed in her mind.

Racing to her clothes chest, Daughtry pulled out the bottom drawer and retrieved her brother's hand-me-down jeans. Disguised in boys' clothes, Daughtry figured she could ride into town and notify the sheriff, as well as the two Monroe families. This would get even more men looking for her father and husband and still wouldn't go against Gavin's instructions that she not join them in the actual search.

Rebraiding her hair, Daughtry coiled it around her head, then pulled on a dark brown hat and surveyed her appearance in the mirror. Noting the curvy appearance of her body in the jeans, Daughtry went to the wardrobe and pulled out one of Nicholas's duster coats.

The coat fell to just above her boot tops, but Daughtry knew it would be better than letting either her father or Nick catch her in town wearing boys' pants. With an apprehensive glance down the hall, Daughtry made her way to the front door.

Walking with determined strides across the corral yard, Daughtry took a rope and singled Nutmeg out of the few remaining mounts. Within a short time, she had the mare saddled and ready, grateful that no one had come to interfere with her plan.

Daughtry covered the distance into Bandelero in half the normal time. She knew she'd pushed Nutmeg to the limits and as soon as the town was in sight, Daughtry slowed the mare to a trot. Nutmeg pranced nervously and whinnied softly at the sights and sounds. Daughtry was amazed at the way the small town was continuing to grow. What had started out as a handful of shops and services was now a bustling town, well on its way to becoming a city.

The sheriff's office was at the far end and Daughtry knew she'd have to ride right through the heart of Bandelero before reaching her destination. Pulling her hat low, Daughtry urged Nutmeg forward, refusing to make eye contact with anyone on the boardwalks.

To Daughtry's utter frustration, the sheriff's office was closed without a single soul to explain his whereabouts. She heaved a sigh and made her way back to Nutmeg, just as a voice called out behind her.

"Sheriff's gone just now, but can I help you?"

Daughtry turned slowly to find Mr. Tate, owner of the hardware store. "I don't suppose you know where he's gone?"

"Daughtry Lucas! Is that you under that getup?" The man's shocked expression almost made her laugh.

"Yes, it's me, but the name is Dawson now. Do you

know where the sheriff is?"

"Sure," Tate replied. "He's gone off looking for your father and some other guy."

"That would be my husband, Nicholas," Daughtry replied. She was relieved to know that the sheriff was already assisting in the search.

"Didn't know you got yourself married," the man said scratching his chin. "Always figured you'd marry one of the local boys."

Daughtry couldn't be bothered with what Mr. Tate thought. Her real concern was what was happening to her husband and father. "If you'll excuse me," she said remounting Nutmeg, "I have things to do." Mr. Tate said nothing as he watched Daughtry settle into the saddle. "Good day, Mr. Tate." Daughtry urged Nutmeg back through town, wondering what she should do first.

Just as Daughtry had convinced herself that contacting Lillie and Dr. Dan would be the best choice, she pulled Nutmeg up short and gasped. The two men who'd taken her father and Nick were riding into town as though they were coming to Sunday meeting.

Without taking her eyes off of the two, Daughtry eased Nutmeg into a slow but steady walk. She had no idea what she was going to do, or how she could manage to capture the men, but Daughtry knew she had to do something.

When the men headed in the direction of the train depot, Daughtry felt herself grow frantic. What if they'd already killed not only Nicholas but her father as well? What if they perceived their job as finished and now they were taking the train back to—wherever?

When the men dismounted and tied their horses to the hitching post in front of the depot, Daughtry began to panic. *What do I do, Lord?* She found her heart racing and, in spite of the cold wind, Daughtry felt sweat on her brow.

The men entered the building and Daughtry quickly dismounted and tied Nutmeg several spaces away from their mounts. Glancing up at the double glass doors of the depot, she could see that the men were deep in conversation with the ticket agent. Without giving it another thought, Daughtry made her way to their horses.

"If they aren't going to leave by train," she mused in a whisper to herself, "they'll come back for their mounts. Either way, they'll be in for a surprise." She quickly slid her hand along the first horse and reaching under his belly, Daughtry loosened the cinch strap. Repeating this action with the other horse, she felt a bit of confidence in her mission. Somehow, she needed to find out what they were doing inside the depot and then she needed to get help.

Daughtry made her way around the building, peering in through the windows to catch sight of the two men. They seemed to be there to use the telephone, and the agent was somewhat disturbed by their request.

Daughtry watched intently, while one man pushed a handful of money across the counter to the agent and waited for his response. Daughtry knew the phone was on the track side of the building and that the agent's bay window was where she'd have her best chance of spying on the two men.

Slipping across the back, barely managing to avoid a man hoisting a heavy crate to the loading platform, Daughtry eased her way cautiously to the bay window. The window was positioned so that the agent could look up and down the track for some distance and Daughtry knew she'd have to keep to the wall beside it in order to avoid being seen. Thankfully, she noted that the two men kept their backs to her when they entered the room and that the telephone was opposite the side she'd chosen to be.

Daughtry felt herself trembling as she strained to hear what the two men were saying. Just then, the heavy blast from the four o'clock westbound blotted out all hope of hearing what the men were saying.

Glancing down the tracks, Daughtry watched as the train eased into the station, blowing off steam noisily. She felt more frustration than she'd ever known possible as she glanced back into the agent's office and found that the men were still on the phone.

"I have to find out what they're up to," she whispered.

People began to leave the train, while others crowded around her to take their place on board. Daughtry felt herself being pushed back through the comings and goings, until she lost her footing and fell forward.

With a shriek of fright, Daughtry found herself caught by strong hands and set back on her feet.

"Whoa, son," a deep baritone voice called out.

Daughtry glanced upward and gasped, while the man staring down at her did the same.

"Sorry, ma'am," the man corrected his mistake, "I guess I mistook you in that garb."

Daughtry still couldn't speak. The man before her was the spitting image of her husband, only his hair was gray and his face betrayed his age. How could it be?

"I—I'm," she stammered. "It was my fault. I apologize."

The man smiled broadly, then reached out to take hold

of the stately woman beside him. "No harm done," he said softly.

Daughtry stared in amazement at the couple. She looked at the woman for a moment and then back at the man.

"Is something wrong, miss?" the man asked her, a look of concern replacing his smile.

Daughtry glanced back at the ticket agent's office and saw that the men were still there. Without hesitation she pushed back her hat and looked into the dark eyes of the stranger. "Do I know you?" she asked boldly.

"I doubt it," the man replied and the woman at his side smiled.

"We're here to surprise our son," the woman said.

"Your son?" Daughtry barely squeaked out the words.

"That's right, perhaps you know where we could find him. His name is Nicholas Dawson. We received a letter from him saying that he's staying with his wife's family. I believe their name is Lucas," the man replied, then shook his head. "Forgive my rudeness, I'm Riley Dawson and this is my wife Alexandra."

Daughtry stared up in dumbfounded silence at her father and mother-in-law. "Oh my," she finally managed to whisper.

"Are you all right?" Riley asked, seeing Daughtry pale at the news.

"I'm afraid so," she whispered, feeling faint. "I have a bit of a surprise for you," she said with a slight smile. "I'm Daughtry Dawson, Nicholas's wife."

Riley's mouth dropped open, while Alexandra's eyes widened and twinkled with amusement.

"You are Nicholas's wife?" Riley questioned.

Daughtry shifted her weight nervously and glanced back

at the agent's office. "Yes, and the fact of the matter is, Nicholas and my father are in trouble and I need your help."

Alexandra instantly sobered and reached out to Daughtry. "What is it? What's happened to them?"

Daughtry quickly explained to her in-laws why she was dressed as she was and how the two men inside the depot were responsible for their son's abduction.

"I need your help, Mr. Dawson," Daughtry said in such a way that Riley couldn't help but put his arm around her.

"Call me Riley," he said softly. "Look, I'll take care of this." He looked past Daughtry to his wife. "You take Zandy and go back to the ranch."

"Zandy?" Daughtry questioned.

"That's what most folks call me," Alexandra stated, trying to keep her voice calm.

"Oh," Daughtry replied with a nod. Then turning back to Riley she shook her head. "I'm not going back. I have to help Nicholas."

"Look, I know you want to help him, but we have no idea what we're going to run into," Riley said firmly.

"I know that half the county is out there looking for them. I can't just sit back and do nothing. Look, those two are leaving. Either help me capture them or stay out of my way." Daughtry's determination caused Zandy to laugh out loud, while Riley rolled his eyes.

"I see our son married a woman just like his mother. Stubborn to the bone and just as beautiful." Daughtry blushed at the half-compliment, but turned to leave.

"Oh, no you don't," Riley said, taking hold of her arm. "You've got yourself a partner."

Daughtry turned and smiled. "Good. I loosened their

cinch straps," she said with a grin. "They ought to just about fall into our arms."

Riley shook his head, while Zandy tried to refrain from laughing. In spite of the danger to her oldest child, Zandy was amused beyond words that he'd married a woman of such character and strength. It served him right, she thought, remembering all his years of stubborn independence.

"They have guns," Daughtry said, while leading Riley and Zandy around the building. "But I figure when they fall off those horses, we might be able to get the upper hand, maybe even get their weapons away from them."

"You leave that to me," Riley said in a voice that made it clear to Daughtry he meant business. She nodded and halted when they reached the front of the depot. The men were still nowhere in sight.

"Alexandra," Riley said, turning to his wife, "you secure our bags and stay out of sight. I'll be hard pressed enough to keep her out of danger's way." He motioned to Daughtry who didn't like one bit that she'd gained yet another guardian.

Zandy opened her mouth to protest, but saw the determination in her husband's eyes and nodded. *No sense in causing a full scale war,* she thought and retreated back to the platform.

Knowing the outlaws wouldn't recognize her or Riley, Daughtry motioned her father-in-law to follow her as the two men came bounding out of the depot. Without any time to lose, Daughtry and Riley flew into action as the men attempted to mount their horses. When the saddles twisted to the side and dumped the surprised men on the frozen ground, Riley quickly grabbed the revolver of the one dressed in black, while Daughtry put her booted foot firmly on the arm of the shorter, squatty man.

"Get up real slow," Riley instructed the men after he had Daughtry remove the other man's weapon. "Where's the jail, Daughtry?"

"Other end of town," she answered, feeling hope for the first time. "Come on, I'll lead the way."

Riley motioned the men forward, while Daughtry apprehensively moved out. The men weren't over their shock as they took hesitant steps forward, but the gun in Riley's hand left them little doubt that he meant business.

A crowd started to gather and follow Daughtry and Riley as they made their way to the sheriff's office. The mumblings and whispers were enough to unnerve Daughtry, but she took a deep breath and forced herself forward. *When this is all done,* she thought, *I may very well faint!*

Mr. Tate was there to greet them, and when Daughtry explained the need to put the two men into a cell, he rapidly produced a set of keys and led Daughtry and Riley into the jail.

Once they had the men behind bars, Daughtry sat down hard on a chair in the outer office, while her father-in-law began to question the men.

"You have my son and his father-in-law," Riley said with a menacing stare at the outlaws. He'd dealt with their kind plenty before, even if it were a lifetime before.

"What if we do?" the short man questioned.

"Well, the way I figure it, you can cooperate and tell me where they are, or I can start shooting parts of your body until you give me the information." Riley prayed his bluff would work.

The man stared at Riley as if trying to decide if he were serious or not. Daughtry held her breath, hoping and praying that Riley wouldn't have to shoot anyone.

"You wouldn't really shoot us," the man in black stated nervously. "Would you?"

Riley fired the revolver into the mattress just to the man's left. He glanced down at the gun as if carefully considering its benefits. "I'll do whatever it takes," Riley answered in a cool, unemotional tone.

Minutes later, Daughtry and Riley emerged from the jail to find the small crowd still lingering to learn what they could. Daughtry refused to listen to Riley's suggestion that he get another man to go with him.

"I know our land better than anyone here in town," she protested with hands on her hips. "And, unless you plan to lock me in a cell with those two, I'm going to find my husband and father."

Riley ran his hand back through his gray hair and stared at Daughtry.

"Remind you of someone?" Zandy questioned, coming up behind her husband.

"Frightfully so," Riley replied with a look at his wife that told her he really didn't mind the comparison. "Poor Nick." Zandy giggled at her husband's mock horror.

"Well?" Daughtry questioned. "Are you coming with me?"

"Of course I am," Riley responded. "Nicholas will have my hide over this and rightfully so, but I'm getting too old to fight the feminine wiles. Could you manage to stop long enough to arrange for Zandy to be taken to your folks' place first?"

"Certainly," Daughtry said with a smile. "My Aunt

Lillie—well she's really not my aunt, but she and my mother are like sisters. Anyway, she lives in that house right over there. She's married to the town doctor, so there's always someone there. Just tell her who you are and what you need. She'll see to it that you get there."

Zandy smiled and nodded, not a bit put off with Daughtry's refusal to take her there herself. Daughtry moved to retrieve Nutmeg's reins and motioned to Riley.

"You'd better saddle up one of their horses, Riley."

Riley gave Zandy a quick kiss, then did just as his daughter-in-law instructed. "Nicholas certainly has his work cut out for him," he muttered under his breath and Zandy's laughter caused Daughtry to wonder at the murmured words.

nineteen

Less than a half-hour after Gus and Jeb had ridden out for town, Nicholas had managed to free himself from the ropes. Crashing the ancient chair's rickety frame against the wall until it fell into pieces, Nicholas had managed to work his arms and shoulders loose.

"If you back up here," Garrett suggested, "I can probably pull those knots free with my teeth."

Nicholas nodded and pushed his hands, still bound behind his back, up to meet his father-in-law's mouth. Garrett worked at the ropes for only a moment before managing to pull the first knot apart. After that it was only a matter of teamwork and they had themselves free.

Rubbing his wrists and the spot in his shoulder that ached from the only sign of age he'd allowed himself—rheumatism—Garrett smiled at his son-in-law. "I guess we'll be quite a surprise for old Gus and Jeb."

"More than they can imagine," Nicholas said, returning the grin. "The way I see it, we'd be wise to lay a trap. There's no way of knowing if they'll come back alone, and I intend to round up every one of those good-for-nothings so I can get on with my life. I can't go on having to look over my shoulder every time a twig snaps, and I'll certainly not subject my wife and kids to it." Looking intently at Garrett for a moment, Nicholas grew sober.

"I'm really sorry for the danger this has placed you and your family in," he began. "I have to admit that one of the

156

reasons I agreed to winter with you here was because I was worried something like this would happen at our place. I figured, and selfishly so, that they'd come around and find our place deserted, with no forwarding address or knowledge of where we'd gotten off to, and they'd give up and go home. I don't want to be responsible for killing any of them, but I won't let them kill my family."

Garrett reached out and put his hand on Nicholas's shoulder. "You did what you had to do. I would have done the same thing and there's nothing to be ashamed of in thinking of Daughtry first." He grinned, breaking the tension between them. "I put her mother first, often to my detriment and, sometimes, my distraction."

Nicholas laughed. "Yes, Daughtry can be a real distraction, too."

"Don't I know it," Garrett said, joining his laughter.

"What are we going to do about this?" Nicholas said, sobering once again.

"We'll have to take them when they come back. We can watch and see if more than just the two of them come back and judge the situation accordingly. The way I figure it, it's going to be about dark before they can make it back from Bandelero. We can use that to our benefit by leaving the place dark."

"Makes sense," Nicholas replied, sizing up the range shack. It was a single room, with little more than fireplace, table, and chair. The other chair, now good for little more than kindling, lay in a heap beside a small metal cabinet. "What's in there?" Nicholas questioned.

"A bit of food, some bandages, that sort of thing. No weapons, except maybe a knife." Garrett strode over to the cabinet and opened it. "Looks like Gus and Jeb cleaned it out. There's bandages and some liniment. Nothing else."

Nicholas nodded and continued to stare out the window. His mind immediately drifted where he didn't want to dwell. Daughtry was somewhere out there. Maybe she was alone and hurt or maybe she'd made it back safely to the ranch. Either way, not knowing was killing Nicholas.

"You love her a great deal, don't you, son?"

Nicholas didn't even smile at the reference. "I do," he whispered. "More than I ever hoped I could love another person."

Garrett came up beside him and put his arm around Nick's shoulder. "Let's pray." With a nod, Nicholas felt hope return.

&

"We're about out of light, Daughtry," Riley called from his mount.

"I know, but we're nearly there," she replied in a breathless manner. "We'll just have to push them a little harder."

The horses, already more than a little weary from their continuous journeys, were sweat-soaked and starting to lather. Daughtry had never abused a mount in her life, but then, she'd never felt the urgency to save another person's life. Nicholas and her father might lie bleeding or half-dead, for all she knew. They just had to get to the ranch shack and see that they were all right. After that, she'd give Nutmeg a well-deserved rest, but not until then.

Riley watched his daughter-in-law with admiring eyes. She was not only at home on the back of her horse, but she seemed oblivious to the chilled winter air and the coming of night. She wasn't a skittish thing and for that Riley was pleased. He couldn't imagine what kind of woman would up and marry his son without any real foundation for their marriage between them, but he was pleased in what he found.

When Nicholas had first written to announce his fulfillment of his father's demands, Riley had been quite taken aback. He'd kept close watch over his oldest son, waiting and praying, hoping that Nicholas would find his way. Then when the letter had come with the papers showing Nicholas's purchase of a small ranch in New Mexico, Riley had seen the first bit of hope for normalcy and a long life for his son.

Without a word to the woman who led them deeper into the mountains, Riley smiled. She was bold and vibrant and beautiful. And, he surmised, she was exactly what Nicholas needed. Here was a woman who knew her own mind and wasn't about to let his son slip back into his old habits of drifting casually through life. Here was a woman to grow a family with—to grow old with.

Daughtry couldn't possibly know what was on her father-in-law's mind. She felt a wave of nausea run through her, causing her to slow their pace a bit. She prayed silently that the feeling would pass, and when it didn't, Daughtry surprised Riley by pulling up quickly.

"Here!" she exclaimed, tossing her reins to Riley. She barely took four steps before losing the contents of her stomach.

Considerably more pale and slightly weak, Daughtry returned to her horse, ignoring Riley's shocked expression. She rinsed her mouth out, then took a deep drink from the canteen before remounting.

Meeting Riley's eyes, she nodded. "We're going to have a baby."

Riley's expression changed from shock to extreme concern. "You can't be out here doing this."

Daughtry shrugged. "That's what my brother said and no doubt what my father and husband will say. I can probably expect my father to suggest a spanking again—that seems to be his answer for wayward children."

"And rightfully so," Riley murmured, refusing to give in to Daughtry's dry amusement. "You could harm yourself."

Daughtry laughed. "I'm a little more concerned about what Nicholas will do when he sees me out here." Urging her horse forward, she grinned over her shoulder. "But I guess it's a little late to start worrying now."

Riley sat for a moment, still stunned by the news. Nudging the horse in the ribs, Riley caught up with Daughtry and spoke. "You amaze me," he said to her.

Daughtry was surprised to hear those words instead of a rebuke. She glanced up, still shaky from her bout of nausea. "Sometimes," she replied. "I amaze myself. I figure God has His hand most firmly on my shoulder, though. I don't doubt for a minute that He led me to town in order to find those two at just the right time. I was the only one who knew what they looked like." She paused, looking skyward. "God keeps pretty busy with me, but then I try to return the favor and keep myself pretty busy with Him."

Riley smiled. His daughter-in-law was a solid Christian; if ever he doubted it before, he no longer did. "Remind me sometime to tell you about how busy He had to keep with me."

Daughtry looked at Riley and nodded. "It's a deal."

❧

The mountain peaks greedily sucked out the last bits of light, just as the range shack came into view. Daughtry and Riley did nothing to disguise their approach. They were hopeful that the noise they made would be welcomed by living, breathing souls.

Daughtry refused to listen to Riley's pleas that she let him enter the shack first. She raced across the ground without even securing Nutmeg to the hitching post. Riley did likewise and was on her heels, fearful that she might find more than she could deal with.

Dear God, Riley prayed, *don't let them be hurt. Don't let them be dead!*

Daughtry burst through the door into the darkness. She opened her mouth to call out to Riley, but someone knocked her down onto the hard wooden floor. While the beast managed to sit itself square on her backside, the cracking thud of a fist to a face left Daughtry little doubt that Riley had been properly subdued.

"Light a lamp," Nicholas called to Garrett who was now nursing his sore knuckles. Daughtry was so stunned she couldn't speak. She began to struggle furiously, which only made Nicholas twist around to clamp a hand to the middle of her back.

"Get off of me, you oaf!" she managed to gasp as her father struck a match to the kerosene lamp he held.

Nicholas's and Garrett's jaws dropped open with the stunned revelation that they'd managed to capture their rescue team. Without thinking to move, Nicholas stared at the crumpled body of his father, now stirring in the doorway. Daughtry started kicking her legs, but the duster wrapped around them sufficiently and saved Nicholas from any blows.

"Well, I'll be," Garrett finally said and motioned to where Riley was struggling to sit up. "You know him?"

Nicholas moaned, but still didn't move. "Yeah, he's my father."

"Figures," Garrett said, rolling his eyes upward.

"Nicholas! You're smashing me into the floor!" Daughtry exclaimed.

Finally realizing what he was doing, Nicholas shifted his weight and rolled to the side of his wife. Daughtry just lay there for a moment, trying to take in enough air to fill her lungs.

"I'd say while you have her down there like that—" Garrett began.

"Don't you dare!" Daughtry interrupted indignantly. "Don't you dare suggest he spank me. I'm not a child! If you two had bothered to look at who was coming...."

Nicholas interrupted as he took Daughtry into his arms and pulled her across his lap. "We did look. We saw that sorrel mare that Gus had ridden out of here and we saw two scraggly looking characters." Nicholas looked Daughtry over from head to foot, then glanced up at his father. "You gonna live, Dad?"

Riley rubbed his sore jaw. "Your father-in-law packs quite a punch."

"Don't I know it!" Nicholas exclaimed, and Garrett turned sheepishly to shrug. "How'd you get involved in all of this?"

Riley tried to smile, but his swollen lip wouldn't allow for it. "Your mother and I came to town to surprise you for Christmas. We ran into Daughtry at the train station where she'd pinned down your captors."

Nicholas turned to see Daughtry looking at him rather smugly. "You went into town wearing boys' pants? After I told you I didn't want to see you doing that?"

Daughtry groaned in exasperation and tried to free herself from Nicholas's grasp. He tightened his hold on her, leaving little doubt that the matter was far from settled.

"I saw the men take you and Daddy," Daughtry explained. "I ran back home and got Gavin and the boys. They're out there somewhere, even now, looking for you two. I couldn't just sit at home and Gavin told me I couldn't go with them."

Garrett looked at Riley with a look that only fathers could share. "She's never been one to follow instruction."

"Well, she's going to learn real quicklike," Nicholas interjected. "Daughtry, you could have been killed. I could have busted you in the jaw like Garrett did Dad. Then what?"

Daughtry opened her mouth to speak, looking first at her husband, then her father, and finally Riley. Finding not even a shred of support, Daughtry crossed her hands against her chest and pouted. "I can't believe you aren't even grateful for the rescue."

Nicholas gently held her under one arm and got to his feet, pulling Daughtry up with him as if she weighed nothing. "I am grateful," he said softly, "but I'd be a whole lot more grateful if you were safely tucked away back at the ranch."

He looked at his father, shaking his head. "I don't suppose she told you that she's expecting?"

Riley chuckled. "She did. Right after she lost her lunch and we were nearly here. Reminds me of your mother," he added with such joy that Daughtry couldn't help but smile appreciatively.

"I take that as a compliment," Daughtry replied. "Your wife is a wonderful woman. I imagine she would have come with us if I'd given her time to change."

At this Nicholas and Riley both laughed, and Garrett shook his head. "Sounds like Maggie. I'm sure if we don't make our way home soon, she'll be leading the searchers for us."

"Those horses are pretty spent," Riley said. "In fact, I think I'd better make sure they didn't wander off too far. In our hurry," he paused with a wink at Daughtry, "we left them to fend for themselves."

"I'll give you a hand," Garrett said, coming forward. "I hope you'll forgive the greeting."

Riley patted him on the back. "Forgiven. From now on, we'll fight on the same side."

"Agreed," Garrett chuckled.

When their fathers had gone outside, Nicholas pulled Daughtry to him so tightly she could scarcely breathe. "I was so afraid you were hurt," Nicholas breathed against her ear. "Thank God you're all right."

"I echo those sentiments myself," Daughtry whispered, lifting her face. "I couldn't just sit at home, Nick. I love you and I had to help. I couldn't have lived with myself if I'd done nothing and lost you."

Nicholas tenderly stroked Daughtry's dirt-smudged cheek. "I love you, Daughtry. My life wouldn't mean much without you in it." He lowered his lips slowly to hers, kissing her long and gently as though gaining reassurance from the action.

Pulling away, Daughtry sighed and leaned her head against her husband's chest. "I like your dad," she finally said. "He's just like you."

Nicholas chuckled softly. "I wouldn't have thought that a compliment a few months back."

"And now?"

"Now, I'm pleased you think it so. He's a good man and I'm proud to be his son," Nicholas admitted.

"You'll work everything out between you?" Daughtry questioned. "I mean the demands he put on you and such. You won't hold a grudge or be angry with him? After all," Daughtry said looking into Nick's dark eyes, "it brought us together."

"No, I'm not angry with him," Nicholas smiled. "Grateful, but not angry."

Daughtry nodded and smiled. "And you aren't angry with me? I mean, I made a pretty big mess of things back at the house. I'm sorry for that, too. I was riding back to apologize when I lost Poco. I just want you to know that it doesn't matter that you didn't love me when you married me. All that matters is that you love me now and that you'll always love me."

Nick kissed Daughtry lightly on the mouth. "I'll always love you, but I may have to tie you to a chair in order for you to bring our child into the world healthy and safe."

Daughtry laughed. "I promise from now on, I'll be good as can be."

"Uh-huh. Sure," Nicholas mused in disbelief, "until the next time."

twenty

Christmas Eve at Piñon Canyon had been a night of precious celebration as far back as Daughtry Lucas Dawson could remember. The house was decorated festively in pine boughs, red ribbons, wreaths shimmering with gold braided ribbons, and a tree that commanded the center of attention in the living room.

Daughtry lovingly touched the ornaments that hung on the tree. Delicate glass spheres, decorated with miniature paintings of the first Christmas, were among her favorites. They were nearly as old as she, and, Daughtry remembered fondly, they were a gift from her father to her mother.

Laughter rang out in the dining room, where most of Bandelero, or so it seemed, had gathered to share in the festivities. When Daughtry's mother had come to New Mexico, soon to be wed to Garrett Lucas, she'd left behind her dear friend Lillie in Topeka, Kansas. But Lillie had soon followed and married Dr. Daniel Monroe, brother to the young pastor, David, who had an even younger wife, Jenny. They were more like a family of closely knit brothers and sisters and their offspring had grown up in a togetherness that seemed natural and secure.

Daughtry had never known a Christmas Eve when they'd not all joined together to celebrate the birth of their Savior. She could still hear the years of gaiety ringing through her memories. She could still feel the warmth that wrapped around her tightly and made her feel that despite what else might happen, in this home, by these people, she was loved.

This year was even more special, Daughtry thought. Nicholas's family was with them. Added to this was the wondrous blessing that Daughtry was carrying her first child. She thought of Mary and how she must have felt as the birth of the Savior to the world approached. What an incredible feeling to know that you carried a life within your body. How much more must it have been for Mary, who carried the world's King.

The boys, now men really, talked boisterously from the dining room, breaking Daughtry's concentration. Anna Maria and Pepita had worked alongside Maggie and Daughtry to bake hundreds of tiny pastries and cookies for the party. Daughtry couldn't help but smile at the thought of her five brothers, not to mention Dr. Dan and Lillie's sons and Pastor David and Jenny's son, Samuel, digging into the intricately woven display of confectionery delights. No doubt they'd give little thought to the arrangement, but Daughtry knew there would be hours of praise for the taste.

Compared to the seeming army of men in the house, Daughtry knew there were only a handful of women. Besides their mothers, Angeline Monroe, Dan and Lillie's feisty daughter, and David and Jenny's quiet little Hannah, now eighteen and twin to Samuel, would round out the party of second-generation New Mexicans. The biggest surprise of all and most pleasantly for the young gentlemen of the family, was Nicholas's dark-eyed sister, Joelle. She came by train only two days earlier and faced the wrath of both Riley and Nicholas at the announcement that she'd traveled alone.

It was of little matter, however, as all of Daughtry's brothers, as well as Samuel, and Angeline's brothers John and James, were quite taken with the beauty, leaving Angeline, who was normally the belle of the ball, with her nose slightly out of joint. No doubt Angeline would work through the competition and find herself the center of plenty of attention.

Daughtry stood alone in the living room and loved it all. She listened to the laughter, the voices, the happiness, and wrapped her hands around her still slender waist. Her child grew here, she thought and smiled. Two warm masculine hands fell over her own and Daughtry leaned back into the arms of her husband.

"I wondered where you'd gotten off to," Nicholas murmured against her ear. "How's my baby?"

"He's fine."

"I meant you," Nicholas whispered huskily.

"I was just dreaming," Daughtry said with a smile.

"Are you sure you weren't trying to figure out what I got you for Christmas?"

Daughtry turned in Nicholas's arms and stared up innocently. "You aren't really going to make me wait until tomorrow, are you?" She batted her lashes coyly and put on her most alluring smile.

Nicholas chuckled. "I do love you, Mrs. Dawson. So very much."

"But you still won't give me my present tonight?" Her voice was pleading like a child's.

"Who can resist such charm and womanly wiles?"

Daughtry laughed and wrapped her arms around her husband's neck. "I promise to make you the very best wife,

Nicholas. I will work hard beside you and together we'll build a ranch every bit as wonderful as Piñon Canyon."

"I've no doubt of it. You seem to make good things happen wherever you go."

"It isn't me," Daughtry replied with a knowing glance upward. "It's Him. God has made all the most wondrous things happen, in spite of the motives we humans attached to them in the first place. He's very good to look out for us that way."

"Yes, He is," Nicholas agreed.

With a tender kiss to Daughtry's forehead, he set her away from him and reached into his pocket. "I was going to wait until tomorrow, but since you are intent on celebrating early...." He fell silent and pulled out a small box. "I'm told this belonged to my mother's mother." He opened the box to reveal an elegantly styled ring. The wide gold band was intricately etched with scrolling and leaves. Set in the very middle was a dark red stone.

"It's a garnet," Nicholas said as Daughtry stared in dumb silence at the ring. He pulled the ring from the box and slipped it on Daughtry's still bare left hand. "I never even thought to send you a ring when I mailed you the proxy." He grinned at her, delighted with Daughtry's complete fascination. "Now you have one and no one will doubt that you belong to me."

"Oh, Nicholas," Daughtry replied, choking back tears, "it's beautiful. It truly is."

Nicholas nodded. "It's only part of the gift, however."

"Oh?"

"Yes," he whispered. "I've already talked with Pastor David."

"About what?" Daughtry asked curiously.

"I want us to marry again," he answered, taking Daughtry's hand to his lips. "Will you marry me in a proper church service, Mrs. Dawson? Marry me in front of all of our family and friends?"

Daughtry began to cry and, not finding the words to answer, she simply nodded her approval.

"Merry Christmas, Daughtry."

Daughtry reached up with both hands and pulled Nicholas's face down to meet hers. She kissed him earnestly on the mouth, her tears falling wet against his face. "Merry Christmas, Nicholas. I love you more with each passing day. I don't see how it is possible to love you more than I already did, but I do. I am yours, now and forever. Forever yours, no matter what the future holds in store."

Nicholas lifted her chin and glanced upward to the ceiling. "Forever His," he whispered in reply, "because He knows exactly what the future holds in store."

A Letter To Our Readers

Dear Reader:

In order that we might better contribute to your reading enjoyment, we would appreciate your taking a few minutes to respond to the following questions. When completed, please return to the following:

> Rebecca Germany, Editor
> Heartsong Presents
> P.O. Box 719
> Uhrichsville, Ohio 44683

1. Did you enjoy reading *Forever Yours*?
   ❏ Very much. I would like to see more books
      by this author!
   ❏ Moderately
      I would have enjoyed it more if _____

   _____

2. Are you a member of *Heartsong Presents*? Yes   No
   If no, where did you purchase this book? _____

   _____

3. What influenced your decision to purchase this
   book? (Check those that apply.)

   ❏ Cover   ❏ Back cover copy

   ❏ Title   ❏ Friends

   ❏ Publicity   ❏ Other _____

4. On a scale from 1 (poor) to 10 (superior), please rate the following elements.

    ___Heroine   ___Plot

    ___Hero   ___Inspirational theme

    ___Setting   ___Secondary characters

5. What settings would you like to see covered in *Heartsong Presents* books?

_____

_____

6. What are some inspirational themes you would like to see treated in future books?_____

_____

_____

7. Would you be interested in reading other *Heartsong Presents* titles?   ❏ Yes   ❏ No

8. Please check your age range:
❏ Under 18   ❏ 18-24   ❏ 25-34
❏ 35-45   ❏ 46-55   ❏ Over 55

9. How many hours per week do you read? _____

Name _____

Occupation _____

Address _____

City _____ State _____ Zip _____

········Presents········

Great Inspirational Romance at a Great Price!

Heartsong Presents books are inspirational romances in contemporary and historical settings, designed to give you an enjoyable, spirit-lifting reading experience. You can choose from 128 wonderfully written titles from some of today's best authors like Colleen L. Reece, Brenda Bancroft, Janelle Jamison, and many others.

When ordering quantities less than twelve, above titles are $2.95 each.

SEND TO: Heartsong Presents Reader's Service
             P.O. Box 719, Uhrichsville, Ohio 44683

Please send me the items checked above. I am enclosing $_____.
(please add $1.00 to cover postage per order. OH add 6.25% tax. NJ add 6%). Send check or money order, no cash or C.O.D.s, please.
      To place a credit card order, call 1-800-847-8270.

NAME _____

ADDRESS _____

CITY/STATE _____ ZIP _____

HPS JUNE